THE UNDEFEATED

ROBERT HARVEY

THE
UNDEFEATED

*The Rise, Fall and Rise
of Greater Japan*

MACMILLAN
LONDON

First published 1994 by Macmillan London Limited

a division of Pan Macmillan Publishers Limited
Cavaye Place London SW10 9PG
and Basingstoke

Associated companies throughout the world

ISBN 0 333 55107 9

1 3 5 7 9 8 6 4 2

A CIP catalogue record for this book is available from
the British Library

Typeset by CentraCet Limited, Cambridge
Printed and bound in Great Britain by
Mackays of Chatham plc, Chatham, Kent

For Oliver, this story of a faraway land

CONTENTS

Foreword ix
Acknowledgements xiii
Japan's Twenty Shoguns, 1868–1994 xv
The Shapers of Modern Japan xvii
Chronology xxvii

PRELUDE
LITTLE BOY AND THE EMPEROR 1

PART ONE
THE MEIJI IMPERATIVE 41

1 Under the Shogun 43
2 Breaking Point 57
3 Return of the Emperor 68
4 The Seeds of Totalitarianism 84
5 Government by Clique 93
6 A Nation of Samurai 109
7 The Monopolists 123
8 Death of an Emperor 132

PART TWO
THE DARK VALLEY 141

9 Emperor in Waiting 143
10 Tokyo Spring 155
11 Into Manchuria 176

12 Butchers in the Snow 192
13 The China 'Incident' 208
14 The Accomplices 227

PART THREE
THE WHIRLWIND 239

15 The Furies Unleashed 241
16 The Unravelling 253
17 The Struggle Within 266
18 Dance of Death 273

PART FOUR
THE UNDEFEATED 293

19 Descent from the Skies 295
20 Democratic Mikado 315
21 Shogun's Showdown 326
22 Return to Arms 339
23 Inner Tensions 351
24 The Democracy That Never Was 381
25 Flight of the Crane 388
26 Greater Japan 405
27 Samurai, Soldiers, Salarymen 416
28 The Juggernaut 446

PART FIVE
THE FAR SIDE OF THE EARTH 459

29 Outsiders 461
30 The Authoritarians 470
31 Return of the God-Emperor 499
32 Not So Sorry 510
33 Return of the Meiji 522
34 The Soft and the Hard 555

Postscript 577
Selected Bibliography 583
Index 607

FOREWORD

ON 6 AUGUST 1993, forty-eight years to the day after Hiroshima, an apparent earthquake reshaped Japan's political landscape: the first opposition administration since 1948 took office. On the face of it this seemed a liberation, a triumph for democracy, proving that even in Japan a change of government was possible, and the people's will could make itself felt. In fact, while representing a major shift in the country's stagnant tradition of rule by the Liberal Democratic Party (LDP), the opposition 'triumph' and change of government was largely illusory.

The general election of the previous month had been characterized by a major shift of votes not from the ruling party, but within the opposition, from the Socialists to the centre, in particular new groupings of disaffected LDP members. These disparate opposition allies took advantage of the LDP's narrow loss of its absolute majority in the lower house to form a 'rainbow coalition' committed to limited political reform; but because the ruling party dissidents held the balance, in practice the government was committed to virtually identical policies on most matters to those of its predecessor. In any event, the country's overmighty bureaucracy and economic bosses would not have permitted otherwise.

Any real innovation would have caused the power behind the new administration, Ichiro Ozawa, one of the LDP's toughest and most skilled power-brokers, to return to his old party, bringing it back to power. The new prime minister, Morihiro Hosokawa, an engaging grandson of the pre-war leader, Prince Fumimaro Konoye, himself descended from Japan's oldest political dynasty was thus a figurehead for a traditional LDP boss and was tossed aside just eight months later. The formation of the government represented a new

ix

stage in the endemic faction struggles within the LDP rather than any real upheaval.

Plus ça change ... The astonishing fact that a power elite has succeeded in presiding over the world's second economic superpower for nearly half a century has aroused much less comment and analysis than it deserves. Most people in the West continue to view the country as essentially benevolent, indeed an ally. This is partly because, in spite of Japan's huge economic presence around the world, the land still seems impossibly remote to Europeans, and even to Americans; partly because most reporting from Japan is confined to the financial pages; and partly because of a quasi-racialist attitude which seems to regard Japan's unique system of government and society as an almost comic curiosity.

Yet those who have witnessed the ravages wrought by authoritarian nationalism this century have good reason for deepening their understanding of Japanese society and politics. I first went to Japan in 1987 as an outsider myself, expecting to find a Western-style industrial nation that was highly modernized and pluralist, if a trifle soulless. In addition, I had long viewed Japan as America's closest and most reliable ally in Asia, barring the odd friction on trade, the only country in the region with a tradition of democracy and free-market economics.

My illusions were quickly confounded, and have since been altogether shattered during six years of travelling to Japan and the research that went into the making of this book. During nearly two decades of travelling the globe as a journalist and politician, one of the striking impressions I have received is of the growing similarity of societies the world over. While huge underlying differences remain, industrialization and the consumer culture have homogenized cities as far apart as Athens, São Paulo, Lagos, Bangkok and now Shanghai.

In Japan, on the contrary, I found very little except technology that bore any resemblance to things anywhere else. Even the first impression of the jumbled, coloured kaleidoscope of modern buildings that make up Tokyo's skyline bears little relation to the more uniform skyscrapers of other modern cities. I found a society in which authority and respect were inculcated from the earliest years; where democracy was a veneer for a highly sophisticated form of government by elites; where the concept of law bore greater resemblance to that espoused by Latin American military dictatorships than by any Western society; and where the economy, far from being a flourishing example of private enterprise, was dominated by state control and cartels.

Most extraordinary of all, the economic system actually worked, indeed excelled, transforming Japan into the post-war world's greatest economic success story and overwhelming established Western notions of the need for free competition. In conversation with government officials and businessmen, I found a feeling of antipathy and even contempt towards the Western values of free markets and individualism which we believe to be universal, based on the reasoning that 'our society works better than yours – so why should we change?'

Of even greater concern I encountered not just ignorance as to the causes of the Pacific War, but an almost universal sense of victimization. A great majority believed that Japan was not to blame for initiating the wars with China, America and Britain. While some on the left were profoundly opposed to the Japanese militarism that led to the war, they shared the fiercely anti-Western attitudes at the far right in their belief that Japan had been monstrously violated by the dropping of the bombs on Hiroshima and Nagasaki. These sentiments, as well as the gradual rolling back of the few reforms that have survived since the American occupation of Japan, are, if anything, on the increase.

All of this, on my first visit, seemed intriguing – as intriguing as the startling originality of Japanese culture, art and history. It also seemed alarming for the country that may become the world's foremost global economic superpower, endowed with a huge global reach, that is increasingly engaged in a trade war with the United States and, to a lesser extent, Europe, and that dwells at the very edge of a continent where several rapidly industrializing countries lacking in democratic traditions are building up their armed forces rather fast.

I resolved to investigate the phenomenon of modern Japan, and to my surprise found myself being carried way back beyond the immediate post-war period to the Meiji era in the last third of the nineteenth century, when Japan made its leap from medievalism – and, some would say, has yet to land in the modern age. To an astonishing extent the goals and roots of today's Japan are firmly embedded in the Meiji era. The pre-war militarist ascendancy was an exteme outgrowth of that tradition, not an aberration, and one which the contemporary elites in Japan barely view as being in error. Of course, many ordinary people do not share these views, and the elites have to take account of this. But the dominant corporatist, nationalist culture is much stronger than in most countries.

America's closest Asian partner for forty-five years, Japan does not really believe that it was wrong to have gone to war with the United States in December 1941. It does not share the same concepts of the rule of law, of democracy, of free enterprise – and despises American culture as *arriviste*. It is astonishingly successful, and increasingly assertive. It seemed a big enough subject to research and write a book about. This is also a journey of exploration inside a country, history and way of thinking entirely different to anything I had ever encountered before, in turn alarming, uniquely cruel, beautiful and utterly charming – but always different.

ACKNOWLEDGEMENTS

I N THE course of over four years researching this book, I have paid three extended visits to Japan, as well as travelling to Hong Kong, Singapore, Thailand, Burma, the Philippines and the United States. I have been given particular help by many friends. My very warmest thanks are reserved for AW and CW, who, as well as proving an invaluable source of information about Japan, gave me immense hospitality and facilities there. In addition, SS-P and DW fired me with their lifelong enthusiasm for Japan, pointing me in many fruitful directions, and, together with GL, read the manuscript and offered invaluable helpful suggestions for research and amendment. I also owe a great debt to DP, PD, RL, DM, SK, CP, KH, TS, HT, KI, YS and TK.

Neither they nor the very many others I interviewed in the course of researching this book are in any way responsible for, or associated with, its views and contents, which are entirely my own. I may not be doing them a service by naming them, so, sadly, will resist the temptation to do them justice.

My special thanks are also due to the Japanese authorities, in particular the Japanese Embassy in London, the Foreign Press Institute in Tokyo, the Press Department of the Japanese Foreign Ministry, the Foreign Ministry itself, the Self-Defence Agency, the Ministry of International Trade and Industry, the Japanese employers' association, the Keidanren, and the Hiroshima Peace Memorial Museum.

I owe a truly huge debt to GA, for all his encouragement, help and perceptive advice, to RP, for his sound advice and excellent editing, and to my tirelessly tolerant assistant, JW. Finally, most of all to my wife Jane, my son Oliver and my mother, who supported me throughout the writing of this book, as well as to C and our friends in Wales, where much of it was written.

Japan's Twenty 'Shoguns', 1868–1994

THROUGHOUT its history, Japan has always had a shogun, a *primus inter pares*, a leader of the dominant elite. This leader has rarely been the emperor, and often, in recent years, not even the prime minister, and has never ruled unchallenged. The real rulers of Japan, over the past century and a quarter, have been just twenty men (although Japan has had more than fifty different Prime Ministers).

MEIJI EMPEROR

Prince Tomomi Iwakura, 1868–71
General Takamori Saigo, 1871–3 (committed suicide)
Prince Toshimichi Okubo, 1873–7 (assassinated)
Prince Hirobumi Ito, 1877–1904 (assassinated)
General Aritomo Yamagata, 1904–13

TAISHO EMPEROR

Prince Kinmochi Saionji, 1913–18
Takashi Hara, 1918–21 (assassinated)

SHOWA EMPEROR

Prince Kinmochi Saionji, 1921–36
General Hideki Tojo, 1936–9
Admiral Mitsumasa Yonai, 1939–40
General Hideki Tojo, 1940–4 (executed)
Nobosuke Kishi, 1944–5

General Douglas MacArthur, 1945–8
Shigeru Yoshida, 1948–54
Ichiro Hatoyama, 1954–6
Nobusuke Kishi, 1956–60
Hayato Ikeda, 1960–4
Eisaku Sato, 1964–72
Kakuei Tanaka, 1972–4
Takeo Fukuda, 1974–8
Kakuei Tanaka, 1978–85

EMPEROR AKIHITO

Shin Kanemaru, 1985–93
Noboru Takeshita, 1993
Ichiro Ozawa, 1993–

THE SHAPERS OF
MODERN JAPAN

MOST WESTERNERS are familiar with a handful of names from the recent histories of the major industrial powers, say Lincoln, Teddy Roosevelt, Taft and Franklin Roosevelt in the United States; Disraeli, Gladstone, Salisbury, Lloyd George and Churchill in Britain; Napoleon III, Talleyrand, Blum, Pétain and De Gaulle in France; Metternich, the Kaiser, Bismarck, Ludendorff, Hitler and Adenauer in Germany; and Garibaldi, Cavour, Mussolini and de Gasperi in Italy.

By contrast, most Americans and Europeans would only be able to identify Emperor Hirohito and, just possibly, Tojo, Japan's wartime prime minister, as that country's giants of the modern period. This is an injustice. In the course of evolving from feudal origins to becoming the world's second most powerful economy, and one of its most significant military powers by the end of the century, Japan has yielded a rich harvest of outstanding, remarkable, colourful, and sometimes terrifying, personalities. The most prominent are, in order of appearance:

MEIJI PERIOD, 1868–1912

Emperor Mutsuhito (1852–1912), the Meiji emperor. 'Restored' to god-emperor status, although accorded little real power, in 1867, at the age of fifteen. Stern but self-indulgent. Embarked on unprecedented journeying to unify his land at the beginning of his reign. He presided over modest industrialization, the introduction of an autocratic constitution, the dissolution of Japan's princedoms and the transfer of the capital from Kyoto to Tokyo.
Ieyasu Tokugawa (1542–1617). The first of Japan's Tokugawa

xvii

shoguns, ruling as much through statesmanship as force, founding a dynasty that lasted 250 years.

Commodore Matthew Perry. Led a flotilla of 'black ships' to Edo (Tokyo) Bay in 1853 and 1854, and, by threat of force, caused Japan to abandon its policy of isolation from the outside world.

Naosuko Ii. Chief counsellor to the Tokugawa shogun who ordered the abandonment of the exclusion policy. Assassinated by nationalists in 1860.

Keiki Tokugawa. Last of the old-style shoguns. Expelled from Kyoto in 1867 and took the decision not to oppose the emperor's forces at Edo. Pardoned by the emperor in 1902.

Takamori Saigo (1827–77). Most prominent restoration military leader, defeating the shogun's forces outside Kyoto. A huge man of humble character, he became virtual military dictator of Japan in 1871–3, almost leading the nation to an early war with Korea. Expelled from power, he led the Satsuma rebellion in 1877, the last stand of the samurai in protest against the decision to introduce conscription. Committed *seppuku* and has inspired the romantic extreme right in Japan ever since.

Tomomi Iwakura. Effective leader of Japan after the Meiji restoration. He was a shrewd court intriguer who mediated between the dominant Satsuma and Choshu clans. An autocratic believer in a strong central state, he started the process of drafting the Meiji constitution.

Koin Kido. The second most prominent samurai in the land after Saigo, he nevertheless threw his weight behind the government in the latter's rebellion of 1877. He died the same year.

Kaoru Inouye. An early samurai leader who founded a prominent Japanese dynasty of politicians and bankers.

Toshimichi Okubo. One of the central core of oligarchs behind the restoration, he switched from being Saigo's intellectual mentor to becoming his most bitter foe. After Saigo's death he briefly became Japan's most powerful leader until his assassination by one of his deceased rival's followers.

Hirobumi Ito (1841–1909). The dominant leader of the late nineteenth century, he drafted Japan's autocratic constitution. A stern, aloof, court bureaucrat, he nevertheless showed enough flexibility to make central rule acceptable in Japan. In his last years, Hirobumi was effectively shunted aside by the rising militarist-nationalist faction headed by General Yamagata and exiled to Korea as resident-general, where he was assassinated by a local nationalist in 1909.

Taisuke Itagaki (1837–1919). Endowed with a splendid white beard and a penchant for fiery rhetoric, Itagaki modelled himself on the great Liberal reformers of eighteenth-century Europe, acting as a major focus for constitutional opposition. However, he took care never really to challenge the foundations of the system, and was frequently enticed into government, leading to charges that he had sold out on his democratic allies.

Aritomo Yamagata. The most controversial of Japan's early leaders. A Choshu samurai of unbending aloofness, he was intelligent enough to realize that Japan must abandon its traditional warrior culture and introduce a huge conscript army to further its nationalist aims. By the turn of the century, with this formidable base behind him, he had become Japan's dominant leader. Following Japanese success in the first Sino-Japanese War, the Russo-Japanese War and the annexation of Korea, his position appeared unchallengeable. The growing unpopularity of the armed forces during the First World War, after in particular Japan's intervention in Siberia, led to a curb in military spending and the assertion of constitutional government against the military. Yamagata sought briefly to extend his influence by opposing the choice of Emperor Hirohito's bride, but lost the struggle and died in 1921.

Masayoshi Matsukata (1835–1924). The inventor of Japan's unique system of state-directed development, he raised funds for the new government after 1868 and introduced land tax reform in 1871. In 1881 he became minister of finance, combining deflationary policies with a squeeze on the countryside that provided the capital for Japan's nascent industries, which were sold off, laying the foundations for the *zaibatsu* conglomerates. Much earlier than Stalin, he created a state-directed model of development economics.

TAISHO PERIOD, 1912–26

Emperor Yoshihito (1879–1926), the Taisho emperor. In stark contrast to his father, Yoshihito was an impulsive, womanizing young man, fond of drink and singing military songs with his cronies, detesting the stuffiness of court life. He was also dominated by his formidable wife. He suffered from meningitis as a child, and his nonconformity became increasingly eccentric. In 1921 Hirohito was appointed Prince Regent as Yoshihito's condition deteriorated into dementia. He died in 1926.

Takashi Hara. Known as the 'Great Commoner', he was the first Japanese prime minister drawn from outside the circles of the ruling autocracy. While in fact a highly conservative politician with his own machine and strongarm men, he did believe in constitutional government and was the protégé of the champion of democracy in Japan, Prince Saionji. Hara engineered Yoshihito's abdication and might have dominated the pre-war period, but was assassinated by nationalists in 1921.

Kinmochi Saionji (1849–1940) The dominant figure of the Taisho period, as he was to be of the early Showa period. The last surviving 'genro' (veterans of the restoration) he long outlived his rival Yamagata. Aristocratic, cosmopolitan, an aesthete, liberal in outlook, committed to deepening democracy, although on occasion haughty and autocratic, he was the dedicated opponent of the nationalists and militarists of the age. He led the opposition to the militarist Katsura government of 1912–13, whose fall resulted in some twenty years of relatively liberal government. Most subsequent prime ministers were his nominees. He dominated the young emperor, although there seem to have been occasions when Hirohito resented this. In the early 1930s Saionji's grasp began to slip, and he narrowly avoided assassination in the February 1936 plot. He always believed Japan's future lay in alliance with the United States and Britain, and died disillusioned in 1940, leaving behind two faithful protégés, Marquis Kido and Prince Konoye – who was to betray his master's ideals.

SHOWA PERIOD, 1926–45

Emperor Hirohito (1901–89), the Showa emperor. Hirohito was a physically ungainly, shy, serious scientist brought up in the shadow of the Meiji emperor, his grandfather, and largely abandoned by his father, the Taisho emperor. Raised in the stern tradition of the court, Hirohito became regent on his father's incapacitation at the early age of twenty, and was emperor at twenty-five. His reign was characterized by a huge frustration with the country's drift towards militarism and war which Hirohito, believing himself to be constitutionally powerless, only occasionally translated into action. In 1928 he reprimanded Prime Minister Tanaka over the assassination by Japanese army officers of the Manchurian warlord Chang Tso-Lin; in 1936 he ordered the suppression of army mutineers involved in the

February coup attempt; and in 1945 he broke the tie among Japan's senior leaders by favouring surrender. He failed, however, to issue a rescript against the drift to war in the period leading up to 1937; and he failed to abdicate after 1945, thereby taking responsibility upon himself for the China and Pacific Wars, and admitting Japan's blame for them. After 1945 he renounced his divinity and under the MacArthur constitution was stripped of his limited formal powers, but earned respect for the crown by journeying across Japan to meet his people. Thereafter he became an increasingly remote figurehead to his people, dying in January 1989 after a prolonged struggle against cancer.

Admiral Kantaro Suzuki. The Imperial Grand Chamberlain at the time of the 1936 coup attempt, he survived several shots to become prime minister between April and August 1945. He was responsible for two fateful decisions: the refusal to accept the terms of the Potsdam Declaration, which led directly to the dropping of the two atom bombs on Japan, and Japan's eventual decision to surrender.

Colonel Tetsusan Nagata. The young lieutenant-colonel responsible for the regeneration of the Japanese armed forces after the First World War. His concept of 'Total War' involved enlisting the entire nation in the war effort, and he advocated collaboration with the *zaibatsu* industrial giants. He was shot by a right-wing extremist in 1935.

General Sadao Araki (1877–1966). The romantic hero of the younger army officers who preached a form of national socialist anti-communism and sought to revive Saigo's samurai tradition. He became minister of war in 1931, preparing for a conflict with Russia. In 1934 he was dismissed and the advocates of war with China rose to the top again. He was sentenced to life imprisonment in 1948 and released in 1955.

General Hideki Tojo (1844–1948). The diminutive, shabby and uncharismatic leader of the Total War group after Nagata's assassination. Descended from a military family, he was economical in speech, and a highly effective commander and administrator, becoming war minister in the years before the conflict, and thus Japan's effective strongman. He advocated war with China and the occupation of South-east Asia, and was the architect of Japan's attack on British and American forces in the Far East. As the war moved against Japan, he amassed ever greater responsibilities for himself, and with the fall of Saipan was finally ousted. After the surrender in 1945 he attempted to kill himself, but was saved for condemnation by the Tokyo War Crimes tribunal and executed in 1948.

Prince Fumimaro Konoye (1891–1945). A scion of the Fujiwara dynasty dating back to the Heian Period, and therefore on casual terms even with the emperor, Konoye was aristocratic, foppish, indecisive, shallow and a flirt with both sexes. He rose to prominence with the publication of romantic ultra-nationalist texts, but was appointed prime minister by Saionji in an attempt to stop the rush to war. He presided over the key decisions to invade China and to occupy Indo-China. After losing office for prevaricating about attacking Pearl Harbor, he turned against the war and believed he would be turned to by the Americans as Japan's national saviour. Instead, on learning he was to be tried as a war criminal, he committed suicide in 1945.

Admiral Isoroku Yamamoto (1884–1947). The brilliant strategist of Pearl Harbor. A convinced opponent of war with America and Britain, he nevertheless planned the surprise attack. He was killed when his aircraft was shot down in 1943.

Marquis Koichi Kido (1889–1977). Under the patronage of Saionji, he moved effortlessly up the ladder of government to become Lord Keeper of the Privy Seal between 1930 and 1937 and between 1940 and 1945. As such he became the emperor's closest confidant. A meticulous, fussy, punctual man, he was vigorously opposed to the militarists and early in the war was actively seeking an end to it. His diary suggested that Hirohito often ignored his advice. In 1945 he narrowly escaped assassination by extreme right-wing officers in the August coup attempt, and he was sentenced to life imprisonment at the Tokyo war crimes trial. He was released in 1955 and lived on another twenty-two years.

General Korechika Anami. War minister at the end of the war, he was a soldier's soldier. Unlike the humourless Tojo, Anami was bluff, popular and not overendowed intellectually. He vigorously opposed the decision to surrender, but, when the emperor so decided, refused to lend his backing to an officers' coup and instead committed ritual *seppuku*. He may have defused a potential civil war within Japan by his sacrifice.

Shinji Yoshino (1888–1971). The architect of many aspects of Japan's post-war economic miracle. He first developed a national industrial policy and a campaign for export promotion; he believed in vigorous state intervention. In 1937 he became minister for commerce and industry, enacting a celebrated law which gave the government virtually total control over production, imports and exports. He was purged during the occupation, but returned in 1953 for a lucrative career in industry, eventually becoming chairman of the Japan Mutual Life Insurance Company.

Nobosuke Kishi (1896–). As significant for his role before 1945 as after. He was Yoshino's devoted pupil. He became the head of the 'reform bureaucrats' committed to state direction of the economy. Kishi's attempts to bring the *zaibatsu* under the government control in 1941 caused his dismissal and the arrest of some seventeen of his associates. However, later in the year, Tojo, who had come to agree with Kishi's view of the need to control the *zaibatsu*, appointed him minister of commerce and industry. The *zaibatsu* resisted government control, but in 1943 Kishi was promoted, in effect to run the Ministry of Munitions and bring the private sector to heel. Astonishingly, Kishi then turned on his old friend Tojo, and after the fall of Saipan openly urged him to sue for peace. The prime minister, enraged at a civilian meddling with military affairs, sought to dismiss him, and possibly to have him arrested and executed, but Kishi refused to resign. When it became clear that he had more support than Tojo, the latter had to go.

Only with the surrender, however, was Kishi able to enact his substantial reforms to both stimulate and guide the direction of the economic miracle. In 1957 he became prime minister, losing office in 1960 amid violent controversy stirred by his contentious attempt to rewrite Japan's security pact with America. Kishi was also responsible for one last bold decision: to initiate the process of opening up Japan's economy to the outside world. Throughout his long, bold and controversial career, his greatest achievement was to be the father of Japan's economic miracle.

SHOWA PERIOD, AFTER 1945

General Douglas MacArthur (1880–1964). The only foreign ruler in Japan's history, MacArthur enjoyed a brilliant, if erratic, career as a soldier, distinguishing himself in the First World War in France, and then becoming America's youngest chief of staff. He left the job for an undistinguished spell as commander of the new Philippine national army, and there in 1941 was surprised by the Japanese invasion force. Retreating to the rocky peninsula of Bataan and the fortress of Corregidor, MacArthur's long stand redeemed him and he fled in 1942 to Australia to become the commander of American forces in the southern Pacific. He staged a drawn-out but brilliant campaign to roll back Japanese conquests, and in 1945 was appointed Supreme Commander Allied Powers in Japan with virtually dictatorial authority. He engaged in a three-year attempt to democratize and modernize Japan's institutions, with limited success. By 1948 his more conservative opponents were beginning the process of rolling back his reforms. With the invasion of South Korea by the North, he led the Americans in a series of brilliant campaigns and blunders before being dismissed for insubordination by President Truman in 1951. He died in 1964.

Shigeru Yoshida. An ebullient former foreign ministry official, Yoshida was prime minister briefly 1946–7, and then from 1948 to 1954. Unashamedly pro-big business, he played a vigorous if losing role in resisting Kishi's economic planning, and more successfully reversed MacArthur's reform programme. He affected an old-fashioned British manner as a means of irritating the Americans, but enjoyed a surprisingly warm relationship with MacArthur. In 1954 he was ousted by yet more nationalist, conservative forces.

Elsaku Sato. The quintessential competent bureaucrat who ran the country during the boom years of the economic miracle from 1964–72. Although the ingredients for the miracle had been put in place by his brother-in-law Kishi, Sato was a much calmer figure and displayed a remarkable talent for conciliating the various groups in Japan during these formative years. Friendly, distant, a little aloof, he had few enemies.

Kakuei Tanaka (1918–1993). Japan's most populist politician since Hara. Born of humble village stock in a remote province, he showed a genius for construction and used his fortune to buy his way into politics and thence up to the job of prime minister in 1972. Although genuinely popular, he fell in a corruption scandal in 1974, but took his revenge by ousting his principal rival, Takeo Fukuda, in 1978, and for the next seven years effectively ran the government, pulling the strings from behind a succession of prime ministers until he was incapacitated by a stroke in 1985. He died in 1993.

Yasuhiro Nakasone. The most stylish of Japan's recent prime ministers. A committed nationalist, he attempted to place Japan's relationship with America on a more even footing and to throttle

THE SHAPERS OF MODERN JAPAN

back government control of industry. He gained a place for Japan on the world stage, but was hampered by his lack of a substantial political base and his dependence on Tanaka for support. He lasted an impressive five years as prime minister.

Shin Kanemaru. Tanaka's successor as Japan's behind-the-scenes kingmaker. Through factional control he manipulated a succession of prime ministers until felled by a scandal in 1993.

Shigeru Sahashi. The toughest of MITI's bosses during the period of the economic boom. He controversially picked fights with private industry and with his supposed political masters, and usually won. He ensured MITI's preeminence throughout the 1960s.

Yukio Mishima. Japan's outstanding post-war novelist. A superb and prolific writer, tackling a variety of controversial themes, he was also a romantic nationalist who staged a ludicrous abortive coup in 1965, committing *seppuku* when it failed.

CHRONOLOGY

Eighth century. Nara Period.

Ninth–twelfth century. Heian Period, dominated between 995 and 1027 by Fujiwara no Michinaga.

1192   Beginning of the civil wars and warrior government.

1568   Oda Nobunaga seizes Kyoto and conquers most of central Japan. First central government in nearly 350 years.

1582   Nobunaga assassinated. Toyotomi Hideyoshi further unifies the country.

1600   Tokugawa Ieyasu seizes control and establishes a centralized military dictatorship under his dynasty that lasts 250 years.

1639   Portuguese expelled and persecution of Christians gets under way.

1641   Japan is closed off to the outside world.

1791–2   American and Russian ships first try to land in Japan.

1853   Commodore Perry lands at Uraga with his 'black ships'.

1854   Perry returns, imposes the Treaty of Kanagawa.

1858   Kanagawa, Nagasaki and Hokodate are opened to foreign trade.

1863   British bombardment of Kagoshima.

1864   First Choshu rebellion.

1867   Choshu and Satsuma armies march on Kyoto, forcing the shogun to flee.

1868   The Meiji emperor is 'restored' and his capital transferred from Kyoto to Edo (Tokyo).

1869	Final defeat of the forces opposed to the restoration.
1871	Feudal princedoms of the *daimyo* formally abolished.
1871–3	Iwakura mission to Europe.
1873	Introduction of conscription. War with Korea narrowly avoided.
1877	Satsuma rebellion of Takamori Saigo is crushed.
1889	Meiji constitution introduced.
1890	The Diet sits for the first time.
1894–5	Sino-Japanese war. Victory for Japan, but unsatisfactory peace agreement.
1902	Anglo-Japanese alliance concluded.
1904–5	Russo-Japanese war.
1910	Annexation of Korea.
1912	Death of the Meiji emperor. Taisho emperor ascends the throne.
1915	The twenty-one demands by Japan on China.
1921	Hirohito becomes regent as his father becomes incapacitated.
1923	Great Kanto earthquake and pogroms on Koreans.
1925	Universal manhood suffrage granted. Repressive peace preservation law also introduced.
1926	Death of the Taisho emperor. Hirohito succeeds to the throne.
1927	Japanese economic depression.
1928	Assassination of Marshal Tso-Lin and failed Japanese attempt to seize Manchuria.
1930	London naval treaty signed. Prime Minister Hamaguchi wounded in assassination attempt and dies a year later.
1931	'March Incident', an attempted coup plot. Occupation of Manchuria. 'October Incident', another coup plot.
1932	Assassination of Finance Minister Inouye. Japanese bombing of Shanghai. Assassination of Prime Minister Inukai.
1934	Another coup plot frustrated.
1936	26 February coup attempt by younger officers fails, but army seizes effective power.
1937	Fighting at the Marco Polo Bridge leads to Japanese invasion of China.
1938	Battle of Changkufeng between Japan and Russia.
1940	Japan joins the Axis with Germany and Italy.
1941	Neutrality agreement with Russia. Tojo becomes prime minister. Japan occupies Indo-China. Britain and the

United States impose an oil and financial embargo. Japan attacks the American Fleet at Pearl Harbor, as well as Hong Kong, Malaya, Singapore and the Philippines.

1942   Singapore surrenders. America and Britain defeated in the Battle of the Java Sea. Japan takes Java, Sumatra and Burma. MacArthur abandons Bataan. The Doolittle Raid reaches Tokyo. The Battle of the Coral Sea checks the Japanese fleet. The Battle of Midway challenges Japanese naval supremacy. The Americans seize Guadalcanal and the Japanese counterattack.

1943   The American invasion of New Guinea and seizure of Woodlark, Kiriwina, Nassau Bay, Salamanua, Finschafen and encirclement of Rabaul. The Battle of the Bismarck Sea.

1944   The Battle of the Philippine Sea. The Americans capture Saipan, Guam and Timor, and the whole of New Guinea. The Battle of Leyte Gulf; the Americans land on the Philippines. Operation Ichi-Go, Japan's last thrust into China. The Tojo government falls.

1945   The Americans seize Iwo Jima and Okinawa. The Japanese thrust into India and are defeated at Imphal and Kohima. The British return to Burma. The saturation bombing of Tokyo. The final occupation of the Philippines. The dropping of the atom bombs on Hiroshima and Nagasaki. Japanese acceptance of the Potsdam Declaration and the surrender. MacArthur becomes supreme commander. Beginning of the purges.

1946   The emperor renounces his divinity. Imposition of the MacArthur constitution.

1947   MacArthur cracks down on the unions.

1948   The *zaibatsu* reforms are put into reverse. Purges are abandoned. Shortlived Socialist-led government.

1950   The outbreak of the Korean War.

1951   MacArthur dismissed. San Francisco Peace Treaty on Japan.

1952   The end of the occupation and beginning of the US–Japan Security Pact. Left–right rioting.

1954   The Bikini Atomic Test, and Japanese reaction. Fall of Shigeru Yoshida.

1955   The formation of the Liberal Democratic Party.

1960   The revision of the US–Japan Security Treaty. Riots in Tokyo and the fall of Kishi.

1970   The suicide of Yukio Mishima.
1972   The rise of Tanaka and the end of bureaucratic rule. The 'Nixon shock'.
1974   The oil shock.
1976   The Lockheed Scandal and the arrest of Tanaka.
1982   Nakasone becomes prime minister.
1986   Tanaka has a stroke and is removed from power.
1987   The fall of Nakasone.
1989   The Recruit Scandal and fall of Takeshita.
1993   Corruption scandal and the fall of Kanemaru. LDP split and return of Takeshita. Fall of LDP and election of Hosokawa, backed by Ozawa, heading 'rainbow coalition' of opposition parties.
1994   Fall of Hosokawa

PRELUDE

LITTLE BOY
AND THE EMPEROR

Absolute power, absolute destruction, is minimalist, like Japanese aesthetics. As modest as two tiny craft, a principal and its escort, drifting across a vast expanse of blue, the noise of their engines rising and falling in the void.

On the fine morning of 6 August 1945, thirteen-year-old Yoshitaka Kawamoto dressed himself in his neat black school uniform, with its flat cap and Prussian-modelled tunic buttoned up to the collar. He was known as a happy, sensible boy, a little shy perhaps, of middling height for his age. He was the apple of his mother's eye, in a family where the father had died young. She saw to it that the impeccable standards of dress and appearance prescribed by the harsh discipline of the school were fully observed. His hair was crew-cut almost to fuzzy baldness, his face scrubbed and washed, his shoes jet-black.

As Yoshitaka affectionately kissed her goodbye and trotted out of the low, wooden house, Mrs Kawamoto's pride must have been tempered with the apprehension of any mother of her generation. She was sad that he was leaving the house, although it allowed her to get on with her chores – as she had not been able to when he was very young. She was concerned, too, that nothing should happen to him on the long journey to and from school, but Yoshitaka was quite grown up by now, and not a child to do foolish things. His mother also entertained a looming fear for the future: at fifteen years of age, boys were expected to go and work in the munitions factories based on the outskirts of town; a couple of years later they would become eligible for military service.

But it was rumoured that the war was ending. Surely it could not continue for four more years? The idea seemed impossibly remote to her on this peaceful August day in the growing heat of the morning. Once during the previous night, she had heard the distant sound of air-raid sirens from Hiroshima, but the family lived too far from the

3

centre to take refuge in a shelter. Two hours later the all-clear had sounded.

Anyway, Hiroshima had never been bombed.

The Kawamoto family lived in a traditional Japanese wooden house on one of the flanks of the mountain range that tumbled down to the placid waters of the Inland Sea like a hand with its five fingers stretched out; Hiroshima was crammed into a couple of gaps of flat terrain between the fingers. As everywhere in the rocky islands of Japan, land was at a premium. The houses and farms were crowded onto whatever spaces the mountains and ocean would allow.

The Kawamotos knew they lived in the loveliest spot of all: they overlooked Miyajima island, a short ferry ride away. There, one of Japan's most spectacular and sacred Buddhist shrines crouched over the water. It was a monastery complex, built out on piles which left only a foot or two of clearance from the surface at high tide. The building was a harmonious, human-proportioned wooden edifice painted in dull red with pleasant, broad rooms for meditation and prayer and narrow, covered catwalks connecting up the different piers; the ubiquitous curving thatch of Japanese Buddhist roofs lent the construction a symmetric harmony.

A stage where Japan's ritualistic Noh theatre was occasionally performed protruded over the water from the left-hand side of the temple. To the right there was a fine, turreted red shrine, resembling a giant carnival hat, dating back only a few years. Young deer roaming in a gully behind the temple were shooed away as dirty pests by local people. The surrounding village was small and poor. The island rose up behind; other shrines, none as important or spectacular as the floating monastery, protruded from the sloping forests above.

The Kawamoto family would have frequently taken the ferry to visit the shrines, to enjoy the peace and because these were sacred places. A few hundred yards from the temple a Shinto arch was skewed lopsidedly into the water, like a monster musical note that had somehow become embedded in the sea.

Yoshitaka would have been taken once at night-time, to witness the lighting of the lanterns at the temple. Ten thousand of them would sparkle out over the still waters of the Inland Sea, giving the monastery the ghostly quality of a mysterious vessel incapable of staying afloat on the darkness of the surface of the water, a myriad of pinpricks of light illuminating mellow red timbers. When the Kawamotos visited the shrine, they had never felt such inner calm:

Yoshitaka had been old enough for some years now to understand such things, to appreciate peace and beauty.

At the same time as Yoshitaka Kawamoto was preparing to set off from his home, Second Lieutenant Morris Jeppson of the US Air Force was making his way along a narrow catwalk in the centre of a B-29 bomber cruising at around 9000 feet at a speed of 205 miles an hour. He was in the bomb bay of the aircraft, which was empty save for a single large metal casing. It was pleasantly cool – 18 degrees Celsius, 66 Fahrenheit. As the aircraft moved evenly along, Jeppson reached the bomb casing and carefully unscrewed three green safety plugs, exchanging them for three red ones. There was no hitch: they fitted perfectly. The world's first atomic bomb about to be used in anger had been armed.

He moved back along the catwalk and reported to Captain William Parsons, the naval officer who was one of the most influential planners behind the Manhattan Project – the programme to develop the world's first nuclear weapons. Parsons was profoundly relieved. The replacement of the safety plug had completed an extraordinary night's work. Less than four hours before he had been down in the bomb bay with Jeppson, who had been holding a torch. Parsons had inserted a charge of high-quality gunpowder wired with an electrical detonator into a breech behind the 'bullet' – a uranium cylinder shaped like a tin of soup some six inches long.

The detonator was programmed to set off the powder, which would propel the bullet down a 52-inch barrel at 900 feet a second into the centre of a uranium ring, and a device made of plutonium-239 would begin emitting neutrons, starting off the chain reaction. After two minutes of preparation Parsons had been ready to perform the most delicate task. He had to assemble the four sections of explosive together, then to connect up the detonator. He had tightened up the breech plate, front and rear. The green plugs had remained in place to ensure that the bomb could not be detonated by an accidental electrical charge. Now it was live.

Parsons in turn informed the mission commander and pilot of the Enola Gay, Colonel Paul W. Tibbets, who turned to gaze in silence at the clear early morning sky over the unending blue expanse of the Pacific. The sun had risen only two hours before in a staggering display of incandescent pink. It was Tibbets who bore the ultimate responsibility for the success or failure of the most important mission ever undertaken by an American aircraft, before or since.

He was a sturdy, good-looking man with an easy, pleasant smile and a deceptive air of quietness and seriousness. He was dedicated, efficient, hardworking, sometimes short and curt with those who failed to impress him, more usually genial and bland. He possessed one of the most distinguished flying records in the US Air Force. He had flown the first B-17 on a bombing mission across the English Channel in the Second World War. He had led the first American raid on North Africa. He had landed General Mark Clark on the airstrip at Algiers under fierce enemy fire. And he had been the chief prototype tester of the B-29 Super Fortress. Now he was on the verge of truly entering the history books – or going down in oblivion – on a mission whose success would be measured by the deaths of hundreds of thousands.

Two hours before, Tibbets had been round the aircraft on a tour of inspection, handing over the controls to his copilot, Captain Robert Lewis. The mission commander encountered Technical Sergeant George ('Bob') Caron, a friend from the old days of the B-29 training programme. After nearly a year of intensive training on this project, Tibbets directly addressed the subject of the mission for the first time. He asked Caron whether he had guessed what they were doing. 'Colonel, I don't want to get put up against a wall and shot,' replied the other wryly.

'Bob, we're on our way now. You can talk.'

Caron asked whether they carried 'a new super-explosive . . . a chemist's nightmare'. Tibbets shook his head.

Caron asked if it was 'a physicist's nightmare'.

'Yes,' Tibbets told him.

'Are we splitting atoms?' Caron asked, recalling a popular scientific magazine he had once read. Tibbets said nothing.

Now that the bomb was fully armed, he switched on the intercom and addressed the crew, answering Caron's question. 'We are carrying the world's first atomic bomb.' He paused. 'When the bomb is dropped, Lieutenant Beser [the radio officer] will record our reactions to what we see. This recording is being made for history. Watch your language and don't clutter up the intercom. Bob,' he told Caron, 'you were right. We are splitting atoms. Now get back in your turret. We're going to start climbing.' A few minutes later, at twenty minutes to seven, the aircraft carrying the bomb, the Enola Gay – named after Tibbets's mother – started to climb to its bombing height of 30,000 feet.

Moments before, First Lieutenant Jacob Beser had frozen as he saw the Japanese early warning signal sweep by the aircraft on the radar, once, twice, and then lock into a constant pulse, indicating that they had a fix. Beser decided not to cause unnecessary stress by informing the crew, or even the captain. There was nothing to be done.

Even at this late stage, Tibbets had no final idea of their objective. It could be one of three cities: Hiroshima, Kokura, or Nagasaki. As recently as 12 May the list had been much longer, with Nagasaki excluded and Yokohama and Kyoto included. On 2 August General Curtis LeMay, chief of staff of the strategic air forces, had dismissed the preferred target of Kyoto. 'It wasn't much of a military target, only a lot of shrines and things of that sort there; and anyway riling people gets you nowhere – it's just not profitable.'

Thus was Japan's Florence spared: destroying the sacred imperial city would have created a vendetta for generations to come. LeMay had told Tibbets that, in view of the large number of troops and weapons concentrated at Hiroshima, it was 'the primary'. Tibbets, relieved, told him he had always preferred it. The following day the list had been finalized. Primary: Hiroshima; secondary, Kokura; tertiary, Nagasaki. All that remained in determining which target the bomb would actually fall upon was whether conditions were right.

Captain Claude Eatherly, a good-looking, voluble Texan, was in charge of the Straight Flush, the reconnaissance flight detailed to check on weather conditions at Hiroshima. The aircraft reached the beginning of the projected bombing run – the 'initial point' – at a height of 30,000 feet, travelling at 235 miles per hour. There was nothing but thick cloud. Moments later, a huge hole some 10 miles wide appeared directly over the city of Hiroshima. The reconnaissance aircraft over Kokura and Nagasaki reported that conditions were faultless there too. The Straight Flush sent a coded message to Tibbets: the weather had determined that the primary target, Hiroshima, had been chosen.

Eatherly, who was under orders to return to base at Tinian Atoll, asked his crew whether they wanted to wait for the Enola Gay's arrival 'and then follow him back to see what happens when the bomb goes off'. Crew members hotly debated the subject. Eatherly suddenly realized that if they didn't get back to Tinian by two o'clock they would miss the afternoon poker game. The flight engineer told the commander they might not have enough fuel to make it, which would force them to land on Iwo Jima. That decided it. Anyway, where was the interest in seeing one bomb drop? 'What would we see?' pointed out Eatherly. For the sake of a poker game, the crew of the reconnaissance plane decided to skip the dropping of the world's first atom bomb on a live target. Hardly less casually did the fates responsible for weather conditions over Japan condemn one city to hell on earth, sparing another. At a height of 26,000 feet, the Enola Gay set course for Hiroshima.

The emotional climate surrounding the dropping of the bomb had begun to take shape more than seven years before, when General Chiang Kai-shek decided to abandon the city of Nanking to the advancing Japanese. The city contained around a million people, two-thirds of them refugees. On the night of 12 December 1937, Chinese resistance ended and the Japanese moved in.

A sixty-two-year-old Chinese railway official described what happened then. 'They shot at everyone on sight. Anybody who run away, or on the streets, or hanging around somewhere, or peeking through the door, they shoot them – instant death.' Three days after the Japanese entered the city, according to Hsu Chuan-ying, there were bodies everywhere. 'I saw the dead bodies lying everywhere, and some of the bodies were very badly mutilated. Some of the bodies are lying there as they were shot or killed, some kneeling, some bending, some on their sides and some just with their legs and arms wide open.' On one street, he started counting the corpses and after reaching 500 decided there 'was no use counting them'.

The Japanese soldiers went into the supposedly protected refugee zone of Nanking and arrested anyone with rough hands, which might have been caused by carrying rifles. Prisoners were arrested and roped together in groups of ten and fifteen and marched away – no fewer than 1500 on a single day. The refugees, themselves in terror thanks to these incursions, could hear machine guns chattering through the night, although there was no fighting in the city.

Rape was the accompaniment to murder. 'The Japanese soldiers – they are so fond of raping, so fond of women that one cannot believe,' said Hsu. 'There was a mass round-up of women between thirteen and forty, most of whom were gang-raped.' Hsu visited a house in which three women, two of them young girls, had been raped. One, he said, had been violated on a table, 'and while I was there blood on the table was not all dry yet . . .' According to international estimates, some 30,000 women in Nanking were raped, and many killed and mutilated afterwards.

Hsu belonged to the Red Swastika, the Chinese Red Cross, and when the Japanese got around to burying the bodies – fearing that their decomposition would create an epidemic – he was appalled by how many were tied together with rope or wire. 'It is our sacred practice to have a dead body all unloosed if it is tied. We wanted to unloose everything and bury them one by one. But with these wires now it is almost impossible to do that. In many cases these bodies were already decayed so we would not be able to bury them one by one. All we can do is simply to bury them in groups.' Hsu reckoned the Red Swastika buried some 43,000 people over the following few weeks, but the real figure was probably much higher, as the Japanese forbade the Chinese relief officials to keep records.

Miner Bates, an American professor at the University of Nanking, gave a picture of the murderous duplicity of the forces that had taken over the city. Posters were put up asking Chinese to volunteer as workers for the Japanese army's labour camps. 'If you have previously been a Chinese soldier or if you have worked as a carrier or labourer in the Chinese army,' said the authorities, 'that will all be forgotten and forgiven if you join the labour corps.' According to Bates, two hundred or so men enlisted on the university campus 'and were marched away and executed that evening'.

Looting was systematic. 'On one occasion I observed a supply column, two-thirds of a mile long, loaded with high-grade redwood and blackwood furniture.' A large number of buildings were burnt: stores, churches, embassies, houses were set alight, their flames illuminating the dark nights while the machines guns chattered. 'We could not see any reason or pattern in it,' said Bates.

It was Winston Churchill, with the characteristic brilliance that underlay an appearance raddled by decades of success, frustration, democratic politics, *bonhomie* and decision-making, who made the most apposite, if crafted, remark about the bomb. The American secretary for war, Henry Stimson, had called on him in his study at Potsdam on Saturday 22 July to hand him a report by Brigadier-General Leslie Groves, chief of the Manhattan Project, charged with creating the first American atom bomb. Churchill, mildly apprehensive on the eve of an election which he believed he would win (and didn't), read the report sombrely. 'Stimson, what was gunpowder? Trivial. What was electricity? Meaningless. The atom bomb is the Second Coming in wrath.'

Churchill in fact knew a great deal about the project, to which British scientists had made a major contribution. But his remarks, even if prepared, had the ring of truth. Churchill's second judgement came later, summarizing what had been agreed at Potsdam about the bomb. The British prime minister asserted that, 'while the final decision lay in the main' with America's new president, Harry S. Truman, Churchill fully supported it. 'The historic fact remains, and it must be judged in the after time, that the decision whether or not to use the atomic bomb to compel the surrender of Japan was never an issue. There was unanimous, automatic, unquestioning agreement around the table.'

How could any man possibly assert such a thing? How could the heads of the most prosperous democratic powers in the world, responsible to their own electorates, arrive at the view that it was permissible not just to develop and produce the most destructive weapon the world had ever known, but that it was acceptable to drop a pair of them, annihilating two cities and killing an eventual total of close to half a million people? How could such a decision have been reached so quickly without more soul-searching, agonizing, debate, or conscience intruding?

Much more than war-battered Churchill, the almost psychopathically unimpressive, anonymous figure of Truman, who just three months and ten days earlier had assumed the presidency, has taken on the proportions of monster of the nuclear age. Was this soft-spoken, tiny Missouri politician pushed into the decision on assuming the presidency by an unstoppable war machine? Was Truman so mean-spirited and provincial-minded that he merely reflected the automatic hatred of the 'barbarous' Japanese as shared generally by most Americans and others in the West? Were the Western leaders unaware of the significance of the nuclear age?

The answer to these questions was that Truman, that shrewd if inexperienced world statesman, knew exactly what he was doing; and that Churchill, his over-experienced colleague, did also. To understand why there was unanimous agreement, it is necessary to go back to the very day when Truman assumed the presidency of the United States.

On 12 April 1945, Truman had been fulfilling his routine duty of presiding over the Senate; when the sitting ended he dropped into the office of the speaker of the house, Sam Rayburn, for a bourbon and water, only to be rung by President Roosevelt's secretary and invited to 'come over'. Once there, he was ushered to the study of Eleanor Roosevelt, the president's wife, who told him immediately that her husband was dead.

Two hours later, at seven o'clock, Truman was sworn in. As

cabinet members filed out, Stimson held back. 'Mr President, I must talk to you on a most urgent matter,' he said. 'I want to inform you about an immense project that is under way – a project leading to the development of a new explosive of almost unbelievable destructive power.' With those cryptic words, the old man left, leaving behind an exhausted and bewildered President in his first hours in office.

Over the next few weeks he was to learn a great deal more. On 25 April Stimson and General Groves arrived for an interview they had requested on a 'highly secret matter'. Straight away, Stimson told Truman that he wanted to discuss a bomb equal in power to all the artillery used in both world wars. He went on, 'Within four months we shall in all probability have completed the most terrible weapon ever known in human history, one bomb which could destroy a whole city. Although we have shared its development with the United Kingdom, physically the US is at present in the position of controlling the resources with which to construct and use it, and no other nation could reach this position for some years. Nevertheless, it is practically certain that we could not remain in this position indefinitely.'

In Stimson's view it was morally essential that the United States win the race for the bomb. 'We may see a time when such a weapon may be constructed in secret and used suddenly and effectively ... with its aid even a very powerful, unsuspecting nation might be conquered within a few days by a very much smaller one ... The world in its present state of moral advancement compared with its technical development would be eventually at the mercy of such a weapon. In other words, modern civilization might be completely destroyed.' He ended by saying that, despite all the drawbacks, he still favoured its being used against Japan. Truman agreed at once on the necessity of continuing the work, but left the final decision on using the bomb against a live target until he was forced to make it.

On 6 July, Truman left for Potsdam. With his wife Bess and his daughter Margaret, he had been attending a concert on the White House lawn given by an army band. As soon as it was over he went indoors, bade the women goodbye, and left for Union Station. Seven hours later a special presidential train drew into Newport News, Virginia, where his heavy cruiser, the *Augusta*, was anchored. On that journey across the Atlantic, under threat of attack by a rogue submarine, he had many hours to ponder the further progress Stimson had reported to him four days before on the development of the bomb, and the suggestion that the Japanese be given one last chance before it was dropped.

Yoshitaka Kawamoto trotted dutifully along the four kilometres of dusty streets to the station. Other diminutive uniformed cadres were also falling into line as instructed, forming an improvised march. Japan was a deeply militarized society, and the discipline of small boys, as Yoshitaka was later to reflect, 'was spartan, with the object of turning us into tough soldiers'. Even so, there was some banter and playful barging about as friends met each other on the way to the station; the friendships formed in youth – the only age when advancement and deference do not determine relationships – are to many Japanese the most lasting, and provide the greatest pleasure in their declining years.

But that morning Yoshitaka was in a serious frame of mind. He was well regarded by the teachers in his class – in as far as their stern injunctions to be aloof from their pupils allowed them to express favour. He had been passing his exams with good marks. The teaching was tough, thorough and unimaginative, a matter of learning by rote, and the punishments were severe. There had been no school treats or holidays during these war years, and Yoshitaka could hardly remember a time when Japan was not at war. If he performed well, he would be able to serve his country, like many of the soldiers who came to the streets of Hiroshima from the nearby base, one of the key supply posts for Japan's overseas army in China.

He would be proud to serve his country. He had been taught from the beginning that Japan's enemies, the Americans and the British in particular, were devils: hardly human at all, barbaric beyond belief. His homeland was under threat from their aggression. He was pleased to be a boy doing well in Hiroshima's best school, with the chance even of becoming an officer in the imperial army. He was in the seventh grade, his first year in middle school. The school had 280 pupils, making it one of the largest in the city. The little train that took the children the 13 kilometres to Hiroshima was rudimentary in the extreme, with narrow wooden benches from which Yoshitaka gazed across to the small wooden ships that plied the Inland Sea against a backdrop of islands and mountains scattered haphazardly across the horizon.

He breathed an inward sigh of relief that he was one of the even numbers in the roll call of his class. The odd-numbered pupils were on duty that day, constructing firebreaks between the rows of wooden houses. Each day the rota alternated between the even and odd numbers. It was hard, back-breaking work, particularly in midsummer. It had been going on for several months, because there were rumours that the foreign devils were to mount air attacks.

But none had come. Some pupils, echoing their parents, complained that the destruction of houses to make room for the breaks was unnecessary – not within earshot of the older boys and the teachers, of course. But Yoshitaka thought that any precaution which could save lives was surely necessary. The homes of Hiroshima, like those almost everywhere else in Japan, were simple wooden structures: a widespread fire would lead to disaster. The teachers said building the firebreaks would mean that a bomb explosion would be a small, contained affair which might burn down a few houses but would not become a general conflagration. The firebreaks were just shallow trenches. Yoshitaka had wondered whether burning material might be swept by the wind from one house to another across the trenches. But there was no wind that day in Hiroshima, and the weather would bring none.

What was Colonel Tibbets thinking about as the Enola Gay climbed the last few thousand feet to its bombing-run height of 30,000 feet? He was a cool-headed man. There is a sense of both detachment and vulnerability about all aerial warfare, which had only been in existence for some thirty years. The detachment lies in the remoteness of the successful air warrior from his victims. Provided the mission is successful, the bomber is as removed from the damage he inflicts as it is possible to be: he sees no carnage, no destruction, no enemy faces, no consequences of his action. Ideally, his war experience is limited to the ground crews on take-off, his own crew in the air, any technical problems that might be associated with the flight, any enemy attack he may come under either from the ground or from the air, the problem of locating his target, and returning safely to base. If unsuccessful, he may face the awesome psychological shock of being blasted from his aircraft just hours away from the comfort of his base to, at best, the harshness of life as a prisoner-of-war or, at worst, death.

Tibbets, a sensitive man, must have been aware of the extent of the destruction he would be responsible for if the mission were successful (although military planners believed that the bomb would cause at most 20,000 deaths – a fraction of the eventual total). He had been chosen for his strength of character. He must have believed, absolutely, in the rightness of his cause. In those last few minutes, any moral doubts were redundant.

So much that could have gone wrong had not. The processes of testing the bomb, picking his team and equipping his aircraft had been accelerated because of the nature of the venture. News of the project his team was engaged upon could easily have leaked out. Some of the scientists on the project had developed qualms of conscience, and sought the intercession of President Roosevelt. Jealous service rivals had tried to get Tibbets's elite air squad disbanded. All these attempts had failed.

Above all, the bomb – dubbed Little Boy by the aircrew – had been loaded without mishap, and the aircraft had taken off. Tibbets remembered how nerve-racking that had been. At 3.30 p.m. on the afternoon of 5 August, the bomb had been loaded onto a trolley, draped with a tarpaulin, and set on a tractor, accompanied by seven military policemen and seven project engineers. Jeeps of MPs preceded and followed the steel cylinder, like the cortège at a military funeral. On reaching the Enola Gay, Little Boy was lowered into a pit, over which the plane was wheeled, then wound up into the bomb bay.

Nearly ten hours later, in darkness, the crew of the flight found themselves running the gauntlet of film crews specially brought over for the occasion by Washington. The captain of the flight, Robert Lewis, made a brief, unemotional speech to his men on the tarmac: 'You guys, this bomb cost more than an aircraft carrier. Don't screw it up. We've got it made, we're gonna win the war, just don't screw it up. Let's do this really great.'

At 2.20 a.m. the crew climbed aboard. Tibbets's greatest fear was that the aircraft would emulate many others in recent missions and crash on take-off in which case 'with this bomb we would lose the whole island'. With its four runways, Tinian Atoll in the Marianas, recaptured from the Japanese, was now the world's largest operational airfield. Little Boy presented a special problem: it was incredibly heavy. The aircraft itself weighed 65 tons and had 7000 gallons of fuel on board; with a twelve-man crew and the bomb as well, it was some 15,000 pounds overloaded. At 2.54 a.m. the plane started to move down the runway. Tibbets's tactic was to build up all possible speed before lifting off. With extraordinary coolness, he refused to open the throttle until the plane had virtually run out of runway. If it did not respond instantly, disaster would have struck. But it rose slowly and smoothly into the air.

Now, so near the target after a long and uneventful flight, so much could still go wrong before the drop. The Japanese might take action; the break in the clouds might have gone; the bomb mechanism could develop a fault. Tibbets knew the dangers, but the greatest – that of crashing on take-off – was already past.

Dr C.R.B. Richards, a British army medical officer, worked in a camp alongside the South Burma Death Railway, on which some 27 per cent of forcibly conscripted prisoners-of-war and nearly half the Asian labourers died. With spades and picks, the workers were forced to remove some three million cubic yards of earth and 230,000 cubic yards of rock. The railway, built to convey Japanese troops to the Burma front and to carry tungsten for use in Japanese munitions, was abandoned and became overgrown after the war.

Dr Richards remembers that camp policy was 'no work, no food'. The camp commander dispatched the malnourished to the hospital, where there was no treatment available. 'I can imagine nothing more appalling than the conditions under which these men lived and died,' Richards later said. 'It was in effect a "living morgue".'

In the camp itself, 'troops were billeted in huts which had been evacuated the previous day on account of cholera deaths. Coolies walked through the huts, spat, defecated and vomited everywhere . . . At Upper Sonkurai camp the latrines were flooded by incessant rain. One of them had broken its bank and a filthy stream oozed through the camp area and passed under the floor of the huts occupied by the hospital . . . The men had nothing to wear except the clothing in which they were captured, and most of that had rotted or perished during the months of the monsoon.' Allied officers who complained were shouted at, insulted, and on occasion beaten with bamboo switches. When a job required more men, Japanese guards would go through the hospital, driving out with sticks anyone who could stand.

Some 3000 of the men in this camp were brought by rail from Singapore to Thailand in trains with 'either non-existent or revolting sanitary facilities'. From the station in Thailand, the prisoners were marched through the jungle in the dark, and severely beaten along the way. Once in the camp they were worked between twelve and twenty hours a day – whenever the rains made it possible. They lived off a little rice and a few bits of fish every day; this was reduced by a third for anyone who fell ill. There were no holidays of any kind.

The target date for finishing the railway was the end of August. A camp survivor said that he had 'gained the impression that everything was to be subordinated to the completion of the line by the end of August, and when this was not fulfilled [the Japanese] became insane with rage'. This officer had been told that 'there was no use quoting the articles of the Geneva convention'.

Disease abounded amid the suffering and squalor. Beriberi, cholera, malaria and dysentery were the commonest illnesses. A British doctor, Major B. L. W. Clarke, remembered afterwards that, at Chungkai Sick Camp, 1400 prisoners out of 8000 had died. He alleges that operations were carried out without anaesthetic or surgical instruments. When five Japanese doctors visited the camp and saw an operation, one fainted and another was sick.

Sungkrai Number Two camp was known as Death Valley. The prisoners lived in huts with dirt floors which turned to deep mud during the rainy season. The hospital was a similar hut, unlit, where those who died at night were not removed until daybreak. Once, thirty-eight cholera victims were left out in the rain for two days before burial. At Tamarkan Camp, a British officer who had acted as an interpreter was beaten and placed in a trench containing six inches of rainwater, infested with mosquitoes. After being threatened with further torture, he tried to commit suicide. He was insane at the end of the war.

In another camp a man with beriberi contracted a kind of elephantiasis that caused his testicles to swell to such a size that he had to carry them in his hands to walk. The Japanese were vastly amused, making him the favourite butt of their jokes before he died in excruciating pain.

Yet the treatment of allied POWs was mild compared with that of Asian slave workers. Indonesians suffering from cholera were often pushed into common graves and buried alive. The healthy among them were regularly beaten, while the women were raped and insulted. One Japanese doctor would beat anyone suspected of having cholera. On another occasion disinfectant was sprayed into the eyes of coolies. 'Coolies are subhuman and not worthy of consideration,' a Japanese doctor explained to a group of Western POWs. Asian labourers in one camp who were unfit for work were injected with a red fluid and died within minutes. At another camp, sick labourers were offered sugar from a tin and died in agony later the same day.

No new clothes were given to the Asians, whose own fell apart and were soon crawling with vermin. Many suffered from virulent skin diseases. Sacks were offered as clothes and blankets for those whose clothes had disintegrated. Apart from burying cholera victims alive, the Japanese would seek to contain epidemics by burning not just the dead but some of the cases considered incurable. 'There are many authentic cases of live cremations,' one witness told the Tokyo war crimes tribunal after the war.

Cases of pure sadism abounded in the Burma railway camps. At Kanburi Number Two Coolie Hospital, according to one witness, 'coolies were kept standing for hours with weights tied to their penises', seemingly for the amusement of the guards. At Kinsayoke Checking Station, coolies being examined for dysentery were 'one after the other kicked violently by the Japanese medical officers'. At Niki Camp, members of a Japanese hygiene unit 'would, during routine examinations, insert glass rods into the vaginas of Chinese women'. At Upper Concuita Camp, 'sick coolies were used for judo practice and thrown over the shoulders of Japanese'. At the same camp, fifty to sixty Asian workers were killed with injections of morphia and potassium permanganate.

On their way to these cesspits of slavery and death, prisoners were forced to travel aboard hellships in which they were kept below deck, without sanitation and on short rations, and were beaten regularly. For example, 1900 American prisoners were confined to the holds of the *Tottori Maru*, a freighter making the journey from Manila to Japan. They were packed together so tightly that a third of them always had to stand. Dysentery was rife because of the filthy food, but there were only six latrines. Many slept in their own filth.

A former prisoner recalls his experience in September 1944 aboard a 5000-ton cargo ship carrying 1750 European POWs, mostly Dutch, 600 Indonesians, and 5500 Javanese labourers. 'We were beaten into the hold . . . crammed together standing upright, since lying down or even sitting was impossible.' The ship was torpedoed off Sumatra and sank in twenty minutes. The few prisoners who survived tried to make for the Japanese lifeboats, 'but instead of taking them in, one of the Japanese chopped off their hands or split their skulls with a huge axe.' The survivors were eventually rescued by a Japanese ship; there were just 276 Europeans, 312 Indonesians and 300 Javanese left.

The town of Potsdam outside Berlin is small, bourgeois and pleasant, endowed with a superb baroque villa, the Sans-Souci Palace, and a comfortable, staid conference centre. In July the weather had been warm and agreeable. As limousines shuttled between Harry Truman's three-floor stucco residence, Winston Churchill's comfortable house and Josef Stalin's fine villa, it was hard to believe that a war which had taken millions of lives had raged all around them and ended just two months before.

On the morning of 17 July, Truman had enjoyed an ample breakfast when a convoy of cars arrived outside his residence. There emerged possibly the most famous living face in the world, a short, plump, genial, boyishly energetic sixty-nine-year-old, Winston Churchill, to pay his respects for the first time to the new American president. Truman had been advised to treat Churchill warily: the British leader, according to the president's advisers, had enormous charm, but was a die-hard reactionary whose main war aim was to restore the status of the British Empire; indeed, Truman had heard from his staff more criticism of Churchill than of Stalin, whom the Americans regarded vaguely as 'a hard nut to crack' but not a particularly sinister figure. The president's advisers had been far more concerned with breaking the stranglehold of British imperialism than with any threat posed by the Soviet Union.

To both their surprises, the plain-spoken Missourian found himself getting along famously with the bluff aristocratic imperialist, who was equally blunt and, rather than using his wartime experience to patronize the inexperienced American, tended to seek and agree with his views. Churchill, desperately frustrated by the way Roosevelt had ignored his concerns about Stalin at Yalta, was keen to recruit the new president to his side. American thinking on the dangers posed by the Russians had evolved just a little since Yalta. Truman was gratified by the way Churchill listened to him. Stalin, who had suffered a minor heart attack, was a day late in arriving at the conference.

After the British prime minister departed, Truman toured the ruins of Berlin, a city reduced virtually to rubble. Later he recalled, rather flatly, that he had seen 'a demonstration of what can happen when a man overreaches himself'.

When the president returned to his villa, Stimson, the secretary for war, was waiting to hand him a telegram from the Pentagon. It read, employing an obvious and tasteless code, 'Operated on this morning. Diagnosis not yet complete but results seem satisfactory and already exceed expectations. Local press release necessary as interest extends great distance. Dr Groves pleased. He returns tomorrow. I will keep you posted.'

Truman replied, 'I send my warmest congratulations to the doctor and his consultant.'

Four days later he received a full eyewitness report from the Manhattan's Project director, General Groves. The world's first testing of an atomic bomb had taken place before dawn on the morning of 16 July at Alamogordo, New Mexico, one of the remotest desert locations. It was cold, and occasional shafts of lightning lit up the desolate eeriness of the place. There were over four hundred people present, most of them around 20 miles away. At 5.25 a.m. the observers lay face down in trenches. Groves was near the scientific director of the project, J. Robert Oppenheimer.

Ten seconds from the intended blast, a green flare shot up; five seconds later, another followed. At 5.30 precisely the words, 'I am become death, the destroyer of worlds,' from a sacred Hindu text, flickered into Oppenheimer's mind as he viewed the first atomic detonation in history.

The *New York Times* observer was to describe the scene later: 'A light not of this world, the light of many suns in one' struck the surrounding hills.

It was a sunrise such as the world had never seen, a great green super-sun climbing in a fraction of a second to a height more than 8000 feet, rising ever higher until it touched the clouds, lighting up earth and sky and all around with dazzling luminosity. Up it went, a great ball of fire about a mile in diameter, changing colors as it kept shooting upwards, from deep purple to orange, expanding, growing bigger, rising as it was expanding, an elemental force freed from its bonds after being chained for billions of years. For a fleeting instant the color was unearthly green, such as one only sees in the corona of the sun during a total eclipse. It was as though the earth had opened and the skies had split. One felt as though he had been privileged to witness the Birth of the World – to be present at the moment of Creation when the Lord said, 'Let there be Light'.

Subsequently, many were to argue that what had been witnessed was the first glimpse of the end of the world.

The explosion had produced a temperature of 100 million degrees Fahrenheit, over three times that at the centre of the sun, and ten thousand times the sun's surface temperature. The light had been brighter than a thousand suns. All life within a mile of the focus of the explosion had been killed; the soil had turned into a white-hot saucer 500 yards in diameter. The scaffolding by the bomb had been vaporized. The billowing nuclear cloud had plumed 40,000 feet into the air; thirty seconds after the explosion, a hurricane-force wind tore through the camp where most of the observers were, followed by a deafening roar. When peace returned, the scientists ran out of their bunkers, dancing and whooping with joy.

When Stimson had finished reading Groves's report to Truman, the president grinned. He had, he said later, 'an entirely new feeling of confidence'. The following day he was told that the bomb would be ready for use by early August. Truman was delighted and calmed after days of increasing restlessness listening to 'endless debates on matters that could not be settled between Churchill and Stalin'. Stimson also showed the report to the British prime minister, and told him that Stalin would be informed of the existence of the bomb without being apprised of details.

Later that day Churchill and Truman met. The British leader told the president that in his view the bomb was 'a miracle of deliverance'. He listed four reasons: it might make the invasion of the Japanese mainland unnecessary; it might end the war 'in one or two violent shocks'; it could – and in this Churchill showed extraordinary perceptiveness – save Japanese honour; and it would avert the need to ask Stalin for help in subduing Japan. Churchill's views complemented Truman's own. The inevitable could be stopped now only by a rare outbreak of good sense on the part of Japan's government.

As he climbed down the iron steps of his railway carriage onto the platform of Hiroshima Station, Yoshitaka Kawamoto was delighted to see Wada, one of his friends. They laughed and chatted, grabbing at each other's satchels as they fell into line together for the short walk to the school. They passed the entrance of the girls' school, speeding up as they went – any boy caught pausing there would get into terrible trouble. The system was strictly segregated, and any contact with the opposite sex except under regulated school or parental supervision was severely punished.

Minutes later, they reached the school, just in time for morning assembly at 8 o'clock. Wada was in a different class, and they exchanged 'see yous' as they joined the ranks of students dictated by grade and seniority standing before the headmaser. As always, they were exhorted to work hard and strive harder for their emperor, the homeland and the war effort. The headmaster told them that the all-clear had been sounded after the air-raid warning of nearly an hour before. Yoshitaka, like many others, had been on the train and not heard it. None of the boys took much notice: air-raid warnings were common occurrences, but nothing ever happened. He had heard older people talking about the fearsome damage inflicted by air raids on Tokyo, but the capital was a long way away.

As the headmaster spoke on the assembly ground outside the school, a single drone could be heard. The eyes of the boys followed the small speck that they knew to be an enemy aircraft. The sky was blue above, although there was cloud in the distance. The tiny insect moving across their field of view was far more compelling, more hypnotic than the headmaster's exhortations. No air-raid alarm sounded, which was curious, but what possible harm could a single aircraft do? It was obviously a reconnaissance plane, and much too high for anti-aircraft fire, of which there was none.

The pupils were divided into two groups, the odd-numbered classmates marching off to join the firebreak construction teams, the even-numbered ones entering the school building. There were forty-nine pupils in Yoshitaka's class, in a long, low room with a single window. A blackboard and teacher's desk stood at one end. The thirteen-year-old took his place standing by his desk, until ordered to sit by the 'elder student' – the senior prefect in charge of the class. He was an odious youth, extremely tough and stern, who would hit virtually every member of the class in a sadistic fury at least once a day, waiting for each to make the mistake or display the minor insubordination they inevitably would.

He ordered them to perform the silent Shinto tribute that was the prelude to lessons every day. Yoshitaka closed his eyes, along with all his classmates, apparently in prayer, but wondering what had happened to that reconnaissance plane that had passed overhead.

The boy thought he heard a noise, the insistent rising and falling hum of an aircraft. He tensed; he heard the prefect telling them to remain with their eyes closed until he returned, and heard the scraping of a chair as the tyrannical senior rose to leave the room – almost certainly to go to the lavatory. Yoshitaka's desk was right in the centre of the classroom, with a row of desks on either side. The window was towards the front.

He opened his eyes, which he had been forbidden to do. If the senior came back quickly – as well he might, he could be setting them up – Yoshitaka would surely be struck severely. A friend near the window called out to him in a quiet voice, so that the rest of the class would not hear, that he could see a B-29. Yoshitaka was excited, craning his head to see the rectangle of sky visible from the window. Other boys were looking too. He rose from his seat to get a better view.

At least 131,000 murders by the Japanese in the Philippines during the occupation between 1942 and 1945 were accounted for by the Tokyo war crimes tribunal. The real figure was almost certainly many times higher. The Philippine counsel at the trial, Pedro Lopez, claimed in his opening statement that for the 'hundreds [who] suffered slow and painful death in dark, foul and lice-infested cells ... the quick, scientific mass extermination in the lethal gas chambers at Camp Dachau would have been a welcome alternative'.

Lopez listed an appalling catalogue: Lucas Doctolero was crucified, nails being driven through his hands, feet and skull, on 18 September 1943. A blind woman was dragged from her home on 17 November, stripped naked and hanged. In Manila, 800 men, women and children at St Paul's College were machine-gunned. At Calamba, 2500 people were bayoneted or shot dead. At Ponson in the south, 100 people were bayoneted inside a church while 200 outside were hunted down like game and killed. At Matina Pangi, 169 villagers were lined up and bayoneted or shot. A Japanese directive commanded, 'When killing Filipinos assemble them together in one place as far as possible, thereby saving ammunition and labour.' Getting rid of the bodies was 'troublesome'. Two recommended solutions were to 'throw them in a river or put them in a house and blow it up'.

For seven days in April and May 1942, 76,000 American and Filipino troops from Bataan and Corregidor were marched 120 kilometres to POW camps. Some 10,000 died. American Staff Sergeant Samuel Moody said that the only food they received on the march were the stalks of sugar-cane they grabbed from the side of the road or the morsels thrown at them by Filipinos. They drank from the water-holes of animals and from ditches. 'We were beaten. The men were bayoneted, stabbed; they were kicked with hobnail boots ... If any man lagged to the rear of the road, fell off to the side, he was immediately bayoneted and beaten.' Bodies littered the road. 'I saw many dead men, many of whom were my friends. I also saw two dead women, one of whom was pregnant. Many times I could look ahead and see my friends stabbed and beaten. Quite often I could hear the groans of men behind me that had received beatings from someone in the rear.'

On 26 July 1945, Japan was given its last chance. In the names of President Truman and the British and Chinese governments – Stalin had been deliberately excluded – the Potsdam Declaration was issued. The main points were, first, a threat:

> The result of the futile, senseless German resistance to the might of the aroused free peoples of the world stands forth in awful clarity as an example to the people of Japan. The might that now converges on Japan is immeasurably greater than that which, when applied to the resisting Nazis, necessarily laid waste to the lands, industry and the methods of life of the whole German people. The full application of our military power, backed by our resolve, will mean the inevitable and complete destruction of the Japanese armed forces and just as inevitably the utter devastation of the Japanese homeland.

Second, there was an offer:

> The time has come for Japan to decide whether she will continue to be controlled by those self-willed militaristic advisers whose unintelligent calculations have brought the Empire of Japan to the threshold of annihilation, or whether she will follow the path of reason.

The conditions followed:

> The following are our terms. We will not deviate from them. There are no alternatives. We shall brook no delay.
>
> There must be eliminated for all time the authority and influence of those who have deceived and misled the people of Japan into embarking on world conquest, for we insist that a new order of peace, security and justice will be impossible until irresponsible militarism is driven from the world;
>
> Until such a new order is established and until there is convincing proof that Japan's war-making power is destroyed, points in Japanese territory to be designated by the Allies shall be occupied to secure the achievement of the basic objectives we are here setting forth;

We do not intend that the Japanese shall be enslaved as a race or destroyed as a nation, but stern justice shall be meted out to all war criminals, including those who have visited cruelties upon our prisoners. The Japanese government shall remove all obstacles to the revival and strengthening of democratic tendencies among the Japanese people. Freedom of speech, of religion and of thought, as well as respect for the fundamental human rights shall be established.

The occupying forces of the Allies shall be withdrawn from Japan as soon as these objectives have been accomplished and there has been established in accordance with the freely expressed will of the Japanese people a peacefully inclined and responsible government.

In furtherance of these aims, the Declaration called for the immediate surrender of all Japanese armed forces – 'The alternative for Japan is prompt and utter destruction.' The declaration reflected some of the infighting between Stimson, the veteran who felt his views were being bypassed, and the new secretary of state, James F. Byrnes, a Democratic Party power broker with little experience of foreign affairs.

As such the document was badly flawed, perhaps fatally so. There was no mention in it of the *sine qua non* for a Japanese surrender: maintenance of the imperial system. Stimson had favoured this, but Byrnes, in deference to American public opinion – two-thirds of which favoured Hirohito's arrest or execution, according to a Gallup poll – was opposed. Stimson, his personal aide, Ambassador Averell Harriman, and Britain's new Labour foreign secretary, Ernest Bevin, all believed, in the latter's words, that 'the emperor was the institution through which one might have to deal to effectively control Japan'.

Truman was more simple-minded: at a party aboard his ship on the return journey, he was exhilarated by the testing of the bomb. America, he said, had 'developed a revolutionary new weapon of such force and nature that we do not need the Russians or any other nation'. The bomb was acquiring an unstoppable momentum. For hard-line Japanese, however, the absence of any reference to the emperor suggested that his office might indeed be abolished – although the more perceptive realized that the omission and reference to the 'freely expressed will of the Japanese people' was an indication that he would be allowed to continue.

The second flaw was the cavalier attitude adopted towards the Russians. Certainly, it seemed like the answer to a prayer for the Americans to be able to contemplate the defeat of Japan without having to ask the Russians for help in opening up a second front to attack Japan from the north. Yet the United States had already begun quietly to encourage the Russians to prepare for the possibility of intervention, in case the option of the bomb was not available in time. The Russians were hardly unjustified in being resentful and suspicious at the way the Americans had behaved, however richly Stalin deserved it for his high-handedness at Yalta.

Finally, the Declaration made no reference to the bomb itself. An obsession with security was partly responsible; the fear of looking ridiculous if the bomb should fail to work was another cause. The Americans were also concerned that they would not be believed if they inserted such a warning. Yet Japanese intelligence was already vaguely aware of the American work on the bomb. While the Japanese would probably have publicly dismissed its existence, privately they might have paused for thought. Certainly, 'prompt and utter destruction' was too vague a euphemism even to hint at the bomb's existence, and was taken to refer to the saturation bombing of Tokyo and other cities.

President Truman had thus made mistakes which compounded the tragedy that followed. The bulk of the blame though, must be ascribed to the Japanese: they missed their chance. As soon as the terms of the Declaration reached Tokyo, they had been delivered by the foreign minister, Shigenori Togo, to the emperor. Hirohito read the Declaration slowly, asking questions. Togo agreed with the emperor that on certain key points the terms marked a substantial climbdown from the 'unconditional surrender' requested in the Cairo Declaration issued by Roosevelt. Hirohito asked whether the terms 'were the most reasonable to be expected in the circumstances'.

Togo agreed that they were: 'in principle they are acceptable'. If that had been the end of it, peace would surely have been achieved and Hiroshima and Nagasaki spared. But at that stage the emperor was not in charge. The cabinet had met earlier and the prime minister, Kantaro Suzuki, a member of the imperial household elite, had decided to prevaricate, probably in the forlorn hope that the Russians would mediate with the Americans. A day later, at a press conference, Suzuki said the government would *mokusatsu* the declaration – meaning that they would 'treat it with silent contempt', 'ignore it', 'kill it with silence'. Suzuki was responding to an officially promoted journalist's question and reading from a prepared text. He had unwittingly pronounced the death sentence on Hiroshima and Nagasaki.

Stimson, in Potsdam, gave the Allies' response: 'In the face of this rejection, we could only proceed to demonstrate that the ultimatum had meant exactly what it said. For such a purpose the atomic bomb was an eminently suitable weapon.'

Harry Truman was famous for the sign on his desk, 'The buck stops here': he alone was responsible for the ultimate decisions. The choice to drop the bomb was the product of multiple complex pressures, arguments, and influences in dynamic tension with one another. Unusually, one of the biggest factors in the process that had led an American President to consider whether a new weapon of such lethal power should be dropped on a centre of population was a name that was to become a byword for American courage and Japanese self-sacrifice: Okinawa. But for the struggle for the island between 1 April and 22 June 1945, the bomb would almost certainly not have been used. Okinawa represented the climax of Japan's policy of intensive resistance to American attack.

Over a year before, in mid-June 1944, the Americans had landed at the island of Saipan in the Marianas. Tokyo, 1300 miles away, came within American bombing range for the first time. By October the Americans had reached the Philippines. There, painfully slow progress was made against Japanese resistance, with Manila falling only in March, and fighting in outlying areas continuing long after that.

In February 1945 the Americans had attacked Iwo Jima – just eight square miles of land. Its importance was to be in providing an emergency landing point for crippled American bombers, 900 miles from Tokyo; the fate of captured airmen in Japanese hands was not calculated to boost the morale of the raiders. The 23,000 Japanese there fought to the last man, inflicting over 20,000 casualties on the Americans and holding up their progress for a month.

At Okinawa the resistance was if anything more intense. The island's significance was that it would be the ideal forward base for invading Japan. Of the Ryukyu Island group, only Okinawa had enough airfields and natural anchorages for the massive concentration of ground forces needed to take the mainland. Okinawa had three-lane airstrips at Naha, Yontan and Kadena, and two smaller ones at Yonabaru and Machinato. There were two fine anchorages on the east side of the island. The Japanese were determined not to give up such a prize lightly. Although they were eventually defeated in the face of overwhelming American superiority, it was at such a cost that the defenders considered it a victory.

The defending force had achieved the aim of considerably delaying the Americans and showing them how costly an invasion of the mainland would be. At that point the purpose of Japan's army commanders was to compel the Americans to abandon their goal of unconditional surrender and negotiate a peace. The kind of carnage that would result from an invasion of the Japanese mainland would, in the view of the commanders, force the Americans to the negotiating table. Japan's leaders were often portrayed as insane fanatics determined to fight to the finish. Yet their objective was not entirely unrealistic. There may have been a point at which the casualties inflicted on the Americans may have forced them to start compromising.

Okinawa rammed the message home. Altogether, the Americans suffered around 20,000 deaths and 53,000 wounded, as well as 26,000 non-battle casualties. No fewer than 763 aircraft were lost and 368 ships knocked out, of which 38 were sunk. The Japanese losses were immense, of course: more than 100,000 dead, and 7800 planes and 16 ships destroyed. Many of their aircraft were lost in kamikaze attacks on American ships. (Kamikaze does not mean suicide, but 'divine wind', a reference to the sudden typhoons that destroyed the last attempted invasions of Japan from the sea, those of the Mongols.) There were more than 1900 such attacks from Japanese aircraft. The large majority failed: some pilots got cold feet, many were shot down, many attacked the first ships they saw – usually minor vessels. The Ohka piloted bomb proved a flop because the aircraft carrying them were sitting targets; the Shinyo suicide speedboats also proved relatively easy to intercept.

Japanese infantry tactics proved to be brilliantly co-ordinated. Okinawa's rocky, rugged terrain turned out to be ideal for defence, and the Japanese made the most of the opportunity: they brought to bear the greatest concentration of artillery encountered by the Americans throughout the Pacific War. A huge network of caves and underground passages provided shelter against the Allied naval and aerial barrage, and gave the advantages of flexibility and surprise. A pattern of the fighting was for the advancing Americans to come under artillery attack, while the Japanese sheltered underground from the bombardment. Then, as the American infantry advanced over exposed ridges, the Japanese would come out of their caves and tunnels and open fire from heavily fortified positions.

The fight for Okinawa would almost certainly have taken a considerably higher toll but for two blunders by the Japanese. Under pressure from Tokyo for a success, the Japanese commander, General Ushijima, launched a disastrous counter-offensive against superior forces which considerably weakened his 32nd Army. A second offensive, this time at the instigation of his chief of staff, Lieutenant-General Cho, who believed that the spiritual superiority of the Japanese army would cause American resistance to crumble, fatally debilitated the Japanese forces. By mid-June large numbers of Japanese were for the first time surrendering, although Ushijima and Cho took their own lives in the classic manner.

The Japanese force at Okinawa had been 110,000 strong. In March 1945 preparations began in Japan for the defence of the mainland – Operation Ketsu-go. It assumed that the Americans would invade Japan's southern island of Kyushu with fifteen divisions in October (in fact America's planned Operation Olympic called for ten divisions to arrive in November). Under Ketsu-go it was intended to muster no fewer than fifty-eight infantry divisions, made up of 2,600,000 from the regular army, backed up by 3,650,000 reservists and a volunteer militia of 28 million. Obviously, not just the militia and reservists but also much of the regular army was poorly trained and ill-equipped. But after Okinawa's 110,000 had shown what they could do, the prospect of an invasion of Japan, and the likely resistance and casualties, was awesome.

At 9.30 a.m. on 16 June, the joint chiefs of staff arrived at the White House to give President Truman the results of a two-day appraisal of the task of invading Japan. General George Marshall outlined the plan for the first attack, Operation Olympic, to go in on 1 November 1945 with 816,000 troops; this would be followed by an invasion of Honshu around Tokyo with 1,172,000 men on 1 March 1946. Stimson told Truman that 'a landing operation would be a very big, costly and arduous struggle on our part . . . The terrain, much of which I have visited several times, has left the impression on my memory of being one which would be susceptible to a last-ditch defence.' The sombre warning given by the chiefs of staff was that a million American lives were likely to be lost in the operation.

A month later, Truman was given an even more dire message by General Douglas MacArthur, the head of American Forces in the

Far East, who was unaware at this stage of the existence of the bomb. He warned that the Japanese could resort to guerrilla warfare in the event of an invasion and that a campaign might last ten years. No estimate of the extent of American casualties could be given; nor was any made of the likely number of Japanese dead and wounded, either by MacArthur or by the Joint Chiefs of Staff. But air raids on Japanese cities had already taken some 700,000 lives before August 1945. Military casualties could be reckoned at upwards of a million, with civilian casualties a multiple of that.

As the Enola Gay reached the initial point, already overflown by the Straight Flush, Tibbets, now piloting the aircraft again, knew they had only three minutes to get to the target. The easy part would be evading any Japanese anti-aircraft fire, finding the target and dropping the bomb. The difficult part would be surviving it. No one could predict how serious the shock waves from Little Boy would be at 30,000 feet. In the plane, Tibbets alone knew of a conversation he had had nearly a year earlier with Oppenheimer, the father of the bomb. The scientist had told him baldly, 'Colonel, your biggest problem may be after the bomb has left your aircraft. The shock waves from the detonation could crush your plane. I am afraid that I can give you no guarantee that you will survive.' His aircraft's most intensive practice had been in executing the turn necessary for a quick getaway, which would be as sharp as safe flying permitted.

With a minute to go, Tibbets ordered 'on glasses'. Nine members of the twelve-man crew put on the thick polaroid glasses they had been issued with to protect their eyes from the nuclear flash. Tibbets, Major Thomas Ferebee, the chief bombardier, and Jacob Beser, the radio officer, kept theirs off in order to do their jobs. They seemed home, they were coming over Hiroshima. 'Stand by for the tone break and the turn,' said Tibbets. Ferebee's bomb aligner focused on the Aioi Bridge, the aiming point. 'I've got it,' said the bombardier, turning on the automatic synchronizer for dropping Little Boy, which let out a low-pitched hum, the 'tone break'.

The die was cast. Little Boy could not be stopped now. At seven seconds past 8.15 a.m. the bomb doors opened and it fell off the retaining hook. The aircraft leapt up 10 feet after shedding its 9000 pound load. Ferebee shouted, 'Bomb away,' and saw it fall. Tibbets rammed the Enola Gay into the right-hand turn he had practised. The crew members were pinioned to their seats by the violence of the movement. Forty seconds later, at 8.16 a.m. Little Boy detonated

890 feet above the ground, just 800 feet from the target bridge, over a clinic.

When Yoshitaka Kawamoto rose from his desk to get a better view of the B-29, most of his friends had their eyes closed in silent tribute, expecting the ruthless class senior to return any minute. An instant later, looking out of the window, Yoshitaka saw 'a pale, intense light, which was bluish in colour'. This eerie experience lasted a full two or three seconds. Yoshitaka remembers hearing nothing. The pressure from the bomb hurled him to the ground. His seated companions were not so lucky: their legs were doubled up and crushed beneath them where they sat.

When Yoshitaka woke up, he couldn't see anything at all. He was in pain, with something very heavy pressing upon him, holding him down. He became aware of the pitiful sound of ten or so injured children singing. He joined in. The boys had been rigorously forbidden to shout things like 'Help me' or 'Save me' in an emergency, so they sang the school song instead. They wanted to alert those outside the collapsed building to the fact that they were still alive. Yoshitaka thought there had been a gas explosion.

One by one, the voices stopped. It became more and more quiet, until only Yoshitaka's voice was left. 'When I realized that I was the only one left singing the school song,' he later told the author, 'you cannot imagine my terror.' At the exact instant of the first explosion, a fireball 84 feet wide formed around a core millions of degrees in intensity. From the Enola Gay, Tibbets said he could savour the brilliance of the explosion. 'It tasted like lead.'

Bob Caron, in his tail gun, blinked at the flash, then opened his eyes and, in his words, took 'a peep into hell'. He observed a huge mass of compressed air that could actually be seen rushing outwards and upwards at the speed of sound towards the aircraft. It looked like 'the ring of some distant planet had loosed itself and was coming up towards us'. The mass of air suddenly caught the plane with a roaring explosion, which Tibbets at first assumed was a direct hit from a Japanese anti-aircraft battery. The plane bounced and jumped violently. Caron yelled, as he saw another circular mass of air accelerating towards the aircraft. 'There's another one coming!' Again the plane was violently shaken.

Tibbets, wrestling with the controls, was calm now. He understood what had happened. 'That was the reflected aftershock, bounced back from the ground,' he told the crew. 'There won't be any more.' The plane had settled, and Tibbets realized they had survived the forces which the scientists had been unable to guarantee would not destroy the plane.

Caron described the awesome sight from his rear turret as the plane moved away. He saw

> a column of smoke rising, rising fast. It has a fiery red core. A bubbling mass, purple-gray in color, within that red core. It's turbulent. Fires are springing up everywhere, like flames shooting out of a huge bed of coals. I am starting to count the fires. One, two, three, four, five, six . . . fourteen, fifteen . . . It's impossible. There are too many to count. Here it comes, the mushroom shape that Captain Parsons spoke about. It's coming this way. It's like a mass of bubbling molasses. The mushroom is spreading out. It's maybe a mile or two wide and half a mile high. It's growing up and up. It's maybe level with us and climbing. It's very black, but there is a purplish tint to the cloud. The base of the mushroom looks like a heavy undercast that is shot through with flames. The city must be below that. The flames and smoke are billowing out, whirling into the foothills. The hills are disappearing under the smoke. All I can see now of the city is the main dock and what looks like an airfield. That is still visible. There are planes down there.

Gradually smoke seemed to be entering the confined space in which he was pinned down in the rubble of the school, and Yoshitaka felt he was stiffening. He understood that the building had been flattened; he knew he was in danger. With a desperate burst of strength, he managed to lift himself out of the debris, pushing aside the rubble. He was in the open air. As he rose, he saw incalculable devastation around him. Above, a huge cumulo-nimbus cloud hung over the city.

Like all the other children of his class, Yoshitaka had been taught an emergency drill. Don't run away, he had been instructed, check for serious injuries first. He found that a piece of wood was stuck in his left arm, which was bleeding. He tried to stem the flow with a rough tourniquet torn from his shirt. His front teeth were bleeding – four of them broken. He was covered in scratches.

The boy stared at the neighbouring wooden buildings, many of them crushed like his school. There were fires all around, rapidly moving towards the nearby wreckage, spreading like liquid, burning the chestnut trees. Yoshitaka wanted to run, but he had been taught not to go alone, to take someone else. So he looked around him. He began to search the rubble of his school in an effort to find somebody alive.

With a start, he found his friend Wada. The boy's skull was split open and one eye had come out of its socket. He couldn't speak, although he was clearly trying to, biting his lip. Like all the other children he had a black identification tag, which he was trying to push with his chin, presumably wanting Yoshitaka to give it to his mother. The boy took it. Wada waved feebly, and Yoshitaka thought his movements were an attempt to tell him to leave immediately. The fires were now approaching. Yoshitaka didn't know where to run, but he headed for the furthest point from the fire. He looked back and saw Wada's one eye still fixed on him. They had been the same age. Yoshitaka still dreams about it.

The fleeing boy was experiencing the stuff of nightmares, a piece of hell come alive. Fires were spreading all around. Amid the smoke and the devastation people wandered, some with skin flayed from the raw and bleeding flesh of their arms and bodies hanging down grotesquely from their fingers and limbs. In the confusion Yoshitaka was surrounded by stumbling figures, shouting out that they should move towards the wind, not away; he didn't know why. As the boy began to run, agonized figures on the ground clutched at his legs and feet, grabbing them feebly. Yoshitaka had to kick them aside in order to continue. Suddenly he saw someone he recognized through the smoke: his school's deputy headmaster, pushing a cartload of injured. He followed the spectral figure with its wheelbarrow of suffering for a moment, until they were swallowed up in the smoke.

Yoshitaka's throat was burning with thirst in the intense heat. He had to drink, desperately. He saw that he had reached the Hiroshima River: he plunged into the water which was filled with a 'truly huge number of drifting bodies'. But he was past disgust: he pushed them aside to make room to stand and drink. It didn't matter, in the intense relief of the cooling water. He climbed out of the river and collapsed on the bank. He was by a bridge some three kilometres from his school.

When the boy recovered consciousness, he saw groups of survivors and relief workers stumbling through the smoke, helping the wounded. They passed him by, oblivious. He viewed the terrible injuries of the survivors, many with their skin blistered. Another cart filled with wounded people was pushed by. He tried at first to get up and help, but he was too weak. Consciousness slipped away again.

He awoke at 7 o'clock that evening in a makeshift hospital ward where the injured lay in rows on the ground. He learned later that army trucks had come through the city shortly after he lost consciousness, and a soldier called Haijan, engaged in the grisly task of sorting the living from the dead, had felt his pulse beating and had put him in a truck filled with barely moving bodies, instead of the one detailed to dispose of the dead.

On the ground about 80,000 – a quarter of the population – were killed instantly or mortally wounded, a third of them soldiers. The clinic directly beneath the blast (at the bomb's 'hypocentre') was razed to the ground, its occupants vaporized. Most of those within a one-kilometre radius died at once or within a couple of days, their skin ripped off and their internal organs severely damaged. Within two kilometres most people were badly burnt. Three or more kilometres away, the injuries were largely limited to skin burns.

The heat was such that granite surfaces within a kilometre of the hypocentre melted; bubbles formed on the surface of tiles less than 600 metres away. The bodies of several thousand soldiers were burnt into the parade ground of Hiroshima Castle; in some cases, shadow imprints of people were all that remained on the ground or on buildings. Hats were burnt into people heads, kimonos printed onto bodies. At the hypocentre itself the blast pressure was 35 tonnes per square metre. The shockwave travelled outwards at 440 metres per second – and was still powerful enough at 30,000 feet to toss a plane about like a leaf. As the column of the explosion rose, it sucked burning air into its base in a nuclear wind which roared across the largely wood-constructed city. Virtually every wooden building within a radius of two miles was burnt.

Anyone within 925 metres of the bomb received a dose of some 700 rads – about 1500 times the normal safe level of radiation – and 100 metres beyond that a dose of 400 rads, at which about half of those exposed usually die. Three-fifths of the deaths at Hiroshima were caused by burns, one-fifth by blast injuries, and one-fifth by radiation. Rescue workers coming into the city experienced residual radiation. An area 19 miles wide was also exposed to a cloudburst which lasted for two hours. The rain was contaminated and black.

Huge numbers suffered from some form of acute radiation sickness over the following five months, usually with nausea, vomiting and diarrhoea, insomnia and delirium, hair loss, internal and external bleeding, inflammation, blood diseases, and general failure of the organs. Keloids – grotesque skin growths – formed one to four months after the explosion. After 1947 leukaemia became common, reaching a peak in the 1950s. After 1960, as the incidence of leukaemia declined, other cancers among survivors increased.

A year after the explosion it was reckoned that 119,000 had died, with 31,000 seriously injured and 48,000 slightly wounded; 4000 people were missing. Some 55,000 buildings were totally burnt and 7000 destroyed by the blast itself. More than four-fifths of central Hiroshima was devastated by the explosion, reduced to a scarred atomic desert.

Yoshitaka Kawamoto's first reaction was that he was incredibly lucky to be alive. Haijan, who had saved the boy's life, passed his bed and patted him on the cheek. He was in acute pain, and desperately thirsty: his throat and mouth were scorching hot. Eventually a medical orderly came down the ward. People all around were crying out for water. As the orderly moved from bed to bed, he nodded or shook his head, permitting his patients to have water or not. Yoshitaka learned later that those the doctors thought were about to die were allowed to have water; those likely to survive were denied it. He never found out why, although the water made people vomit and probably weakened them. A soldier took pity on the boy as he pleaded for water and went to a nearby ice box, finding a piece of ice for him to suck on.

At eight o'clock Yoshitaka was examined again, and the decision was made to transfer him, along with other badly injured victims, to an uninhabited island in Hiroshima Bay. Dazed and uncomprehending, he was brought ashore to a dismal tent-city of the injured and the dying. There he lay for several days, growing weaker on the pitiful rations of food and water the injured were given. Around him, thousands died. He could only presume his end was not far off.

Weeks later, his mother reached him. Living so far from the hypocentre of the blast, she had survived it unscathed and immediately gone searching for her son. It had taken many days of touring hospitals; eventually she heard of the camps on the islands in the bay and hired a fishing boat to visit them one by one. When she found him she took him away to a house in the hills beyond Hiroshima. He was a piteous figure: ten days after the blast he had lost all of his hair; his face and body were black for three months, while he bled regularly from his nose and mouth. He vomited constantly.

For a year, Yoshitaka lay at death's door. There were no medicines and food was short. His mother sought to cure him with herbs and root extracts. Later he would claim that his mother's love 'was the medicine'. He had been incredibly fortunate – to have been just 800 metres from the hypocentre of the world's first atomic explosion and lived. He was the only one of 49 members of his class still alive forty-five years later, and one of only 4 survivors out of the 280 pupils of his school.

After the occupying forces arrived in Japan, he was astounded to see friendly soldiers from Australia and New Zealand; he had been taught that they were devils. Nearly half a century on, as director of Hiroshima's Peace Memorial Museum, he asserts that 'We have to know the experience of history – not just that of Hiroshima, but the other history of Japan's actions before and during the war. We have to understand our mistakes. We have to understand the atrocity of war.' Coming from him, the sentiment is not banal.

The story of the second bomb can be told more briefly. At 1.56 a.m. on 9 August, another B-29 called Bock's Car took off from Tinian Atoll carrying a plutonium bomb slightly more powerful than the one dropped on Hiroshima. The aircraft's usual pilot, Fred Bock, was flying an observer plane behind. In his place was Major Chuck Sweeney, a cheerful Boston Irishman, and the bombardier was Captain Kermit Beahan. The bomb, nicknamed Fat Man because of its shape, was targeted for Kokura.

Fate rolled its dice, however, and spared the city. With the bomb doors open at a height of 31,000 feet, Beahan looked for the target point – the city's arsenal. But industrial haze and smoke from a fire obscured it. 'No drop,' he shouted. Once again they flew over the target area; once again the view was obscured. Anti-aircraft fire opened up. The plane went over a third time, as Japanese fighters began to climb into the sky. Beahan could still not see the arsenal through the haze. 'No drop,' he called again.

Sweeney decided to make for the second objective – Nagasaki, Japan's historic centre of Christianity. Sweeney had only enough fuel to make a single run over the city before he returned to land on Okinawa. Puffy white clouds had moved in over Nagasaki, but a break showed the outline of the city stadium. Beahan trained his bombsight on it. Fat Man fell for forty seconds before detonating at twenty past eleven in the morning.

The hypocentre of the blast was the Urakami branch of Nagasaki prison, where 134 prisoners and wardens were vaporized. Some 30,000 people were killed instantly, and 120,000 were to die altogether. Unlike Hiroshima, only 16 per cent of the victims were involved with the war effort, and only 3 per cent were soldiers. Nagasaki was, in effect, Mitsubishi's company town: out of 1700 in its steelworks, 1000 died.

The most vivid eyewitness description of the afterblast came from Tatsuichiro Akizuki, a local doctor:

> The sky was as dark as pitch, covered with dense clouds of smoke; under that blackness, over the earth, hung a yellow-brown fog. Gradually the veiled ground became visible and the view beyond rooted me to the spot with horror.
>
> All the buildings I could see were on fire: large ones and small ones and those with straw thatched roofs. Further along the valley Urakami Church, the largest Catholic church in the East, was ablaze. The technical school, a large two-storey wooden building, was on fire, as were many houses and the distant ordnance factory. Electricity poles were wrapped in flames like so many pieces of kindling. Trees on the nearby hills were smoking, as were the leaves of sweet potatoes in the fields. To say that everything burned is not enough. It seemed as if the earth itself emitted fire and smoke, flames that writhed up and erupted from under ground. The sky was dark, the ground was scarlet and in between hung clouds of yellowish smoke. Three kinds of colour – black, yellow and scarlet – loomed ominously over the people, who ran about like so many ants seeking to escape. What had happened? Urakami Hospital had not been bombed – I understood that much, but that ocean of fire, that sky of smoke! It seemed like the end of the world.

The plight of the victims was pitiable:

> Ten or twenty minutes after the smoke had cleared outside, people began coming up the hill from the town below, crying about and groaning, 'Help me, help!' Those cries and groans seemed not to be made by human voices; they sounded unearthly, weird. About ten minutes after the explosion a big man, half-naked, holding his head between his hands, came into the yard towards me making

sounds that seemed to be dragged from the pit of his stomach. 'Got hurt sir,' he groaned; he shivered as if he were cold. 'I'm hurt.'

I stared at the strange-looking man. Then I saw it was Mr Kenjiro Tsujimoro, a market gardener and a friendly neighbour to me and the hospital. I wondered what had happened to the robust Kenjiro . . . His head and his face were whitish; his hair singed. It was because his eyelashes had been scorched away that he seemed so bleary-eyed. He was half-naked because his shirt had been burned from his back in a single flash . . .

After Mr Tsujimoro came staggering up to me, another person who looked just like him wandered into the yard. Who he was and where he had come from I had no idea. 'Help me,' he said, groaning, half-naked, holding his head between his hands. He sat down, exhausted. 'Water . . . water . . .' he whispered . . .

As time passed more and more people in a similar plight came up to the hospital – ten minutes, twenty minutes, an hour after the explosion. All were of the same appearance, sounded the same. 'I'm hurt, hurt! I'm burning! Water!' They all moaned the same lament. I shuddered. Half-naked or stark naked, they walked with strange slow steps, groaning from deep inside themselves as if they had travelled from the depths of hell. They looked whitish, their faces were like masks. I felt as if I were dreaming, watching pallid ghosts processing slowly in one direction – as in a dream I had once had in my childhood.

These ghosts came on foot uphill towards the hospital from the direction of the burning city and from the more easterly ordnance factory. Worker or student, girl or man, they walked slowly and had the same mask-like face. Each one groaned and cried for help. Their cries grew in strength as the people increased in number, sounding like something from the Buddhist scriptures, re-echoing everywhere, as if the earth itself were in pain.

To quantify human suffering and death seems obscene. To weigh one person's life is a task for God, not man. To weigh the fates of hundreds of thousands goes beyond blasphemy, it might seem. Yet for the practical purpose of reaching a decision in war, men, however inadequate, have to make such judgements all the time.

So it was with the decision to drop the bomb. At one level, anyone introducing a weapon capable of destroying the world, and of contemplating the destruction of 120,000 people at a stroke, is flouting every bound of conventional humanity. Yet if there is every reason to believe that the lives of countless more will be saved by such actions, there may be felt to be little alternative.

Such inhuman calculations are the very essence of decision-making in war, although probably no single decision has yielded so drastic a result in so short a space of time as that to drop the bomb. The politicians and generals waging war find it difficult to ascribe different moral values to different weapons. Although the bombs inflicted a particularly ghastly kind of death on many people, it is hard to suggest that the injuries were worse than those inflicted by, say, conventional ordnance or incendiaries in the 'normal' course of war.

There was much concern among the scientists who helped to perfect the new technology about its use against a country that was a long way from acquiring similar technology. Yet victory through the ages has gone to nations with more advanced weaponry. The view was taken in Washington that the development of nuclear technology was inevitable: better that responsible, democratic hands should wield it first. The technology could not be suppressed, but those that might be tempted to use it irresponsibly could be deterred.

When Truman had to make the decision whether or not to drop the bomb, he was doing so in the harshest circumstances possible: a world at war. However agonizing the decision, it would be hard to find a more clear-cut rationale than the situation in which the American president believed he found himself. His first duty in war was to proceed to victory at as limited a cost as possible to his own countrymen and soldiers. That is not the only duty, of course: even in armed conflict certain rules have to be respected (for example, regarding the treatment of civilians and prisoners-of-war), and a democratic leader has a duty to wage war as humanely as possible.

The nature of the Second World War was such that the decision had already been taken that the mass-bombing of civilian populations was permissible. That had been a quantum leap – but it had been decided upon virtually as soon as bombing began to play a major part in warfare. One statistic may help to place even the horror at Hiroshima and Nagasaki in perspective. By mid-June, as a result of the saturation bombing of Tokyo, strategic bombing had killed 760,000 people, injured at least 412,000, destroyed 2 million dwellings and rendered 9–13 million people homeless. These figures are well above the totals for Hiroshima and Nagasaki.

The circumstances that Truman had to consider seemed clear cut. There was no reason to expect anything other than last-ditch, bitter resistance to any invasion of Japan. The Americans expected to suffer upwards of a million deaths as a result of the invasion; Japanese casualties were likely to be very much higher. The battle of Okinawa had already displayed the savagery of the resistance likely to be encountered in an invasion. Further saturation bombing raids in advance were likely to take many more lives than even the previous ones had. And the Japanese had been offered, and had rejected, a last chance to settle – although in hindsight there had been serious errors in the nature of the offer made.

Last but not least, the enemy had waged an aggressive war in which millions had died in open conflict, had savaged millions of others to death through brutal occupation policies, and had shown none of the natural constraints to prisoners and subject peoples that could be expected of humane combatants. To persuade such an enemy to talk was not an option considered by Truman. The weakest link in this powerful chain of reasoning was whether a serious attempt at a negotiated peace with Japan would have produced results not far different from the eventual terms of surrender and occupation. General MacArthur later asserted that Japan could have been blockaded navally into submission.

Truman had been given what he considered to be an instrument likely to end the war. He believed that use of that weapon would cause suffering only a fraction as great as that which would accompany a messy landing on Japan; even after the bombs were dropped, the Japanese army wanted to fight on, but was overruled by the emperor. Truman felt he would have to answer to the American people had the bomb not been used, and a million of his countrymen and several million Japanese had died in an invasion. In the circumstances, it seemed that no other decision was possible. What Truman could not have guessed, but Churchill had grasped, was that in dropping the bomb he had also performed an incalculable service to the very elements of the Japanese power structure most responsible for the whirlwind of carnage unleashed by the Pacific War.

PART ONE

THE MEIJI IMPERATIVE

One night, at a late hour [an old merchant] was hurrying up the Kii-no-kuni-zaka, when he perceived a woman crouching by the moat, all alone, and weeping bitterly. Fearing that she intended to drown herself, he stopped to offer her any assistance or consolation in his power ... Then that O-jochu [honourable damsel] turned round, and dropped her sleeve and stroked her face with her hand; – and the man saw that she had no eyes or nose or mouth, – and he screamed and ran away.

From 'The Story of Mujina', *Kwaidan*,
compiled by Lafcadio Hearn

I

UNDER THE SHOGUN

THE FUTURISTIC twentieth-century shriek of the world's first nuclear blast might seem light years away from a world in which great lords flounced about on huge medieval palanquins while citizens prostrated themselves on their faces or risked having their heads smitten from their bodies by strutting warriors in masks and armour. Yet barely three-quarters of a century – the span of a lifetime – separated the two in Japan.

In November 1867 came the watershed that is commonly accepted as the starting point of Japan's modern history. It underpinned the country's emergence as a military and industrial power of the first rank, culminating in the demonic, murderous frenzy of the Pacific War, the bombing of Hiroshima and Nagasaki, and the country's resurgence forty years later to economic superpower status. The event that is as significant to modern Japan as the English and American Civil Wars, the French and Russian Revolutions, or the unifications of Germany and Italy were to those countries was the deposition of the country's 250-year-old military dictatorship, the Tokugawa Shogunate, and the restoration of the emperor to formal power. It is commonly viewed as the moment when feudal Japan gave way to modern Japan – the creation of a strong central state with a proper constitutional structure buttressed by the forces of industrialization and middle-class prosperity.

In fact, it was a unique kind of upheaval. It was not a revolution by Japan's disaffected, emerging middle class, as happened in many other countries, but a reversion to power of the most anachronistic class in all Japan – the increasingly downtrodden and redundant class of samurai, hailing back to the Middle Ages. It has been deemed an aristocratic revolution, yet the samurai were less

43

aristocratic in the sense of representing the country's traditional landowning class than a privileged caste defining itself in terms of ancient status and special privileges, rather than wealth and land.

The fact that this rather quixotic, too-grand-to-work class was behind Japan's transformation into a modern state has defined the peculiar direction of the country's development this century. It is rather as if the fox-hunting squirearchy of England, the grandees of the old Confederate South in America, or the landowning gentry of Russia had taken up the banner of social revolution and modernization. To understand how Japan's most anachronistic class seized power in 1867, precipitating a brief but bloody civil war that put into place a pure authoritarianism that has endured through victory and defeat for a century and a quarter, a brief sketch of Japanese society on the eve of universal male suffrage in Britain and on the morrow of the American Civil War is necessary.

Japan's creation myths bear setting out. In the beginning was the Plain of High Heaven, on which dwelt the gods, among them Izanagi and Izanami, who between them gave birth to the islands of Japan. Izanami died, while Izanagi, as she was washing her eyes and nose, gave birth to three children, the gods of Sun, Moon and Storm. The Goddess of the Sun was Amaterasu Omikami, who was appointed to rule the Plain of High Heaven. Her brother Susanowo-no-Mikoto, His Swift Impetuous Male Augustness, was furious. He also lusted after his sister. When he made advances he was thrown out of her rooms.

He retaliated by throwing excrement over the dining-room where she was celebrating the ceremony of the first fruits. He broke down the divisions of the rice fields, and finally – the ultimate insult – flung a rotting piebald horse which he 'had flayed with a backward flaying' into her chamber through a hole in the roof. Amaterasu fled into a cave and the world was plunged into darkness.

The gods, appalled, assembled outside the cave and erected a sacred tree into which they placed a jewel in the upper branches and a mirror in the middle branches. They then summoned Ama-no-Uzume, the Heavenly Alarming Female, who performed a wild dance. As the Kojiki, the book of the creation recounts (in Basil Hall Chamberlain's translation):

> Her Augustness the Heavenly Alarming Female, hanging the heavenly clubmoss of Mount Kagu as a sash, making the heavenly

spindle-tree her head-dress and binding the leaves of bamboo grass in a posy for her hands, laid a tub before the door of the heavenly rock dwelling and stamped till she made it resound. Doing as if possessed by a deity and pulling out the nipples of her breasts, she pushed her skirt-string beneath her private parts. Then the Plain of High Heaven shook and the eight hundred deities laughed together.

Amaterasu, hearing the commotion, peeped out of the cave, caught sight of her reflection and, fearing she was to be supplanted by the brilliant beauty in the mirror, came out, whereupon she was seized by the gods and returned to shine in the heavens. Susanowo was expelled from heaven, ending up in the Land of Darkness; there he killed a monster and found a sword in one of its tails. This he presented to Amaterasu.

In keeping with the Japanese notion that there is no good or evil, Susanowo is still worshipped as Japan's most popular deity. According to the legend, Amaterasu's great-great-great-grandson became the first emperor of Japan after bitter fighting which ended with his establishing a palace in Yamato, south of Kyoto, in 660 BC. Thus Japan was founded by a ruler descended from the gods and whose heirs were to continue supposedly in unbroken succession to govern Japan to this day. His subjects were the descendants of the god Susanowo, placing the Japanese above all races in being directly descended from the gods.

For the best part of two millennia, Japan has been aggressively reclusive. A collection of mountainous islands off the coast of Asia, plagued by earthquakes and volcanic eruptions, it was populated originally by colonists from mainland Asia, probably Korea, who displaced the native Ainu people. For centuries an expanding population dwelt on this rough, inhospitable land. Although national unity proved difficult to impose upon a disparate and remote territory, a regionally based social structure emerged in which medieval warlords, who alone had the right to bear arms, presided over a destitute and wretched peasantry. Japan was an overcrowded and barren group of islands, where order could be kept only by the ruthless exercise of force. Its nearest neighbours were deeply hostile. The national character has been shaped at least as much by its geography as by its history.

Japan's relations with the outside world were characterized by intense suspicion and insularity punctuated by occasional intervals of outward-looking curiosity. Underlying the hierarchical nature of Japanese feudalism lay the Shinto religion, a primitive cult of multiple deities which glorified war, sacrifice, and suicide, revolved around respect for the god-emperor, and lacked any underlying humanistic tradition. Japan acquired some ethical grounding, however, with the spread of Buddhism, Confucianism and, eventually, Christianity from mainland Asia. The rather bleak countenance of Japanese society was leavened by a purist tradition of arts and aesthetics dating from the Heian period of the eighth to the twelfth centuries. This was Japan's golden age, taking its name from the capital, now Kyoto, under the Fujiwara dynasty.

The dynasty ruled according to a fantastic system of government – 'marriage politics'. The emperor's brides were chosen exclusively from among Fujiwara girls. The head of the family was almost always the father-in-law or grandfather (sometimes both) of the reigning sovereign. By the tenth century the Fujiwaras had the emperor entirely in their grasp. He came to the throne as a youth and was married to a Fujiwara girl; their son would become crown prince. The emperor was forced to abdicate, usually at the age of about thirty. The son would succeed, and the cycle would start again.

The greatest Fujiwara, Michinaga, saw no fewer than four of his daughters married to emperors, who in turn produced three more emperors. By the end of his life, Michinaga was the father-in-law of two emperors, grandfather of a third, grandfather and great-grandfather of a fourth, and grandfather and father-in-law of a fifth. Emperors frequently had to marry an aunt, and were not, of course, consulted about the matter.

Another remarkable feature of politics during the Heian period was that death by no means diminished a man's power. Take the case of the Fujiwaras' great rival, as cited by Ivan Morris in *The Court of the Shining Prince.*

> Michizane's death in exile was far from being the end of the career; in fact his greatest success came after. In the years following his demise there was a series of catastrophes in the capital – droughts, floods and fires; his chief Fujiwara adversary and the crown prince both died prematurely. All this was attributed to the curse of Michizane's angry ghost, and efforts were made to placate him. The documents relating to his exile were burnt, while the minister himself – now twenty years under the sod – was restored to his former post and promoted to the Senior Second Rank. Even this was not enough to appease the ghost, and seventy years later Michizane was elevated to the supreme post of prime minister.

Heian society, like that of Japan ever since, was obsessed with rank and status. There were ten court ranks, the first three divided into senior and junior, the others into upper and lower. There were some thirty ranks altogether, apart from the four reserved for princes of the royal blood.

The main division was between the third and fourth ranks. Those who belonged to the top three ranks were known as *kugyo* (high court nobles) and acquired all the most valuable privileges. Members of the fifth rank and above were appointed by the emperor; those beneath were appointed by the Great Council of State, and lacked many important privileges, such as the right to appear in the Imperial Audience Chamber. Strikingly, court rank determined both one's post in the government and one's wealth; in China and imperial Rome the reverse was true. Entry into the rank hierarchy was decided exclusively by one's family connections.

Members of the first five ranks were paid from special grants of rice land (the source of just about all wealth during this period), ranging from about 200 acres for the senior first rank (prime minister) to about 20 acres for the junior fifth rank (minor counsellor). Their children were admitted into the rank system when they came of age. Anyone of the fifth rank or above could wear ceremonial dress and had special allowances of silk and cloth. Guards and messengers were assigned to him, as well as 'sustenance households', groups of peasant households, ranging from about 4000 for the prime minister to about 900 for a member of the third rank, which paid him feudal dues.

The codes and imperial edicts rigorously set out the standard of living appropriate to each rank – the height of one's gatepost, the type of one's carriage, the number of one's outriders. Costume was rigidly defined by rank, down to the type of fan one could hold: 25 folds for the first three ranks, 23 for the fourth and fifth, 12 for the sixth and below.

Even Emperor Ichijo's pet cat was given the theoretical privilege of wearing the head-dress (*koburi*) appropriate to the fifth rank and above, and was known by the title of Myobu, which applied to ladies of medium rank.

Small wonder that Morris concludes that if a visitor from England in the eleventh century were deposited in the city of Heian,

He would have been confronted with a world totally different from anything he knew, a world which culturally was many centuries in advance of his own and which in customs, beliefs and social organisation was more alien than anything that Gulliver discovered on his travels. For Japan one thousand years ago had developed in a pattern that was almost totally unrelated to the experience of the West.

In the strictly deferential nature of rural society, and in the several centres of authority, lay the origins of two distinguishing characteristics of modern Japan: the subservience of Japanese workers at the bottom, and the dispersal of authority at the top. The institution of emperor, deified under the Shinto religion, provided the national focus for a country that was, to all intents and purposes, a federation of independent baronial states. The emperor, for all the reverence surrounding his status, was largely impotent, confined to the religious capital of Kyoto while shoguns ruled in his name. At times the emperor's influence was more marginal still, and power even more diffused. Unlike China's emperors, frequently overthrown in the course of history, the Japanese imperial dynasty remained unbroken through two millennia because it remained 'above the clouds' – without real power.

Vastly to oversimplify a long and convoluted period of history, Heian Japan was followed by an age dominated by battling regional warlords, still owing theoretical allegiance to the emperor, and subsequently, in the sixteenth century, the advent of the shoguns – ruthless military dictators. The social historian Takeo Yazaki casts light on the absolute stratification of society under the shogunate:

The neo-Confucianist philosophy known as *Shushigaku*, based on the ideas of a medieval Chinese Confucian scholar, Chu Hsi, was authorized as the basic content of education in the *bakufu* (The Shogunate) and no other schools of thought were presented. One of the principles of *Shushigaku* was that a person's fate and fortune were determined by the social conditions of his birth. No one could, nor should he try to, alter his inherited station in life, a notion uniquely tailored for the stabilization of authority in a feudal social order.

The strata motif of society resulted in many differences in living conditions of the warriors. This was evident in the style of houses, areas allowed for residential lots, and even the location of residences, not to mention actual incomes and the different levels of culture enjoyed. If this was true within the warrior class, how much more pronounced were the differences between them and the lower classes of farmers, artisans and merchants. Preservation of the varying social and cultural levels appropriate to each class, and to each grade within the classes, depended upon maintenance of the radical differences in political and economic power that existed between the warriors and their inferiors. Only when changes occurred in the economic structure did cracks appear in the stratified edifice of status that so clearly separated the rulers from the ruled.

Although shogunal Japan gave the appearance of extreme backwardness, it was in some respects more advanced than the 'imperial Japan' which succeeded it. Yet one of the rare visitors before 1867 would have witnessed scenes that had more in common with the medieval pageantry of Europe than a modern society.

The history of Japan between 1600 and 1850 was a tale of two cities: the nominal capital, Kyoto, and the real capital, Edo (the modern Tokyo). The main road between the two, the Tokaido, was a bustling highway along which the princes of Japan, the *daimyo*, passed in procession, borne aloft in palanquins before which ordinary mortals prostrated themselves in total abjection – or risked death if they did not. The *daimyo* were invariably accompanied by large bands of retainers and samurai, with their two swords, short skirts and butterfly shoulders, and their hair grown long and twisted tightly together in a tail protruding forward like a giant proboscis over otherwise bald skulls. The road was also frequented by pilgrims visiting Kyoto's temples, as well as a mass of commercial traders, actors and working labourers who needed permission to cross the roadblocks set up by the shogunate.

It took a week to travel between Edo and Kyoto. The contrast between the two could hardly have been more pronounced, even then. Kyoto was a sprawling, wealthy city on a wide plain between two mountain ridges. It straddled a river feeding a network of canals (which were not extensive enough to make it the Venice of Japan; Florence is a better comparison). The ubiquitous simplicity of Japanese wooden houses extended across the plain in a fine gridlock of streets and buildings. Beyond, particularly on the eastern side but also huddled beneath the western ridge, were some of the most evocative temples and shrines in Japan. It was a city where the creative energies of artists under the patronage of a formal and indolent aristocracy were producing some of the world's sparsest, most contrived art.

The four centres of power in Kyoto may be symbolized by its finest attractions. At the centre was the Imperial Palace, set in a vast and pleasant park alongside two lesser residences. Although more recent than one might think, the palace itself was a classic example of the mixture of grandeur and simplicity that Japanese aristocratic art has made its own. The grandeur lay in its scale: the extensive gardens, the great compound, more than a mile in its perimeter, enclosed by a low wall of superb elegance and simplicity that extended into the distance with seemingly perfect linear perspective. Inside, the buildings were wooden with thatched roofs in the classical style. Even the inner ceremonial hall, the Shishindon, and the emperor's private residence, the Seiryoden, displayed no over-ornamentation or vulgarity of the kind so common across the rest of Asia.

Inside, the emperor's apartments consisted of low, latticed rooms with decorated screens adorned with refreshing blue paintings of Mount Fuji and the Inland Sea. The furniture was beautiful but sparse in the extreme, with tatami mats, lacquer screens, and the odd storage cupboard. The Japanese today make much of the human dimensions of the building; indeed, its low outside wall can easily be scaled. The palace was to become an important symbol of the emperor's formal power. As the centuries went by, successive emperors were looked upon as the supreme spiritual leaders of their country, while real authority lay with a succession of extremely tough temporal rulers.

The most striking illustration of temporal rule comes from the second of Kyoto's four powers, less than a mile from the Imperial Palace. Nijo Castle was the residence of the founder of the Tokugawa dynasty, Ieyasu Tokugawa, a brilliant strategist who broke with the Japanese tradition of relying on pure force, substituting guile. The castle, built during the sixteenth century at a time when most of Europe's rulers had long since abandoned such fortifications, radiates sheer military brio. Surrounded by a wide moat, with walls ten feet thick made of giant, beautifully interlocking stones reminiscent of the Inca architecture of Peru, it exudes a grim determination to resist attack. Within the compound of the castle lie a succession of inner courtyards surmounted by over-ornate Chinese gates whose complexity and gilt inlays are in stark contrast with the purism of the Imperial Palace.

Inside the main residence of the shogun is an astonishing wooden building that must qualify as one of the wonders of the East: although as simply laid out as the palace, it presents a succession of corridors and long rooms decorated with some of the most exquisitely coloured panels in the world. Beautifully executed paintings of tigers and horses in turquoise grass formed the backdrop to the exercise of power by the real rulers of Japan for 250 years.

In an inner room the shogun would receive his nobles, prostrating themselves like the lowest labourer, their foreheads touching the ground. The ever-present danger of assassination for Japan's temporal ruler was underlined by the so-called 'nightingale floors' of the castle, carefully constructed so that the boards would squeak loudly against one another to give warning that someone was approaching. Within the immense compound a huge military tower overlooked the pleasant Japanese garden. Nijo Castle was a carefully conceived and strongly fortified enclave from which the shogun dominated Japan until the move to Edo, which marked the passing of all real power from Kyoto.

The third power of Kyoto is symbolized by what is arguably the finest Buddhist temple in the country, the Kiyomizu, a wooden structure built in the sixteenth century upon a giant platform of crisscrossed timbers that extends outwards from an almost vertical hillside hundreds of feet above Kyoto. While the superbly crafted temple architecture, with its intricate, overlapping wooden eaves and carefully carved edgings and traceries, provides an endless source of wonder, what is also fascinating about this prime Buddhist temple is its vulgarity. Above its central shrine, a wooden platform with an endless plethora of tokens, good-luck charms, lanterns, candles, trinket stalls and statuettes provides an awesome display of the idolatrous pandering to mass taste indulged in by popular Buddhism.

It is not hard to see, viewing the golden figurines of the nearby Sanjusangendo Hall, why Buddhism sought to remedy its corruption through ornamentation by creating such elite, spare expressions of art and meditation as the Zen garden of Ryoanji. In truth, to anyone but the purist, the garden is a ghastly disappointment. Surrounded by a low, red-roofed wall, it consists of some fifteen rocks set in a bed of white gravel which is carefully raked each day by monks. The gravel is said to represent water, the rocks mountains or clouds, edged by green moss. For the truly contemplative, the rocks are merely objects of meditation in an atmosphere of abstract calm. Carl

Andre's controversial Tate Gallery bricks are positively dynamic in comparison.

If the contrast between the Kiyomizu and Ryoanji is one between the earthly approach and the inner life of Buddhism, the much-rebuilt Heian Shrine in north-west Kyoto presents its own stark affirmation of Japan's native Shinto religion against the imported Buddhist presence that has so often dominated but never suppressed it. The Heian Shrine is immense, a huge red and green building embracing an enormous open colonnade with such fineness of proportion that its sheer scale is tempered by harmony. At the north end lies the sanctuary, where to the eerie sounds of gongs and twanging instruments, ceremonies of slow and laboured ritual are conducted by priests in traditional droop-sleeved robes. Wound tendrils of hair protrude forward across their foreheads like the antennae of strange insects.

Behind the elegant lines of the courtyard lies one of the most elaborate and delightful Japanese gardens ever conceived, an entrancing landscape of rocks, shrubbery, mosses, trees, cherry blossom, lichens, lilies, ponds, bridges and lanterns, waterfalls and water channels – everything, in short, except flowers. The garden is a culture park, every element of which is designed as part of a composition complementing the rest: nothing is left to chance. Far from being a triumph or even a celebration of nature, it glorifies man's dominance over nature, a victory of the intellectual and reflective qualities of the mind over the arbitrariness of the surrounding world.

As at the heart of every Japanese garden, there is water – water coursing down gentle steps, water flowing over carefully cleared riverbeds, water caressing exquisitely positioned stones, water dripping into old stone basins, water surrounding an island of pines in a park. The Heian Shrine's pond is truly beautiful, a harmonious arrangement of small islands and trees in the tranquil stillness of a reflecting surface of glass.

A garden, too, is the saving grace of the fourth landmark in Kyoto's gridlock of powers. This is the Kinkakuji, the Temple of the Golden Pavilion, originally built as part of the villa of a fourteenth-century shogun. Recently rebuilt after its destruction by fire in 1950, and now covered with gold leaf, it represents an extreme of vulgarity that is at direct variance with most of Kyoto's architecture. Only its position in a tranquil pool backed by a pine-faced rock garden saves the structure from grossness. (It is evident – and a relief – that beneath the spare asceticism of much of Japanese art lies the same craving for ostentation that characterizes most Western societies.) The garden, where workers are to be seen carefully removing every weed with exquisite care so as not to disturb the mossy ground around, represents the traditional Japanese attempt to curb the pavilion's flamboyance. One of the most classic tea-houses in Japan is located here too: it is an exceptionally modest wooden hut. The deceptive roughness of the place underpins a rite that embodies the entire contrived spartanism and complex, unspontaneous simplicity that lie at the heart of the Japanese social ethic which much of Kyoto still embodies.

The ceremony, called the *chanoyu*, 'hot water for tea', embodies the rite of *wabi*, cultivated poverty, in which the wealthy and privileged could share a social encounter with different classes (although never the truly poor). The ceremony takes place in accordance with severe rules laid down by schools descending from the sixteenth-century tea-master, Sen no Rikyu. The essence of the ceremony is the idea that people of different backgrounds can briefly escape from the bustling outside world into an inner world of contemplation and pure manners and thought. Guests will pass first through the *amigasa-mon* (woven umbrella gate) into the tea garden (*roji*) and into the inner garden (*uchi roji*), where there is a classic stone arrangement and a basin containing water, with which the guests rinse their mouths and hands. These rites should be performed with economy and grace, as befitting all tasks, even the simplest.

To enter the tea-house itself, guests have to pass through a tiny opening, designed to compel warriors to shed their swords (and give the obese an uncomfortable moment). Inside there is a piece of calligraphy on a long scroll in an alcove, which guests study before proceeding to a small sunken hearth, around which they sit. The host arrives – a little late, one might think – and guests make polite conversation about the preparations and discuss the thought embodied in the scroll, according to an etiquette which limits not just the subject of conversation but also the tone of speech and gestures. A ritual light meal is then served on a tray bearing covered bowls of rice, soya, fish and vegetables, as well as Japan's powerful rice wine, sake. After eating, the guests leave the tea-room briefly, returning to discover that the scroll has been replaced by a flower in a vase. They then drink thick, slightly frothy tea, elaborately prepared, first from a central bowl and then from individual bowls, before departing, again with stylistic formality.

The tea ceremony was the centrepiece of Japan's samurai culture. Warriors, paradoxically, glorified its peaceful, non-martial nature.

More predictably, warrior themes dominated the purist Noh theatre; inspired the screen and panel painting of the Tosa and Kano schools; influenced the obsession with all things Japanese, including landscape painting, books, silks and ceramics; dominated the literary tales of the time, the *gunkimono*, of which *The Tales of Heike*, with its bittersweet view of life, is the classic; and shaped the architecture of the period, the fortified hilltop castles. Helmets, swords and arms were fashioned to the best standards of workmanship and design.

Japan's aristocratic war culture was an extraordinary achievement, creating whole epochs such as the Heian, absorbing the refined traditions of Chinese art while grafting onto them an elaborate rustic Japanese notion that glorified the simple and imperfect. It was a sensitive cult of perfectionism, often drawing on popular cultures, but refining them into the kind of pure elitism that only a system of virtually absolutist entrenched privilege based on caste can cultivate.

By the early seventeenth century, Kyoto's world of ruthless aesthetic purism, of glorification of the warrior myth, of tough-minded aristocratic supremacy and contempt for the merchant and middle classes was already all but dead in terms of real political power, although it continued to hold sway throughout the Japanese countryside and in the small towns. The Tokugawa shoguns, far from representing the forces of feudalism out of which the 1868 restoration of Meiji Japan wrenched the nation, were in fact its first modernizers. In moving the capital from Kyoto to Edo (later Tokyo), the shogun was consciously recognizing the shift of authority from the elitism of the rural aristocracy to the new moneyed merchant classes.

In contrast to the formalistic, ritual splendour of the imperial capital, Edo became a thriving city based on commerce, a racy urban lifestyle and an ostentatiousness that thumbed its nose at the spartan rule of Kyoto and the countryside. Where Kyoto was restrained, stratified, elegant, dignified, respecting the code of contrived simplicity, Edo was commercial, raucous, extravagant, fun.

The *ukiyo*, the 'floating world', had come into being, 'a world of fugitive pleasures of theatres and restaurants, wrestling booths and houses of assignation, with their permanent population of actors, dancers, singers, story-tellers, jesters, courtesans, bath girls and itinerant purveyors, among whom mingled the profligate sons of rich merchants, dissolute samurai and naughty apprentices'. In the floating world, money dominated: the merchant lorded it over the warrior. Prostitutes, doctors, writers and painters predominated over imperial servants and police.

Of course, behind this exotic scene was a hard-working, thriving city where extremes of wealth and poverty prevailed. But there could be no greater contrast than that between aristocratic Kyoto and bourgeois Edo. The samurai class retained its contempt for the merchants, the lowest of Japan's four traditional classes – the others were the warriors, the peasants, the artisans; yet in practice, as the new economy flourished, it was not long before many samurai and even the great *daimyo* princes became indebted to the merchants.

Edo was thus a *nouveau-riche* city *par excellence*, a huge sprawl of modern wooden housing where the conventions and extreme formalities that governed Kyoto and the countryside no longer existed. Japan, under the tough-minded absolutism of the Tokugawa shogun, had moved from the feudal age to the bourgeois age; what no one could have predicted was that the country would – in a limited but important sense – return to the feudal age with the Meiji restoration.

The shogunate was a ruthless military dictatorship, but it never crushed the feudal magnates it had subdued. As time passed, the shogun had lived increasingly in Edo, within a moated and walled compound larger than the one in Kyoto. At the time of the move, in 1590, Edo was a small castle town; by 1750 it had expanded into a city of more than a million people. While the hereditary shogun gradually lost power to his advisers, as the emperor had in an earlier age, the system maintained a rigid system of control. In one sense, that succeeded: the shogun unified the country through the crudest of methods, compelling the noblemen to submit to his demands through a calculated policy of deliberately impoverishing them, through taxes and other means, and by hostage-taking: their wives and children were compelled to live in Edo, where the *daimyo* were obliged to visit them every other year. In addition, the nobles had to perform military service and force their retainers to do so.

Thus the Tokugawa shogunate, through its 250-year tenure, reined in the power of the feudal princes, who up to then had been dominant in Japan, without destroying them. A unique tension came into being. One of the country's chief characteritics was its mountainous nature, which permitted it to be carved up into a series of autonomous *daimyo* fiefdoms. Those fiefdoms were incapable of mounting a challenge to the administration in Edo because of the latter's strong-arm methods. The shogun was the undisputed master of the land, and capable occasionally of replacing insubordinate princes with his own nominees; but provided the feudal lords behaved themselves, they were allowed to run their virtually self-governing princedoms. This pattern of autonomy by competing great houses ultimately held in check by ferociously feudal rule from the centre was to become a distinguishing feature of Japanese society, even into the twentieth century.

Beneath the *daimyo* were the local worthies, the samurai, a class of warriors comprising fully 10 per cent of the population, utterly superior in outlook and increasingly impoverished economically. Their official status could not be grander: they were permitted to wear swords and to kill anyone they pleased – in practice, commoners who did not show the proper respect. Yet after the centralization of authority around the shogun, the wars between rival *daimyo* that were the samurai's main *raison d'être* dwindled away; their masters were increasingly squeezed by the taxes of the central government; and many were displaced for showing insubordination to the shogunate. The samurai were traditionally debarred from making money for a living and the class as a whole became poorer and poorer, some 400,000 of them becoming dispossessed *ronin*, wandering the country in search of a lord to serve. They could earn a living only by becoming intellectuals and bureaucrats, professions which were not dishonourable for their caste.

Whereas the shogun whittled away at the authority of the old feudal lords and samurai, he proved unable to rein in the growing power of the merchant classes: by the end of the eighteenth century, two hundred or so merchant houses of enormous wealth had emerged. In the early seventeenth century Mitsui came into being as a high-interest lender, then a hundred years later established a chain of shops. Increasingly, the new rich became the lenders and paymasters of the old classes, struggling to keep up under the squeeze imposed by the shogunate.

2

BREAKING POINT

I T WAS astonishing that the whole house of cards, built upon
shifting ground, lasted as long as it did. By 1850 the new urban
classes had not only antagonized the samurai, but had piled huge
new burdens upon the broken backs of the peasantry. The seething
ferment of despair that existed among the lower orders in both town
and country (four-fifths of Japan's 30 million people lived in the
countryside) was the most unsettling factor. Like a Japanese volcano,
it erupted with increasingly unpredictable, unchannelled frenzy
throughout the last years of the shoguns, as economic development
came to be based on the growing exploitation of the masses. Few at
the top of one of the world's most hierarchical societies showed any
concern for this human misery; but many understood the threat that
it posed, and what might happen if static Tokugawa society did not
reform itself.

The lot of the peasantry around the middle of the last century
was one of almost unbelievable misery, tending what has been
described as the most exacting crop in the world, and dominated by
the most ferocious system of servitude ever devised. This system was
defined by what may be Japan's most significant cultural characteristic: collectivism. The point has been made by Karl Wittfoegel, the
scholar, among others, that oriental despotism was forged by the
need of societies in the East (and, indeed, one in the West – Inca
Peru) to create absolutist, collectivist social systems to manage crops
which depend for their irrigation on the efforts of a whole community. Of few countries is this truer than for Japan, a harsh
mountainous land where rice could be grown only through intensive
and back-breaking shared labour. In the 1920s, Robertson Scott
published a terrifyingly vivid glimpse of the squalor and drudgery

57

involved in that most picturesque of activities, the planting and harvesting of wind-rippled green paddy-fields:

> It is because more than half the paddies are always under water that rice cultivation is so laborious. Think of the Western farm labourer being asked to plough and the allotment holder to dig almost knee-deep in mud. Although much paddy is ploughed with the aid of an ox, a cow or a pony, most rice is the product of mattock or spade labour. There is no question about the severity of the labour of paddy cultivation. For a good crop it is necessary that the soil shall be stirred deeply.
>
> Following the turning over of the stubble under water comes the clod-smashing and harrowing by quadrupedal or bipedal labour. It is not only a matter of staggering about and doing heavy work in sludge. The sludge is not clean dirt and water but dirty dirt and water, for it has been heavily dosed with manure, and the farmer is not fastidious as to the source from which he obtains it. And the sludge ordinarily contains leeches. Therefore the cultivator must work in sodden clinging cotton and leg coverings. Long custom and necessity have no doubt developed a certain indifference to the physical discomfort of rice cultivation. The best rice will grow only in mud and, except on the large uniform paddies of the adjusted areas, there is small opportunity for using mechanical methods.

After this the rice must be planted, transplanted, weeded four times, harvested, threshed, winnowed and polished, the latter taking anything between 200 and 1000 blows of the mallet, depending upon the quality required. All these things require an intensive team effort, none more so than the levelling of the ground necessary to grow the rice (the ground must be absolutely even, or part of the crop will be dry and part saturated by water), the building of low banks of water around the paddy-fields, and the irrigation of the field to replace water lost through evaporation, leakage or in transit.

The system that kept the peasantry on the rice paddies before 1867 was among the most elaborately and fiercely repressive the world had ever seen. There were at least four levels of oppression: the hierarchy within the family, the hierarchy within the village, the hierarchy of economic dependence – usually between landlord and tenant – and the hierarchy of central government over local community. When all are considered together, the mysteries of Japanese politeness and deference become easier to understand, while it is remarkable, not that the Japanese peasantry laboured for so long under conditions of such extreme misery, but that it did so often manage to raise the standard of revolt.

For Japan's samurai, the notion of *noblesse oblige*, of kindness and concern for one's social inferiors, was utterly alien. Within the family, wives showed absolute respect to their husband, children to parents – particularly the father, younger brothers to elder brothers, girls to boys. Even grown-up children continued to respect their fathers, while parents could break up the marriages of children as old as forty. Elder brothers had total control of younger ones until the latter set up their own households – if they ever did, for many lingered on as unpaid servants of their older brother's family. Women walked behind their husbands and were lower in status, even if they were permitted to perform actions like going shopping, which was prohibited in most other Asian societies.

Marriages were arranged by families and were very rarely the product of spontaneous attraction between people. Subject to the iron rules of deference, families were probably more internally democratic than it might seem. Indeed, the Japanese obsession with consensus building, and with the whole family agreeing upon and supporting a decision – what a Westerner might call collective responsibility – which now governs the largest businesses has its origins in the rules governing family life. Nevertheless, the system was fundamentally patriarchal and authoritarian.

The next unit of control was the village. Each village had a headman, elders, and 'delegates', as well as being divided into arguably the most important nucleus of Japanese life – a system of 'five-man groups'. The headman was charged by the central government with keeping accurate records of the village census, levying the rice tax on the village, spending on public works, adjudicating disputes, keeping order, and repressing violence. He was a kind of combination of mayor and sheriff. He was assisted by the elders, three or four from the most prominent families in the village. The delegates were the spokesmen of ordinary villagers – a kind of parish council. So far, so reasonable.

The five-man group, to which every peasant family belonged, was a special Japanese refinement. The group was a collective entity each of whose members was regarded as responsible for the misdeeds of another: thus it was in the interest of each member of the group to ensure that his fellows behaved themselves. As every family member was regarded not as a separate individual but as a member of the family, so every family was regarded as part of its group, which was regarded as part of the village collective. Individuals had no existence outside the group.

The formal body that drew up the rules affecting the village and administered punishment was the village assembly: the principal punishment consisted of ostracism, *mura hachibu*, where the offender's family is ignored by the fellow-villagers except for the purposes of helping fight a fire or attending a funeral. This punishment could be given out for disclosing village secrets, or for being generally obstreperous. Worse still, villagers could be banished altogether for such crimes as stealing, harbouring criminals, and committing arson: to be turned into an outcast, in a society extolling mutual dependence, where a person's worth is defined by membership of a group, is an awesome fate. Not only could the members of the offender's five-man group also be punished for the crime, but so could the immediate neighbours and even the three families directly across the street.

The real power in the village lay in the hands of the *miyaza*, the Shrine Association. This was made up of the village's oldest and wealthiest families, which chose the headman and the elders and was largely self-perpetuating.

Finally, the young people of each village were regimented through 'age groups', to which teenagers belonged until they were married or reached their early thirties. The groups were run by the older members, and the male groups had authority over the female groups, even having full sexual access to them, which neither the girls nor their parents could deny. The age groups could ostracize erring members or, in a particularly Orwellian twist, gather outside an offender's home and shout a list of his or her family's misdeeds, along with ritual abuse.

A further level of control was economic: by some estimates there were more tenants than private owners at this period in Japan's history. Although under the Confucianist ideal the landlord was obliged to provide benevolence and protection to his tenants, in practice their dependence on his good temper was virtually total, usually magnified by debts to him; beneath these two were the *genin*, 'low persons', a kind of landless labourer. (It should be remembered that all these classes stood below the samurai, who had the right to behead any of them if he wished.)

The fourth bond of subjection was that of the village itself through the samurai, to the local feudal lord, who himself was subject to the Tokugawa shogun. In practice, provided a village paid its dues, it was permitted virtual self-government. Yet certain general laws applied to the peasantry as a whole. As the historian Harumi Befu wrote:

> First, the state manifestly existed for the benefit of the ruling class, and therefore other classes, including the peasants, existed to support the ruling class. Hence the oppressive measures to keep the peasants at the bare subsistence level, taking away every bit of surplus they produced. Second, the peasants were considered by nature stupid, needing detailed regulations for conduct. Third, the society was conceived of in absolutely static terms in which the peasantry had a definite position defined by the ruling elite: hence the numerous regulations aimed at maintaining and emphasising the status relation of the peasants to other classes, especially to the ruling class. Fourth . . . to the Tokugawa administration, law and morals were both bound up with the concept of government. Hence the moralistic admonitions intermingled with legal codes and the moralistic tone of legal codes.

In a 1960s study of the Japanese village in the seventeenth century, Thomas Smith concludes:

> The persistent docility of the peasantry, in a country where even today they number almost half the population, is a fact of obvious and immense significance . . . this political and social passivity has provided an extraordinary solid base for authoritarian government and support for social policies of the most conservative order for the past four centuries at least. To inculcate and enforce such discipline among peasants who, in general, have been held consistently at the ragged edge of starvation implies some extremely efficient system of social and political control . . . Despite the spectacular changes effected in other spheres, the Meiji restoration passed over the village without disturbing the distribution of power or the system by which land was exploited. Thus the Japanese landlords of modern times, taken as whole, were not a new and precariously dominant group thrown up by the impact of capitalism on the village but a class whose habit of power goes back to the formative period of Japanese feudalism.

A deeply conservative government of hereditary military oligarchs rigidly enforcing central control upon the country's traditional feudal fiefdoms; a static and miserable peasantry; a thriving and uncontrollable urban melting pot: these were the three principal characteristics of Tokugawa Japan by the early nineteenth century. It was a remarkable achievement for one family to have held sway over such a country for two and a half centuries, particularly as it derived its legitimacy through force, not heredity or popular acceptance. When the end came, it did so because the forces opposed to the status quo had reached a critical mass.

There were three principal factors. First, the reaction of the peasantry and the urban proletariat to the rapacious exactions of the ruling elite and the merchant class had grown so great that fierce uprisings, brutally put down, had become endemic. Second, the shogun's policy of excluding the outside world was no longer practicable – indeed, it seemed likely to lead the country towards the kind of colonization by the Western powers already under way elsewhere in Asia. And third, the dispossessed samurai class and the more remote of the chieftains – the 'outer lords' as opposed to the 'inner lords' (who were largely Tokugawa trusties) – saw their chance of revenge against hated central oppression.

Some bitter and bloody fighting was to mark the end of the Tokugawa regime. Yet, by the standards of civil wars and revolutions elsewhere, its inner decay was such as to dispatch it fairly quietly. The Tokugawa were not removed by a revolution, because the pressure came from the old aristrocratic classes and minor gentry, not from below; still less, as the subsequent legend has it, were they ousted by a 'restoration of the emperor', who for centuries had enjoyed no power, even though the coup was formally carried out in his name. The upheaval was primarily a reaction by the most conservative forces in Japanese society to a military dictatorship that had presided over unprecedented change. When those forces took control, they instituted a number of huge reforms across the surface of Japanese society designed primarily to turn a backward and corrupt society into a nation of the front rank. But because these new authorities were drawn from Japan's most conservative class, they also acted to preserve and even consolidate the hierarchical and static structure of Japanese society beneath the surface.

It was rather as if the enlightened, Tolstoyan part of the provincial nobility of Russia had taken control of the Tsarist court from the corrupt noblemen at the centre. Missing out on an experience shared at some time in the past three hundred years by Britain, France, Germany, Italy, Spain, Russia, China, and even America (if its revolution can be defined as partly a middle-class one), there was no push from below. The urban middle class, which was small, did not take part, while the peasantry was cowed and brutalized into submission. The modernization of Japan after 1867 – which, as this book will argue, laid down the precise foundations of a social and political structure barely interrupted by the upheavals of the 1930s and 1940s – was accomplished by the aggrieved descendants of Japan's old feudal classes.

This was to have a decisive influence on Japan's extraordinary trajectory across the twentieth century. Japan has been labelled, with less than total exaggeration, the world's only example of working communism; it could equally, and with much greater accuracy, be called the world's only example of working feudalism. In 1867–8 the forces of feudalism overthrew an unpopular militaristic central state and its mercantilist allies, and substituted a unique blend of economic progress and political regression based on a rigid hierarchy which, astonishingly, was to stand the test of time.

The growing revolt of the peasantry against Tokugawa Japan was caused by the wilful exploitation of the new capitalist classes. The ruling classes were becoming increasingly indebted to the newcomers, and were passing on an ever greater proportion of their costs and taxes to those below. In addition, rice prices suffered from feverish speculation as the economy grew more complicated. A feudal lord, in order to pay some of his debts, would halve the pay of his farmers, who would insist in turn on greater yields for less pay from the peasants. In addition, there were spectacular crop failures: a single famine in mid-century caused a million deaths. It became common practice for peasant families to abandon their children outdoors to die, while girls were commonly sold to the brothels of Edo and Osaka.

In the first hundred years of Tokugawa rule the countryside had been relatively settled: there were only 157 outbreaks of rural unrest throughout the period. Over the next fifty years to 1753 there were 176 cases, and in the remaining century of the shogunate there were some six uprisings every year. The uprisings usually took the form of a mass gathering by a mob and a march on the house of the feudal lord, while buildings belonging to the wealthy were sacked. Sometimes the rioters had their demands granted; sometimes they were brutally dispersed by the soldiers. Almost always the peasant leaders were hideously treated – decapitated, crucified, boiled in oil or banished.

In the cities, there was simple class-based unrest as the poor took out their anger on the homes of the rich. In the last 150 years of Tokugawa rule there were more than 200 urban riots, some 35 of them during the final decade. The most serious, at Osaka in 1837, was headed by a former policeman, Heihachiro Oshio, who led thousands of townspeople and peasants in several days of looting. They were joined by thirty samurai, using primitive guns and hand grenades. When the riot was put down amid considerable bloodshed, Oshio committed suicide. The growing levels of discontent expressed in these riots caused many members of the ruling class to conclude that the static dictatorship of the shoguns could not continue for ever.

The discontent of the samurai was less evident, but no less acute. Stranded on fixed incomes, many had lost their feudal lords and become leaderless outlaws, forbidden by caste from making their own living. It was permissible for the younger children of merchants to marry into the samurai, and thus gain status while injecting capital into this noble, pauperized class. But most samurai formed a huge reserve – perhaps as many as two million – of disenchanted people trying to earn a living from the jobs in government they were forced to take up. The authorities were all too conscious of the dangers they presented: in the cities, the town heads (*nanushi*) kept a constant watch on their activities. By the mid-nineteenth century the position of the samurai was quite desperate.

The loaded gun pointed at the head of the shogunate was a new Japanese nationalism bred of the evident failure of the government's policy of excluding all outsiders from the country. As early as 1816, the eighth shogun had relaxed the ban on some imports, yet most trade remained forbidden and Christianity banned. British, American and Russian ships frequently appeared in Japanese waters, were given supplies and then were sent on their way. Only the long-standing Dutch colony at Nagasaki was allowed a foothold.

During the first half of the nineteenth century, though, overseas interest in Japan increased. The Russians, who had colonized Siberia, looked to Japan for supplies. The British, having defeated China in the Opium War of 1842 and been given a lease over Hong Kong, were looking to Japan for trading possibilities. As the contest between the two imperial powers developed, the Russians in 1852 decided to send four ships under Admiral Putyatin all the way from

Europe to Japan to secure a privileged commercial treaty. When the Russian flotilla arrived at the port of Nagasaki in 1853, they were astonished to learn that an American squadron under Commodore Matthew C. Perry had already arrived in Edo Bay.

The importance of Perry's arrival on Japan's history should not be overstated; the system was largely dying from within. Yet the visit of the four 'black ships' – two driven by steam – represented the arrival of messengers of death for the *ancien régime*. The steamships were symbols of a world progress which had bypassed Japan entirely. They also starkly underscored the vulnerability of Edo itself: all the city's food supplies came by sea from the north and the west. Indeed, this mountainous nation of semi-autonomous fiefdoms depended upon the sea for an enormous amount of its essential transport.

Perry was a tough-minded sailor in his late fifties who understood that the Japanese were impressed by power rather than conciliation. An unfortunate incident had occurred in 1846 when Commodore Biddle had made the first major American approach to Japan, trying to be conciliatory. Biddle was jostled by a Japanese seaman and accepted an apology; a Japanese diplomat later told an American senator that they did not fear American vengeance after that, as an American commander had failed to punish an ordinary seaman who had treated him disrespectfully.

Perry was determined to have none of that. He treated the emissaries sent by the Japanese to his ship with contempt, insisting on leaving a letter from his president that amounted to an ultimatum demanding the opening of trade relations, and promising to return a year later with a large fleet of ships. Perry had been assured by his American masters that 'any departure from usage, or any error of judgement he may commit will be viewed with indulgence'. After delivering his missive, the commodore sailed up the bay, ignoring Japanese warnings, to a position from which it was clear that he could shell the outlying parts of the city; he then departed in grand manner.

A month later, Admiral Putyatin's less impressive force arrived and, being much less tough-minded, was kept kicking its heels in Nagasaki for three months. The two visits convinced the Japanese that their policy of total isolation was no longer workable. The Americans had come because they needed access to supplies for ships employed in the lucrative trade with China; in addition, they were unhappy with the dismal reception accorded their shipwrecked crews in Japan, who endured months of ill-treatment before being repatriated. The United States, with the opening up of California and the Gold Rush of 1849, had become a Pacific-oriented nation.

Underlying this was the feeling that Japan, an isolated and backward country, was ripe for the commercial picking. An unedifying scramble was under way between three major powers – America, Britain, and Russia – two of which were about to go to war with each other in the Crimea. Within a matter of months, Japan came to see the utter helplessness its policy of isolation had led to: it was a nation undefended, without a navy, as ready for absorption by the colonial powers as China had been. For once, the clichéd metaphor of an ostrich sticking its head in the sand as its defence against outside danger was apposite.

The Japanese government's response to the Perry mission was a frantic attempt to rearm. Gun batteries were erected along the shoreline near Edo. But when Perry arrived as promised with seven ships in 1854, he delivered his ultimatum: either the Japanese accept his terms, or military operations would begin. Already intimidated by the return of the Russians to Nagasaki a month earlier, Japan acceded in March 1854 and signed the treaty of Kanagawa, opening up the ports of Hakodate and Shimoda for supplies and trade. The Japanese drew consolation from the fact that these ports were far from Kyoto and Edo. The following October, a British contingent under Admiral Sterling arrived in Nagasaki and extracted agreement to call there and at Hakodate.

A month later the tireless and luckless Admiral Putyatin had sailed into Osaka Bay, close to the imperial capital at Kyoto, causing consternation among the Japanese. After sailing out, Putyatin's ship, the *Diana*, was badly damaged in a giant whirlpool caused by an earthquake, and eventually sank. To the Japanese, this was a sign of the wrath of the gods at their concessions to the barbarians. But Putyatin and his men were rescued and treated with courtesy, and negotiations between Japan and its powerful northern neighbour were soon concluded with the partition of the Kurile Islands and the large, mainly uninhabited, island of Sakhalin, to the satisfaction of both sides. Moreover, the Russians were given landing rights at Shimoda, Nagasaki, and Hakodate.

By the end of 1855 a formal treaty had been signed with Holland, and the following year America's Townsend Harris became the first resident foreign diplomat in Japan, using his position to extract privileged terms for the Americans while playing on Japanese fears of the British – the major naval power in the Far East. He sought an audience with the shogun himself, and in December 1857, bearing a presidential letter, he became one of the first outsiders to be brought into the presence of the ruler, the somewhat precious Iesada Tokugawa, who told him that 'he was pleased with the letter sent with the Ambassador for a far distant country, and likewise pleased with his discourse. Intercourse should be continued for ever.'

The shogun's decision was in reality dictated by his chief counsellor, Masahiro Abe, who was nothing if not a realist. 'Everyone has pointed out that we are without a navy,' he told the shogun, arguing that there was no alternative but to make as few concessions as possible from an extremely weak hand. Masuhiro's successor as chief counsellor was Naosuku Ii, *daimyo* of Hikone, who was even more aware of the frailty of Japan's position. In 1858 he agreed to the so-called 'unequal treaties' by which Edo and other ports were opened up to foreigners, imports were taxed at a low level, and nationals from the eighteen countries signing the treaty were exempted from being bound by Japanese law. The treaties were very close to being a colonial diktat and one, moreover, carried out in the name of a virtually powerless shogun, in defiance of the openly stated wishes of the emperor, around whom outraged Japanese nationalists had begun to congregate. The treaties caused an outcry and the beginning of a campaign whose rallying cry was, 'Return the emperor! Expel the barbarians!' – which was later to become the slogan of the Meiji restoration. Naosuku Ii responded with savage repression.

3

RETURN OF THE EMPEROR

IN JANUARY 1860, as the chief minister's palanquin trundled down the steep hill alongside the moat that surrounded the stubby walls of the shogun's castle in Edo and turned in deep snow to enter the Sakurada Gate, Ii was attacked by a group of nationalist fanatics and stabbed to death. It was the first of the nationalist assassinations that were to plague Japanese politics for the best part of the next hundred years.

With Ii's death, the shogun and his regime were on the ropes, and they knew it. By 1862 they had been forced to abandon the rule that compelled the *daimyo* to spend every other year in Edo; the family hostage system was also ended. Meanwhile, the Choshu clan of 'outside' lords had begun a full-scale insurrection in the west, enlisting peasants and townsmen as warriors, violating the old castle system which decreed that samurai alone could bear arms.

The insurrection formally began when the Emperor Komei in Kyoto, growing ever bolder as he was chivvied by aristocratic admirers into pushing the crumbling Tokugawa regime over the brink, abruptly issued an edict to the shogun telling him to expel foreigners from Japan the following year. The shogun assured the foreign community that the edict would not be enforced; but fanatics began to attack outsiders with increasing impunity, fired by the knowledge that they were carrying out their divine emperor's will. In Yokohama and Edo, some foreigners were stabbed to death.

In September 1862 an Englishman, Mr Richardson, was attacked as he travelled along the Tokaido highway between Edo and Kyoto. The culprits were retainers from Satsuma, which was also in virtually open rebellion against the shogun. The British responded with fury, sending a squadron to bombard, and virtually flatten, the capital of the Satsuma clan at Kagashima. In June 1863 came the deadline for the expulsion of the 'barbarians', and Choshu shore guns on the Shimonoseki Straits opened fire upon American, French and Dutch ships, the Americans and the French firing back. In September 1864 the imperialist powers finally lost their patience, and a combined British, Dutch, French, and American fleet destroyed the Choshu batteries, reopening the Straits.

Yet even the colonial powers were aware that Japan was falling apart. Large parts of the country were effectively independent of the centre: the shogun held sway only around Edo, and the loss of tributes from the rebellious regions was further squeezing an economy already in serious financial difficulties. The British minister, Sir Harry Smith Parkes, carefully watched the direction of events and initiated contacts with the ignorant, rebellious young extremists from the provinces – in marked contrast to the French, who remained closely allied with the shogun.

In 1866 the young Shogun Iemochi died, and his guardian, Keiki Tokugawa, came to power. The same year the former rival armies of Satsuma and Choshu concluded a secret alliance in which the Tosa and Hizen clans also joined. Even part of the merchant class, notably the Mitsui family, sensing which way the wind was blowing, joined forces with these aristocratic backwoodsmen. The Emperor Komei himself was believed to have given this pact his backing. A year later he too was dead, and his fifteen-year-old son, Mutsuhito, succeeded him as the mystically divine Meiji Emperor, spiritual ruler of the Japanese. He now embodied the hopes of all his fellow countrymen who were anxious to rid the nation of its crumbling military dictatorship.

In November 1867 matters came to a head. Two armies of the Satsuma and Choshu moved into Kyoto, in preparation for an attack on the shogun's palace, Nijo Castle. Learning of their approach, Shogun Keiki also formally received an ultimatum from the head of the Tosa clan demanding that he restore 'the governing powers into the hands of the sovereign and so lay a foundation on which Japan may take her stand as the equal of all other countries'.

At night, Keiki fled his palace to Osaka, to escape the attack he believed to be imminent. There his loyalists persuaded him that they had sufficient strength to launch a counter-offensive to 'rescue' the emperor from the capital's new masters. In January 1868 the shogun's armies advanced on Kyoto, but were halted at the towns of Toba and Fushimi. A pitched battle ensued. On the second day, a large part of the shogun's army went over to the emperor, and the following day the shogun's remaining forces were routed. Keiki took a boat from Osaka to Edo where, with good grace, he bowed to the inevitable and decided that Edo Castle, despite its formidable defences, should be surrendered. Only in Ueno, in the eastern sector of the city, was there some resistance to what were no longer rebel, but imperial forces.

Many clans loyal to the Tokugawa fought on, however. At Wakamatsu and then at Hokkaido, fighting continued until well into the following year. Keiki himself was spared, perhaps because he had tried to damp down futile resistance, and was received in audience by the emperor in 1902.

The final chapter in Japan's Tale of Two Cities was about to be written. In the autumn of 1868 the youth who had inherited Japan paid a formal visit to Edo, the shogun's capital. It was a brilliant, last display of the old Japan. This is how a contemporary observer described it, as the Ho-o-ren or 'phoenix car' approached:

> This is a black lacquered palanquin, about six foot square and with a dome-shaped roof; the front is closed only by curtains, and in the centre of each side is a latticed window, through which it was possible to see that it held no one. The Mikado is supposed to travel in it, but has really a more comfortable palanquin . . . the bearers of the car which is carried high upon their shoulders and on a frame which raises it six feet from the ground were . . . all dressed in bright yellow silk . . . There were fully 60 of them immediately surrounding the Ho-o-ren, and the effect of the group, with the brilliant sun lighting up the sheen of the silk and the glitter of the lacquer, was very gorgeous and indescribably strange, comparable to nothing ever seen in any other part of the world.
>
> And now a great silence fell upon the people. As far as the eye could see on either side, the roadsides were densely packed with the crouching populace, in their ordinary position when any official of rank passes by . . . [As] the phoenix car . . . with its halo of glittering attendants came on . . . the people without order or signal turned their faces to the earth . . . [No] man moved or spoke for a space, and all seemed to hold their breath for very awe, as the mysterious presence, on whom few are privileged to look and live, was passing by.

The following spring the court moved permanently to the shogun's castle at Edo, which became the Imperial Palace. Edo was renamed Tokyo ('Eastern Capital'). The spiritual ruler of Japan was now also to be its temporal ruler.

How would the emperor exercise real power under the new dispensation? Two things were certain: first, all official power in Japan was henceforth to be wielded solely in his name. While this had been nominally true in the past, no observer of Japan was under any illusion that the emperor had possessed real political authority of any kind under the shogunate. Second, the new order was to be modelled on the basis of other consitutional monarchies in the rest of the world that had been investigated by the Japanese.

The decisions of the government would be referred to him, and he sat in on its discussions, even if he usually took no active part. Writers in the late twentieth century have frequently tried to compare the position of the emperor during the crucial years leading up to the Pacific War to the previously purely spiritual authority he exercised in the centuries before the Meiji restoration, but the comparison is false. The emperor's position after the restoration was entirely different to that before. He was now the formal pinnacle of power: the senior ministers reported to him, he appointed the prime minister and oversaw key decisions, and he presided in person over all the great activities of state. The contemplative hermit of Kyoto was no more.

None of this is to suggest that he became Japan's dictator, personally responsible for the decisions affecting Japan up to 1945; even the shogun had, after a time, become a creature of his advisers. In fact, the emperor's power was something entirely new: he stood at the apex of an absolutist system of respect, and was supposed to have the powers of a European monarch (the Japanese believed this essential to success in the modern world, without knowing exactly what those powers were); yet he was hedged about with the kind of entourage and overmighty advisers that had been a feature of Japanese politics since time immemorial. To some extent the character of the new central authority of the state was to be shaped by the personality of the emperor himself. Spiritual and temporal power in Japan had converged in a youth barely past puberty who possessed the aura of a god and the authority of a king, running Japan from the single capital of Tokyo.

*

The teenager who had been raised to supreme authority in 1863 had been placed there by others, a curious collection of backwoods 'outside lords', a group of young idealists and samurai nationalists, and a motley gang of malcontents and opportunists. The driving force behind the Meiji restoration, as already noted, was the warrior caste. The historian T. C. Smith, among others, argues forcefully that this made Japan's entry into the modern era unique. Because that new ruling class was 'aristocratic', it was much less defensive about its privileges than an elite threatened by revolution from below would have been. Indeed, despite its nominally superior status, the samurai order was dispossessed and impoverished, compelled to join bureaucratic posts under the brutal shogunate while resenting the great wealth of the merchant class. The warriors were naturally discontented, angry with their lot in life and determined, on gaining power, to transform the higher echelons of society. Smith's argument bears quoting at length:

On the one hand were a few thousand families of superior lineage and a very large income, with imposing retinues and magnificent houses, who in practice, though not in law, monopolised the important offices of government; some offices in effect became hereditary. On the other hand was the bulk of the warrior class, numbering several hundred thousand families, who were cut off from high office and lived on very modest incomes; many in real poverty, pawning their armour and family heirlooms, doing industrial piecework at home to eke out small stipends, and resorting to such pitiful tricks as sewing strips of white cloth to the undersides of their collars so people might take them to be wearing proper undergarments. As warrior mothers proudly taught their children, a samurai might have an empty belly but he used a toothpick all the same.

But it was not so much the contrast between his own and the style of life of his superior that moved the ordinary warrior to fury. It was, rather, the impropriety of the merchant's wealth. Surely it was a perversion of social justice that the warrior, who gave his life to public service, should live in want and squalor, while men who devoted themselves to money-making lived in ease and elegance, treated him with condescension and even rudeness, and in the end not infrequently found favor with the lord.

The merchant was not to blame since he merely followed his nature. Though he was feared and hated for that, ultimate responsi-

bility lay with the effeminate high aristocrats who, through idleness
or incompetence, failed to use their inherited power for the proper
ends of government.

Smith argues that Japanese society evolved very differently
precisely because the revolution was aristocratic rather than
democratic:

First, a point so obvious that it need only be mentioned in passing:
the aristocratic revolution, despite the civil equality and economic
progress it brought, has not made for a strong democratic political
tradition – but the contrary.

Second, more than any other single factor, perhaps, that revolution helps explain Japan's rapid transition from an agrarian to an
industrial society. How different the story must have been had the
warriors behaved as one would expect of an aristocracy, if they
had used their monopoly of political and military power to defend
rather than change the existing order.

Third, as there was no aristocratic defense of the old regime,
there was no struggle over its survival, no class or party war in
which the skirmish line was drawn between new and old, revolutionaries and conservatives, There was, of course, a tension
between traditional and modern, Japanese and Western, but not a
radical cleavage between the two by ideology. All parties were
more or less reformist, more or less traditional, and more or less
modern; excepting perhaps the Communists, whose numbers were
insignificant, no pre-war party thought of the past, as such, as a
barrier to progress . . .

Fourth, status-consciousness is relatively strong in Japan in part
because there was no revolutionary struggle against inequality, but
for that reason class-consciousness is relatively weak. Those attitudes are by no means contradictory. The nervous concern of the
Japanese for status is quite consonant with their relatively weak
feelings about class – higher ups to some extent being looked on as
superior extensions of the self.

Smith's analysis is acute and convincing, except in one respect:
an aristocracy, in the European sense, usually applies to the few
thousand principal families in the land – in Japan's case the *daimyo*
and their chief followers. The samurai were formally deemed aristocratic and were intensely status-conscious, but in their numbers and

lack of landed wealth, they closely resembled much more the English landed gentry than the aristocracy – as they also did in moral outlook.

Of the extraordinary representatives of the class that now were to lead Japan from the thirteenth century into the twentieth in just fifty years, four stand out: one was the great military leader of the uprising, Takamori Saigo, soon to become a noble anachronism, the head of the Satsuma forces and standard-bearer for the samurai. A large, outspoken man with the bluff appearance of a modern sumo wrestler, he was intensely admired by his troops and not over-respected for his intelligence.

Another was Tomomi Iwakura, the wily court intriguer of the Meiji period, and arguably the main force behind the Meiji constitution. Koin Kido was a prominent samurai with a much greater intellect than Saigo; his support for the regime proved decisive at its moment of greatest danger. Kaoru Inouye was one of the most enlightened of the early samurai leaders.

Four other men were to dominate the late Meiji period. Hirobumi Ito emerged as the country's Bismarckian autocratic prime minister after most of the first generation of leaders had departed from the scene, struggling to limit the extent of popular participation while modernizing the country at breakneck speed. Taisuki Itagaki was as respected for his personal appearance and magnificent beard as for his romantic espousal of opposition causes. Itagaki was to become an eighteenth-century-style leader of the opposition, both pushing the cause of more representative government and defying more radical pressure for popular change. Another late Meiji statesman (of whom more later) was General Aritomo Yamagata, the founder of the modern Japanese army. Finally, Kinmochi Saionji was to become Japan's major voice for common sense and moderation in the early twentieth century.

At the peak was the Meiji emperor. He was a squat, astonishingly energetic man with pouting lips and a sullen expression, like a bulldog's, but betrayed by a receding lower chin. His thick black hair combined with his precocious maturity to give him a ferocious look that, as he grew older, inspired affection rather than fear. His taste for court cronies and concubines grew with time, but he never became dissolute. Mutshito, Emperor Hirohito's grandfather, had been born in 1852 and was to perform a far larger political role than any of his forebears for centuries. Such few eyewitness accounts as have been handed down say he was gruff, occasionally kindly, with a strong constitution.

These were the men who had taken over a backward, isolated country on the further fringes of the civilized world in the second half of the century. At the time, there was nothing about Japan to suggest power or success. It was an irrelevance, a string of inhospitable islands off the coast of Asia, useful as a staging post for sorties to the Asian mainland by the colonial powers. The only reason that Japan had not been colonized, probably, was that the major powers – Britain, America, and Russia – thought it hardly worth the effort. There could have been little in the early days of the Meiji reign to reassure those who had seized power that Japan was destined for anything more than a lowly international role.

Within a matter of months, the men who had freed the country from the grip of a crushing and oppressive military dictatorship found themselves embattled on at least three fronts. First, they discovered that Japan was far weaker internationally than they had feared – as naked a nation as it was possible to be. One of the chief motives behind the restoration had been to 'expel the barbarian'. The new rulers quickly realized that the only way of doing so was to become stronger than he, and this could be achieved only through copying his secrets and his methods. The idea of excluding him was hopelessly outdated, and a passport to becoming his servant, just as China, which for centuries had believed its culture to be superior to any other, was being mercilessly despoiled by the colonizers' military and organizational superiority.

The second front was economic: the country was facing financial ruin, and only the most radical of initiatives would permit it to escape the clutches of a parasitic bureaucratic class, with its mercantilist retainers, squeezing the lifeblood from its hard-pressed rural producers. Thirdly, the very class which had propelled the new regime to power – the warriors, the samurai – was one of the biggest drains on state finances. The country's new rulers had to find some way of dealing with the expectations of the samurai that their time had come again, for they could no longer be supported by the state as non-producers. Only two solutions seemed possible: the destruction of feudal privilege so that the samurai might make money just like everyone else, which would create intense resentment among those that failed; or the deflection of their warrior energies abroad.

*

The first problem was overcome by a move that was extraordinarily bold by Japanese standards. In 1871, the new regime decided to send a mission abroad to find from foreigners the best way of mobilizing the country into the industrial age. Having learnt the lesson that the exclusion of outsiders had been the cause of their political backwardness, and flying in the face of the popular anti-foreigner sentiment that had brought the new regime to power, the government sought deliberately to copy the methods of the countries that were more powerful than the Japanese so as, eventually, to be able to surpass them. The Japanese chose to prostrate their proud culture to the barbarian – unlike China, which scorned the West and had suffered accordingly.

Iwakura himself chose to lead the two-year mission, which consisted of a hundred senior officials; Ito, his successor as the most powerful man in Japan, accompanied him. Left behind as virtual military dictator alongside the eighteen-year-old emperor was Saigo. There must be room for speculation that what in fact had happened was the temporary consolidation of the restoration by its military wing, which was only too delighted to see the senior civilian statesmen away for so long; however, Saigo, for all his personal magnetism, was not the kind of leader appropriate to transforming Japan in the long term.

The travellers had a mind-bending experience. The particular fields of study for the group were industry, education, and constitutional law. On industry, one member of the group wrote back from London, 'Factories have increased to an unheard-of extent, so that black smoke rises to the sky from every possible kind of plant ... This is a sufficient explanation for England's wealth and strength.' Kido was fascinated by the education system in America: 'From now on, unless we pay a great deal of attention to the children, the preservation of order in our country in the future will be impossible ... To prevent trouble in our country ten years from now, there is only one thing to do and that is to establish schools worthy of the name.' He was also interested by parliamentary government: 'The people have parliamentary representatives whose duty is to inspect everything that is done and to check arbitrary proceedings on the part of officials. Herein lies the best quality of these governments.'

The Japanese behaved as though they were visitors from outer space seeing civilization for the first time. In a sense they were: the shogunate had kept them isolated from the world for centuries. Yet the purpose of this venture was to bring Japan up to date, able to compete with the outside world. In spite of the strength of feeling against the repressive inefficiency of the shogunate, no one had considered a radical transformation of the structure of Japanese society itself, far less its uniquely Japanese social mores, beneath the top layer. The shoguns had tried to isolate Japan. This had failed, and the world outside was now so much more advanced that it could invade and colonize Japan whenever it chose. Therefore Japan had to catch up and surpass the world, to prove itself. A new, modern administration was required. But all this was to be done to protect Japan's essential traditions and way of life.

After nearly two years abroad, the travellers returned in 1873 laden with ideas only to face an immediate and dramatic political crisis involving the key institution of the restoration – the samurai – and the new regime's incipient imperialism. Saigo, the strongman, was responsible. The new regime had been eager to flex its muscles abroad and occupy the energies of the restless samurai. Accordingly, the restorationists looked to revive what they believed to be an unequal treaty with their weak neighbour to the west, Korea.

The Koreans responded with dismissive contempt. Saigo proposed that he should visit Korea and challenge the regime there over its attitude; then, if he were insulted or killed, Japan would have a pretext for invading. On the return of Iwakura and the others, a hasty debate took place about the merits of this expedition. Japan's 'peace' leaders agreed that the country was far from being able to afford a major war which would also deeply antagonize Russia. Reconstruction came first.

It was significant that even the peace party did not dispute the rightness of emulating the world's major industrial powers by launching Japan's own programme of colonization; they objected only to the timing. The debate was an angry one, and Saigo resigned from the government. The following year angry samurai staged a 'punish Korea' uprising in sympathy with him. Two years later two further rebellions by samurai broke out, and in 1877 Saigo himself headed a major uprising in Satsuma that threatened the very survival of the new regime.

At stake in Saigo's uprising was not just the fate of Korea, but that of the entire samurai class. The warriors felt, with good reason, that they had been responsible for the 1867 coup and the restoration of the emperor. Yet Japan's new rulers quickly recognized that, although they had an obligation to defend the interests of the class, in its present form it had become an anachronism, a drain on resources, and was an obstacle to the creation of a modern state.

One of the most remarkable features of the restoration had been the speed with which the regime turned on its former supporters. Japan could become powerful only if, in place of an arbitrary government presiding through a system of hostages and blackmail over a group of feudal princes, a proper central state was set up. In 1871 the triumphant lords of Choshu, Satsuma, Tosu, and Hizen had formally surrendered their lands to the emperor. The declaration was memorable and historic and it prompted – as it was designed to do – similiar avowals from the rest of Japan's feudal lords, who would otherwise face the new regime's wrath. Henceforth, individuals would possess their property not as of right, but on sufferance from the state (the emperor), who could claim it at any time. In fact, this seemingly selfless principle was not as altruistic as it seemed. The *daimyo* were given generous compensation and became governors of the provinces they ruled; only after their passing did centrally appointed prefects take formal control of local government in Japan.

Moreover, in proportion to their support for the Meiji restoration, the great *daimyo* houses were given shares in the spoils of the new economic order. Thus were laid the foundations for the *zaibatsu*, the Japanese conglomerates that were to become the world's largest single concentrations of authoritarian economic power by the turn of the century. Many of the old princes were also absorbed into the higher reaches of government, and the senior samurai were designated a new 'gentry' class.

The new administrators modelled the state initially on that of eighth-century Nara Japan. A council of state was set up having supreme decision-making powers, with the wily Iwakura as its chief member, as minister of the right – the prime minister. With the *daimyo* finally abolished, there was no need for their retainers. Samurai hereditary income was curtailed and then paid off in a one-time grant; samurai privileges in legal status, dress, surnames and forms of address disappeared, as did the right to kill commoners who failed to show the proper respect.

Samurai were forbidden to carry their swords. The monopoly of armed power was transferred to the regular police and the armed forces – up to then the Imperial Guard of some 11,000 men. The final blow came with the introduction of conscription, and in 1872 the mobilization of a 'nation of samurai' in place of a privileged caste. The obvious intention was to assemble a loyal armed force around a desperately weak emperor who would otherwise be prey to insurrection by any leader who could muster the warrior class behind him.

Predictably, samurai resentment exploded. In 1877 Saigo placed himself at the head of a force of tens of thousands at Kyushu. The government sent a large force, including newly trained conscripts, commanded by one of the most dangerous, colourful and controversial figures in modern Japanese history: General Yamagata of Choshu – Satsuma's traditional rival – who was to become the founder of the modern Japanese army. Fighting was fierce and bitter, with 30,000 casualties inflicted on both sides. The samurai, although the better fighters, were poorly equipped. Yamagata later declared that his army proved that 'the Japanese, whether of the military class or not, originally spring from the same blood and when subjected to rigid discipline could scarely fail to make soldiers worthy of the renowned bravery of their ancestor.'

The Saigo uprising, the last fiery eruption of old Japan, would influence generations of extreme right-wingers over the next eight decades – and beyond.

Saigo himself had been born in Satsuma, one of the remotest provinces of Japan, mountainous, large and barely loyal to the shogun under its defeated rulers, the Shimazus. Some two-fifths of its people were samurai; the rest of the population had to work hard to support this unproductive class.

Saigo was the eldest of seven children, the son of the lowly head of accounts for the lord of Satsuma, who was also a sumo wrestler. The youth was huge for a Japanese, with an enormous appetite. He was seven feet tall and some 240 pounds in weight, and said to be too fat to mount a horse. As a young man he was considered slow-witted, and became a sumo wrestler himself. At school he was admired for his independence and physical courage, as well as his fiery temper, which could suddenly rise to the surface. He was also modest and generous.

Saigo had a maudlin streak: he was deeply distrustful of his fellow man and self-doubting, as can be seen in his early writings. In a letter, he wrote, 'Now I have finally discovered that human beings cannot be trusted. They are as changeable as the rolling eyes of a cat. To my amazement some people on whom I had relied as kindred spirits have made unfounded accusations against me.'

In his twenties, Saigo went to work for the lord of Satsuma, and on the death of his master was so grief-stricken that he tried to commit suicide with his friend, Genssho, a priest. Ivan Morris takes up the story:

A few months later, when Genssho reached Kagoshima as a fugitive from the *bakufu* police, Saigo arranged that they would escape at night by boat and end their lives together in the sea. When the boat was about a mile into Kagoshima Bay, the two friends went to the prow. The other men on board supposed they had gone to admire the magnificent moonlit scenery, but in fact they were exchanging farewells and writing their obligatory death-poems. These preliminaries completed, Saigo and his friend leapt off the gunwale. A contemporary print shows the white-robed priest and his young samurai companion as they are about to hit the water: their grim, determined faces are brightly illuminated by the full moon, while further back in the boat a companion sits playing the flute, serenely unaware of the tragedy that is being enacted a few feet away.

Shortly after the loud splash was heard, the crew sighted the two bodies and, having hauled them out of the water, brought them to a hut near the shore. The priest did not respond to attempts at artificial respiration; the burly young samurai, however, was still alive . . .

For the next few years, Saigo suffered severe hardship as a prisoner in exile under the new, unsympathetic lord of Satsuma. But in due course he was pardoned and given the job of Satsuma war secretary, eventually leading the joint Satsuma–Choshu forces that defeated the shogun's army in 1868. After the victory, Saigo, defying all conventions, retired to rural life in Satsuma. In 1871, however, he was prevailed upon to join the central government. A year later he became commander of Japan's armed forces.

His existence remained spartan in the extreme. He preferred to eat from a common bowl with his soldiers and veterans, rather than attend state banquets. He dressed simply in plain cotton cloth and wore sandals or clogs on his feet; he was once accosted as he walked barefoot in the imperial palace by a police guard suspecting that he was an intruder. He detested Westerners, and never travelled abroad; he disdained urban living and wealth. Saigo became a focus for all the forces opposing the modernization of Japan, remaining faithful to the reactionary principles of the restoration of 1868. He became the dominant figure in the land on the departure of the Iwakura mission to Europe; but a former friend of his, Count Toshimichi Okubo, vied for power with him, and when Saigo overreached himself in actively courting war with Korea, Okubo emerged the winner.

Okubo was to be the key figure in the next stage of the Meiji restoration. He pressed for the confiscation of the feudal domains and the removal of samurai privileges, and established a fiercely centralizing government run by a dominant bureaucracy. He favoured rapid technological advance. He ruthlessly crushed opponents and criticism, enacting a rigorous censorship law in 1875. He himself dressed in full Western clothing, with a huge breastful of medals and sashes, his hair and sidewhiskers groomed in imitation of a Victorian gentleman. He was the apotheosis of the Meiji autocratic bureaucrat, who knew what was best for his country and never bothered to obtain popular consent – the root cause of Japan's problems to the present day.

Okubo came to detest the populist, plain-speaking Saigo, now a focus for samurai opposition to the regime. Power in Edo was firmly in the hands of Okubo and Prince Yamagata, the head of the new army, who had antagonized the samurai by introducing universal conscription, undercutting the samurai's traditional exclusive right to bear swords. As samurai unrest grew and Saigo languished in exile, the government grew increasingly nervous.

The spark for the uprising was unwittingly provided by the government itself in January 1877, when it attempted to smuggle out most of Kagoshima's arsenal in an attempt to prevent Saigo's increasingly militant followers from laying their hands on it. News of the government's pre-emptive strike leaked out, and young samurai seized the imperial arsenal first in an open act of rebellion. That was enough for Saigo. He had a meeting with the young hotheads, exposing them to the full force of his fury but agreeing to place himself at their head. At court, he was promptly stripped of his titles and decorations and denounced as a traitor and an enemy of the emperor. The government mustered an army of 40,000 men to face the 25,000 rebels assembled by Saigo.

The warrior-rebels decided to seize the initiative by attacking the town of Kumamoto, in central Kyushu. They marched through the snows of February, growing stronger in number by the day. But Kyushu Castle was one of the three most impregnable fortresses in

Japan, built on a formidable rock. With great difficulty, the 4000 loyalist defenders held out against Saigo's superior forces day after day, until a large relief force arrived.

Saigo's men withdrew, with the imperial army in pursuit, escaping first to the south, then to the town of Nabeoka in the eastern corner of Kyushu island, where they were surrounded. However, with a small contingent, Saigo managed to fight his way through enemy lines to make the hundred-mile journey back to Kagoshima, the capital of Satsuma. But Kagoshima had fallen into the hands of the imperial forces, who were backed up by warships. Saigo had by this time lost around 25,000 men, while the imperial army had lost around 6000.

With his tiny band of a few hundred, the rebel leader succeeded in fighting his way back into the capital, routing the government force. However, the main imperial force soon arrived and surrounded the town. Saigo held on for two weeks, before retreating to a cave near Shiroyama overlooking the bay and the volcanic island of Sakurajima. There he received a passionate entreaty from General Yamagata, the commander of the loyal forces:

How worthy of compassion your position is! I grieve over your misfortune all the more intensely because I have a sympathetic understanding of you . . . Several months have already passed since hostilities began. There have been many hundred casualties every day. Kinsmen are killing one another. Friends are fighting against each other. Never has there been fought a more bloody internecine war that is against all humanity. And no soldier on either side has any grudge against the other. His Majesty's soldiers say that they are fighting in order to fulfil their military duties while your Satsuma men are, in their own words, fighting for the sake of Saigo . . . But it is evident that the Satsuma men cannot hope to accomplish their purpose, for almost all the bravest of your officers have been killed or wounded . . . I earnestly entreat you to make the best of the sad situation yourself as early as you can so as, on the one hand, to prove that the present disturbance is not of your original intention and, on the other, to see to it that you may put an end to casualties on both sides immediately. If you can successfully work out remedial measures, hostilities will soon come to an end.

But Saigo was fated to play his tragically Japanese role to the end, to inspire generations of future self-sacrificial warriors. He and his companions spent the moonlit night of 23–24 September 1877 composing such poems as:

> If I were a drop of dew, I could take shelter on a leaftip,
> But being a man I have no place in this whole world.
>
> Having fought in the Emperor's cause
> (I know my end is near)
> What joy to die like the tinted leaves that fall in Tatsuta,
> Before they have been spoiled by autumn rains!

At four in the morning the government attack began. Saigo descended the hill and was hit by a bullet; he was carried down further, until he told his faithful retainer, 'My dear Shinsuke, I think this place will do.' Then he cut open his stomach and had his head cleanly cut off by Shinsuke. The head was later found by the Imperial forces and presented to Yamagata. 'Ah, what a gentle look you have upon your face,' he exclaimed. Saigo's rebellion had been hopeless from the start, a last sacrificial death-spasm of old Japan.

Two sinister threads lead from that clash into the history of Japan this century. First, the tradition of samurai fanaticism, of extreme nationalism with the objective of rescuing the emperor from his evil advisers, was established and confirmed by Saigo's quixotic rebellion. He provided the role model for succeeding generations of the extreme right; the kamikaze pilots regarded the 'death-defying' Saigo as their precursor. Second, the foundation of the new Japanese army, opposed by the samurai class and conscripted largely from the grinding poverty of the Japanese peasantry, was laid. The new army was a levelling one in which formal class distinctions were abolished and, in theory, it was possible to rise from the ranks to the top; in practice it remained very status-conscious until war decimated the higher ranks. Indeed, the class divisions of the army were to prove part of the dynamic rush to disaster of Japanese militarism in the 1930s.

4

THE SEEDS OF
TOTALITARIANISM

FTER THE triumph over the samurai in 1877, there followed a
thirty-year period in which the new regime set out to consolidate itself and lay down the defining characteristics of the
Meiji era that marked the emergence of modern Japan. These were:
the creation of the emperor myth; the establishment of a modern
centralized administration modelled on French and British lines; the
drawing up of a unified education system; the consolidation of a
state religion; the setting up of a national army; the construction of
a modern industrial society; and finally, based on the self-confidence
engendered by industrial success, the evolution of an aggressive and
expansionist foreign policy modelled on what the Japanese believed
to be the example of European colonialism.

The combined effect of these radical transformations was to
make Japan perhaps the most efficient authoritarian society the
world has ever known. For the Japanese managed to graft the
totalitarian methods of the twentieth century, amplified by modern
communications and education, upon a system that – because Japan
had undergone no revolution – was still intensely hierarchical in
nature. Japanese society, as has already been noted, was based on
obeisance from top to bottom, extending from family to village to
central government. Improved modern methods of authoritarian
control, plus a modern army and secret police, as well as the
indoctrination made possible by the education system, combined to
produce a terrifyingly effective pyramid of pure power.

The greatest flaw in the post-Meiji Japanese system was that, in
spite of its rigidly hierarchical nature, at the very pinnacle there was
a crisis of authority. The ship of state was formidable and mono-
lithic, but there was no one at the helm – or rather there were several

people disputing supreme authority. To change the metaphor, inside the bristling headgear of samurai armour, there was nothing, no controlling eyes or brain – which perhaps made the structure of Japanese power all the more sinister.

By vesting absolute authority in a figurehead – the emperor – who did not exercise full power, other sources of real legitimacy were denied control. Sovereignty in Japan was not vested with the people, or with parliament, or even with an oligarchy, but in the hollow shell of imperial power, which in practice meant those who happened to have the ear of the throne. This was jealously fought over, and Japan prospered best when there was paralysis at the top – something as true of the pre-war as of the post-war period. But when one of the factions close to the throne grew too strong, it obtained control of a system of awesome power: in the wrong hands, the destructive force of the body politic could be truly fearsome. This was the constitutional structure forged by the aristocrats who created Meiji Japan. Its major institutions, as we shall see, have shown astonishing durability and continuity through the traumas of economic collapse, war, atomic destruction, reconstruction and the attainment of superpower status.

The emperor was now at the heart of the political culture. Prior to the Meiji restoration, the office had been passive and mystical. The few foreigners with experience of Japan under the shogun hardly ever heard the emperor mentioned; his practical duties were limited largely to the performance of certain ritual functions at the heart of a stagnant aristocratic court at Kyoto. In order to stage the coup, the 'outside lords' who came to power after 1867 looked to cast the emperor in a more active future role, endowed not just with divinity but with supreme political authority.

The 'above-the-clouds' figure in Kyoto was at first transformed into a more modern kind of monarch, travelling the country to unify the nation. In 1872 the emperor embarked upon the first of six 'Great Circuits' across the country: ships, horses, palanquins, and his own two feet carried him from one end of his domains to another, up steep mountain paths and across major rivers. Kaoru Inouye, one of his chief advisers, argued that 'the emperor's visiting all parts of Japan not only infects the people of the Empire with virtue, but also offers the opportunity of displaying direct imperial rule in the flesh,' thus strengthening the imprint of monarchical government. The young Emperor Mutsuhito was accessible, stayed in people's houses and inns, and was the subject of obeisance and veneration by thousands of subjects eager to see him in the flesh. Perhaps the founders of Meiji Japan intended initially to make him the kind of constitutional monarch they had observed in Britain – loved and respected, but ultimately merely the pinnacle of a system which was firmly in the grasp of government, politicians, and people. Not until Hirohito's travels after the Second World War would a Japanese emperor be so human, so close to his subjects.

As the emperor grew into adulthood it became clear, moreover, that he at least was unlikely to be purely a puppet of his senior advisers. The extent to which Mutsuhito was involved in day-to-day decisions is a closely guarded secret, even now. Formally, he had no authority to intervene in decision-making: he merely approved the decisions of his Council, which was later transformed into his Cabinet. But as he outlasted his senior advisers, his views came to count for more and more. Nor was Mutsuhito a withdrawn or quiet personality. He made clear his passionate interest in two areas of policy. Education was one consuming field of concern; the other was war, where it is doubtful that major decisions could have taken place against the express disagreement of the emperor.

Mutsuhito presided over two wars: the first Sino-Japanese War and the Russo-Japanese War. As the first conflict broke out in September 1894, the imperial headquarters moved south to the port of embarkation for the troops, Hiroshima, 'to oversee the imperial affair of war'. For eight months, it was reported, the Meiji Emperor lived the life of his troops, experiencing 'imperial simplicity' (shisso), living in a small room, sitting on a three-legged stool, wearing out his clothes. 'Unheeding of the inconvenience, the emperor works day and night at military offices, rises at six, retires at midnight and even when resting listens to his aides experienced on military matters.' The emperor gave more than 800,000 cigarettes to the troops, as well as 7000 gallons of sake. Until recently, the emperor was lauded for his 'guiding role' at Hiroshima.

Almost exactly a decade later, in the Russo-Japanese conflict of 1904–5, the war leader re-emerged into prominence. Instead of leading a life of privation, this time the emperor was credited with most of the decisions affecting war and peace; he also wrote no fewer than 7526 poems on the subject (mercifully, not least for him, only four lines long) during the year and a half of war. These include such classics as 'When I think of those in battle, I have no heart for the flowers' and 'Crush the enemy for the sake of the nation, but I never forget to have mercy' – a sentiment Tolstoy criticized as self-contradictory in a celebrated literary duel with the Japanese writer Tokutomi Roka.

It was not just in the field of education and war that the emperor abondoned his official 'above the clouds' status to deal with earthly matters. After a violent outbreak of rioting, which in 1911 resulted in several executions, the crown was responsible for a grant of 1.5 million yen for drugs and medicines for the very poor in order to convey the message that, in the words of the official announcement, 'as economic conditions change, the hearts of the people are steadfast'. Not just by donations to the poor, but by exhortations to hard work, good manners, simple living, and strenuous effort did the emperor actively exhort his people to overcome hardship without recourse to extremism.

Yet virtually no student of the period regards the emperor as having exercised direct day-to-day political power: that lay in the hands of the Choshu and Satsuma clan chieftains, who alternated as effective prime minister with remarkable regularity. They used the imperial institution in a much more actively political way than before. While the emperor had influence and was certainly prepared to make his own views known, he neither initiated nor controlled policy.

Emperor-worship was also proselytized intensively as part of the nationalist creed that ushered Japan into the twentieth century. The extent to which respect for the emperor was inculcated, not just as a matter of political culture but as a deep-seated obligation upon ordinary Japanese, cannot be exaggerated. The Japanese system of *on*, 'obligations passively incurred', with which, like original sin in the Christian religion, every Japanese is born, related not just to one's very reason for existence, but to one's parents, one's older brother or sister, one's teachers, and one's work, as well as society, symbolized by the emperor.

Of these *ko-on*, obligation towards the emperor, was the highest of all, and no man could begin to repay it in full. Duty to the emperor far eclipsed that to Japan as a country, or to the government. While historically such obligations had always existed, Meiji Japan laid special stress upon them because the emperor was the sole source of its legitimacy. Japan had until then been a divided country whose allegiance to its feudal lords was all-important. A set of national values engendered by overseas threats had been virtually non-existent; very few Japanese were even aware of an outside world. Its intrusion fuelled nationalist sentiment, while the growing severity of taxation helped to erode the feeling of loyalty to one's feudal lord. The Meiji restoration therefore capitalized upon an latent loyalty to a 'divine emperor', transforming it into the very lifeblood of twentieth-century Japanese nationalism.

The high-profile leadership role accorded the emperor under the Meiji regime required a sharp break with the past – indeed, it was almost a desecration of the previous tradition that the emperor was so divine as to take no part in politics. This sat awkwardly with the fact that the oligarchs wanted the emperor to do their bidding and not make any real choices. So monarchical absolutism was never really exercised throughout the Meiji period, even under Japan's most powerful emperor. It has been argued, indeed, that in those areas where the emperor did assume major responsibility – education, war, and social control – the emperor's personal feelings were paramount. Even if this is true, the throne's concerns were extraordinarily convenient to the ruling oligarchy, whose policies the emperor's personal interventions helped to boost.

In the 1880s the Meiji Emperor, after his initial descent to earthly status, visiting his people and sharing the experiences of his soldiers, began to rise again 'above the clouds', becoming more and more remote. This may be a reflection of his own autocratic, tough personality as he aged. Almost certainly, though, it was also part of an attempt by the Meiji authorities to return him to his godlike role now that their rule was consolidated. Once again he was to act as symbol for the nation rather than its ruler. The more self-confident the Meiji oligarchs became, the less important the emperor was to buttressing their status and the more important as a symbol of national unity in whose name they chose to act. The cult of the emperor was hyped as never before. The emperor became the distant father of his people. He appeared only at grand functions like diplomatic receptions and troop manoeuvres, and no longer visited the houses of ordinary mortals.

The bureaucracy around the throne grew tighter. The Imperial Household Ministry, the Kumaisho, became remarkably powerful. Two men dominated the ministry in the later Meiji period: Hisamoto Hijikato, who was minister from 1887 to 1898, and Mitsuaki Tanaka, who ran it from 1898 to 1909. The two men considered themselves the most powerful ministers in the land. Yet in practice the greater power was wielded by the effective prime ministers and strongmen of the country: Hirobumi Ito, Japan's tough-minded autocratic leader, who was close to Hijikata, and Yamagata, the country's effective military leader, a Bismarckian figure who was a friend of Tanaka's. The emperor himself was closer to Ito, and had some sympathy for his attempts to create a constitutional, even genuinely parliamentary structure for the regime.

By contrast, Yamagata was a military autocrat who was slavishly loyal to the imperial system and fought by every means available to emphasize its all-powerful status to the Japanese people. Like many ordinary people, Yamagata worshipped daily at the shrine of the emperor. It was Yamagata who was responsible for the growing distance of the subjects from their emperor, having been impressed by the way the Tsar of Russia was kept remote and mysterious from his people (hardly a fortunate comparison, as events turned out).

Yamagata was to be the most powerful man in Japan for years to come, the creator of its military machine and an autocrat of unbending sternness. Yet he was from the first uncharismatic and unappealing in the extreme: thin and stiff, deeply reserved, and troubled by ill-health, born of samurai stock, he had the characteristic Japanese hatred of the foreigner. When a British vessel raided a village for fuel and water, Yamagata wrote: 'The ugly English barbarians behaved with extreme disorder and uncontrollable couthness . . . When we unsheath our swords and kill them, they . . . will be thrown into the deep sea like bits of seaweed.' He was brave, and was badly wounded in the forearm while commanding a Choshu fort attacked by French ships.

As a young man Yamagata was a member of the *kiheitai*, 'shock troops': an entirely new concept in which groups of samurai formed the nucleus for a military force of commoners. The idea was that the ancient privileged caste of samurai were too few to resist the foreigners making military incursions into Japan, so the ancient privileges of the caste had to be shared with commoners – under samurai control, of course. This *kiheitai* was at the centre of Yamagata's subsequent vision of a national conscript army run at the top by Choshu samurai, but soldiered by conscripted commoners.

An emperor worshipped by many Japanese as a living deity, who had replaced the shogun as the supreme political arbiter, was the first underpinning of modern Japan. It was easy enough to see why the emperor had been so important in 1867, when the shogun was deposed. His authority alone had been superior to that of Japan's absolutist ruling family for two and a half centuries. He was a unifying symbol of his country, and, because he had been so rigorously excluded from political power in the past, a popular one at that. He was not identified with oppression, or with a particular political standpoint.

But why, from being an accessible and attractive young monarch, had he been elevated once again to the status of demigod by the closing stages of the Meiji period? The period has been compared to the Victorian age in Britain, but in almost every respect the comparison is false. No person of the slightest influence in Britain believed that the monarch, whose authority had been chipped away over three centuries of parliamentary struggle, was all-powerful, and few ordinary people did. In contrast, by the end of the Meiji period, its leaders were seeking to boost the monarchy to divine status again.

They did this because of their own lack of legitimacy. Certainly, as an aristocratic, bureaucratic elite of high intelligence, they put into place a highly effective administration which brought Japan into the modern era. But, like any bureaucracy, it was seen as self-appointed. Civil servants, however brilliant, energetic, and well-intentioned, cannot run a country without some form of legitimacy which makes ordinary people accept their right to govern. Sheer ability has never been enough.

In world history, there have been three major sources of legitimacy: heredity, popular support and coercion (and a few minor ones like theocracy). Although Yamagata was essentially a military autocrat and might have been able to rule Japan through force, the country had not yet reached a stage where terror underpinned government. With the collapse of the shogunate, most of the forces of argument, criticism and democracy that had raised their heads everywhere else in the world appeared in Japan.

The bureaucratic class was not only loath to surrender its control of the country; it believed deeply that no country could be run by democratic means, through popularly elected, corrupt and squabbling politicians. At most, politicians should be permitted to provide a minor check to the power of the executive, to provide an illusion of popular participation. So the bureaucracy looked to the monarchy and the system of respect that permeated Japanese society to buttress its legitimacy, which otherwise was based on nothing. Japan's self-perpetuating elite used the prestige of the emperor to conceal the fact that it had neither a true monopoly of military force – as the shoguns had had – to control the country (the armed forces never regarded themselves as subject to the bureaucrats), nor a popular mandate. The imperial system became the clothing for autocratic, bureaucratic rule, often well-meaning, always intolerant of criticism.

In the emperor's name, a struggle was to be waged during the last Meiji years against genuine democratic and constitutional forces; Japan was not so bizarre a country that it failed to harbour its own advocates of parliamentary constitutionalism. The Victorian age in Britain, like Japan's Meiji period, was one of great self-confidence and commercial and imperial expansion. Yet in some respects the Victorian age represented the attainment of maturity for Britain's economic and constitutional development: the successful pioneering of industrial technology and economic theory, more than a century before, had come to fruition. Moreover, Britain's parliamentary tradition, evolved over several hundred years, had reached the stage where the middle classes could demand and obtain universal male suffrage.

By comparison, Japan's economic and constitutional evolution was concertinaed into just four decades: the country proceeded from feudalism and an economy which depended very largely upon agriculture to a centralized bureaucratic state and considerable industrial power in the space of little more than a generation.

Even at the beginning of her reign, Queen Victoria was largely a ceremonial figurehead, the limits of whose power were clearly understood. Yet in the Japanese context it was as though, by the end of her reign, Victoria had suddenly been invested with the divine right of kings, and a small clique acting in her name had crushed the forces demanding popular participation and constitutional rule.

Closer comparisons can be drawn with Napoleon III's France and the Kaiser's Germany. In neither case, however, was the monarch endowed with godlike powers, and neither had the dynastic legitimacy to aspire to them. It is impossible to imagine Frenchmen or Germans committing suicide for Napoleon or Wilhelm in the way the Japanese did for their emperor until the end of the Second World War. The legend that the emperor was descended from the Sun Goddess, and was therefore divine, was tied up with the claim that the imperial line of succession had been unbroken throughout Japan's history. This was then inculcated by all modern means of communication into ordinary people. It was as if the Führer or Duce cult of a Hitler or Mussolini had become welded to a historical legitimacy endowed by thousands of years of history, with the spiritual authority of a living god.

The emperor principle was certainly an ancient Japanese tradition, but it was only during the Meiji period that it was propagated to the point where the vast majority of Japanese literally worshipped the emperor as a father figure of love and respect to whom they had virtually limitless obligations; when someone spoke on behalf of the emperor, moreover, he had to be obeyed. The Meiji rulers – in particular during the later period when the armed forces were becoming more powerful – thus forged from existing Japanese tradition a potent weapon of absolute rule such as had never existed before in the country's history. The Meiji autocrats had set themselves a task of forging national unity in a country driven by intense internal rivalry, and turning it into a commercial and military giant.

Japan's history this century has often been seen in terms of a steadily evolving constitutional experiment, hijacked during the 1940s by a radical band of extremist officers. In fact, in terms of emperor-worship (as in so many other fields), the foundations of absolutism and militarism were laid down under the Meiji emperor, and it is possible to argue that it was the constitutionalists who hijacked the state for a few years during the 1920s. The Meiji restoration was to establish the main lines of Japanese politics up to 1945, and to a significant extent thereafter.

The imperial family had its origins in the distant past; the modern imperial myth dates back no further than 1868. The extremists of the 1930s were to be justified in arguing that they were faithful in most respects to the emperor system and to the nationalist model created by the Meiji period, although in no sense were they being faithful to Japan's earlier history of internal introspection and imperial impotence. The road to Pearl Harbor began in the late nineteenth century, not during the 1930s.

5

GOVERNMENT BY CLIQUE

FROM THE start, brave men tried to challenge the new authoritarians. The standard-bearer of constitutional reform and liberalism in Japan was Taisuke Itagaki, an elegant, attractive personality with the finest flowing beard ever seen in Japanese politics. However, he was hardly a revolutionary figure. One of the oligarchy's most prominent members (although not a member of the dominant Choshu or Satsuma clans), he sided with Saigo in sharp disagreement with the government's refusal to go to war with Korea in 1873. In 1874, he became leader of the opposition, calling for the establishment of an elected assembly; he knew that this had already been considered as a necessary façade of modern government.

The document drawn up by Itagaki was nevertheless a memorable plea for constitutional government. It complained that 'administration is conducted in an arbitrary manner, rewards and punishments are prompted by partiality, the channel by which the people should communicate with the government is blocked up and they cannot state their grievances'. It demanded that, as in other countries of the world, 'the people whose duty it is to pay taxes to the government possess the right of sharing in the government's affairs and of approving and condemning'. The document countered with almost unassailable logic the oligarchy's argument that Japan needed as much time as the West had had to develop its own forms of democracy:

> The reason why foreigners have perfected this only after the lapse of centuries is that no examples existed previously and these had to be discovered by actual experience . . . If we can select examples from them and adopt their contrivances, why should we not be

successful in working them out? If we are to delay the using of steam machinery until we have discovered the principles of steam for ourselves, or to wait until we have discovered the principles of electricity before we construct an electric telegraph, our government will be unable to set to work.

Leading Japanese politicians denounced the document with outpourings of unashamed reaction. There was great danger, avowed one, in giving power to a people whose intelligences were insufficiently developed 'for they do not know how to exercise them duly, and hence fall into licence'. Itagaki, however, had made it clear that he was not contemplating giving the vote to the lower orders: 'We would only give it in the first instance to the samurai and the richer farmers and merchants, for it is they who produced the leaders of the revolution of 1868.'

Itagaki's movement, the Jiyuto, or Liberal Party, was led largely by discontented samurai, some of them officers, some of them idealists, and supported by the malcontents of that class as well as by peasant proprietors, tenants, and the urban poor. One of the peculiarities of the Jiyuto was the moderation of its leadership and the radicalism of some of its followers, such as those who in 1884 staged a violent uprising in Chichuba Province, as a result of which the moderate Jiyuto leaders agreed to disband the party. There is no real mystery about this, however: Itagaki and other leading nobles and merchants believed in a more constitutional and considerate form of government. In no sense did they favour social upheaval – indeed, they were as violently nationalist and imperialist in outlook as the oligarchy itself.

Radical groups flocked to the opposition banner only to discover, as has happened throughout Japan's history, that no real change in the system was possible. The tradition of revolutionary violence dates from this period. The Japanese far left became violent and anarchistic precisely because it could see no way in which the political system could be reformed except through bloody revolution. The very hopelessness of its cause drove it to desperate tactics (just as the far right, which realized it could not topple the regime after Saigo's defeat, decided to use terrorism to influence the climate of opinion in its favour).

Meanwhile, the Liberal movement was riven by internal rivalries, inadequate leadership and the opportunism of its leaders, who were frequently wooed into government. Other movements lacked any solid base among the urban bourgeoisie and proletariat; the government moved with ruthless alacrity to destroy any manifestation of working-class solidarity. The Liberal movement increasingly came to appear as no more than a group of aristocratic and samurai malcontents who were not, however, in fundamental disagreement with the system. Of course, they were supported by the various groups in society – and there were many – at the receiving end of Japan's system of enforced industrialization: principally the peasants, who were mercilessly taxed to provide the capital for industrialization, and the urban workers.

Under prodding, the government had agreed in 1881 to provide the semblance of constitutional rule by promising to draw up a constitution and summon a parliament by the year 1890. When the parliament finally met, it proved to be powerless. Democracy was stillborn in Japan. The architect of the constitution had been Hirobumi Ito, now virtually prime minister and current leader of the oligarchy. In March 1882 he set off on a trip to Europe to study constitutions there. Prince Kinmochi Saionji, another prominent courtier who was to become the attractive voice of reason and moderation in Japanese politics right up to the Pacific War, was dispatched specifically to study the French constitution.

Ito first went to Berlin to study with two prominent German jurists, Rudolf von Gneist and Professor Lorenz von Stein. The two advised him that constitutions should be ratified only by the court, not by people, that Parliament should have no authority to ask questions about the armed forces and the prerogatives of the imperial household, that elected representatives should be refused the power to question ministers, and that if they rejected a budget, the previous year's budget should come into force. These German sages also considered that cabinets should not be drawn from political parties, that universal suffrage should not be introduced, and that only the government should be granted the power to initiate legislation.

On a brief stopover in England Ito was delighted to receive such advice, and was dismissive of Herbert Spencer's lectures on representative government. 'The tendency in a country today is erroneously to believe in the words of British, French and American liberals and radicals as if they were golden rules, and that leads virtually to the overthrow of the state. In looking for principles and ways of combating this trend, I believe I have rendered an important service to my country, and I feel intensely that I can die a happy man,' Ito wrote in 1881 before beginning to draft the constitution.

(The nature of the political debate in Japan is illustrated by the fact that Ito was a relative liberal compared with the tough-minded Yamagata.)

When the draft constitution was ready, it was entrusted not to a constitutional council but to the privy council – the highest bureaucratic power in Japan. The people were being handed crumbs from the table of the ruling elite. In 1889 the constitution was promulgated. It formalized the huge extension of central government power at the expense of local autonomy that occurred in 1874 when the Department of Home Affairs took over the whole semi-autonomous structure of local government. Henceforth the department, the Naimusho, would have authority over local taxes, schooling, hospitals, public works, ports – virtually the whole range of local government functions. The usually indirectly elected headmen and councils were merely given the right to rubber-stamp the decisions of the bureaucracy.

At a national level, a parliament was set up along strictly German lines with the power to reject the budget – but the government retained the right to introduce that of the previous year. Ministers were responsible to the emperor, not to parliament. However, the Diet (the lower house) had to approve all measures before they became law. However, to its credit, even with such limited powers the Diet in its first two years attempted to block the government at every turn. The government, now instituted as an elderly cabal of the most senior civil servants – the *genro* – and a cabinet, responded by attempting to discredit Parliament. In addition, the army, an emerging power in the land, viewed elected politicians with open contempt.

The aristocratically constituted upper house of peers was able to block most initiatives emanating from the lower house; and the latter was undermined by having its sittings restricted and through systematic bribery. Parliament was convoked by the emperor in late December, and promptly adjourned through the New Year's holiday to 20 January; it was frequently shut down by imperial order for a fortnight; and its sittings were restricted to three afternoons a week. Most years it sat for only forty days altogether. A contemporary observer, Walter McLaren, described the situation thus:

> By deserting their party principles, as outlined in 1890, and by selling their support to the oligarchy, the parties have immensely strengthened the latter's position, and at the same time postponed

the realisation of a responsible government for a generation or even longer . . .

The epidemic of bribery and corruption in the Diet in 1898 and 1899 was the result of the peculiarities of the Japanese political system and the Japanese character. If the representatives of the people in the lower house were unable to control the policy of the government, they could at least, by refusing their consent, prevent the government from carrying out its measures; therefore the government was forced to purchase a sufficient number of votes . . . Hence in 1898 Yamagata for the oligarchs and Hoshi Totu for the kenseito (the main opposition party) arranged terms satisfactory to everyone concerned. In return for the votes of the party and the enactment of its own programme of legislation, the government handed over valuable considerations in franchises and money . . .

Few party politicians have made as immense fortunes out of bribes as have the cabinet ministers, and it is only necessary to point to the list of Japanese millionaires to prove the point. A few of them are businessmen – the Mitsuis, the Iwasakis, Okura, Shibusawa, Furukawa, Yasuda – others are descendants of the great daimyo families, who at the beginning of the Meiji era were already in possession of great wealth, and the remainder are the so-called elder statesmen and cabinet ministers. These latter were originally in almost every case either poor samurai or the sons of men of very modest fortune, and have all their lives been in the service of the state, drawing small salaries. Their present immense properties are not the result of savings wisely invested, but of speculations and bribery.

In short, the political system set up by Meiji Japan consisted of an oligarchic bureaucratic elite which ran the country in the name of the emperor, occasionally according to his wishes, trampling on the rights of a parliament elected on only a limited franchise, buying and selling deputies with contempt. Moreover, few governments in the world were as clearly run from the centre – that is, by the bureaucracy – as was Japan's after local government reform. The representatives of the people were pushed into a distant third place towards the end of the nineteenth century by the emergence of Japan's military class.

Before looking at military power, however, the role played by two of the most powerful institutions of authority utilized by the Meiji autocracy need to be examined. These are education and religion, which together gave Japan's rulers a degree of thought control over the people that the Nazis never came near, and which even Stalinist Russia failed to match.

The creator of Japan's education system, which has proved remarkably durable for a century, was Arinori Mori, the Meiji government's most celebrated education minister. His views were to be hotly contested by a senior imperial adviser, Eifu Motoda, to whom Mori's precepts were dangerously liberal. Motoda believed in instilling children with absolute loyalty to the emperor and with carrying out the world 'mission' of the Japanese nation; Mori believed in a more moderate form of nationalist indoctrination, and in the benefits of military training. Mori was assassinated by a fanatical right-winger suspicious of his 'liberal' Western ideas, but the minister's system lived on.

Some idea of the 'liberality' of Mori's ideas can be gained from their origin. In 1867 he spent a year in the United States, where he fell under the sway of Thomas Luke Harris, a Christian fundamentalist who had established the Brotherhood of the New Life Colony in Amenia and Salem-on-Erie in New York State. The bases for these colonies were discipline, hard physical labour and absolute subservience to the creator. 'Duty, friendship, and obedience', the slogan of Harris's colonists, was transplanted into the Japanese school system – with obedience, of course, reserved for the emperor.

The system Mori gave his country was essentially a dual one: through primary and secondary education, a degree of indoctrination and toughness was introduced that smothered all independent thought and critical attitudes. At university level, freedom of discussion and lax discipline were permitted. The theory was that the elite alone should be permitted the luxury of independent thought – this would be necessary to them in later life; the ordinary person was cudgelled into a wholly dependent way of thinking.

There was an intermediate educational milieu, from which the Japanese middle and management class emerged: the 'normal schools', where military discipline was strictly enforced. The Tokyo High Normal School, for example, was run by Colonel Yamakawa. Students were kept in barrack-like dormitories, and were forced to take part in five or six hours' military discipline every week. Mori believed that 'military training must be carried out for the sake of physical development'.

Even so, Mori's ideas were denounced as wildly radical by

Motoda, who took advantage of the emperor's interest in education to persuade him to make a tour of primary schools in 1878. As intended, the emperor returned horrified by the spread of knowledge, albeit introduced by severe rote methods, at the expense of the Confucian virtues of submissiveness and loyalty. The emperor promptly issued a rescript – an imperial edict – attacking Mori's methods. Written by Motoda, it was as remarkable for its reactionary banality as for the fact that it was to become an almost sacred text in the schools, kept in its own shrine in each school, and read with trembling reverence by every headmaster to his pupils. The introduction to this gospel ran as follows:

> In recent days, people have been going to extremes. They take unto themselves a foreign civilization whose only values are fact-gathering and technique, thus violating the rules of good manners and bringing harm to our customary ways. Although we set out to take in the best features of the West and bring in new things in order to achieve the high aims of the Meiji restoration – abandonment of the undesirable practices of the past and learning from the outside world – this procedure has a serious defect: it reduced benevolence, justice, loyalty and filial piety to a secondary position. The danger of indiscriminate emulation of Western ways is that in the end our people will forget the great principles governing the relations between ruler and subject, and father and son. Our aim, based on the ancestral teachings, is solely the clarification of benevolence, justice, loyalty and filial pity . . .
>
> While making a tour of schools and closely observing the pupils studying last autumn, it was noted that farmers' and merchants' sons were advocating high-sounding ideas and empty theories . . . Moreover, many of them brag about their knowledge, slight their elders and disturb prefectural officers. All these evil effects come from an education that is off its proper course . . . Agricultural and commercial subjects should be studied by the children of farmers and merchants so that they return to their own occupations when they have finished school and prosper even more in their proper work.

The rescript itself, a kind of divine credo which schoolmasters on occasion killed themselves for stumbling over, ran thus:

> Know ye, our subjects!
> Our imperial ancestors have founded our empire on a basis

broad and everlasting and have deeply and firmly implanted virtue; our subjects, ever united in loyalty and filial piety, have from generation to generation illustrated the beauty thereof. This is the glory of the fundamental character of our empire, and herein also lies the source of our education. Ye, our subjects, be filial to your parents, affectionate to your brothers and sisters; as husbands and wives be harmonious, as friends true; bear yourselves in modesty and moderation; extend your benevolence to all; pursue learning and cultivate arts, and thereby develop your intellectual faculties and perfect your moral powers; furthermore, advance the public good and promote common interests; always respect the constitution and observe the laws; should any emergency arise, offer yourselves courageously to the state; and thus guard and maintain the prosperity of the imperial throne, coeval with heaven and earth. So shall ye not only be our good and faithful subjects, but render illustrious the best traditions of your forefathers.

The way here set forth is indeed the teaching bequeathed by our imperial ancestors, to be observed alike by their descendants and subjects, infallible for all ages and true in all places. It is our wish to lay it to heart in all reverence, in common with you, our subjects, that we may all thus attain to the same virtue.

This was the most important imperial promulgation between 1868 and 1945. Three things stand out: it lays central stress on hierarchical family loyalty; it requires 'subjects' to pursue 'the public good', with the emphasis on social rather than private obligation; and firmly demands subordination and devotion to the state and the throne 'coeval with heaven and earth'. Many of its exhortations are admirable, of course, such as that enjoining husbands and wives to be harmonious and friends true. But as the incantation of pure authoritarianism – which in thousands of schools throughout Japan it literally was – it takes some beating.

Mori, in the preface to the rescript, had been given the black spot of imperial disapproval; on the day of the promulgation of the new constitution, 11 February 1889, he was assassinated. The essence of the system from then on was not the learning of knowledge in the parrot-like form favoured by Mori, but service to the emperor. The regulations for the teaching of history insisted that 'the essential aim of teaching Japanese history is to make children comprehend the fundamental character of the emperor and to fashion in the national spirit ... Children should be taught the outlines of the establishment of the Empire, the continuity of the imperial dynasty.' Geography was taught to make children understand 'how our country stands in the world, and to instil in their minds a love of their country', and so on.

A terrifying degree of formality was inculcated into Japanese school life: the emperor's birthday, the ceremonial assemblies surrounding the reading of the imperial rescript on education (which had to be carried reverently in white gloved hands and read to perfection), the display of imperial portraits, the raising and lowering of the flag – all were carried out in the manner of sacred ritual.

Loyalty to the emperor; obedience; physical and military training; strict learning by rote: these were the cornerstones of the Japanese education system. While it all sounds harsh in the extreme, and its principal purpose was to produce citizens loyal to the emperor who would function like automatons in the national interest, it should be remembered that it replaced a virtually nonexistent system and reached the masses, and that education in the outside world was almost as tough, if more liberal-minded in subject matter.

A feature of the Japanese system that might be described as progressive – although it also reflected Japan's obsession with hierarchy at all levels – was its 'meritocratic' nature. While Japan remained an oligarchy at the highest levels, and real power was confined to a ruling elite of traditional families and friends, both aristocratic and from the richest merchant classes, the intention was to create a measure of competition which would allow the best and the brightest to come forth and serve in the higher administrative posts. This created a highly structured society, and plagued education with the frenzied competition that was one of its most unattractive features. It was also, though, a laudable attempt to create a genuine meritocracy.

The system provided for six years of elementary schooling followed by streaming at the age of eleven or twelve. There was intense pressure at this stage, because it was virtually impossible to move to a higher stream from a lower one later on. Those destined for higher education went on to middle school, if they passed their exams; those who failed went to advanced primary, continuation, vocational, technical and normal schools. After five years at middle school, pupils were futher streamed to go into 'higher' schools, which prepared them for university.

Only one in thirteen middle-school graduates could expect to go on to a higher school, and only one in twenty-five to the prestigious schools which led on to the imperial universities. In the 1920s, of the 70,000 middle-school graduates a year, only 5000 would get into one of the higher schools. With such few openings, pressure was intense and the competition for exams overwhelming. Passing or failing decided whether a pupil was to enter the country's upper middle class in government or business, or be confined to the lower strata of society. Those that failed could stop their studies, go to a normal or military school, or go to a college or technical school, which might train a man up to be an engineer, a doctor, or an architect. The few that succeeded went to university on completing their courses.

Those entering one of the elite schools, such as the Tokyo First High School, were guaranteed a place at Tokyo Imperial University, the top university, which in turn guaranteed them a senior post in business or government. For girls, who were rigorously separated from boys at an early age, the highest possible aspiration was to go to a college or technical school. Much has been made of the meritocratic bias of the new system; indeed, it was a major improvement on the one it had replaced. But money was necessary to purchase enough days of cramming to get into the best schools, as were connections to help with places, and bribes to help students through exams. University itself was extraordinarily relaxed, and a degree virtually guaranteed: it proved to be the one extended holiday in the competitive life of the Japanese achiever.

The Japanese system was thus defined from the start by elitism and status. Ordinary school-leavers went on to become manual workers, middle-school graduates to do white-collar work (the production channel in industry or the lower administrative class in government), and university graduates went to higher executive channels of business, industry or the bureaucracy. There was virtually no interchange between the three: people were pigeon-holed for life.

The structure of Meiji society consisted, then, of a tiny controlling and competing bureaucratic and business elite possessing immense hereditary wealth; an upper class made up of the best administrators and bureaucrats; and a huge white-collar class distinguished from an equally large blue-collar class. There was virtually no middle class. Indeed, the structure was not all that different from that of pre-Meiji Japan in a non-industrial context: a privileged few lording it over the rest, but now with the distinction that able men in the lower reaches of society could make it all the way up the ladder to the top rung but one – an advance not to be dismissed.

*

The second main instrument of ideological control used by the Meiji government was religion. What happened in Japan may be unique; it was partially attempted by the Islamic countries which this century have sought to base their authority on religious rule. In Japan after the restoration, a hotchpotch of local superstitions that barely deserves the name of religion was promoted above the advanced and meditative creed that most Japanese believed in – Buddhism – and turned into the religion of the state. When, inevitably, this attempt to impose religion upon the people failed, the new religion was used for secular goals – to underpin the supremacy of a political system deriving its authority from emperor-worship.

The resurgence of Shinto under the Meiji government has usually been portrayed as the reassertion of a native religion against the corrupting foreign influence of Buddhism and, to a lesser extent, of Christianity and Confucian ethics. Nothing could be further from the truth. By the time of the Meiji restoration, few educated people regarded Shinto as a coherent religion at all. It was the umbrella term under which was drawn together the huge wealth of superstitions and myths that made up Japan's popular peasant culture. There was no body of doctrine, no central organization, no real priesthood, no sense of ethics or beliefs to Shinto – merely a plethora of animist gods and a cult of ancestor worship centred around the emperor.

Buddhism and Confucianism, and to a lesser extent – because of the official resistance to it – Christianity, had been necessary to fill the moral and intellectual vacuum left by this jumble of legends and ritualistic devotions to particular shrines, which were the independently run focuses for worship. The Meiji imposition of Shintoism was as if a government had come to power in London in the middle of the nineteenth century wanting to revive the legend of King Arthur and his court as a national religion; or the government of Norway had resurrected the myth of Thor; or the one in Greece that of Mount Olympus. Even these stories had greater plausibility and sophistication than Japan's ancient folk-myths, although the beauty and poetry of the latter were sometimes unsurpassed. Prince Inouye, one of the Meiji era's foremost statesmen, argued that 'as a religion, Shinto is primitive. But it is not merely a religion; in relation to Japan's *kokutai* [national spirit] it is related to Japan's future as a nation.' He insisted that 'Shinto as vulgar Shinto is mere superstition, but as the ancestor worship of Japan, it possesses great power.'

Both remarks illustrate the real aim of the government in raising Shinto to its new pedestal. First, to impose an authentically national religion upon a people. To most thinking Japanese, the native beliefs were so crude as to have been subordinated by Buddhist and Confucian ethics from China. Second, to resurrect the imperial institution's sacred role. Both were political objectives. They ran up against the simple fact that anyone with a religious disposition of any sophistication in Japan was more likely to be influenced by Buddhism, which indeed had been intelligent enough to tolerate and absorb Shinto beliefs, thus defusing any potential conflict between the two. Ordinary Japanese were permitted to believe in both, one more satisfying on an intellectual and moral plane, the other more so on a superstitious plane.

By 1868, Shinto existed only as a congregation of shrine priests associated with more or less popular shrines that existed to allow contact with *kami*, a vast pantheon of spirits inherent in nature. These spirits could be summoned to help people, or might require entertainment or purification rituals to appease their anger. Any person, living or dead, or any place or any object could be worshipped as *kami*, which were popularly said to number eight million gods. They lived in the sky, in trees, in rocks, in waterfalls and on islands, as well as being the embodiment of emperors, nobles, and courtiers, or even simple ancestors. Deer and foxes acted as their messengers, and priests interpreted their wills. An enormous amount of Shinto ritual consisted of incantations to the *kami*, who were emotive rather than moral or rational in their behaviour.

The Meiji government, activated by the direct political need to place the emperor at centre stage, promptly sought to disentangle Shinto from Buddhism by issuing an edict to that effect in 1868. What had happened, in many cases, was that Buddhism respected Shinto deities and shrines as lesser gods and places of worship; now it was the turn of the subordinate Shinto priest to be the master. A massive pillaging of Buddhist temples got under way. Buddhist priests were defrocked, their lands confiscated and their status wound down. All Japanese were instructed to register with their Shinto shrines, in order to give the priests direct control over the people. The same year the Department of Divinity was set up as the highest organ of government. The Meiji Emperor personally began to visit the great shrines, particularly the Ise shrine, the most revered of all. National rites and ceremonies were created, supplementing the extensive variety of local customs.

Quite quickly, however, the attempt to subordinate Buddhism began to founder. It became apparent that Buddhist precepts and

Confucianist thought had a much greater hold over the majority of thinking Japanese than did Shintoism, although most continued to have some respect for the old superstitions. Ritual was not enough: Japan still had a spiritual hankering for a set of values, and the appeal of Buddhism showed no sign of falling apart. The Department of Divinity's status was damaged; later it was abolished as the new Meiji rulers realized they could not simply order ordinary Japanese to suppress their inner beliefs. Instead, the Meiji rulers tried turning Shintoism into an arm of the state.

In 1870 the Great Promulgation Campaign was launched, using Shinto priests as a means of propagating a series of views designed to enhance the support of ordinary people for modern, imperial Japan. The main tenets of the campaign were: first, respect for the gods and the laws of the country; second, making clear the Principles of Heaven and the Way of Men; and third, reverence for the emperor and obedience to the will of the court and those who acted in his name. The campaign had a significant internal impact, but Buddhist priests withdrew when they saw that the Shinto clergy were using it to assert their supremacy, and it gradually withered for lack of popular support. Prominent intellectuals were devastating in their criticism of Shinto clerics.

To many educated Japanese, it seemed absurd that animist myth should be elevated to a position of superiority over the profundities of Buddhist teaching. In fact, Shinto was so shallow in both its pastoral and its moral role that it proved unable to compete intellectually with the great religions. As merely an assertion of crude paganism, it could regard other religions as foreign imports, and fall back upon its role as custodian of the sacred shrines and upon the pure ritual of its ceremonies. It was uncomfortable in any pastoral role, reluctant to carry out funerals because of the 'polluting' effect of the dead. The obsession with purification and cleanliness was, of course, a feature of many early creeds, which sought to enforce minimum standards of hygiene in very primitive conditions.

The obvious failings of Shinto were such that, with only a small popular following, it took refuge in asserting that it was not a creed at all, but above religion, and therefore should enjoy powers that no religion had. In fact, Shinto administrators virtually called for this in their manifesto of 1874, which requested the establishment of 'national teaching' and the reinstatement of the Department of Divinity as the supreme organ of government. The memorial argued that there was no need for religion because the emperor, being divine, fulfilled that role: government in effect was a religion, and loyalty to it was observance. The memorial gives an insight into the Shinto mentality at the time:

> National Teaching (*kokyo*) is teaching the codes of national government to the people without error. Japan is called the divine land because it is ruled by the heavenly deities' descendants, who consolidate the work of the deities. The Way of such consolidation and rule by divine descendants is called Shinto . . . The Way of humanity in the age of the gods is nothing other than Shinto in the world of humanity. Ultimately, Shinto means a unity of government and teaching . . . [The Department of Divinity should be restored in order to make it clear that] the National Teaching of the imperial house is not a religion because religions are the theories of their founders. The National Teaching consists of the traditions of the imperial house, beginning in the age of the gods and continuing throughout history. Teaching and consolidating those traditions for the masses are inseparable from government, related as the two wheels of a cart or the wings of a bird. The National Teaching is Shinto . . . and Shinto is nothing other than the National Teaching.

The plea for national teaching and the reinstatement of the Department of Divinity fell on deaf ears. One thing the government was not prepared to do, just because the emperor, now restored, had been the supreme religious deity, was to place the reins of power in the hands of obscurantist clerics. Instead, the oligarchy was prepared to use the creed for its own purposes, and fall in with the idea that Shinto, not being a religion, was above religion. Shinto's role became that of exalting the shrines, of which Ise and the shrines to the war dead were to become the most important. Shinto became an extension of the Japanese colonial and militarist ethic in the Meiji period. In addition, the hierarchical ranking of shrines and shrine registration became another means by which the government could keep an eye on the good behaviour or otherwise of ordinary people.

To honour the war dead, twenty-six special shrines were set up, the main one being the Yasukuni Shrine in Tokyo, as well as local shrines, 'nation-protecting shrines' and lesser war memorials. The immense significance of the Yasukuni Shrine is expounded by Helen Hardacre in her pioneering work on Shinto – an area previously virtually off limits to Western analysts:

The Yasukuni Shrine received respect exceeded only by that accorded to the Ise Grand Shrines. The special status of this shrine derived from the fact that the emperor himself paid tribute to the souls of the war dead. The significance of enshrining the soul of a human being in Yasukuni is that the rite of enshrining is an apotheosis symbolically changing the soul's status to that of a national deity. Accordingly it ceases to be a mere ancestor of some household and instead attaches to the nation. When the emperor paid tribute at Yasukuni, the head priest handed him a sprig of the sakaki plant, which he held for some time, eventually returning it to the priest to place upon the altar. In no other place did the emperor so honor the enshrined souls of commoners. For this reason it was believed to be a great honor to be enshrined there.

Only those who died in battle were exalted there; the wounded were considered disgraced. The essence of the shrine was the glorification and honour of death in battle. Emperor Meiji, who visited the shrine seven times around the beginning of the Russo-Japanese war and led a massive celebration afterwards, was devoted to it. His son Taisho went twice, and Hirohito no fewer that twenty times before 1945.

By 1900 the annual festival of Yasukuni had become a huge jamboree with fireworks, horse racing, sumo wrestling, Noh drama and geisha dancing. There was even a popular board game, whose main objective was to land on a square called 'death', which brought the player to enshrinement at Yasukuni. For many ordinary families, enshrinement at Yasukuni for a soldier was the highest honour possible, bringing greater status than any achievable in life. One father visiting his son's memorial at the turn of the century was recorded by a foreign observer as saying:

> I married very young and for a long time had no children. My wife finally bore a son and died. My son grew up fine and healthy. Then he joined the emperor's forces and died a manly death in southern Kyushu in a great battle. When I heard that he had died for the emperor, I cried with joy, because for my warrior son there could be no finer death.

Another shrine that attracted a national following was that of the Meiji Emperor himself in Tokyo. The cult of shrines was also imposed upon the conquered Japanese territories. By 1943 there were 137 set up in Manchuria, 368 in Korea, and 18 in Taiwan. The shrines became a focus for schoolchildren, who at a ludicrously early age were taught the honour of dying in battle. Children's allegiance to the emperor, as already noted, was enshrined in every school through the emperor's photograph and the imperial rescript on Education, which were both kept locked in a special room, to be taken out only on ceremonial occasions. When the rescript was read, it was paraded, Shinto-style, to a special space with fresh gravel and adorned with red, white and blue curtains, while rice cakes were offered to it as though it were a god.

The intolerance of the Shinto forces behind the Meiji restoration became immediately apparent when it was found that in the neighbourhood of Urakami, near Nagasaki, many Christians had been practising their faith in secrecy for more than two hundred years, in violation of the Buddhist–Shinto credo that banned the religion. The governor of Nagasaki promptly arrested and tortured sixty-eight of the Christians to try and get them to renounce their faith. All 4000 members of the community were banished to distant places of exile, many of them dying in the process. These actions caused revulsion around the world, and it was probably this reaction that prompted the Meiji leaders to enshrine religious freedom in the 1890 constitution, although only partially.

However, Shinto zealots had every opportunity to make life difficult for the Christians. In a famous incident in 1890, a Christian teacher called Uhimira Kanzo refused to bow before the newly promulgated Imperial Rescript on Education; he was dismissed and pilloried in the press as proof that Christianity was unpatriotic. In 1899, General Yamagata proposed a law which gave the state far-reaching powers to control all independent religious activity, on pain of imprisonment or heavy fines. The Diet refused to pass this at first, and only in 1940, at the height of militarist zeal, was it fully enacted.

6

A Nation of Samurai

THE CREATION of the emperor myth, the setting up of a modern central state, the establishment of a modern education system, and the consolidation of Shinto were the first four great enterprises of the Meiji period.

The fifth was the creation of a Japanese national army, a terrifying incubus that was to grow alarmingly in size and power until it suffocated most other institutions and combined with the industrial giants to bring about the country's ruin in 1945.

The origin of the national army has already been touched upon. It emerged, tentatively, as the answer of Japan's modernists to the continuing threat posed by the samurai armies of the provincial princes. To break their stranglehold on armed power in Japan, to suppress the numerous peasant revolts, and to project the country's power more forcefully in resisting predatory foreign powers, a conscripted army was introduced; this so violated Japanese tradition that it inspired the last great rebellion, that of Takamori Saigo, in 1877. Although another conspiracy had been unearthed in 1872–3, it was after Saigo's revolt that the great expansion of the Japanese army under Yamagata began, not because the government feared it could not control future uprisings (the danger was past), but in an unashamed attempt to lay the groundwork for Japan's colonial expansion. Indeed, Saigo's revolt was the last occasion on which the samurai, or any of the outlying *daimyo* – now stripped of their armies – were to challenge the power of the state.

By this time the number of peasant revolts was also falling off. They had, in fact, posed a major problem to the new government, although because they were a challenge to the authority of the whole ruling class, they never came close to overthrowing the state and were brutally put down. Unlike in Russia, Japan's ruling class never saw the need to give an inch to peasant demands, and showed no hesitation in applying force. The existing army had been more than sufficient for the purpose; the aim of expanding it after 1877 was very different. General Yamagata put it with characteristic bluntness in 1883. It was a preparation, he said, 'for war on the mainland of Asia ... In the meantime the high-handed attitude of the Chinese towards Korea, which was antagonistic to the interests of Japan, showed our officers that a great war was to be expected sooner or later on the continent, and made them eager to acquire knowledge, for they were as yet quite unfitted for a continental war.'

The new army was organized along Prussian lines. It drew its conscripts largely from the peasant and industrial classes; the higher up the social ladder, the easier it was to escape conscription through bribes and connections. Most well-to-do families had one younger son in the armed forces, and these were likely to be professional officers. The senior jobs in the army went almost exclusively to samurai from the Choshu clan, and those in the navy to samurai from the Satsuma clan. From the very beginning of the modern Japanese armed forces, the generals and admirals were men who regarded themselves as the makers of modern Japan and the forces behind the emperor, and thus not subordinate to any of the institutions created by the new regime.

This was to have momentous consequences: they owed their allegiance to no one. Even the emperor was, in their view, their creation, although they showed formal obeisance to him. The armed forces were a race apart in another respect as well, for although they had come into being as a counterpart to the samurai they were now largely officered by ex-warriors who regarded themselves as a superior class, and who held civilian politics – indeed, all aspects of civilian society – in contempt. This was reflected in the Meiji constitution, which showed that even Yamagata was not unaware of the perils of an overmighty army.

The war minister remains a figure of immense contradictions. For many post-1945 historians he was the devil incarnate, the man who created Japanese militarism. Certainly he was among the most autocratic and martial of Meiji statesmen. But he nevertheless firmly believed in the oligarchic system that had come into being in 1868, and feared that the army could align itself with political movements, or, worse, become divided along partisan lines. Thus he was the man behind the bible of modern Japanese militarist thought, the Imperial Rescript to Soldiers and Sailors, which enjoined them 'neither to be led astray by current opinions nor meddle in politics but with single heart fulfil your essential duties of loyalty'.

The advice was two-pronged. First, soldiers should not get mixed up in social causes such as the popular rights movement of 1880–81, which were dangerously liberal and democratic; second, the armed forces should not be made use of by an aspiring shogun figure to install military government to restore order. Imperial loyalty (*chusetsu*) was more important than the maintenance of order in Japan. Unwittingly, Yamagata thus forged the chief weapon of military intervention, for now the armed forces were subject not to parliament, or even to the civilian government, but directly to the emperor – giving them unrivalled access to the ultimate authority. The army regarded itself as outside and above politics.

Yamagata, who in the late Meiji period was often effectively running the country, had the same attitude to the bureaucracy, which he considered more important than mere politicians. He obtained an imperial ordinance which referred with utter contempt to the political parties. His idea was of a detached bureaucracy serving the emperor, while alongside it the non-political armed forces in his service served the nation's interests abroad. Beneath both was parliament and the political authority, which served only to act as a sometimes tiresome obstacle to government, but one necessary to ensuring the allegiance of the people. It barely occurred to him that the army might some day vie with the bureaucracy for the emperor's ear. The soldiers would surely obey injunctions to loyalty.

The model for Japan's army was Germany's. The army was advised by Major Jacob Meckel to set up a general staff along German lines, with a head reporting directly to the commander-in-chief, the emperor. The war minister also had direct access to the throne, but his principal role was to reconcile the needs of the military with the demands of the civilian government. Yamagata underlined the importance of the chief of staff's function by actually resigning as war minister to assume the job in 1878. Military men had a disproportionate influence on government until 1898, holding a majority of cabinet posts until then, and only just under half thereafter.

An imperial ordinance of 1900 decreed that the minister of war and the minister of the navy had to be drawn from generals and admirals on the active service list. Thus cabinets could be brought down if either service withdrew its minister, and this was to become of increasing importance during the heyday of Japanese militarism.

The navy was given its own general staff in 1891, and direct access to the emperor after the Sino-Japanese war. From the first, the army was more interested in territorial expansion, the navy in keeping the sea lanes open for trade: it became the 'moderate' wing of the armed forces.

Yamagata built up the army with quite remarkable speed. By 1895 it consisted of some 240,000 men, half of them reserves (conscripts were required to spend seven years with the reserve after completing military service). The core consisted of 78,000 men equipped with modern arms and professionally trained. Officers were drilled in strategic planning, intelligence work, mobilization, communications and supply. The navy by that time had twenty-eight steamships, totalling 57,000 tons in weight, and Japanese shipyards were beginning to build major warships with rapid-firing guns and torpedoes.

By the last decade of the nineteenth century, when the rest of the world's industrial powers were beginning to doubt the virtues of imperialism, one of the most backward nations had thus acquired the means to embark upon a period of sustained expansion. About this fateful course to suffering and disaster, it should be said that some of Japan's motives in adopting imperialism were as defensible as those of some of the older colonial powers.

There were four main motives behind Japanese imperialism. The first was defensive. Up to 1868, Japan lay like some prostrate hedgehog before the major imperial powers. The 'defence' adopted by the shogun had been to curl up in a prickly ball, expunge all foreign influences and pretend that the outside world did not exist. The arrival of predatory American, Russian, British and French warships destroyed any illusion that Japan could resist the major powers militarily; its only protection now was its lack of resources, which made it an unattractive prize.

The second was economic: it took only a brief experience of industrialization in the second half of the nineteenth century for Japan to realize that it lacked the necessary ingredients – raw materials and markets – for its industrial base. Marxist historians have long argued that Western imperialism derived from the need of countries sated with capital to find new outlets, by exporting to dependencies overseas. For Japan, the security of its supplies of raw materials and its overseas trade became a simple matter of national economic survival. Once Japan had industrialized, it had to safeguard essential imports and markets in a hostile world where both were threatened by predators. That the world was unfriendly, no Japanese doubted: the colonial powers were not going to permit Japan free trade in Asia, which they dominated, without a struggle.

Third, there was a curious mixture of ideological, racial and anti-colonial reasoning which was not entirely without moral force or logic. Japan saw itself as an Asian country, albeit one vastly superior to the rest. The Japanese viewed the depredations imposed upon Asia by the colonial powers – America, Russia, and Britain – with deep distrust, and came to see their mission as to liberate the continent from those powers and impose an authentically Asian form of dependence upon them – one based on their concept of filial loyalty, the benevolent subordination of countries to their 'father', Japan. What they failed to appreciate was that many Asians might consider the relationship of total subordination of children to their father and of subjects to the emperor in Japan not the ideal substitute for Western colonialism – indeed, possibly a worse alternative. But Japan's concept of 'co-prosperity' was certainly an authentically Asian solution.

Fourth, and less forgivably, there was a feeling in Japan that, as a nation which in the space of two generations aspired to become one of the world's great powers, an empire was its due, just as it was for any major industrial power. The great empty spaces of Manchuria and other parts of Asia beckoned. Japan had to fight for its own sphere of influence, or it would inevitably be squeezed out.

Japanese imperialism was thus buttressed by a formidable logic, although one that was perhaps out of step with world history. The Japanese statesmen who travelled to Europe failed to appreciate the growing influence of public opinion in the democracies, which had sparked a decline in imperial interest, while anticolonialist movements were breaking out throughout their possessions, increasing the costs of remaining there. Japan was like an adolescent eager to stake out its own territory just as other nations began to outgrow the urge. Japan's intellectual immaturity, far from being entirely reprehensible, was to combine with its political underdevelopment to create the tragedy of the Pacific War. There was nothing unreasonable or even megalomaniac about Japan's quest for overseas possessions: it was logical, even defensible.

This becomes obvious once one considers the arguments put forward by Yamagata and circulated on at least two occasions. In

1888 he argued that, with the completion of the Trans-Siberian Railway in Russia and the Pacific Railway in Canada, a major clash would ensue between Britain and Russia. He believed that the Russians would invade Korea which then, as throughout history, was the Asian bridgehead to Japan. 'It is our policy to maintain Korea as an independent nation without ties to China and to keep Korea free of occupation by one of the great nations of Europe.' Alongside this fear, Yamagata believed that China, like Japan, might undergo a process of modernization and, from a position of dominating Korea, threaten his country. It was important, therefore, that Japan had the military strength to exert its own claims as Russia, Britain, and China struggled for dominance of the region.

Two years later, Yamagata argued that Japan's real frontiers 'of interest' extended beyond the country's shoreline: 'If we wish to maintain the nation's independence and to rank among the great powers, it is necessary to step forward and defend our line of interest, to be always in a favourable position, and not satisfied to defend only the line of sovereignty. Our line of interest is really in Korea.' He extended this notion to arguing that Japan, rather than any of its rivals, must become dominant in East Asia and 'ride the wave of victory' there.

For all the pretexts, it is hard not to view Japan's position as one of unashamed aggrandizement and opportunism: at a time when most Asian societies were a shambles of decadence and exploitation, Japan was the only country to have got its act together – and was intending to roar into the vacuum. These views, moreover, were being expressed by the country's major 'Victorian' statesman fifty years before the militaristic 'aberration' of the Pacific War.

Yamagata's theory was set out even more explicitly in 1877 by the man who was to become Yamagata's chief of staff. He argued that there was a clear possibility that one of the Western powers which had already largely subdued China would launch a direct attack upon it, thus threatening Japan's independence. The only possible retaliation was to strike into China on two fronts: a land offensive against Peking from the north and a siege of Shanghai from the sea. The objective would be not to seize China, but to trade these two captured towns for an 'independent' Manchuria, which would in effect become a Japanese protectorate; to create a similar protectorate over southern China; and to take over Taiwan and northern China. Thus, just two decades after the Meiji restoration, senior army officers were entertaining ideas of a large empire in Asia in order, as they saw it, to forestall the designs of other empires upon the region.

The first flashpoint for the growing forces of Japanese imperialism and militarism was Korea, as it had been in 1873. As Japan's closest neighbour on the Asian mainland, separated only by the narrow Korean Straits, it had always been a bone of contention between China and Japan. Initially, Korea and Japan had been allies because they had both been victims of the system imposed by China on anyone who traded with that alarmingly decadent country. After the Meiji restoration, Japan promptly sought to impose its own commercial terms on Korea and, when rebuffed, shrank from war.

Just two years later, in 1875, Korean shore batteries opened up on Japanese ships – probably as a result of provocation by the latter – and Japan's fleet set sail, demanding that Korea's ports grant preferential trading rights. The intimidated Koreans acceded, and the Chinese retaliated by seeking preferential trading agreements between Korea and the West, as a subtle ruse to secure Western support should Japan invade Korea. In Korea itself views became increasingly polarized between those who favoured the status quo, who were pro-Chinese, and the pro-Japanese modernizers. In 1884 the latter carried out a coup in Seoul with the help of the Japanese legation. Only Hirobumi Ito's cool head in promptly denying that the Japanese government had been involved avoided hostilities. The uprising was suppressed.

Ten years later, when Japan was much more self-assured militarily, a new spark was found. The Koreans asked for Chinese help in suppressing a group of armed insurgents, whereupon the Japanese promptly sent in their own forces and demanded that the Korean government undergo a thoroughgoing reform. The Koreans and Chinese indignantly rejected this, and on 1 August 1894 war was declared.

Japan's first imperial adventure was under way. It was characterized by a string of popular successes that sent national pride soaring. The Japanese quickly surrounded and took Seoul; by mid-September they had taken Pyongyang in the north. A month later Japanese armies had moved into southern Manchuria, north of Korea, and then into the Liaotung Peninsula, taking Port Arthur, its capital, by the end of November. The successes were so overwhelming (and were supposedly under the emperor's personal direction from his headquarters at Hiroshima) that the Japanese public became convinced that it was only a matter of time before the country took its proper place in the front rank of nations. Ostensibly, Japan secured a satisfactory peace agreement at Shimonoseki in April. Korea was freed from its vassal status to China and concluded a close alliance with Japan. The Liaotung Peninsula and Taiwan were ceded.

Having spectacularly won the war, Japan proceeded quickly to lose the peace. The major colonial powers – Britain, Germany and France – were alarmed by the speed of the Japanese victory. In addition, the palsied weakness of imperial China, which the major powers had preferred to administer through the treaty port system rather than invade, was exposed. On 11 April 1895 the Russians pressed France and Germany to join in the 'triple intervention', which demanded the return of the Liaotang Peninsula to China, for fear that Peking would otherwise be under constant threat from Japan. The Russian foreign minister, Sergei Witte, wanted to avoid what he saw as the strong possibility that 'the Mikado might beat the Chinese empire and Russia would need hundreds of thousands of troops for the defence of her possessions'.

Faced by this ultimatum from three great powers, the Japanese had no alternative but to leave. The Russians also brought intense pressure to bear to reassert Korea's independence in fact as well as in name; the Japanese were again forced to agree. The first expedition to the Asian mainland had thus ended with military victory and diplomatic defeat at the hands of the imperial powers – a combination calculated to leave Japan with both an appetite for further intervention and a lasting resentment of its colonial adversaries.

The Korean campaign deeply affected the recent attempts to set up constitutional government in Japan; the voices of democracy had no choice but to join in the popular patriotic battle-cries. Meanwhile, the successes of the army and the navy had become the stuff of legend: in particular, the heroic march on Weihaiwei in nightmare conditions after a landing at Port Arthur became the first of Japan's modern military myths. The journals of an obscure second lieutenant, Nanbu Kijiro, were devoured eagerly by a Japanese public which had never before savoured military success. 'As far as one could see, snow covered the Shantung Peninsula. It was biting cold. Beards hung like icicles, frozen from the chin. To combat frostbite, all extremities had wool protective covers. But the cold iced even our bone marrow. The horses were too cold to continue. We walked . . . In this way we marched for several days.' Weihaiwei was seized after three weeks of these grim conditions. A legend had been born, that of Japanese endurance and invincibility.

A further feature of Japan's first overseas military intervention deserves mention. Although Japanese imperialism was understandable in the context of the struggle for domination in Asia after the country had emerged from isolation, the Japanese had acted in Korea (as they were to act on subsequent occasions) on the flimsiest of legal pretexts – that Chinese troops had been brought in to crush a local rebellion. There was no legal justification for what they did. They simply considered Korea to be fully within their sphere of influence, so it was necessary to keep out their rivals if they were to establish an enormous integrated economic zone that would furnish Japan's requirements. It is hard to see any real difference between the justification of this war and that of any other of Japan's colonial wars in terms of national security. The road to Hiroshima began at Seoul.

The opportunity for Japan to revenge itself on Russia was not long in coming. The Russians now started to overreach themselves, moving forces into the Liaotang Peninsula: the reality that China was now under their guns prompted a desperate scramble between Russia, Germany and France effectively to divide the country. Russian interests clashed directly with those of Japan: they included a proposal to build a railway line across Manchuria linking Vladivostok to the Trans-Siberian Railway, with a spur running south to Port Arthur. The Liaotung Peninsula was granted to Russia under a twenty-five year lease just a few years after Japan had had its military conquest of the region overturned. Russia now effectively controlled Manchuria, which was of immense strategic importance to Japan. Russia did not actually dominate Korea, viewed by Japanese defence planners as 'a dagger aimed at the heart of Japan' and, increasingly, as a strategic extension of Japanese territory. But that might quickly follow.

After the humiliation of 1895, Japan's statesmen sensibly responded to this Russian bullying by seeking alliances with the other imperial powers. It quickly found a friend. Britain and the United States had both remained cautious as Russia, France and Germany greedily carved up the Chinese mainland. Chary of major continental involvement, the British in particular prepared to lend support to the American idea of the 'open door': the new partition of China would be recognized, in effect, provided Britain and the United States were given free access to the region for trade.

But the British were profoundly uneasy about the expansion of Tsarist power in the area, and feared that Russian control over Manchuria would exclude British commerical interests. By 1902, the Japanese had taken advantage of this unease. In September of that year the Anglo-Japanese alliance was signed, by which the British effectively promised the Japanese that they would not join any anti-Japanese coalition of the kind that had occurred with the 'triple intervention' of 1895. This was a massive relief for Japan, which had spent the previous seven years doubling the size of its armed forces for what it regarded as an inevitable clash with Russia. It meant that it no longer need fear conflict with the most powerful naval force in the region.

But war with Russia was inevitable. By 1902, the Japanese army had defined Korea as an essential foreign interest. 'For the long-range policy of our country,' stated a memorandum of the general staff, it was essential that Korea become 'part of the Japanese empire'. The Russians, far from being content with their gains further north, made it clear that they intended to contest this. As far back as October 1895, the Japanese minister in Korea had been implicated in an attempted coup in Seoul in which the country's queen, who hated the Japanese, was murdered. The king escaped to take refuge in the Russian legation.

Hirobumi Ito attempted to limit the danger of open war by agreeing, in effect, to respect Korea's neutrality with Russia. General Yamagata, dispatched to attend the coronation of Tsar Nicholas II, reached an agreement by which Korea was placed under an informal joint protectorate of the two nations, which were permitted to maintain armies in the country. The next few years saw frenzied attempts by the Japanese to set up economic ties to advance their interests in Korea. There is evidence that, as the century ended, Russia was getting less interested in its competition with Japan in Korea and more concerned with its rivalry with Britain in China.

In 1900, the Boxer Rebellion broke out across China. The Japanese co-operated with the British in suppressing the revolt, while at the same time preparing to exploit it in their own imperial interest from their base at Formosa to make a salient into Fukien Province, a 'southern option' for expansion which excited many Japanese military and business leaders. At the last moment, the initiative was called off for fear of offending Japan's ally, Britain.

The Boxer rising had another effect as well: the Russians moved in large numbers of troops to defend their interests in Manchuria. For Yamagata, among others, this was tantamount to a declaration of war. It was clear, he argued, that Russia was undertaking a 'primitive occupation' of Manchuria; China's partition was 'inevitable'. In 1901, Japanese Prime Minister Taro Katsura argued that Russia 'will inevitably extend into Korea and will not end until there is no room left for us'. His foreign minister claimed that, 'If Manchuria becomes the property of Russia, Korea itself cannot remain independent. It is a matter of life and death for Japan.' Although over the next three years the Japanese energetically sought the withdrawal of Russian troops from Manchuria by diplomatic means, there was no progress on the central issues. Japan had already decided to launch a war against Russia. In December 1903 the cabinet reviewed the issue, and in early February the following year land and sea forces attacked Korea in a massive onslaught against the Russian forces.

Japan's navy bombarded and quickly bottled up the Russian Far Eastern Fleet in Port Arthur, while the army attacked the city from the land. A major offensive was staged in April against Liaotung, spearheading the campaigns against Russian ports in Manchuria. Contrary to Japanese war mythology, the offensive was successful only in preventing the Russian navy from posing the kind of danger to the Japanese navy that might have crippled the war effort. The first battles stretched out into the kind of prolonged and bitter trench warfare that the world was to see much more of in the First World War. The Battle of Liaotung took two months to win, but Port Arthur fell only after a year.

In March 1905 the Japanese and Russian forces engaged in the Battle of Mukden, where 250,000 Japanese engaged 350,000 Russians with no decisive result. The Russian Baltic Fleet, which had sailed halfway round the world to lift the blockade on Port Arthur, arrived in May in the Tsushima Straits, where it was attacked by the Japanese fleet under Admiral Heihachiro Togo in one of the most decisive naval engagements of modern times. The victory that had eluded Japan on land was won at sea. The Japanese were already seriously worried about the huge casualty rate and enormous cost of the war; but the Russians, for whom the war had until then been little more than a side-show, took advantage of an American offer of mediation to attend the Portsmouth Peace Conference of August 1905.

There the Russians made major concessions. Japan was given complete freedom of action in Korea, as well as the Liaotang lease and control of the spur railroad from the Chinese Eastern Railway at Harbin down to Port Arthur. In Manchuria the Japanese secured the total expulsion of Russia and won significant concessions for themselves from China, which formally had possession of the country, but stopping short of exclusive control.

Japan had fought its first major war in Asia as an ambitious and powerful country, and won – although not overwhelmingly – against one of the major colonial powers. It had initiated the fighting, but its aim, to prevent Russian domination of Manchuria and the Korean peninsula, was one which had aroused sympathy in Britain and America. Japan was viewed as a 'plucky little country' which had taken on the Russian bear. Russia's behaviour in China had been sufficiently bullying to give Japan the benefit of the doubt. The outcome of the war was in effect to add another colony, Korea, to the one already occupied, Formosa, and to whet Japan's appetite for further gains in Manchuria. Internationally, Japan's alliance with Britain and the general distaste for Russia had earned the country a considerable measure of support: outsiders saw Japan's motives as partially anti-colonial, not colonial and bullying in themselves.

At home, the huge number of casualties had sent the cult of war shrines into a frenzy, encouraged and financed by the state, while jingoism reached new peaks of fervour and anger after the 'disappointing' terms of the Portsmouth peace treaty. While the war was under way, party politics had virtually ceased: from being an oligarchy dominated by Ito, Japan had become a virtual military dictatorship dominated by Yamagata and his protégé Taro Katsura. Ito himself was dispatched afterwards to the important but subordinate post of Japanese resident-general in Korea. In 1907, with a staff of around 70, a police force of just 250, and two detachments of soldiers, he descended on Korea's 'Emperor' and forced his abdication. An insurrection broke out which was ruthlessly suppressed, and provided Japan with the excuse to annex the country formally. In October 1909 Ito paid a visit to Harbin and was assassinated by a Korean nationalist. So ended the life of the most influential Meiji figure of them all – a Bismarck considered too soft by his contemporaries in government.

By August 1910, Korea had been formally absorbed into Japan. In Manchuria, Japanese business, at the government and army's prodding, had already begun a concerted assault on the region's natural resources. This quickly offended both the Americans and the

British, who were wedded to the 'open door' policy. By 1906 that irritation had grown to such proportions that Ito had formally to remind the army chief of staff, General Kodama, that 'Manchuria is in no sense Japanese territory. It is simply part of Chinese territory. Since there are no grounds for exceeding our authority in a place which is not our territory, there is no need to create a colonial ministry to harbour such duties. The responsibility for ruling Manchuria rests with the Chinese government.'

This was a dangerous moment for Japan in its international behaviour. The Meiji restoration had succeeded in forging a strong national army and navy, as well as a belief that to survive internationally the country must expand. Both the Sino-Japanese war of 1895 and the Russo-Japanese war of 1905–6 had been wars started by the Japanese, each of which had yielded a colony: Formosa first, Korea second. The army was now arguing that the conquest of Manchuria was necessary for the country's security, while business leaders also pressed for its annexation.

The navy, which as we have seen was independent of the army and also directly answerable to the emperor, had entirely different views. It believed that, for a group of islands like Japan, territorial conquest was much less important than domination of the seas, and that war with the country's main naval rivals, the United States and Britain, was inevitable. Indeed, for a moment after the Russo-Japanese war there was serious friction between Japan and Theodore Roosevelt's America; a 'world tour' by the American fleet failed to impress the Japanese, however, which had as many ships in the western Pacific as the Americans.

Thus there were three separate directions in which Japan's new-found imperial destiny was spurring the country to further conflict: to move into Manchuria, to move into Fukuoka in southern China, and to take on the 'open door' powers. As Meiji Japan entered the first decade of the twentieth century in a cacophony of jingoistic nationalism, it was impossible to predict that a brief flurry of enlightenment – which would come to be seen as a period of decadence and weakness by a later generation of militarists – would soon effectively bottle up the forces of Japanese imperialism for almost two decades.

In the decades to come, democracy would try to find roots, Emperor Hirohito would come to the throne, and the uniquely authoritarian, powerful society created by the Meiji oligarchy would show the faintest sign of finding some kind of maturity – or 'illustrious harmony', the name chosen for Hirohito's reign, the

Showa period. It was economic crisis that checked the momentum of colonial expansion in 1910, just as it was economic crisis that was to spell the end of Japan's 'spring' in the late 1920s. It is to the origins of one of the most powerful economies the world has ever seen, which were put in place by the Meiji regime, that we now turn.

7

THE MONOPOLISTS

THE JAPANESE government of 1868, faced with a primitive agricultural economy, a reasonably wealthy merchant class and virtually no industry at all, adopted a radical approach to the Japanese economy. It did something quite new, an example to be followed first by the Soviet Union in the 1920s and 1930s, and then by most other developing economies. For obvious reasons, Russia's communists never acknowledged their debt to Japan (even if they were aware of it). Yet the model for crash industrialization under state direction was established not by Joseph Stalin but by someone who is not a household name at all: Masayoshi Matsukata, a wily bureaucrat who was responsible for the formation of the great Japanese companies that today bestride the world. Matsukata came from a lower samurai family in Satsuma, becoming a provincial governor immediately after the restoration, charged with the task of obtaining funds to support the industrialization of Japan.

In 1871 he moved into Ito's private office to work on local tax reform. A visit to France shortly afterwards impressed him with the *dirigiste* methods of government finance there. In 1881 he became minister of finance at a time of dire financial difficulty caused by two problems: the massive printing of money immediately after the Restoration, partly to finance the cost of putting down the Satsuma rebellion, and the assault on Japan's home market by foreign companies now that tariffs had been removed. Matsukata formulated the policy of the state incubating Japan's new industries before selling them off to private buyers.

This interventionism stemmed largely from necessity: the country's merchant class was deeply reluctant to invest. The merchants, nurtured in the sheltered autarchy of Tokugawa Japan, were remarkably conservative, their house rules warning them not to diversify into new lines, not to depart from traditional procedures, and not to be disrespectful to the ancestors who had set up the business. In addition, very few merchants supplied foreign buyers or knew anything about machinery. Apart from the wealth of the merchant class, there was virtually no capital available for industrialization. Matsukata's ruthless solution was the land tax, which squeezed the peasantry to devastating effect. Again, this was precisely the model fastened upon by Stalin and most developing countries: milking the agricultural sector to provide capital for industry. Another rationale was that the surplus population in the countryside would then flock to the cities to make up the new industrial workforce.

In a third respect Stalin would follow the example of Japan. The classic 'natural' process of industrialization was for light consumer industries such as textiles to come into being to satisfy local demand for goods such as clothes; as they grew and spread, heavy industries providing the machinery for them were created. The Japanese started with heavy industry, partly because this was a wholly new industrial model, partly because the first priority was to set up Japan's war machine. Engineering works, furnaces, arsenals, foundries and shipyards were already being built up at Satsuma and Choshu from the mid-nineteenth century: when the 'outside lords' took power, they insisted on the national expansion of major chemical industries – sulphuric acid works, and glass and cement factories.

One feature not to be reproduced in Stalin's Russia was the astuteness of the Meiji oligarchs in realizing that, as they had no technology base of their own, they had to learn their methods and techniques wholesale from the West. There was no false pride in Japan, of the kind that led China for centuries to reject the modernizing influence of Western technology. Arsenals sprang up in Nagasaki under Dutch supervision; the French managed the Yokusaka shipyard, arsenal and ironworks; and the English administered other shipyards. As light industries such as textiles began to grow up in the 1870s and 1880s, the English managed the Kagoshima spinning mill, the French the Tomioka and Fukuoka plants and the Swiss and Italians the Maebashi Filatures. Bright young Japanese were soon able to absorb the new skills as they took over factory management from the foreigner.

State control was not confined to providing money for industrialization. It was also used to force companies engaged in 'destructive' competition to merge. As early as 1880, the government was drawing up strategic plans for industrial development. Matsukata continued to provide large subsidies to industries to help them fight foreign competition. The government's share of Japanese capital formation never fell below 40 per cent throughout the last two decades of the nineteenth century.

Where Japan openly diverged from future socialist models was in selling off many of the industries the government had put on their feet, except for those connected with defence. The process began with the Regulations on the Transfer of Factories enacted in 1880, which stated that 'the factories established for encouraging industries are now well organized and business has become prosperous; so the government will abandon its ownership of factories, which ought to be run by the people'. The cotton spinning mills set up at Hiroshima and Aichi under English management were among the first to be sold off, to the Hiroshima prefecture and the Shinoda company. The Shinagawa Glass Factory was sold to the Ishimura company, the Shimmachi Spinning Mill and the Fukuoka Filature to Mitsui, and so on, most of the sales taking place in the early 1880s.

The government's first priority had been to attract members of the unemployed and restless samurai class to manage the new companies. 'In trying to create employment for the samurai, we must give prime importance to the development of industry,' one prominent minister wrote. Yet while many Japanese found employment as managers in the new industries, the companies were sold, at ludicrously low prices, almost exclusively to a tiny financial cabal consisting of the more adventurous merchants and the more entrepreneurial among the camp followers of the Satsuma and Choshu aristocrats.

Four giant combines established positions of immense financial and industrial prominence during this period: Mitsui, Mitsubishi (which snapped up the major shipyards), Sumitomo, and Yasuda, which branched into banking and commerce. The lesser groups were put together largely by ex-*daimyo*. Known as the *zaibatsu*, these giant oligopolies would lead economic development in an entirely new direction, skewing the Japanese model into something quite unique. There would emerge a powerful business class, resembling the semi-independent princedoms of the past, which was to challenge government for dominance not just of the Japanese market economy, but of the international marketplace.

The peculiar nature of the *zaibatsu* was shaped by the shortage of capital for industrialization. Because the capital was put up not by a variety of private investors but by the government, the *zaibatsu* were shaped rather like big government departments, with a pyramid peaking at the summit. The enterprises were usually family-run at the very top, with various systems of control. Just beneath the families were holding companies which had direct financial control of the numerous member companies. The holding companies managed a network of subsidiaries, interlocking directorates, stockholdings, margin guarantees, and loans from the banks.

The Mitsuis, a family of bankers and traders going back to the sixteenth century, were the most powerful. The eleven branches of the Mitsui family were represented on a family council which was presided over by the eldest son. A huge base of retainers was selected and carefully trained for their complete loyalty. The Mitsuis helped to finance the Meiji restoration, and many have suggested that the company was in some respects the maker of the coup, rather than merely its chief economic beneficiary. Certainly Mitsui was richly rewarded: the major family companies – Mitsui Gomei, the Mitsui Bank, Mitsui Bussan, and Mitsui Kozan – vastly expanded their holdings, from commerce, banking, and mining into textiles, shipping, warehousing, sugar, metals and machinery. By 1937 the company had a staggering market value for the time of $470 million in 1937 values and controlled an empire worth several billions.

Mitsubishi's fortune was largely founded on shipping; it was controlled by the two Iwasaki families, whose elder sons alternated in the post of chief policymaker. By 1944 Mitsubishi had control over a quarter of Japanese shipping and shipbuilding – an immense business; a third of electrical equipment; half of flour milling; nearly two-thirds of the production of sheet glass; a third of sugar production; and around 15 per cent each of coal and metal production, warehousing, bank loans and cotton textiles.

Sumitomo was almost entirely owned and run by the head of the family and specialized in mining and equipment. By 1945 the company had investments of some $100 million in more than a hundred and twenty companies and thirty industries. Yasuda specialized in banking, and had assets of only $35 million by 1945, with direct ownership of $110 million worth of subsidiaries, yet through its stockholdings the financial giant controlled assets of at least $10 billion. Banking was a major growth area for all the *zaibatsu* during the depression, when they swallowed up small struggling banks. In 1939 the seven big private banks held nearly 60 per cent of the total assets and deposits of all banks; four of the seven were Mitsui, Mitsubishi, Sumitomo and Yasuda.

The *zaibatsu* existed alongside an economy of tiny firms and family-based component suppliers, which were entirely dependent upon them and enjoyed no security of contract comparable to that of employees of the big companies. This made the *zaibatsu* all the more dominant; there was no strong backbone of middle-sized business in Japan. The economic dominance of this handful of companies straddling commerce, industry and banking had enormous benefits in terms of economies of scale, long-term planning, the ability to raise capital, to switch between a failing sector and a newly prosperous one, to cushion company employees from the effect of recession, and to crush competition and suppress trade unionism whenever necessary. Equally, the disadvantages of this system for those outside the *zaibatsu* are readily apparent.

There is a great controversy as to whether the *zaibatsu* houses continued to benefit from government favours and direction and whether they were the creatures of the state or its masters. The straightforward explanation seems the best: government was fully involved in the nineteenth century, providing capital and subsidy, showering favours upon its privileged supporters in the financial and industrial elite.

It is hard to appreciate adequately the suffering of the workforce as Japan underwent its first, accelerated industrial revolution in a society in which workers had no political voice and enjoyed little sympathy from the class that ran their lives. The peasant class felt the squeeze in two ways. First, there was great agrarian distress as a result of the steep tax increases: no fewer than 368,000 peasants were forced off the land for non-payment of taxes between 1883 and 1890. The number of tenants in seven prefectures increased from 34 per cent in 1883 to 42 per cent in 1887. Miserably destitute peasants, unable to make a living from the land, trekked to seek work in textile factories, cement works and foundries. When a new factory was set up, its agents scoured the countryside, often targeting localities that had some connection with the boss, for workers who were obliged to labour in conditions no better than those of eighteenth-century Britain.

Workers had no contracts and were expected to work whenever required, at any time of the day or night, for wages so low that long hours were essential to their survival. Many returned to the country-side, only to find there was nothing there to provide them with a livelihood. Many who persisted in their jobs quickly became ill and died of tuberculosis and other diseases. They were generally housed in dingy dormitories. Housing conditions were insanitary and over-crowded, the food was poor, and the pay low. Many women in the textile industries fared no better.

There was some social mobility, nevertheless. It was just possible for a bright youth to become an apprentice at the age of fourteen or fifteen with a merchant shop – a chance to escape dirt-poverty by climbing from the lowest rung in the ladder. At the age of seventeen a boy could become a *chuzo*, clerk, after an initiation ceremony in which he would have been given a kind of frock-coat called a *haori* and a tobacco case; he would then be given authority over a younger boy. Between the ages of twenty-one and twenty-five he might qualify as a manager. Ten to thirteen years later he was allowed to marry and live outside the dormitory, being given proper robes. Even in the entrepreneurial sector of the econ-omy, absolute hierarchy prevailed, as did the tradition of servitude to one's business master, who controlled every aspect of the young trainee's life.

For all the underlying change of the Meiji era, Japan's industrial revolution was in its infancy. Between 1870 and 1923 the economy grew at a rate of around 2.5 per cent a year, which probably made it the fastest growing in the world. Growth was in spurts, with short, sharp recessions in 1890, 1900–01, and 1907–8. Growth was very largely engineered by government spending, which tripled between 1890 and 1900, then more than doubled again from 183 million yen to 338 million yen in 1910. Defence spending multiplied seven times between 1870 and 1923. With the expansion of heavy industry beginning to get under way through government sponsorship, the percentage of the workforce in industrial employment rose from 31 in 1890 to 44 in 1915. Most industry, however, was now light industry, with textiles accounting for a third of manufacturing output and half of exports up to 1914. Half of all family labour consisted of women textile workers. By 1912, 44 per cent of the gross national product was still derived from agriculture.

The number of industrial workers had increased nearly 20-fold between 1888 and 1909 – but the figure is less startling when one considers there were only 136,000 industrial workers to begin with, and only 2.5 million in 1909 (there were 8 million by 1935). The cities were being transformed: the proportion of the population living in cities of more than 50,000 inhabitants nearly doubled over the same period, from 7 to 14 per cent. Tokyo's population virtually doubled; Osaka's rose to 1.5 million. As the number of workers grew, so did the first faint stirrings of industrial militancy. By 1907 strikes were becoming commonplace. They were met, as might be expected, with the threat of dire repression, coupled with a conscience on the part of some Meiji leaders that growing inequality was a problem that would have to be addressed.

As far back as 1901, Yamagata's minister of home affairs, was drawing up a package of suppressive measures. The Public Peace Police Act of 1900 had been introduced to ban the Social Democratic Party on the day it was founded. In 1905 social dissent in the cities reached new dimensions, albeit over a patriotic issue: the Treaty of Portsmouth, widely regarded as a sell-out after the Japanese victory over Russia, was the subject of angry rioting in Hibiya. The following year there were violent demonstrations against rises in tram fares, and in 1907 strikes mushroomed, starting at the Ashio copper mine, spreading to the Koike coal mines, the Uraga docks and the Horonai mines. Again, the Public Peace Police Act was invoked.

The Act was to form the basis for government repression throughout the period. It provided for the filing of a report with the police whenever a political association was formed; assemblies had to be reported three days in advance; outdoor mass demonstrations had to be reported twelve hours in advance. The police had powers to prevent any of these taking place. Article 17 of the Public Peace Police Act prohibited the 'seduction or incitement' of others:

> (1) In order to let others join, or prevent others from joining, an organisation which aims at collective action concerning conditions of work or remuneration; (2) In order to let the employer discharge the workers, or to let him reject an application for work or to let a worker stop his work, or to let him refuse an offer of employment with the view to organising a lockout or strike; (3) In order to compel the other party to agree to the conditions of remuneration.

It is not hard to see that these provisions could be invoked to thwart virtually any attempt to form a trade union. The result was the Chinsen Ki, the Period of Submersion, during which, because unions could not legally be formed, demonstrations usually took violent form, with company property being destroyed and burnt. In

1909, 12,000 miners ran riot at the Ashio copper mine, burning housing, throwing bombs, and smashing lamps; the riot was finally suppressed by three infantry companies from the Takasaki Regiment's headquarters. In 1911 a celebrated tramway strike on New Year's Day in Tokyo ended with most of the strikers' demands being met, but also with the imprisonment of forty-seven of their leaders.

Unsurprisingly in this climate, the repression led to the formation of an underground socialist movement. The suppressed Social Democratic Party re-emerged as the Japan Socialist Party, permitted to organize by the enlightened Saionji government in 1906. However, rivals and more extreme offshoots also came into being: Denjiro Kotoku led an anarchist wing, while Sen Katayama led the first Communist Party. The low boiling point of the autocracy towards these new groups was demonstrated first by the Red Flag Incident of 1908, and then by the Great Treason Incident of 1910–11, when Kotoku and eleven other socialists were condemned to death for allegedly plotting against the emperor. It seems clear, on later evidence, that the charges were a complete fabrication, and used as the pretext for a general crackdown on the labour movement. Katayama left the country in disillusion in 1914.

Yamagata formulated a crushingly authoritarian decree in 1910 that marked the formal banning of socialism in Japan:

> In considering the changes in popular sentiment that occur in modern society, the people begin by claiming political rights and, once they are allotted these, they demand food and clothing and wish for the wealth of society to be equally apportioned. Realizing that such demands are incompatible with current national and social institutions, they turn their efforts to the destruction of the foundations of the state and society. Herein lies the genesis of what is called socialism. Its immediate causes are the extreme division between rich and poor and the marked changes in ethics that accompany the modern culture.
>
> It is now urgently necessary both to construct a policy that will remedy this affliction at its roots and also, for the sake of national and social self-preservation, to exercise the strictest control over those who espouse its doctrines. The spread of this infection must be prevented . . . it must be suppressed and eradicated . . . The first essential in the eradication of socialism is the diffusion of full and complete national education and the cultivation of moderate thought. After that the next task is material relief in the form of what is known as social policy.

The various remedies suggested by Yamagata included 'excluding individualism', promoting 'healthy thought', and 'expanding vocational education to eliminate the educated unemployed idlers'. Yamagata's ideologues argued that to prevent 'socialism becoming anarchism as the common flu turns to pneumonia', as well as 'individualism, internationalism . . . husbands addressing their wives with the horrific "*san*", and the light Japanese cuisine being overwhelmed by heavy Western food, the country must return to traditional ancestral values. One would be hard put to find as classic a statement of authoritarianism as Yamagata's document anywhere in the world, even at that time.

8

DEATH OF AN EMPEROR

I N 1906, THE powerfully built fifty-three-year-old Emperor Mutsuhito, who fought shy of routine medical check-ups and refused to have any thorough ones, began to suffer from diabetes and kidney failure. He spurned proper examinations or treatment, and continued with an unchanged diet as his condition steadily deteriorated over the next six years. On 12 July 1912, while attending graduation day at Tokyo Imperial University, the emperor suddenly complained of feeling tired and short of breath. He underwent his first intensive examination, which revealed that he was suffering from uraemic poisoning – which in those days was fatal.

A second opinion was sought from two specialists from the Tokyo Imperial University; as they were not allowed to examine the emperor because they lacked a formal court title, they were officially appointed 'imperial aides' at an emergency ceremony. They were not permitted to give him any kind of injection, however, as his body was divine. When news of the emperor's illness got out, crowds assembled in front of the palace to pray. The tramcars outside slowed down, and blankets were wrapped around the rails to muffle the noise. Theatres closed their doors. On 30 July he died.

It had been one of the most remarkable reigns in world history, wrenching Japan from the thirteenth century and forcing it into nineteenth-century industrialization in just thirty-five years. The *Daily Telegraph* at the time captured the hyperbole of the age:

> Thus ends the era of Meiji, the reign of 'enlightened peace'. Japan was an unknown, hidden land, trampled under the heels of a feudal militarism, and the sport of a succession of shoguns when His

Majesty, in his 15th year, ascended the throne occupied in unbroken line by his ancestors since the days when Tyre and Sidon were in their glory, Carthage was flinging her yoke over the inhabitants of North Africa, and the wise men of the East were still straining their eyes for the Star of Bethlehem. The Emperor has passed away, in his modern palace in Tokyo, in the full knowledge that under his inspiration, and with the devoted aid of his statesmen, the red disc of the national flag which, in the words of a great Japanese, was the wafer over a sealed island, has become the emblem of the confident hope of a united nation which has won its place among the Great Powers of the world. In the history of civilization, there is nothing more wonderful than the evolution of this island kingdom.

The death of the emperor was accompanied by three remarkable rites of passage, each of which symbolized different aspects of the Meiji transformation – and showed its limitations. The first was the funeral itself, an astounding pastiche of ancient and modern Japan. The ceremony began at eight o'clock on the night of 13 September. Temple bells tolled 108 times, cannon boomed in the distance, and the processional dirge sounded as the emperor's cortège emerged from the imperial palace into the eerie torchlight of a Tokyo night. Hundreds of thousands took to the streets to watch the procession of 20,000 file past.

The carriage itself was immense, attended by mourners in traditional court dress. Following them came attendants with bows and halberds, fans and staffs, imperial princes, the palace staff, the *genro* (council of elders), members of the government, senior civil servants and noblemen – many eschewing drab top hats and tails to revert to traditional pre-Restoration splendour – and members of the two houses of the Diet in tails 'like river loach after goldfish, or penguins after golden pheasants', as one observer remarked.

Two hours after it set off, the procession reached Aoyama parade ground where, watched by assembled ambassadors and dignitaries, trumpets were sounded and the new Emperor Taisho, Prime Minister Saionji, and Imperial Household Minister Watanabe all spoke briefly. The coffin was then put on the funeral train for Kyoto. The train left at two the next morning; subjects bowed and prostrated themselves beside the line as it passed by. When the train reached Kyoto the following afternoon after its 340-mile journey, the body was taken to the imperial tomb at Momoyama.

*

The second incident was a true throwback to Japan's Dark Ages. Just before the funeral cortège left the Imperial Palace, General Maresuke Nogi and his wife Shizuko, the emperor's most trusted military aide and guardian to his grandson, Hirohito, seated themselves in front of the imperial portrait in their spartan home less than a mile from the funeral site at Aoyama.

The general, it is believed, stabbed his wife in the heart with a short sword, perhaps because she could not go through with the act of ritual suicide. Then he cut a horizontal gash in his abdomen and tried to sever his head, leaving it partly attached.

They left notes which spoke of 'following the lord' – an ancient feudal practice called *Junshi*, leaving this world to guard the emperor on his journey through the afterlife – which had been outlawed as far back as 1663. Nogi's note also spoke of his shame at having lost the imperial colours during fighting in the Satsuma rebellion of 1877. A possible unspoken motive was the loss of Nogi's two sons in the Russo-Japanese war, after which the general is said to have asked the emperor for permission to kill himself, but was refused; with the emperor dead, he had been delivered from his obligation to stay alive.

The suicides caused major controversy, overshadowing the funeral itself. On the one hand, admiration was expressed that the traditional ways of Japan had not come to an end with its passage to modernity. On the other, a dozen other people promptly followed the general's example and committed suicide. People argued that the old, savage Japan should not be glorified in this way. In fact, the suicides represented a reassertion not just of the spirit of *bushido*, the warrior spirit, but the revival of certain notions in the armed forces. Those who denounced Nogi's death as quixotic missed the point: in the new Japanese armed forces, such notions represented the new spirit. And the army was still extremely powerful in Japanese society.

The third event, which followed shortly after the emperor's death, was the opposite of Nogi's *seppuku* in that it offered a hopeful indication that Japan was entering the modern age. The armed forces were, as ever, pressing for an increase in military spending, citing the danger of a war of revenge by Russia, as well as the world tour of the American fleet; the army also argued that with Korea and southern Manchuria to protect, Japan was overstretched. Two more divisions were required on top of the existing nineteen. But in 1911, when Saionji had formed his second cabinet, he insisted on rigorous fiscal conservatism to deal with the incipient threat of inflation.

In May 1912 the army, under a new war minister, General Uehara, and with the support of Prince Yamagata, demanded funding for one of the two divisions. Saionji refused and Uehara resigned – the first time the army had tested its privilege of withdrawing its support from a civilian government and thus bringing it down. Yamagata prevailed on the ailing emperor to appoint his protégé, the prickly, starchy General Katsura, as prime minister. The stakes were the highest possible: could the military dictate to a civilian government? The army was making an outright bid to assert its supremacy. To Katsura's astonishment, the navy, which bitterly opposed the army's grab for power, refused to appoint its own minister to his government – taking a leaf out of the army's book and also threatening to bring him down. Yamagata and Katsura insisted that the *genro* force the navy to fall into line, which it did with bad grace. But the Diet flatly refused to ratify the increased defence budget.

Katsura held on for fourteen months of bitter argument. Then, in a memorable debate, Yukio Ozaki, one of Japan's most prominent opposition politicians, furiously assailed the military chiefs and the Choshu oligarchy in particular: 'They always mouth "loyalty" and "patriotism" but what they are actually doing is to hide themselves behind the throne, and shoot at their political enemies from their secure ambush. The throne is their rampart. Rescripts are their missiles.' The government was formally censured in parliament. Katsura obtained an imperial rescript requiring the Diet to revoke the censure motion; this was clearly unconstitutional, and the Diet refused. Even Yamagata could see that by bringing the throne so openly into the political arena, Katsura was doing it harm. He was forced to resign, and the navy chief, Admiral Yamamoto, took office.

The crisis constituted a turning point: a first check on the arrogance of the army and of the Choshu oligarchy; the first real assertion of parliamentary power; the first bringing down to earth of the imperial institution which, under a new, inexperienced monarch, had been unofficially castrated in terms of political power; the first time the power of the elder statesmen had been blocked. The army had been squarely defeated, and the pool from which service ministers might be drawn was broadened to include retired or inactive general officers – that is, officers who might no longer do the bidding of the high command of the time.

*

The Meiji Empress did not long outlive her husband, dying on 11 April 1914. A great shrine to both their names was built in 1920 (it was destroyed during the Pacific War and rebuilt in 1980). The Meiji outer garden, home of Tokyo's main sporting centre, also contains a large, bleak building of reinforced concrete and marble, the Memorial Picture Gallery, which houses an extraordinary collection of large canvasses that portray the emperor's reign.

It is a fascinating tableau of Japan's history during the fateful first forty-five years of its modern era. The evolution from traditional clothing, prostration, palanquins and kimonos to the frock-coated, top-hatted, crinolined court of the later Meiji period is beautifully illustrated, never more so than in the painting of the promulgation of the new constitution, in which the emperor (whose features as a living god could not previously be painted) appears in a Western-style uniform surrounded by generals and tail-coated senior attendants. In fact, the painting shows only the outward ceremony. Earlier, a purely Japanese celebration had taken place. The emperor had placated his sacred ancestors by declaring at a formal Shinto ceremony that the new constitution had been enacted to preserve the ancient forms of government bequeathed by them to the country. Shinto priests also reported to the Ise shrines and to the gods of the founder of the imperial line, Jimmu, and Meiji's dead father, the Emperor Komei. Yet the external appearance was new, modernizing, Western.

Only a mile away, the same duality repeated itself: down the slope that led to the Imperial Palace, with its formidable moat and walls, a giant *mélange* of a palace had been built for Crown Prince Yoshihito. Its outside walls were based on Buckingham Palace, its inner courtyards on Versailles. The vulgarity of the thing was apparent to the Meiji architects, especially when contrasted with the simplicity and beauty of the Imperial Palaces. One was for show, reflecting Yoshihito's tastes, pandering to the foreigner; the other was Japanese.

Today, the visitor to the mausoleum, the memorial picture gallery, is given an explanatory leaflet. This asserts, accurately, that 'the Emperor Meiji enhanced the national power of Japan greatly'. It goes on to claim that:

> During the Meiji era Japan flourished under the benign rule of the Emperor Meiji, who promulgated the Meiji constitution, promoted friendship with overseas countries, and developed the nation in every cultural field. It was the most glorious of all periods in more

than 2000 years of Japanese history, a period during which the foundations of modern Japan were laid.

It was Emperor Meiji who, as the leader of this colourful early period of Japanese history, devoted himself wholeheartedly to increasing the prosperity and peace of the nation. Consequently, Emperor Meiji was regarded by both Japanese and foreigners alike as a truly great emperor.

Empress Shoken gave skilful aid to the Emperor, and the Empress during this eventful and difficult Meiji period was lauded as the model of the Modern Japanese Woman ... May their great achievement for the world's peace and welfare be remembered for ever!

It is remarkable enough that such fawning nonsense can be shown to present-day visitors to a country that believes itself to be the most advanced in the world. Anywhere else, a nation – particularly one with a deeply controversial history – would limit itself to a bald statement of fact. Yet more remarkable is the distortion of history it represents. The Meiji period can in truth be described as a great one for Japan, but peace, friendship, and welfare were hardly its principal triumphs. In fact the achievements of the Meiji oligarchs were little short of miracles – but they were deeply flawed and stunted too.

An aristocratic caste, largely from two Japanese provinces, had taken charge of an impoverished, overpopulated, inward-looking country run by a corrupt, hereditary military dictator. In the space of three generations they had imposed on the country one of the most ruthless systems of political centralization ever created, founded a cult of emperor-worship, resurrected an ancient national religion and turned it into a kind of compulsory pagan folk cult, and fashioned a means of mass indoctrination through education.

They had transformed Japan from an agricultural country into a formidable industrial power by squeezing the already wretched peasantry until their ribs squeaked. They had created a huge and imposing modern army which they unleashed to great effect as the vanguard of Japanese imperialism. With a defensiveness bordering on paranoia, they had lashed out at the first signs of class revolt. The system that the feudal lords created behind the cloak of modernistic imperialist rule was that of an aristocracy, an oligarchy, using all the means of a totalitarian state to preserve its power. The course that led to the country's national suicide in the Pacific War was set in Meiji times.

The myth was later to be assiduously propagated – and is still being advanced – that the Meiji period had laid the foundations of constitutional, democratic, peaceful rule from which Japan inexplicably departed in the 1930s. In fact, it was the decade and a half following the death of the Meiji Emperor that was the real aberration in Japan's history, as a variety of pressures brought the country to a form of constitutional rule that was always desperately precarious.

The 1930s saw the reassertion of traditional Meiji values: monopolistic capitalism, militarism, unbridled colonialism, religious and educational indoctrination, and a hierarchical authoritarianism which nurtured the extremism that ended at Hiroshima and Nagasaki in August 1945. Japan's militarists, while most directly responsible for the Pacific War, did not seize power in a vacuum; as much responsibility rests with the power structure which for its own purposes appeased, sought to use, and even abetted the militarists. That power structure and ideological backdrop were fashioned in the Meiji period.

Yet while historians tend to lay the blame for what happened in the 1930s as the 'dark valley' of militarism, they can be almost as dismissive of the 1920s period of *ero*, *guro*, and *nonsensu* – erotica, grotesquerie and nonsense – under the new Taisho Emperor, whose weakness and illnesses seemed to personify his short rule. The decade and a half following the death of the Meiji Emperor is widely dismissed as a kind of Japanese Weimar Republic, but in fact it laid the basis for Japan's greatest spurt of industrial development, as well as its only real experience in pre-war democracy. The refreshing freedom of that experiment stands in stark contrast with the disastrous constitutional legacy left by the Meiji autocrats, who had always despised the very concept of democracy. It foundered because of the enormous strains produced when Japan's industrial revolution collided with world recession. It is no coincidence that the imperial throne was at its weakest during that period.

To revert again to the comparison between the Meiji period and the Victorian age: the latter's imperialism coincided with the coming to maturity of Britain's industrial society and its parliamentary and democratic institutions. The middle class was firmly in control and extending the franchise to the working classes. In Meiji Japan, an aristocratic clique harking back to feudal morality was in control, dominating the bureaucracy and the army, reluctant to share power, sheltering behind the throne, embarking upon a full colonial adventure just as other countries, for a variety of reasons, were thinking about withdrawing from their colonies.

The advent of the electric light, the steamship, the train, and the assembly line concealed methods of thinking that went back centuries and a system of government that was in many respects a regression from the rule of the shogun. Feudal lords had forged the conditions of a modern national state. During the Taisho period, for the first time in the history of Japan, they were to face a challenge from beneath. In these years, too, Hirohito was to reach his maturity.

PART TWO

THE DARK VALLEY

He heard voices talking in the grove; and he went in the direction of the voices – stealing from shadow to shadow, until he reached a good hiding place. Then, from behind a trunk, he caught sight of the heads – all five of them – flitting about, and chatting as they flitted. They were eating worms and insects which they found on the ground or among the trees . . . the head of the aruji, followed by the other four heads, sprang at Kwairyo. But the strong priest had already armed himself by plucking up a young tree; and with that tree he struck the heads as they came, knocking them from him with tremendous blows.

From 'The Story of Rokuro-Kubi', *Kwaidan*, compiled by Lafcadio Hearn

9

EMPEROR IN WAITING

ON 29 APRIL 1901 a boy was born to Princess Sadako, the wife of Crown Prince Yoshihito, Emperor Meiji's son, after less than a year of marriage. The boy was called Hirohito. Hiro means 'affluent'; an ancient Chinese text suggested that if a country was affluent, its people would be at peace. Hito was the customary imperial name, meaning humane or generous. The infant was, in addition, given the princely name of Michinomiya. Prince Yoshihito wrote the first name, while the imperial household minister wrote the second; they were ceremonially laid on the baby's pillow, while the names were announced at three shrines in the palace gardens. Hirohito was looked after by his mother and wet nurse at the crown prince's palace.

Seventy days after the birth, the baby was sent away to be raised by another family, as was the cold custom in the imperial family and among the higher aristocracy. It was believed that a child might be in danger from the rivalries of the principal ladies in the household; toddlers anyway got in the way of court proceedings, and adult ways and courtesans were not good for an infant's character. General Oyama, a distinguished officer, was asked to take in the boy. He refused: the responsibility would be too great, and he would be expected to commit suicide if the child fell ill and died.

Count Sumiyoshi Kawamura, a venerable former navy minister, was approached next. He accepted. On 7 July the baby was brought to his villa in Azubu, two miles from the crown prince's residence, and accommodated in a specially built pavilion in the garden. A wet nurse and a doctor and nurse from the Imperial Palace were in attendance; the general's wife and daughter were ever present. A courtier, Osanaga Kanroji, who wrote an account of Hirohito's early years, bears testimony to the seventy-year-old's devotion to his charge. The old man decided to instil in the child 'a dauntless spirit to withstand all hardships' and to remove 'traces of arrogance and egotism'. He arranged for an English governess to give the boy 'an independent spirit, a sympathetic heart and a sentiment of gratitude'. Little more than a year later the boy was joined by a younger brother, Prince Chichibu.

When Hirohito was not yet four years old, Kawamura died, and his widow petitioned to be relieved of her heavy responsibility. The two princes were transferred to a building in the gardens of the crown prince's palace. Less than two years later a special kindergarten was set up near by. It consisted of three rooms in the classical Japanese style with tatami mats and sliding panels that could be removed to open up a large space. Cotton cushions were tied around the pillars to prevent accidents. Five children, all a year older than the little prince, so as to advance his development, were selected to be his companions.

Hirohito was a prematurely grave, excessively clumsy child. Kanroji recalled, 'He looked formal and serious in his youth, neither smiling nor laughing. He did not appear to take any joy in either exercise or play.' He was awkward: 'The young Prince Hirohito was not particularly well co-ordinated. It even took him a long time to do up the buttons on his Western-style clothes. It was most irritating to stand by and watch him, and one wanted to reach out and help. But one could only stand there patiently, and the more one stared at him, the more he fumbled. We have the expression "twice more than others", but for His Majesty, it was "three times more".'

The boy suffered from increasingly obvious minor disabilities. He was very shortsighted, which being made to concentrate on distant objects for hours at a time (thought to be a remedy) did nothing to improve. He walked with a shuffle and had a slightly curved spine, which gave him a stoop; sitting in a specially designed chair failed to cure this. He was small and weak, yet usually well disposed to his playmates, sometimes taking the blame for them – as he could not be punished – while on occasion acting the boss and insisting on taking the role of commander-in-chief in war games. He was cosseted and pampered to protect him from physical harm, his aides picking him up when he fell and catching him on one occasion when he jumped from a wall. Two years later, he was sent to the Peers' School, which catered for children from the highest ranks of Japanese aristocracy.

The principal of the school was General Maresuke Nogi, for-merly commander of the Third Army in the Russo-Japanese war, and a personification of everything that was worst and best in Japan's aristocratic warrior tradition. He is said to have been the main influence on Hirohito's early life: certainly the emperor was to retain a long affection for Nogi, although it is doubtful whether, in later years, the more widely experienced Hirohito took the general's purist militarism all that seriously. During the siege of Port Arthur, Nogi had not just presided over the bitterest struggle in the war; he had insisted on the highest standards of discipline and humanity from his troops, severely punishing any transgression against civilian life and property. He showed that, given the right leadership, the Japanese were capable of civilized conduct in war – something seriously called into question half a century later.

The grizzled old warrior was personally approached by the emperor to become the school's head, in order to transform it from a playground for rich children into a suitable stable for an emperor. The general himself lived in a small two-storey wooden building, and was prey to that occasional tiresome disease of the very rich or very important: stinginess, a trait he inculcated into Hirohito as the downside to his modesty. Nogi, as might have been expected, paid special attention to his charge. Every day after class the principal would see his imperial pupil off home, straightening his cap, adjusting his salute, giving him a lecture. Once a week the boy received special instruction from the head; in addition, Nogi would often attend Hirohito's classes, making him thoroughly nervous.

During his five years at the Peers' School, however, the prince gradually overcame his early disabilities. He was forced to undertake rigorous physical training, including cold showers, and to participate in athletics and fencing, as well as swimming – at which he became quite good, and later enjoyed. He also became relatively proficient at that sport of the elderly or indolent, golf. The general's uncon-cealed bias against the pleasures of life rubbed off on Hirohito, who was never to over indulge himself sensually, as had his grandfather and father, but to prefer retiring, solitary activities.

Hirohito's over-dependence upon Nogi stemmed from his virtual lack of family life, apart from the attention of dedicated attendants; this was quite usual in Japan's aristocratic circles. His grandfather, the emperor, was distantly genial towards him, smiling at him when the occasion permitted and sometimes encouraging him in his sporting activities. Although gruff and fierce in appearance, the emperor was reputed to have a small army of concubines, and a penchant for poetry and good claret. He alternated between being a jolly old soul and a severe patriarch.

His son, Yoshihito, was weak-willed and from an early age had showed signs of mental instability. Mutsuhito treated his son with formality and distance: he was clearly a major disappointment. Crown Prince Yoshihito was an absentee father: as he reached maturity, he spent as little time in Tokyo as possible, avoiding its severe winters, scarcely seeing Hirohito. He was also an insatiable drunk and womanizer, carrying his father's tastes to extremes. On a memorable occasion Hirohito, at the tender age of four, was plied with sake by his father until he fell in a stupor. The young prince claimed later that he never touched alcohol from that day. Certainly he never became a womanizer, thus breaking with the aristocratic tradition of his family.

In his cautious tastes, he was to forge an ideal for Japan's emerging middle classes that was to stand the throne in immensely good stead. An emperor without the discretion and common sense that Hirohito displayed throughout his life would almost certainly not have received the support necessary to weather the typhoons of the 1930s and 1940s. His own character and the training of his early youth were to create one of the world's first modern 'bourgeois' monarchies whose exemplary behaviour made it difficult for opponents of the throne to find their target.

Six weeks after the Meiji Emperor's death – itself a traumatic event for Hirohito – Nogi appeared after a long absence abroad at the residence of his imperial pupil, his beard untidy, his appearance unkempt, his eyes dull and sunken. He gave the boy two books on the duties of the throne and lectured him, as usual:

> I am not dissatisfied with your progress while I have been away, but I ask you to study harder. You are now the crown prince, the youngest of the officers of the army and navy and the future commander of the nation. I beg you to attend to your military duties and to take care of your health, no matter how busy you are. Please remember that my physical presence is not necessary for me to be with you in your work. I shall always be watching you and your welfare will always be my concern. Work hard, for your sake, and the sake of Japan.

The same night, in front of the imperial portrait, Hirohito's surrogate father committed suicide, in the terrible manner already described. The prince was just eleven years old. On hearing the news, he is said to have remarked with remarkable sang-froid – or perhaps numbed by the shock – that 'Japan has suffered a regrettable loss'. The boy was now without a mentor. His father was by now impossibly remote; his mother, beautiful, intelligent, and a Fujiwara princess scarred by the tragedy of her marriage, had never played much part in his life.

The prince spent two more years at the Peers' School before the decision was made to create a special school around him. It was argued that he must be spared the bullying and other risks of being sent to an ordinary institution. The school was set up in the grounds of the Togu Palace, well away from the venality of the Akasaka Detached Palace, with its air of Versailles decadence revolving around Yoshihito. Hirohito's new mentor was Admiral Togo, the hero of the naval war with Russia. He was cast in a very different mould from the austere Nogi. A cheerful extrovert who enjoyed fraternizing with his men, he was put in charge of a boy who was at an age when children are much more likely to ask questions; Hirohito was to be much less influenced by him – indeed, according to some accounts he viewed the admiral with contempt.

Seven years of schooling followed, in the company of five other pupils chosen to give Hirohito companionship. His curriculum was a standard high school one: he dropped music, arts and crafts, and composition, at which he did badly, in favour of horseback riding and military science, both of which were to be useful in his later life. He was taught French badly and learned ethics under a famous scholar of the period, Shigetake Sugiura. Although not as absurd a figure as is sometimes made out, Sugiura was an ardent advocate of the Meiji doctrine of the inherent superiority of the Japanese over other races, particularly the 'decadent' Chinese.

The crown prince was also introduced to his lasting passion, science: Professor Hattori, his biology teacher, inspired him by taking him out in a boat for specimen-collecting trips off Hayama, the imperial family's resort. At the age of seventeen he was to achieve one of his life's ambitions when, walking along the beach at Numazu, he spotted a large red prawn. It was a new discovery, to be named *Sympathithae imperialis*. He was confirmed in his interest in marine biology, and under his tutor made a further contribution to the science by discovering several rare shellfish from a specially built boat.

Hirohito was hardly an extrovert, yet he was not as cold and peculiar as some biographers make out. His love of science was commendable and unusual at the time; certainly no previous emperor had displayed such an interest. He was hard-working and disciplined, if not brilliant in his studies. He was a good student of military history. He was not keen on extramural activities, but this was hardly a disadvantage for an emperor who was to preside over the most intensely hard-working urban civilization in world history. The household was desperately keen that he should not take after his dissolute father, whose character took the imperial influence in politics into as sharp a decline as Emperor Mutsuhito's had elevated it.

From the first Hirohito displayed much less of an interest in sex than had either his father or grandfather. At the age of fifteen he made love for the first time, to a concubine sent by his father. A year later he was already being prepared for marriage. In traditional Japanese style, he had no say in choosing his betrothed, who was selected by the senior members of the imperial household ministry. She was Princess Nagako, the fourteen-year-old daughter of Prince Kuniyoshi Kuni, from a family which had frequently intermarried with the imperial line. She was small, full of charm, intelligent, and cheerful – neither a beauty nor a wallflower.

She was also of the Satsuma clan, which quickly aroused the fury of the still powerful founder of Japan's military machine and head of the rival Choshu clan, General Aritomo Yamagata. It was soon put about that colour-blindness ran in Nagako's family on her mother's side. The argument advanced by Yamagata, then a peppery octogenarian, and others was that any son of the marriage would be expected to serve in the armed forces; learned articles were written asserting that colour-blindness was hereditary, and that a son born with it would fail the new military test to screen officers against the defect.

The bride's indignant father, Prince Kuni, was interviewed and advised by Yamagata and Prince Fushimi, the imperial household minister, to withdraw his daughter from the match. He flatly refused, writing at once to the emperor with the threat of major scandal and his own suicide. 'It was the imperial house itself that asked for my daughter's hand,' he pointed out. 'If the engagement is to be broken, it should be done by the imperial house. And I'd like to add that if that comes to pass, I shall be forced to answer to the insult to me and my family by first stabbing Nagako to death, and then committing suicide myself.' He produced evidence to show that neither his wife nor daughter was colour-blind. The prime minister, who as a Choshu was on Yamagata's side, responded angrily that this was rude behaviour and not something the imperial family should be subjected to. Yamagata wrote back coruscatingly, but Kuni promptly informed the empress, having become convinced that Yamagata was doing no more than attempting to sabotage the marriage in order to further the claims of one of his own relations.

Yamagata at this stage made a fatal mistake. He suggested that Hirohito should go on a trip abroad, partly to get him out of the way of this court crisis, partly to broaden his horizons. Right-wing opinion was outraged at this proposal that a future emperor should so depart from tradition as to leave Japan. Yamagata's 'treachery' in suggesting such a thing became confused in the public mind with his intrigues at court, and demonstrations were held in favour of Prince Kuni and his daughter. When Yoshihito was finally consulted on the matter by Baron Nakamura, minister of the royal household, the emperor said elliptically, 'I believe that even science is fallible.' The emperor had overruled his advisers, and Nakamura resigned.

The surprising thing about this extraordinary episode of soap-operatic family intrigue was not that it happened; such goings-on are common in many wealthy families, and probably take place in most royal circles. The remarkable feature of the whole affair was that in 1918, just three-quarters of a century ago, such goings-on could ever become a matter of major political debate. The abdication crisis in England is hardly a parallel: at stake then was whether the head of the English Church could marry a divorced woman, an issue which tested the very limits of the moral tolerance of the times. In the West, the possible colour-blindness of the king's spouse would surely have merited little more than a mention in a gossip column, even in 1918. The technological achievements of Japan at this time stand in marked contrast to the mores of society beneath.

Hirohito's trip abroad proved to be a milestone in his development. The great debate accompanying the decision to send him now has a faintly comical quality. The prime minister was in favour of it, because he believed a modern monarch should have knowledge of the world outside. The dispatch of a Japanese fleet to escort the crown prince was also intended to underline Japan's new-found importance in the world. However, the ultra-nationalist right was aghast that he should have any contact with 'barbarians'. In addition, his father the emperor was ailing, and it was feared that he might die while Hirohito was abroad. Immediately after an emperor's death, an accession ceremony is traditionally carried out during which the successor inherits the imperial regalia – the sword, the jewel, and the mirror – yet it would take weeks for Hirohito to return from Europe to carry out this essential function. Some suggested that the crown prince should show respect by not travelling while his father lay ill; others, that there might be threats to the security of the crown prince abroad.

Yet on 3 March 1921, Hirohito left Japan aboard the battleship *Katari*. His little squadron called at a host of ports, all of them, except Okinawa, British dependencies: Hong Kong, Singapore, Colombo, Aden, Suez, Port Said, Malta and Gibraltar, and was accorded a twenty-one-gun salute at each. He basked in the new world status of Japan, but must have been left with an awesome impression of Britain's imperial power. He relished the freedom the journey gave him after the rigours and formality of the Japanese court and of his schooldays.

On 7 May, Hirohito arrived at Portsmouth where he was greeted by the twenty-seven-year-old Edward, Prince of Wales – tall, cheerful and informal. Together they boarded the state train, and travelled to Victoria Station, where they were met by King George V, the Duke of Connaught and the Duke of York (later George VI). Hirohito spent three days at Buckingham Palace, where he was befriended by the Prince of Wales and was much taken by his relaxed approach and teasing of stuffy palace officials; even the king treated him as an equal. He was accorded a state dinner and an informal family lunch, at which the king advised him frankly about the duties of a sovereign.

For a further four days he was the guest of the government at Chesterfield House, meeting the prime minister, David Lloyd George; royal writers were to write patronizingly of the tact with which the 'heir to the most ancient and historic throne in the world' dealt with 'the nephew of a cobbler from a distant Welsh village'. Later he travelled to Scotland to go shooting at the Duke of Atholl's estate at Blair Castle, and joined in dancing the reels with local people. Hirohito considered this 'genuine democracy without class distinction' – which gives a flavour of just how stratified contemporary Japan was.

On 30 May Hirohito returned to his ship for the short journey to Le Havre. He duly saw the sights of Paris, including the Champs Elysées, the Eiffel Tower and the Bois de Boulogne. He went shopping, handling money for the first time, and buying a bust of Napoleon to add to those of his two other heroes, Lincoln and

Darwin. At Versailles he saw a performance of *Macbeth*. He also visited Verdun and the Somme, the recent spilling ground of so much blood; he wandered among the blackened trees and wooden crosses. 'War is truly a cruel thing; anyone who admires war should come and see this place,' he remarked. He went on to Belgium and Holland and to Italy, where he had an audience with the Pope.

Hirohito returned to Yokohama on 3 September, to a rapturous welcome. His father had not died in his absence, but his deterioration was plain to see. Hirohito and the Emperor Yoshihito had never been close, but there is little reason to suppose that the young man did not feel some affection for his father – particularly after the emperor's intervention on the side of human feeling in the matter of his bride.

Yoshihito's short reign had been disastrous for the court's influence. As a child he had suffered from meningitis, which appeared to have triggered off a progressive mental deterioration. As a young man he had overindulged his sexual appetites, and was a hard drinker. He was fond of dressing up in Western-style military uniforms, consciously imitating the wax moustache of Kaiser Wilhelm II, and gave extravagant parties at his massive folly, the Akasaka Detached Palace. It was hard to begrudge him the pleasures of his short life. By 1916 he had grown increasingly eccentric. During one military parade he struck out at soldiers with his riding crop, told a soldier to dismantle his pack, then repacked it himself, and embraced the officer. On another occasion he rolled up his prepared speech for the opening of the Diet and peered through it at members of parliament.

He had not always been a drunken, selfish debauchee: as a young man he had shown some independence of spirit, slipping out of the imperial summer house at Numazu Detached Palace to visit a local family, the Uematsus, where he would be given tea and cakes. He was clearly bored by the business of government, although perfectly capable of taking decisions. When his advisers came to see him he would often offer them a handful of cigarettes, saying, 'That's for all your effort. Now, here, have a smoke.' He enjoyed reading poetry and singing military songs, or attending small impromptu concerts of martial music staged by his guards. The empress had developed from being a beautiful young woman into a formidable personality in her own right, and her husband would sneak into the pantry for a cup of sake, telling the servants not to say anything to his wife.

THE UNDEFEATED

Hirohito's mother was a formidably beautiful and intelligent woman, brought up in great simplicity on a farm. Akihito's tutor, Elizabeth Gray Vining, one of the few Westerners who met her in later life, offers this portrait:

She was a tiny lady, with a bright eye, a rather hawk-like profile, an expression of great sweetness, and an immense dignity. She was wearing a black silk dress with a V-neck filled in with a high-collared black lace guimpe, and little black kid slippers with jet beadwork on them showed under her long, full skirt. The only light note in her costume was a diamond and platinum pin at the point of the V in her dress. Inevitably she made one think of Queen Victoria, although there is nothing in the records to suggest that Queen Victoria was slender or that she had a sense of humour, which the Empress Dowager unquestionably had. The conversation never lagged. The Empress Dowager was in command of it throughout. Charming, vivacious, low-voiced, she asked questions, and introduced topics, her fingers turning and moving in her lap.

As Yoshihito's illness worsened, he became known as 'the tragic emperor'. Takashi Hara, the prime minister, who along with the two remaining genro (elder statesmen), Prince Yamagata and Prince Saionji, was charged with the problem of the emperor's deterioration, became concerned that there was a danger to the throne. For one thing, the cult of emperor-worship had reached new heights; as yet the public knew nothing of Yoshihito's medical condition, but his lapses might become common knowledge. For another, the existence of a weak emperor meant that unscrupulous courtiers might try to influence his wife. 'Recently it has got to the point where one must do everything through the empress, and I am very concerned about the abuses that this might lead to in the future,' Hara remarked.

With painstaking thoroughness, Hara went through the processes of persuading first the emperor himself, then his wife, then the Imperial Family Council, then the Privy Council, that the emperor must give up his powers to his son, who could then become regent. On 4 October, shortly after Hirohito's return to Japan, the shocked Japanese public learnt for the first time of the remarkable mortality of the 'divine' emperor.

This skilfully handled crisis coincided with the death of Prince Yamagata, one of the two remaining genro. An increasingly crusty old man, he had played a huge role not only in shaping Japan's emerging military class, but also in determining the authoritarian nature of its constitution. If any one man can be held responsible for the rigidity of the political system that was eventually to lead to the Pacific War, it was Yamagata. The effect of his death on the army was to be far-reaching: it at once removed the most powerful military figure at court, making the armed forces anxious about their possible loss of influence there; and it undermined the disciplinary hierarchy of the institution. Yamagata, for all his faults, was the only military authority who could keep the generals in check. Now there was no one to take over this essential function.

Japan was entering uncharted and turbulent waters. In a bitter foretaste of things to come, on 4 November the prime minister was assassinated by an eighteen-year-old right-wing fanatic. The remaining *genro*, Prince Saionji, as well as Hirohito himself, decided to go along with Hara's plans to make the young man regent of Japan at a ceremony on 25 November. Although Yoshihito, the Taisho Emperor, was to live for another five years, from that moment on Hirohito was in effect the apex of the emperor system and the absolute ruler of Japan in the public eye – even if he was far from being so in reality.

In defiance of those who viewed Hirohito as a dour young man with a prematurely aged outlook, he had acquired a cheerful new self-confidence as a result of his European trip. He went to the races in Tokyo, visited the rather tame nightclubs of the aristocracy, ate bacon and eggs for breakfast, and wore plus-fours at golf. In December he invited a group of young friends and a host of geishas to a homecoming party, opening a stock of Scotch whisky given him by the Duke of Atholl. The bright young things danced and listened to music, after Hirohito's welcoming remark, 'For the next two hours please forget that I am crown prince. Let us not stand on ceremony.' The palace chamberlains were shocked by the disrespect shown to Hirohito. The elderly Saionji, who had overseen the European trip, summoned him to give him a stern telling-off for his behaviour. The timid Hirohito was crushed by the rebuke and never gave a similar party again. It had for a moment seemed that the light of popular participation and liberalism might shine upon the towering structure of mystical authoritarianism for a brief instant at the very outset of the rule of this mildly open-minded young man; but it was not to be.

The youth who in effect ascended the throne in 1921 was in direct contrast to the grandeur of the office itself. He was introverted, retiring, and not a forceful personality. He was of only moderate intelligence. His boyhood development had been almost unbelievably stunted, giving him very little knowledge of conditions in his country; his foreign tour, contrived as it was, provided him with the only broad experience he had ever enjoyed in his life. He was, however, somewhat determined in character, a trait which had enabled him to overcome some of his physical defects and to spend long hours studying. After his brief partying, he became dutiful in the extreme. His two main interests remained science and military history, while his upbringing made him deeply nationalist and racist in nature. His outlook was leavened by the modern ideas of some advisers, notably Hara, before his death, and Saionji, who for a time became his closest mentor.

Hirohito approached his rule with formality, but also with a refreshing lack of pomposity and stuffiness, and an open mind towards the introduction of more democratic principles into a ramrod-straight society. While little is known of his views at the time about Japan's imperial destiny – if he had any – his visit to the battlefields of the First World War had made a major impression on him. There was certainly nothing about this quietly spoken, pleasant, dutiful young man to suggest that, in the words of one recent critical biographer, he would emerge as 'a cunning waverer and opportunist who used his military machine to conquer half the earth without ever taking full responsibility for its misdeeds'. The adversity and struggle that had shaped the lives of his two fellow figures of hate from the mid-twentieth century, Hitler and Mussolini, hardly applied in Hirohito's case. He was to display much greater political skill than first seemed likely, in defending Japan's interests at a time of great suffering for his nation. But it is to the system itself and to Japan's evolution as a society and economy that one must look for explanations of the next two decades, not to the inadequate individual at the nominal pinnacle of authority.

10

TOKYO SPRING

T HE UNDISTINGUISHED reign of Emperor Yoshihito had
seen even more change and dislocation in Japanese society
than there had been during the Meiji period. In the space of a
decade, the centralizing, absolutist nature of the Japanese state was
transformed radically in four separate ways that promised an
unravelling of the whole authoritarian structure. First, the period
saw a rapid spurt in Japan's economic growth, dwarfing the light
industrialization of the Meiji period. Second, the power of the
Japanese army was momentarily checked and then reversed as a
coalition of interests reacted powerfully against its growing overseas
appetites. Third, economic and social change unleashed the first
serious pressure for political reform in Japan from below. Fourth,
the power of the emperor himself declined sharply, although this
was not reflected in the cult of emperor worship, which certain
interests were cultivating intensively at the time.

All of these things were in their way encouraging developments
and might, under normal circumstances, have led to the emergence
of Japan as a young constitutional democracy. It was the country's
bad luck, and to an even greater extent for the rest of the world, that
the experiment was so quickly to go sour and that the system set up
by the Meiji oligarchs was so fatally skewed against normal constitutional evolution. Out of this emerged the horrors of the 1930s and
early 1940s.

The First World War had been the forge which produced Japan's
greatest rush to twentieth-century industrialization. After some loss
of confidence and a short economic crisis, it became apparent that
while overseas competition was declining, as the European powers
turned their attention to vastly increasing war production, there was

a huge demand for munitions and war supplies that Japan could meet. In just five years between 1914 and 1919, the number of factory workers in Japan increased from 1.1 million to 1.8 million. Electric power generation increased by 34 per cent, electric motor capacity by no less than 200 per cent, and the capacity of the copper industry by 44 per cent.

Although Japan had to import nearly all of its local coal and iron, its steel industry was largely created during the First World War. Japan had only eight steel plants with an annual combined capacity of more than half a million tonnes in 1914; by the end of the war it had fourteen (as well as 166 smaller plants), with another three large plants set up in Korea and Manchuria. The output of pig iron had increased from 240,000 to 580,000 tons, and that of rolled steel, forgings and steel castings from 255,000 to 550,000 tons.

Japan's economic growth was accompanied by a huge penetration of Asian markets while the European powers were otherwise engaged. To achieve this, the Japanese had skilfully entered the war on the side of Britain and France: the purpose was to secure lucrative defence contracts and to enlarge the country's toehold in China. Within three months of the beginning of the war, the Japanese had seized German possessions in the Shantung Province, embarking upon the seizure of Tsingtau.

New Prime Minister Shigenobu Okuma and Foreign Minister Takaaki Kato were determined not to miss the opportunity provided by the First World War to attempt to turn the whole of China into a protectorate. After the fall of Shantung, the Japanese believed they had a stranglehold on decadent China, and issued an ultimatum, the Twenty-One Demands, against the advice of Britain, their principal ally at the time. Among the demands was, predictably, the extension of Japan's rights in southern Manchuria, but the ultimatum went on to require that China expel all foreign military and political advisers; that the Japanese police be given authority over certain areas of the country; and that China purchase more than half of its war material from Japan. The demands amounted to nothing less than an attempt to reimpose the old treaty port system on China, and although Japan eventually settled for less, it indirectly threatened to withdraw from the war effort against Germany unless its aspirations were recognized. Britain did so, even though its colonial interests there were compromised.

Meanwhile the Japanese also moved in a new direction, occupying a host of German-controlled islands in the Pacific – a move whose sole purpose could only be to extend the strategic reach of the Japanese navy. These included the Marianas, Palau, the Carolines and the Marshalls. Studies were now initiated into the commercial possibilities of the South Seas, including Southeast Asia. The same period saw the birth of the concept of the Greater East Asian Economic Co-Prosperity Sphere. Japan argued that, once China saw the advantages of stable government and prosperity to be derived from greater association with Japan, it would join in resisting any post-war attempt by the British to regain their influence.

One prominent businessman close to the government argued that Japan must now try 'to develop the limitless natural resources of China and the industry of Japan by co-ordinating the two, so as to make possible a plan for self-sufficiency under which Japan and China might become a single entity'. The remarkable mushrooming of Japan's imperial ambitions at this time once again underlined the continuity between the ideals of the Meiji Emperor and that of his successor, the Taisho Emperor. Now that Korea had been swallowed up and Manchuria's eventual annexation was virtually taken for granted, Japan's ambitions were in China and South-east Asia.

Yet the immediate impact of the Twenty-One Demands was on opinion abroad, particularly in the United States, which for the first time began to formulate an image of Japan as a regional bully; the Americans were also alarmed by Japan's move into the western Pacific. Even Yamagata realized that Japan had overstepped the mark, and had the foreign minister replaced.

While Japan's imperial aims thus grew during the First World War, the prestige of the army itself actually began to decline. It was a long time now since significant victories had been achieved. The army had been routed in its attempt to dictate its own budget in 1913, and there were other much more pressing demands on the public purse. At the time of Yamagata's death, the armed forces were becoming deeply frustrated: they had not taken part in the 1914–18 war; they feared their power was under challenge; and they believed Japan to be on the brink of a militarist, imperialist destiny which civilian politicians were too feeble to take advantage of.

The third element of the transformation accompanying Hirohito's accession was the growth of industrial militancy. This was fuelled by the accelerating pace of industrialization and the conditions of unbelievable penury in which workers were kept. Conditions had not improved since the 1880s: in order to bring quick profits, workers were treated as slaves in all but name in many factories: female employees were literally penned into company compounds and not allowed to leave more than a couple of times a month. 'Dormitory workers', as they were called, were not permitted to strike and could be punished physically for absenteeism. They could be asked to work day or night, and even had their leisure hours strictly controlled. The food was meagre, the sanitation non-existent, the quarters crowded, the bedding shared.

In the mines, conditions were, quite literally, satanic. Baroness Ishimoto, a social reformer, provided an unforgettably harrowing description of her visit to a mine in about 1917. The men earned about $20 a month at contemporary rates of exchange, the women $10. Some thirty miners died on average for every million tons of coal mined (in England the comparable figure was ten).

While I was down at the Miike mines, wives and daughters of miners went down in a half-naked condition, mingling with the naked men labourers. They followed the men and carried out the coal as the men loosened it with their picks. It was ridiculous to expect morality in such circumstances. Women who worked in the darkness had a pale complexion like the skin of a silkworm; they spoke and acted shamelessly, the last sign of feminine dignity sloughing off. Often pregnant women, working until the last moment, gave birth to children in the dark pit.

It would be hard to tell the difference between the lives of pigs and the lives of these miners. Certainly the human beings were living like animals in barns. Their barns were built on the bare hill in rows, barrack fashion, out of poor rough boards roofed with thin sheets of zinc. One barrack was usually divided so as to house from five to seven families. Each one of these booths was about twelve feet square, separated from the adjoining booth by thin boards. The average size of one family was five or six members and there was only one lavatory for a whole row of barracks. There was neither gas nor water service. It might be bearable in winter to live in a booth crowded with five or six people, but how could one stand the summer heat of south Japan in such conditions? . . .

Women who were already fully tired from their long day's labour in the mines returned home to carry pails of water from a distant well to their kitchens. They cooked, washed and nursed like other women whose energies are spent only on such domestic tasks. Naturally they were abnormally exhausted and nervous.

They often beat their impatiently hungry children who could not wait for their mothers to cook the meals.

Given such conditions, it was not surprising that when the economic boom showed signs of faltering, the 'rice riots' of 1918, beginning as a series of raids on the houses of rice dealers, brought down the government of Count Masatake Terauchi; his replacement was the first commoner to run Japan, Takashi Hara. At least a hundred people were killed and thousands arrested before the army regained control. Hara had been Prince Saionji's successor as leader of the Seiyukai Party – although, surprisingly, he had enjoyed a good relationship with Yamagata. The 'Great Commoner' was quite unlike his contemporary in Britain, David Lloyd George. Although in rivalry with the army faction, he was profoundly illiberal in his attitude to the unions and mass movements, and engaged a gang of *soshi*, professional bullies, that to some extent mirrored the fascist toughs in Italy.

However, he was a genuinely popular figure. His assassination in 1921 ended the career of the one civilian leader in a position to wrest power on behalf of the people from the three groups that dominated Japanese life – the bureaucracy, the army, and the economic plutocrats. Above these three groups the crown was undergoing a period of exceptional weakness. The Emperor Yoshihito lacked all personal authority, while the hold of the powerful oligarchic ministers of the Meiji period was visibly weakening: only Saionji was still alive, and the new generation of bureaucratic leaders lacked the authority of their predecessors.

The great flaw in the huge apparatus of power erected by the Meiji regime was beginning to become apparent. Japan had been ruled since 1868 by a mixture of hereditary right and brute force, the oligarchs shielding their rule behind the emperor's mantle of authority. With the emperor weakened and their own power in sharp decline, some enlightened members of the oligarchy like Saionji recognized the desperate need for greater legitimacy based on the consent of the people. Otherwise – and particularly if civil disorder broke out throughout Japan, as it was beginning to – the armed forces would step in.

There was no special reason why the armed forces should display restraint in Japan. Traditionally the samurai class had been powerful; sovereignty in Japan resided not in parliament, nor the people, nor even the bureaucracy, but in the person of the emperor, the commander-in-chief of the armed forces, to whom they owed direct allegiance. The oligarchs who had constructed modern Japan had jealously vested sovereignty in the emperor in order to deny it to the people, to preserve their elitist power in a unique combination of the führer principle and absolute monarchy. They failed to see that anyone else who gained the ear of the emperor could perform exactly the same feat and govern through him. Because sovereignty was vested in a largely powerless individual, it could be hijacked more easily than in any country of the world. It can be said with pardonable exaggeration that the army had only to cultivate a constituency of one.

A vacuum had already developed by the 1920s with the declining power of the bureaucratic class; the throne needed another prop. Moreover, the emperor, being a callow young man, was anxious to reassert royal authority after a decade of decline following the death of the impressive Meiji Emperor. It was almost certainly unrealistic to have expected Hirohito alone to have resisted the army's irresistible march to power over the next fifteen years, and the new regent, although commanding respect, was hardly an overwhelming personality.

It might be asked whether Hirohito actually connived in the army's accession to power, in order to strengthen the power and authority of his own office, and also because he saw such a development as desirable. If he did, he bore at least the guilt of complicity in the rise to power of the militarists; it is here, not in his acts during the war years, that the principal question of his culpability arises. Was he an accessory, or even an active accomplice in the army's seizure of power in an attempt to reassert the superiority of a throne sadly diminished in authority, if not in glory, by the disastrous reign of his father? The answer to this question is fascinating and complex. Yet more even than Hirohito, it was Japan's industrial–bureaucratic class that must take the prime blame for permitting the tiger of militarism to enter the very heart of Japanese government, as a survey of the fifteen years leading up to the Pacific War shows.

Certainly what is beyond doubt is that the seeds of militarism were sown by the haughty, self-perpetuating oligarchic group of selfish old bureaucrats who were unwilling to place power in Japan on any kind of popular pedestal. Even the military classes looked more democratic by the late 1920s than the collection of crusty old princes and their camp followers that had governed Japan for more than sixty years. It would not be surprising if the young emperor, tired of being lectured to by old men, did not partially share that view.

Saionji alone showed some awareness of the danger. In an article written for a French newspaper in 1918, he made a passionate appeal for moderation and good sense in domestic and foreign affairs:

> In the age of staggering progress in which we live, it is the duty of men of all walks of life and all races to help in the destruction of all those elements, like Prussian militarism, that could halt or even delay civilisation's progress . . . This message cannot lend itself to any ambiguity . . . The peace that must emerge from the [Versailles] conference must not just be a European peace, but well and truly world peace and it must be kept for ever. Humanity must be able to draw lessons from the mistakes of the past, if it is to live in happiness and rich and eternal peace.

He campaigned relentlessly for Japan's inclusion in the Versailles process, that peace before its time, when a starry-eyed American president sought to impose order upon the cynicism of the old world, and was cheated. For Japan, Versailles represented the height of idealism.

But the sad truth was that Saionji was a *passé* figure, even then. His days of real power were over, and his influence as Japan's representative at Versailles, and then as *genro* and adviser to the emperor, was confined to court circles. With the exception of Saionji and a small group of liberal activists like Prince Inouye, the aristocratic class itself had hobbled Japan's constitutional development before it could begin to modify the institutions created in the 1868 Meiji restoration. Enlightenment was stillborn. When the bureaucrats were seen to be the anachronism that they were, modern forces seized power; the most powerful of these was the army.

A large part of the aristocratic class, moreover, sympathized with the army and particularly with its overseas aims. The roots of Japanese colonialism lay firmly in the Meiji period. For seventy years, Japanese colonial policy was to be one of consistent expansion and occasional retreat when it had overreached itself, sometimes forced out by its rivals. But as conquests were made and militarism grew, there was no sign of political opposition in Japan from any except Saionji and a handful of others – or from public opinion, on the few occasions it was consulted. Most of the governing class believed Japan had a right to an empire, the bigger the better; were convinced of their racial superiority over the countries colonized; and felt they were fulfilling an idealistic mission in expelling the West from Asia. As later election results were to show, ordinary Japanese were not particularly keen on carrying these ambitions through the trials of major war. But there was a consensus among the governing class. The differences that existed within that class were ones of tactics, direction, and perceived dangers, not of political objectives.

Over the first fifteen years of Hirohito's rule, two streams tumbled in an unstoppable torrent from the same source in the Meiji period: the ascent of the armed forces to power, and the expansion of Japan's colonial ambitions. These two streams ran side by side; it was not that one was the source of the other. They ran parallel, until they converged in the thunderous cataract of war.

The reign of the young regent began on a note of youth, hope and optimism that the dark undercurrents of politics did not justify. On 12 April 1922 Hirohito's young friend, the Prince of Wales, came to Japan on a state visit, to be greeted by the same shy young man he had encountered in Buckingham Palace – but this time endowed with the formidable authority of the regency. Edward was taken to Hakone, Kyoto, Nara and Nagashima, displaying an easy lack of concern with convention that shocked many Japanese, particularly on one occasion when he posed as a coolie.

At the time there seemed every prospect that the reign would be one of increasing prosperity and calm. Japan's industrial base was larger than ever before. Its arts and society were undergoing an unprecedented enlightenment. Universal male suffrage was only three years away, and for the first time parliamentary institutions were making themselves felt in the life of the nation. Internationally, Japan seemed intent on pursuing its aims through peaceful means. There was little hint of the terrifying stampede into the vortex of repression, fear, suffering, and military defeat to come. What could transform this industrious, punctilious society of over-mannered, anxious-to-please, seemingly Western-oriented workaholics into a barbaric engine of war, the like of which the world has seen only in Nazi Germany? Prince Edward, visiting Japan, undoubtedly found Japanese deference and politeness profoundly comical; he cannot have found them threatening and dangerous.

In reality, the dangers existed long before Hirohito ascended as regent, and the brief hopes of the 1920s were no more than fleeting glimpses of a better world for Japan. The façade of Japanese constitutionalism was extraordinarily weak, like the flimsy, ubiquitous wooden houses in which ordinary Japanese lived. When times were good and the economic climate was favourable, it survived; when the winds of depression raged, it was to blow over with absurd ease, like those other ill-grounded regimes of Weimar Germany and the Third Republic in France. When the constitutional façade was gone, only industry and militarism were left, snarling at each other in a naked power struggle, with the bureaucrats left as feeble umpires on the sidelines.

Because the militarists, unlike the industrialists, had some genuine popular support for two simplistic messages that resembled those of Nazi Germany – nationalism and crude egalitarianism at a time of great economic and social privation – it is not surprising that they won in the end. In particular, the *zaibatsu* were identified with the exploitation that had provoked such wretchedness among the population. In true style, the *zaibatsu*, recognizing their imminent defeat, decided to go along with the militarist tide, surrendering to *force majeure* and hoping to profit thereby – and then, after the war, rapidly distancing themselves.

But this is to anticipate events. The real blame lay with those who, to entrench their own privileges, created a system that was not founded on popular or even middle-class support; indeed, the *zaibatsu* themselves, who were originally the extension of aristocratic authoritarianism into industrial and economic life, undermined any possibility of creating the solid middle class that is the bulwark of a democratic society. As in virtually no other industrial nation, it was not only political power that was concentrated in the hands of a very few; so was economic power. In Japan there were just the industrial oligarchs and the toiling masses, as in some awful Marxist caricature, with precious little in between. In contrast to the traditional Marxist picture, the oligarchs were so relentless in suppressing every expression of popular and left-wing opposition that they could be challenged only by right-wing, nationalist populism – which made a powerful impression on ordinary people, certainly securing more support than the hated *zaibatsu* bosses could command.

One astute contemporary observer, T. A. Bisson, summarized the power structure in Japan in an article written in December 1944:

> Democratic forces that were attempting to express themselves in the twenties, and for a time seemed to be succeeding, were in

reality held in careful leading strings by the dominant groups . . .
The controlling force in modern Japanese society has never
expressed itself exclusively through a single group. No one political
vehicle through which power is solely conducted exists in Japan or
can exist under the present system. Not the dominance of one
group interest but the accommodation of several, all within a single
dictatorial coalition, is the typical expression of the Japanese
system.

Political decisions are reached and effected through a consensus
which takes into account the opinions and reflects the immediate
and continuing shifts in power of four main groups: the bureaucrats (including those surrounding the emperor), the military
services, the business interests, and the party leaders. Normally,
each of these four groups occupies a well-defined sphere within the
cabinet or the administration as a whole.

In the usual carve-up of power, the military leaders held the army
and navy ministries, the general staffs, and other organs of the
supreme command. The *zaibatsu* held one or more of the economic
portfolios, for instance the Finance and the Commerce and Industry
ministries. The party leaders held at least two of the following four:
Railways, Communications, Agriculture and Forestry and the
Interior. The bureaucrats held the Foreign Ministry, some of the
economic portfolios and sometimes the Home Ministry. Outside the
cabinet, they also ran the imperial household, as well as the
presidency of the Privy Council.

William Lockwood brilliantly sketched the sheer power of the
zaibatsu and their importance in the development of Japanese society
between the wars:

> Probably no other modern industrial society organized on the basis
> of private property has offered a comparable display of the
> unrestrained 'power of bigness', employing all the devices of
> monopolistic control. The single qualification – and an important
> one – would seem to be the comparative rarity of actual market
> monopolies in individual products. Usually two or more of the
> giant combines were found in more or less active rivalry with each
> other and sometimes with a host of small producers. The same
> combines, however, tended to dominate a number of fields of
> industry and trade . . .
>
> The institution of the *zaibatsu* contributed greatly to the rapid
> accumulation of capital in modernization of technology which

underlay Japan's industrial development. It enabled Japan to reap certain economies of large-scale organization even where the production unit remained small; it placed the direction of large sectors of the economy in the hands of able technicians and executives employed by the combines; it afforded a device by which industrial investment was accelerated through the ploughing back of huge profits accruing to the owners.

On the other hand, if the concentration of control in Japanese industry and finance was progressive in these technical aspects, its social aspect was less admirable. It was one of the factors perpetuating inequalities of income and opportunity in modern Japan almost as wide as those of feudal times. It carried over into modern industry the tradition of hierarchical status and authoritarian control which was inimical to political and social democracy. By hampering the pervasive growth of independence and individual initiative in economic life it reinforced other circumstances militating against the emergence of a broad and sturdy middle class, or a vigorous trade union movement. And in politics, the plutocratic alliance of the *zaibatsu* and the political parties contributed eventually to the defeat and discrediting of parliamentary government after 1930.

Like some terrible omen of the times to come, Hirohito's early regency was marked by a massive earthquake, on 1 September 1923. In Yokohama and Tokyo, devastation was immediately followed by raging fires. Yokohama was destroyed altogether, while half of Tokyo was razed to the ground. The death toll was 100,000. The giant catfish under Japan that, legend had it, rears up in anger when the humans above displeased it, had wreaked a terrible vengeance.

Worse was to come – a portent of the nationalist frenzy that was to follow: the police used the disaster as a pretext to crack down on a supposed conspiracy between Korean nationalists and Japanese communists to set up a revolutionary government in the aftermath of the earthquake. Many were arrested and many murdered, as angry mobs sought out Koreans – the only significant immigrant community in Japan. Although the government was almost certainly not responsible for the massacres, it bowed to the pervasive racial and anti-communist sentiment of one sector of Japanese opinion.

Tokyo was rebuilt within three years, partly through foreign generosity. The walls of the Imperial Palace had remained standing, but little else: huge modern houses now flanked wide avenues, while the familiar wooden houses were now found only on the surrounding hills. Japan to this day has little sense of permanence about its housing, and a remarkable fatalism in the face of disaster – which helped the nation as much during the war as after the bombing of Hiroshima and Nagasaki in 1945.

The impact of the earthquake was to be partially assuaged in the public mind by an event of national celebration: Hirohito's wedding, repeatedly postponed, first through the opposition of Yamagata and then by the earthquake. On 26 January 1924, six years after the original engagement, the twenty-two-year-old Hirohito and his nineteen-year-old bride were married at the Imperial Palace in Tokyo; not until May did public festivities take place, in deference to the suffering caused by the earthquake. In August the royal couple went on a month's honeymoon, after which they moved into the huge, over-the-top Akasaka Detached Palace, where Hirohito's father had spent so much of his short life.

The homely Nagako and the shy Hirohito were close from the first, spending much time together: she playing the piano for him and singing, the two of them listening to records together. The Garden of the Four Seasons, to the south of the palace, where trees and plants bloomed throughout the year, became a favourite promenade. Hirohito set up a little laboratory in the grounds of the palace, complete with a shed for raising animals and a field for growing plants. It seemed that he was at the height of his personal happiness. On 6 December 1925, a baby girl was born to the royal couple.

It was ten days after Princess Teru Shigeko was born that the incapacitated Emperor Yoshihito collapsed with a stroke. Another followed; he could no longer walk or talk properly. A year later, on 25 December 1926, he died of pneumonia at the age of just forty-seven, during a fierce thunderstorm. The same night, Hirohito was given the sword and jewel of office – two of the three insignia of the throne, supposedly bequeathed by the Goddess Amaterasu – while another ceremony was held in the imperial sanctuary before the sacred mirror, which could not be moved.

The actual coronation of the new emperor took place two years later, in November 1928. It was a staggering occasion, befitting the figurehead that the Meiji rulers had turned into a godlike, all-powerful entity, and the leader of an increasingly self-assertive, nationalist country, and went on for eight days. The coronation banquet itself lasted a whole day and was attended by 4000 guests.

The Japanese people showed a remarkable acquiescence towards the occasion, in spite of acute economic difficulties.

They seemed particularly to warm to the simplicity of the imperial couple. Many had heard of one of Hirohito's first reforms within his own household: he had abandoned the aristocratic ranking of ladies-in-waiting, a hotbed of courtly intrigue, making them all equal and permitting commoners to serve for the first time. He insisted, too, that ordinary Japanese, not classical courtly Japanese, be spoken in the palace. Above all, he showed that he and his wife would be a faithful couple, not a nominal one with the emperor indulging in his concubines, as his father and grandfather had before him. He seemed in spirit with the times, reflecting a kind of divine simplicity magnified many times by the state propaganda machine. He was twenty-seven at the time of his coronation; before that, although he was privy to the great decisions of state, it would be absurd to suggest that he had had much influence on them.

Yet the same year two incidents occurred that cast his role in a new perspective. The first, a truly sinister display of the power of imperial devotion, occurred at the great coronation day parade on 1 December 1928, when more than 70,000 students and young people congregated in front of the huge walls of the Imperial Palace, beyond the moat. In the freezing December evening, as rain fell, the royal tent was suddenly dismantled. It was announced that the emperor would appear without protection, in sympathy with the young people here. Promptly the students began removing their overcoats in reciprocation.

When Hirohito arrived at 2 a.m., he was wearing a military cape. Seeing the youngsters without their coats, he promptly stripped off his own, and the well-fed minions in attendance were obliged to follow suit. For nearly an hour and a half the emperor stood unprotected, saluting thousands of youths marching without their coats. As a display of the loyalty inspired by the emperor and of ludicrous, self-abasing stupidity by both him and his subjects, it was a foretaste of events a decade later.

The second incident instead redounded to Hirohito's credit. He had by now been the nominal head of his country for nearly six years, still strongly supported by the liberal Prince Saionji, whose mind belied his age, although his political power had sharply diminished. The prince profoundly loathed militarism, and had outlived his rival Yamagata. Saionji had openly criticized Hirohito's 'lack of courage'. Prince Kuni, Hirohito's father-in-law and a liberal aristocrat, had said in his dying words to his daughter, the empress, 'The reigning emperor is rather weak-willed at times. Therefore he will need your support. Be strong! Be strong!'

Hirohito was young, impulsive, fed up with being criticized for indecision, and of a reasonable liberal caste of mind when, in the first fateful step towards Japan's military armageddon, the Manchurian warlord Chang Tso-lin was assassinated in 1928 by Colonel Komoto, a senior Japanese staff officer. The young emperor had already insisted that 'a real military expansion' into Manchuria 'would antagonize the Chinese', and had opposed it.

The prime minister of the time, General Giichi Tanaka, summoned by the emperor after the assassination, promised to take action against its perpetrators. Hirohito told him that 'no matter what sort of man Chang Tso-lin may have been, he was the designated authority in Manchuria. It was very wrong of the army to have any hand in his assassination.' Tanaka prepared a full report on the incident, which turned out to be no more than a whitewash. Hirohito was furious. He asked the prime minister, 'Does this not contradict what you told me before?' Tanaka replied that he could 'offer a number of explanations for that'. 'I have no wish to hear your explanations,' the emperor said sharply, and left the room. The prime minister promptly resigned, having no choice after such an imperial snub.

Years later Hirohito was to regret his show of anger. 'I was too young at the time,' he said. In fact, the Meiji constitution had firmly instructed the emperor to follow the prime minister's advice on political issues. One minister at the time complained that 'to treat the nation's prime minister so lightly, even once, is a serious matter. It would have been proper to remonstrate with His Majesty over this.' Hirohito had behaved like a hotheaded young man, in defiance of the constitution that shackled him to impotence yet used his awesome imperial office as its backbone. He was chastened by the experience.

But he had been wise, humane, and right. His was the human heart that beat faintly at the centre of a monstrous system that acted in his name; he was all-powerful in theory, yet his own wishes hardly mattered. He had kicked against the system, and had been slapped down. This already timid individual was to be much more circumspect in future about challenging the powers that be. Only twice more was he to show any real personal initiative; and indeed a constitution which accorded him such huge formal authority and so little real power was at heart contradictory and deeply unstable. There was to be a terrible and ironic personal tragedy in the emperor's powerless opposition to the policies carried out in his all-powerful name.

The events of the 1920s and 1930s now unfolded like a Shakespearian tragedy to their final denouement. Japanese imperialism was firmly anchored in the ideals of the Meiji oligarchs, but there had been major divisions of policy on how fast and how far to proceed. The attempt by Saigo to spur Japan into Korea had led briefly to civil war; yet Korea had in the end been occupied under more favourable circumstances. The Sino-Japanese and Russo-Japanese Wars were both imperialist ones, ending in qualified victories for Japan.

There was general agreement among the ruling groups in Japan – the bureaucracy, the armed forces, and the business leaders – that further expansion was desirable, but no clear idea as to the best way of achieving it: the navy and many businessmen, for example, favoured expansion southwards; the army favoured further expansion deep into China. For the moment caution prevailed. Under Japan's brief phase of parliamentary government, the middle-class electorate showed little inclination to be sucked into war – and, briefly at that time, public opinion counted for something. Business was cautious; the international climate was wrong. Japan's First World War allies had grown suspicious, and the British and Americans were still the major naval presence in Asian waters.

Politically, moderates under the influence of the business elites headed the government. After Hara's assassination in November 1921, four short-lived governments followed each other in swift succession before two major parties crushed the nominees of what was left of the Meiji bureaucracy in the general election of 1924. These were Takaaki Kato's Kenseito Party, and the assassinated Hara's Seiyukai Party. In fact, each party was heavily dominated by the *zaibatsu* – Mitsubishi and Mitsui, respectively. In the delicate power balance within Japan, it would be fair to say that real power had for the first time passed to big business in alliance with what little influence public opinion possessed.

The bureaucrats were on the defensive, although still entrenched in the ministries and, in particular, the imperial household. Their leader, the remaining *genro*, Prince Saionji, was however on the side of reform. Beneath him, higher and middle echelons in the bureaucracy seethed at their loss of control. They also resented the challenge to Japanese society represented by the forces of modernization and 'licentiousness', and Japan's overseas moderation. The third power, the armed forces, was for the moment neutralized, but it harboured some of the most radically reactionary forces in Japanese society.

Kato and his successor as head of the Kenseito, Reijiro Wakatsuki, were resolved to pursue Japan's quest for greater overseas influence by peaceful means. Kijuro Shidehara, the foreign minister, had moved to dispel the extreme suspicion of Japan generated by the notorious Twenty-one Demands on China. Japan's new policy of non-interventionism was helped by the disastrous experience of Japan's expedition to Russia during the civil war there in 1918. In alliance with the Americans, a 70,000-strong force had blundered about, trying to secure national interests rather than defeat the Red Army. The Japanese had been given instructions to 'facilitate the activities of Japanese officials and civilians' engaged in the 'conduct of business and the development of natural resources.' They were to 'enhance Japan's position in its future competition with the Western powers in China'.

Exasperated and pushed back by the Russians, the Americans withdrew in 1920. Alone and facing huge casualties for questionable objectives, the Japanese retreated from the Amur River in 1922, and in 1925 evacuated northern Sakhalin, leaving behind them the enmity of the Soviet state. This military débâcle contributed to the low public standing of the Japanese army at the time. A moderate minister of war, General Ugaki, was appointed in 1924 to cut the army's strength by no fewer than four divisions.

Meanwhile, in China, Japan's previous aggression had made it enemies on all sides. In addition, its trade objectives there were coming into conflict with those of the United States. The British had refused to renew the Anglo-Japanese alliance on the ground that Japan showed 'little chance of industrial survival unless she can obtain control over the resources of China' – and that would endanger Britain's own commercial activities there. Japan's international emissaries spoke bitterly of 'the attempt to oppress the non-Anglo-Saxon races, especially the coloured races, by the two English-speaking countries, Britain and the United States'.

Yet Japan did not dare take on such enemies. Kijuro Shidehara, the foreign minister, argued eloquently in favour of the extension of Japanese influence by non-military means. 'Japan, being closest to China, has an advantage by way of transport costs and she also has the greatest competitive power because of her wages. It must therefore be a primary priority for Japan to maintain the great market of China.' Iwane Matsui, of the Japanese general staff, insisted that Japanese policy was 'to substitute economic conquest for military invasion, financial influences for military control and achieve our goals under the slogans of co-prosperity and co-existence'. This was hardly the language of peaceful diplomacy, but it did mark a greater degree of Japanese caution than in the past.

The Tokyo spring of parliamentary democracy and restraint abroad contained the seeds of its own destruction. Four forces were to crush it with devastating and unerring precision: the first was the growth in right-wing political extremism; the second, tied to this, was the fatal identification of the business groups with the main democratic political parties; the third was the economic crisis that began in 1927; and the fourth was the rebirth of Chinese nationalism after decades in which that huge, decadent sluggard of a country had been picked at like some putrid carcass by predatory colonial outsiders.

The growth in right-wing political extremism had a variety of causes. It had a long pedigree, dating back to the existence of the unemployed samurai class who had been behind the restoration of the emperor in 1868, and had then been stripped of its perks. The breeding ground was the city of Fukuoka, the closest point in Japan to the Asian mainland: the starting-point for the invasion of Korea by the Empress Jingu, and for the attacks mounted by Hideyoshi in 1592, and the main operational base during the Russo-Japanese War. Fukuoka samurai had left their castle city to stage an attack on the home city of the Meiji statesman Tomomi Iwakura as recently as 1874.

In 1881 a mass of samurai secret societies coalesced to form the Genyosha, dedicated to reverence of the Emperor, to furthering the interests of the nation, and to the rights of the people. The Genyosha did not believe, after Saigo's defeat in 1877, that an armed uprising was an option: the purpose of the society was to bring together like-minded extreme nationalists, particularly in the bureaucracy and the army, to promote their common aims. There were a huge number of these, and the Genyosha was, literally, masonic in its network, furthering the business interests of its members, seeking intermediaries to act for sympathetic military and civilian leaders and, not least, resorting to systematic terror in pursuit of its aims.

Mitsuru Toyama was the Genyosha's best-known leader. Born

of an improverished samurai family, he spent his youth in tea-houses and brothels; quite early on, he established for himself a curious autonomy and immunity from the law that allowed him to patronize not just home-grown terrorists but right wing revolutionaries overseas. His two unwavering ideals were implacable opposition to Western interests and hatred of communism. In 1892 he reached an agreement with the government by which he was assured that it would pursue a strong foreign policy and increase military spending in exchange for Genyosha support. Toyama's strong-arm methods, with the assistance of *soshi* (toughs) from neighbouring areas, terrorized Fukuoka Province; the election was the bloodiest in Japanese history, with dozens killed and several hundred wounded.

The police and the Home Office closely co-operated with him, which was convenient as the police could not be seen to launch attacks on public meetings themselves, but instead would turn up later to restore peace, arresting the victims of the attacks. At cabinet level, an unofficial alliance existed between the Interior, War and Navy ministries, who were happy to use the services of the Genyosha. The organization also provided the army with an unofficial foreign intelligence service. Contacts with anti-Manchu secret societies, nationalist groups in colonial territories and dissident Muslims in Central Asia were established and developed. In 1882 Toyama, with the help of the Kumamoto Soai-Sha ('Mutual Love Society'), sent over a hundred young men to China to gather information.

Parallel to the growth of the Genyosha (literally, 'Dark Ocean Society') and the Kokory-ukai ('Black Dragon Society') was that of a clique of extremist philosophers, of whom the best known was Ikki Kita, later dubbed the father of Japanese fascism. Kita was an intellectual, not a man of action like Toyama. His book, *A Plan for the Reorganisation of Japan*, published in 1923 and promptly banned because of its egalitarian views, might be described as 'socialist–imperialist'. He seized upon the two most populist creeds of the time, the yearning for equality and the desire for national self-assertiveness, and welded them together even more closely than Hitler and Mussolini would manage. He sought the establishment of a 'revolutionary empire of Japan' through a military *coup d'état*, which would be founded on the indissoluble bonds between the emperor and the armed forces, and whose mission would be to further Japanese expansion abroad.

Domestically his programme was radical. Politics would be suspended and the corrupting barriers between the emperor and his people done away with. The rich would be expropriated of their land and financial dominance. The economy would be state-controlled and placed on a war footing. Land reform would be introduced in order to give protection to tenant farmers. Profit-sharing and an eight-hour day would be introduced into industry, and civil liberties would be permitted.

Kita's international views displayed the same kind of crazy, simple-minded plausibility. Britain, 'a multimillionaire standing over the whole world', and Russia, 'the great landlord of the northern hemisphere', needed to be expelled by the Asian nations, headed by Japan. 'Our several hundred million brothers in China and India have no path to independence other than that offered by our guidance and protection.' Japan should 'lift the virtuous banner of an Asian league and take the leadership in a world federation'. Japan was not acting entirely out of altruism, of course: one reason for this struggle was that, for Japan, 'great areas adequate to support a population of at least two hundred and forty or fifty millions will be absolutely necessary a hundred years from now'. Even some recusant communists followed a similar line of thinking: Japan, on one account, had the task of leading 'a progressive war for the people of Asia' against British and American capitalism.

Kita's ideas can be clearly traced in two later expressions. In the army, the Imperial Way Faction, led by General Sadao Araki, who became war minister in 1931, paid unashamed homage to them. But they became fashionable even in much more aristocratic circles. Prince Konoye of the venerable Fujiwara family, later to be a bitterly controversial prime minister, argued as far back as the 1920s that Britain and the United States were pursuing policies to keep down the 'have-nots', condemning Japan 'to remain forever subordinate to the advanced nations'. It would be necessary, he concluded, 'to destroy the status quo for the sake of self-preservation, just like Germany'.

The Imperial Way Faction had enormous influence among junior officers. Many believed passionately in what became known as the Doctrine of the Showa Restoration: the argument that, just as after the Meiji restoration the feudal princes, the *daimyo*, had had to surrender their lands to the emperor, so now must the 'feudal' industrial princes, the *zaibatsu*, surrender their wealth to the emperor. Such views were equally popular among the army officers from the traditional samurai background and those from a peasant background who had come up with the introduction of conscription. They were to comprise a pure form of nationalist communism, based on racism and imperialism.

The appeal of these ideas owes a great deal to the fact that the authoritarian system of Japan moved with such relentless intensity against any formal mass movement of the left. The radical right – preaching social equality, nationalism, the unity of the Japanese people under the emperor's mantle, hatred of capitalism, whether home-grown or from abroad, and the wish to lead the peoples of Asia in a crusade against the West – had come up with a vision of genuine mass appeal, particularly to the huge swathes of Japanese society that had suffered the ravages of industrialization and depression, many of whose sons had been conscripted into the army. In Japan, the radical alternative to rule by big business and the bureaucracy became the egalitarian right, because the egalitarian left had been suppressed. This, in turn, was to alarm Japan's ruling class, and helps to explain why they abandoned all good sense and calm in the whirlwind of events that began in the 1930s.

The ties between big business and the political parties were, of course, to be fatal for the latter and nearly so for the former. As long as Japan's economy was booming, such ties were acceptable. Elections were financed by large gifts from the *zaibatsu*, and politicians used open bribery to get themselves elected. The two leading parties traded accusations of corruption. The *zaibatsu* themselves were far from popular among the workers they employed and among the small business interests they habitually squeezed and crushed. In the countryside – whence the bulk of soldiers were recruited – the powerful urban economic interests were identified not just with economic exploitation, but with the introduction of a new Japanese order that had destroyed centuries of tradition. W.G. Beasley, the chronicler of Japanese imperialism, put the new mood succinctly:

> As Japanese society became more bourgeois, so nationalism became in one of its guises a critique and a lament: that landlords had become absentees, exploiting villagers; that businessmen were *nouveaux riches*; that politicians were party men, seeking only power; that none of them put the nation first. At schools and universities, it was said, the young were being taught to esteem individualism, which was a Western word for selfishness.
>
> In these circumstances, nationalism became critical of contemporary leadership . . . This involved, *inter alia*, a return to the same kind of ambitions overseas and the same kind of imperialist policies in pursuit of them as had developed in the Meiji era. Nationalism was also revolutionary, however. It denied the validity of much

that had been done in the name of modernisation in the past; demanded once again a complete reordering of society, effected by force in the emperor's name; and condemned the whole world order as unjust. It therefore called upon Japanese to carry through to completion the tasks which the Meiji leaders had left half-done, both at home and overseas. The heroes it chose were the 'men of spirit' of the 1860s, who had helped to bring the Tokugawa down. Its methods, like theirs, were terrorism and the *coup d'état*. Patriotic assassination, never absent for long from modern Japanese politics, became frequent and respectable again.

11

INTO MANCHURIA

FOR JAPAN the financial crash came earlier and ended sooner than elsewhere. In 1927 a minor bank failed; thirty-six more followed, bringing down scores of small firms with them. The *zaibatsu* gobbled up many of the hapless victims. The crisis stemmed to a great extent from the *zaibatsu* domination of the banking system, which had favoured an expansionary monetary policy even when this could not be sustained by real economic growth. The Wakatsuki government fell, and Giichi Tanaka of the opposition Seiyukai Party came to office. This first economic upheaval had the effect of beginning to discredit party politics, while increasing public hostility and contempt for the *zaibatsu*, particularly among the military class and the oppressed but conservative peasantry.

The crisis coincided with the challenge to Japan abroad. Many army officers were appalled by the government's hands-off approach to China, but in the same year it became apparent that Chiang Kai-shek's Nationalist forces had gained control of the Yangtze Valley and were moving north to consolidate their hold over the country. The Japanese for the first time feared that a strong China was on the cards, which would undoubtedly threaten their interests in Manchuria. In the circumstances, many officers felt it would be a dereliction of duty to continue Shidehara's policy of conciliation. The whole simplistic swirl of foreign policy weakness, corruption, democratic politics, big business exploitation, and economic crisis began to fuse into a single obsession in the Japanese military mind: something must be done. Of course, any society has its extremists, and should be capable of putting them down.

Indeed, the first confrontation between the established order in

Japan and the militarists ended in victory for the former – but of so marginal a kind that it merely spurred on the subsequent challenges. The initial battle for the control of Japan between the establishment and the far right was joined over the assassination of the Manchurian warlord, Chang Tso-lin.

Chang, the 'Old Marshal', had been a loyal protégé of Japan's, a formidable and unscrupulous military leader in southern Manchuria from around 1920, controlling the southern city of Mukden. Chang had been supplied with Japanese arms, and was ready to co-operate with the Japanese; he was also firmly anti-Russian. However, he was deeply ambitious, and wanted to take over all of China. Japan's government at the time resolved to make him the puppet ruler of Manchuria, while discouraging his aims to the south. Accordingly, Japanese advisers were attached to Chang's staff, as much to keep an eye on him as to prop him up. Japanese troops were soon fighting alongside Chang when rebellions threatened. The alliance had all but made Manchuria a Japanese protectorate by December 1925. With some 100,000 Japanese lives already lost protecting Japanese interests there, and with so many subjects and commercial interests at stake, the Japanese forces, the Kwantung Army, became an occupying presence.

Within these constraints Chang showed a measure of independence, setting up a Chinese-style education system to rival the Japanese one, and permitting Chinese firms to compete with Japanese, while renewing his interest in the rest of China. In 1926 he was self-confident enough to move down from Manchuria and occupy the capital, Peking. This alarmed the Japanese, who at this stage had no wish to get sucked into China's civil war and who did not want to make enemies of the man who might emerge as China's strongman, General Chiang Kai-shek – even though they viewed him with deep suspicion.

General Tanaka, Japan's new prime minister, tried to deal directly with Chiang, securing a promise that his forces would stop short of Manchuria. When the generalissimo nevertheless attacked early in 1928, Japanese troops engaged his army. Chiang's forces advanced relentlessly on Peking, and Tanaka was forced to issue an ultimatum declaring that Japan would resist any encroachment on Manchuria with all the forces at its disposal. Simultaneously Chang was told that he must withdraw his forces from Peking into Manchuria, or risk having the border closed against him by the Japanese; this he did. The Japanese informed Chang that he would not be allowed to move south again. Their clear objective was to hold on to Manchuria and prevent its absorption into China's civil war.

There followed one of the most puzzling incidents in the history of Japanese imperialism. As the defeated warlord returned from Peking to Mukden, a bomb was placed under his train on the orders of Colonel Daisaku Komoto, a senior officer of the Kwantung Army. Chang was seriously injured by the blast, and died shortly afterwards. At first Chiang Kai-shek was blamed; later the explosion was widely interpreted as providing a pretext for the Japanese invasion and annexation of Manchuria now that the only Chinese leader with any real authority there was dead. The incident was significant as the first example of the Japanese army apparently acting off its own bat, without reference to the high command in Tokyo, much less the government or the emperor.

On this occasion, the tactic badly misfired and proved highly counter-productive. Neither the Kwantung Army nor the Japanese high command made any move. Chang's son, Chang Hsueh-liang – the 'Young Marshal' – took over his father's army and promptly started to pursue a policy of opposition to Japanese interests, reaching an agreement with Chiang Kai-shek in December, no doubt spurred by the widespread rumour that the Japanese had in fact murdered his father. In China, there were boycotts of Japanese goods. A railway system favourable to the Japanese was ripped up by the Young Marshal. The Japanese were forced back on the defensive, and in June 1929 they grudgingly recognized Chiang Kai-shek as the legitimate ruler of China.

In Japan, Colonel Komoto's insubordination infuriated the emperor and led him to demand punishment for those responsible. When Tanaka proved unwilling or unable to deliver this, the emperor's cold fury caused him to resign. There remains the intriguing possibility that Komoto had, after all, been acting with some kind of secret directive from the government: Chang had become a serious embarrassment to the Japanese and an obstacle to normal relations with China; his removal made possible agreement with Chiang Kai-shek. If Komoto – who narrowly escaped court martial – was acting under government direction, the primary objective was a moderate one. If, as is more likely, he was not, his gross insubordination had failed. The army hotheads, it seemed, had been rapped over the knuckles.

*

The setback to their cause was temporary: the beginnings of Japan's grim aberration, of the rush to extremism and madness, were only months away. The emperor, as weak as any constitutional monarch, was being steered by moderate party politicians, who were accused on all sides of corruption, believed to be in the pay of the detested business corporations, with only the flimsiest figleaf of popular legitimacy. The country's huge conscript army was as powerful as it had ever been, and longed for the opportunity to intervene and give direction to Japan's affairs, now so feebly run by the politicians. In particular, as the military men saw it, such few colonial possessions as Japan had were in danger of being taken over by the renascent Chinese, aided by Russian Bolshevism and British and American imperialism. The army believed itself capable of winning any war it embarked upon: what were the politicians waiting for?

In Manchuria, where so many Japanese lives had been lost and so many interests and, indeed, so much *lebensraum* were at stake, the politicians were permitting the creation of an anti-Japanese state which in 1930 firmly declared its allegiance to Chiang Kai-shek, who would presumably want to push the Japanese out. The army, which regarded itself as the direct descendant of the main Choshu faction behind the Meiji restoration, had direct access to the emperor, bypassing the cabinet, and considered itself above the decisions of the government. The emperor was a young man under the influence of 'defeatist' advisers; loyalty to him did not entail allegiance to the corrupt influences around the throne, as numerous 'loyal' samurai rebellions in the past testified. Japan's samurai purity was being corrupted by urban and internationalist influences.

While there undoubtedly were some moderate senior army officers, and some constitutionalists among them, these views were held not just by junior hotheads but by many senior members of the general staff. What happened over the next couple of years has often been described as the action of a few extremists. All the evidence suggests, however, that the general staff was directly implicated. The army had resolved to take control not just of foreign policy but of the government: a military *coup d'état* was under way, albeit in fits and starts, with half-cock conspiracies and subterranean plans of action. By 1932, no government could be formed without the acquiescence of the service ministers, and those ministers refused to endorse any government headed by a party politician – that is, elected by popular mandate.

Democracy, which had so tentatively taken the stage as the

oligarchs relaxed their grip a decade earlier, was dead, and in its place was dictatorship by a military clique riven by rivalries between services, ranks, and personalities. It is hard to describe the three-year agony that led to this as one huge conspiracy; the process was too messy. But undoubtedly the great majority of senior and middle-ranking officers, a large part of the bureaucracy, and a fanatical minority of civilians had precisely this objective in mind: to fill the empty, bristling helmet of samurai armour that was the emperor system with a fighting brain to replace the feeble and venal politicians then in control.

Two events shattered what restraints might have acted to curb army and civilian nationalists. The first was petty and absurd; the second, deserving of sympathy. In 1930, at the London Naval Disarmament Conference, the Japanese delegation, which included the navy minister, agreed to a limit on the number of Japanese warships in the Pacific which was at once strongly contested by the naval general staff. Prime Minister Tanaka had resigned following the emperor's criticism of his failure to prevent the assassination of Chang Tso-lin. His successor was the leader of the opposition, a feisty old man, Osachi Hamaguchi, known in political circles as 'the Lion'. His war minister was the moderate General Ugaki, one of the last constitutionalists to hold the post. The government was tainted by being closely connected with Mitsubishi. The foreign minister, Jinnosuke Inouye, was the son-in-law of the head of that family, but had a reputation as a brilliant and honest economist in his own right.

Hamaguchi, who was acting as navy minister in Tokyo, immediately endorsed the recommendation of the London Agreement, which also must have given satisfaction to Inouye, who wanted to cut military spending. The nationalists were appalled, claiming he had acted unconstitutionally in ignoring the views of the naval general staff (although the navy minister himself had signed the agreement). Senior army officers were appalled that their rival service appeared to be losing its autonomous power of political decision-making to the despised civilians.

Much more seriously, and almost simultaneously, the world depression arrived. Japan had already had a foretaste of this in the 1927 wobble, and as a result was in a better position to face it than most countries in the industrial world. The view that the militarists seized power because of the strains induced by the depression is facile and demonstrably untrue. Yet the slump struck Japan in three very specific ways. First, it dealt a body blow to Japanese exports, which plunged between 1929 and 1931. In America the silk market collapsed, threatening many small farmers in Japan and plunging the north of the country into desperate povety; this was further compounded by the failure of the 1932 rice crop, which led to a major famine. Farmers staved off hunger by selling their daughters to the brokers that travelled the countryside on behalf of the big city brothels. The self-appointed representatives of the rural communities were the extreme nationalists who had hijacked the aspirations of Japan's traditionally miserable and repressed peasantry from the genuine peasant leaders so vigorously persecuted by local authorities and central government alike.

Second, the depression also dealt a serious blow to the credibility of the monopoly capitalists who dominated the political parties. In fact, urban Japan was much less hard hit than rural Japan, and was to recover quickly. But to the most radical sector of public opinion – the hard-hit peasantry and their right wing champions – the corruption and domination of the oligarchic monopolies were never more apparent. With their rotten, greedy, exploiting ways, they could no longer even point to success as their pretext for eroding Japan's traditional way of life.

Third, the peaceful approach to trade liberalization and negotiation was now exposed as a hollow sham: as countries rushed to put up trade barriers in the wake of the great depression, Japan had nothing to gain by continuing to endorse open-door and treaty port systems – which it had always suspected were the shabby devices of Western colonial exploitation in the first place. Its policy henceforth would be one of creating its own self-sufficient trading bloc and expelling foreign colonialists from Asia. One prominent Diet member argued in 1931 that 'economic warfare' was leading to the creation of 'large economic blocs'. Japan must create its own, using force to assure 'its rights to a bare existence'.

The army decided to act. The brush-dry tinder of Japanese extremism had been ignited by a fierce economic depression that was most affecting the class from which its junior officers were drawn – the peasantry, bitterly opposed to urban cosmopolitanism. The emperor must be rescued from his corrupt advisers. The nationalists acted on three fronts: through domestic terrorism, through preparation for a coup which intimidated successive civilian governments into virtual submission, and through the pursuit of an independent, aggressive policy in Manchuria.

*

It is hard to exaggerate the climate of fear into which Japan was plunged by the whirlwind of far-right terror that was unleashed in 1930. In November of that year, Hamaguchi was shot by a far-right terrorist in the gothic splendour of Tokyo Station – nine years after Hara's assassination. Shidehara, who had returned as foreign minister, became acting prime minister until the following April, when Hamaguchi bravely returned to office in spite of his injuries, only to have to give way to Foreign Minister Wakatsuki. 'The Lion' died shortly afterwards.

Only months after the assassination attempt, a group of senior army officers was discovered to be plotting a coup designed to put the War Minister, Ugaki, at the head of a military government. In March 1931 the moderate Ugaki learned of the plot, which became known as the 'March Incident' and denounced it. The conspirators included Major-General Kuniaki Koiso, later to become prime minister, and the vice-chief of the general staff. On this occasion, as on others, many senior officers were involved, and all went virtually unpunished. The 'October Incident' followed months later: the plot this time was to blow up the entire cabinet and set up a military junta. Senior officers were again involved, and it was exposed only when some got cold feet. The ringleaders were held for a day or two, then posted away from the capital.

Unsurprisingly undeterred, the assassins and the plots soon started again. Early in 1932, Inouye, the former finance minister linked to Mitsubishi, and Baron Dan, chief director of its rival Mitsui, were assassinated by members of a fanatical right-wing sect calling itself 'the League of Blood'. On 15 May, seventy-five-year-old Prime Minister Tsuyoshi Inukai, who had succeeded Wakatsuke, was shot down in his official residence by nine young cadets. The killers were given prison sentences that tapered off within a few years with their release. Early in 1934 a plot was discovered to bomb the cabinet of Inukai's successor, Admiral Saito, and to set up a cabinet headed by an unnamed prince of the imperial house. In August the following year the deputy minister of war, Major-General Nagata, was slain by a sword wielded by a lieutenant-colonel. All of this was but a build-up to the most celebrated coup attempt of them all, that of February 1936.

This catalogue of terror and military fanaticism illustrates the conditions under which Japan's responsible decision-makers laboured from 1930 onwards. Right-wing murderers, aided and abetted by sympathizers in the police, the ministry of home affairs, the army, the bureaucracy, and the judiciary waged war on those of a different persuasion. The courage of those who fought back is to be commended. It is going too far to say that murderous extreme right-wingers actually took over the government in the early 1930s, but rarely have fanatical assassins so influenced a climate of opinion that to give authority to the armed forces seemed the only way both of appeasing and containing them. The goon squads of the right were the gallery to which the military figures who became progressively more in charge as the 1930s progressed were forced to play. Certainly, many senior military men worked hand in glove with the extremist groups that nurtured the killers and coup-plotters.

More to the point, decisive action against them was virtually impossible. Who would order such action – tottering civilian cabi-nets or military-dominated administrations that owed their existence to the climate of fear? Who would carry it out – the home affairs ministry, the police, the judiciary, or the army, infiltrated by the secret societies? Once again, it is hard not to look to the Meiji oligarchs for responsibility, in failing to set up the independent organs of state and the popular and middle-class institutions needed to smother the actions of what, after all, was only a small minority. The left was ruthlessly suppressed, while the threat was coming from the right.

Internationally, the day Japan embarked upon the fateful course that led to Hiroshima and Nagasaki, and the day the outside world came to learn of the extraordinary tensions in what to outward appear-ances was a rather earnest industrial power, was 18 September 1931, the start of the 'Manchurian Incident'. This was far from being the spontaneous affair later alleged. The view taken by the principal planners of the Kwantung Army, Seishiro Itagaki and Kanji Ishiwara, had for some time been that Japan's presence in Manchuria was deteriorating dangerously. The young Marshal, Chang Hsueh-liang, was now formally committed to Chiang Kai-shek and was spreading anti-Japanese propaganda. Chinese commercial interests were com-peting against Japan in Manchuria, and winning. Manchuria's treasure-trove of food, raw materials and *lebensraum* was in danger of being lost by default – or at least by the pussyfooting of Shidehara at the Foreign Ministry.

Throughout the summer, campaign plans were drawn up in consultation with the general staff in Tokyo. It is highly disingenuous to say that Japan's senior military figures were ignorant of these preparations. By the beginning of September there was some evidence that Japanese Foreign Office officials in Manchuria, as well as senior government circles, were buzzing with rumours about the military preparations. Both Prime Minister Wakatsuki and Foreign Minister Shidehara protested energetically to the new war minister, General Minami, and also to the emperor. At the instigation of the *genro*, Prince Saionji, Hirohito sent for Minami and flatly instructed him that the army must be restrained.

Minami thereupon behaved with all the deviousness that might be expected from one fully in cahoots with the army in its plot to seize Manchuria. He sent a letter to the commander of the Kwantung Army instructing him to abandon any plans for 'direct action' against the Chinese. Major-General Yoshitsugu Tategawa was instructed to carry the message. A less suitable candidate could hardly be imagined: he had been implicated in the March Incident and was closely involved with the army nationalists. Instead of going by air, he travelled by boat to Korea and then by train to Mukden. There he was met by a colleague who had also been involved in the March Incident, and taken to a geisha house where he got drunk, his letter still upon him.

The same night the Manchurian Incident began. The Kwantung Army commander, Shigeru Honjo, claimed that the Chinese had planted a bomb on the South Manchurian railway north of Mukden. In fact, it was detonated by the Japanese. Even in the unlikely event that the Chinese had been responsible, the reaction of the Japanese was grotesquely out of proportion: it consisted of a full scale attack on Chinese troops in Mukden. Within hours the city itself had been occupied after heavy fighting. Honjo, in a clearly premeditated move, was already rushing reinforcements to Mukden and asking the Japanese army in Korea to send men. Changchun to the north was taken hours later. Then, at last, General Tategawa delivered his letter.

On 20 September the war minister, the chief of staff and the director of military education went to the emperor to get him to rubber-stamp the occupation of Manchuria and the crushing of Chinese resistance there. They insisted there could be no going back. By the end of the year, virtually the whole territory was under Japanese control; Chang Hsueh-Liang had fled south of the Great Wall of China, and the feared Russian invasion had not materialized. The Wakatsuki government was left spluttering in embarrassment and fending off a great storm of international opprobrium. Prince Saionji's second-in-command complained afterwards that 'from beginning to end the government has been utterly fooled by the army'.

Toshiaki Kawahara, in his biography of Hirohito, paints a pathetic picture of the emperor at the time:

> Hirohito's military attaché was about to enter the emperor's chambers one day during this period when he heard a sad soliloquy from beyond the door. 'Again, again . . . they're at it again. Once again the army has gone and done something stupid, and this is the result! Wouldn't it be simpler just to give Manchuria back to Chang Hsueh-liang?' The aide was left with a vivid image of his troubled sovereign, alone in his room, pacing back and forth, muttering to himself. Indeed, it was the emperor's habit to wander up and down the room, talking to himself, when he was troubled or upset about something.

From the course of events, the only conclusion is that the whole occupation had been plotted by officers on the spot, with the approval and connivance of the army high command, headed by the minister of war, General Minami. The incident of the courier, the advance planning, the preparations for reinforcement, the immaculate nature of the campaign itself, its prompt endorsement by the military chiefs in Tokyo – all these suggest connivance from top to bottom. Equally it is impossible to doubt the sincere opposition of the prime minister, the foreign minister and the emperor to the venture. Japan's foreign policy was now out of control, being spearheaded by unbridled army action in defiance of the constitutional government, and even of imperial wishes. The coup against civil authority had begun, although it was not yet completed. It could still be turned around.

The consequences of the occupation of Manchuria were quickly felt. In February 1933, the Lytton Commission set up by the League of Nations to investigate the causes of the Manchurian Incident discreetly but firmly censured Japan, and at the General Assembly of the League later in the year, Japan was condemned for its actions by forty-two votes to one (Japan's). The Japanese delegation promptly walked out. Manchuria was renamed Manchukuo and the last Emperor of China, Pu-yi, installed as head of state. Pu-yi was treated as a joke by the Kwantung Army commanders who really ran Manchuria, and was humiliated on his one visit to Tokyo in 1935, being kept apart from his family and treated as a clear subordinate of Hirohito. His palace was an old salt exchange.

In the international community Japan was treated with extreme suspicion, which seemed further justified by the country's slide towards war with China. By the time of its withdrawal from the League, Japanese army units had advanced on Jeihol and Hopei Provinces, with the pretext of securing Manchuria's defences. Deeply concerned by the trend, in 1932 Hirohito had asked Prime Minister Tsuyoshi Inukai to initiate contacts with China behind the army's back. The emperor warned Inukai that 'the army's interference in domestic and foreign policies, and its wilfulness, is a state of affairs which, for the good of the nation, we must view with apprehension'. A small mission was dispatched to China, but the army learnt of the arrangement through a sympathizer, the chief cabinet secretary.

Meanwhile, Inukai was preparing, with the emperor's agreement, an imperial rescript to restrain the armed forces in Manchuria and China. It was feared that such a rescript would lead to outright disloyalty and perhaps mutiny by many of the younger officers engaged in the campaigns there; many court officials were reluctant to approve the idea, while even the moderate Prince Saionji feared the effects of the emperor descending into the political fray. Nevertheless, it seems certain that a command was being prepared when, with perfect timing, Inukai was shot dead. Hirohito never again considered the idea of issuing a rescript.

Admiral Saito, Inukai's replacement, was the first of a succession of prime ministers who believed that the military tiger should be ridden rather than restrained. 'Everything will be all right,' Saito remarked shortly after taking office, 'so long as we old men are here to put on the brake.' However, the extent to which Japan's imperial aims were expanding in accordance with the army's wishes was revealed in December 1934, when a memorandum was drafted for the cabinet by the Army, Navy and Foreign Ministries which stated that China was to be brought into a grouping, along with Manchuria, with Japan as the 'nucleus'. Non-interference in Chinese affairs must cease, according to this document. Japan must 'exploit internal strife' in order to overcome China's 'anti-Japanese attitude'. Chiang Kai-shek must be induced to appoint persons friendly to Japan to certain offices within his government.

A year later, China's border provinces with Manchuria were placed with the control of a separate regional government under Japanese domination, the Hopei-Chahar Political Council. The

Japanese empire had grown a little bigger for 'defensive' reasons. The Japanese justified their expansion by claiming that there was no recognizable political authority in China at all. Yet it is beyond doubt that as things were Manchuria could have been defended against any conceivable military attack from China. Japan quite simply did not need a new buffer strip along the boundaries of its buffer Manchuria, taken to buffer Korea, itself a buffer against aggression. In fact, this theory of accumulating buffers was spurious. Japan's absorption of a slice of China was naked imperialist aggression, pure and simple, and sanctioned by the highest authorities in government, albeit reluctantly so by the emperor.

Hirohito at that stage seemed to be almost alone in trying to take a stand against the militarist tribe: the bureaucracy and the officials of the imperial household seemed resigned both to a continuing expansion of the Japanese empire abroad and the growing extremism in Japan's domestic political scene. A loyal supporter of the emperor's, Dr Tatsukichi Minobe, then Professor of Constitutional Law at the Tokyo's Imperial University, had been trying to redefine constitutional law in order to limit the powers of absolute authority. He came under sudden right-wing fire in February 1935.

What was at stake was whether the Japanese state had any existence outside imperial authority. If it did, there were constitutional limits to the power of the emperor and, more important, the army would be subservient not only to the emperor but to the state. If it did not, whoever acted in the name of Hirohito was absolute. A book of Minobe's, in which he suggested that while the emperor was the highest organ of the state, he was 'not the sole fount of authority within the state', was furiously attacked by right-wing members of the Diet. 'There is a state because there is an emperor, not an emperor because there is a state', thundered the leader of the ruling party.

Hirohito commented later:

> When it comes to the larger debate over whether sovereignty lies with the ruler or with the state, this emotional argument over whether the organ theory is good or bad is really quite foolish. I myself am inclined to believe in the sovereignty of the state over that of the ruler, mainly because the latter view can all too easily lead to despotism. In a country like Japan, where ruler and nation are one and the same, what is wrong with the organ theory? Many

187

people are criticising Minobe these days, but there is nothing disloyal about him. Is there anyone else of his stature these days? It is sad, indeed, that such a fine scholar should be treated in this manner.

Once again, Hirohito's instincts were admirable, but in seeking to defend his friend in terms acceptable to his opponents, he appeared to be trying to have it both ways. A theory that sees ruler and nation as one and the same is just as potentially despotic as the concept of an absolute emperor; indeed, it is hard to see the distinction between the two. Minobe was forced out of his chair and narrowly escaped assassination; another advocate of moderation had been removed. Members of both major political parties cautiously supported overseas expansion in the prevailing climate, while the opposition Social Democrats split, one faction supporting expansion. The repression of any parties further to the left remained vicious and uninhibited.

Even as late as the winter of 1935, Japan's road to disaster seemed neither clear cut nor inevitable. The country was pursuing a policy of opportunistic expansionism in China, a chaotic, war-torn and disintegrating state. A new outbreak of war there seemed increasingly likely; the gathering clouds over Europe made it increasingly unlikely that the European powers would continue to protect their interests in China. The country with the most direct stake in China's future those days was the United States; another country seriously affected and highly uneasy about Japan's growing influence on the mainland was its traditional enemy, Russia. It was to be a great irony of history that Russia, the country that at all stages Japan most feared, was the only major power that Japan did not fight until the very last days of the Second World War. Japan regarded the Americans and British (wrongly, as it turned out) as much lesser threats, and for that reason was later prepared to risk conflict with them. War with America and Russia seemed possible in the mid-1930s, but still a fairly remote prospect, provided Japanese incursions into China were slow and circumspect.

In domestic politics, the unstable balance between the three main factions surrounding the throne – the militarists, the *zaibatsu* and the bureaucrats – had been thrown out of equilibrium. The political parties were now no longer players. Elected only on a restricted suffrage, they were regarded as the corrupt pawns of the *zaibatsu*; they performed only a minor role when governments were formed. The bureaucrats were no longer the *primus inter pares* of the emperor's advisers: the wise old men of the Meiji era were reduced to one – Saionji, now in his dotage. The others lacked influence and any sort of popular support. A large part of the bureaucracy was loyal to *zaibatsu* interests, and a large part to the armed forces.

The only real hope of restraining the growing power of the armed forces in shaping foreign policy lay in a firm line being taken by the country's industrial elite, the *zaibatsu*, who – as subsequent events were to show – were nearly as powerful as the militarists. Had the *zaibatsu* joined with the emperor, the constitutional part of the bureaucracy, and the political parties in offsetting the dominance of the militarists, then a measure of balance could have been restored to Japanese government. Hirohito and the constitutionalists, who could scent danger, were too weak to perform the task alone.

Equally, the militarists, although powerful and much feared as they unleashed their campaign of terror in concert with their civilian allies, were not powerful enough on their own to take full control at the helm of the Japanese state. The Japanese cabinet, formally at least, could make a decision only if it acted unanimously. The army, although increasingly in the vanguard, needed at least the passive acquiescence of the civilian powers. While the latter could not restrain the army from acting independently, neither did they need to give their approval to its actions. Understanding this, the senior leaders of the armed forces went to some lengths to act within the boundaries set by the Meiji doctrine of cautious imperial expansion – even to the extent that the army high command became an object of contempt and distrust among the impatient junior officers.

In 1935, the watershed was reached. What tilted the balance of these forces was the remarkable decision by the *zaibatsu*, hitherto in rivalry with the armed forces, to support the militarists. The authoritarian nature of the Meiji constitution was tailor-made for permitting a small group to hijack the formidable authority of the Japanese state; the second essential ingredient for the militarists' seizure of power and prosecution of the Pacific War was an alliance with the *zaibatsu*, who thus became one of the guilty parties in the creation of Japan's aggressive war machine.

The debate on how the militarists came to dominate Japan has been much less wide-ranging than the one over the causes of the Nazis' rise to power in Germany. The broad historical consensus is that, acting against Japan's other power groups, the militarists were solely responsible for the 'dark valley', seizing power through terrorism at home and waging aggressive campaigns abroad. Interest has also focused on the emperor's responsibility, the view recently gaining ground that, contrary to conventional wisdom, Hirohito was implicated more than previously assumed. Yet, as can now be seen, the emperor's ability to control events was highly circumscribed, and limited to one or two missed opportunities for taking a firm stand against over-zealous subordinates. The evidence suggests that the militarists achieved their dominance of Japanese politics through a tactical alliance with the *zaibatsu* and part of the bureaucracy. Japanese politics traditionally required a consensus between the three major power centres – and the politicians no longer had much influence. The consensus was achieved largely before the war, with only the emperor and a small minority of constitutionalists objecting.

Hirohito's public position embodied the Japanese consensus and overruled his privately voiced objections. Believing he lacked the authority to block cabinet decisions, he went along with them, which is certainly deserving of the charge of complicity, although not of instigation or support. More damningly, he felt – perhaps because he believed he would run a real risk of deposition or assassination – that he could not make use of his direct line to the militarists as commander-in-chief of the armed forces, a peculiarity of the Meiji constitution. However, the reverse certainly applied: the armed forces made use of their direct line to the emperor to bypass the civilians in the cabinet, and to use the stamp of his supreme authority as a cover for their actions. The emperor certainly deserves the charge of weakness, but not of evil intent.

The central blame lies with the armed forces and the *zaibatsu*. It was the alliance of the militarists with the business interests that provided the force necessary to drive Japan towards world war. Only in 1936 did events begin decisively to move this way, although right up to the Japanese invasion of Southeast Asia in 1941 the war with America and Britain could have been averted. In the five years after 1936 there was no carefully laid plan by the Japanese to take over Asia and crush Chinese, American and British power in the region; rather, a series of monumental errors drove forward Japanese expansionism, culminating in the most monumental mistake of all, the Pacific War. Japanese policy throughout the period was less a matter of clear-cut command and rational choice than a series of jerky, puppet-like reflexes by institutions driven by a combination of ignorance of the outside world and programmed reactions that did not admit of the possibility of retreat, compromise, or error. The Japanese walked into the war like a clockwork toy that could not be stopped, capable only of being deflected from one objective to cause mischief in another direction.

12

BUTCHERS IN THE SNOW

THE KEY moment was 26 February 1936. During the early hours of the morning, a heavy fall of snow deepened the huge drifts already buttressing the thick walls of the Imperial Palace. The scene was one of desolation and tranquillity, with barely a person to be seen or a vehicle on the road. Many of the principal officials of the court were long since in bed. Two senior figures, Grand Chamberlain Kantaro Suzuki and the Lord Privy Seal, Admiral Saito, recently demoted from prime minister, had been attending a dinner party at the American Embassy, after which they stayed on for a film, *Naughty Marietta*, a light comedy.

At the dinner they had discussed the results of the parliamentary elections, just five days earlier. These had been remarkable. In the last opportunity before the Pacific War for popular consultation, Japan's limited electorate had shown its preference, even in a climate of hysterical nationalism, not for the extreme right but for the more moderate of the two main parties, the Minseito, which won 205 seats to the Seiyukai's 174; the small parties of the legalized left also did well. If it had been left to ordinary Japanese there probably would have been no Pacific War; but their influence was slight.

At about two in the morning, in the guards' barracks closest to the Imperial Palace, members of the First Army Division and the Third Regiment of the Imperial Guard were summoned to their parade grounds. Four officers were in charge of these detachments: Captain Teruzo Ando, Captain Shiro Nonaka, Lieutenant Yasuhide Kurihara and Captain Ichitaro Yamaguchi. Ando was duty officer for the Third Infantry Regiment that day, and Yamaguchi duty officer for the First Infantry. The regimental commanders had gone home that evening.

A large part of the First Army Division was known to be seething with right-wing discontent, and the whole division was accordingly to be transferred to Manchuria in April to lessen any danger from that quarter. Most of the soldiers were from miserably poor backgrounds, peasants' sons who had only just joined the army and had expected a grim winter. They had been given the rudiments of training, and been taught that they must obey the orders of their officers just as if they were obeying the emperor himself. The soldiers were told they were going to the Yasukuni Shrine, or embarking on night manoeuvres. Blindly these illiterate, brutalized young men did as they were ordered. Some 1300 were assembled at various points around the Imperial Palace.

At four in the morning, under cover of darkness, the soldiers divided into nine squads and embarked upon a carefully planned rampage of murder. One group went to the residence of the war minister, General Yoshiyuki Kawashima. They were challenged by the duty guard officer; he told them the general had a cold. The young officers stormed into his bedroom and read him a copy of their manifesto, the Great Purpose:

> With due reverence, we consider that the basis of the divinity of our country lies in the fact that the nation is destined to expand under imperial rule until it embraces all the world ... It is now time to expand and develop in all directions ... Self-seeking refractory men ... encroached on the imperial prerogative, obstructing the true growth of the people, themselves driven to the utmost depths of misery, making our country an object of contempt ... words fail to express our anger at such wickedness ... It is clearer than light that our country is on the verge of war with Russia, Britain and America who wish to crush our ancestral land ... We are persuaded that it is our duty to remove the villains who surround the throne.

In retrospect, many observers believed that Kawashima had been apprised of the plot in advance and supported it. For almost every act of insubordination by junior officers there seemed the possibility of acquiescence and even instigation by senior officers; it was always convenient for them to test the waters of insurrection and then wash their hands of responsibility in the event of failure. In any event, Kawashima did not resist, and did not overtly oppose the plot. He was to become a kind of hostage and mediator for the rebels, receiving visits from a host of senior officers over the next three days.

A second group of mutineers occupied the police station directly across the road from the Imperial Palace, forcing the policemen on duty there to surrender. A third group went to Admiral Suzuki's residence. He awoke at the commotion and tried to seize his sword. 'Are you His Excellency?' a soldier asked. Suzuki asked why they had come.

A sergeant said, 'No time. We're going to shoot.'

'Go ahead and shoot,' said Suzuki irritably. Three officers shot him, then one knelt by the body to deliver the *coup de grâce*.

His wife screamed, 'Don't do it, I'll do it,' and he desisted. Instead, the three then knelt in front of the body and saluted it.

Captain Ando told the hysterical Mrs Suzuki, 'I am particularly sorry about this but our views differ from His Excellency's, so it had to come to this.' Suzuki, remarkably and fatefully, was to survive to become the man charged with the distressing patriotic responsibility of Japan's surrender in 1945.

A 300-strong contingent surrounded the prime minister's residence, killing four policemen at the gate. The premier, Admiral Keisuke Okada, who was in his dressing-gown, took refuge in a disused storeroom while his brother-in-law, Colonel Matsuo, attempted to ring for help, then fled the house. He was caught by the soldiers, mistaken for the prime minister, and put up against a wall and shot. Okada emerged from his hiding-place, and two maids concealed him in a cupboard under a pile of laundry. Another detachment of rebels arrived at the foreign minister's house, found him asleep in bed, and shot him three times, slashing at him with a sword as well.

About 200 soldiers surrounded the house of the Lord Privy Seal, Saito. He was shot down in his nightgown while his distraught wife attempted to protect him with her body. They fired again and again, riddling his body with bullets and wounding his wife with their swords. General Watanabe, the inspector-general of military training, was shot down at his home and his throat cut. Outside Tokyo, a former Lord Privy Seal narrowly escaped assassination when his granddaughter warned him and led him up a hill in the dark, losing his pursuers below. Saionji, who was also on the death list, had been tipped off beforehand and had taken shelter in the house of his local police chief.

Half an hour later, the emperor was awoken to hear of the

carnage. 'So they've finally made their move,' he remarked. His chief military aide, General Shigeru Honjo, witnessed a rare display of imperial rage. When the war minister, General Kawashima, arrived at the palace, having been escorted through by the rebels surrounding the gates, he told Hirohito, 'The conduct of these officers is indeed disgraceful; yet it arises from their sincere devotion to Your Majesty and to the nation. It is hoped that Your Majesty will understand their feelings.' He insisted on reading the rebels' manifesto to the emperor.

Hirohito was furious: 'They have murdered our closest advisers. What possible justification can be found for the brutality these officers have shown, no matter what their motives? We order the immediate suppression of these rebels.' Honjo suggested the emperor might reconsider the word 'rebels'. 'Soldiers who act without our orders are not our soldiers. They are rebels,' retorted the emperor. As the prime minister was believed to have been killed, the emperor appointed the minister of home affairs to run the government and accept the resignation of the cabinet. When General Kawashima resigned, he wrote to the emperor implying that he knew nothing of the plot. Hirohito exploded. 'Does the war minister think that this letter absolves him? It's this kind of thinking that makes the army so bad.'

Meanwhile, Okada's son-in-law, after donning the obligatory topper and morning dress, managed to reach the Imperial Palace to inform the emperor that the prime minister was still alive and in hiding behind rebel lines. Hirohito was delighted. He had ordered Kawashima flatly to 'end this incident as soon as possible'.

Yet, although it seemed just possible that the senior military leadership knew nothing of the intended coup, their immediate reaction was to support it. Kawashima issued a statement saying: 'The motives behind the uprising have been made clear to the emperor. We recognize that your acts are a manifestation of your loyalty to the state.' General Sadao Araki, the army's most controversial right-wing general, labelled the insurgents 'restoration troops'. By the evening the rebels were elated with such formidable backing from the high command. It seemed that the senior generals behind the emperor were unwilling to take them on, and would eventually accept the position; it was important that they should remain in position until a military government took over.

Hirohito, who all day had been grumbling at General Honjo, was appalled at the attitude of the army high command, which now issued a statement blithely saying that Tokyo had been placed 'under the jurisdiction of the First Division'. Honjo, who may have been implicated in the coup, failed to tell the emperor the news that nothing was being done to control the rebels, adding to his frustration and fear that his opposition to the coup was not being relayed to the outside world.

The following morning martial law had been declared by Lieutenant-General Kashii, who himself was in sympathy with the insurgents. He insisted that 'all occupying troops must return to their original corps. These are His Majesty's orders.' The impatient Hirohito had meanwhile summoned a meeting of the senior princes of his household. He suspected that at least one of them was in league with the plotters, who would not scruple at deposing or even killing him and installing a successor. The finger pointed at his younger brother, Prince Chichibu, the commander of the Eighth Division at Hirosaki, nearly 500 miles north of Tokyo.

Chichibu had befriended Captain Ando in a previous command, and both admired Ikki Kita's right-wing diatribe, *A Plan for the Regeneration of Japan*. The news that Chichibu was coming on his own initiative to Tokyo had caused considerable disquiet among the emperor's retainers. Professor Hiraizumi, a right-wing but loyal theorist from Tokyo Imperial University, was sent to meet the prince at Minakami Station; the professor accompanied the prince to Ueno Station, where two truckloads of the Imperial Guard were waiting to ensure that he had no opportunity to talk to the rebel leaders. There was no contact either on the journey to the Imperial Palace, and when he saw his brother at last over a meal, the prince assured him he had no connection with the plot – as was later confirmed by one of the plotters. It was said afterwards that the prince had changed his mind on hearing of the murders; another explanation is that he realized Hirohito had sufficient force on his side to prevail. Later in the day the emperor met other members of the imperial family, asking them all to pledge their allegiance.

Meanwhile, the desperate Honjo continued to plead the rebels' cause, almost certainly reflecting the views of the entire army high command. The insurgents 'should not necessarily be condemned . . . because they were thinking of the good of the nation.'

Hirohito replied angrily. 'How can we not condemn even the spirit of these criminally brutal officers who killed my aged subjects who were my hands and feet? To kill these aged and venerable men whom I trusted the most is akin to gently strangling me with floss-silk.' Their only excuse, in the emperor's view, was they had not acted 'for selfish reasons'. In response to the emperor's orders, some

25,000 men had at last taken up positions surrounding the rebels, with machine guns and tanks at the ready. The First Fleet had been assembled in Tokyo Bay with its guns trained on the rebel positions.

By the morning of the third day, the rebels were dispirited and desperately cold. The forces arrayed against them and the emperor's implacability told them that their days were numbered. One ring-leader asked, through an intermediary, whether an imperial messenger might be sent to witness their ritual suicide. The response was fast and furious. As Honjo reported, 'His Majesty is extremely angry. He said that if they wanted to commit suicide, they should go ahead and do it, but sending an imperial representative is out of the question. Furthermore, he said that if the division commander had done nothing about the incident, he does not know where his duty lies. I have never heard His Majesty issue so stern a censure. He gave strict orders that the rebellion be suppressed immediately at any cost.'

Leaflets were dropped by aircraft over rebel positions. They urged bluntly, 'Return to your units. It is not yet too late. All who resist are rebels. We will shoot them. Your families weep to see you becoming traitors.' Japan's best-known radio announcer, Shigeru Nakamura, reinforced the message:

> You may have believed that the orders from your superiors were right and in obeying them absolutely, your motives were sincere. However, His Majesty the Emperor has recommended all of you to return to your home units ... You must not defy His Majesty for, in doing so, you will be branded traitors for all time. Since even as I speak it is not too late, lay down your arms and return to barracks. If you do, your offences will be pardoned.

Tanks rumbled ominously through the streets. In dribs and drabs rebel units began to disperse, and no attempt was made to stop them. Captain Nonaka, the most senior, shot himself. Ando tried to kill himself. Other officers surrendered, believing they would be treated leniently, as was the precedent; in fact the main plotters were quietly executed under the express orders of the emperor.

The danger was past: the plot had collapsed. Hirohito had for the first time emerged as a true leader of his country. There can be no doubt that his steady nerve had largely contributed to the demise of the coup. In the days after the coup, its extensive ramifications became apparent. Prince Chichibu was clearly implicated. The emperor's secretary, Marquis Kido, had privately worked against the plot beforehand, but did not inform the emperor of what he knew. Kawashima was implicated, and Honjo may have been. A major shake-up of the senior ranks of the army now took place in which several thousand unsuitable officers were purged.

Yet in spite of the strong hand he seemed to hold, Hirohito now flinched. According to Honjo – who was replaced shortly afterwards – Hirohito told him of the need to accommodate 'the urgent demands of the military to some extent to avoid a repetition of the tragedy'. Later, he said that 'since we fear a repetition of this kind of incident if we do not accede [to the army's demands] we want to take their view into consideration'. The emperor, it seemed, had won a battle only to lose the war.

How had this extraordinary reversal come about, just after his most dramatic display of decisive action? Later he was to admit, 'In some sense I was violating the constitution in my rebuke of Prime Minister Tanaka at the time of the Chang Tso-lin incident, and in the stand I took in the 26 February Incident.' On both occasions he seems to have shrunk from the consequences of his boldness with remarkable speed. In fact, the 26 February revolt was a much more complex affair than at first appeared. It reflected the state of undeclared civil war within the army over foreign policy objectives, the state of the nation, and control of the armed forces themselves.

As in some elaborate conspiracy theory, the outcome of the 26 February Incident was that although the visible coup had been crushed, in fact a military coup had taken place unnoticed on a much wider scale. Far from proving that the government had reverted to the control of the civil authorities, the slow response of the armed forces to the emperor's desperate appeals for action exposed how dependent he was on their support: the military chiefs who had eventually come to rescue him after three tense days in which he was virtually a hostage of the extremist officers now held him, and what remained of constitutional government in Japan, in the palm of their hands.

There had been complicity by senior army men in the coup, who certainly knew it was coming and did nothing to stop it when the attempt was made. They could pose as the men who rushed to the emperor's defence – but not before he was given convincing evidence of just how defenceless he was without their protection. In addition, permitting the abortive coup to take place had the considerable advantage of allowing the junior officers who had been an irritation to the generals for more than a decade enough rope to hang themselves.

The impact of the real coup – the coup behind the coup – was felt immediately. From then on the political parties ceased to enjoy any effective power; the bureaucracy was sidelined; the emperor's protests were barely heard; and his every decision was shaped by the fear that extremist militarists would stage another coup, and this time no one would come to save him. The choice of prime minister, while not actually dictated by the army, became irrelevant: real power was in the hands of the war minister, whose threat to resign was invariably enough to bring the moderates to heel. The prime minister was not an outright army nominee until the 1940s, but he might as well have been, because the real prime minister – in both defence and domestic matters – was the war minister.

The struggle within the army which surfaced in the attempted coup of February 1936 dated all the way back to the aftermath of the First World War. Japan had played no part in that war, except to take the profitable role of chief armourer to the Western powers – which had caused mixed feelings among its allies, the British and the French. Admiral Jellicoe, the British naval commander, commented acidly that, 'apart from the selling of guns and ammunition to the Russians and ourselves, Japan is not taking a full share in the war'.

In addition, the Japanese army was hopelessly out of gear with the new concept of 'total war' that had been experienced in Europe. Having taken no part in the war, and failed to modernize its strategy and equipment, the Japanese army, built up by Aritomo Yamagata, which had considered invading Manchuria while its allies were otherwise occupied in the European war, had declined from first to second rate.

Worse followed immediately. Under the pressure of economic crisis, defence spending had slumped from nearly half the budget to around a third between 1921 and 1923. In any event, the disastrous Japanese intervention in Siberia had muddied the image of the military class. Public opinion had been revolted by the expeditionary forces' association with Major-General von Ungern-Sternberg, the 'cruel baron' commanding one of the White Russian armies, who pledged to carve out a Greater Mongolia, restore the empire of Genghis Khan, and plant an avenue of gallows from Mongolia to

China. Stopped short of these objectives, his forces hanged Jews, dismembered people, and roasted deserters alive. When Prince Saionji came to power in Tokyo, favouring the end of militarist competition between nations and espousing the principles of Versailles, the army was deeply resentful and feeling sorry for itself.

In these inauspicious conditions, the army began planning for the future. Yamagata, although still alive, was no longer in charge of day-to-day policy. His successor and protégé, General Katsura, was unpopular and lacked his authority. One of the most important of the new generals was General Ugaki, the moderate, down-to-earth minister of war who, in October 1926, set up an Equipment Bureau, designed to look at 'the conversion of the industrial reserves of the nation to a war footing'. The objective was to follow Lloyd George's example in setting up a Ministry of Munitions, and to prepare Japan for the time when the whole of the nation's resources would have to be harnessed to the demands of modern war. The army, which as we have seen considered itself the vanguard of imperial Japan, had been infuriated by the way industrial interests had decided to give low priority to munitions production because it was unprofitable.

During this period the tension and competition between the armed forces and the industrial conglomerates was at its highest (the bureaucracy still loftily considered itself above both). The Japanese army wanted to modernize, and to be capable of harnessing the economic resources of the nation in the likely event that the country would have to go to war within a matter of years. The man in charge of the new bureau was Tetsusan Nagata, a brilliant staff officer, who in 1928 published the book that was to dominate Japanese military thinking over the following decade, *Total National Mobilization*, which argued the case for the creation of a 'garrison state' calling upon every last resource of the nation in the event of war.

The Resources Bureau, a kind of co-ordinating and planning adjunct (the equivalent of the British Committee for Imperial Defence), bringing together the prime minister, military ministers and the principal economic ministers, was set up at the same time. A national plan in the event of war was devised. In 1929 a series of exercises began to provide Japanese soldiers with the necessary experience of war: factories produced war material at full capacity; bombers buzzed the Osaka region, while anti-aircraft fire blazed across the skies.

The Nagata plan, however, required partnership with the most powerful force in Japan: the *zaibatsu* industrial moguls. General Ugaki had spoken in 1929 of the need to tighten 'the links between military forces and the industrial world'. In exchange for the *zaibatsu*'s help, the army was prepared to hand over its control of huge areas of war production. A historical compromise took place: the army's ambition to use military force to secure raw materials and markets in order to compensate for the loss of those abroad through the erection of tariff barriers during the depression became attractive to both the *zaibatsu* and parts of the bureaucracy. The Important Industries Control Law was drafted to provide government support and rationalization for certain industries considered important to the war effort.

The partnership between the two was thus cemented: the military establishment was for the first time working hand-in-glove with the *zaibatsu*, and the two together were now more powerful than either the bureaucrats or the government. Indeed, what gave the armed forces new impetus was the conversion of the industrialists to their cause through the collapse in world free trade. The industrialists saw that military conquest was needed to secure supplies and markets; the armed forces saw that the industrialists were needed to provide the economic underpinning of the plans for total war.

The dominant group in the army which favoured this approach was later to be derisorily labelled the 'Control Group' by its opponents. Nagata was its focus; around him he built up an informal apparatus called the Issekikai, a kind of loose secret society within the military. It included a young officer called Hideki Tojo, later to become Japan's most notorious wartime prime minister; Tomoyuki Yamashita, the 'Tiger of Malaya'; Daisaku Komoto, the celebrated assassin of Chang Tso-lin; and two officers, Kanji Ishiwara and Seishiro Itagaki, architects of the Manchurian Incident. So influential and senior had these officers now become that, although young rebels to begin with, they could now be said to represent the mainstream of establishment military thought.

Their views were to predominate in the build-up to the Pacific War and thereafter. While the interpretation of young hotheads leading their elders astray may have been true at the time of the Manchurian Incident, it certainly was not in the later 1930s. The high command, with a few notable exceptions, was fully informed and aware of most of the major military actions that took place after 1936. The Issekikai was so close to the high command that even in the early 1930s it is hard to believe that both Chang's assassination and the Manchurian Incident did not have the approval of senior figures in the War Ministry – although not of the civilian cabinet or the emperor himself.

What the Control Group, the army high command, and their new allies among the *zaibatsu* could not have predicted was the rumbling discontent among the lower ranks of officers which threatened in the 1930s to ignite into a military coup, resulting in the imposition of an authentic kind of Japanese fascism and social revolution. A brand of egalitarian anti-*zaibatsu* socialism combined with fanatical nationalism and devotion to the emperor had already been preached by Ikki Kita in his book, *A Plan for the Reorganisation of Japan*. Kita's advocacy of a Showa restoration to overthrow the 'business *daimyo*' and parcel out their fiefdoms to the emperor, just as the nobles had done in the nineteenth century, had led to the book's initial suppression. Although they were violently anti-communist, business and government leaders feared that Kita's doctrines could find deeper roots in Japan than 'alien' communism, which was anyway being ruthlessly suppressed by the police.

Kita's theories found fertile ground among the junior ranks of the officer corps in the later 1920s and early 1930s. The Japanese army had undergone a profound social transformation since Yamagata's reforms. From being an elite commanded by samurai of Choshu descent, it was now a largely conscript army, only 15 per cent of whose officers were of samurai descent (although this included many of the most senior officers). The Choshu were only a small minority among these. The ranks of the army were drawn from the very poorest parts of the population, from the remote mountain regions – the people worst hit in the slump of the 1920s. A much resented class distinction therefore existed. The younger officers, reflecting the extreme resentment among their men, deeply disliked the more glamorous officers and their failure to proceed with such enterprises as the occupation of Manchuria. The junior officers held parliamentary government in deep contempt, viewing it as a nest of corruption, manipulated by the *zaibatsu*.

Above all, they hated the *zaibatsu*, with whom the army commanders in the mid-1930s – once the Young Turks of their day, now the military establishment – had now forged a pact. The *zaibatsu* represented the huge impersonal economic forces which had brought radical change to the previously static and peaceful Japanese countryside, first draining away the young men into an alien and immoral urban life, then emptying the villages of their young women, who were sold by starving peasant farmers into a life of prostitution in the cities. It was in reaction to this pact between the military and the *zaibatsu* establishment that the young officers' movement, now dubbed the Kodo-Ha – 'Imperial Way' school – virtually seized power within the army in 1932.

The key organizer of the faction was the charismatic Mitsugi Nishida, a disciple of Kita's. The hero of the Imperial Way group, which considered itself the direct descendant of Saigo's romantic samurai tradition – even though very few of its supporters were of warrior descent – was General Sadao Araki, the head of the Kodogikai, a 40,000-strong civilian–military organization. He had argued the case for the invasion of Manchuria after the assassination of Chang Tso-lin. He was a brilliant man, highly civilized with a tough exterior: he had strong, broad features and a handlebar moustache. He served as a young man in Russia and loathed communism, which he viewed as the principal threat to Japan. 'There is a shining sun ahead for Japan in this age of Showa,' he proclaimed. The aborted coup in October 1931 had as its aim the installation of Araki; in an astonishing move to placate the dissidents in the armed forces, he was appointed war minister in December of that year.

The new minister had radically different plans to those of Nagata and the Control Group. He believed that war with Russia was imminent, and devoted himself to the immediate and short-term rearmament of Japan to strike north against the Russians. He drove a coach and horses through Nagata's painstaking, long-term preparations, breaking off the alliance with the *zaibatsu*; Nagata himself was transferred out of Tokyo to become a regional commander. Araki revived the traditional art of sword-making, to provide individual swords soldiers could be proud of, rather than the mass-produced kind introduced by Yamagata. Japan's agents were sent abroad to make large-scale purchases of arms and equipment.

The *zaibatsu* were thrown into confusion and fear by this unexpected turn of events. On the one hand, they welcomed the new government's repression of communist agitators; on the other, talk of social revolution, equality, and the Showa restoration alarmed them, as did the decision to freeze them out from developing Manchuria. There seemed to be the prospect of a government along National Socialist lines which would introduce widespread nationalization. It is hard to exaggerate the loathing felt by junior officers for the *zaibatsu*, who were believed to be linked with international Jewry, communism, and foreigners generally. The radical officers were capable of unleashing violently anti-elitist forces in Japan.

Hirohito and the bureaucracy also distrusted the younger officers. However, in spite of their extremism, they did not share the
Control Group's addiction to war with China, being satisfied with
the occupation of Manchuria and favouring instead the occupation
of resource-rich Siberia. In Manchuria there was a genuinely idealistic attempt to keep the *zaibatsu* out: the Kwantung Army, in which
Imperial Way officers were predominant, preached the principle of
'state capitalism'. This failed, largely because the army lacked the
resources to develop Manchuria on its own, so a new industrial
conglomerate, Nissan, was set up to develop the region. Nissan
differed from the old *zaibatsu* in having been founded on genuine
principles of joint-stock ownership, with shareholdings distributed
among thousands rather than a single family. But a prominent
minority of the old *zaibatsu* bought Nissan shares through intermediaries. In Northern China, the Imperial Way group was unable to
keep out the *zaibatsu*, which ran the region's mines through the
North China Development Company.

The young officers thus posed a real major threat to the most
powerful interests in Japan: the now hugely swollen *zaibatsu*, which
had gorged themselves on the smaller companies during the recession; the bureaucracy and imperial court; and the senior army
establishment (not to mention the navy). It is a remarkable irony of
history that had the Imperial Way faction prevailed, Japan might
have gone to war with Russia, not China, during the 1930s. In the
climate prevailing then, it is hard to see that either America or
Britain would have shown any readiness to go to Stalin's aid. The
Pacific War might have been averted; indeed, Hitler might have
decided to open up a second front in the east, rather than attack
France.

The Imperial Way faction did not prevail. The gigantic interests
it had upset combined to fight back. Araki, caught between the
pressures from below and the hostility of Japan's most powerful
groups, fell ill and was forced to accept a nominally superior job as
supreme war councillor, relinquishing the War Ministry to General
Saburo Hayashi, from the Control Group; he promptly sent for
Nagata. Collaboration with the *zaibatsu* resumed, the total war
programme was put back on the rails, and the focus of Japan's
policy shifted back from the 'strike north' option of war with Russia
to the 'strike south' option of war with China. The junior officers
were seething, all the more so when one of their number was
replaced as Inspector-General of Education. A lieutenant-colonel

burst into Nagata's office on 15 August, 1935 and shot dead the *éminence grise* of the Japanese army.

From that moment on, both sides prepared for a showdown. The army establishment, with the backing of the *zaibatsu*, waited for the young officers to overreach themselves and provide an excuse for their suppression as an organized group within the army. At the same time, the military establishment was aware that by rushing to the aid of the civilian authorities when a coup was staged, it would effectively be confirmed in control of the nation, along with its *zaibatsu* allies, who were persuaded of the economic benefits of the army's policy of expansionism. Unaware that they were about to fall into a trap, the Imperial Way officers launched their conspiracy – and were suppressed, while being used as fall guys for the army elders' seizure of power.

With the crushing of the February coup, the Control Group was firmly in charge. A massive purge ran through the army to rid it of the Imperial Way faction. The war minister was given the power to appoint, transfer, promote and demote every officer in the army. Army ministers were henceforth to be chosen from the ranks of active generals, making it impossible for governments to find retired generals who disagreed with current military thinking to do the job. The army had not been so centralized since its birth under Yamagata. The first army minister after the coup was Hisaichi Terauchi, a formidably tough-minded man who immediately set out the three missions of the army as enforcing discipline, safeguarding national defence and reforming the administration. The main purpose of the last task was to make money available for military expansion.

The new prime minister, Koki Hirota, was a former foreign minister and nominee of Prince Saionji, whose power was all but at an end. When he formed his cabinet, he found Terauchi exercising a veto over each of his appointments. 'The military is like an untamed horse left to run wild,' Hirota told a friend. 'If you try to stop it, you'll get kicked to death. The only hope is to jump on it from the side and try to get it under control . . . Somebody has to do it. That's why I've jumped on.' He didn't stay on for long; while he did, it was all he could do to stay in the saddle. He resigned after only a few months.

Saionji, flexing his old, tired counsel of moderation for the last time, tried to install one of Japan's constitutionalist generals, Ugaki, as prime minister. In an attempt to intimidate him, the Kempeitai, the sinister riot police, stopped Ugaki while he was on his way to see the emperor. Ugaki pressed on, but the army refused to nominate a minister of war to serve with him. One of Terauchi's cronies now took control: this was General Saburo Hayashi, a tough-minded soldier with no political skills, whom both the main parties joined in opposing. Faced by outright political opposition in parliament, he resigned after just four months. This was a partial defeat for the army: if the civilians could not have their preferred candidate, they could at least block an out-and-out military reactionary.

A compromise was needed: this turned out to be Prince Fumimaro Konoye, surely one of the most inappropriate choices ever made for a nation at a time of extreme crisis. Konoye's basic qualification for the job, from the army's point of view, was that he was a rabid nationalist and a political lightweight with no support in parliament. Related to the emperor and descended from Japan's oldest family, the Fujiwaras, he had considerable influence at court. Yet his ideas were shallow and silly, and he lacked any popular power base; he was merely, at first, a useful front man for military rule. Later, he acquired the courage and wisdom of experience. He had a weak and attractive personality; idle and easygoing, he treated the emperor as a chum, which endeared him to the friendless Hirohito. He was tall, good-looking, and a womanizer (and probably bisexual), as well as a hypochondriac.

Sir Robert Craigie, British Ambassador to Japan in 1937, commented:

> Time and again one was impressed by acts of statesmanship, only to be irritated just as often by his apparent lack of firmness in leadership, and his failure at times of crisis to use his strong personal position to curb the extremists. His Japanese friends were completely baffled by many of his actions, wondering whether he really stood for what he was supposed to represent – a moderating influence – or whether, unknown to his more responsible friends and followers, he was a totalitarian at heart and rather enjoyed giving the army its long rope.

For the political parties, his attraction was that, although a rather eccentric nationalist, he was not in the army's pocket. He was reasonably intelligent and, like many without a political power base, believed he had more political authority than he had – although he was not so obtuse as to fail to understand when he was being manipulated, which provoked frequent crises of conscience, usually overcome. He was fated to be prime minister when the two key decisions were made that led to the Pacific War; like Germany's pre-Hitler Chancellor, Franz von Papen, he was destined to be the doormat for his country's warmongers.

With the seizure of power by the Control Group, which was committed to the annexation of China and supported by the major *zaibatsu*, events moved rapidly. A statement of principles was drawn up, known as the Foundations of National Policy. This asserted that Japan must 'eliminate the tyrannical policies of the powers in East Asia' and substitute 'cordial relations . . . founded on the principles of coexistence and co-prosperity'. Economic expansion was to be achieved by creating a strong coalition between Japan, Manchuria, and China. While the views of the Imperial Way faction urging war against the Soviet Union were now discredited, the army recognized the need to leave forces in Korea and Manchuria that were big enough to deter the Soviets from attacking. The army must also be strong enough to retain 'ascendancy in the Pacific', said the principles. 'Self-sufficiency' was required in important resources and materials needed for the nation's defence and its industry. As far as the Japanese army in China was concerned, this represented a green light to move ahead and conquer the country; the Chinese reached much the same conclusion as well.

13

THE CHINA 'INCIDENT'

THE RESULT was the celebrated clash at the Marco Polo Bridge, just north of Peking, on 7 July 1937. It is more difficult on this occasion to blame the Japanese unreservedly for starting the fighting. Both sides had decided the time had come for a showdown. Chiang Kai-shek, overconfident but rightly suspicious of Japanese intentions, was spoiling for a fight. Equally, the Japanese felt the time had come to teach China a lesson: unless the cocky generalissimo was dealt with head-on he might become a more formidable foe. They believed that China would collapse under a Japanese onslaught like a paper tiger – the Japanese chief of staff, General Sugiyama, assured the emperor that the campaign there would take a month to finish.

The *zaibatsu* favoured war with China in order to secure their industrial schemes in the north of the country and, ruthlessly, to destroy the Chinese capacity to resist militarily and compete economically further south. Some generals favoured war in order to subdue the minor nuisance to the south before undertaking the far more hazardous task of confronting the colossus to the north. For Japan, the Chinese adventure was to be the biggest miscalculation in its history.

The Marco Polo Incident itself was trivial. Just before midnight, as a small group of Japanese soldiers under the command of Captain Setsuro Shimizu were resting on the banks of the Yuntung River, a volley of shots rang out. One Japanese private went missing in the dark. The shots may have been fired by Chinese nationalists, but more probably were the work of Communist agitators intent on making mischief for Chiang Kai-shek. The missing private turned up shortly afterwards, but the Japanese took advantage of the incident to demand a Chinese withdrawal from the strategic Marco Polo Bridge and the railway bridge beside it. The Chinese refused. The Japanese tried to search a small town at their end of the bridges, only to be fired upon by Chinese troops. Gunfire and casualties began to multiply.

On learning of the incident, Chiang Kai-shek declared privately, 'The time has come now to make the decision to fight.' He announced that his country had reached its 'final critical hour'. The Japanese were no less ready to make a stand. The high command considered it would be wise to move against China now, while Russia was in the throes of one of Stalin's great purges. Chiang Kai-shek's recently concluded agreement with the Communists to fight the Japanese had strengthened him and made the latter nervous.

The fighting quickly spread. The extent of Japanese war preparations was revealed by the speed with which troops were rushed from Korea and Manchuria. General Sugiyama, minister of war in Prince Konoye's government, poured in troops from the mainland. Konoye, with the support of the navy and foreign ministers, tried to object. Hirohito asked plaintively, 'Isn't this the Manchurian Incident all over again?'

Sugiyama threatened to resign, bringing down the cabinet, if he was overruled. He got his way; the armed forces could hardly have staged a more blatant seizure of power if they had grabbed control by force. The emperor, prime minister and cabinet were all shown to be less powerful than the army. Japan was under a military dictatorship. Only the *zaibatsu* could have frustrated the armed forces by denying them the essential supplies they needed; but at this stage big business stood four-square behind the army, seeking to secure its interests in northern China as well as to destroy strategic competition from the Chinese.

Whatever the rights and wrongs of the Incident itself, Japan's actions from then on amounted to outright aggression. Talks between the two countries broke down after a few weeks, and more fighting broke out after Chinese militia at Tungchow rebelled against their Japanese officers and massacred two hundred civilians. In August fighting broke out between Japanese and Chinese forces in Shanghai, and Japanese reinforcements were rushed into the city in an engagement that lasted three months before the Chinese were expelled.

The fighting was full-scale, and there could be no pretence that it was not co-ordinated from Tokyo: the officers in the field were not the primary instigators of the war against China. It was to last for eight years and claim the lives of some 3.2 million Chinese soldiers and perhaps as many as 10 million civilians; the Japanese lost around 1 million in the fighting. It was to be the greatest single conflict the world has ever seen, before or since.

The war was initially fought on two fronts: in the north, and around Shanghai. By November 1937 the Japanese army was already down the Yangtse, driving towards the Chinese Nationalist capital of Nanking, a bustling city in a loop on the southern bank of the river with a permanent population of around 250,000 people, but now also teeming with three times that many refugees. Nanking was a cultural centre, with a university and several institutions of higher learning. Chiang Kai-shek decided it was too exposed, however, for serious resistance, and his soldiers, along with about half the city's inhabitants, withdrew to regroup in the interior. On 12 December the last Chinese detachments fled, and the following day the Japanese moved in. There followed one of the worst atrocities of modern times, in which tens of thousands were murdered and as many women raped in an orgy of carnage and lust that went on for days.

Prince Konoye and other Japanese leaders believed that Chiang Kai-shek would sue for peace after the fall of his capital and offered the Chinese stringent terms, which one part of the Nationalist leadership was disposed to accept. If so, the China 'Incident' would have been won reasonably satisfactorily by the Japanese in five months – although not the one month promised the emperor.

Yosuke Matsuoka, Japan's notorious foreign minister under Konoye, summed up the Japanese attitude to China:

China and Japan are two brothers who have inherited a great mansion called East Asia. Adversity sent them both down to the depth of poverty. The scapegrace elder brother (China) became a dope fiend and a rogue, but the younger (Japan), lean but tough and ambitious, ever dreamed of bringing back past glories to the old home. He sold newspapers at street corners and worked hard to support the home. The elder flimflammed the younger out of his meagre savings and sold him to their common enemy. The younger in a towering rage beat up the elder – trying to beat into him some sense of shame and awaken some pride in the noble traditions of the great house. After many scraps, the younger finally made up his mind to stage a showdown fight. And that is the fight now raging along the North China and Shanghai fronts.

Chaing Kai-shek spurned the proposals, and in January 1938 the Japanese announced there would be no further negotiations. The Chinese secured a minor success in Shantung in April, but their main army was nearly encircled by a brilliant Japanese flanking manoeuvre at Hsuchow on the Peking–Nanking railway. The Japanese continued to push ahead, with a fair degree of success that year.

But an unpleasant shock was to await them. Confident of defeating China, the Japanese began to turn their attention to their more serious foe, Russia. That summer the Japanese came close to a major engagement with Russian forces at Changkufeng Hill, near the border of Korea, Russia, and Manchuria. At this stage the war was being fought by the army under a new war minister, General Itagaki, virtually without reference to the civilian cabinet. But the emperor retained some influence. Appalled by the prospect of war on two fronts with China and Russia – which some generals favoured, believing they could beat both – he summoned the war minister and the army chief of staff. Although Hirohito's powers were severely limited, with the onset of war he had formally taken up his role as commander-in-chief. As Toshiaki Kawahara recounts:

> In response to the prospects of a long-term conflict, a military headquarters was set up in the Imperial Palace, and inevitably the emperor was kept very busy. Night and day he was beset by worries over the outcome of the military action, and began to look haggard. Hirohito was a man of delicate sensibilities. Worry soon took its toll, and as he so often did in such circumstances, he began talking to himself. Sometimes, when reports from the field were good, he would feel even more exhausted – perhaps due to the sudden release of tension.

The military chiefs, while contemptuously brushing aside the objections of Konoye's civilian cabinet, could not be quite so dismissive of the emperor's mood. He made his anger known on the occasion of the clash with Russia. 'Really, the army's behaviour is outrageous,' he told General Itagaki. 'Be it at Lukouchiao at the time of the Manchurian Incident, or just recently at the Marco Polo Bridge, they ignore the orders sent out by central command and all too often go their own way, employing despicable, inexcusable methods. They are our forces, yet we find their conduct disgraceful, not to say impertinent. Henceforth not one soldier will be moved without our explicit orders.'

Itagaki was shaken. 'I can never enter His Majesty's presence again. I must resign.' The chief of staff, Prince Kan'in, also sought to quit. Prince Konoye persuaded them to withdraw their resignations. Had they not done so, the government would have fallen and an outright military coup might have followed, which the emperor was determined to avoid at all costs.

This incident encapsulated the dilemma and tragedy of Hirohito's personal responsibility for events. There can be little doubt of his opposition to the steady escalation of Japan's military involvement in Asia, which was voiced at virtually every step forward (although not in the decision to go to war with America). Usually, Hirohito objected for sound pragmatic reasons, but this did not make him a calculating opportunist. Such justifications were the only ones likely to cut much ice with the armed forces; a general statement of principle against expansionist policies would have been brushed aside as a sign of weakness. However, when it came to outright confrontation, the emperor was now to back down on every occasion until 1945 because he believed he could better influence events at the centre of power than by being cast out (he believed that his assassination or enforced abdication in favour of the more pliant Prince Chichibu was always a possibility). He may have been right.

Yet in giving way, he lent his immense personal authority to militarist-inspired decisions as effectively as if he had been deposed and a new emperor found. He could not escape his share of responsibility – which might, indeed, be considered greater than that of any of his subjects – for decisions which he privately opposed but publicly approved. As it is, we shall never know what might have happened had the emperor placed his massive prestige on the line in opposing one of the key decisions about the army, denying them the imprimatur of acting in his name, because he never tried to do so. In failing to do so, he became the army's reluctant tool, and history has to assign to him a major portion of the blame for the course Japan was now to follow.

The army, in fact, obeyed the emperor's will and pulled back from confrontation with the Russians. The wisdom of his counsel was to be underlined within a year, in May 1939, at one of the most far-flung, desolate places on earth. The Nomonhan region, on the border between Manchuria and Outer Mongolia, was a large, undulating grassy plain. Mongolian forces began to stage incursions across the Halha River, which the Japanese had designated the boundary of Manchuria. The Russians may have been testing Japanese resolve on ground of their own choosing. The Kwantung

Army took the bait and rushed forces to the border, launching a major expedition to cut Mongolian and Russian supply lines. Soon a full-scale engagement was under way between Soviet and Japanese forces involving aircraft, tanks and heavy artillery.

The contest was unequal from the start: the Soviets had overwhelming force and much better transport facilities. They pushed the Japanese back to the Halha River. In spite of the success by the air force in destroying 120 Soviet planes at Tomsk – thereby risking an escalation of the conflict into a full-scale war between the two nations – the Japanese suffered an overwhelming and humiliating defeat, their routed army losing some 20,000 dead and the same number of injured at the hands of Soviet forces commanded by the most brilliant of their military leaders, Marshal Zhukov.

It was Japan's great good fortune that the Soviet Union was in no mood for full-scale war. The Japanese puma had attacked and, with one great swipe from the Russian bear, had been bloodied and repulsed. The incident persuaded the Japanese high command of the need to pursue softer options further south. It should have alerted the militarists to the fact that when confronted with a force as well prepared as itself, the vaunted invincibility of the Japanese war machine soon evaporated. The clear superiority established in the early months of the Pacific War was to be against soft, ill-defended, unprepared targets, thus inevitably limiting success in the long term.

In China, the war continued through 1938 with a string of Japanese victories, although none of them decisive. They captured Hangkow in the autumn and landed at Bias Bay in the south to seize Canton with remarkable speed. At this stage, Chiang Kai-shek was again expected to sue for peace, and the Japanese hinted they were ready to reach an agreement. Through the conflict, Japan showed no desire to occupy the whole of China – probably an impossible objective – merely to turn it into a vassal state. To their astonishment, Chiang rejected their terms from his new capital of Chunking, although some of his lieutenants made their peace. The war settled into a longer, slower phase of Japanese advances and Chinese retreats, with fewer dramatic victories and Japanese forces continually harrassed by Mao Tse-tung's Communist guerrillas. The Japanese always had the upper hand; but final victory remained utterly elusive.

This is not the place for a full history of the awesome conflict between China and Japan. But its outline can briefly be sketched.

The Japanese armies were far better equipped, professionally trained and disciplined than the Chinese. From the first, the Chinese were hampered by a chaotic command structure of virtually independent warlords under Chiang Kai-shek, ancient equipment and a virtually non-existent air force, a festering civil war between the Nationalists and the Communists, and the readiness of huge numbers to desert.

However, the Chinese had long-term strategic advantages. They had a virtually limitless pool of manpower and an enormous hinterland that repeatedly absorbed the punches of the Japanese armies. As was to happen in subsequent wars, the sympathy of the populace and the rough terrain permitted continuous guerrilla warfare against the Japanese – especially when Mao's Communists joined the fray. In addition, as Japan's vicious war of attrition spread, with the intention of terrorizing the Chinese population into surrender, it had the opposite effect: many fought back just as viciously and resorted to a scorched-earth policy as the invader approached. The Japanese were usually the better tacticians, especially at the beginning of the war, but suffered from sticking strictly to the rule book. The Chinese were hampered in turn by shambolic and often disastrous generalship, but their tactics improved as the war continued, and occasionally they displayed a brilliant ability to improvise and to outmanoeuvre the enemy. The war went through five phases.

The first phase (1937–8) was marked by the Japanese thrust into North China following the 'China Incident' at the Marco Polo Bridge, which was largely provoked by Japan, and by the Chinese seizure of the Japanese enclave in Shanghai to the south, intended to provoke Japan into retaliating by doing battle on Chiang Kai-shek's favoured territory. This reasoning was sound – an attempt to get the Japanese to overextend themselves on two massive fronts – but the Japanese fought with such skill and ruthlessness that three-fifths of Chiang's crack soldiers, 50,000 men, were killed, 10,000 of them officers. The Japanese lost somewhat fewer. The centre of Shanghai was devastated by the most concentrated bombing the world had ever seen.

In the north, meanwhile, Japan's forces engaged in a massive offensive which took them from Peking, across the Great Wall, through to Shanxi Province in the west and down to the Yellow River in the south. In this initial phase of fighting the Japanese staged spectacular advances, only occasionally suffering setbacks such as the defeat at Pingxingguan in September 1937, which enormously heartened the beleaguered Chinese. By December the Chinese were compelled to withdraw from the Nationalist capital, Nanking, and the city was occupied amidst a carnival of Japanese butchery. After the fall of Nanking, the Japanese believed Chiang would surrender; their strategy had been 'quick war – quick settlement'; but the Chinese failed to oblige, and meanwhile the Japanese had given them sufficient respite to entrench themselves at Wuhan – one of the biggest mistakes of the war.

The Japanese now embarked on the second phase of the war (1938): the drive to subdue the huge swathe of territory between their two great thrusts from Peking and Nanking. Their target was Xuzhou, the meeting point of the north–south and east–west railway lines. An epic battle took place around the city and around Wuhan itself. The Japanese came up against unexpectedly fierce resistance at the village of Taierzhang and were forced to withdraw. Chiang, however, failed to pursue the retreating army, permitting the Japanese to regroup. Some 400,000 Japanese now faced some 600,000 Chinese. After bitter fighting the entire Chinese force was threatened with encirclement, but the Chinese withdrew their armies in secret, virtually intact.

Although Xuzhou was a major victory for the Japanese, it had for the Chinese the same symbolism as Dunkirk would have for the British: their beseiged army had escaped the trap. By May 1938 the Japanese were approaching Wuhan, determined to catch the main Chinese army. The latter imaginatively flooded the approaches by breaking the dykes of the Yellow River, and blunted the Japanese offensive. However, the Japanese were adept at using river craft, and meanwhile staged a massive encircling operation through the mountains to the east of the city, pitting some 400,000 men against a Chinese army of 1,600,000.

On 25 October Wuhan fell, but once again most of the huge Chinese force escaped with their arms and equipment intact up the Yangtze gorges, which formed a natural defensive barrier against the Japanese. With the fall of Wuhan, one of Chiang's chief lieutenants, Wang Jingwei, defected to the Japanese, who considered the war all but won – although having taken a year longer than expected. Chiang now controlled only the barren west and south of the country.

However, the generalissimo again refused to negotiate, and the Japanese found themselves largely unable to move forward, confined instead to a defensive holding operation across the immense swathe of territory they had captured. This was the third phase (1938–41) in which, broadly, the Japanese held the main cities along the coast and the main lines of communication inland, but did not control the interior. As Mao put it, 'China is like a gallon jug which Japan is trying to fill with half a pint of liquid. When her troops move into one section, we move to another. And when they pursue us, we move back again.'

Japan's previously unchallenged control of the air now came under attack as the Soviet Union poured in 70 planes a month to reinforce the 400-strong Chinese air force (headed by Chiang's wife!). The generalissimo's capital of Chungking came under relentless Japanese bombing, but only the civilian population suffered, as the troops were evacuated to caves and well-entrenched fortifications outside the city. As the stalemate persisted, a mass of minor engagements took place, with the Communists harassing the Japanese in the north and the Nationalists in the centre. The Japanese attempted to break through in the south, moving into Hunan Province and down towards Canton, but were blocked by the Chinese at Changsha, with both sides suffering enormous losses.

Towards the end of 1939, the Japanese tried to break out of the impasse through a flanking movement south of Chungking into the mountains around Yichang; these were taken, after several months of fierce fighting, in June 1940. The main Japanese strategy was now to cut the Chinese supply routes from Indo-China and Burma, which they did with the occupation of French Indo-China and, after Pearl Harbor, the invasion of Burma.

After Pearl Harbor, the war entered its fourth phase (1941–4). China had at last acquired formal allies: the Americans and the British. The flow of supplies increased, and the Americans were soon fully engaged in intercepting Japan's naval supply routes to its forces in China. In addition, the Americans provided a much better air force, the 'Flying Tigers', under General Claire Chennault. A much more mixed blessing was Chiang's new chief of staff, General 'Vinegar Joe' Stilwell, an abrasive officer of limited experience but considerable knowledge of China, who insisted on a massive redeployment of Chinese troops into Burma to help the beleaguered British.

In the spring of 1942, the Japanese took advantage of the extended Chinese lines to launch major attacks against the weakened Chinese armies in the south and to cut off a large part of the Chinese army in northern Burma, inflicting a massive defeat. However, the Chinese position held at Changsha. At about the same time the Japanese prepared a massive attack on Sichuan Province, Chiang's last stronghold, but had to call this off as the tide turned in the Pacific.

The war now continued as a stalemate, with often very large and futile offensives being fought: for example, the Japanese reprisal attacks after the Doolittle bombing raid on Tokyo cost some 250,000 lives. The Chinese Communists, meanwhile, continued to stage a relentless guerrilla campaign in the north. In the south, the Japanese launched a ferocious attack on the Chinese, briefly capturing the town of Changde in a bid to prevent any further Chinese attempt to reopen the Burma road (their main supply line from Burma to Chungking, the capital city since 1938). This failed and, under advice from Stilwell, Chiang – to the dismay of many of his generals – diverted his crack troops down to the south-west again. In June the town of Myitkina with its strategic airfield was taken from the Japanese, and from then on the Chinese scored a string of successes in Burma.

However, the operation had severely weakened the Chinese position in eastern China, and Japan now staged a series of major offensives in Hunan and Kwangsi Provinces – Operation Ichi-Go – the fifth and final phase of the war (1944–5). The attack was bold and imaginative; even Changsha was finally captured. If Japan had not been reeling from losses elsewhere, the war in China might finally have been won. In October 1944, Stilwell was at last fired for this gigantic strategic mistake. By December the Japanese had cut a corridor through into Indo-China and occupied virtually the whole of south-east China. Only as Japan's supplies and forces began to dwindle under the pressure of the allied offensives in the Pacific War did the Japanese effort in China flag, and the Chinese begin to regain lost territory. China had virtually lost the conflict by 1944, after having remarkably staved off defeat in 1938.

The epitaph on Japan's war with China must be that, while the Chinese fought with tenacity and, on occasion, brilliance, the Japanese very nearly won against near impossible odds and terrain. As with the Pacific War itself, the Japanese defeat was largely a consequence of over-extension and over-ambition, a case of a cat trying to eat a panda.

Three features of the war deserve attention. The first is that, from an economic viewpoint, the war did not deliver the goods. For decades the Control Group of the Japanese army had pressed for the creation of a Japanese-dominated 'Co-Prosperity Sphere' with China as the obvious economic framework for the development of the Far East. In the years since the world depression had closed off international markets, the *zaibatsu* had come to believe that China could provide the resources necessary for continued economic growth. However, the immense dislocations of the war and the hostility of the Chinese prevented the emergence of a new market for exports on the mainland. Even the development of natural resources in the areas the Japanese controlled proved disappointing, with industries and mines lying idle for much of the time.

This led the *zaibatsu* to look with new favour on the arguments being put forward by the navy and some in the army that Southeast Asia was a more promising prospect for economic penetration, in terms both of the treasure chest of oil and raw materials there, and of better markets. It was argued that Japanese supremacy through domination of the sea lanes was more attainable than victory in the vast land war in China. Thus Japan's gaze shifted first from Russia to China, then from the latter to Southeast Asia.

Second, even as late as 1940 there was no reason to suppose that Japan was on course for war with the United States and the other Western powers. Certainly the Japanese army and navy had been greatly strengthened to deal with such a contingency; but the objectives remained confused, and conflict was far from inevitable. The invasion of China had been an opportunistic one based on a gross miscalculation of the country's military weakness, entered into almost by accident. The war had provoked no more than occasional outbursts of indignation from Western foreign ministers and the press; yet no major country was going to fight for China, in spite of the vast scale and horror of the carnage there. If Japan had concentrated on China alone, it would probably have prevailed in the long run, and created a huge Asian empire.

Instead, just four years after embarking on all-out war with China from which it could not now extricate itself, Japan initiated the most far-flung of its imperial ventures yet – into Indo-China. This time the move had the backing not just of the hotheads on the spot, the army hierarchy in Tokyo, and the *zaibatsu* establishment, but also of the navy (which had been deeply critical of the Chinese war), Prince Konoye and his cabinet – and the emperor. The invasion of Southeast Asia led directly to war with America, which the Japanese failed to foresee. The entire Japanese establishment deserves the blame this time (indeed, sections of the army were the most reluctant participants, because the adventure was a diversion from

China and depended too heavily on the hated navy's ability to keep open supply-lines at sea).

A third key aspect of the Sino-Japanese War was its systematic brutality. The Rape of Nanking gave only a foretaste of this, being the rule rather than the exception. The angel of death now took flight across China. The town of Pingting, said an eyewitness, was turned into a base 'sending soldiers north and south, east and west . . . Those coming from the front would rest a day or so and rape and loot . . . Anyone whose clothes had any resemblance to those of a soldier was killed on the spot without questions.' At Wuhu during the first week of occupation, 'the ruthless treatment and slaughter of civilians and the wanton looting and destruction of the homes of the city far exceeded anything ever seen in my twenty years' experience of China . . . The soldiers seemed especially to seek Chinese women for violation.'

At Kaifeng 'women dare not go on the streets as they are attacked even in broad daylight in their homes, or dragged off the street to their homes by Japanese soldiers. I never guessed I would ever come into contact with such awful wickedness that is occurring day by day. Multiply anything you have heard about them by 20 and it is only half the truth. Small boys are kidnapped and along with young women are shipped by train to the east . . .'

At Kihrien, 2000 civilians were killed. 'I never thought I should witness such suffering and live.' In Hangchow: 'Our beautiful Hangchow soon became a filthy, battered, obscene place . . . a city of dread . . . robbery, wounding, murder, rape and burning . . . Japanese military police did their best to help us foreigners but for the city at large there was no help.'

Terror in the towns and villages of the Yangtze basin combined with the destruction of homes, of food stocks, and of the means of making a living to create a sea of refugees. Of the million people in Nanking, 750,000 fled before the imperial army. Perhaps as many as 20 million Chinese were forced to seek survival elsewhere, and no one knows how many died.

No single explanation accounts for the astonishing scale of the atrocities. There were at least eight major factors:

(1) Racism. This undoubtedly played a major role in the attitudes of ordinary Japanese. However, Japanese attitudes towards the Chinese were somewhat ambivalent. Towards other Asian races

pure contempt was displayed: the peoples of Southeast Asia were beyond consideration, barely human at all. Westerners were viewed with hatred inspired by their colonial record. They were inferior, but had subjugated much of Asia and so were regarded with some awe, not least for their sheer physical size; this was supposedly offset by the superior intelligence of the Japanese and their unique minds. The Chinese had long been viewed as Japan's cultural siblings and rivals: they had Confucianism and Buddhism in common. Perhaps because of this the Japanese army was particularly intent on establishing its superiority through mass murder.

(2) The amorality of Japanese religion and ethics. Because Shintoism laid no stress on the individual conscience, but rather on conforming to a collective view within a hierarchy headed by an emperor and rigorously structured beneath him, there was no room for the individual to question the will of the collective. Right was what a soldier was ordered to do; to disobey was to do wrong. There was no overriding moral absolute to set this against.

(3) The brutal way of life of the ordinary Japanese peasant, who made up the bulk of the rank and file of the imperial army. Certainly the utter impoverishment of Japan's peasant families, coupled with the tradition of absolute subservience to the authorities in the villages, helps to explain the routine sadism and lack of humanity of ordinary soldiers. The essence of the Imperial Rescript to Soldiers and Sailors was an injunction to absolute loyalty. Loyalty was their essential duty, and 'duty is weightier than a mountain, while death is lighter than a feather.'

(4) The indiscipline of the Japanese army. The army expanded with astonishing speed before 1937 growing from twenty-four divisions to thirty-four the following year, forty-one in 1939, and fifty in 1940. Previously soldiers had had at least two years' training; now they received a month or two of basic training before being put into the field.

(5) The Japanese army's predilection for rape, particularly in China, was a product of the wretchedly low status accorded Japanese women – women of other races were viewed with complete contempt. The situation became so bad that the Japanese authorities began to round up whole villages of women, setting up brothels in Korea and some parts of China, thus limiting off-duty activity. The Korean 'comfort girls', whom it was established in 1992 served in government-organized bordellos, were

expected to service anything up to ten to twelve Japanese a day. For the ordinary soldier, rape was one of the few pleasures in a comfortless and deprived life in which he could expect to reap very few of the spoils of war.

(6) Military training, which in Japan, as might be expected, went to extremes in exaggerating the standard military drill of dehumanizing the individual, humiliating him and forcing him to conform to the wider group purpose of winning a war. This leads to inevitable excesses in any war, from those perpetrated at My Lai in Vietnam to the more systematic atrocities carried out by Soviet Forces in Afghanistan or by the Serbs, and others, in Bosnia. Yet nowhere – except perhaps in the still inexplicable holocaust in Cambodia in the 1970s – were they on such a vast scale as those inflicted by the Japanese on the Chinese and during the Pacific War.

(7) The nature of the fighting. There can be no doubt that the war in China was of a particularly vicious and bloody nature. The Chinese Nationalists fought savagely and gave little quarter; and when Mao's guerrillas entered the fray, they conducted a no-holds-barred campaign of a kind that left the Japanese defensive, frightened and vicious. The traditional response to such tactics – whether in China, or later in Malaya and the Philippines – was to terrorize the villages that supported the guerrilla fighters, usually by massacre and burning, or by extracting information by torturing captured insurgents.

The desperation of the ordinary soldier should not be underestimated: according to a military surgeon stranded in the Philippines, Tadashi Moriya, there were two ways to avoid starvation. One was bats:

We tore off the wings, roasted them until they were done brown, flayed and munched from their heads holding them with their legs. The brain was relishable. The tiny eyes cracked lightly in the mouth. The teeth were small but sharp, so we crunched and swallowed them down. We ate everything, bones and intestines, except the legs. The abdomen felt rough to the tongue, as they seemed to eat small insects like mosquitoes. We never minded that, and devoured them ravenously . . . Hunger is the best sauce, indeed, for I ate 15 bats a day.

An officer reported he saw a group of soldiers cooking meat. When he approached, they tried to conceal the contents of the mess tin, but he had a peep of them. A good deal of fat swam on the surface of the stew they were cooking, and he saw at once that it couldn't be the karabaw meat. Then I had the news that an officer of another unit was eaten up by his orderly as soon as he breathed his last. I believe the officer was so attracted to his orderly that he bequeathed his body to his servant, and the devoted orderly faithfully executed the last will and testament of his lord and master and buried him in his belly instead of the earth.

(8) Japan's *bushido* creed was harsh in the extreme: death was viewed as beautiful, beheading a noble way to die, surrender as deeply shaming and those who engaged in it beneath contempt.

All these played their part in creating the savage fury of bloodletting that marked the Japanese army's rampage through China; the worst and most extensive mass murder and carnage in the history of humanity.

Yet the underlying explanation is that the perpetration of atrocities was systematic, a deliberate tactic ordered from above. The evidence for this seems overwhelming. First, at the outset of the war with China, when many of the worst atrocities, including the Rape of Nanking, took place, the Japanese army was not noted for its indiscipline. Indeed, the vigorous purge of junior officers carried out after the attempted putsch of February 1936 meant that it was more centralized than ever before: atrocities on the scale that occurred could not have taken place without the knowledge and tacit approval, if not outright orders, of the authorities at the top, although there were certainly officers that disapproved of and condemned these actions.

Second, the *bushido* tradition in fact advocated respectful, even chivalrous treatment of the enemy. Nogi's behaviour to his defeated Russian foes in the Russo-Japanese War was the most recent example. There was room for mercy in the creed of *bushido* – but not in the eyes of the Japanese army commanders determined to win the war with China. *Bushido* was perverted in the military training of the 1930s. Its self-sacrificial doctrines were retained, while its code of honour was discarded in favour of a much more modern code: that of 'total war', which envisaged treating not just soldiers but whole nations as combatants, and favoured using every method available – including torture, murder, deceit, and boobytrapping –

to win. The total war theorists, at the very summit of the Japanese army, believed there were no limits to combat – a thoroughly twentieth-century doctrine with no connections at all to traditional *bushido*.

Several participants in the Rape of Nanking alleged that they were acting under orders; and one of the underlying concepts behind the 'China Incident' was the Japanese idea of a 'war of punishment', inflicting brutality on a massive, organized scale. Anything that could hasten victory was permissible, and deliberate savagery was believed to be a tactic that would spread sufficient terror to do just that. But this was seriously to misunderstand the Chinese character. Brutality convinced the Chinese that surrender to the Japanese would be a more terrible fate than continued fighting, and resistance was stiffened. Certainly, even after the Control Group purged the Imperial Way rebels and centralized decision-making, the Japanese army was more prone to being led from below than most.

Yet some form of responsibility can be ascribed. Take the Rape of Nanking. To this day, it is not clear who in fact gave the orders for the mass murder, rape and looting that engulfed the city as it was abandoned by Chinese Nationalist forces. In the post-war investigations, the Japanese generals implied that the carnage was either on a much smaller scale than is commonly supposed, or that it was instigated by troops on the ground. Was it the ordinary soldiers? Was it the NCOs and middle-ranking officers? Was it the divisional commanders in the field, General Kesago Nakajima, Major-General Heisuke Yanagawa, and Prince Asaka (Hirohito's uncle by marriage)? Was it General Matsui, the commander-in-chief in China? Was it the army high command in Tokyo? What did the government and the emperor know?

From the available evidence it is possible to make a reasonably precise judgement about which of these links in the chains of command were involved. Given the prevailing conditions of discipline at the time – and the Rape of Nanking occurred before the degeneration of the Japanese army and intense military pressure of the following few years – it seems certain that ordinary soldiers were not acting under their own initiative. The scale of the pillaging, the length of time it went on for, and the absence of disciplinary action against the ranks all point in the same direction. Similarly, nowhere before had NCOs and middle-ranking Japanese officers felt free to permit their men to go on a rampage. A Japanese private, Shiro Asuma, and other Japanese ex-servicemen insisted after the war that they were acting on orders from above.

The three main divisional commanders were certainly aware of what was happening, and are believed to have issued the specific orders to do it. General Matsui, who was condemned to death by the Tokyo war crimes tribunal for his part in the Rape was, in historian Edward Behr's view, 'the one Japanese general who was appalled by the Nanking atrocities and did his best to prevent them'. In fact, Matsui's role was more ambiguous. Not being a divisional commander on the spot, he lacked the necessary authority to rein in his generals. Indeed, Nakajima, Yanagawa and Asaka were all intimately connected with the Control Group and the Issekikai, the army within an army that now effectively ran Japan, whose most prominent member was General Tojo. It is possible that Matsui was in effect powerless, and too frightened to challenge the authority of the emperor's uncle. In his pre-trial evidence, Matsui denied that the Rape ever took place.

What is incontrovertible is that from the first day not only the world press (although not the censored Japanese press), but also the Japanese Foreign Office was flooded by descriptions of the Rape and vigorous protests. No fewer than seventy representations were forwarded to the Japanese embassy in Nanking by the International Rescue Committee. A note dated 27 December – ten days after Matsui admits he entered Nanking – said bluntly: 'Shameful disorder continues and we see no serious efforts to stop it. The soldiers every day injure hundreds of persons most seriously. Does not the Japanese army care for its reputation?' The embassy officials were visited by scores of foreigners and were largely excused from blame. Miner Bates, an American professor at Nanking University, testified that, 'These men were honestly trying to do what they could in a very bad situation, but they themselves were terrified by the military and could do nothing except forward these communications through Shanghai to Tokyo.'

The messages certainly arrived in Tokyo and were the object of intense diplomatic concern there. According to Bates, the American embassy in Nanking had shown him messages from the American ambassador in Tokyo, Joseph Grew, 'in which he referred to these reports in great detail and mentioned conversations in which they had been discussed between Grew and officials of the Foreign Ministry, including Mr Hirota'. Apart from the Japanese embassy – which was next door to the university campus, where many of the worst atrocities occurred – the American, British and German embassies were sending a stream of messages which were forwarded to Tokyo. Counsellor Hidaka of the Japanese embassy protested in person to General Asaka and sent a report to the Foreign Ministry, which was forwarded to the Ministry of War and the general staff.

The carnage was no spur-of-the-moment matter, but continued for at least a fortnight. During that time, there is no record of orders having been issued from Tokyo to stop it, although eighty officers were transferred from Nanking a couple of months later. Almost certainly, the emperor in his new war headquarters must have learnt of the Rape. Foreign Minister Hirota and Prime Minister Fumimaro Konoye were informed but were powerless to stop it.

It seems likely, from all the evidence, that the Rape of Nanking was ordered by the Control Group in Tokyo, now committed to winning the China conflict in as short a time as possible through the 'war of punishment' tactic. Those orders were directly executed by the divisional commanders in the field. Matsui – powerless, it must be assumed – turned a blind eye, and later joined in the general conspiracy of silence to deny that the Rape had ever occurred (he thus bears a major responsibility). It seems probable that the emperor and prime minister protested so violently that an official inquiry followed – much too late – and those chiefly responsible were transferred, while their superiors remained in office.

However, there was no change of policy. Atrocity followed atrocity across China, although no single incident was as widely observed internationally and independently reported as the Rape of Nanking. Large numbers of prisoners were taken, and most were executed or became forced labourers. This was logical to the Japanese military mind: prisoners were beneath contempt, deserving only death for failing to fight to the end, Chinese ones doubly so. Besides, the army, which had very few supplies and was expected as a matter of policy to live off the land, lacked the wherewithal to feed them. Nevertheless, the decision to call the war an 'incident' was at least in part a hollow attempt to justify the most flagrant violation of human rights and the Geneva Convention. Responsibility for this must extend all the way up to the government in Tokyo and to the emperor himself.

Two further atrocities of the Sino-Japanese war bear comment. First, there was Japan's notorious Unit 731, set up by imperial decree as the Epidemic Prevention and Water Purification Supply Unit under General Shiro Ishii. The real purpose of the unit was to develop methods of scientific, chemical and bacteriological warfare, testing these on human beings. Between 3000 and 10,000 died in its horrific experiments, in some of which prisoners were dissected alive. These experiments, mirroring similar ones in Germany, were pretty useless to the Japanese war effort. (One remarkable Japanese air-raid which dropped infected rats in fact caused nearly 2000 Japanese deaths.) But they marked a peculiarly grisly turn of the screw. It seems certain that Hirohito personally supported the Unit, although there is no clear evidence that he knew of its experiments on humans. If he did, he may have considered it to be just another necessary evil of war. General MacArthur was later to invite obloquy by failing to prosecute the Unit's chiefs after the war, and helping himself to the data from their experiments.

Another repugnant aspect of the war was the Japanese army's resolve to finance a large quantity of its costs through the drug trade. This decision was taken at the very top. The China Affairs Board, set up by Prince Konoye, oversaw not just the China Development Board, but a $300 million annual trade in opium deliberately revived in China by the Japanese army as a means of both raising money and demoralizing the Chinese population. Although narcotics were almost extinct in central China itself in 1917, the Japanese in Manchuria took over the Young Marshal's lucrative drugs business, set up huge poppy plantations, and ran and licensed the dens that sold heroin (there were some 600 in Peking alone).

The conclusion is inescapable. Although most of the horrors associated with Japan's war in China were instigated and carried to extremes by Japanese armies in the field, most were approved by the Control Group in Tokyo. Both in Tokyo and in the field, the war of punishment was deliberate policy. Funding it through the opium trade was deliberate policy. The press-ganged brothels were official policy. The attempt to subdue all of China was deliberate policy. All these decisions were taken at the highest level of the army, and any opposition from the civilian government was ignored. To those actions he knew of, the emperor grudgingly gave his consent because he had no power of veto; he may have even believed in the necessity of some of them. There can be no doubt that he approved of the decision to go to war with China – albeit with the usual reservations. He made clear his view that the conflict must be brought quickly to an end.

14

THE ACCOMPLICES

MUCH MORE serious than the issue of responsibility as applied to the largely powerless emperor, dragged along in the wake of his government's decisions, was the role of the other major players in 1930s Japan – the *zaibatsu*, which alone had the power to block Japan's march to war. The evidence suggests not just acquiescence by the *zaibatsu*, which now had a virtual stranglehold over the Japanese economy, but their active encouragement. The business interests, starved of overseas markets, were determined to find new ones and to secure supplies of strategic raw materials with the help of their military friends.

The *zaibatsu* had revived their alliance with the Control Group, helping them to crush the hated Imperial Way hotheads in the army (whose policy of waging war with Russia might, ironically, have averted the Pacific War altogether). The mainstream of the army, hand in glove with the *zaibatsu*, took the decision to go to war and use the hellish methods with which it was prosecuted. And the *zaibatsu* were left to run the huge body of forced labour in the mines and factories of occupied China. They also ran the narcotics trade: Mitsubishi controlled supply and distribution of drugs in Manchuria, while Mitsui controlled it in south China, the two squabbling for control of the rest of occupied China.

By 1939, as war broke out in Europe, however, the outcome of the war in China had proved a disappointment both for the army and the *zaibatsu*. China's treasure-chest had been smaller than the *zaibatsu* had been led to expect: raw materials were barely available outside Manchuria. The Chinese market, except for opium, provided poor pickings: a proper manufacturing base was lacking, and in that impoverished, war-torn, terrorized land, consumption was low. The war had deprived Manchuria, with its abundant raw materials, of its labour force: most of Mukden's factories were idle. Some 500,000 Japanese had died in two years of fighting.

Given time and effort, Japan would probably have secured all of China. But the bogging down of the army in China and the poor economic returns made the *zaibatsu* impatient. They turned to their closer ally, the traditionally weaker power in the Japanese military establishment, the supposedly 'moderate' navy. At that stage, the die was cast. As late as 1939 the Pacific War was entirely avoidable: America was not willing to fight for China, however savage and large-scale the fighting there. But with the *zaibatsu*'s decision to align with a minority of the army and the bulk of the navy in their grand vision of a 'southern strike' into Southeast Asia, war became inevitable. Ironically, the China-obsessed mainstream army leaders joined the civilians and the emperor in worrying deeply about the consequences of such an extension of the war. Prime responsibility for the invasion of Southeast Asia – which caused the Pacific War – thus lay with the navy and the *zaibatsu*.

The catalyst for Japan's ill-starred venture into Southeast Asia was the trend of the war in Europe. Japan's attitude to Europe was entirely opportunistic. Its military alliance with Britain had fallen apart after the First World War, and with its walk-out from the League of Nations relations between the Western powers and Japan were now wary and suspicious. This encouraged the Japanese to make common cause with Germany and Italy, the Axis powers who also were in bitter rivalry with Britain, France, and the United States and shared Japan's deep distrust of the Soviet Union. The Japanese persuaded themselves that they shared a common cause with Germany and Italy as 'have-not-nations' in opposition to the British and American 'empires'. In 1936 the three signed the Anti-Comintern Pact, directed against the Soviet Union.

The Japanese military attaché in Berlin, Lieutenant-General Hiroshi Oshima, pursued a vigorous policy of friendship with Hitler, whom he deeply admired, even suggesting at one stage that Japan would join Germany in fighting Britain and America. 'Perhaps we could call on the war minister to reprimand him,' commented an exasperated Hirohito, who was unenthusiastic about an alliance with Germany. On another occasion the emperor buttonholed the war minister. 'Is it not a usurpation of imperial authority for the military attaché to promise, on his own, our military co-operation with Germany? I am further disturbed by the fact that the army seems to support him on this issue, and I am displeased that you have failed to bring the matter up at cabinet meetings.' Nevertheless, Germany and Japan seemed to be drawing ever closer together.

In August 1939 Hitler dropped a bombshell by concluding a non-aggression pact with Japan's foremost enemy, the Soviet Union, which could now reinforce its armies in the east to face Japan. The shocked Japanese prime minister, Baron Hiranuma, resigned, remarking that 'the situation in Europe has taken a strange and complex new turn'. Hirohito, who had long distrusted the Germans, argued forcefully, 'In foreign affairs our goal should be maintaining a harmonious relationship with England and the United States. Furthermore, the foreign minister should act in a manner more clearly consistent with constitutional provisions.' The foreign minister at the time was a departure from the moderate tradition of that institution: Yosuke Matsuoka was a verbose nationalist, who had also engineered the appointment of one of his military allies, General Hata, as the new war minister. Relations between Germany and Japan were now severely strained for a time.

But in the early summer of 1940, as Hitler's armies overran continental Europe, Japan was eager to join the winning side. There were two immediate consequences: first, the triumph of the Nazis in Europe suggested to the Japanese that the façade of parliamentary democracy – and by now in Japan it was no more than that – was outmoded. Totalitarianism was seen as the new wave. Prince Konoye, prime minister once again, formally dissolved the political parties and set up a mass movement 'designed to assist the imperial throne'. In fact the parties had long counted for little, and Japan had been a virtual military dictatorship since 1939; but now even the pretence was gone. Second, in September 1940 the tripartite Axis Pact was signed. The essence of the pact for Japan was that it committed Germany to coming to its aid in the event of an attack by the United States. Defeat in France had virtually removed Japan's other Far Eastern rival, Britain, from serious challenge in the Pacific; at the same time Britain had bowed to Japan's demands to close one of the main supply routes to Chiang Kai-shek's beleaguered army in China – the Burma Road.

Hirohito was unhappy with the Axis Pact, remarking, 'even if we wait to see what happens between Germany and Russia, there will still be time for an alliance,' and insisting, 'surely the United States will embargo imports of oil and scrap iron to Japan by way of retaliation. What will happen then?' Another time he said angrily, 'No matter how you look at it, this will be ruinous for the army. They won't wake up to the situation until Manchuria and Korea have been lost.' With Britain crippled and America neutral, Japan began to consider the feasibility of further colonial advances, even though it had yet fully to absorb China. Japan was behaving rather like a beast of prey which, having half devoured one victim, is suddenly diverted by the presence of other plump, defenceless animals grazing nearby.

In June 1941 Germany, which had been urging Japan to strike against British and French interests in Asia, invaded the Soviet Union. The Japanese were delighted: with Britain, France and The Netherlands now on their knees, their Asian interests were ripe for the picking; the Soviet Union's attentions were now entirely taken up in Europe. America would not risk war with Germany by seeking to block Japan's aims in Indo-China and the Pacific. It was now or never: here was an opportunity to create a truly awesome empire in southern Asia that was too good to miss. The region had oil, tin, bauxite, nickel and rice – all the things most desperately needed by Japan's expeditionary force in China and, more importantly, by the *zaibatsu*, who took the view that, with Japan's export earnings at an all-time low and no money available to buy raw materials, they had to be seized instead.

A month after the launch of Hitler's Operation Barbarossa offensive into Russia, the Japanese made their move, little foreseeing that it would make war with the United States inevitable. There is no doubt, though, that Hirohito was genuinely troubled by the venture. He told the Lord Privy Seal, Marquis Kido, who had emerged as his chief adviser, that, 'I am not at all pleased when we act on our own and take advantage of the other side's weakness like a thief at a fire. However, in order to deal with the unsettled conditions we find in the world today, it would not do to be beaten because we failed to attack when we had the chance ... I only hope you will show prudence in the execution of your plans.'

The army and the navy, meanwhile, had joined with the *zaibatsu* in a nearly unstoppable alliance. The navy's War Guidance Office had long been advocating the 'strike south'. 'Finally, the time has come,' it declared. 'This maritime nation, Japan, should today commence its advance to the Bay of Bengal. Moss-covered tundras, vast barren deserts – of what use are they? Today people should begin to follow the grand strategy of the navy.' Yamamoto prophetically told Konoye in mid-1941: 'If I am told to fight, regardless of the consequences, I shall run wild considerably for the first six months or a year, but I have utterly no confidence for the second and third years. Now that the situation has come to this pass, I hope you will work for avoidance of an American–Japanese war.'

Like the British in Burma, the Vichy government in France had been bullied into closing the supply route across Indo-China to Chiang Kai-shek's forces. Nevertheless, in July 1941 Japanese forces occupied French bases in southern Indo-China; the Vichy government had conceded, having little alternative. It seemed that the occupation could be only be a prelude to the invasion of Malaya, the Philippines and the Dutch East Indies. The British responded by promptly reopening the Burma Road to China in a gesture of defiance against Japan's unprovoked expansionism. The Japanese were later to claim that this made the occupation of Malaya and the East Indies inevitable. But in this case the chicken seems clearly to have preceded the egg: they had no pretext for occupying French Indo-China in the first place, because both the British and French supply routes to Chiang had already been closed. The United States, Britain and The Netherlands responded by imposing an embargo on the supply of oil, iron and steel from any of their territories or dependencies to Japan. Japanese assets in the United States were also frozen.

It took some time for the Japanese to realize that America was serious: their reaction then was to conclude that war with the United States was inevitable – and that the Americans had brought it on themselves. Admiral Nagano, the naval chief of staff, summed up the Japanese view at an historic cabinet meeting on 3 September: with the country now starved of oil, the allies could only become stronger and Japan weaker. 'Although I am confident that at the present time we have a chance to win the war, I feel that this opportunity will disappear with the passage of time.' Tojo was less certain, believing that victory was by no means assured, but that Japan had no other choice. The emperor prodded Konoye into a frantic last-minute effort to talk peace with the Americans.

It was to become apparent over the next few months, however, that the Japanese were right about one thing at least: peace was now impossible because the Americans were resolved to maintain sanctions except in the unlikely event of Japanese capitulation to humiliating demands. In occupying French Indo-China, the Japanese had miscalculated disastrously (although they would plead that there had been no clear-cut signal from Washington to lay off). That single act, taken with the approval of all Japan's main power centres – the emperor and his household (grudgingly), Prince Konoye, the cabinet, the army, the navy, the *zaibatsu*, the bureaucracy – represented the crossing of the Rubicon.

Why did the United States, which had watched in passive disapproval while Japan's massive war effort against China proceeded, react with alacrity and firmness to the Japanese occupation of French Indo-China which, almost alone of the advances of the past decade, took place with the acquiescence of the country concerned and largely without bloodshed? Two explanations have about equal weight. With the move into Indo-China, Japan now clearly threatened Southeast Asia; it was against America's strategic interest that Japan should not just dominate the western Pacific, but be able to call upon huge supplies of strategic raw materials. Yet there was a second reason. Roosevelt was by now anxious to enter the European war, having been convinced by Churchill of the dangers of German hegemony over continental Europe. This partly explains why the Americans were prepared to tolerate the war with China, but not the invasion of Indo-China. Roosevelt must have known that the imposition of sanctions rendered war virtually inevitable; and the Japanese attack on Pearl Harbor, coupled with Hitler's ritual declaration of war on America (which was not necessary under the Axis Pact, since Japan had not been attacked), made it possible for the United States to enter the European war promptly. That this was uppermost in Roosevelt's mind is supported by the way most Americans forces were swiftly assigned to the European theatre, not to the Far East – much to General MacArthur's disgust. Roosevelt was to treat the war with Japan almost as a sideshow. Confident that he would prevail there in the end, the American president's initial attentions went far beyond Asia.

This helps to explain why, in the four months leading up to their entering the war, the Americans behaved – just as the Japanese claimed – in a pretty intransigent fashion. None of this excuses Japan, which had embarked on a series of large-scale, unprovoked aggressions against its neighbours, of which the invasion of French Indo-China, by no means the worst, was the critical move. But it does explain why, from July 1941, war with America was more or less inevitable. The four months after the embargo was imposed were marked in Japan by frantic preparation for war coupled with Hirohito's equally frantic search for peace. The emperor's motives were twofold: manifest reluctance to resort to war, and his considerable doubts that Japan would win. Admiral Nagano, the naval chief, had told him in July that a total victory was out of the question;

'Indeed, we're not even sure of winning.' On 6 September the draft plans for war were approved before the emperor. But he insisted that every last diplomatic effort be made.

The following day the cabinet approved two fateful resolutions. First, 'in order to preserve the Empire's self-sufficiency and self-defence, Japan is determined not to back away from war with the United States, Britain and the Netherlands; consequently, war preparations are to be completed by the end of October'. Second, 'parallel with the above, and in an effort to satisfy the Emperor's demands, Japan will exhaust all diplomatic means with respect to the United States and England'.

The head of the privy council, standing in for the emperor, addressed a number of questions to the navy minister on behalf of Hirohito. The emperor had been advised not to put these questions himself. After they had finished, he angrily drew out a poem by the Meiji Emperor:

> I believed this was a world
> In which all men were brothers
> Across the Four Seas.
> Why then do the waves and winds
> Arise now in such turmoil?

The military chiefs assured him they would make an effort for peace. Prince Konoye had been pressing for a summit with Roosevelt, which the Americans played along with for a while, to buy time, although they suspected that the Japanese intention was to 'spring a Munich'.

However, the Americans were being simultaneously appraised of Japanese preparations for war by MAGIC, the name given to a remarkable breakthrough in cracking Japanese communications codes which was to serve superbly throughout the Pacific War. In September, Roosevelt drew up terms for a settlement which the Japanese could not accept. The Americans emphasized that they required a withdrawal not just from Indo-China, but from China itself. Konoye's fall-back position was to offer a retreat from Indo-China in exchange for lifting the embargo, in other words a return to the status quo before July. The prime minister had a secret meeting with the American ambassador in Tokyo, Joseph Grew, to press for the summit; Cordell Hull, the American secretary of state, was unimpressed.

On 12 October Konoye met Tojo, the war minister and by now

the acknowledged chief of the Control Group in the army, and urged him to withdraw 'some' troops from China. Tojo flatly refused, and it is certain that the Americans would have rejected such a half-measure. By then it seems that Hirohito himself had accepted that war was inevitable, telling Kido realistically that 'in the present conditions I think US–Japanese negotiations have little hope of success'.

On 14 October, Tojo sent an ultimatum to Konoye, urging his resignation for his failure to report that there were serious divisions within the navy as to the advisability of war (Konoye suggested that the navy as a whole was against war, something Tojo disputed). Konoye, faced by the prospect of the government falling, recommended that a moderate, Prince Hikashikuni, succeed him. This relative of the emperor's later claimed that he told Konoye to go ahead and form another government, sacking Tojo. This would have called the army's bluff. It might also have led to the outright military coup that the emperor feared above all else. Instead, Hirohito appointed Tojo as prime minister, with the memorable remark to the snake-like Kido, who had proposed the war minister, 'It is just as they say, you can't control a tiger unless you enter its lair.'

Hideki Tojo was the son of a famous general under the Meiji Emperor. Even for a Japanese, he was short. He made a virtue of dressing as unprepossessingly as the ordinary Japanese soldier: unpolished shoes, baggy pants, un-ironed uniform. He was in striking contrast to his predecessor as war minister, General Araki, an inspired and loquacious public speaker. Tojo would speak, briefly and exactly to the point. He was both an able administrator and an effective field commander. He first rose to prominence as head of the military police in the Kwantung Army in Manchuria, becoming commander of Japan's mechanized forces in China and then being promoted to vice-minister of war in Konoye's first cabinet. His abilities impressed Konoye, and he was appointed air force chief, immensely strengthening that arm. Konoye appointed him war minister in his second and third cabinets, under pressure from army extremists.

Tojo was highly effective, reimposing discipline on the faction-ridden army, dissolving the separate infantry, cavalry and artillery divisions, as well as the engineering and air commissariats, so that the army was more unified and able officers could be transferred from one branch to another at speed. Tojo's experience in China had taught him the value of air power, mechanization and blitzkrieg tactics, and he introduced a 'modern weapons' department into the army. He had a brilliant military mind, and was a masterly strategist. He was tough, determined, utterly loyal to Japan and the emperor (and therefore somewhat lacking in imagination) – and, by any measure, a psychopath.

Konoye later sadly told his aide that he had been let down by Hirohito:

> When I used to tell the emperor that it would be a bad thing to start the war, he would agree with me, but then he would listen to others and afterwards tell me I shouldn't worry so much. He was slightly in favour of war and later on he became more war-inclined. Eventually he started believing that I was no expert on strategy or military matters generally. As prime minister, I had no authority over the army and there was only one person I could appeal to: the emperor. But the emperor became so much under the influence of the military that I couldn't do anything about it.

Konoye's verdict is damning, but also self-serving. The truth was a little more complex. It is true by this stage Hirohito was reconciled to war: he had displayed his own sometimes prescient doubts about the recklessness of the military, and he now accepted, in view of America's refusal to back down, that his country could not yield and save face. In this he reflected the views of almost everyone but Konoye – the man who nevertheless had presided over Japan's decisions to invade China and to occupy Indo-China.

Japan was far advanced with preparations for all-out war long before Pearl Harbor. In July 1940, the manufacture of luxury goods was prohibited; the sale of stocks of luxuries was stopped in October. Non-essential industries were prepared for the quick shift to war production. Eighteen months before Pearl Harbor, driving for pleasure was banned. In mid-1941 private cars were stopped from using the streets. Rubber-soled *tabui* had disappeared from the shops two years before the war in order to accumulate reserves of rubber; oil and iron ore were also being stockpiled. For several years, useful materials like metal plumbing fixtures were being stripped from private homes. Nails, bottle caps, spectacle frames and hat pins were seized. Two weeks before Pearl Harbor, members of the powerless Diet were forced to use buses to get to their sessions. Other signs of war preparations were the absence of coffee; the extinguishing of neon lights in the Ginza, Tokyo's central shopping district; the introduction of 'Service Day for the Development of Asia', a kind of family fast-day every month; and a ban on the polishing of rice (which made it smaller). In 1940 rice, salt, sugar, matches and other daily necessities had been rationed – even though the war with China did not justify these measures. Women were forbidden to wear smart clothes or style their hair.

By 2 November 1941, Hirohito was meeting with his chiefs of staff over the direct operational planning for war. When Japanese negotiators met the Americans on 7 November, their demands had stiffened perceptibly. On 26 November the Americans reiterated their demand to the Japanese for withdrawal from both China and Indo-China. Roosevelt warned his top admirals to prepare for war. Henry Stimson, the American secretary of war, recalls that Roosevelt told them, 'We were likely to be attacked as early as next Monday [1 December] for the Japanese are notorious for making an attack without warning.' Roosevelt believed this would come in the southern Pacific, because Japanese ships were assembling at Shanghai.

At a fateful meeting of senior statesmen on 29 November, Konoye was bafflingly, perhaps duplicitously, ambiguous:

> I deeply regret that I have not been able to do anything towards the adjustment of Japanese–American relations despite my efforts from last April onwards. I beg to express my appreciation to the present cabinet for zealously striving to attain this end. To my great regret, I am forced to conclude, on the basis of this morning's explanation by the government, that further continuation of diplomatic negotiations would be hopeless . . . Still, is it necessary to go to war at once, even if diplomatic negotiations have been broken off? Would it not be possible, I wonder, while carrying on matters as they are, to find a way out of the deadlock later by persevering to the utmost despite the difficulties?

All the other senior men present spoke against war. Hirohito's doubts were raised at this eleventh hour by Prince Takamatsu, his younger brother, who reported to him on 30 November that the navy 'will be very pleased if a war can be avoided'. The emperor promptly summoned the navy minister and chief of staff as well as Tojo, and was assured that they had no doubts. Kido reported, 'When the emperor questioned them, they answered with conviction, so he told me to have the prime minister proceed as planned.' The decision to go to war had in effect been taken. Some time between early September and the end of November, the emperor's mind had been decisively changed in favour of war; he may have been persuaded by what he saw as the obduracy of the Americans. There can be no doubt that, with the exception of a few elderly bureaucrats and a minority within the navy, all Japan's power structures were now reconciled to the inevitability and desirability of war. The decision to go to war was a national one, not that of a militarist clique. Hirohito must have known of the impending attack on Pearl Harbor. At a meeting on 2 December, Nagano and Sugiyama told him that the night of 8 December provided the best opportunity because, among other things, it was a Sunday, when the Americans would be at ease and their ships in port. Now, 8 December was a Monday in Tokyo and the rest of Asia, and a Sunday in Hawaii, the other side of the International Date Line. Some present-day Japanese historians say that Nagano informed Hirohito that the attack would be on a Monday, when Americans would be weary after Sunday revels, which seems a tall story.

On 2 December 1941 Admiral Yamamoto, commander of the Japanese fleet and one of those who harboured the most serious doubts about the desirability of war, sent out his coded order, 'Ascend Mt Nitaka! 1298', meaning that the attack on Pearl Harbor was on for 8 December. The Japanese fleet had already left the Kuriles and was in the northern Pacific. At 6 p.m. Washington time, President Roosevelt followed the advice of a last-minute intermediary and sent a personal message to Hirohito asking for a withdrawal from Indo-China without spelling out the need for a withdrawal from China. The note was held back by Japan's military censors, reaching the American ambassador in Tokyo, Joseph Grew, 12 hours later. At midnight on 8 December, Tokyo time, he tried to relay the message to the emperor but, absurdly, was told by the foreign minister that Hirohito could not be disturbed.

The Japanese declaration of hostilities against the United States was transmitted to the Japanese embassy in Washington, to be handed over at 1.00 p.m. the following day. Supposedly because of delays in the transmission, it was in fact handed over to Cordell Hull by the Japanese ambassador, Admiral Nomura, at 2.20 p.m. Half an hour before, Hull, along with Roosevelt and the Navy Secretary, had been apprised of the Japanese attack on Pearl Harbor.

PART THREE

THE WHIRLWIND

The usual offerings had been set before the corpse; and a small Buddhist lamp – *tomyo* – was burning. The priest recited the service, and performed the funeral ceremonies – after which he entered into meditation ... when the hush of the night was at its deepest, there noiselessly entered a Shape, vague and vast and in the same moment Muso found himself without power to move or speak. He saw that Shape lift the corpse, as with hands, and devour it, more quickly than a cat devours a rat – beginning at the head, and eating everything, the hair and the bones and even the shroud. And the monstrous Thing, having thus consumed the body, turned to the offerings, and ate them also. Then it went away, as mysteriously as it had come.

From 'The Story of Jikininki', *Kwaidan*,
compiled by Lafcadio Hearn

15

THE FURIES UNLEASHED

JAPAN'S DECISION to start the Pacific War has been portrayed in conventional history as the hijacking of a nation by a militarist class, prepared to stoop to treacherous surprise attack at Pearl Harbor in the pursuit of an insanely ambitious Asian empire. The Japanese themselves have done little to dispel this myth, because, if it were true, it would mean that the post-war cure for Japan's ills was simply to diminish the armed forces to a point where the seizure of power by them would become virtually impossible – which in fact is what happened after the Pacific War.

The reality differed in almost every point from the conventional accounts. Territorial expansion in Asia had been a goal not just of the militarist class but of virtually all of Japan's ruling elite since Meiji times; the chief argument between the country's radicals and moderates had been over where to expand and when. The militarists became more powerful in Japan's system of competing elites, not just through intimidation and brute force – although there was plenty of each – but because the overwhelming consensus among the elites had moved in the direction of the military solution. In particular, the *zaibatsu* had decided in the mid-1930s that only territorial expansion could make up for the markets and supplies of raw materials lost during the world depression.

The decision to invade Indo-China, taken on the cold grounds of military opportunity and strategic necessity, was the most moderate of the three courses the Japanese believed lay open to them – the others being to attack the Soviet Union or to concentrate all their resources on finishing off China. The occupation of Indo-China had the backing not just of the army (and power after 1936 was largely in the hands of the dominant faction of senior officers, not the

241

reckless commanders on the ground who had played a major part in the invasion of Manchuria), but of the 'moderate' navy, the *zaibatsu* bosses, a majority of the bureaucracy, and even, eventually, the emperor. That occupation rendered war inevitable.

The Japanese were wholly unprepared for the American response, which they interpreted as a declaration of economic war. Their attitude was not, indeed, unreasonable. In return for lifting the state of economic siege, which the Japanese believed would slowly strangle their economy and fighting ability, the Americans had demanded humiliating terms. If the Americans persisted in their attitude, and they did, the Japanese saw no alternative to war – and the ingredients of this were surprise, tactical boldness and extreme ferocity. There was indeed a good deal of treachery behind the preparations for the 'day of infamy', as Roosevelt dubbed Pearl Harbor: in particular, there were the diplomatic feints and the failure to convey the declaration of hostilities until after the attack.

Yet the history of warfare is littered with such deception. For a country that believed it had to fight for its very survival, observation of the diplomatic niceties and the loss of the element of surprise in staging an overwhelming pre-emptive strike were unlikely to be part of Japanese strategy. Pearl Harbor was to be a day of infamy as much for the woeful state of American unpreparedness as it was for Japanese treachery. Japan's attitude to war was a reflection of the elite consensus – only the voters, who had virtually no power in Japan during the 1930s, had their doubts – and was based on a perfectly logical unfolding of events. In December 1941 the Japanese believed they had no alternative but to fight, although they were far from certain they could win.

Tojo had expressed misgivings, and Admiral Yamamoto, in charge of the planning of Pearl Harbor, had openly disagreed with the decision to fight the United States. 'A war between the United States and Japan would be a major calamity for the world,' he had written. He considered that the possibility of such a war was 'outrageous . . . However with the understanding of the navy minister and the chief of general staff it is also necessary to make preparations for whatever the navy is to undertake.' He added:

> In order to fight the United States, we must fight with the intention of challenging practically the whole world. In short, even if a non-aggression pact is concluded with the Soviets, the Russians cannot be entirely relied upon. While we are fighting the US, who can guarantee they will observe the pact and not attack us from the

rear? At any rate, as long as matters have come to this point, I shall extend my utmost efforts and will probably die fighting on the battleship *Nagata*. During that time Tokyo will probably be burned to the ground.

While Tojo nevertheless relished the prospect of war, Yamamoto and most of the leaders of the Japanese army and naval establishments believed that, while war was dangerous for Japan, there was no alternative but to proceed. The same logic applied to Japan's strategy and war aims. These have been widely described as hopelessly over-ambitious and over-extended, encompassing an empire that was to make Ancient Rome look modest, reaching as far as Burma in the west, New Guinea in the south and half of the Pacific in the east; the seeds of its collapse seemed inherent in the very speed and scale of the invasion. Yet in practice the reckless Japanese strategy may have been the only one possible for a country which had made the 'outrageous' decision to go to war with the United States in the first place.

The peculiar circumstances of 1942 should also be borne in mind. At the time it seemed not impossible, even probable, that Britain and Russia would be defeated by Germany in Europe and that the United States – upon which the Germans had declared war – would be forced by the prospect of a war on two fronts to sue for peace.

The strategy consisted of three elements. The first was a massive seizure of land and territory in the south – Malaya, the Philippines, and the Dutch East Indies – to coincide with the destruction of the American Pacific Fleet at Pearl Harbor, and also the seizure of Wake Island and Guam; the second, the creation of a series of fortified garrisons on the islands of the central Pacific to deter American attack; and third, a strategy of consolidation. The plan was based on the fact that, while the eastern Pacific between America and Hawaii was empty sea, the western Pacific was pockmarked with islands which could provide a defensive ring. If Japan held these, it could beat off American attacks and strike at any force attempting to sail to Australia and New Zealand.

Central to the success of all the operations was the success of the attack on Pearl Harbor; if the American Pacific Fleet were allowed to escape, most of Japan's operations in the south, which depended on supplies across the sea, would be vulnerable.

The Japanese need not have worried. American complacency was, in truth, infamous. Through the intercepts of the MAGIC code-breakers, who had plugged into virtually all Japanese naval communications in the Pacific area, the Americans knew that a Japanese attack was likely: the only dispute was over the probable target. By any standards the huge naval base at Pearl Harbor must have seemed the biggest and most tempting. In spite of the diplomatic feints, it was evident that negotiations were stalling and that war was approaching: this justified placing all American forces in the region on a state of maximum alert. It is true that the Americans expected an attack further south. Moreover, the Japanese went to elaborate and ingenious precautions to seize the initiative to stage their attack, including the maintenance of radio silence throughout the fleet as it approached Pearl Harbor. The fleet also stayed just behind a storm and cloud weatherfront then rapidly crossing the Pacific, which shielded the ships from aerial observation.

Yet when the 183 torpedo and dive-bombers of the Japanese carrier fleet took off early in the morning of 7 December, they could hardly believe their luck. As the Japanese had expected, the Americans were in a low state of preparedness. The day before, General Walter Short, the commander of ground and air forces in Hawaii, had received an alert from his intelligence officer that a coded message had been sent out by a presumed Japanese spy: 'The flowers in bloom are fewest out of the whole year. However, the hibiscus and the poinsettia are in bloom now.' The message may have referred to the fact that the American aircraft carriers had set sail, while virtually the whole of the rest of the fleet was in port.

Short, who had previously received a secret warning from Washington that the Japanese were about to strike, concluded that his subordinates were 'too intelligence-conscious', then set off for a gala evening at the Schofield Barracks Officers' Club. Admiral Husband Kimmel, Commander of the Pacific Fleet, was attending a small dinner party at the Halekulani Hotel after spending the afternoon considering why the Japanese were changing their codes so often, and why their carrier fleet had disappeared.

At 9.30 that evening, General Short left the Officers' Club and drove back along a road with a broad view of Pearl Harbor, blazing with lights below. The American Pacific Fleet was at anchor and at peace. 'Isn't that a beautiful sight,' he remarked. 'And what a target they would make.'

Just before four o'clock in the morning a Japanese submarine was sighted in the approaches to Pearl Harbor. This was so extraordinary that the ship that had made the sighting did not report it to base. More than two and a half hours later, a midget submarine was spotted and sunk. A few minutes after this, a white sampan was spotted inside the restricted approaches to Pearl Harbor, but it quickly surrendered. At seven o'clock another submarine was detected. Not until fifteen minutes later was a senior officer informed of these incursions.

Earlier, the harbour's outlying radar had picked up the presence of a truly massive number of aircraft approaching Hawaii. At the Opana radar station near Kahuku Point on the northern tip of Oahu, Privates Joseph Lockard and George Elliott were idly observing the radar screen. Walter Lord, in his graphic account of Pearl Harbor, *Day of Infamy*, takes up the story from when the two men picked up the approach of a huge flight of planes – like 'a pinball machine gone haywire' – 137 miles to the north, 3 degrees east, and telephoned Private Joseph McDonald at the radar information centre. McDonald took the message to Lieutenant Kermit Tyler.

Helpfully he explained that it was the first time he had ever received anything like this – 'Do you think we ought to do something about it?' He suggested they call the plotters back from breakfast. They didn't get too much practice and this certainly seemed 'an awful big flight'.

Tyler was unimpressed. McDonald returned to the switchboard and called back Opana. This time he got Lockard, who was excited too. The blips looked bigger than ever; the distance was shrinking fast – 7.08 a.m., 113 miles ... 7.15 a.m., 92 miles. At least 50 planes must be soaring towards Oahu at almost 180 mph. 'Hey Mac!' he protested when McDonald told him the lieutenant said everything was all right. Then Lockard asked to speak directly to Tyler, explaining he had never seen so many planes, so many flashes, on his screen. McDonald traipsed back to Tyler. 'Sir, I would appreciate it very much if you would answer the phone.'

Tyler took over, listened patiently, and thought a minute. He remembered the carriers were out – these might be Navy planes. He recalled hearing the radio on his way to work, remembered that it stayed on all night whenever B-17s were in from the coast – these might be Flying Fortresses. In either case, the planes were friendly. Cutting short any further discussion, he told Lockard, 'Well, don't worry about it.'

When the bombers with their Zero escorts arrived, 780 of the anti-aircraft guns on the ships were unmanned, and only 4 of the 31 army batteries were operational. Commander Mitsuo Fuchida wrote afterwards as they flew over 'Battleship Row': 'Even in the deepest peace, I have never seen ships anchored at a distance of less than 500 to 1000 yards from each other. The picture down there was hard to comprehend.' At 7.49 a.m. the Japanese attack began. Within moments the battleship *Arizona* had blown up, *Oklahoma* had turned turtle, and *California* was sinking. Perhaps the most poignant moment of the raid took place on the battleship *Nevada*, where band leader Oden McMillan waited to play morning colours at eight o'clock:

> The band crashed into the 'Star-Stangled Banner'. A Japanese plane skimmed across the harbor . . . dropped a torpedo at the *Arizona* . . . and peeled off right over the *Nevada*'s fan tail. The rear gunner sprayed the men standing at attention, but he must have been a poor shot. He missed the entire band and marine guard, lined up in two neat rows. He did succeed in shredding the flag, which was just being raised.
>
> McMillan knew now, but kept on conducting. The years of training had taken over – it never occurred to him that once he had begun playing the National Anthem he could possibly stop. Another strafer flashed by. This time McMillan unconsciously paused as the deck splintered around him, but he quickly picked up the beat again. The entire band stopped and started again with him, as though they had rehearsed it for weeks. Not a man broke formation until the final note ended. Then everyone ran wildly for cover.

A second wave of bombers came in at nine o'clock. The *West Virginia* was blown up, while the *Maryland*, *Tennessee* and *Pennsylvania* were badly hit; the *Nevada* was grounded. Eleven smaller ships were hit, and 188 aircraft were destroyed. The main naval dockyards and oil storage tanks were wrecked. The only failure for the Japanese – and it was a major one – was the absence of America's carrier fleet. It had been a brilliant attack. The fact that it violated the Hague Agreement of 1907 which specified that hostilities could not begin without a formal declaration of war was of only academic interest to the Japanese. Tojo was later to admit that even the message delivered to Cordell Hull, which had been delayed until immediately after Pearl Harbor, was only a 'final note', not a declaration of war under the convention. America's indignation at Japan's failure to comply with the legal formalities stemmed in large part from its own glaring inability to protect its own fleet.

In the first few months of the war, everything went Japan's way. The day after Pearl Harbor, the British battleships *Prince of Wales* and *Repulse*, accompanied by several destroyers, set out for Singapore to intercept Japanese forces being landed on the Kra Peninsula, the thin slice of land between Thailand and Malaya. Japanese fighter-bombers found the ships and in two hours sunk them both. 'In all the war, I never received a more direct shock,' Churchill admitted afterwards. Guam, meanwhile, had fallen to Japanese forces. Wake's defenders fought back heroically, but in a fortnight the island fell after supplies had failed to get through. The garrison at Hong Kong put up an epic struggle, and lasted out until Christmas Day. The Gilbert Islands soon fell.

Just four days after Pearl Harbor, the Japanese launched their first offensives: against Malaya and the Philippines. The Japanese deployed speed, courage, and tactical brilliance throughout the Malaya campaign, landing at a series of points along the undefended coast. The defenders, mostly ill-trained Indian troops under British command, were demoralized to find that Japanese forces had thrust between them and their supply base at Singapore, threatening to cut them off, and all too often fled south in confusion to avoid such a fate. In fact they could probably have resisted by retreating deeper into the peninsula and outflanking the smaller Japanese forces. But by 15 January the Japanese Twenty-Fifth Army had advanced 400 miles in five weeks and was within 100 miles of the apparently impregnable British stronghold of Singapore.

On 31 January the last British troops in Malaya retreated across the causeway between Singapore and the mainland. The British force on the island was a massive one: around forty-five battalions, outnumbering the Japanese army's thirty-one, under the control of General Arthur Percival. Singapore's garrison had, however, been supplied with the wrong ammunition, which rendered the batteries facing the Malay coast virtually inoperative. The more impressive sea batteries were redundant because the threat came from the coast of Johore, just a mile to the north.

On 8 February the Japanese attacked in overwhelming strength against Percival's forces, which were necessarily strung out across 30 miles of vulnerable shoreline. The overstretched defenders on the north-west coast of the island were overwhelmed and fell back. A week later the Japanese had advanced to secure control of the reservoirs on which the city, whose population was now swollen by refugees to a million, depended. The following day Percival surrendered, and was photographed carrying the Union Jack in defeat, in what was to be labelled the greatest disaster in British military history.

It certainly was a defeat: 130,000 troops had yielded to a force half their number. Yet it is hard to see what else Percival could have done. To have fought on would have been to invite a lingering and horrific end for his forces, with no hope of relief. Just conceivably, a swift counter-offensive when the Japanese landed, or before the water shortage began to bite, might have been possible against the numerically inferior enemy forces; but the Japanese had the advantage of higher morale and superior momentum. The real lesson of the defeat was the danger of depending on 'fortress' bases, particularly ones as exposed as Singapore: an 'impregnable' garrison was much more vulnerable, once its supply lines were cut off, than a series of bases. This was a lesson the Japanese themselves were to learn later in the war.

Percival's defence of the island can hardly be classed as imaginative or heroic. But the superior determination, mobility, firepower and sheer energy of the Japanese forces had put the defenders off balance in much the same way as Hitler's blitzkrieg tactics had in Europe. Dunkirk was a defeat, although the evacuation of the British Expeditionary Force rendered it heroic. For Singapore's defenders there was no such consolation, only shame and the horror of becoming prisoners of the Japanese (many Indians taken there went over to the Japanese forces).

Japan's invasion of the East Indies had begun on 16 December. Japanese tactics consisted in amphibious landings along the whole 2000-mile length of the East Indian archipelago: Borneo and the Celebes were attacked in January, Timor and Sumatra in February, Java in March. The fighting was wholly unequal from the start. The Dutch defenders were ill-equipped and outnumbered, and had very little support from the local people. Small detachments of Australian troops provided the only semblance of a struggle. But the great bulk of Australia's forces were fighting with the British in the Middle East and in Malaya. In fact, there was now only the thinnest of lines of defence between the invading Japanese and Australia.

On 27 February the Japanese fleet appeared off Java with the clear intention of effecting a landing there. What remained of the Allied naval force in the region had assembled under Admiral Doorman to attack the Japanese fleet. The two fleets met in the Battle of the Java Sea, which began late in the afternoon: two heavy and three light cruisers and nine destroyers on the Allied side confronted two heavy and two light cruisers and fourteen destroyers on the Japanese side. After a massive exchange of fire, the Japanese used long-range torpedoes to force the Allied fleet to break away from the engagement. In darkness, Doorman sent half of his fleet to refuel, but retained the other half in an attempt to attack the Japanese and prevent them from landing. He bore down on part of the fleet, only to be surprised by the rest of it, which ambushed his ships with their torpedoes. It seemed the Japanese were unstoppable at sea, as well as on land. What neither side could know was that the Battle of the Java Sea was to be the only decisive Japanese naval victory throughout the Pacific War.

Within a fortnight, Java surrendered. Sumatra capitulated soon afterwards. In Burma the flimsy British military presence threatened to collapse almost as easily, but General Alexander was determined to fight back. He had no option, however, in the face of Japanese superiority but to stage a 600-mile retreat – the longest in British history – across Burma, pursued by the Japanese, who were stopped from chasing him into India only by the monsoon.

It is not hard to see the explanation for the spectacular Japanese successes in just four months. They had the advantages of surprise; of well-disciplined, well-armed fighting men willing to endure extreme physical hardship; and of a brilliantly conceived and executed strategy of amphibious warfare. With the exception of the garrison in Singapore, their opponents were ill-prepared, ill-equipped, unsupported, and strung out in small bases which could be picked off at will. The Allies had little air support; after the destruction of the American Pacific Fleet, Japan could move virtually at will through these South Sea island paradises, soon to be turned into living hells. Doorman's defeat represented the end of the last substantial naval force in the region capable of withstanding the Japanese. With Penang, Hong Kong, Singapore, Bataan, Rangoon and Malaya under their control, with India and Australia under threat, with all the oil, rubber, tin and bauxite that they needed, with Britain and America humiliated, the Japanese triumph had been as spectacular as any in the history of warfare.

They stumbled over only one obstacle in the hurricane fury of

their advance: the Philippines. Even there, the culpable unpreparedness of their enemy and the fury of their attack at first seemed to
repeat the pattern of Pearl Harbor and Singapore. Their onslaught
was to be only marginally affected by the fighting in the Philippines,
yet out of it was to grow a legend which did as much as anything to
affect the course of the Pacific War and of Japan's post-war history.

When Pearl Harbor was attacked, the American commander in the
Philippines was General Douglas MacArthur, a sixty-one-year-old
former chief of staff recalled from semi-retirement to co-ordinate the
defence of the islands. MacArthur had been transferred from the
American army in order to set up a Philippine Defence Force for his
old friend Manuel Quezon, the country's leader, in advance of
America's granting of independence to the archipelago. He received
little support from Washington, and by late 1941 his task was only
half complete. By December he was in charge of some 134,000
troops, only 12,000 of them American, equipped largely with First
World War Enfield rifles, 100 or so light tanks and no artillery. The
air force consisted of around 70 fighters, 32 bombers just sent to the
islands, and some 40 creaky Philippine aircraft. The defence strategy
for the islands consisted of 'Plan Orange', by which a defending
force would retreat to the mountainous Bataan Peninsula on Manila
Bay, its purpose being to deny access to the enemy.

Just four hours after the attack on Pearl Harbor, a radar base at
Luzon had picked up approaching Japanese aircraft. The fighters
and bombers were scrambled into the air to avoid attack; the
Japanese bombed nothing. The raid was almost certainly a feint. By
the following morning the Philippine 'air force' had returned to base.
At noon a massive surprise attack by the Japanese destroyed 18
bombers and all 70 fighters. After that any threat to Japanese sea
lanes was over; worse, the defending American force had no air
cover and the 14 remaining American planes were flown to Australia
to avoid destruction. The raid had been the worst setback in
MacArthur's career. On 12 December the absence of air cover
caused the surviving Anglo-American fleet to be dispatched to the
East Indies, where they were savaged in the Battle of the Java Sea.

On 22 December the Japanese Fourteenth Army under
Lieutenant-General Masaharu Homma landed at Lingayen Gulf,
some 110 miles north of Manila, with 100 landing-craft and some
80,000 men. The Filipino defenders were routed, but fell back in
good order to one of the few defensible parts of the archipelago, the

Bataan Peninsula, leaving vulnerable Manila in their wake. In all, some 80,000 Filipino and American troops made it there, together with 26,000 refugees. MacArthur himself went to the island fortress of Corregidor, off Bataan, a rocky protrusion covering about two and a half square miles, bristling with guns and mortars and riddled with tunnels which housed around 10,000 defenders. Bataan, by contrast, was some 30 miles long and 15 miles wide, just a couple of huge jungle-clad mountains.

There the defending forces, surrounded and bombarded under what until then seemed the hopeless leadership of MacArthur, provided the first real show of resistance to the Japanese in the Pacific War. Bataan was pounded day and night, as was Corregidor. It became increasingly apparent that promised help from the United States would not arrive – for the good reason that, with the Japanese controlling the Pacific sea and air lines, it would have been highly dangerous to send it. In spite of dwindling food supplies and relentless attack, the Filipino and American forces held out month after month, to the surprise of all observers. MacArthur refused to leave Corregidor until personally ordered to by Roosevelt. The American commander captured some of the flavour of the resistance:

> Our troops were now approaching exhaustion. The guerrilla movement was going well, but on Bataan and Corregidor the clouds were growing darker. My heart ached as I saw my men slowly wasting away. Their clothes hung on them like tattered rags. Their bare feet stuck out in silent protest. Their long bedraggled hair framed gaunt, bloodless faces. Their hoarse, wild laughter greeted the constant stream of obscene and ribald jokes issuing from their parched, dry throats. They cursed the enemy and in the same breath cursed and reviled the United States; they spat when they jeered at the Navy. But their eyes would light up and they would cheer when they saw my battered, and much reviled in America, 'scrambled egg' cap. They would gather round me and pat me on the back and Mabuhay Macarsar me. They would grin – that ghastly skeleton-like grin of the dying – as they would roar in unison 'We are the battling bastards of Bataan – no papa, no mama, no Uncle Sam.'
>
> They asked no quarter and they gave none. They died hard – those savage men – not gently like a stricken dove folding its wings in peaceful passing, but like a wounded wolf at bay, with lips curled back in sneering menace, and always a nerveless hand reaching for that long sharp machete knife which long ago they

had substituted for the bayonet. And around their necks, as we buried them, would be a thread of dirty string with its dangling crucifix. They were filthy, they were lousy and they stank. And I loved them.

For a brief period, a lull set in. The Japanese were exhausted and had not expected MacArthur to continue resistance; the besieged of Bataan were running short of food and water, and by mid-February barely half were fighting fit. MacArthur was criticized for digging in on Corregidor and failing to visit Bataan.

On 11 March, MacArthur left on a fraught and dangerous journey by sea and air to Australia, apparently believing in the heat of battle that he would be able to muster the forces to return and relieve the garrison at Bataan. When he reached Adelaide, the gaunt and haggard general made his most famous statement:

> The President of the United States ordered me to break through the Japanese lines and proceed from Corregidor to Australia for the purpose, as I understand it, of organizing the American offensive against Japan, a primary objective of which is the relief of the Philippines. I came through and I shall return.

In fact, he found not a single combat division in Australia, and very few aircraft capable of penetrating enemy territory, let alone reaching the Philippines. On 8 April the remaining forces in Bataan surrendered and, although earning a salute from the Japanese, were hurried on the notorious 'death march' overland to prison camps. Corregidor finally fell on 6 May. Japan was now in undisputed control of all of East Asia. Australia lay vulnerable to the south; Chinese forces continued to resist to the west. The same month, American code-breakers learnt that the Japanese were planning an invasion of Port Moresby, on the southern coast of New Guinea, which they feared would presage an attack on Australia itself.

In May 1942 it seemed to the Japanese that all their efforts had been rewarded with success. The British and the Americans had been routed, and the Russians had not entered the war against them. Japan's allies in Europe were victorious – the Japanese were on the winning side. A quarter of the world had been conquered in less than six months.

16

THE UNRAVELLING

THE SAME month, as the last beleaguered survivors of the Philippines surrendered, came the first indication that the Japanese might not after all be militarily superhuman or invincible. One of America's foremost aircraft carriers, the USS *Hornet* had succeeded in bringing a number of B-52 bombers to raid Tokyo, the spectacular Doolittle raid, which shocked the Japanese high command; most of the pilots ran out of fuel and crash-landed in China. On 7 May two other carriers, the *Yorktown* and the *Lexington*, were sent to intercept the Japanese invading force near Port Moresby. In the Battle of the Coral Sea, the Japanese carriers *Shoho* and *Shokaku* were badly damaged, while the *Lexington* had to be abandoned. The attempt to capture Port Moresby was blocked. Yamamoto was now determined to provoke a naval battle in order to destroy America's carriers. His fleet set sail for the island of Midway, near Hawaii, with the intention of provoking an American response. As he expected, the Americans decided to make a stand.

By this time the Americans had assembled a fleet which, although smaller than the Japanese one, was respectable. It consisted of three carriers, bearing some 180 aircraft, with cruisers and destroyer escorts. The Japanese had five carriers, with superior battleship escorts, and some 272 aircraft. However, the Americans also had Flying Fortresses stationed on Midway itself. The battle began with a Japanese air raid on Midway, which resulted in the destruction of two-thirds of the fighters stationed there. The Americans responded by playing for time as they brought up their carrier fleet, using the few remaining aircraft at Midway to launch attacks on the Japanese fleet. Thinking they had caught the Japanese napping, American torpedo bombers homed in on the Japanese, only to be shot down by Zero fighters; the Japanese fleet remained largely intact.

During the second wave of American bombing, largely by accident, thirty-seven Dauntless dive-bombers from the USS *Enterprise*, which had temporarily got lost, turned towards the scene of the fighting to see the Zero fighters engaged in action with the torpedo-bombers. Their chief, Lieutenant-Commander Wade McClusky, personally led his aircraft in a surprise attack on the vulnerable Japanese carriers. Three of them were destroyed in the space of five minutes; the fourth fled, only to be found that same afternoon and sunk.

The Battle of Midway marked the turning-point in the naval war. With America's far superior war production machine, the odds were lengthening against Japan in the long term. Over the following two years, the Americans were to produce twenty carriers against the six produced by the Japanese. Midway had been a close-run thing, a battle won almost by accident, but it signalled to the Americans that victory in the Pacific was possible. It showed that there was good reason to divert precious war resources to the Pacific theatre. And at that stage the Americans made a number of crucial decisions that were to determine the course of the Pacific War.

The first was to aim for Japan itself as the central strategic objective. From then on, there was no intention of merely rolling back the Japanese conquests: the aim was nothing less than to strike at the home islands themselves and extract an unconditional surrender. The strategy was to neglect the limbs, and strike at the heart. And from then on the Japanese goal of a negotiated settlement was hopelessly unrealistic.

This led to the second key choice, of how to get there: along the rocky and desolate atolls of the northern Pacific, or by regaining the major islands of the East Indies now held by the Japanese? Finally, there was the fiercely controversial strategy adopted by Roosevelt to concentrate the bulk of American forces in Europe – even though the Japanese attack on Pearl Harbor had triggered the American entry into the war and threatened American interests most directly.

The first choice – to aim for Japan itself – won enthusiastic support. The second created a major inter-service row that at times threatened seriously to damage the American war effort in the Pacific. At the heart of it was the decision to give MacArthur, who had expected control of the entire Pacific area of operations, only half the cake: the chief of naval staff, Admiral King, insisted on setting up a separate Pacific Ocean Area Command under Admiral Chester Nimitz. MacArthur later wrote angrily:

Of all the faulty decisions of the war, perhaps the most inexplicable one was the failure to unify the command in the Pacific ... It cannot be defended in logic, in theory, or even in common sense. Other motives must be ascribed. It resulted in divided effort, the waste, diffusion and duplication of force, and the consequent extension of the war and added casualties and cost. The generally excellent co-operation between the two commands in the Pacific, supported by the goodwill, good nature, and professional qualifications of the numerous personnel involved, was no substitute for the essential unity of direction of centralized authority. The handicaps and hazards unnecessarily resulting were numerous, and many a man lies in his grave today who could have been saved.

In addition, MacArthur volunteered to serve as the subordinate commander, despite his seniority, if the commands were unified. The crucial Battle of Leyte Gulf was nearly to be lost as a result of faulty co-ordination between the two commands. The division of commands meant that while Nimitz and the navy pressed for an 'island-hopping' strategy across the northern atolls to Japan, MacArthur remained committed to the southern route, which also led to the Philippines, to which he had a close emotional attachment and had vowed to return. Later, MacArthur was bitterly to accuse the navy of failing to send him support and supply ships when he needed them, and of wasteful frontal assaults on minor island targets where the Japanese were well dug in. Against that, the protagonists of island-hopping, the navy, could argue that their route to Japan was much more direct and involved assaulting much smaller garrisons than that proposed by MacArthur.

In the end, a messy compromise was reached between the northern and southern routes. MacArthur had the best of the argument, convincing the joint chiefs of staff that victory over Japan was not possible without ending Japanese control of the major islands flanking the Pacific: 'island-hopping' would merely lead to an over-extension of American forces, making them vulnerable to attack from the Japanese-occupied west. Moreover, the large American armies needed for the occupation of Japan could not be moved into place without control of the major territories necessary to support them; an army could not live off barren rock.

There was a great deal of special pleading on both sides. But it is hard not to conclude that while a thrust along the line suggested by MacArthur was essential, the northward route was not in fact indispensable – although there was something to be said for the two-pronged attack eventually adopted (it threw the Japanese off balance and confused them – they could never be sure where to concentrate their forces). Almost certainly, MacArthur was right in urging a unified command: ironically, the American row exactly mirrored Japan's notorious inter-service hatreds and preference for different avenues of military advance.

The navy was given charge of the first major American advance in the war, the attack on Guadalcanal, the strongly fortified Japanese outpost of eastern New Guinea, while MacArthur was given charge of the invasion of New Guinea itself and the attack on Japan's command centre in the south, Rabaul. Even as MacArthur began to plan his campaign, American tactics were thrown into confusion by a major Japanese landing at Buna with the objective of crossing the nearly impenetrable mountain jungle of southern New Guinea in order to seize Port Moresby, the capital. Simultaneously, the Japanese responded furiously to the almost unopposed American landing on Guadalcanal: the Japanese regarded this as a major test of their strength, and threw in everything they could.

The capture of Port Moresby would bring Japan even closer to Australia and provide air bases capable of striking into the Northern Territory. MacArthur was determined to avoid this at all costs. It had seemed impossible that the Japanese could cross the rugged and ferociously hostile Owen Stanley Range. Now a force was sent under General Blamey to cross the jungle-clad mountains from south to north, and try to cut off the supply line of the invaders. Almost simultaneously, the Japanese were ordered to return to Buna, as troops were rushed to the battle at Guadalcanal. The Japanese fought a desperate race back to Buna to avoid being outflanked by Blamey's forces, and in fact broke through to form an enclave along the coast. With incredible difficulty the Americans managed to overwhelm this enclave, and won their first land battle against the Japanese, at a cost of some 3000 dead and more than 5000 wounded.

Meanwhile, Guadalcanal had become an epic. After establishing their beach-head, the marines had to be supplied down a treacherous channel through which ships came under fire on two sides. On 8 August the Japanese surprised an American flotilla, sinking four cruisers and destroying another. The Americans hit back on 24 August, sinking a carrier, a cruiser and a destroyer. However, Japanese reinforcements poured in as the fighting spread across the island, and became ever more intense and bloody. In October the Americans ambushed one of the Japanese carrier convoys known as the 'Tokyo Express'; two days later the Japanese came off best in the Battle of Santa Cruz. In November, during the Battle of Guadalcanal, the Japanese were bloodied; a fortnight later, the Japanese failed in a major attempt to intercept the American supply convoys to Guadalcanal. Only in February, after frenzied fighting, was the struggle brought to an end when the Japanese force was evacuated.

The tide had turned, painfully and bloodily, in the Allies' favour. There was to be much criticism of their decision to battle so hard for Guadalcanal and at such appalling cost, not least from MacArthur. Yet at that stage in the war a grim battle of attrition against the Japanese was almost necessary, in order to drive home the message that they were after all not invincible. After Guadalcanal, the imperial army would never again take the offensive in the Pacific. It fought bitterly to hold on to what it had acquired.

In the new American tactics, a small force of bombers would attack under cover of a small fighter force to seize an airfield from which to stage the next advance. Naval forces under this newly provided air cover would regain the sea lanes. This 'triphibious' approach had the advantages of avoiding frontal attacks and huge casualties, bypassing Japanese strongpoints and neutralizing them by cutting off their lines of supply, and thus isolating their armies and starving them in the battlefields: to 'hit 'em where they ain't'. MacArthur angrily criticized the shortage of aircraft carriers. Because no offensive could proceed without proper air cover, and because there were so few carriers, the American advance was limited to the speed with which air bases could be established on land. Colonel Matsuicho Juio, senior intelligence officer of the Eighth Army Staff later recalled:

> This was the type of strategy we hated most. The Americans, with minimum losses, attacked and seized a relatively weak area, constructed minefields and then proceeded to cut the supply lines to troops in that area. Without engaging in a large-scale operation, our strongpoints were gradually starved out. The Japanese army preferred direct assault, after the German fashion, but the Americans flowed into our weaker points and submerged us, just as water seeks the weakest entry to sink a ship. We respected this type of strategy for its brilliance because it gained the most while losing the least.

The next target was Rabaul, with its large naval base, airfields, and supply depots. MacArthur was determined to engage the enemy as infrequently as possible as he moved up the coast of New Guinea, leap-frogging to the next airstrip and leaving Japanese forces out-flanked with their supplies cut off. In fact the campaign proved much slower and more arduous than expected, requiring a series of landings and difficult amphibious operations. But one by one, his targets were picked off. Woodlark, Kiriwina, and Nassau Bay were seized virtually without casualties. MacArthur's forces then marched on Salamanua, a major base which the Japanese evacuated. Thanks to a brilliant encircling move, MacArthur then forced the Japanese to withdraw also from Lae. The Japanese put up stiff resistance at Finschhafen, which fell on 2 October. The bulk of New Guinea was now in Allied hands.

Meanwhile, a parallel assault was being mounted by naval forces along the Solomon Island chain to the east. The Russell Islands fell in February, New Georgia in June, and Vella Cavela in August. Japanese counterattacks were unsuccessful. By October the Allies were ready to attack Bougainville, the final stepping stone to Rabaul. The US Navy was poised to form one part of the pincer, and MacArthur's forces the other, in Operation Cartwheel, which was intended to surround the Japanese stronghold.

The American air force was now securing victories through a new policy of low-level bombing. In the Battle of the Bismarck Sea, Flying Fortresses sunk four destroyers and a convoy of transport ships. In another aerial engagement in April, Admiral Yamamoto was shot down. MacArthur's advance was then slowed by a prob-ably unnecessary landing on southern New Britain; his Australian forces became bogged down in arduous fighting on the Huon Peninsula.

At Teheran at the end of 1943, Stalin, Roosevelt and Churchill approved a new strategy which allocated greater resources to the Pacific War, and persuaded Admiral Nimitz to go on the offensive in the northern Pacific, in open competition with MacArthur's forces further south. The general was meanwhile given specific goals: the seizure of Kavieng, New Ireland and Manus, to encircle Rabaul further. Meanwhile, Nimitz wasted no time in making a landing on the Marshall Islands, in January 1944, and seized its westernmost island, Eniwetok, in a bloody battle in February.

MacArthur decided to bypass Kavieng, leaving it to wither on the vine, and seize Manus, which he did with relatively light casualties. By this stage tens of thousands of Japanese had been killed, while some 100,000 had been left behind by the Allied advance. American planners then decided that an outright assault on Rabaul, which was encircled, was unnecessary – it too could be neutralized by air bombardment and bypassed. MacArthur was instructed to seize the Admiralty Islands and advance a full 600 miles to Hollandia, along the coast of northern New Guinea. At the end of March his air force caught the Japanese air force at Hollandia napping, and destroyed 300 aircraft; then, with a huge invasion fleet, the Allied forces landed there, taking the Japanese entirely by surprise and forcing most to flee to the hills.

The Japanese, horrified at the two-pronged attack, now resolved to try and contain it with one major gamble: to try to lure American naval forces into a trap, where the Japanese could make use of their control of air-space and the protection of shore-based guns. The project was called Operation A-go. However, the American naval forces made no moves towards the Japanese fleet, preparing to concentrate on island-hopping in the north. On 19–21 June, the Japanese fleet, which had decided to pursue the Americans, met its match. The Battle of the Philippine Sea, which became known colloquially as the Marianas Turkey Shoot, saw the sinking of three Japanese carriers, with two others severely damaged; 330 Japanese planes were lost.

Immediately afterwards, Saipan in the Marianas was landed upon, and after a fierce battle was seized; in July, Guam and Timor also fell after heavy fighting, in which 60,000 Japanese and at least 5000 Americans were killed. The Japanese fleet was now no further threat for several months. MacArthur's forces now moved forward much faster and more self-confidently, to Biak and Noemfoor Island in Geelvink Bay, and Sansapor at the top of the Vogelkop Peninsula. The Americans now effectively controlled the whole of New Guinea, and were only 500 miles from the Philippines.

The joint chiefs of staff were reviewing the situation. With the seizure of the Marianas, which brought American aircraft within strategic bombing distance of Japan, they saw little reason to get bogged down in a long campaign to liberate the Philippines. Better for MacArthur's land forces to be brought under Nimitz's control, Formosa to be seized, and an invasion of Japan proper to be prepared. On 26 January Roosevelt travelled to Pearl Harbor to meet MacArthur, the only senior commander who recommended landing in the Philippines.

MacArthur was by now a legendary figure in America, as much for his Bataan campaign as for his penchant for wading ashore under enemy fire on the occasion of major landings. Now he made a theatrical entrance alongside the cruiser *Baltimore*, carrying the President, arriving in a large open-backed limousine with a police escort. He wore a brown leather services jacket, dark glasses and his 'scrambled egg' floppy campaign hat. He was applauded by the sailors as he came on deck to meet Roosevelt for the first time in seven years. MacArthur was shocked by the change in the President's appearance. 'He was just a shell of the man I had known.'

Admiral Nimitz was already there. He was much less enthusiastic about the naval strategy for seizing Formosa than MacArthur was about seizing the Philippines. MacArthur stated the moral obligation to free the Philippines, but he had more important and rational arguments to hand as well:

> I was in total disagreement with the proposed plan, not only on strategic but psychological grounds. Militarily I felt that if I could secure the Philippines it would enable us to clamp an air and naval blockade on the flow of all supplies from the south to Japan, and thus, by paralysing her industries, force her to early capitulation. I argued against the naval concept of frontal assault against the strongly held island positions of Iwo Jima or Okinawa. In my argument, I stressed that our losses would be far too heavy to justify the benefits to be gained by seizing these outposts. They were not essential to the enemy's defeat, and by cutting them off from supplies, they could be easily reduced and their effectiveness completely neutralized with negligible loss to ourselves. They were not in themselves possessed of sufficient resources to act as main bases in our advance ... To bypass isolated islands was one thing, but to leave in your rear such a large enemy concentration as the Philippines involved serious and unnecessary risks.

MacArthur's arguments won the day: in September, instructions were issued for American forces to aim for the Philippines. It was to remain MacArthur's conviction to the last that a direct invasion of Japan was unnecessary – as indeed were the atomic bombs dropped in order to make such an invasion redundant. With its fleet on the defensive and the Philippines in American hands, he declared, Japan could be strangled economically, becoming the biggest of all examples of his wither-on-the-vine philosophy, and forced to sue for peace.

This view was to be set aside the following year, presumably because it would take too long and almost certainly require a negotiated settlement with Japan. MacArthur was forced to acquiesce reluctantly in the decisions of his superiors. When he became Japan's viceroy for six years, he attempted to put into practice those reforms of Japan's authoritarian warrior society that he believed would justify the sacrifice at Hiroshima and Nagasaki; even in this, however, he was frustrated. One of the most intriguing questions about the Pacific War is whether MacArthur's strategy of slow strangulation might have worked.

For the moment, his policy to liberate the Philippines had been adopted. As American forces prepared for the landings there, the Japanese rounded up their remaining naval forces for a final attempt to stop the invasion: a large Japanese fleet opposed the American fleet at Leyte Gulf in October. The battle, the largest in world naval history, raged for several days and was a close call for the American fleet, part of which had been mistakenly sent off on a wild-goose chase in search of the Japanese carriers, largely as a result of poor co-ordination between Nimitz's forces and MacArthur's. In the end, however, the Japanese lost four carriers, including their flagship, three battleships, six heavy cruisers, three light cruisers and ten destroyers: the fleet was all but destroyed.

The way was now open for the landings on Leyte. MacArthur waded ashore, as was his wont, on 20 October 1944. The landing proved remarkably successful, but the Japanese followed up with four counter-offensives, throwing so many aircraft into the fighting that American control of the air seemed in danger. For a while it looked as if the offensive was stalled, until American aircraft succeeded in sinking a major Japanese convoy carrying reinforcements to Leyte in November. Even so, the Americans remained bogged down in a massive quagmire of mud for several weeks until MacArthur came up with a bold plan to stage a further landing in December at Ormoc, behind Japanese lines. The landing was successful and panicked the Japanese. The impasse was broken.

The same month, the small outpost of Mendoro was attacked and seized with high casualties. An invasion force of 200,000 men was assembled to move on Luzon, the main Philippine island. The Japanese were now fighting a war of attrition, to delay invasion of the home islands. The American fleet supporting MacArthur, under Admiral William Halsey, suffered several setbacks: a typhoon wrecked several ships; an attack on Formosa's airfields was frustrated by the weather; and in January a series of kamikaze attacks sunk a battleship, two cruisers, and a destroyer. But the bulk of the forces landed without opposition.

The Japanese garrison of 27,500 men retreated to mountain strongholds in the centre of the island. Even against light resistance, though, the Americans made slow progress as General Krueger, their commander, feared a break-out from the mountains to cut him off in the rear. MacArthur compelled Krueger to move faster on Manila, where the Americans feared that thousands of prisoners-of-war were about to be butchered. Two further landings were staged to complete the encirclement of the capital. In a spectacular raid, a contingent of MacArthur's army rushed into central Manila, scattering the Japanese forces, to free some 5000 prisoners.

However, the fight to rid the capital of its 20,000 troops, the recapture of Corregidor and Bataan, and the attempt to get the Japanese out of the central mountains were to take several bloody months. The casualty rate was high: some 45,000 Japanese lost their lives, compared to 14,000 Allied troops. With the southern Philippines liberated, Borneo fell also.

After the conclusion of the epic battle for the Pacific, Japan's struggle in the western part of its empire was almost a sideshow. In April 1944 the Japanese launched Operation Ichi-go to try to regain the initiative in China. This proved so successful that it seemed that Chiang Kai-shek's forces might at last be overwhelmed, although they just managed to hold their own until the end of the war.

Another offensive, U-go, had as its objective a thrust from Burma into India, as a pre-emptive strike against what seemed to Japan to be an inevitable British offensive after the successful penetration by Orde Wingate's Chindits. On 6 March General Mutaguchi, surely the most inept Japanese commander of the war, led a major Japanese force across the Chindwin River into India, making for Imphal and Kohima, two cities that commanded the approaches to the Indian plain. General William Slim, the British commander, had expected such a thrust and his defences were well established in the two cities. Try as they might, the Japanese could not take them in spite of the closest and fiercest fighting of the war. On 22 June, after the monsoon had arrived, Mutaguchi finally conceded defeat and led his bedraggled forces back across the swampy roads into Burma before they became impassable. Only 20,000 out of 85,000 survived from the original invasion force.

The final chapter in Japan's encirclement began in February 1945 with the invasion of Iwo Jima by Nimitz's marines. The operation, to secure a few square miles of territory, was appallingly costly: nearly 7000 Americans died and 20,000 were wounded, while all 21,000 Japanese defenders were killed. Okinawa was next. On 1 August the first contingents of what would eventually amount to a force of 250,000 men landed to take on the deeply entrenched Japanese army of 50,000 men.

The battleship *Yamato*, with an escort of a cruiser and eight destroyers, set out on a suicidal mission to delay the American landings. On 7 April she was located by American aircraft and pounded mercilessly, before capsizing with 2300 sailors on board. The cruiser and five of the destroyers were sunk. Thus ended the last naval engagement of the Pacific War. More effective were the attacks by 900 kamikaze aircraft, which wrecked three destroyers and two ammunition ships. Over the following five months, the Americans lost fourteen destroyers and some 5000 dead at sea.

The American advance across Okinawa was painfully slow, as the Japanese resisted bitterly, ridge by ridge. About 4000 Japanese uncharacteristically surrendered in June, although 110,000 others had perished. The Americans lost 21,000 men altogether. MacArthur had argued against frontal attacks on the islands, saying they were inessential to his strangulation plan. In fact the other American commanders had resolved to use Okinawa's anchorages as the staging-point for their invasion of Japan – which in the event was rendered unnecessary by the use of the atomic bombs. The fury of the Japanese resistance at Okinawa and Iwo Jima was the prime argument for dropping the bombs. MacArthur was dryly to observe that the total killed on both islands was greater than in the whole of his campaign from Papua New Guinea to the Philippines.

The epitaph on the Pacific War must be that Japan's defeat was inevitable, written in its very successes early on. The Japanese had played for the highest stakes: by destroying the American fleet at Pearl Harbor, they had ensured that the war would be fought to the finish. They grossly underestimated the American will to resist, believing that their superior motive would overcome the spirit of the supposedly pampered and indolent Americans. They also underestimated the power of American industry to produce ships and guns at a vastly faster rate than they could themselves. As a group of offshore islands, Japan was especially vulnerable to naval attack to cut off its supply routes, and, once the tide had turned in the sea war, Japan's defeat was only a matter of time.

The early Japanese successes were secured by surprise, fanaticism, lightning tactics, and above all the softness of their targets. They had caught the Americans unprepared, sleeping at anchor. They had exposed the weakness of the British forces in Asia while the bulk of the country's war effort was concentrated in Europe. The Dutch were a walk-over. Only the Australians put up serious resistance. The local populations of the areas they occupied did not support their old colonial masters, and were at worst hostile to them and at best indifferent, except in the Philippines. (In fact the Japanese occupation decisively weakened the hold of the colonial powers in the post-war period.) Having for the most part secured easy victories across a land empire one and a half times larger than that of Nazi Germany at its most extensive, they were highly vulnerable to heavy attack. Only ferocity and determination prevented greater Japan from collapsing much more quickly than it did.

That said, both MacArthur and Nimitz staged tactically brilliant campaigns, reversing the Japanese occupation much faster than Washington dared hope. Japan's six-month wonder would have ended much more quickly had the Americans given strategic priority to the Pacific campaign. Instead, Roosevelt had from the first accorded priority to the European threat – even though it was Japan's attack that caused the United States to enter the war. Accordingly, only twenty-nine divisions of some half a million men were to serve at any one time in the Pacific theatre, only a third of them full combat divisions. Japan had around the same number engaged in the Pacific War and a further two and a half million or so committed to China. By contrast, in Europe the United States fielded four million men. There were around the same number of British forces, and twelve million Soviets, ranged against ten million Germans.

The position in Europe was so desperate and critical that Roosevelt's decision was understandable. In retrospect, though, had American forces been more evenly divided between the two theatres, the American success in the Pacific might have been much speedier. It was all the more remarkable that MacArthur and Nimitz achieved so much with so little – virtually an even fight with the occupying Japanese. Although overwhelming American firepower played a major part in the final stages of the war with Japan, that was far from being the case at the beginning. The Americans won a hard and fair fight. The two key questions as far as American strategy was concerned were whether anything was achieved through having competing lines of approach, and whether a policy of economic strangulation would have worked.

17

THE STRUGGLE WITHIN

RINCE KONOYE, who had made the decision to invade Indo-China, resigned after failing to prevent its inevitable conse-quence – a headlong rush by Japan into the Pacific War. Poacher turned gamekeeper Tojo, who had led the Japanese cabinet from behind as war minister, now became prime minister with the task of carrying through the decision to go to war. The illusion was created that Japan was now turning into a military dictatorship. In fact, with the exception of Tojo's appointment, the government remained much the same as it had always been – a mixture of interest groups: the armed forces, the economic superbosses, and the bureaucrats.

Tojo was firmly in the driving seat, but the *zaibatsu* in particular were always in a position to block government decisions. Tojo, in fact, depended upon the goodwill of the *zaibatsu* to meet the huge demands of modern warfare. Three months before Pearl Harbor, after a year of intense debate, the *zaibatsu* had scored a spectacular victory in opposing an attempt by some military leaders to subject them to the control of wartime bureaucracy. Indeed, the Major Industry Association Ordinance was drawn up appropriating power over specific industries to the Industrial Control Associations, in effect giving the cartels absolute control over war material, labour and capital in their industries, with instructions to rationalize smaller firms. This was like appointing a wolf to round up a flock of sheep.

The *zaibatsu* now had the power to gobble up or render dependent their small competitors, and they did so, vigorously. The big four *zaibatsu* doubled their percentage of production from 12 to 24 per cent in the four war years after 1941 – absorbing hundreds of smaller firms. The war years also produced a much larger reliance on heavy industry to produce war material; by the end of the war, heavy industry accounted for four-fifths of Japan's industrial output, compared with around half at the outset. Heavy industry was entirely dominated by the *zaibatsu*.

With Japan's early war successes, the *zaibatsu* moved in behind the soldiers to control the mineral treasures of the East Indies and channel raw materials to Japan. As we have seen, the 'total war' group in the Japanese army, which was now in control and whose senior representative was Tojo, believed in close collaboration with the *zaibatsu*. The group recognized that it would achieve its expansionist aims only in alliance with the cartels. In turn, the *zaibatsu* recognized that their interests could be furthered only by cooperation with the army, in importing the raw materials and finding markets through conquest that had been denied by world recession. The partnership was one of mutual dependence.

As the war developed, however, Tojo and the other military chiefs began to look for a system of central control of production that would result in less autonomy, profiteering and stockpiling by the *zaibatsu*. However, the cartels fought back bitterly to retain their growing share of the spoils. Early in 1943 Tojo sought a measure giving him special powers over the economy, but he was forced to accept a series of reforms giving the *zaibatsu* greater powers than ever. First, his cabinet was enlarged to include more representatives from business. Second, an advisory council of seven leading cartel representatives was set above him. Third, the *zaibatsu* were given control of the administration of a new ministry of munitions, nominally headed by Tojo but in fact run by the deputy minister, Nobusuke Kishi, later to become a post-war prime minister. Fourth, a Mitsui executive, Ginjiro Fujihara, was appointed to the cabinet in November 1943 as a kind of *zaibatsu* minder for Tojo.

Under the new provision, big business's control over the economy was actually strengthened. Increasingly it began to seem that the *zaibatsu* dictated politics to the military, rather than the other way round. But there is no evidence to suggest that they were a restraining influence on the armed forces of the period – the high noon of Japan's aggression abroad – until late in the war.

The other powers in the land – the bureaucracy, the imperial household and the emperor himself – were steadily declining in influence. Despite Hirohito's reservations about the desirability of war, after the decision to go to war had been made he seemed to regard it as his duty to dedicate himself to prosecuting the war effort as vigorously as possible. Many observers of Japan have noted as a national characteristic the ability to press for one course of action, be frustrated, then prosecute the reverse course with equal fervour. The emperor was in this mould, which in truth is also a characteristic of a weak mind not overendowed with intelligence.

The exasperation with Hirohito that both Konoye and Kido felt during the war, when the emperor who had had such misgivings about going to war seemed at times to be in thrall to Tojo's fervour, is thus explained, and not in terms of an evil or Machiavellian personality, which there is nothing in Hirohito's actions before or after the war to suggest.

Kawahara, his biographer, writes:

Hirohito had signed the declaration of war on December 8th [1942], in spite of his reservations, under pressure from the military. After hostilities began, he felt duty-bound to support the war effort. He put aside his former misgivings and, along with the nation, concentrated on the task of defeating the Allies. After the outbreak of the China war, Hirohito had given up golf; thereafter he also gave up horseback riding. Apart from a visit to the Grand Shrine at Ise and one to the Nasu Detached Palace, Hirohito did not leave Tokyo until the war ended. He lost seven or eight kilos, as he subsisted on wartime rations. Towards the end of the war, when the news was all bad, he suffered a nervous breakdown. He would forget that he had watered his plants and water them again. He took to pacing up and down his room, and railing impotently against the military, to the despair of his aides.

It is certainly true that Hirohito did his best for the war effort and indulged in celebrations at Japanese victories; little else could be expected of the head of a nation at war, with soldiers dying in his service, even if he believed that conflict had been the consequence of misguided policies. Short of abdicating, Hirohito could hardly have indulged himself in open criticism or expressions of sadness at Japanese victories. Kido, his chief adviser, found him 'poised and serene [with] not the slightest anxiety in his behaviour' following Pearl Harbor. The emperor was 'very cheerful after the fall of Singapore, attributing the successes of the operation to advance planning'.

Yet in February 1942, only three months into the war, Hirohito was talking of peace, although more as one dictated to the Allies than as the consequence of negotiation. Still, in Japan's jingoistic climate it was a surprising thing to do. He told Kido: 'Let us not lose any opportunity to end the war. It would not be good for humanity if the war were prolonged and the tragedy spread. If it does go on, the Army will get worse. We have to consider the situation carefully and plan accordingly.'

Hirohito's prime reservations about the war were concerned with its winnability, not its morality. There is no record of whether the emperor was aware of the atrocities committed in China, Malaya and the Philippines, although he showed no emotion to Kido when informed of the Bataan death march afterwards.

With the Battle of Midway, the tide began for the first time to turn in the direction Hirohito had always feared; but he remained cool. 'It's really regrettable. It's a shame. But I've given orders to the chiefs of staff not to lose our sense of combat, not to become passive as far as operations are concerned.' Early in 1943 Buna was lost. Hirohito remarked that the operation 'must be rated a failure but if this can be the basis of future success it may turn out to be a salutory lesson'. By April 1943, Hirohito was striking a more querulous, gloomy note:

> You make all sorts of excuses like thick fog and so on, but this should have been taken into consideration beforehand. I wonder if the Army and the Navy talk to each other at all?. . . We can't win with this kind of lack of co-operation. If we go on fighting like this we will only make China rejoice, confuse neutrals, dismay our allies and weaken the Co-Prosperity Sphere. Isn't there any way, somehow, somewhere, of closing in on a United States force and destroying it?

Two months later he told Tojo harshly, 'You keep saying the imperial army is invincible but whenever the enemy lands, you lose the fight. You have never been able to repulse an enemy landing. If we don't stop them somewhere, where, I ask you, will it all end?' After the Japanese withdrawal from Guadalcanal, the emperor scolded, 'The military underrated the Allies; their sacrifice was in vain.' Hirohito undoubtedly reflected the views of both the bureaucracy and the imperial household. But for long no criticism of the war effort was to be heard from the *zaibatsu* ministers in the government, whose alliance with the armed forces remained intact as defeat followed defeat.

However, the search was on for a way to extract Japan from the war. By early 1944 this involved Kido as well as the almost disgraced figure of Konoye, for some time an advocate of early peace. The emperor, having been a relatively late convert to the war, now seemed reluctant to believe it was definitely lost: he persuaded Tojo, who was growing ever more isolated, to take on the roles of foreign minister and war minister in order to streamline the Japanese war effort. Presiding over this immense bureaucratic empire, Tojo had no alibis when Nimitz's forces astounded Japan by taking Saipan in mid-1944. The Americans were now within bombing distance of Japan itself. In the emperor's eyes the army had made a severe mistake in committing Japan to defend Rabaul in the south and neglecting the defence of Saipan, close to home and much more important strategically. Tojo had no choice but to resign after the fall of Saipan as his cabinet enemies, now joined by the *zaibatsu* representatives, combined to force him out.

At this stage, Kido and Konoye were discussing ways of initiating peace talks, and even of forcing Hirohito's abdication in favour of his youngest brother, Prince Takamatsu, who, unlike the more bellicose Chichibu, had always inclined towards the peace faction; but they merely represented a tiny minority in the government. A moderate, General Koiso, was appointed to succeed Tojo. With the beginning of the Allied campaign to liberate the Philippines and start massive aerial bombardment of Tokyo, all hope of turning the tide evaporated. The question for the armed forces, their *zaibatsu* allies, and the bureaucracy was how to secure the best possible peace terms.

In January 1945, it seemed that Hirohito too was beginning to favour talks, albeit very late in the day: 'Now a decisive battle will have to be fought on Leyte as Luzon has been lost . . . We will have to conceal this from the people . . . It's reported that the US Army intends to land at Luzon. The war situation in the Philippines is extremely grave.'

In March the saturation raid on Tokyo was staged which killed some 100,000 people (more than were to die at either Hiroshima or Nagasaki). Eight days later, Hirohito toured the city and remarked sadly to Kido: 'After the Great Kanto Earthquake, everything was so totally, cleanly burnt and destroyed that one did not feel a sense of shock. But this is far more tragic. It pains me deeply. Tokyo has become "scorched earth".'

In May a large part of the Imperial Palace was burnt down, although the shrine of the sacred mirror was spared. The Meiji Shrine was destroyed the same night. The government now had to confront reality. Tojo and the army continued to urge resistance, arguing that America could be lured into a truly bloody invasion of Formosa which would force them to negotiate terms. Tojo also tried to secure the appointment of General Hata, the war minister, as prime minister, to succeed the caretaker Koiso. Hirohito, knowing that a new prime minister would have to assume responsibility for the surrender, compelled a distinguished elder statesman, Admiral Kantaro Suzuki, survivor of the death squads of the February 1936 coup, to take the job. All but the army were now reconciled to the inevitability of defeat.

In these dark days, one section of the elite was still carefully protecting its interests. The *zaibatsu* had turned decisively against the war. For them the danger had begun with Tojo's attempts to wrest control of war production from them at the height of the Pacific War, which they bitterly and successfully resisted. They were now appalled by the destruction wrought by the B-29s upon their property, and feared that workers would begin to revolt. They pressed for the 'nationalization' of industry and for setting up an 'industrial army' among the workforce subject to military discipline, and thus banned from strikes or absenteeism.

Under the terms of the nationalization proposal, the state agreed temporarily to underwrite the major industries and to restore them to the *zaibatsu* after the war; formal ownership would remain in *zaibatsu* hands, as would operating control of the companies concerned. The state would be responsible only for their losses and the costs of reconstruction. Army officers were given the task of organizing a huge civilian militia into which the whole nation was effectively conscripted, to prevent any insurrections against the elites responsible for having reduced Japan to rubble. T. A. Bisson, the American economist, argues that the *zaibatsu*'s representatives nevertheless remained in control of the two cabinets that followed the fall of Tojo, and that they hugely increased their share of plant and capital at the expense of the smaller producers.

One further absurdity was now to ensue: Japan had lost most of its empire and was cut off from its forces in those areas isolated by the Allied advance. The country was now being subjected to the most awesome and savage punishment. Saturation bombing raids carried out from American and British carriers, as well as the Marianas, Iwo Jima and Okinawa, had destroyed nearly half the built-up area in sixty cities. The large urban sprawl from Tokyo to Yokohama lay in ruins; Sosaka, Nagoya and Iwaki were devastated. In addition, America's submarines were waging a remorseless war of attrition, virtually completely cutting Japan's external lines of supply. There was not the slightest chance that Japan could break out of its encirclement. Its major industries had virtually come to a halt, its fleet was confined to port, and it was dangerously short of supplies and spare parts. Yet, though their country lay in ruins around them, Japan's army chiefs would still not admit to their own people that the country was defeated.

Suzuki, the new prime minister, was no friend of the militarists, but he too felt unable to accept the inevitable, and clutched at one last straw. That straw was Russian mediation on Japan's behalf. It was a ludicrous hope: the Russians were Japan's traditional worst enemy. Suzuki offered to hand over to Russia southern Sakhalin, the northern Kuriles, and northern Manchuria, as well as a handful of cruisers and raw materials from the south (which the Japanese could not however deliver, as the supply lines there had been cut). The hope was that, in return, Stalin might be induced not just to mediate with the West, but also to provide Japan with desperately needed oil for the last battle which, the Japanese believed, would compel the Americans to accept a negotiated peace.

Suzuki's proposal was a non-starter. The Soviet Union had long looked upon Japan with intense suspicion; they had already agreed at Yalta to declare war on Japan after Hitler's defeat. They stood to gain much in such a war. When Suzuki took office, the Soviets told him they would not renew their neutrality pact with Japan. The prime minister pleaded with them to reconsider, and would accept neither the repeated rebuffs nor the sound advice of the Japanese ambassador in Moscow. In July, with the fall of Okinawa, the government tried to send Prince Konoye, one of their elder statesmen, to Moscow to seek Soviet mediation with America. The Soviets brusquely brushed the proposal aside, although Stalin reported it to Roosevelt at Potsdam.

There the Allies drew up their proposals for unconditional surrender, making some modifications to their original terms: they hinted that the office of emperor might, after all, be permitted to survive. The offer was not spelt out, however; nor was there any explicit warning of the possible dropping of the atomic bomb. Suzuki, while working towards Japanese acceptance of the Potsdam declaration in cabinet, referred to its terms with disdain at a press conference. Truman would wait no longer.

18

DANCE OF DEATH

O N 6 AUGUST, 'Little Boy' was dropped on Hiroshima. When Hirohito heard reports of the destruction there, he was, for the first time since February 1936, goaded into decisive action, overruling the views of his advisers, the army and the cabinet:

> No matter what happens to my safety we must put an end to this war as quickly as possible, so that this tragedy will not be repeated ... Since it has reached the point where such new weaponry is being deployed, we cannot continue this war any further. It is impossible. We no longer have the luxury of waiting for an opportune time to begin negotiations.

On 8 August the Soviet Union declared war on Japan, and their armies swept brutally into Manchuria, quickly gaining total control: the Kwantung Army melted before them. The Manchurian Incident had at last turned full circle: nemesis was complete. The following day, 'Fat Man' was dropped on Nagasaki. Incredibly, even though Japan was surrounded on all sides, confronted by the Soviet Union, America and Britain, and was now losing Manchuria in addition to the rest of the empire, even though many major cities had been reduced to rubble, even though two atomic bombs had been dropped, the country was still not to yield without a struggle. Many senior army officers really did seem to believe that annihilation was preferable to surrender. The next few hours were to be the emperor's finest, after a bad war, and the army's most demented.

The chief, bitter protagonist of peace was Shigenori Togo, the foreign minister, who was utterly outspoken and unfearful in his quest. He was arrogant, intellectually self-confident, and at sixty-two a comparative youngster in Japanese politics. Seventy-seven-year-old Suzuki, the prime minister, a moderate from the imperial household elite, was verbose, sleepy-headed, vague and often indecisive. They were the only two civilian members of Japan's top policy-making body at this stage, the Supreme War Council. Incredibly, the day before Nagasaki this group had failed to meet because one of its members had 'more pressing' business than to discuss war and peace.

At eight o'clock on Thursday 9 August, Togo had arrived at Suzuki's house. The day was already hot. Suzuki agreed that the council must meet, and Togo went to call on his sole military ally, the navy minister and former premier, Admiral Yonai. The council met at eleven o'clock, just half an hour before the Nagasaki bomb exploded. Suzuki opened the proceedings by recommending that the government accept the terms of the Potsdam Proclamation. Yonai, the moderate who years earlier had been forced out of office as prime minister because he opposed the alliance with Germany and Italy, also urged acceptance. Togo's position was well known. The only condition the moderates sought from the Allies was some reassurance on the position of the emperor.

The other three flatly opposed surrender unless a number of other conditions were met as well: a nominal occupation force, Japan's right to try its own war criminals, and the demobilization of Japanese troops by their own officers. The purpose was clear: to try to preserve the illusion to the Japanese army and people that the country had not in fact surrendered. Face was still everything – even worth fighting to the death for. The leader of the hardline faction was, unsurprisingly, the war minister, General Anami, a stolid serving officer of no great imagination, lacking in Togo's messianic fervour, but respected by his men. The army chief of staff, General Umezu, and the navy chief, Admiral Toyoda, were also opposed to surrender.

Togo angrily rebuffed Anami, saying the Allies would refuse to negotiate such terms. Umezu retorted that the Japanese had not yet lost the war and could still inflict great damage on the enemy. Togo answered that Japan would certainly not be able to withstand a second assault. At one o'clock the council adjourned, deadlocked. At half past two a meeting of the full cabinet began. Togo again argued the case for peace. Anami replied with stubborn self-delusion:

We cannot pretend to claim that victory is certain, but it is far too early to say that the war is lost. That we will inflict severe losses on the enemy when he invades Japan is certain, and it is by no means impossible that we may be able to reverse the situation in our favour, pulling victory out of defeat. Furthermore, our army will not submit to demobilization. Our men will not lay down their arms. And since they know they are not permitted to surrender, since they know that a fighting man who surrenders is liable to extremely heavy punishment there is really no alternative for us but to continue the war . . . We must fight the war through to the end, no matter how great the odds against us.

He was supported by the conservative home affairs minister, Genki Abe, who said he could not guarantee civil peace if the order was issued to surrender. However, the *zaibatsu* ministers were unanimously in favour of peace. The ministers of agriculture, commerce, transport and munitions argued that the country was now finally exhausted. At ten o'clock the cabinet adjourned, having failed to resolve its differences and reach the necessary unanimity.

There was nothing for it. Togo and Suzuki realized that the emperor would have to intervene – even though there was no provision in the constitution for him to do so. At ten minutes to midnight, the emperor arrived to take his place at a further meeting of the Supreme War Council, which was also attended by the cabinet secretary, Sakomizu, and the president of the privy council, Baron Hiranuma. They met, in uniforms and morning suits, in a hot and stuffy 18-foot by 30-foot bunker. Togo once again set out the case for surrender; Anami for fighting on. Hiranuma, a silly old man, aligned himself with the hardliners, though he had no formal vote. Anami settled back in his seat with satisfaction; the war party was beginning to prevail.

Suzuki rose suddenly: 'Your Imperial Majesty's decision is required as to which proposal should be adopted,' he said. Anami was caught off guard. The emperor, speaking as prearranged, declared that continuing the war could only result in the annihilation of the Japanese people and an extension of the suffering of all humanity. It was obvious that Japan could no longer fight, and its ability to defend its own shores was doubtful. 'That it is unbearable for me to see my loyal troops disarmed goes without saying . . . But the time has come to bear the unbearable – I give my sanction to the proposal to accept the Allied Proclamation on the basis outlined by the foreign minister.' Then he left the room. Suzuki proposed that

His Majesty's decision be adopted as the decision of the council. There was no dissent from Anami.

At around two in the morning the cabinet met and resolved to accept the Potsdam Declaration, 'with the understanding that the said declaration does not comprise any demand which prejudices the prerogatives of His Majesty as a sovereign ruler'. That morning, Anami summoned his senior officers. 'We have no alternative but to abide by the emperor's decision,' he said. 'Whether we fight on or whether we surrender now depends on the enemy's reply to our note. No matter which we do, you must remember that you are soldiers, you must obey orders, you must not deviate from strict military discipline. In the crisis that faces us, the uncontrolled actions of one man could bring about the ruin of the entire country.' An officer asked if the war minister was actually contemplating surrender. Anami slammed his swagger stick down on the table. 'Anyone who isn't willing to obey orders will have to do so over my dead body,' he told his men – and in Japan this was no mere figure of speech. Japan waited for the reply throughout the following day, and were still waiting on the morning of 11 August.

That morning, a group of hard-line officers met to consider the next step. Lieutenant-Colonel Masahiko Takeshita, General Anami's brother-in-law, presided. Among the officers present was a pale, thin-faced fanatic, Major Kenji Hatanaka. It was resolved that the Imperial Palace be seized and the emperor placed under the 'protection' of the hard-liners. Suzuki and Tojo were marked down for assassination, as was the emperor's chief adviser, Marquis Kido. It was February 1936 all over again.

Just past midnight on 12 August, the Allies' reply was heard: the Japanese acceptance was agreed to, on the condition that the Japanese government and the authority of the emperor would be 'subject to' the Supreme Commander of the Allied Powers. Anami and Hiranuma saw Suzuki immediately afterwards and persuaded him that this demand was unacceptable and that Japan must fight on. Togo was appalled when he heard that the prime minister had changed his mind, and had Kido summon the elderly Suzuki to tell him that surrender was the express wish of the emperor. Suzuki bowed to imperial authority, and reversed himself once again.

Meanwhile, Anami, who had been put under intense pressure from his fanatical juniors, was wondering whether to ask Japan's senior officers to appeal as a body to the emperor to reject the Allied terms. To his astonishment, General Umezu, the army chief of staff, then told him that he had changed his own hard-line opinion and now favoured surrender. But by the next day, 13 August, Umezu had reverted to his previous position, and the Supreme War Council was again divided, three–three, on whether to accept the Allies' final terms. The cabinet also split along predictable lines.

Throughout the day, rebellious groups of officers began to get organized. A number of them went to see General Anami, requesting that martial law be declared and the Allied terms rejected. The war minister was non-committal. At ten-thirty the following morning, the Supreme War Council was again convoked. Once again, the split was three–three. The emperor now spoke, while those present sobbed quietly. It was an absolute pronouncement from what the Japanese labelled the Voice of the Crane (an imperial command which, like a crane, could still be heard in the sky after the bird has passed):

> Although some of you are apprehensive about the preservation of the national structure, I believe that the Allied reply is evidence of the good intentions of the enemy. The conviction and resolution of the Japanese people are, therefore, the most important consideration. That is why I favour acceptance of the reply . . .
>
> If we continue the war, Japan will be altogether destroyed. Although some of you are of the opinion that we cannot completely trust the Allies, I believe that an immediate and peaceful end to the war is preferable to seeing Japan annihilated. As things stand now the nation still has a chance to recover.
>
> I am reminded of the anguish Emperor Meiji felt at the time of the Triple Intervention. Like him, I must bear the unbearable now and hope for the rehabilitation of the country in the future . . .
>
> As the people of Japan are unaware of the present situation, I know they will be deeply shocked when they hear of our decision. If it is thought appropriate that I explain the matter to them personally, I am willing to go before the microphone.

Following the meeting, Anami informed his brother-in-law, Takeshita, that he would abide by the imperial decision. In addition, he would not resign from the government – thus drawing upon himself the final responsibility for the army's acceptance of the emperor's decision. Had he resigned, the government would have fallen and the country been plunged into chaos. Whether Anami secretly accepted that Japan had no realistic alternative, but had been going through the motions on the army's behalf, or whether he felt he must obey a direct command of the emperor, can only be surmised. The war minister summoned another meeting of his senior officers. The atmosphere in the room was electric.

> The army . . . will be like the rest of the country, obey the emperor's command . . . one of a soldier's chief virtues is obedience. The future of Japan is no longer in doubt, but nor will it be an easy future. You officers must realise that death cannot absolve you of your duty. Your duty is to stay alive and do your best to help your country along the path to recovery – even if it means chewing grass and eating earth and sleeping in the fields!

The cabinet spent most of the remainder of the day arguing fruitlessly about the exact wording of the surrender. The argument was over the phrase, 'the war situation grows more unfavourable to us every day', favoured by the navy minister, Admiral Yonai, and 'the war situation has not developed to Japan's advantage', favoured by General Anami. Both were massive understatements; in the end, Anami's wording prevailed.

That night, at around eleven o'clock, Hirohito himself twice recorded the imperial rescript announcing surrender. It was another act of outstanding bravery. No emperor had ever broadcast before, no ordinary Japanese had ever heard the voice of their living god. In doing so, Hirohito was to render it impossible for ordinary soldiers to claim they had not received his direct order to surrender; it could not be argued that 'treacherous' advisers had issued the order in his name. The message itself was astonishing. It was the first time in Japan's thousands of years of recorded history that the nation had been defeated and was to undergo occupation: the concept of Japan's invincibility was threatened by the broadcast; surrender up to that point had been considered an act of shame beyond measure. But if the emperor ordered it, even the unthinkable could be borne – indeed, it became the duty of ordinary Japanese.

The announcement was carefully crafted in order to preserve the country's self-respect. More than that: it was the birth of the myth of Japan's undefeat, which was to become as potent and dangerous as the legend that arose in Germany after the First World War, that of the *Dolschstoss* – the Stab in the Back – according to which the German armies marching back in 1918 had not lost the war, but merely been betrayed by treacherous civilian politicians. Out of this seed of untruth was born the dark avenging angel of Nazism a generation later. The argument that Japan's armies had not been defeated, merely forced to yield by the atomic bomb – the 'new and most cruel bomb' – was born in the emperor's surrender broadcast. It is worth setting out in full:

> After pondering deeply the general trends of the world and the actual conditions obtaining in our empire today, we have decided to effect a settlement of the present situation by resorting to an extraordinary measure.
>
> We have ordered our government to communicate to the governments of the United States, Great Britain, China, and the Soviet Union that our government accepts the provisions of their Joint Declaration.
>
> To strive for the common prosperity and happiness of all nations as well as the security and well-being of our subjects is the solemn obligation which has been handed down by our imperial ancestors and which lies close to our heart.
>
> Indeed, we declared war on America and Britain out of our sincere desire to ensure Japan's self-preservation and the stabilization of East Asia, it being far from our thoughts either to infringe upon the sovereignty of other nations or to embark on territorial aggrandizement.
>
> But now the war has lasted for nearly four years. Despite the best that has been done by everyone – the gallant fighting of the military and naval forces, the diligence and assiduity of our servants of the state, and the devoted service of our one hundred million people – the war situation has developed not necessarily to Japan's advantage, while the general trends of the world have all turned against her interest.
>
> Moreover, the enemy has begun to deploy a new and most cruel bomb, the power of which to do damage is, indeed, incalculable, taking the toll of many innocent lives. Should we continue to fight, not only would it result in an ultimate collapse and obliteration of the Japanese nation, but it would also lead to the total extinction of human civilization.
>
> Such being the case, how are we to save the millions of our subjects, or to atone ourselves before the hallowed spirits of our imperial ancestors? This is the reason why we have ordered the acceptance of the provisions of the powers of the Joint Declaration.
>
> We cannot but express the deepest regret to our allied nations of East Asia, who have consistently co-operated with the Empire towards the emancipation of East Asia.

The thought of these officers and men as well as others who have fallen in the fields of battle, who have died at their posts of duty, or who have met with untimely death and all their bereaved families pains our heart night and day.

The welfare of the wounded and the war-sufferers, and of those who have lost their homes and livelihood, are the objects of our profound solicitude.

The hardships and sufferings to which our nation is to be subjected hereafter will certainly be great. We are keenly aware of the inmost feelings of all of you, our subjects. However, it is according to the dictates of time and fate that we have resolved to pave the way for a grand peace for all the generations to come by enduring the unendurable and suffering what is unsufferable.

Having been able to safeguard and maintain the structure of the imperial state, we are always with you, our good and loyal subjects, relying upon your sincerity and integrity.

Beware most strictly of any outbursts of emotion which may engender needless complications, or any fraternal contentions and strife which may create confusion, lead you astray and cause you to lose the confidence of the world.

Let the entire nation continue as one family from generation to generation, ever firm in its faith in the imperishability of its sacred land, and mindful of its heavy burden of responsibility and of the long road before it.

Unite your total strength, to be devoted to construction for the future. Cultivate the ways of rectitude, foster nobility of spirit, and work with resolution – so that you may enhance the innate glory of the imperial state and keep pace with the progress of the world.

The broadcast must stand as one of the most dishonest utterances by any head of state in human history, outside the annals of Nazi Germany. The government, rather than the emperor, was of course responsible for its contents. But a number of points stand out immediately. First, there is no mention of a surrender. In fact, Japan is presented as taking the initiative: 'to effect a settlement of the present situation by resorting to an extraordinary measure'. For simple Japanese, who depended on official lies and propaganda for information, it would be hard to resist the conclusion that Japan itself had initiated the quest for peace out of its own sense of humanity. Further, the emperor merely accepted the provisions of the Joint Declaration by the Allies. For all the remorse shown, this might have been a commercial transaction. To ordinary Japanese who wished to delude themselves (a great many, to their credit, did not), this was no surrender.

Second, Japan emphatically denied having done any wrong. On the contrary, it had declared war on Britain and America out of a 'sincere desire to ensure Japan's self-preservation and the stabilization of East Asia, it being far from [their] thoughts either to infringe upon the sovereignty of other nations or to embark on territorial aggrandizement'. Even for someone who accepts the Japanese version of events – that its legitimate colonial expansion had inadvertently over-provoked the Western powers – this statement is a startling piece of effrontery. It would be hard to view the creation of what was probably the largest (if one of the shortest-lived) empires in human history as not infringing upon the sovereignty of others or engaging in territorial aggrandizement. For Japan to express its regret to its 'allies' in East Asia for surrendering to them and' the West, after fifteen years of systematic murder, rape and looting was barefaced to a degree. Japan was apologizing for removing the jackboot from the necks of its colonies.

Third, Japan did not acknowledge military defeat, only that the war had 'developed not necessarily to Japan's advantage', while world trends had turned against its interests. The string of devastating reversals along two fronts in the Pacific and a third in India and Burma might never have happened: what had happened was that a 'new and most cruel bomb' had been deployed which might lead to the obliteration of the Japanese nation. Undefeated in the field, morally in the right, Japan had to yield before the inhuman atomic perfidy of the enemy. The country had its alibi for defeat.

Finally, the Japanese were exhorted to enhance the 'innate glory of the imperial state' – the very regime that had led them to the present humiliation and devastation. Thus ordinary Japanese, cocooned from reality by wartime propaganda, were now to believe that the Pacific War was largely the consequence of Western hostility to the peaceful, idealistic Japanese state which had been intent on liberating the peoples of Asia; and that Japan had sued for peace in the interests of avoiding overwhelming human suffering after the horrific nuclear attacks at Hiroshima and Nagasaki, which wholly eclipsed any alleged excesses by the Japanese forces in the past. Japan, of course, had not been decisively defeated. The bombs had purged the nation of both the shame of defeat and its guilt for starting the war and committing innumerable atrocities on a scale never seen before.

Throughout the broadcast there was no hint of guilt, regret, remorse, or acknowledgement of error. Japan was not to blame for the war, but its course had gone a little wrong recently and the bomb threatened the nation with extinction. So peace had been agreed upon. That was all. The bombs wiped the slate clean: they were as cathartic and purgative of shame and guilt for the nation as committing suicide would be for an individual. Those blinding flashes of bluish white light and the immense suffering they caused were as cleansing and 'beautiful' a method of absolving a nation of guilt as the rites of *seppuku* for a warrior who had been defeated or dishonoured.

The tapes were hidden carefully away, and the emperor left the broadcasting studio with tears in his eyes. But apparently he had little to cry about, for Japan had not acknowledged its surrender. It is legitimate to suppose that the whole huge pretence was not merely the necessary face-saving for a people brainwashed into thinking that loss of pride was all, but rather that the vast majority of ordinary Japanese knew defeat for what it was, yet preferred to go about it with dignity, rather like a businessman who has suffered financial ruin, but still puts on an impeccable suit and dutifully leaves for the office each morning. There must certainly have been an element of this for ordinary Japanese. Yet the sheer extent of the lie leads to the conclusion that a large part of the Japanese establishment had, in spite of all the evidence to the contrary, come to believe its propaganda: that Japan could have fought on had the bombs not been dropped; certainly many senior army officers did. Japan was undefeated, and could still hold its head high.

The text of the broadcast actually went too far, in the opinion of one section of the army, who sought to stop it going out. The conspirators, led by Major Hatanaka, had a simple plan: to use the Imperial Guards, the emperor's personal bodyguards, to seize control of the Imperial Palace and isolate the emperor; to block the surrender broadcast; and to win over the Eastern Army, which commanded Tokyo and its surroundings. The first snag, however, was that the commander of the Imperial Guard, General Takeshi Mori, would not join the conspiracy. Hatanaka soon sorted that out: at one o'clock in the morning he went into Mori's office and shot him; another insurgent decapitated his brother-in-law, who was also there. The conspirators attached the dead commander's seal to their orders for securing the palace, which were promptly carried out.

Lieutenant-Colonel Ida, the top-ranked conspirator, was sent to secure the support of the Eastern Army, which he failed to obtain. The duty officers preferred to wait until General Tanaka, the commander, who had gone to bed, turned up in the morning. Meanwhile a number of senior officials were rounded up and imprisoned in a shed. Lieutenant-Colonel Takeshita was sent to secure the support of his brother-in-law, the war minister, General Anami, who just at that moment was preparing to kill himself in atonement for assuming the responsibility of surrender on behalf of the Japanese army.

There was a mixture of Shakespearian tragedy and almost comic pathos about the scene as Takeshita was invited by his brother-in-law to join in a heavy drinking session while he prepared himself for death. Madness raged outside, while Anami grew more and more drunk, and Takeshita prevaricated, unable to find the courage, in the presence of imminent death, to urge the minister to join the coup. Some two hours of steady drinking and talking later, Lieutenant-Colonel Ida went to the war minister's residence to find out what had delayed Takeshita. The official Japanese account picks up the story:

'Now come on,' said Anami, 'pull yourself together, and let's drink our sake. I don't know how long it will be before we have our next sake party together – in some other place.' He laughed heartily at his joke.

The others joined him. The drinking resumed. Anami's round face grew rosier.

'If you drink too much,' said Takeshita, in a worried tone, 'your hand might slip, you might not succeed in killing yourself.'

'Don't worry,' Anami replied genially. 'I haven't drunk too much yet. Besides, drink helps because it improves the circulation – the blood will flow more quickly. And don't forget I'm a fencer! Fifth grade. No, I'm not likely to fail. Relax!' Anami's hearty laugh rang out.

His guests smiled, as etiquette demanded.

In the meantime, Marquis Kido's house had been attacked. At four in the morning General Tanaka, the loyal commander of the Eastern Army, arrived at his office, arrested those of his officers who were in on the plot, and then drove to the Imperial Palace. By now the party sent to kill Suzuki was on its way to his private house. By a matter of minutes, because the rebels took a wrong turning, Suzuki escaped the trap and fled to the house of a friend. The infuriated soldiers burnt Suzuki's house down.

At last, some time after five o'clock, General Anami committed *seppuku*:

The war minister rose and put on a white shirt. 'This was given to me', he said, 'by the emperor when I was his aide-de-camp. He had worn it himself. I can think of nothing I prize more highly – and so I intend to die wearing it.'

Anami then pinned his decorations to a dress uniform and put the uniform on, after which he removed it, folded it properly, and laid it in front of the Tokonoma. 'When I am dead,' he said, 'will you drape the uniform over me?'

Takeshita nodded, unable to speak; Ida felt his eyes fill with tears.

Anami took a photograph of his second son, Koreakira, who had died at the age of twenty-one during the China Incident, and placed it on top of his folded uniform in front of the Tokonoma . . .

When Takeshita returned, after seeing Okido, he paused in the corridor, behind the kneeling, but upright figure of the war minister. Then Takeshita also dropped to his knees. Anami had drawn the dagger across his belly and was now, the dagger in his left hand, looking for the carotid artery on the right side of his neck.

Anami began to sway. The dagger swept across his neck, and a torrent of blood pulsed out. Yet Anami's body was still erect.

'Shall I help you?' asked Takeshita, in quiet, almost inaudible tones.

'No.' There was nothing unusual about the war minister's voice; he might have been answering the most ordinary of questions. 'Leave me.'

Takeshita went out into the garden. Ida lay sobbing on the bare ground.

More than an hour after he had committed his act of *seppuku*, General Anami still knelt in the same place, his body still erect. The blood still flowed from his wounds.

'Aren't you in agony?' Takeshita whispered.

But there was no reply. The war minister seemed to have lost consciousness. Takeshita took the dagger that lay beside him and thrust it deep into the right side of Anami's neck. The body fell.

General Tanaka, meanwhile, had brushed past the armed sentries at the palace and told the rebellious officers there they were now under his control. He then marched into the *gobunko*, the imperial library, where the emperor had been sleeping lightly through the night, oblivious to the events around him. The building had been shuttered and barred by the flapping, elderly imperial chamberlains. Tanaka was allowed in when he informed them that the coup was over.

Major Hatanaka, whose men had failed to find the tapes of the imperial broadcast, had by now broken into the offices of the broadcasting station in an attempt to seize ten minutes of air time. After Tanaka had freed the emperor and apologized for the 'disrespect' his late arrival might have caused him, bowing five times, he also found Kido, who had been hidden in a small room under the imperial household ministry. Hatanaka, having failed to intimidate the broadcasting staff into giving him air time, returned to the outside of the Imperial Palace with a fellow conspirator, Lieutenant-Colonel Shiizaki, one on a motorcycle, the other on a white horse. They tried to distribute leaflets calling for a general insurrection.

Shortly before noon, when the emperor's announcement was due to be broadcast, Hatanaka shot himself on a patch of green near the palace's Sakashita Gate. Shiizaki stuck a sword into his stomach, and then shot himself in the head. Major Koga, Tojo's son-in-law, who had been guarding the body of General Mori through most of the night, cut his stomach open in the shape of a cross.

Colonel Ida, who had so often pledged to commit suicide, was placed under guard, and failed to do so. Takeshita, Anami's brother-in-law, lived on to become a senior general in Japan's post-war Self-Defence Force. The heroic Tanaka shot himself through the head on 24 August, possibly because he felt responsible for the air raid damage to the Imperial Palace and the Meiji Shrine. Sporadic resistance continued around the country after the emperor's broadcast, particularly at Atsugi air base, at which General MacArthur was shortly to land. But on the whole, the docility with which the imperial army submitted to the emperor's command to surrender was remarkable.

Japan's death throes had been agonized and protracted. The tragi-comedy of the coup attempt had demonstrated two things: how only a handful of strategically placed officers could influence not just the direction of the army, but the destiny of the Japanese nation (it was remarkable how men like Hatanaka and Ida, with the support of only a tiny number of officers, had nearly wrested power from the central government). And now in spite of the fanaticism of a few at the head of the army and further down, the overwhelming majority were only too ready to cast aside a lifetime's training and lay down their arms. The long-standing fear of the emperor and his moderate advisers that any real opposition to the army vanguard would result in civil war was shown to have been unfounded. This raises the question of whether an imperial rescript against the militarists in the late 1930s might have worked; the emperor and his advisers were perhaps the victims of their own trapped and timid perceptions in the Imperial Palace hothouse. The emperor's command had, in the end, been obeyed.

How can the emperor have felt, during that long night before Japan's surrender, while unknown to him the shades and spirits of Japan's dying army grappled for its soul, only to be chased away by the morning light, and his minister of war ritually drank sake and prepared to commit suicide? The immediate outlook could not have been bleaker for that remote, detached, shy little man with his rarefied tastes, suppressed emotions and sudden bursts of anger. He had recovered from his nervous breakdown in the middle of the war, and was now leading a life of spartan simplicity, rising at seven to wash, read the newspapers, pray, and eat a breakfast of black bread and oatmeal; then working until noon, and eating a lunch of cooked vegetables and dumpling soup. Afterwards he would return to work and take a short walk. He had no real friends and neither smoked nor drank; his family had been moved out of Tokyo, and he turned in early each evening.

He slept lightly, and the image must surely have recurred to him that night of the destruction of Tokyo, which he had witnessed from one of the few constructions left standing amid the burnt-out shells of the wooden buildings of the capital. More than 100,000 had been killed in Tokyo alone, while a million and a half had been rendered homeless. The majority of people were sleeping in flimsily constructed shelters of corrugated iron and charred wood. Closer to home still, on 24 May the Imperial Palace had been hit. The main part of it dated from 1884, and had taken four years to build, out of cypress wood. It had beautifully painted doors, screens and ceilings, with chandeliers imported from Europe. The main building was entirely gutted, its copper roofs collapsing in upon its treasures. Thirty-three firemen had died trying to put out the blaze.

Six months earlier, the emperor had moved his quarters into the *gobunko*, with its underground shelter 100 metres to the north-east. Hirohito had been heartbroken as the fire raged; his main concern had been to protect the palace shrine, some 200 metres to the west of the main palace.

Surrounded by a devastated city, in a nation ravaged by war and two atomic bombs, he was an emperor whose empire was in ruins. He bore the ultimate responsibility. Most of the ideals he personified had been destroyed. Japan, the land of the select, was about to be occupied by barbarians; the Japanese empire was eliminated; the 'unbeatable' Japanese army was conquered. His country was enduring unprecedented hardship and suffering, even for a land that was no stranger to natural calamities.

He had come to office with high aspirations to return the imperial throne to its former position of influence after the rule of his idiot father, under whom the palace had been a playground for competing court factions and grubby civilian politicians. Hirohito had tried to do his duty, to restore the authority of himself and his imperial household at the apex of the huge bureaucratic–authoritarian structure of the Japanese state. But events had conspired tragically against him.

On three occasions in his rule he had exercised direct imperial authority: when he had dismissed the prime minister after the murder of Chang Tso-lin; during the February 1936 revolt; and again now, at the time of surrender, to prevent Japan's darkest hour from turning blacker still. Saionji and the others had advised him that to interfere more would prejudice his throne, his life even. He should have acted to issue a rescript to halt Japan's drift towards war in the mid-1930s, as Prime Minister Inukai had advised. That was when the slide could have been stopped.

The slide had been the culmination of a mass of errors which seemed inevitable at the time. There was the crown's refusal to permit the growth of truly representative institutions, for fear that they might have been manipulated by the left during the dangerous period of the late 1920s. There was the decision to curb the insolent young officers of the Kwantung Army in Manchuria, which merely gave power to their superiors in Tokyo, who were just as determined to embark on a course of imperial expansion – in the disastrous direction of China. There was the fatal alliance of the army and the *zaibatsu*, born largely of the consequences of world recession, which was too strong for the emperor or his household to resist.

There was the fateful decision to invade China itself, starting a war that the chief of staff, General Sugiyama, had promised the emperor would take a month to win, and was still unwon after eight years and millions of casualties. There was the navy's new strategy, and the cockiness of the admirals in believing they could destroy the American fleet and force Roosevelt to a negotiated settlement. There was the awesome miscalculation of the Konoye government that the invasion of Southeast Asia would be quietly accepted by the international community. So many miscalculations by the armed forces, by his advisers.

Hirohito's own instincts had usually been right, but they had not prevailed. He had been right to try to stop the armed forces seizing the initiative in foreign policy. He had been right in his doubts about the China war. He had been right to worry about the consequences of invading Indo-China. He had been right to try to avert the Pacific War through diplomatic means, for fear that Japan would not in the end prevail. Only at the height of the madness of war, as the tide turned against Japan, had he somehow become convinced by Tojo that if Japan redoubled its efforts it might win, buttressing the war party to the extent that even the faithful Kido had despaired and considered the desirability of forcing him to abdicate. Yet Kido failed to understand that it was Hirohito's sacred duty to his ancestors and Japan's soldiers to pursue the war to a successful finish once it had been declared. He had had no alternative. Now all was in ruins.

Yet he was no longer the pathetic, guilt-ridden figure of preceding months. With the decision to surrender, he was more at peace than he had been for years. His country had at last turned the page: there was something to look forward to, peace was about to come. He believed that Japan could recover, as it did from earthquakes and all other kinds of natural disaster. He could not have faced the judgement of his ancestors had he been called upon to account for his reign thus far: even his demented father, Taisho, had presided over an era of peace and prosperity in contrast to the hurricane rule of his son up to 1945.

But the emperor still had a chance to restore his country to greatness. With the dropping of the bombs, the enemy had assumed the entire burden of blame for Japan's defeat on its own shoulders. True, the war had not been going well – all Japanese recognized that. Yet the country had not been defeated, even though it could not hope to prevail against the new weapon. There would now be misery, suffering and humiliation throughout the land, particularly for the army. Who knew how the barbarian conquerors of Japan would behave in occupation? But Japan had salvaged its natural honour. It could be no part of *bushido* to undergo complete national self-immolation against impossible odds. With the imperial system preserved and honour intact, Japan could be rebuilt.

As General Anami prepared for death that night, he left two suicide notes of no great moment. As an afterthought, he wrote on the back of the second, 'I believe in Japan's sacred indestructibility.' He told his brother-in-law afterwards, 'It's true. The dead are dead, the living face hardships that are beyond our power to foresee, but if they work together, and if each does what he can, I believe that Japan will be saved.' Like Hirohito, he knew that the atomic bombs had given Japan the fresh start it needed to recover and rebuild.

The emperor was a light sleeper, but he slept more soundly than on any night in recent months, satisfied to have exercised his imperial power so decisively in the cause of saving Japan's honour and of saving lives.

The three other men most implicated in the tragic events of the past eight years slept less soundly. Tojo was fatalistic about defeat: he had never been certain that Japan would prevail, although he was satisfied that he had done his best, and that there had been no alternative to Japan's 'defensive' war. He believed that if he had been empowered to continue the war with all of Japan's resources – which the greedy *zaibatsu* had denied him at the last minute – then the war could have continued to go Japan's way even up to late 1944. He felt no sense of personal dishonour. This hard, brilliant man was touched now by personal tragedy: the participation of his son-in-law, Major Koda, in the conspiracy to frustrate surrender – which Tojo so admired, but knew was doomed to failure – had been followed by the inevitable *seppuku* and the grief of his daughter. Tojo was steeling himself for his own nearly successful suicide attempt.

In the vaults of the Imperial Household Ministry, Marquis Koichi Kido had spent much of that night fearing for his life. He was a favourite target of the conspirators, he knew that. He had no way of telling how much support they had. He had felt all along that he had done his duty: advising the emperor about the need for peace and the destructive consequences of war, keeping him advised of the reality of things against the crude propaganda of the armed forces. He had been surprised at how little the emperor had listened to him over the last two years of the war; Hirohito apparently had been convinced by the army that the war could be won.

All the same, the Lord Privy Seal had advised Hirohito not to exercise his power at the wrong time. Kido's prime objective was to protect the integrity of the throne. There was a time when he had toyed with the idea of persuading Hirohito to abdicate in favour of a more decisive regent, probably Prince Takamatsu. In the end it had proved impossible. He had done his best. The decision to surrender had represented the culmination of everything Kido had worked for for two years. Now it seemed possible that the imperial institution would survive. That was all that mattered. He might now be murdered by the rebels, or executed by the occupation forces. He had little about which to reproach himself before his ancestors.

Former Prime Minister Fumimaro Konoye, for his part, spent the night of the coup attempt in hiding; he had known of the planning of the coup the day before and had communicated his fears to his political ally, Marquis Kido. Konoye had never entirely liked the dispassionate, meticulous, fastidious court bureaucrat. This prince of Japan's most ancient line, the Fujiwaras, was given to flamboyance, self-confidence, elegance. Konoye was the stage aristocrat, blessed with brains, good looks and royal blood.

He had been prime minister when Japan made its two most disastrous decisions – the invasion of China and the invasion of Southeast Asia – that had led directly to all-out war and defeat. In retrospect he knew they had been mistakes, but at the time he believed there was no alternative. They were not his fault. Any political leader had to deal with the practicalities, with the possible, not with the ideal. He had tried to take the military in hand, indeed had twice resigned when the struggle became a vain one, when the zaibatsu lent their support to the military. He had sought to mitigate the worst consequences of military mistakes.

Now, with peace in the ascendant, Konoye foresaw a major role for himself after the war. Earlier than anyone, he had courageously spoken out against the war, fearing that it would discredit Japan's institutions and pave the way for a communist takeover of the country. From 1942 onwards he had worked consistently for peace; he was sure the occupation forces would recognize his contribution. He was the natural figure to preside over occupied Japan and see the country through its most difficult ordeal. He prepared himself for the role.

He never imagined that MacArthur and the occupying authorities would view him with distaste, as one of the chief connivers in Japan's aggressive wars, and later indict him for war crimes. When he realized what was to happen, he killed himself: no prince of the imperial blood could submit himself to the indignity of a public trial. Konoye left a copy of Oscar Wilde's *De Profundis* on his deathbed, with certain passages underlined:

> I must say to myself that I ruined myself, and that nobody great or small can be ruined except by his own hand. I am quite ready to say so. I am trying to say so, though they may not think it at the present moment. This pitiless indictment I bring without pity against myself. Terrible as was what the world did to me, what I did to myself was far more terrible still.

Konoye, Kido, Tojo, Hirohito. The devious happy-go-lucky aristocratic nationalist, intelligent enough to foresee the disaster which he nevertheless played a leading role in leading Japan towards. The fussy bureaucrat who advocated peace yet could not persuade his emperor – and least of all the military–*zaibatsu* alliance that dominated Japanese politics – to embrace it. The fanatical, hard army officer who pressed for war even as he saw its potentially disastrous consequences. The all-powerful emperor who lacked the power to stop a great swathe of the world being terrorized in his name. The gambler, the courtier, the martinet, the recluse. Four men who did their duty, had immense power, and presided over the greatest interlude of suffering the world has probably ever known. Four men with different shares in that terrible and awesome responsibility. Unlike those crude European despots, Hitler and Mussolini, all four were civilized, erudite, intelligent, three of them from the highest families in the land. They were not obvious villains at all.

Within months, one would die at his own hand, another would be hanged, a third would be sentenced to life imprisonment, and a fourth – the most culpable of all – would be confirmed in office as head of the Japanese state for another forty-four years. That night, none knew their fate. Of the four the happiest was certainly Hirohito, who believed that Japan could now rise again.

The mistakes of the past, the humiliation of defeat, the allegations of cruelty and torture had all been eliminated in the purifying flash of the atomic bombs over Hiroshima and Nagasaki. Just as the noble self-sacrifice that General Anami was inflicting upon himself that evening would cleanse all stain upon his honour and that of the army he led, so the suffering of the two obliterated cities had wiped out the shame of Japan. Not only the country, but the old order, could now survive. Japan had not been defeated. Japan had done no wrong. The tenacity with which this palpable untruth was to be held and embroidered over the next half century served only to demonstrate its importance as the ideological cornerstone of the post-war Japanese state.

PART FOUR

THE UNDEFEATED

In the depths of the mirror [the train window] the evening landscape moved by, the mirror and the reflected figures like motion pictures superimposed one on the other. The figures and the background were unrelated, and yet the figures, transparent and intangible, and the background, dim in the gathering darkness, melted together in a sort of symbolic world not of this world. Particularly when a light in the mountains shone in the centre of the girl's face, Shimamura felt his chest rise at the inexpressible beauty of it . . .

It was then that a light shone in the face. The reflection in the mirror was not strong enough to blot out the light outside, nor was the light strong enough to dim the reflection. The light moved across the face, though not to light it up. It was a distant, cold light. As it sent its small ray through the pupil of the girl's eye, as the eye and the pupil were superimposed one on the other, the eye became a weirdly beautiful piece of phosphorescence on the sea of evening mountains.

From Snow Country by Yasunari Kawabata

19

DESCENT FROM THE SKIES

O N 30 AUGUST 1945, less than a month after Little Boy was
dropped, one of the most remarkable acts of courage
displayed in the Pacific War, exceeding any throughout a
long career of bravery, was performed by a sixty-five-year-old
general and a handful of American officers and soldiers. A C-54
aircraft, the Bataan, took off from Okinawa into a clear blue sky.
On board were the commander of American forces in the Far East,
General Douglas MacArthur, and his chief aides.

If he was nervous, MacArthur tried not to show it. He paced up
and down the aircraft, talking of his priorities and the awesome
powers that in a few hours were to pass to him. He dictated staccato,
apparently random thoughts to his secretary.

> First destroy the military power . . . Then build the structure of
> representative government . . . Enfranchise the women . . . Free the
> political prisoners . . . Liberate the farmers . . . Establish a free
> labour movement . . . Encourage a free economy . . . Abolish police
> oppression . . . Develop a free and responsible press . . . Decentral-
> ize the political power . . .

Could he, for the first time in modern history, accomplish that
miraculous phenomenon, the successful occupation of a defeated
nation?

It amounted to a blueprint for the reshaping of a whole oriental
society. In fact, this extensive list of priorities had been transmitted
to MacArthur the day before from Washington under the title,
'Initial post-surrender priorities for Japan', reflecting years of planning at a high level and bearing President Truman's personal stamp

of approval. MacArthur then took a nap. His faithful ally, General Courtney Whitney, described by his detractors as a 'stuffed pig with a moustache' and generally viewed as pompous and rude, woke him up to admire what MacArthur commented under his breath was 'beautiful Mount Fuji'. The plane began its descent to Atsugi air base.

The danger of landing with only minimal protection in the heart of the Kanto Plain, where 300,000 well-armed Japanese troops were stationed, many refusing to acknowledge defeat, was only too apparent. Atsugi had been a training base for kamikaze pilots, many of whom had refused to surrender. A mutiny after the emperor's broadcast had sputtered on for days. Only a couple of small American advance parties had preceded MacArthur.

Yet MacArthur ordered his own party to take off their guns before the aircraft landed. He believed that if the Americans arrived unarmed they were less likely to be attacked; moreover, it would impress on 'the oriental mind' that the Japanese had been defeated. MacArthur would come as a conqueror, not as a fighter.

The showman with dark glasses and corncob pipe, who had probably been as responsible as any for Japan's defeat, descended from the aircraft and set foot on enemy soil. Awaiting him was, according to Whitney, a collection 'of the most decrepit-looking vehicles I have ever seen – the best means of transport the Japanese could round up for the trip into Yokohama'. MacArthur was given the place of honour in an ancient American Lincoln; the other American officers climbed aboard the cars behind, some twenty American soldiers joining the convoy immediately after the commander-in-chief.

A fire engine 'that resembled the Toonerville Trolley' started with such a loud backfire that the Americans ducked. Then, like 'a sequence in a dream fantasy', in the words of MacArthur's aide, General Eichelberger, the clapped-out procession of clattering, sputtering vehicles started the 20-mile drive to Yokohama along a gauntlet of Japanese soldiers – two divisions of some 30,000 men – with their backs to the procession, either out of respect or contempt, no one quite knew.

Two days later, on a cloudy Sunday morning, MacArthur's naval rival, Admiral Nimitz, climbed aboard the massive 45,000-ton battleship *Missouri* anchored some 18 miles out in Tokyo Bay. Under a huge Stars and Stripes, the Japanese delegation stood on the crowded deck, watched by thousands of American seamen and cameramen finding angles from every conceivable part of the superstructure.

The Japanese delegation was less impressive than MacArthur might have expected. The emperor, of course, would not attend. The prime minister, Prince Higashikuni, was the emperor's uncle and had used his royal blood as a pretext for staying away. His deputy, and the real power in the government, Prince Konoye, also made his excuses. The short straw was drawn by the foreign minister, Mamoru Shigemitsu, a tough old idealist who had lost a leg in a bomb attack fifteen years before, and who, appropriately enough, was a vigorous anti-militarist. For the army, General Yoshijiro Umezu, the chief of the army general staff, the figure who had vacillated and then urged Japan to fight on, had been ordered to attend. When he had first heard this he had gone pale with anger and threatened to commit *seppuku*, until the emperor himself prevailed upon him to go.

The Japanese looked grim and diminished in their morning dress and top hats and uniforms, standing stiffly to attention as an American army chaplain said a prayer and a tinny 'Star-Spangled Banner' was played. They were joined by MacArthur, Nimitz, Halsey, Wainwright and Percival. One of the Japanese delegates, Toshikazu Kase, recorded how it felt for him.

They were all thronged, packed to suffocation, representatives, journalists, spectators, an assembly of brass, braid and brand. As we appeared on the scene we were, I felt, being subjected to the torture of the pillory. There were a million eyes beating us in the million shafts of a rattling storm of arrows barbed with fire. I felt their keenness sink into my body with a sharp physical pain. Never have I realized that the glance of glaring eyes could hurt so much.

We waited for a few minutes, standing in the public gaze like penitent boys awaiting the dreaded schoolmaster. I tried to preserve with the utmost sang-froid the dignity of defeat, but it was difficult and every minute seemed to contain ages. I looked up and saw painted on the wall several miniature Rising Suns, our flag, evidently in numbers corresponding to the planes and submarines shot down or sunk by the crew of the battleship. As I tried to count these markings, tears rose in my throat and quickly gathered to the eyes, flooding them.

MacArthur was now placed in one of the most remarkable positions of any man in world history. As Supreme Commander of

Allied Powers (SCAP also the title of his administration) he had been given sole charge of a country of 75 million people with a unique tradition of obeisance, deference, and hierarchy; he was the first foreign ruler and occupier in 2000 years of Japanese history. His absolute power from that day can be paralleled with that exercised by Pizarro in Peru, Cortes in Mexico and Clive in India after defeating absolute systems of government. He was perhaps the only example of a true viceroy, appointed to rule over another land – and a huge one at that – in America's history of generally avowed opposition to colonialism. MacArthur was Japan's new shogun, dwarfing the emperor in power. He had charged himself with no less a task than the transformation of a warlike, despotic state into a modern democracy. He embarked on the task with vigour.

The first of MacArthur's reforms were retributive. The Tokyo war crimes tribunal was a costly fiasco, dubious in law and picking on a handful of scapegoats, deserving of punishment though they may have been; by its end, MacArthur had recognized it as such. The supreme commander also made little secret of his distaste for war reparations. Many economists, Keynes among them, had identified the reparations exacted from Germany as a major cause of the Second World War.

In 1945, President Truman had appointed Edwin Pauley, a former Gulf Oil magnate and Democratic Party fundraiser, not just to exact reparations but to reform the industrial structures of Germany and Japan. Pauley drew up ambitious plans to transfer basic industries from Japan to Southeast Asia, arguing that 'as Japan began to recover there would be more local strength' to prevent aggression for economic motives. The idea was to redress the uneven balance between Japan's industrial strength and that of the Asian mainland. The specific intention was to transfer iron and steel mills from Japan to Manchuria, which had the necessary raw materials of coal and iron ore; this would give China the kind of industrial production which Japan would be forced to respect.

Pauley and his chief adviser, Owen Lattimore, a respected Asian expert, concluded early on in the occupation that MacArthur, who resented their intrusion on his turf, was little disposed to help them. In December 1945 Pauley advanced a programme to seize 'Japanese excess capacity' which might later contribute to 'economic imperialism'. He called for the seizure of twenty-seven of the most important machine-tool manufacturers, which accounted for roughly half of

Japan's total production, as well as restructuring the aircraft, ball-bearing, and shipping industries and slashing steel production from 11 million tons to 2.5 million. Truman promptly approved the reforms, saying that 'these should be implemented as soon as the necessary details are worked out'.

The programme was quite clearly punitive, and almost certainly unworkable, as it would impose restraints on industrial development that no country could accept in the long term. MacArthur was deeply opposed to it from the first. Under duress, he agreed to transport a million and a half machine tools to mainland Asia, but carried the Pauley reparations package no further. The recipients of Pauley's initial generosity began to quarrel bitterly among themselves.

In 1947, with the Truman administration beginning to have second thoughts, another mission led by Clifford Strike, a prominent engineering manufacturer, suggested that it was 'neither sensible nor desirable' to adhere to the Pauley programme. Japan had to be left with 'enough industry so that the Japanese economy will be self-sustaining'. Strike argued that Japan had little if any excess industrial capacity. Pauley indignantly retorted that Strike's recommendations would amount to a 'complete repudiation of US reparations policy'.

In October 1948, American officials stressed that those countries still seeking reparations should begin to move Japanese industrial plant to the former colonies under a tight timetable. Most were physically unable to do this, and the reparations programme was terminated. It had achieved almost nothing, it was opposed from the beginning with eminent good sense by MacArthur and, if carried through, would have been thoroughly bad policy. Nevertheless, so far as the success of one of the main objectives of the occupation was concerned, the scorecard so far was nought out of two.

The next of MacArthur's reform objectives was to be the most important of all: a concerted assault upon the four elites of Japanese power – the military cliques, which MacArthur wanted to destroy; the monopolist *zaibatsu*, the enemies of a 'free economy'; the country's 'oppressive police state'; and the bureaucrats, whom MacArthur sought to weaken by decentralizing political power. All four groups, moreover, were to be the targets of a massive purge of those primarily involved in the militaristic rush to disaster in the 1930s and 1940s.

MacArthur subsequently argued that he considered the purge a mistake from the first: he 'doubted its wisdom'. However, an order issued by him and his staff in January 1946 contained a strong commitment to weed out the guilty men among the ranks of politicians, bureaucrats, military officers, corporate executives, local government officials, teachers, theatre producers, film-makers, educators, university professors, and police chiefs. No fewer than 2.5 million people were to be affected. Those purged were accused of:

> participation in, or support of, military aggression and overseas imperialism; dissemination of ultra-nationalist propaganda; claims of ethnic superiority and attempts to act on them – assuming leadership of other Asiatic races, for example, or excluding foreigners from trade and commerce; advocacy of totalitarianism; the use of violence and terror to achieve political ends and crush opposition to the regime; an insistence on the special status and prerogatives of the soldier.

The subjects' public views during the era of Japanese expansion in the late 1930s – and dating sometimes as far back as 1931 and the Manchurian Incident – as well as during the Pacific War were under inspection.

A further objective of the purge was the destruction of Japan's numerous far-right societies and the banning of their members from government employment. These included not just the Black Dragon Society (known officially as the Amur River Society), but such bodies as the Bayonet Practice Promotion Society, the White Blood Corpuscle League, the Anti-Foreigner Similar Spirits Society, the Society for the Ultimate Solution of the Manchurian Question and the Imperial National Blood War Body.

Everyone in Japan in the offices affected was asked to fill out a questionnaire, detailing military service, membership of political organizations, and past careers. A central screening committee examined the completed forms. However, the penalties for covering up past misdeeds were not severe. By 1947/8 the questionnaire was no longer required, and only outside evidence could disqualify a person from office. SCAP, moreover, sought to ensure that those removed did not return to their jobs, debarred them from other types of work, and prohibited their relatives from holding similar offices and thus acting in their stead. The Japanese argued that this amounted to visiting the sins of the fathers upon the sons.

There can be no doubt that the effects of the initial purge were fairly severe. The Home Ministry lost 34 senior officials, and the imperial household 118, 170 peers were removed from the upper house, while only 10 per cent of Diet members were deemed eligible for re-election in April 1946. The purge was implemented with special harshness in the army, the former enemy of the civilian ministries, which were now in charge of carrying out SCAP's edicts. Yet the impact was largely confined to old people whose careers were coming to an end; within a year or two evasion through anticipation (and early retirement) or failure to screen effectively was widespread.

In October 1948, an order, which effectively marked the death-knell of the MacArthur reforms, put the purge into reverse. Several 'relatively harmless' purged individuals were permitted to return to public office, including most of the businessmen affected. An Approved Persons Board began making reinstatements – 150 in the first fourteen months of office, some 10 per cent of those applying, rising to 30 and even 90 per cent in subsequent years.

By 1951 some 177,000 people had been de-purged – more than two-thirds of the original total. Many of the rest were now past retirement; only 9000 people remained on the banned list. The Potsdam Declaration had specified that 'there must be eliminated for all time the authority and influence of those who have deceived and misled the people of Japan'. Only a tiny proportion were in fact eliminated. By 1952, there were 139 former victims of the purge in the house of representatives, and two years later one of their number, Ichiro Hatoyama, became prime minister. Denazification in Germany was a much more thorough and lasting process. Mac-Arthur had tried, and had been frustrated.

The attempt to single out individuals to blame for Japan's wartime excesses involved a measure of rough justice, and was arguably less important than the reforms needed to transform the armed forces, the police, big business, and the bureaucracy.

The most thorough and successful reform was, of course, of the army. This was achieved in three ways: writing into the constitution a specific clause, Article Nine, by which Japan 'renounced war'; disbanding the imperial army; and ensuring that the new army was a largely passive organization imbued with democratic values. The insertion of the 'no war' clause into Japan's constitution was one of MacArthur's prime achievements, yet he denied the responsibility was his at all, crediting instead Prime Minister Shidehara.

To the Americans it was essential that the clause appeared to originate from the Japanese, otherwise it might be repealed after the occupation ended. Shidehara and some of his peace party may genuinely have thought the article desirable, and it was supported by a large swathe of public opinion in Japan, which was understandably sickened by war and resented the army as a force of oppression. MacArthur himself at the time leaned to the view that Japan was in no danger of attack from Russia, as long as the Soviets understood that America would retaliate overwhelmingly. He considered that a police force and a symbolic American presence would be enough to secure Japan's defences. He believed Japan should be supported through American bases at Okinawa and the Pacific, which could best deter the Soviets if necessary. Provided Japan was not altogether demilitarized, he did not believe the Soviets would attack.

The 'no war' provision was a remarkable one in any constitution, doubly so in Japan's. It read:

> Aspiring sincerely to international peace based on justice and order, the Japanese people forever renounce war as a sovereign right of the nation and the threat or use of force as a means of settling international disputes.
>
> In order to accomplish the aim of the preceding paragraph, land, sea, and air forces, as well as other war potential, will never be maintained.

The disarming of Japan was achieved through prodigious organization by MacArthur's forces. The demobilization and repatriation involved some seven million Japanese. In addition all arsenals, ammunition dumps and advance depots had to be located; much of this was booby-trapped against an American invasion and highly volatile. Ammunition frequently exploded, parachute flares ignited and on one occasion a cave full of propellant charges blew up, killing dozens of Japanese workmen. Another massive explosion took place at Tatayama airfield, where an ammunition dump blew up.

Tanks, guns, anti-aircraft equipment and aircraft were cut open with blowtorches. Ships were distributed among the victorious nations; some were scuttled or used in American atomic tests. Some 120,000 bayonets and 81,000 rifles were taken by the Americans. All of Japan's air defences and combat aircraft were destroyed. Military airfields were to be turned over to agricultural purposes, and no Japanese was permitted to pilot even civil aircraft. The vast and formidable arsenal of civil defence equipment was confiscated, including baseball bats, crossbows, guns, plumbing pipes, explosive arrows, and primitive bazookas. There can be very little doubt, though, that in the fortnight between Japan's surrender and the beginning of the occupation, quantities of munitions were spirited to secret depots in the hills with the intention of providing an arsenal for a future 'secret army' akin to that in Germany after the First World War. In the event, none was needed.

SCAP also sought to enforce a policy intended to prevent Japan from rearming: no reserves, no arms imports, and no arms production were permitted. Atomic energy equipment was confiscated, nuclear scientists were arrested, and all nuclear-related material was seized. Japan's four cyclotrons were destroyed on Washington's orders – to MacArthur's fury. A ban was imposed on all industrial activity geared to war and a ceiling set on the production of steel, oil, railway equipment, ball bearings and machine tools. These levels were set at a tenth of the levels of the Japanese armaments programme of the 1930s. Finally, the Americans formally disbanded the Japanese army, navy and air force.

All three of these far-reaching attacks on the militarists were to prove partly illusory, although it would be wrong to say that they had no effect. The constitutional ban on war, it turned out, was far from being a prohibition on defence spending. Vice-President Richard Nixon was to call it, with dismaying candour, an 'honest mistake' as early as 1953. MacArthur made it plain at the time: 'Should the course of world events require that all mankind stand to arms in defence of human liberty and Japan comes within the orbit of immediately threatened attack, then the Japanese, too, should mount the maximum defensive power which their resources will permit.' MacArthur was soon to recommend that a defence force of ten divisions be set up, with corresponding sea and air arms. However, the importance of Article Nine as a block on Japan's path to remilitarization should not be underestimated: the bitterest political clashes and the worst street fighting of the post-war period were to revolve around this very issue, and that of the relationship with America. These issues were to divide Japanese society as no other, tearing away the façade of Japan's so-called 'consensus' for a time.

The destruction of the *matériel* was, of course, irreversible. But some was saved, and the long-term bans on stockpiling, importing and producing ordnance and weapons, even in some limited respects for nuclear purposes, were ignored by the end of the occupation –

not least by the Americans, who needed supplies for the Korean War. They could not be enforced on post-occupation Japan. The limits on heavy-industry production were similarly ignored.

Behind the scenes, moreover, at least one part of the occupation forces ensured that the dissolution of the Japanese war machine was only partially successful. The man who achieved this was General Charles Willoughby, head of military intelligence (G2) and the occupation's most powerful military commander after MacArthur. Willoughby was born of a Prussian military family, as Charles von Tscheppe-Weidenback. He was tall, good-looking, authoritarian, and possessed of a powerful temper. After Japan's defeat, for Willoughby, the prime task was to fight communism; he considered the anti-militarist provisions of the occupation wasteful. His sympathies often lay on the borderlines of fascism. He argued that Mussolini had been right to invade Ethiopia, thus 'wiping out a memory of defeat before re-establishing the traditional military supremacy of the white race'. After retiring in the 1950s he served as an adviser to Spain's General Franco – the 'second greatest general in the world'.

Willoughby set up a 'loyalty desk' inside SCAP to scrutinize the civilian machinery of the occupation bureaucracy and to weed out 'leftists and fellow-travellers'. His unit succeeded in forcing out several reformers: the great Japanese scholar and economist, Thomas Bisson, was hounded out of SCAP and lost his job at Berkeley after the occupation. Willoughby also supported Joseph McCarthy's witch-hunts by providing 'evidence' of the 'guilt' of some of his political opponents inside SCAP. Within Japan in 1947, he admitted later, he had acted under a top-secret Pentagon order to preserve the nucleus of the Japanese general staff and to maintain the records of the army and navy. This ran directly counter to SCAP's official instructions.

By January 1946 there were still some 190 Japanese generals and admirals pursuing 'occupation objectives'; many were engaged in the process of 'historical research' on a major project set up by Willoughby in co-operation with General Seizo Arisue, head of Japanese military intelligence at the end of the war. The results never emerged. Arisue and another senior officer, Takushiro Hattori, former private secretary to Tojo, were engaged in setting up what was in effect their own general staff of fifty or sixty senior officers throughout Japan. Further down the ranks, 'local assistance bureaus' were set up consisting of entire companies supposedly engaged in helping demobilized soldiers, but in fact acting as clandestine army units. 'Farms' were also set up by veterans along military lines, consisting of entire military detachments staffed by officers. Tanks were used as tractors, education was militaristic, and army drill was still maintained, as was discipline.

Willoughby himself took control of records set up by the former army authorities which fully documented the soldiery of the old imperial army. When the time came to recreate a Japanese army, the men and materials were in place. The whole process irresistibly recalled the setting up of Germany's secret *Wehrmacht* after the First World War. Prophetically, the London *Times* had predicted on 27 August 1945 that:

> The way is . . . opened for the propagation of the myth, which proved so formidable a factor in the rise of the Third Reich, that the army had not been conquered, that the war was lost by poor civilian morale caused by the Allies' employment of an unfair weapon . . . It will be strange indeed if the Japanese General Staff does not endeavour to 'go to ground' as the German General Staff did in 1918.

At the same time the Japanese government had already decided 'informally' to maintain a 'police force' of 25,000 men and to set up a gendarmerie of the same size. Hitoshi Ashida, a leading politician who was chairman of the constitutional amendments committee of the House of Representatives, argued at the time that 'paramilitary' forces were needed to protect Japan from left-wing subversion and civil unrest. By 1948, American Defense Secretary James Forrestal had ordered the Department of the Army to commence limited rearmament in Japan.

General William Draper, a leading member of Forrestal's team and a staunch anti-communist who had also pressed for Germany's enlistment in the anti-communist struggle, claimed in March 1948 that there was a 'general trend in recent department thinking towards the early establishment of a small defensive force for Japan, to be ready at such times as the American occupation forces leave the country'. MacArthur's former Pacific War aide, General Eichelberger, argued that 'dollar for dollar, there is no cheaper fighting man in the world than the Japanese. He is already a veteran. His food is simple.'

That summer the authorities decided in principle to set up a force of 150,000 troops to engage Russia in what many American planners saw as an inevitable war on two fronts – Europe and Asia.

However, just the act of setting up such an army could provoke the Soviet Union; it was therefore necessary to label this a 'national police force'. An American military report at the time pointed out that 'even though created originally for the maintenance of domestic law and order, an augmented Civilian Police would be the vehicle for possible organization of Japanese armed forces at a later date and could initiate manpower registration records.'

There is evidence to suggest that both MacArthur and Prime Minister Yoshida bitterly resisted the pressure from Washington for rearmament. MacArthur suggested that the Japanese

> would not be willing to establish an armed force of their own unless we forced them into it. This we should not do . . . Japanese rearmament is contrary to many of the fundamental principles which have guided SCAP ever since the Japanese surrender . . . abandonment of these principles now would dangerously weaken our prestige in Japan and place us in a ridiculous light before the Japanese people.

As late as 1950, MacArthur argued that for Japan to have an army would cause 'convulsions' in Australia, New Zealand, Indonesia, and the Philippines. Yoshida was an out-and-out opponent of the militarists, though highly conservative politically. Both believed that America could deter the Russians in the Pacific much more effectively from the Pacific islands.

However, with the outbreak of the Korean War, MacArthur's rearguard action against the Pentagon was no longer tenable. In July 1950 he ordered Yoshida to set up a 'National Police Reserve' of 75,000 men to stand in for the first division of the American Eighth Army sent to Korea. Willoughby proposed that Colonel Hattori be put in charge of the new force, but MacArthur refused. The force was created without reference to the Japanese parliament. It was dressed in American-style uniforms, based in American barracks, and trained by American instructors. Three thousand senior ex-officers were recalled, and most of the men were former veterans. The 'police' were equipped with rifles, light machine guns, mortars and light tanks. Willoughby described it as 'the army of the future'.

In 1951 John Foster Dulles, in charge of negotiating the peace treaty with Japan, pressed for American bases in the country and the setting up of a Japanese army of 350,000 men, as well as an Asia–Pacific defence pact. In April that year, Truman fired MacArthur, and in September the peace treaty granting Japan its independence was signed. It recognized Japan's 'right of individual or collective self-defence', provided for the country to enter into collective security arrangements with its Asian neighbours, offered Japan American protection in the event of attack, and gave America the right to station forces in Japan indefinitely.

Yoshida insisted that as the American umbrella would not last for ever, 'we must undertake to build up a safe defensive power of our own gradually'. In August 1952 the National Supply Agency was set up to plan for Japan's defences under a 'civilian' head with a decidedly dubious pedigree. He was Tokutaro Kimura, a former member of many right-wing secret societies, who had been purged by MacArthur and only two years before had sought to set up a 'Patriotic Anti-Communist Drawn Sword Militia'. Two months later the National Police Reserve was expanded to 110,000 men and merged with Japan's burgeoning naval force into the National Security Force. The 'police force' now possessed medium tanks and heavy artillery.

In March 1954, the Mutual Defence Association Agreement was signed between America and Japan. The same year, the Diet passed the law officially establishing Japan's new armed forces. The Self-Defence Agency Law created the Japanese Self-Defence Agency, which was a ministry of defence under another name. The Self-Defence Forces Law set up permanent armed forces, which already existed in embryonic form. The army alone was to be 130,000 strong, although three conditions remained: that it would be a professional army, with no conscripts; that it would not be sent overseas; and that it would be under civilian direction.

The navy, like the army, had been assiduously preparing for its return to the national stage. Admiral Kichisaburo Nomura was the man who held the flame aloft in the dark days following Japan's surrender. He was also the celebrated ambassador to the United States who delivered Japan's declaration of hostilities after the attack on Pearl Harbor, and the butt of American fury at the time. Barely a year after the Japanese surrender, Nomura drew up proposals for a Japanese coastguard force to cope with a severe outbreak of piracy along the coast from China, Russia, and Korea. MacArthur had responded at once, and by March 1948 a 10,000-man Marine Safety Board was set up, later to become the Maritime Safety Agency. Two years later, Japanese minesweepers helped the Americans to clear a path for a landing north of Wonsan in Korea – the first time Japanese armed forces had been used for any purpose abroad after the Pacific War. In October 1951 the Americans offered the Japanese eighteen frigates and fifty landing-craft as the nucleus of a new Japanese navy.

In 1952 the restrictions on the construction of war materials were relaxed, and the industry was going at full throttle by 1953. In January of the following year the Air Self-Defence Force came into being and pilots were permitted to train again. The turnaround in America's initial solemn commitment never to allow Japan to rearm was virtually complete: the three services had been brought back into being, staffed largely by the officers and men of the old imperial armed forces.

In four significant ways, however, the position of the armed forces was now very different to what it had been before the Pacific War. First, they had been demoted to being the most junior of the three main partners in government (the bureaucracy, the economic giants, and the armed forces). Second, they remained objects of intense suspicion among ordinary Japanese. For decades after the Pacific War, it was a sign of relatively low social status to belong to the armed forces; to that extent pacifists had made much of the running among post-war Japanese. Third, the constitutional prohibition against waging aggressive war committed the armed forces to be scrupulous about avoiding overseas entanglements. Fourth, defence spending in Japan, while far from small, remained a relatively low priority in comparison with that of other major industrial nations.

Thus, while MacArthur's attempts to neutralize Japan, turning it into the 'Switzerland of Asia', as he called it, had foundered just three years after his departure from Tokyo, it can be said that his efforts were not entirely in vain. Japan, while far from disarmed, would remain a hesitant military power for decades to come. MacArthur's wholesale opposition to Japanese rearmament was genuine, and reflected his background and judgement of the country and the dangers rearmament might pose; he was virtually alone on the American anti-communist right in holding the view he did. He was overwhelmed by an unstoppable coalition between the anti-communists now dominant in Washington, their followers under his own command, industrial interests and the Japanese establishment. On this issue, he went down fighting, and still managed to achieve some of his original goals.

The assault by MacArthur on the anti-democratic parts of Japan's internal security apparatus – the various police forces – did not entirely fail, either, although it was heavily modified with the passage of time. Even MacArthur admitted the 'extraordinarily difficult' nature of the problem. The 'Thought Police', responsible for internal repression and the detention of some 60,000 dissidents, had been well entrenched in the Home Affairs Ministry. The civilian police, who were less feared, had been ruthless in the suppression of public meetings and worked in league with the right-wing secret societies. The Kempeitai were a kind of local gestapo who acted with the maximum brutality against dissidents.

One of MacArthur's first acts had been to free the country's political prisoners, who had been held in conditions of horrific suffering. His second objective was to break the centralized stranglehold of the Home Affairs Ministry and strengthen the power of local government. He demanded the decentralization of the police forces, as well as, of course, the outright abolition of the Kempeitai and Thought Police.

Every town with a population of more than 5000 was given the right to have its own police force which was no longer answerable to the central government. This created a mass of problems: some towns could not afford a proper force, and police pay fell accordingly, leading to corruption; it was hard to co-ordinate between rival forces. Indeed, after the occupation the Japanese government moved quickly to recreate a national police force, of a rather more responsible kind than before – although not entirely devoid of the characteristics of the pre-war period. Local autonomy as decreed by MacArthur in other spheres of administration was more successful, building upon the traditional Japanese unit of the village; but the Home Affairs Ministry regained a considerable measure of control after the occupation ended.

MacArthur's attempts to tie down the bureaucracy were confined to constitutional reform designed to make it accountable to parliament. This was only partially successful, although the changes secured were significant. By and large the power of the bureaucracy was hardly diminished by the occupation. In some respects it was considerably strengthened because it doubled in size and regained its top position among Japan's elites: the armed forces were now discredited, and the *zaibatsu*, suffering from wartime devastation, were keeping their heads down.

The American assault upon the third leg of power in Japan – the *zaibatsu*, who had steadily increased their stranglehold over the

Japanese economy before and during the war – was much more determined, and led to the greatest controversy surrounding the occupation. The *zaibatsu* shared equal responsibility with the armed forces for Japan's slide towards war. It was the profound conviction of most of the reformists within SCAP that, unless the great combines were broken up, real democracy in Japan was impossible and no middle class would be created, much less a free-market economy. Indeed, the supporters of SCAP's principal reformer, General Courtney Whitney, probably placed more emphasis on this than on any other change.

The economist Thomas Bisson, later pilloried and hounded by Willoughby, argued convincingly that the *zaibatsu*, far from opposing Japanese aggression, helped to channel its direction to serve their interests – into China and Southeast Asia in particular. During the period of wartime mobilization, he argued, they used the 'control associations' to establish a stranglehold over raw materials and further increase their control over industry. Contrary to the *zaibatsu*'s attempt to pin all wartime responsibility on the armed forces, they worked hand in hand with the military to mould Japan's economy for war during the pre-Pearl Harbor years. 'If the *zaibatsu* are permitted to survive the conditions of defeat, they will continue to dominate Japan's postwar government. With the experience gained in this war, they will be able to prepare even more thoroughly for their next attempt to conquer East Asia by force of arms.'

Between 1931 and 1941, the *zaibatsu*'s share of key industries related to war preparation rose from 15 per cent to an astonishing 72 per cent. By 1945, the ten biggest *zaibatsu* controlled three-quarters of industry, finance and commerce in Japan – possibly more, through the skilful manipulation of financial holdings, than at the height of the Meiji period. Another American economist working for SCAP, Eleanor Hadley, pointed out that Mitsubishi's family holdings in relative terms were 'the equivalent of a single American conglomerate comprising US Steel, General Motors, Standard Oil of New Jersey, Alcoa, Douglas Aircraft, Dupont, Sun Shipbuilding, Allis-Chalmers, Westinghouse, A T & T, RCA, IBM, US Rubber, Sea Island Sugar, Dole Pineapple, US Lines, Grace Lines, National City Bank, Metropolitan Life Insurance, Woolworth Stores and the Statler Hotels'.

MacArthur himself was in no doubt about the malevolent effects of the *zaibatsu*. 'The world', he argued, 'has probably never seen a counterpart to so abnormal an economic system. It permitted the exploitation of the many for the sole benefit of the few. The integration of these few with government was complete and their influence upon government inordinate, and set the course which ultimately led to war and destruction.' MacArthur took the bull by the horns in October 1945, asking the four major giants of Japanese business and industry – Mitsui, Mitsubishi, Sumitomo and Yasuda – to submit plans for their own dissolution. The idea, as ever, was to give the impression that the Japanese had virtually administered their own reform, as well as to evoke the principle at the time of the Meiji restoration, when the *daimyo* offered their lands to the emperor.

Needless to say, the proposal drawn up by the companies, the Yasuda Plan, was almost wholly cosmetic. They proposed that the holding companies of the four corporations be dissolved, and that family members resign from the boards of major subsidiaries. Family shares in the holding companies would be sold to a 'liquidation commission', and the proceeds invested in ten-year bonds as compensation for the losses suffered by the families. Although superficially attractive, the flaws were obvious from the start: there was nothing to prevent people acting for the families at one remove buying up the shareholdings. The subsidiaries were to remain intact. No attempt would be made to break up the smothering monopolies that the subsidiaries exercised over Japanese industry and commerce.

Shigeru Yoshida, Japan's post-war prime minister, lent his backing to the plan. He asserted that the *zaibatsu*, far from profiting from the war, had been kept out of Japan's conquered lands by the jealous army, and also that the *zaibatsu*'s investment in wartime production gave rise to meagre profits. This had been true only of Manchuria. MacArthur, his hands full, initially welcomed the Yasuda Plan and issued SCAPIN 244, which liquidated the holding companies as proposed. But the supreme commander had his doubts, and either on his own initiative or in response to the concerns of the 'China crowd' in Washington, who were appalled by the limited nature of these reforms, asked for an advisory group of anti-trust experts to be dispatched from Washington.

This group, under the chairmanship of Professor Corwin Edwards, took only a few months to reject the Yasuda Plan. Edwards was convinced of the need to reform the *zaibatsu* – 'the guys principally responsible for the war . . . and a principal factor in the Japanese war potential'. For decades the *zaibatsu* had enforced 'semi-feudal relations between employer and employee, held down wages, and blocked the development of labor unions'; they had retarded 'the rise of a Japanese middle class', which was necessary as 'a counterweight to military despotism'. The low wages permitted ordinary Japanese had stifled domestic consumption and led to the drive for exports. The power and influence of the giant industrial combines made them primarily responsible for Japan's atrocious behaviour overseas.

Edwards was no fellow-traveller, or even a radical. He vigorously opposed nationalizing the *zaibatsu* or promoting worker control. Instead, he advocated selling stock to small firms and controlling the old monopolies with rigour through anti-trust legislation limiting the size, scope, and ownership of the new businesses. MacArthur, although at first hostile to the Edwards reforms, which he viewed as a criticism of his own measures, was soon an enthusiastic convert to the cause.

The three principal recommendations of the Edwards mission, if fully implemented, would almost certainly have revolutionized the Japanese business world. First, the holding companies were to be dissolved, along with their subsidiaries; the leading *zaibatsu* bosses were to be prohibited from reacquiring them. Second, a Holding Companies Liquidation Commission was set up to dissolve any over-large enterprise: it proposed to break up 325 of Japan's biggest companies in the first instance. Third, a Fair Trade Commission was set up to implement a new anti-monopoly law outlawing 'unreasonable restraints of trade' and unfair methods of competition, in an assault on the huge, intricate network of *zaibatsu* control: the inter-corporate security ownership, family ties and interlocking directorates. All shareholdings in the companies defined as being an 'excessive concentration' of economic power were to be sold by the Liquidation Commission on the open market, at very low prices, in order to encourage the spread of small and medium enterprises and individuals. A crushing levy of up to 100 per cent on war profits was imposed, with steep increases in inheritance tax, and the economic assets of fourteen leading *zaibatsu* families were to be frozen in preparation for sequestration (although this in fact happened to only fifty-six people).

On paper, this was an imaginative and ambitious programme, and undoubtedly MacArthur's heart was in it. But a victory against the towering combines of Japanese business power was far, far harder to achieve than one against the war machine. MacArthur's frontal assault was first softened and absorbed by the concealed resistance of the Japanese bureaucrats who were supposed to implement the reforms, but were in fact very close to the *zaibatsu* themselves; it was then lost in the jungle of Japanese business practices, which were virtually incomprehensible to the outsider; and it was finally repealed when Japanese business found allies among American business and right-wingers who waged a vicious propaganda battle that ended up depicting MacArthur – of all people – as being the dupe of socialist and communist forces.

Two further major assaults on economic privilege were undertaken by MacArthur. The first was to be one of the few really lasting achievements of the occupation, and was also to have a profound effect upon the country's political system. The plight of the peasants in Japan was a wretched one: most worked in the service of small farmers as poor as themselves. One prominent member of SCAP, Edwin Martin, described the position succinctly:

> So long as the 47 per cent of the Japanese people living on farms are barely able to survive, they will continue to be a source of cheap labor and cannon fodder. They will be an uneducated and dissatisfied group, seeking a way to better their lot without too much regard for the morality of the means, or understanding of the probable consequences of their acts.

Once again the Japanese administrators formulated wholly inadequate proposals. MacArthur demanded more far-reaching action. Absentee landlords were expropriated, their land being purchased by the government and sold to tenants at pre-war prices – in effect, the land was given away. Owners were allocated 7.5 acres for their own house, and were allowed to rent out 2.5 acres. These patches might seem ridiculously small, but in mountainous Japan only 2000 farmers had more than 100 acres, and few had more than 10; a 7.5 acre farm was a respectable size (this gives an idea of the sheer scale of rural poverty). Over the years of the reform almost a third of all land was expropriated in this way, benefiting a similar proportion of Japanese peasants.

For the first time, the new rural class was not living at levels of absolute poverty and became deeply conservative, transferring its allegiance to right-wing parties and becoming one of their chief props. Japan thus neatly sidestepped what was to be the source of major political instability in the rest of Asia – the existence of a peasant underclass – and also buttressed the country's ruling parties. Later, the existence of these hundreds of thousands of smallholders, whose rice prices were supported by governments which owed their existence to the peasants, would bring its own problems. But at the time, MacArthur's land reform was successful in improving the lives of millions of wretchedly poor Japanese, undermining the militarist class which had been rooted in the peasantry – and bolstering conservatism.

The final area of change touched an area of intense controversy: the power of organized labour. Politically repressed and fragmented into small-scale unions that were usually merely a tool of management, trade unionism was practically non-existent at the end of the war. Idealists in SCAP considered this an affront to the natural rights of labour. The Civil Liberties Directive of 4 October 1945 ordered the Japanese government to abolish all laws restricting freedom of the press, thought, speech, religion or assembly. This permitted unions to begin organizing. With MacArthur's decision to free political prisoners, many communists and former union leaders emerged from jail.

In December 1945, a law was passed guaranteeing Japanese workers the right to organize trade unions, to collective bargaining, and to strike. No fewer than fourteen labour relations bills were passed, setting up all the customary machinery of Western industrial relations, including labour exchanges, vocational training and arbitration machinery. In April 1947 the Labour Standards Law was enacted, setting out minimum standards for safety, hygiene, wages, overtime, working hours, holidays, sick leave and accident compensation. Forced labour was abolished, and the employment of women and children was regulated.

Between 1945 and June 1949 the number of union members rose from just 707 to 6,655,483. Two giant union federations sprang into being: Sodomo, the Socialist General Federation of Trades Unions, and Sanbetsu, the Communist National Congress of Industrial Unions. The new laws were enforced, and quickly led to the equivalent of an earthquake in Japan's deeply conservative social structure. This enabled MacArthur's right-wing critics in Washington to pillory him and force him to change course in such a way as effectively to smother the power of organized labour in Japan almost as completely as in pre-war years.

20

DEMOCRATIC MIKADO

T HE THIRD major category of reforms after the punitive measures and the attacks on Japan's vested interests, were constructive. Chief among them were MacArthur's attempts to modernize the constitution, to institute rule by representative, decentralized government, to create a genuinely free press, to liberalize education, and to separate religion from state.

MacArthur's new constitution was the most dramatic direct imposition of American power during the occupation. As in other matters, MacArthur wanted the new constitution to be drawn up by the Japanese so as to endow it with wider authority. Virtually as soon as the occupation began, in October 1945, a group under Prince Konoye, the deputy prime minister, began to examine constitutional reform. Within weeks, however, it became clear that Konoye himself might be indicted as a war criminal, and his group was quietly wound up.

A new body was set up instead under the minister of state, Joji Matsumoto, a prominent opponent of the militarists in the pre-war period. Along with many other members of the old oligarchy he believed that Japan's problems had arisen because of the militarists' departure from the spirit of the Meiji constitution. To him, constitutional reform meant reasserting the supremacy of the old Meiji institutions. On 1 February 1946 the Matsumoto committee's recommendations were released to the press. They fell far short of American intentions for democratic reform.

Two days later, MacArthur, backed by a firm directive from Washington, ordered a group under General Whitney to draw up their own proposals for a draft constitution. The two worst features of the Matsumoto committee's proposals were, in MacArthur's

315

view, the continuing power vested in the emperor and the refusal to submit legislation to proper parliamentary control. MacArthur insisted on three main points: the emperor could stay on as head of state, but must be responsible to the people; feudal institutions – such as the peerage – must be abolished; and war was to be proscribed. The members of the political branch of SCAP worked on the few books and constitutional treatises they could get their hands on; one drew on extracts from a book by Abraham Lincoln; another drew on the writings of the Abbé Sieyès; another found an authority on constitutional law in the library of Tokyo University. Within ten days they had assembled the outline of a constitution for a nation of 75 million people.

The methods used to ensure Japan's acceptance of the draft were those of Al Capone. At 10 a.m. on 13 February, General Whitney led a delegation of his constitutional committee to the home of Foreign Minister Shigeru Yoshida, who was waiting with Matsumoto, his secretary, Jiro Shirasu, and a Foreign Ministry official. According to the American account of the meeting:

> General Whitney sat with his back to the sun, affording best light on the countenances of the Japanese present who sat opposite him. He cut short any analysis of the Matsumoto draft by stating flatly that it was 'wholly unacceptable to the Supreme Commander as a document of freedom and democracy' and gave the Japanese 15 copies of SCAP's own draft. At 10 o'clock General Whitney [and his aides] left the porch and went out into the sunshine of the garden as an American plane passed over the house. After about fifteen minutes Mr Shirasu joined us, whereupon General Whitney quietly observed to him, 'We are out here enjoying the warmth of atomic energy' – which Whitney later described as a 'psychological shaft'.

This was pressure of the crudest kind. At ten minutes to eleven Whitney returned to the house and told the Japanese that unless they adopted the SCAP draft, two things would follow: the question of the emperor would be reviewed, including the possibility that he might be tried as a war criminal; and SCAP would submit its proposals to a referendum, which might undermine the power of the conservative clique then in control. 'Mr Shirasu straightened up as if he had sat on something. Dr Matsumoto sucked in his breath. Mr Yoshida's face was a black cloud,' summarized Whitney. 'The Japanese acted as though they were about to be taken out and shot.'

The constitution, crude though well-intentioned, contained the essential underpinnings of democracy. The Diet was set up as Japan's sole legislative body, and was given the final say in approving the budget, as well as powers of scrutiny over the cabinet, a majority of whose members now had to be drawn from the Diet. An independent judiciary was established with the power to review all legislation passed by the Diet. Local government was to be decentralized and elected. A bill of rights was drawn up, enshrining freedom of speech, thought, religion, assembly and the press. Discrimination on grounds of race, nationality, creed or political opinion was outlawed. Universal suffrage was introduced. Women were given the right to vote and the right to choose their husbands, as well as to divorce.

Above all, the emperor was stripped of his temporal power. On 1 January 1946, he issued a rescript which has been interpreted as a renunciation of his divinity: 'The ties between us and our people have always stood upon mutual trust and affection. They do not depend upon mere legends and myths. They are not predicated on the false conception that the emperor is divine.'

The rescript was believed to have been suggested by a tutor in English to Crown Prince Akihito, Reginald Blyth, who acted as a kind of intermediary (and even spy) for SCAP in the emperor's household. Harold Henderson, head of the Education, Religion and Fine Arts Department of SCAP, actually dictated it to Blyth. To this day, the Japanese insist that the rescript was largely the work of Prime Minister Shidehara. On Kawahara's account: 'For years the target of attacks by militarists and right-wingers for his pro-Western sympathies, Shidehara saw the concept of a divine emperor as not only antiquated but also as the cause of great suffering.'

On 28 December he showed the finished draft to Hirohito, who nodded his approval, saying it was 'just fine', though he wanted to add as a preface a reference to the Emperor Meiji's Charter Oath of Five Articles, which had set the guidelines for the Japanese state in 1868. The completed rescript, published and broadcast on 1 January 1946, has come to be known as 'The emperor's proclamation of his humanity'. The rescript was far more limited than it appears on first reading. The emperor remained at the centre of Shinto worship, as he had before; as far as the Shinto priests were concerned, there was no change in their treatment of him. Moreover, Hirohito's unbroken connections with his distant ancestors had not been changed; he had merely divested himself of the concept that he was a living god – which had been played up by the militarists, but was not at the centre of the Meiji notion of the imperial ascendancy.

The constitution made him subordinate to the will of the people: authority flowed from them to him, not the other way round. Government was 'a sacred trust of the people, the authority for which is derived from the people, the powers of which are exercised by representatives of the people, and the benefits of which are enjoyed by the people'. However, the new constitution was Mac-Arthur's constitution, imposed upon the Japanese people. What gave it strength was the support it secured among ordinary Japanese, who relished their new role in checking and controlling their masters of many centuries. This upheaval, in practice, was to be remarkably circumscribed, but the democratization of Japan was to be one of MacArthur's finest achievements.

The house of Hirohito, indeed, had fallen on difficult times. Stripped of his divinity, a servant of the people, Hirohito found himself for the first time having to campaign actively for the survival of the institution he embodied: acceptance of the monarchy was no longer unchallenged. In this, he resembled the young Meiji Emperor, who had to fight so hard to earn support for his authority throughout the land. It is hard not to view Hirohito's postwar performance, which re-established the authority of the monarchy, as his finest hour. His modest, bumbling public image came into its own.

With the concept of *lèse-majesté* abandoned, the emperor came under fierce personal attack from left-wing opponents, as well as caustic derision from foreign journalists: this was to work almost wholly in his favour. But for the great mass of ordinary Japanese, it was enough that the emperor had descended from the clouds and sought their approval. In the desperate times after the war, his shabby appearance and humility exactly matched the mood of the day and reflected the suffering of the people.

His household was reduced from 8000 to 1000, after General Whitney told the emperor's staff, 'We've no room for royal parasites here.' One imperial official's wife described the plight of these rejected courtiers: 'Everyone lived on the black market. One sold what precious possessions one still possessed, article by article, in exchange for food. We called it onion-skin living. An appropriate description. Each layer of your belongings you peeled off and sold made you weep.' The emperor's advisers propagated the image of an ascetic emperor – which was nothing less than the truth. He had cut down to a single meal of rice a day. His daughters were photographed washing dishes.

Hirohito and his advisers recognized that the emperor must now be exposed to the people, in a series of walkabouts in towns and factories around the country. For a man in his mid-forties who had never had any contact with the common people, his decision to do this was not without courage, and it must have been painful at first. He still shrank from physical contact with his subjects, preferring to bow, and his conversation was appallingly stilted. Huge crowds turned out to see him: at Kawasaki, Osaka and Nagoya, people thronged as though he were a presidential candidate, treading on his toes, clawing at his clothes. Hirohito and his entourage frequently camped in government offices, classrooms and railway carriages. He was to all intents and purposes running for re-election.

He often went several days without bathing. On one occasion, an innkeeper in Kawajima refurbished the baths in his honour and invited local dignitaries to take their baths in the same water used to cleanse the emperor. However, Hirohito was tired and went straight to bed; instead, two of his doctors decided to have a bath. The furious innkeeper pulled the plug on them, while a host of local worthies stood by in disappointment.

Hirohito's personal discovery of the most banal aspects of everyday life was to make his conversation on the itinerary unintentionally funny. On one occasion he remarked, 'The inns are really designed so that it is easy for people to stay in them.' As he surveyed the ruins of Hiroshima, he observed, 'There seems to have been considerable damage here.' His remark on the condition of the peasantry has become a classic of royal insensitivity and pathos:

> Peasants in their own way lead happy lives. One cannot say that members of the aristocracy are always happy. I enjoyed freedom when I was on a tour of Europe. The only time when I feel happy is when I am able to experience a similar feeling of freedom . . . so peasants should think about the pleasantness of nature out there for them to enjoy and not merely dwell on the uncomfortable aspects of their lives.

With his tireless journeying in his shabby and ill-fitting clothes, the emperor won the hearts of his people. Feudalism was so deep-rooted in Japan that it was enough that their god had come to them; that he was an awkward and uninspiring person did not matter.

*

Hirohito's campaigning partly restored his reputation; but behind the scenes in Japan there was a lively debate, from which he emerges with less credit. Although much of the material about this remains secret, it seems that an influential part of court opinion (indeed, possibly a majority of the emperor's advisers) favoured his abdication as soon as a decent interval had elapsed after 1945, and when the war criminals' trials were over. The reasoning was that his stepping down should be seen not as an act of the occupation, but as a decision by the emperor himself.

There was precedent: Hirohito's father, Mutsuhito, had entrusted his powers to his son as regent when he became too incapacitated to continue in office. Hirohito's abdication would have been difficult to handle because his son Akihito was still a minor; yet the throne had formally been stripped of its powers. Any regent – probably one of the emperor's brothers, not necessarily Chichibu, who was ailing and had been implicated in a number of pre-war right-wing plots – would have had a purely formal role to play in government.

By abdicating, Hirohito would have performed a selfless act and formally accepted all responsibility for the events leading up to the war. Of course, he would not have performed the supreme sacrifice of those executed as war criminals. Yet his penance would have been of the same order, by imperial standards. Truly, Japan would then have been purged of its war guilt. Even if abdication was not on the cards, there were many who believed he should have formally issued a rescript accepting responsibility for the war.

The debate emerged in public when, in May 1948, the chief justice of the supreme court, Shigeru Mibuchi, said: 'If at the end of the war the emperor had of his own accord issued a rescript accepting responsibility, it would have moved the Japanese people very deeply.' Hirohito defended his decision not to abdicate to a palace official: 'I am like a canary whose cage has been opened and someone says, "Fly away!" Where should I fly to? If I have a song to sing, why should I waste it on places where the wind may blow it away?'

A month later, the president of Tokyo University, Shigeru Nanbara, was more outspoken still:

> I believe the emperor ought to abdicate. And I am not the only one; this is an opinion shared by educators throughout Japan, from elementary school teachers to university professors. The only thing is, he needs to consider the repercussions this would have among

the Japanese people, and should time his announcement carefully. His abdication should be carried out without any pressure from politicians or citizens. It should be a spontaneous act that comes from within himself.

Even as loyal a supporter of Hirohito as Kawahara concludes:

That Hirohito escaped trial at the Far Eastern War Crimes Tribunal was solely because it was politically expedient for America and the Occupation forces. But this by no means absolves him . . . there is a feeling that if he had apologised and taken public responsibility just after the war, the matter would be behind Japan . . . I suspect that when all is said and done, historians will have this to say about Emperor Hirohito: he may have been of pure and noble character, but for some reason he never found it in himself to accept responsibility for the war.

The point is a crucial one, and not merely of academic or historical interest. Hirohito's refusal to abdicate reflected the behind-the-scenes argument about not just his own, but Japan's guilt. His chief advisers believed that while there had indeed been an unpardonable excess of militarist zeal, Japan was largely forced into the war by forces beyond its control and that it had nothing to apologize for – except losing, against virtually impossible odds. But the road to war was taken not by the militarists alone, but by a consensus of all of Japan's elites following a logic established in the Meiji era. The bureaucratic elite, once more in the ascendant, chose not to apologize for the war because it still believed that the decision to wage it had been the only one possible; one must assume that Hirohito shared that view.

The continuation of Hirohito in office graphically underlined Japan's refusal to accept responsibility for the war, echoing the surrender broadcast and foreshadowing every subsequent refusal to apologize. Hirohito's decision not to go was no mere act of omission, but a positive assertion that Japan felt it had done no fundamental wrong. Given the readiness of the Japanese themselves to accept Hirohito's abdication after a decent interval, and the historical precedents, MacArthur's dire warnings about the dangers of insurrection and communism can be dismissed as pure hyperbole. The right could argue that the war had changed nothing: the continuity of Hirohito's rule had been maintained, and indeed had prevailed against the country's military occupiers.

The survival of the emperor contributed to the myth of undefeat that was to spring up after the war, the national refusal to face up to responsibility and indeed to gloss it over and to justify the actions that led up to war. Had the emperor accepted responsibility not just in the privacy of MacArthur's office – which he did – but publicly, and renounced his throne, the Japanese people would have been given an incontrovertible demonstration that the country had been wrong to initiate the Pacific War. Instead, just as in the surrender broadcast, he admitted no guilt and nor, therefore, did Japan. Once again, Hirohito, for all his private common sense, had failed his people. For the American occupiers, it was remarkable that the man in nominal charge of the war effort should have been allowed to stay, breaking precedent not just with the fall of the Kaiser and the Austro-Hungarian emperor after the First World War, and of Hitler and Mussolini in the Second, but of the treatment of defeated enemies virtually throughout history.

Hirohito's survival in office had another impact, equally profound but more subtle. It suggested to many in the Japanese hierarchy that although the form of government had changed, its substance – the hierarchical pyramid of power – had not. It was all very well for a foreign-dictated constitution to assert that Hirohito's authority derived from the will of the people. But Japan's vast panoply of authoritarianism and deference had traditionally depended very little on the written word – still less on one imposed by outsiders. If the majority continued to believe in the emperor's status as the pinnacle of authority in Japan, then the situation was much as before.

The emperor's power had always been symbolic, justifying the awesome cataract of subjugation of the system beneath him. He was now more powerless still, but if the symbol stayed, so did the system. Of course, government could now be removed by election; but Japan's democracy was quietly modified to ensure that the same conservative forces remained permanently in office. Hirohito had been largely a figurehead before the war, although he did have some powers in reserve (which he proved deeply reluctant to use). After the war he was formally deemed a figurehead, and stripped of those powers. But behind the scenes it is hard to believe that he did not act much as before: exercising his influence through his advisers, and occasionally venturing a private opinion which would certainly carry great authority. However, his government and advisers would now have been extremely careful not to divulge the existence of such views and opinions.

*

MacArthur's three other constructive reforms were to free the press, to liberalize education, and to separate religion and state, a process already begun by the imperial rescript renouncing his divinity. Freedom of the press was enshrined in the constitution, and it was to work in practice in a very circumspect way. The reforms of education and religion – the two great propaganda bulwarks of the militarist state in the 1930s – were ambitious and, like so much else about the SCAP programme, only partially successful. The reform of education was one of the central planks of MacArthur's reforms. Even before SCAP had stated its demands, some 116,000 teachers were sacked and large numbers of new teachers brought in, many of them victims of past militarist purges.

In April 1946 a teachers' manual was issued preaching revolutionary doctrines for education: it suggested teachers use their own initiative in the classroom, experiment with new methods and encourage pupil participation. In addition, the Ministry of Education set up a programme of 'teacher reorientation', which included a five-week course of lectures on the militarists' role in the pre-war period. Under the terms of the reform as dictated by SCAP, education now existed to promote the individual; the Ministry of Education's monopoly over teachers, textbooks and the curriculum was to be eased, and local education boards were given responsibility for these matters; and pupils were given a freer choice of subjects. The Meiji education structure was reformed: there were now to be six years of elementary education and three of middle school, which were compulsory, plus the option of three years at senior high school – the American system at the time. History and geography courses were shorn of their nationalist overtones, and *shushin* – moral teaching – abolished altogether and replaced by civic and social study courses.

Competitive sports replaced co-ordinated exercises, while schools were now told to pay attention to weather conditions and to the stamina and ages of children when compelling them to take part. Five- to eleven-year-olds were no longer to be taught judo, kenyo, kyudo, 'walk with measured tread', 'warships', 'play at soldiers', and 'fish torpedoes'; their elders were reprieved from learning 'halberd practice', 'navy march', 'stronghold of iron', 'shout of triumph', 'bayonet exercise', and 'hand-grenade throwing'.

The Ministry of Education's monopoly on textbooks was abolished in 1948; instead a 'textbook authorization committee' allowed independent authors to write them, and schools made their own selection. In practice, the ministry retained the power of veto over the contents of textbooks. Moreover, it proved far easier to reform Japan's education system on paper than in reality. Many old teachers quietly returned to the schools. Although the militarist message was no longer preached, most teaching was to remain rigid and unimaginative, and discipline was to stay strict. The textbooks were to remain far from satisfactory, particularly in relation to accounts of the Pacific War.

There was intense pressure from the Christian evangelist groups, to which MacArthur paid particular attention, for the radical transformation of state Shinto. As one Christian critic explained it, Shinto is:

> the only religion in the world which constrains its followers to practice every vice recommended by Satan. No other religion, no matter how barbarous may be its adherents, glorifies lying, cheating, stealing, rape, plunder and pillage on the wholesale scale of Shintoism. No other barbarous religion outlines a religious and racial destiny which contemplates the extermination of the entire remainder of the human race.

MacArthur saw his task as being to strip Shinto of its militarist trappings, and to ensure the separation of religion and state. In the Shinto directive of December 1945, he cut off government funding for Shinto and its shrines; made illegal the semi-compulsory shrine levies on ordinary Japanese; forbade public servants from attending ceremonies in an official capacity; and curbed Shintoist indoctrination in the schools.

Pupils were no longer required to bow towards the Imperial Palace, while the shrines at which the Imperial Rescript on Education and the emperor's portrait were kept were removed. Schoolchildren were no longer forced to go on compulsory trips to Shinto shrines, which were also prevented from employing former soldiers as priests. Government officials were forbidden to participate at military funerals. The national holidays celebrating Shintoism were abolished.

However, SCAP was scrupulous in not seeking to eradicate Shintoism as such. MacArthur himself, with his fervent Christian beliefs, embarrassed his own officials by invoking Christian ideals throughout the occupation – in which he seemed to be in conflict with the attempt to separate religion and state. He encouraged missions from American Bible societies to distribute the Good Book.

At one stage, MacArthur told the young Billy Graham that the emperor was considering becoming a convert to Christianity, and taking his people with him; later there were rumours that Hirohito was thinking of becoming a Catholic. In fact, Christianity made relatively few converts during the occupation: the Catholics increased their numbers from around 20,000 in 1941 to 157,000 in 1951.

MacArthur messianically exaggerated the number of converts to Christianity. On one occasion he claimed there were two million Japanese embracing 'the Christian faith as a means to fill the spiritual vacuum left in Japan's life by the collapse of their past faith'. This Christian spearhead 'would transform' hundreds of millions of backward people in Asia. In 1947 he hailed the fact that three major Asian nations had Christians as their leaders – in Japan, the socialist Tetsu Katayama, in China, Chiang Kai-shek, and in the Philippines, Manuel Roxas. Yet all three soon lost their jobs.

MacArthur's zeal probably did little harm; the Japanese may even have been impressed by his religious faith. The great failing of his reforms in this sphere, as in others, was believing that awe for the emperor and ingrained beliefs could be eliminated at the stroke of a pen. But the Shinto–militarist association was driven underground, and many ordinary Japanese were probably glad to be rid of it. However, many thousands still subscribed to it openly, waiting for its time to return.

Press reform too was a strictly limited affair. At first, at the end of the war, there was a sigh of relief when Japanese military censorship was lifted and newspapers revelled in a new-found freedom to publish. But although MacArthur established press freedom, he imposed his own more relaxed controls. 'News must adhere strictly to the truth . . . there should be no destructive criticisms of the Allied Forces of Occupation,' went one SCAP directive. American black-marketeering, theft, rape, and drunkenness were subjects that could not be discussed, although some Japanese euphemisms for American soldiers got through: 'blue eyed nationals' and 'men with nine-inch footprints' were described as committing such crimes. American censorship extended to emotional descriptions of Hiroshima and Nagasaki; overall, it proved a poor example for the Japanese press, which was to exercise a curious kind of self-censorship in reporting, as though it feared the consequences of excessive frankness.

21

SHOGUN'S SHOWDOWN

TOWARDS THE end of 1947 and at the beginning of 1948, it was possible still to be optimistic about MacArthur's attempts to reshape Japanese society. A truly remarkable and energetic effort had been mounted against the worst features of Meiji and militarist Japan. In most fields reform was quite popular – Japanese obeisance had been so deeply inculcated over hundreds of years that there was little opposition to relaxing the grip of the master classes. In many areas the reforms were superficial and naive, but in others they were subtle and well constructed.

Yet there were enormous forces seeking to obstruct the best attempt that has ever been made to give Japan a genuinely reformist administration. The bureaucratic and business communities obstructed change by every means possible; in America, business and simple-minded military officers viewed the reforms in Japan with intense suspicion. But for the right's high regard for General MacArthur, the hero of the Pacific War, the backlash would have come much sooner and been much more severe (which was almost certainly why the State Department favoured his appointment in the first place).

Meanwhile, the clouds of the Cold War were gathering; this led to an immense simplification of America's world-view. On the one hand the subdued 'China crowd' in the State Department were now the targets of attack by the 'Japan crowd', which regarded them as fellow-travellers, and believed that America's best friend in Asia was the Japanese right. On the other hand, SCAP's reforms, which were no more than the introduction of full democratic rights into a system that stretched back to the Middle Ages, could be portrayed as damagingly subversive.

In addition, Japan, in dire economic difficulties, was assailed by a wave of strikes and left-wing agitation in the immediate aftermath of the war. This was hardly surprising, now that the left had regained its freedom, although the stability of the Japanese state was never threatened. The unrest played into the hands of MacArthur's critics. To retain his balance, MacArthur was forced to tack sharply to the right – but not quickly enough for many in Washington, who began to undermine his power. The whole reform process began to unravel, to the advantage of the elites responsible for the Pacific War in the first place.

MacArthur's enemies had first begun to join forces in Washington in 1947. The initial shot was fired by Harry Kern, *Newsweek*'s foreign editor, who had been pro-Japanese throughout the 1930s and blamed Chiang Kai-shek, absurdly, for manoeuvring Roosevelt into forcing Pearl Harbor upon the Japanese. Kern was a small-minded right-winger who believed that MacArthur's reforms would hand Japan over to the communists. *Newsweek* launched its campaign in January 1947, criticizing the economic purge which drove some 30,000 'active, efficient, cultured and cosmopolitan' managers from office and which would destroy the basis of 'the entire Japanese economic structure'. This would play into the hands of the Soviets: 'We Americans could have all Japan working in our interest' but instead were now 'engaged in wrecking the country so as to leave it as an eventual prize for the Russians.'

Kern's principal ally was a New York lawyer, James Kauffman, who at the start of 1947 was commissioned by the American business community in Tokyo to write a report which was bitterly opposed to MacArthur. Kauffman obtained a copy of FEC 230, which contained MacArthur's anti-*zaibatsu* reforms, and bitterly attacked these as 'socialist and unAmerican'. The country was in deep trouble 'much to the delight of senior Russians who are attached to the Soviet Embassy in Tokyo'. In similarly crude terms, Kauffman went on: 'The high command in Japan has failed to take advantage of the services of experienced businessmen which have been offered. It has accepted the advice of mediocre people and listened to the siren song of a lot of crackpots ... not only financial institutions, but all business is to come under the knife of the economic quack.' A copy of the report was leaked to *Newsweek*, which indulged in similar polemics.

The third of MacArthur's principal enemies was the under-secretary for war, General William Draper, whom Kern tried to promote as an alternative supreme commander to MacArthur. Draper sent a copy of the still classified anti-*zaibatsu* report to Senator William Knowland, who denounced it in the senate. He also circulated a memorandum, apparently originating within SCAP, attacking MacArthur as vain and stupid and interested in Japan only as a stepping-stone to the presidency of the United States.

MacArthur's reply was vigorous and intelligent: for him the *zaibatsu* were the bitter opponents of free enterprise. The real conflict in Japan, he said, lay 'between a system of free competitive enterprise . . . and socialists of one kind or another'. The monopolists were a form of 'socialism in private hands'. Thus he cunningly and accurately stuck the collectivist label on the big business interests being promoted by Kern. Draper, as army under-secretary, persuaded his boss, Kenneth Royall, to deliver a celebrated speech in San Francisco on 6 January 1948 arguing that the reforms should be put into reverse, and that the assault on business there should be brought to an end.

America's interest, Royall argued, was to build a Japan 'strong and stable enough to support itself and at the same time . . . serve as a deterrent against any other totalitarian war threat which might hereafter arise in the Far East'. The army had quite clearly decided that American policy towards Japan must be reversed in the interests of the struggle against communism. It must be assumed that President Truman had some advance knowledge of such a key speech.

MacArthur, however, firmly defended his position:

> Traditionally [a people] exploited into virtual slavery by an oligarchic system of economic feudalism under which a few . . . families directly or indirectly have controlled all of the commerce and industry and raw materials of Japan, the Japanese are rapidly freeing themselves of these structures to clear the road for the establishment of a more competitive enterprise – to release the long suppressed energies of the people towards the building of that higher productivity of a society which is free.

'Amazing strides', said MacArthur, had been made towards industrial rehabilitation and recovery.

By January 1948, however, a prominent member of the State Department, W. W. Butterworth, had joined the army's opposition to SCAP reform. He argued that Japan would have to recover 'through the normal operation of merchant greed, not idealist reforms'. In February, MacArthur reacted to the combined assault on him by the army, the State Department, a large part of the American media, and the senate by attacking 'the traditional economic pyramid' and suggesting that unless the *zaibatsu* were reformed, 'there is not the slightest doubt that their clearing away will eventually occur through a bloodbath of revolutionary violence'.

The law on deconcentration was pushed through the Diet. Around three hundred companies, controlling over half of Japan's commerce and industry, were earmarked for possible dissolution. MacArthur's enemies reacted furiously. George Kennan, the State Department's highest flier, who had joined their number, visited Japan and issued a forty-two-page commentary attacking SCAP as a parasite gorging on Japan, taking up a third of the country's budget; he argued against radical reform. Draper and Percy Johnston, chairman of the Chemical Bank, led a delegation to Japan in March which argued passionately that Japan must be made economically 'self-supporting as soon as possible', and that the reforms, the anti-*zaibatsu* law, and the purge must be ended.

MacArthur was defiant and firm: he told Sir Alvary Gascoigne, the head of the British mission, that 'America's tycoons', such as Royall and Draper, opposed the anti-*zaibatsu* law because they thought it would hinder their own business interests. MacArthur insisted that he would not obey orders from 'a mere under-secretary'. But the supreme commander's position was already being undermined from within, through no fault of his own: Japan's economy was a shambles; and union militancy was growing to a level at which it could be portrayed as a serious communist threat.

MacArthur, in truth, had hardly been slow to respond to the problem of the unions. As far back as spring 1946, 'production control' – the seizure of factories and mines by workers who formed co-operatives to manage them – was under way. In April and May of that year large demonstrations had taken place, with workers demanding bigger fuel rations, wage increases and the resignation of the government. On 19 May a huge crowd outside the prime minister's residence and in front of the Imperial Palace alarmed the authorities. MacArthur issued one of the toughest proclamations of his period of office, a warning against mob disorder or violence by 'undisciplined elements' threatening order in post-war Japan. The Japanese government must act, he warned, or SCAP would. The government accordingly took measures against the far left. Later MacArthur denounced 'strikes, walkouts, or other work stoppages which are inimical to the objectives of the occupation'. Union leaders were threatened with arrest. MacArthur was exceeding his brief: the principal targets of the occupation were supposed to be Japanese militarists, not union members, and most of the strikes in Japan were peaceful. Moreover, MacArthur's declaration had clearly violated the new right to strike. On 1 January 1947 he banned a one-day general strike as a 'deadly socialist weapon'.

His authority began to falter decisively only in the spring and summer of 1948, when he rashly allowed his name to go forward for the Republican nomination for president. He had a flimsy campaign organization, and on the eve of the Wisconsin primary he came under attack from a rising star, Senator Joe McCarthy, as an old man hopelessly out of touch with American politics. At the Republican convention, MacArthur won just seven votes on the first ballot. The general's many enemies were jubilant, and for the first time MacArthur's fighting spirit seemed to ebb.

In spring 1948 a Deconcentration Review Board set up by Draper, with the backing of the army and the State Department, went through the three hundred plus companies targeted by the occupation. Virtually every one was exempted from the anti-trust legislation. Edward Welsch, helplessly in charge of the Anti-Trust and Cartels division of SCAP, concluded bitterly that:

> What was initially considered . . . a major objective of the occupa-
> tion [had] become . . . a major embarrassment . . . Without for-
> mally questioning the desirability or broad purposes of the policy,
> it was decided to take measures which would minimize the actions
> prepared for carrying out the policy. The facts of the last war faded
> . . . and conjectures on the next war took their place.

MacArthur was so scathing about the army department's wish to set up a Japanese army, however, that even Draper backed off. At the same time it seems clear that MacArthur was coming close to some kind of emotional breakdown as his plans were emasculated and his power savagely reined back. He fervently tried to prove his anti-communist credentials by beginning what was described by a British embassy observer as an 'almost hysterical . . . witch-hunt' in Japan. The press became shrilly anti-communist and anti-labour.

General Willoughby was the driving force behind the campaign, through his counter-intelligence corps. CIC argued that the strikers were being idealistically motivated: the truth was that Japan's precarious economic condition, as well as rising prices and food shortages, had led to a growing number of strikes and demonstrations. But MacArthur's response was decisive: public sector workers were finally stripped of their right to strike and bargain collectively, with the threat of 'anarchy, insurrection and destruction' being cited by the authorities. When the Japanese government implemented these measures, there were walk-outs throughout the country. SCAP instructed the government to arrest the strikers, trade union activists and communists. Even the British, usually America's allies on the Far East Commission, were appalled by this resort to frankly dictatorial powers.

When Sir Alvary Gascoigne, regarded as a close friend by MacArthur, protested to the supreme commander, he 'shouted at me without stopping for one and three-quarter hours. MacArthur accused the British of taking sides "with the Kremlin" and of "betraying" America. Britain was helping the Russians to "corrupt labour and cause disruption and chaos".' Sir Alvary described the meeting as his 'most painful duty in Japan'.

> The press was absolutely forbidden to publish anything other than favorable stories on SCAP. When he or SCAP were criticized in United States newspapers, he (or Whitney) would draft and send verbose and baroque replies – even to the smallest and least significant journals – often unwisely adding fuel on a fire that would have died of its own accord. The staff treated MacArthur with awed reverence . . . MacArthur himself would say that, 'My major advisers have now boiled down to two men – George Washington and Abraham Lincoln.'

At about the same time – early 1948 – SCAP shifted the focus of its purges from right to left: some 10,000 suspected communists were removed from the public sector, the media and the education system; around the same number were relieved of positions in industry.

In June 1950, as tensions over Korea mounted, MacArthur purged the whole central committee of the Japan Communist Party, as well as the editorial staff of *Akahata* ('Red Flag'), the party newspaper, which was banned shortly afterwards. The US chamber of commerce distributed pamphlets entitled 'How to Spot a Communist' and 'Communism: A World Threat'. In alliance with Willoughby's anti-communist crusade was the Special Investigation Bureau, staffed largely by former members of the Thought Police, which expanded from 150 members in 1948 to 1700 under Mitsu-sada Yoshikawa.

SCAP's lurch to the right was accompanied by a similar one in Japanese politics that was to define the political complexion of the country for the next forty years. The emergence of a communist threat – both the real one in Asia and the imagined one in Japan – as well as the dramatic change of direction in Washington prompted Japanese conservatism to reassert itself. The Social Democratic Party, which had enjoyed a brief spell in power during the occupation, split, never to return to power again. The middle-of-the-road Ashida cabinet fell, and the Liberal Democratic Party was formed by a merger of the two main right-wing parties, coming to power under its tough-minded leader Shigeru Yoshida.

The mould of Japanese politics was thus set for decades to come. MacArthur was belatedly to claim the credit over the next few months for crushing communism, breaking the power of the unions and splitting the socialists. In fact he had been largely forced to do so by Washington. Japan had harked back to pre-war oligarchic Meiji rule with the virtual collapse of MacArthur's power; from 1948 on, he was largely a figurehead, just as the emperor had been over the previous two years. The new shogun, always exerting his power discreetly during the occupation, was Yoshida. MacArthur may have tried to convince himself that the move to the right was really necessary in view of the challenges within Japan. Yet he cannot really have believed this: he had fought long and hard for real change in Japan during the period when he was the most powerful man in the country.

The intense bitterness he felt at the turn of events is reflected in his reminiscences, which make virtually no mention of how his reforms were turned upside-down. Like the idealist he fundamentally was, he boasts of his programme of change as though it had actually been effective. MacArthur, who had won so many battles, had been decisively defeated by a large and formidable combination of con-servative and military enemies in Washington, by Willoughby's fifth column within the SCAP hierarchy, and finally by the most formid-able power of all, even in national defeat – the Japanese ruling class, determined to frustrate any real change in the system of government established by the Meiji oligarchy. The Japanese elite effectively obstructed most, though not quite all, of the significant reforms.

On the most crucial issue – the dissolution of the *zaibatsu* – there had been no visible progress at all by the end of the occupation.

The Japanese economic and industrial structure was virtually the same as during the middle of the Pacific War, when the *zaibatsu* were considerably more powerful than they had been during the 1920s. The Japanese economy was still dominated by a handful of massive, furiously competing, yet also co-operating economic giants, reborn as Keiretsu. Virtually the whole of Japan's economic success was governed by this single fact during the post-war years.

As for the other traditional centres of power in Japan, the bureaucracy had survived virtually intact, and was to re-embark upon a new golden age of oligarchic dominance, while the militarists had been relegated to a much lower place on the ladder of power – but had by no means been eliminated, as had been the intention. A fourth estate had also entered into the power structure: the political class, while much more significant than before the war, was in no sense truly sovereign. In any democracy, it is true that the elected politicians are usually only the first among equals at a table which also accommodates the bureaucracy and the business class, the trade unions, the armed forces (and the security services), and the press. In Japan the model was fatally skewed, even after MacArthur's frenzied attempts to reform it: the *zaibatsu*, by virtue of their huge concentration of economic power, and the bureaucracy were clearly at the top of the pecking order, with the political leaders a distant third; the armed forces were now fourth. Neither the unions nor the press counted for anything.

The final verdict on MacArthur, Japan's flawed but remarkable shogun, must be favourable. He came from a deeply conservative background, the US army. He had fought the Japanese with tenacity and brilliance. Yet in his stewardship he not only resisted the attempt by many of his fellow countrymen to give the Japanese a taste of their own vengeful values, but made the only attempt in the country's history to introduce the kind of democratic, popular values that might block the awesome hold of its traditional power structures. For over two years he fought with remarkable vigour on behalf of the idealists beneath him. He was crushed by an unholy alliance of the Japanese private sector and bureaucracy, genuine anti-communists in his own administration, and the military–industrial complex in the United States. His subsequent attempts to suggest that he agreed with these three groups did him no credit, and must have been regretted later. As in Bataan, he lost against overwhelming odds. But, as there, what survived from his struggle was by no means negligible: the relegation of the army to lower status and the tenacious flowering of democracy, in particular.

On 11 April 1951, MacArthur was dismissed by Truman as America's Korean War commander on the grounds of alleged insubordination. This is no place for a history of the war. Suffice to say that both the Korean War and the dismissal of MacArthur were to have enormous reverberations in Japan, effectively shattering the huge prestige that America enjoyed since those first, uncertain days of the occupation, replacing it with ill-concealed contempt in a large part of the ruling elite and public opinion. The importance and immediacy of Korea for Japan remained unchanged now as throughout Japanese history, particularly the Meiji period.

The war was a subject of grave concern: for years the peninsula had been viewed as 'a dagger at the heart of Japan', an essential part of the archipelago's security: the prospect of a communist victory there – and a Chinese communist one at that – was unthinkable to the Japanese government. In fact, the Korean War transformed Japan's strategic position. The Americans could only justify staying on there in terms of the danger of a communist occupation of Japan. Japan, moreover, had been used as the jumping-off point for American forces going to Korea. From an enemy, it had been transformed into a valuable ally.

The Korean War also had a remarkable indirect effect on Japan: it provided the kick-start needed for Japan's ailing economy: as in the First World War, Japan's munitions industry underpinned economic recovery. Finally, America's failure to dislodge the communists from the Korean peninsula raised eyebrows in Japan – for the first time, there was a question mark over the invincibility of the superpower that had defeated them. Japan in the past had successfully conquered Korea, defeating both the Russians and the Chinese there. The United States could not do so: this lent credence to the view that Japan lost the Pacific War only because it was overstretched and because of the atomic bomb.

MacArthur's fall was, if anything, even more traumatic for the Japanese. The national deference to hierarchy had led them to look upon him as a kind of benevolent despot, a figure even more powerful than the emperor, and more remote still. He seemed to most Japanese almost omnipotent. Kawahara depicts the impact of his fall upon Hirohito:

> It was as if the sky had fallen. The Japanese, who are brought up to be submissive to authority, had eventually come to respect the supreme commander of their former enemies. When Hirohito was

334

first informed of the news at a little past 4 p.m. on April 11, 1951, he simply sat and stared into space for a long time. Later, when he received more details from Grand Chamberlain Mitani, he seemed genuinely surprised again, saying 'So it's really true . . .'

Six years before, in 1945, the emperor's fate had been in MacArthur's hands. And now the general had been relieved of his command with just one telegram from the President of the United States.

Much had changed in the six years of occupation: Hirohito initially declined to make a farewell call on MacArthur, suggesting that MacArthur should visit the emperor. When this was refused, Hirohito called on MacArthur, now a private citizen, for the sixth time at his American Embassy residence, as a token of his appreciation and respect. But the emperor stayed away from the departure ceremonies, headed by Prime Minister Yoshida. MacArthur was regarded with some affection by the Japanese, who nevertheless rejoiced in his fallen status as heralding the end of the occupation, and were later incensed when he described their political sophistication as being that of twelve-year-olds. MacArthur was never quite forgiven for that gaffe.

There were some immediate fears in Japan that the occupation might not now be so benevolent; for MacArthur had proved himself a true friend of the Japanese people. At the same time the emperor and political leaders must have realized that no future occupation leader would be as powerful as MacArthur. The time was fast approaching for Japanese politicians to take their destiny in their own hands. General Matthew Ridgway, the new supreme commander, was an easygoing personality with a fine record of bravery and none of the political complexity or subtlety of MacArthur. He was content, by and large, to leave politics to the politicians.

Two immediate consequences flowed from the war and from the manner of MacArthur's dismissal. The Americans began to consider as a matter of priority how to wind up the occupation; and Japanese politics, which had already lurched sharply to the right in 1948, were now confirmed in their drift towards anti-communist conservatism. Up to now, the occupation had been prolonged largely because of the country's dire economic straits and because MacArthur's powerful enemies in Washington were determined to undo his work. The supreme commander, although in charge, had indeed sought an end to the occupation as far back as 1947, so that there would be no chance to undo his reforms.

There is some evidence to suggest that the delay in Japan's economic recovery until the change of direction the following year was substantially a result of the direct refusal of the *zaibatsu* to invest and engage in economic activity until the threat posed to their interests by MacArthur and the SCAP reformists was removed. In 1948 the anti-*zaibatsu* reforms were abandoned, and Japan's bosses, in alliance with their friends in Washington, emerged victorious. Economic recovery got under way, sharply accelerated by the Korean War. In 1949 a prices and wages policy imposed by SCAP helped to stabilize the economy. By the following year, many companies were at least partially solvent, and by 1951 industrial production had returned to the level of the early 1930s. Almost certainly, recovery would have come three years earlier had the *zaibatsu* not been determined to pursue MacArthur and, in effect, to engage in an investment and production strike (as they did unpatriotically against militarist attempts to take them over during the Pacific War).

With MacArthur's removal, there was no longer any need to prevaricate: the Americans could safely negotiate a peace treaty with the Japanese and end the occupation. There remained one problem. America's Far Eastern allies, given so limited a role throughout the occupation, were not disposed to end it unconditionally as they continued to regard Japan with deep suspicion. The British pressed for economic restrictions on Japan's growth; the Chinese were deeply hostile; Australia and New Zealand would only consent if the United States signed a formal security treaty with them; the Philippines required a similiar defence agreement; and the Soviet Union flatly opposed any end to the occupation.

The chief American negotiator of the peace treaty with Japan was John Foster Dulles, an arcane but senior Republican serving a Democratic administration and thereby ensuring a bipartisan policy. Dulles got on famously with Hirohito as well as the Japanese government. He toyed with three chief options. The first was a direct American guarantee of Japan's security, with an agreement by the Japanese not to rearm. The second option was the militarization of Japan so as to ensure that the country could defend itself. The third was a formal guarantee by America, the Soviet Union, Britain and China to respect Japan's neutrality provided the country did not rearm at all. The Russians and the Chinese naturally favoured the latter. The communist countries joined America's allies in vigorously opposing the second option, which was favoured by the Americans. The first option was adopted as a compromise that failed to satisfy only the Soviets, and then not too seriously.

It was also the choice favoured by most senior Japanese, giving them the best of all possible worlds. Rearmament would have been cripplingly expensive, in Japan's parlous economic state, and would have aroused the immediate hostility of most of Asia. An American guarantee would enable Japan to concentrate on economic recovery from behind a shield. For the Japanese right, it had the advantage of guaranteeing American support in the event of communist attack; prior to 1948, the Pentagon's strategic thinking was that Japan was unnecessary to the defence of the Pacific, and could be happily left neutral. American strategy in the Pacific was tied to an arc of islands south of Okinawa. For the left, it kept Japan's militarists in check, however ritually they might denounce the presence of American 'imperialists' in Japan.

The foundations for Japan's post-war rise to economic super-power status were being laid. Japan would become a 'pacifist commercial democracy'. The Americans were reasonably happy, but they wanted to enlist Japan as a major ally against the Soviet Union – something that never really happened. The Philippines, and Australia and New Zealand, were largely satisfied that Japan would remain under some American restraint, as US bases would remain there and the country's growing army would be held in check. The Japanese carefully sided with neither Nationalist China nor Communist China, which half-pleased the latter. Only the Soviets were angry, with Andrei Gromyko, their delegate to the San Francisco Peace Conference, on 8 September 1951 vigorously attacking the agreement.

Forty-eight nations signed the treaty. Under its terms, Japan fully accepted the wholesale dissolution of its former empire. Korean independence was restored, while Japanese claims to Formosa, the Pescadores, southern Sakhalin and the northern Kuriles were re-nounced. American control of the Ryukyu islands, in particular Okinawa, was recognized by Japan. There were no economic restraints placed upon the country, and its right to self-defence was recognized. In the treaty's preamble, the United States agreed that 'in the interests of peace and security, [it] is ... willing to maintain certain of its armed forces in and around Japan, in the expectation, however, that Japan will increasingly assume responsibility for its own defence against direct and indirect aggression'. On 28 April 1952, the day before the emperor's birthday, the occupation ended and Hirohito, albeit hedged in by the new Japanese constitution, was formally ruler of his land again.

The peace treaty was enormously satisfactory to the Japanese, and in particular to the outstanding leader of the immediate post-war period, Shigeru Yoshida (although it was actually negotiated with the country's sole, and very short-lived, Socialist administration). Yoshida's views coincided with those of MacArthur, whose closest Japanese confidante he was. His role was to be pivotal in defining both the country's new political colouring after the Americans had gone, and the new pattern of power-sharing between the main forces in Japan: the bureaucracy, business and the politicians. After MacArthur's departure, Yoshida was unquestionably the dominant figure in Japan, and the biggest shaper of post-war Japanese society.

22

RETURN TO ARMS

JAPANESE POLITICS after the occupation seemed on the surface to plunge into a dark age of unending factional squabbles within the Liberal Democrat Party presided over by a succession of shuffling, obscure politicians. The country that underwent one of the most vicious, dramatic and sinister power struggles in the world before the war now seemed a paragon of dullness: a single party ruled throughout the post-occupation period, giving Japan a stability unprecedented in any major industrial democracy. A natural consensus seemed to have evolved around the idea that Japan should be under-armed and pro-American, and should pursue economic expansion without looking back.

This political stability underpinned astonishing growth. A prominent architect of the post-war economic boom in Japan quipped years later that the businessmen had been responsible for 70 per cent of the Japanese economic miracle, and the bureaucracy for 70 per cent. That added up to 140 per cent, so the politicians were responsible for minus 40 per cent. Yoshida was to define his view of commercial reconstruction taking precedence over political power thus: 'Just as the United States was once a colony of Great Britain but is now the stronger of the two, if Japan becomes a colony of the United States it will eventually become the stronger.' This view seemed ludicrously far-fetched at a time when Japan was still half-devastated and half-starved, possessing a fraction of the natural resources of the United States. It does not seem so implausible now.

In fact, beneath the surface of Japan's external consensus and tailcoat intrigue, there was a political ferment. The policy of subservience to the United States was by no means quietly accepted by large parts of Japanese opinion. The right saw it as humiliating, the

339

left as immoral. If either had triumphed, the course of Japan's post-war politics would have been very different. Yoshida's policy prevailed for decades because it persuaded most influential Japanese that it was by far the best tailored to Japan's self-interest. During the post-war years, however, the country twice came perilously close to open insurrection, and several times to takeover by the extreme right. The balance remains precarious. Japan lives under a volcano, Mount Fuji. It is dormant, not extinct.

America withdrew from Japan in 1952 leaving a country which had agreed, in effect, to act as a stationary aircraft carrier for the projection of American forces in the Far East, and which looked in return for protection against the Soviet Union under the American defence umbrella, both conventional and nuclear. The phrase used to describe this policy was 'pacifist commercial democracy'. It squared many circles: it tapped the absolute hatred of many Japanese for war after the shattering experience of the bombs and defeat; it gave the Japanese time and money to concentrate upon their economic reconstruction and regeneration; it allayed the fears of Japan's Asian neighbours, ever suspicious of the country that had launched a war that killed millions; and it placed Japan at the front rank of nations resisting what seemed an irresistible tide of communism flowing through the region.

The creator of Japan's post-war security arrangements, Shigeru Yoshida, was not, however, anything like a pacifist himself: he was an immensely able right-wing politician. He was also a remarkable personality: although deeply conservative, he had been an outspoken opponent of the Pacific War as early as 1941. As a member of the Yohansei group of conservatives in the armed forces, the business community and the bureaucracy, he was in the minority at the time: he had helped to draft the first memorandum submitted by Prince Konoye advocating an end to the war in early 1945. The memorandum suggested, in the most conspiratorial terms, that Tojo and his supporters were radicals seeking to reshape the Japanese economy and society on the Soviet model. The alleged evidence for this was Tojo's attempt to force big business to accept the domination of the Ministry of Munitions – something which had automatically taken place in war in such countries as Britain and Germany.

In fact, the *zaibatsu* beat off the challenge; at that stage, after years of channelling and benefiting from the direction of Japanese militarism, the big corporations had become increasingly opposed to Tojo. When military defeat came in Saipan, the conservatives and the *zaibatsu* were instrumental in his fall. The *zaibatsu* continued to prosecute the war, because they were not against the fighting as such; their prime concern was to resist Tojo's apparently 'socialist', anti-business tendencies, which seemed to hark back to those of the Imperial Way group during the 1936 uprising. Konoye echoed Yoshida's arguments in pointing out to the emperor that military defeat was as nothing compared to the prospect of 'leftist revolution'.

There was a lurking fear among intelligent conservatives in Japan that the intensely hierarchical nature of society laid it open to hijack by the communists, whose ideal structure of society it mirrored. If the communists secured control, they could slide in at the top more easily than in any country on earth, simply by taking advantage of the methodical brainwashed mindset of Japanese before the war to propagate their own ideas: the people of Japan might then have become the most formidable shock troops of global communism. Konoye and Yoshida insisted that the militarists were door-openers for the communists. 'Wiping out' militarist training and carrying out the reconstruction of the military were 'the peculiarities and prerequisites for saving Japan from communist revolution'.

The army replied by having Yoshida arrested in April 1945. He was entirely acceptable to MacArthur as prime minister after Shidehara in 1946 for a year, and then again after the historic defeat of the moderate left in 1948, winning four more elections before being forced out in November 1954. Yoshida was a tough-minded, cantankerous, even eccentric personality, glorying in representing a straightforward throwback to the half-democratic and capitalist Japan of the 1920s. A former ambassador in London, he was sixty-seven when he first became prime minister; he wore a pince-nez and wing collar, preferred English tailored tailcoats and suits, puffed at cigars and rode in an elderly Rolls-Royce, partly as a way of irritating the Americans. Known to the Japanese admiringly as 'one man', he was happy to refer to the country's trade enemies as 'a bunch of bastards', to theorists on MacArthur's staff as 'quite peculiar types' or 'red subversives', and to form a covert alliance with General Willoughby.

However, his opposition to the power of the armed forces and his insistence that Japan rebuild before rearming led him both to support Article Nine of the new constitution and to articulate the theory of the country as a pacifist commercial democracy. Yoshida argued that, while Japan regained its economic strength, so too it could forge its political authority. He deeply admired the Meiji leaders for expanding Japan's influence without drifting into war with Britain or America.

He wrote that it was by this means that 'a small island nation in the Far East came in half a century to rank among the five great powers of the world'. He favoured the *zaibatsu*, the aristocracy, the old education system and the authority of the emperor. He argued that the Americans were operating on an 'erroneous assumption that we are an aggressive people of ultra-militarist tendencies to be refashioned into a peace-loving nation'.

Yoshida later openly boasted of how he had outwitted the Americans. The occupation, he said, 'was hampered by its lack of knowledge of the people it had come to govern, and even more so, perhaps, by its generally happy ignorance of the amount of requisite knowledge it lacked'. He noted that on one occasion SCAP had issued a directive ordering a purge of all 'standing directors' – that is, any director – of Japanese firms. The Japanese chose to translate this as 'managing directors' – a fraction of the total. Thus, said Yoshida, 'we were able to save many ordinary directors who might otherwise have been so classified from the purge'.

Yoshida was indeed a passionate supporter of big business. He was asked in 1945 whether action should be taken against the *zaibatsu*:

I answered that it would be a great mistake to regard Japan's financial leaders as a bunch of criminals, that the nation's economic structures had been built by such old established and major financial concerns as Mitsui and Mitsubishi, and that modern Japan owed her prosperity to their endeavours, so that it was most doubtful whether the Japanese people would benefit from the disintegration of these concerns.

I explained further that the so-called *zaibatsu* had never worked solely for their own profit, but often at a loss, as for instance during the war when they continued to produce ships and planes on government orders regardless of the sacrifices involved; that the people who had actually joined hands with the militarists and profited from the war were not the established financial groups, but the new rich who were alone permitted by the military to conduct business in Manchuria and other occupied territories to the detriment of the old established concerns; and that those who had most heartily welcomed the termination of the Pacific conflict were the leaders of these old established concerns that had laid the foundations of their prosperity in time of peace and had never felt at ease in their relations with the military clique who had become masters of the nation for the duration of the war.

Yoshida's views soon came under fire from both left and right. The left, reinforced by the colossal pacifist sentiment in post-war Japan, argued that Japan should opt for 'total neutrality' and abandon its subjugation to the United States, preferring an equality of relations with America, the Soviet Union and China. On the other side, Yoshida was viewed with intense suspicion by many unreconstructed conservative politicians. The militarists had good reason for hating him, but they were no longer so powerful. Yoshida himself came from the most liberal agency of the bureaucracy: the Foreign Ministry. But he was acute enough – unlike his pre-war predecessors – to see that the bureaucracy itself needed a wider power base from which to dominate Japanese politics. He did two things to try to secure one: first, he carved out an alliance between the ruling conservative party – the Liberal Democrats – and the *zaibatsu*. Second, he encouraged senior bureaucrats to run for public office, as a kind of climax to their careers. The old party bosses, themselves largely the creatures of the *zaibatsu*, intensely resented his attempt to infiltrate bureaucratic control into politics. But in the early stages of Yoshida's dominance they had no choice but to rally round him, in the face of the threat from the left.

On May Day in 1952, the annual left-wing demonstrations degenerated into savage violence. Rioters set fire to American cars parked by the palace moat, while fierce battles with the police ensued. It marked the beginning of a major left-wing campaign against the 'problem' – the argument that although the occupation was formally ended, in practice it continued with the presence of thousands of American servicemen and the subordination of Japan's foreign policy. A constant outpouring of press reports alleged excesses by American servicemen, including their supposed penchant for turning the areas around their bases into centres of prostitution.

In 1954 an American hydrogen bomb was set off at Bikini, and a small Japanese fishing boat was caught in the radiation; unfortunately this became apparent only after part of the catch had been sold. There was a widespread panic among this fish-loving people, and for a while seafood virtually disappeared from their tables. The Americans suggested that the boat had violated the warning zone around the test site, but this was later found not to be the case. A wave of anti-Americanism swept Japan. Yoshida's brand of pro-Americanism was put on the defensive, and his chief rival on the right, Ichiro Hatoyama, put an end to his ascendancy the following year.

Hatoyama was a politician of the old school, which argued that Yoshida had practised a policy of 'subservience' to America. It was decided to put the bureaucrats that Yoshida represented in their place. Moreover, he was determined to revise the constitution: 'The present constitution', he said, 'was imposed on us in English when neither the government nor the people had freedom. It must take a very patient man to be grateful to it. It was drawn up with a view to sapping our strength.' He believed in full Japanese rearmament. In addition he wanted the police force centralized and the unions brought to heel even more than they already had been.

Finally, he wanted Japan to resume relations with the Soviet Union as a means of ending its dependence on America. Yoshida's attitude to the *zaibatsu* had been to co-operate, considering them essential to the economic regeneration of Japan after the war, while dominating them: indeed, the power of the state was at a zenith immediately after the war, because the *zaibatsu* needed state assistance in reconstruction. Hatoyama's attitude was one of straightforward partnership with big business.

When the divided Socialists came together in 1955, so did the two main conservative parties, in the Liberal Democratic Party (LDP). Hatoyama wrote into the party's programme the goals of constitutional revision and rearmament. The ruling party was now committed to restoring Japan as a major military power, and one independent of the United States. But it was blocked by the fact that the opposition had more than a third of the seats in parliament: a two-thirds vote was required for revision. Hatoyama's attempt to restore relations with the Soviet Union largely failed: there was no peace treaty and no territorial settlement, because the Russians showed no willingness to return the occupied Kuriles. Diplomatic relations were, however, normalized.

Hatoyama's successor was Nobosuke Kishi, the former minister of munitions in Tojo's government and originally regarded as a war criminal by MacArthur. Kishi was originally a super-bureaucrat whose commitment to economic recovery was second to none. He understood how to manipulate the power centres of Japan – the bureaucracy, the *zaibatsu*, the militarists and now the new one, the politicians – as did virtually no one else, and was the first represent-ative of the desire to return Japan fully to its pre-occupation values.

He wanted nothing less than to renegotiate the 1951 security treaty with the United States to give Japan an equal say, as well as constitutional revision to permit full rearmament. This was opposed by the United States, by Japan's Asian neighbours, and by the Soviets and the Chinese. But what stopped him in his tracks was a massive display of opposition from ordinary Japanese, mobilized by the left-of-centre parties. When, in 1960, some four million people took to the streets and serious rioting followed, President Eisenhower's visit to Japan had to be cancelled. It was one of the few times in Japanese political history that popular opposition had been massively felt, and had been successful. Kishi managed only to push through a mildly amended security treaty, and resigned in humiliation.

From that moment on the LDP retreated into its shell and espoused the Yoshida programme: alliance with the United States, gentle but steady rearmament, and an all-out effort for economic growth to double the national income. Political controversy was to be eschewed. Japan had moved perilously close to outright confron-tation between the elites and the people, and for once the elites had retreated. Defence spending was even reduced as a proportion of gross domestic product (GDP) – which, however, was growing fast – from 1.2 to 0.8 per cent.

Eisaku Sato, a later prime minister and brother of Kishi, even held the view that Japan should not possess, manufacture or admit nuclear weapons – which seemed a rebuff aimed at the Americans, whose aircraft carriers regularly carried them into Japanese ports. It was not widely believed that the Americans removed their weapons before docking, even after Sato's pronouncement. Sato also publicly endorsed the MacArthur constitution: 'The spirit of the constitution has become the flesh and blood of the nation,' he declared.

The security equation remained largely unchanged throughout the early 1960s. However, as the United States found itself increasingly trapped in the quagmire of Vietnam, the certainties that bound the Japanese government to its closest ally began to erode. While left-wing Japanese eagerly indulged in ritual criticism of United States imperialism, the right was far from certain that Vietnam was a clear-cut case of America fighting the good fight against communist insurgents. Gradually many Japanese conservatives began to identify with the small Asian nation fighting, and indeed prevailing, against the might of the United States. This demonstration of American weakness caused many to question, once again, the whole basis of Japan's security dependence on the United States.

Two further shocks followed: after America's withdrawal from Vietnam, the Americans began to voice doubts about their commitment to Korea and the Philippines. The Japanese feared they were about to be abandoned, when they had deliberately remained under-armed and dependent upon the United States. In 1971, moreover, President Nixon floated the dollar, which was a decision primarily motivated by the need to reduce the value of the currency against the yen, as Japan was then flooding America with imports. This was seen, rightly, as a direct slap in the face.

Professor Tetsuya Kataoka, a leading Japanese political scientist, summed up the importance of Vietnam to the Japanese political elite as follows:

A question may naturally arise: will the search for a new role take Japan on the path to revanchism? Will not Japan, no longer believing in the verdict of the Tokyo trial *in toto*, be bent on revenge against the United States? . . .

An intelligent American – not a wide-eyed revisionist – in the post-Vietnam era may realize that the verdict of the Far Eastern Military Tribunal had all the one-sidedness of victor's justice. It was to Japan what the verdict of the counterculture has been to America and her history. To say, therefore, that a majority of the Japanese today do not believe in that verdict is far from saying that they feel they were simply right, or that they seek revenge . . .

But the most important factor may be one that the Japanese are not clearly aware of. In all the post-war years, the Japanese have harboured hidden resentment towards their former conqueror, who has been ahead of them in almost everything they have done, be it entrepreneurship, inventiveness, or, not least, war-making. In this view, America's bungling and subsequent humiliation in a war of succession to Japan's former possession might have constituted a comeuppance. The way some conservative Japanese cheered on the Vietcong after the Nixon shock suggests that the Vietcong had become their proxy against white men – even though they knew full well that that was an illusion. In a way, Hanoi's victory constituted that perverse justice that George Kennan spoke of, and it wiped the slate clean of war-related emotion.

The leadership of the LDP, however, did not react with a prompt reversion to Kishi's policies. Instead it began a steady return to the old pre-war Japanese values, most notably in the increasingly revisionist attitude towards the Pacific War. This was best illustrated in an interview in 1969 with Kakuei Tanaka, who was to become one of the most powerful post-war prime ministers:

I don't think World War II was such a simple war in the history of the Japanese nation. During the occupation it was simply regarded as a war of aggression by Japan, and that was that . . . At that time, we Japanese had virtually no natural resources. There were some hundred million of us then, and when we tried to obtain cheap imports we were kicked around by the high tariffs. We tried to emigrate elsewhere, and we were slapped with exclusion. Our export goods were discriminated against. Didn't we hit the very bottom in the Depression? Still, we went on to assault Imphal, Guadalcanal . . . and tried to take one-third of the earth. That was aggression. That was going too far. But after the Sino-Japanese war, everything that came thereafter including the days when the Japanese nation was spitting blood – 'Was that not a war of aggression?' – you say in one sentence and demand my answer. That's very difficult.

In the mid-1970s, Takeo Fukuda, a close friend of Kishi's, briefly came to dominate the LDP. In 1978 Fukuda raised the issue that had been dormant for nearly two decades: that the defence of Japan must be brought to the forefront of political debate. That seemed to lift the lid on a Pandora's box of long-suppressed views. Defence Agency officials, as well as Fukuda, argued that although Japan would continue to respect the principles of nuclear disarmament, the country was not constitutionally barred from possessing nuclear weapons, cruise missiles or bacteriological weapons. Only intercontinental ballistic missiles were absolutely aggressive in intent.

Fukuda then paid an official visit to the Yasukuni Shrine. Yasuhiro Nakasone, one of Japan's most tough-minded right-wingers, felt free to address students at Tokyo University about the repeal of Article Nine. The chairman of Japan's joint chiefs of staff, Hiro Omi Kurisu, attacked the concept of 'defensive defence' which had dominated Japanese thinking for twenty years. He suggested that the position was untenable: officers from the Self-Defence Force might, in any confrontation, be forced to shoot first because of their inherent weakness, which would be constitutionally illegal. This proved too much even for Fukuda, and Kurisu was dismissed.

The deputy minister of defence had already, in 1973, questioned the very basis on which defensive thinking rested. Takuya Kubo enunciated the 'standard defence forces concept' which viewed the Self-Defence Forces as no more than a trip-wire should an emergency arise:

> the standard defence force is assumed to be an adequate screen behind which the country can mobilize if a threat greater than 'limited and small-scale aggression' is encountered. In that event, the standard defence force will also enable Japan to fight a holding action until American defence forces arrive and join with Japanese forces to expel the invader.

What this means is that Japan would be ready to mobilize and put a much larger army into the field at short notice if the country was seriously threatened. Fukuda's faction contained the largest number of MPs belonging to the Blue Storm Society, which is tough-minded on domestic and foreign issues. Even further to the right of him, Nakasone was soon to become prime minister, after Fukuda's unexpected departure from office.

The underlying trend in Japanese attitudes to defence through the post-occupation years is patently clear. Yoshida set the course, from which one prime minister after another has attempted to strike out in a rightward direction – towards less reliance on the Americans and building up Japan's own armed forces. However, every time the overwhelming logic for keeping a low defence profile so as to proceed with economic growth and co-operation with the rest of Asia has prevailed. Kishi tried dramatically to break out of the confines of this policy, and came a cropper. Fukuda and Nakasone proceeded much more slowly – and achieved more as a result. But if the LDP hierarchy is straining at the leash on defence issues, it can be imagined how high nationalist feelings run among the rank and file.

How far had Japan gone towards rearmament by the time Nakasone became prime minister? The answer must be a long way, but not as far as it could have. By the mid-1980s, Japan's defence budget was the eighth largest in the world. The armed forces' strength was around 240,000 men, with an army the size of Britain's and 650 combat aircraft. It deployed as many ships as the Americans in the East Asia region, and more aircraft. It had pretty good equipment, including F-15 fighters, Chinook helicopters, Hawkeye early warning systems and Hawk missiles. In addition Japan had a large military aerospace industry and arms manufacture was growing, particularly of ship-to-ship missiles, and micro-electronics.

Japan's peaceful nuclear programme was accelerating fast, and a debate was under way about the desirability of acquiring 'small-size nuclear weapons'. In spite of the size of the defence budget, Japan's average spending in the mid-1980s was still below the guideline figure of 1 per cent of GDP. If this were tripled to the level of defence spending by, say, West Germany, it would enable the Japanese to dispense with the American defence umbrella. Japan would be in a position to acquire at least 16 aircraft carriers, 34 attack destroyers, 85 ordinary destroyers, a further 350 fighter aircraft and five to six times as many tanks. If defence spending were raised to the American level, 6 per cent of GDP, Japan would be only a short head behind the Americans as a global military power.

After Kishi's defeat in 1960, Japan resolved for three decades to keep defence spending down, so as not to annoy America and the rest of Asia, on which its trade and protection depended – even though the gut feeling of most leading Japanese politicians was that the country should go its own way and rearm as it pleased. By the mid-1980s, Prime Minister Nakasone was trying to resist the traditional policy of Japan's elders in arguing that the country's best interests were secured through a policy of manic economic growth and reliance on the military protection of others – even though Japan's defences were far from inconsiderable.

Tetsuya Kataoka argued most eloquently for a revived, autonomous 'Gaullist Japan':

A gnawing sense of doubt is spreading in Japan about the U.S. will to honour its commitments to defend East Asia. Japan would rather not speak of it for fear of damaging America's credibility, because as things stand today Japan has no other recourse than alliance with the United States. Japan simply must assume that the full panoply of American arsenals will be first coming for her defence . . . Someday a security crisis is going to knock on Japan's door. One of two things will follow: Japan will fail to overcome that crisis, in which case her pacifism will confirm itself; or she will meet the crisis successfully and in doing so will shed her pacifism . . .

The Japanese problem arises from the contradiction of her being an unarmed economic giant, and this is to a degree a reflection of the contradiction in US policy towards her. But so long as the American presence in East Asia was dominant, the contradiction did not matter much. The United States could have it both ways with Japan: demanding mutuality in the alliance while obliquely warning against autonomy. But the most pertinent question that is raised today is not whether a militarily autonomous Japan poses a danger to the United States, but whether the United States can go on performing the task of protecting Japan. To say the least, US policy towards Asia had become fluid in the 1970s. The United States threatened to end the alliance with Japan in 1971; she retreated from Vietnam; she has begun withdrawing from South Korea; and she has abandoned Taiwan.

The United States can no longer have it both ways regarding Japan's defence or status. The United States must either offer a reliable guarantee of Japan's security that includes the security of her last outer defence in Korea, or she must allow Japan to shift to a more independent posture. To lull the Japanese with an illusion of security only to awaken them with a rude shock would be to invite serious consequences.

These words are almost as pertinent today as when they were written.

23

INNER TENSIONS

THE TWO great post-war battlegrounds between left and right were to be fought on the issues of trade union power and, of course, rearmament. Both were won by the right, on the industrial front crushingly so, on the military front on points.

As we have seen, SCAP's reforms had been vigorous on the industrial front, partially liberalizing the union laws, only to suffer a reverse with the strike called on 1 February 1947, which was banned by MacArthur after a large demonstration had been called in Tokyo two days earlier. Yoshida was exultant; SCAP reformers like Eleanor Hadley were dismayed, arguing that 'the unions were only doing what they had been told they had a right to do and then this right was arbitrarily cut off'.

The popular pressure was now coming to boiling point, and in May Yoshida was forced into opposition, his Liberal Party – the successor to the pre-war Seiyukai Party, backed by Mitsui – losing power to a weird coalition between the Socialist Party and the far-right Democratic Party (formerly the Minseito, backed by Mitsubishi). The Socialist-led government floundered as it tried to control inflation and unemployment; by October 1948 Yoshida was back in power. He had been given the backing of Washington to introduce the 'Dodge Line', a series of swingeing austerity measures involving the loss of 250,000 jobs and large lay-offs in the private sector, presided over by Joseph Dodge, president of the Bank of Detroit. Meanwhile, trade unions were ruthlessly purged and the Communist Party virtually banned.

But the battle with the unions was far from over. In the late 1940s to mid-1950s, there were strikes in the coal, electric power, steel, and car industries. The struggle was to come to a head in the summer of 1953, when the car workers' union federation, Zenji-Roren, went on strike against three companies, one of them Nissan. The company's response was ferocious: there were pitched battles between strikers and police, helped by their traditional underworld allies. Nikkeiren, the employers' organization, arranged a massive bank loan to Nissan and won the agreement of rival firms not to take up the Nissan market share during the strike. A further blow to the strikers came when those loyal to the management formed a union under the slogan, 'Those who truly love their union love their company'.

After three months the strike collapsed. Nissan was never again to lose a single day's work through industrial action. It had been a crushing defeat for the unions. Nobutake Shikanai, the Nikkeiren boss, considered this a crucial turning-point in Japan's post-war history: 'If the management side had lost, then in Nissan and elsewhere the communist-led unions would have had a big say in the running of the country, and Japan would have lived in misery.' The labour struggles were 'like an infectious disease which, once contracted and survived, leaves the individual stronger and immune from the disease. Today's success was achieved only by the blood, sweat and tears that were shed on both sides in those years.'

There were similar confrontations at Toyota and other companies. In 1960, miners at the Mitsui coal mine at Miike in Kyushu went on strike against pit closures for nearly a year. The strike was terminated through sheer violence: the police and local toughs attacked hundreds of miners with wooden staves and drove them out of the mine. The less militant steel unions were brought into line somewhat less violently. Union membership, which had peaked at 40 per cent in the mid-1950s, declined. By the early 1960s it was estimated that the cost of strikes in Japan was running at around one-seventh that in the United States. In the public sector militancy continued, spearheaded by Sohyo, the Japanese General Council of Trades Unions; but most strikes were limited one-day affairs seeking the right to strike, which periodically closed Tokyo's transport system. However, strikes remained formally illegal in the public services.

The power of the left in industry was thus ground down with all the relentlessness displayed by the imperial army facing the peasant revolt of Shiro more than three hundred years before. On the other great issue of the day, Japanese rearmament and the American connection, the struggle was to be even more bitter and protracted. In December 1954, Yoshida's remarkable seven-year ascendancy came to an end and his right-wing rival, Ichiro Hatoyama, finally pinned responsibility upon him for a scandal involving contracts in the shipbuilding industry. By any standards, Yoshida had been a brilliant post-war leader for Japan; by any standards too, he had been deeply conservative, a representative of the bureaucratic class in the best traditions of Meiji authoritarianism who had attempted to seed a generation of successors throughout the political system.

However, his immediate successor, Hatoyama, was much further to the right – a traditional nationalist political boss. When in 1955 Japan's two main socialist parties came together, Hatoyama's Democrats grudgingly agreed to ally with the Liberals to form the LDP, whose rule was to continue unbroken until 1993. The party's 'mission' committed it to amending the constitution, in particular Article Nine, repealing the laws passed under the occupation and seeking 'the eventual withdrawal of the foreign armed forces from Japan'. Its constitution roundly denounced 'the mistakes of the occupation policies' as a result of which 'the natural sentiments and patriotic feeling of the nation were unjustly impaired and the natural power of Japan was weakened'.

Thus the party that has ruled Japan for four decades was officially committed from its inception to reversing such few changes as the occupation had succeeded in imposing on society, to rearmament and to the eventual removal of American forces from the country. The only obstacle to rearmament was the necessity of securing left-wing support for a two-thirds majority to amend the constitution – which was not forthcoming. The ruling party was pledged, in fact, to returning society to something close to the position before the war – a war in which the ruling elites would admit to having done no wrong. While Japan has in fact slowly drifted to the right in accordance with these goals, the reason why LDP leaders did not fully succeed was a ferocious rearguard action by the left, buttressed by a huge swathe of public opinion.

Hatoyama, as we have seen, was deeply conservative, but too cautious to seek a sharp rightward move on the more sensitive issues. His successor, after a short interval, was anything but restrained. Nobusuke Kishi had been the architect of Japan's state-directed development model, first experimented with during the war when he was minister of munitions, then fully applied immediately after the war. It was as if Albert Speer instead of Ludwig Erhardt had become chancellor of Germany. The new prime minister in fact represented a compromise between the two main strands of the LDP: the *toha*, career politicians, and the *kanryoha*, the more moderate bureaucratic followers of Yoshida. Kishi was a right-wing bureaucrat.

He was to precipitate the most savage right–left confrontation in Japan's recent history. It was won – inevitably – by the system, but it did act as a red warning light against too obvious an attempt to return Japan to its militarist past. After the Kishi experiment, consensus was to return under governments usually – although not invariably – dominated by the bureaucratic establishment. After the Kishi experience, *toha* leaders like Yasuhiro Nakasone who sought to steer the nation on a more nationalist right-wing course were kept in check.

Kishi arrived in office determined to secure a revision of the 1951 security treaty. After protracted negotiation he succeeded in obtaining a draft from the Americans that placed Japan on a more 'equal' footing and appealed to Japanese nationalists. The United States was now committed 'in accordance with its constitutional practices and processes' to defending Japan, and America's remaining rights to interfere in Japanese affairs were removed. The new treaty, however, aroused fury on the left. Nasashi Ishibashi, a former Socialist leader, denounced the treaty for committing Japanese troops to be used 'in effect as frontline troops for American military strategy'. In early 1960 a huge wave of agitation broke out against the new treaty when it was submitted to the Diet for ratification. The Diet and the American embassy were constantly besieged by thousands of snake-dancing demonstrators. Street battles with the police broke out every few days.

On 19 May opposition members grabbed hold of the seventy-six-year-old speaker of the Diet and carried him to the basement of the parliament building in an effort to forestall a vote on the treaty. LDP members seized him back, while the police held back left-wing deputies. With the left physically barred from entering the chamber, the debate was resumed and the treaty ratified by LDP members alone. This was too blatant a violation of the 'consensus' that theoretically governed Japanese politics, and there was widespread public outrage. Newspapers called on the government to resign. As many as 13 million Japanese signed petitions calling for an election, while 6 million stopped work.

By the following month the situation was getting out of hand. When the advance party for President Eisenhower, due a week later to sign the treaty, arrived in Tokyo, their car was surrounded and demonstrators pounded on the roof; the occupants feared the car would be turned over and those inside pulled out. The delegation led by presidential press secretary James Hagerty had to be flown by helicopter to the safety of the American embassy. The presidential visit was cancelled.

Extremists were now beginning to seize the initiative from the official opposition. The student federation, Zengakuren, resolved to 'block the treaty revision by physical means and overthrow parliament'. On 15 June, students surrounded the Diet and broke into the grounds. They were eventually repelled by a massive police attack in which one student was killed. After that, order was restored and the strikes were called off by moderate Socialist leaders, who agreed to return to the Diet, which they had been boycotting. On 23 June the treaty was finally signed, but Kishi, who had lived in constant fear of assassination and was under massive police protection, was forced out of office less than a month later and then stabbed in the leg by, ironically, a right-wing fanatic.

The debate over the security treaty was to be a milestone: once again, the system had crushed a large populist movement, plunging many Japanese into apathy at the hopelessness of any attempt to obstruct the will of the oligarchy. On the other hand, the sheer scale of the protests had alarmed the elites and put them on notice that they must be more cautious. The next prime ministers, Hayato Ikeda and Eisaku Sato, were to concentrate single-mindedly on economic growth at the expense of any more controversial political initiatives.

The left-wing upsurge had added a new urgency and a flavour of extremism to the political situation. On the far left, factions from the protest movement now drifted into outright confrontation with the government, and even into terrorism. On the far right, secret societies made their reappearance. In October 1960 the Socialist leader, Inejiro Asanuma, was stabbed to death on a public platform by a young right-winger. The following year a seventeen-year-old broke into the house of a publisher who had produced an 'insulting' work of fiction about the crown prince; the youth stabbed a housemaid to death and injured the publisher's wife. Bin Akao, the leader of the far-right Patriotic Party, insisted that the right had 'no choice but to resort to violence to fight back' against the 'communist-dominated' press. Such threats forced the already cautious Japanese press to censor itself for fear of causing offence to the far right.

During the 1960s, with the Americans mired in Vietnam, the left found a new cause to rally behind; but the demonstrations were smaller and more ritualistic, held under the umbrella of the Citizens Council of Peace in Vietnam. A more lively issue was the decision to build Narita Airport on farmland 35 miles outside Tokyo, which drew together an unlikely combination of the far left, environmentalists and local farmers, who refused to budge. This combination forced the government repeatedly to slow the pace of construction, and the airport was limited to a single runway. No bullet train connects Tokyo to the airport, which still subjects all passengers to a gamut of security checks – for fear not of international terrorism, but of anti-Narita protests.

Another issue that erupted during the late 1960s was widespread student protest against the conservative ethos of the education system and the absence of real democracy in Japan. This blended with demonstrations to pressurize the United States into returning Okinawa to Japan. Parts of Tokyo University were seized and police used water-cannon and helicopters to restore order. A spin-off from the student protests of the 1960s was the United Red Army, which probably consisted of no more than a hundred or so hard-core terrorists at any one time, and paralleled the Baader–Meinhof gang in West Germany and the Red Brigades in Italy. In March 1970, some of its members succeeded in hijacking a Japan Air Lines plane to North Korea.

In 1972, a URA cell was uncovered in the mountains some 100 miles north of Tokyo: two policemen were killed in the ensuing siege. It was found that fourteen members of the group had been tortured and killed for 'ideological crimes' a few weeks before. The same year, URA terrorists in collaboration with a Palestinian group shot dead twenty-four people at Lod Airport in Israel. A tremendous explosion at Mitsubishi Heavy Industries killed eight people and injured three hundred. Another group, the Chukaku-ha (Central Core Faction) distinguished itself with spectacular, but usually ineffectual, missile attacks against the Imperial Palace, the American embassy and other targets.

On the right, extremist splinter groups continued to terrorize opponents, usually through intimidation, at the lower level of politics: buses, trucks, and even armoured vehicles blaring out right-wing messages and festooned with slogans became a common sight in Japan. There were occasional outrages, like the attempt on the life of the mayor of Nagasaki in 1991, who had suggested that the emperor might have been responsible for the war, or against members of the press deemed to have offended the right. In 1992 a twenty-four-year-old extreme right-winger fired three shots at Shin

Kanemaru, Japan's top political boss, from a range of 20 feet. They missed, but conjured up images of the pre-war period.

With the end of Eisaku Sato's eight-year premiership in 1972, Japanese politics underwent a sea change, as significant as the fall of the Kishi government in 1960, but which went almost unnoticed outside the country. Sato was the quintessential bureaucrat: a man in Yoshida's mould, as moderate as Liberal Democrat politics allowed, essentially a technocrat and manager – a leader of whom the Meiji leaders would have been proud. Power since the war had alternated between the conservative professional politicians and the bureaucrats, with the latter usually emerging on top. Yoshida, Kishi (although a deeply nationalist bureaucrat), Ikeda and Sato were all cut from the same bureaucratic cloth, and had dominated Japan for twenty-two of the twenty-seven post-war years; Katayama, the only professional politician among them, survived for just two years. In political terms, the conservatives dominated the party for five years, compared with nineteen years of 'moderate' rule.

Moreover, it could be argued that, towards the end of Sato's premiership the prime minister was, by and large, the supreme political authority. Although his position was that of holding the ring between the interests of the bureaucracy and the *zaibatsu* (and to a limited extent he also represented public opinion), he was the final arbiter of Japan's course. Yoshida, with his role in shaping the nation's political system, Katayama with his right-wing views, Kishi with his attempt to strike out in a nationalist direction, and Ikeda and Sato with their concentration on economic growth at the expense of everything else, each made their mark on Japan in different ways. They were all recognizably their own men, each ruling for between two and eight years.

Between 1946 and 1972, the question of who rules Japan could not be posed: the top political authority was recognizably the prime minister, combining as he usually did the highest position in the bureaucracy with supreme political legitimacy. Although the country was far from being a democracy in every sense of the word, the political authority, responsible to parliament, was the highest in the land.

In 1972 all this changed for the worse. From then on, the average survival span for a prime minister was to be two years. Over the next twenty-two years Japan had twelve prime ministers, compared with just six in the preceding twenty-four years. The premiership came to oscillate between nationalist conservatives and bureaucrats, this time with the former in the ascendant: there was a marked shift to the right. However, frequent changes of prime minister reflected the fact that the job was no longer the most important in Japanese politics or society: all too often, real power was held by someone behind the scenes pulling the strings. This sharp decline in democratic responsibility in Japan marked a return to the old tradition of a shogun as the power behind the throne. Voters could not tell where real power lay, so their already tenuous contact with the political authority was further frayed.

One of the most binding forms of democratic control is the ability of voters to choose between different leaders, or different sets of leaders. In Japan, it now became far from clear who the real leader was (and more often than not, identifiably popular leaders were promptly removed from office by jealous colleagues). Most of the blame for this deterioration in modern Japanese politics can be pinned on one man: Kakuei Tanaka. After his baleful presence had done its worst, the LDP was to end its gentlemanly jousting for consensus and degenerate into a bitter Tammany Hall struggle between factions, occasionally to be flushed clean by judicial investigation and public indignation, until the slime of patronage and corruption politics built up again.

Of course, there was corruption long before Tanaka: it was built into the system. But he made it the very purpose of politics itself. In many ways Tanaka, when he first came to the fore, was an attractive figure and a relief for Japanese weary of the University of Tokyo Law Faculty tradition of elderly autocrats that had dominated in the past. Refreshingly, he was a man of the people – born of a peasant family in one of the poorest villages in one of the most remote regions of Japan. He went to elementary school, then worked as a ditch-digger in the paddy-fields. At the age of sixteen he left for Tokyo to set up his own small construction firm. During the Pacific War the business boomed (as a private in Manchuria he had fallen ill early on in the war), and by 1943 it was one of Japan's fifty largest construction firms. With a solid financial footing, Tanaka tried to buy his way into politics. In 1947 he was elected a Democratic Party candidate, crossing the floor to the Liberal Party the following year.

At just thirty years old he became vice-minister of justice under Yoshida. A few months later he was charged with bribery – taking money from local coal owners for opposing plans to run down the mines. He was found guilty by a lower court, but was acquitted by a higher one. Soon he was rising fast within the party, becoming minister of posts at the age of thirty-nine, minister of finance at forty-four, minister of international trade and industry at fifty-three, and finally prime minister at fifty-four – a remarkably young age for a Japanese premier. His wealth also mushroomed, as a result of property development, usually in areas where government took an interest and he appeared to have advance knowledge of official intentions. This large fortune provided him with the means to set up an enormous network of patronage, dispensing funds to deputies belonging to different factions.

The sheer scale of Tanaka's machine did not become evident until much later. Industrialists were forced, by promise of favours or threats of penalties, to give huge sums to the machine, which used dummy organizations to bank the proceeds, failing to report them to the tax authorities. Firms, as well as industrial and professional associations such as the body representing Japan's doctors, poured money into the funds, which were then used to buy Tanaka support in the Diet. In a single year Tanaka personally bought stock worth $425 million, although his declared income was only $260,000.

Tanaka had transformed Japanese politics into a cynical game of buying deputies, exploiting its corrupt tendencies to the extreme. He represented the crudest kind of populist response to stifling elitist politics. He had a genuine popular appeal: he often wore a kimono and wooden sandals, and carried a large white fan. Japanese fondly nicknamed him 'the builder', the 'kingmaker', 'the shadow shogun'.

In fact his boss-style, bribery-based brand of politics was precisely the kind of demagoguery to which the Japanese system, with its shallow foundation in popular legitimacy, laid itself open. Just as the autocrats of the pre-war period could be shoved contemptuously aside by the populist miltarists, so was the aloof bureaucratic generation of the post-war period susceptible to being swept away by a free-spending populist thug like Tanaka. He bought his way into the premiership, and there was nothing the fuming elitists of the bureaucracy or the LDP could do about it. He revealed how easy it was for a crook to commandeer a political system which was not founded on democracy.

This had two results. First, it debased Japanese politics, spawning imitators; all sides now copied his methods to buy and retain power. Second, it caused the real power-wielders of Japanese society – the bureaucracy and the *keiretsu* – to distance themselves further from political power, and thus from any vestige of popular responsibility; they viewed the politicians with outright contempt, bypassing them and resolving their differences elsewhere. Political power mattered much less than before, because parliament was now run by men who lasted only briefly in office, could be manipulated by their civil servants, and were largely intent on making money and rising up the greasy pole, rather than taking responsible decisions. In fact, subsequent events suggest that Tanaka the populist strongman so alarmed and disappointed the elites that they actively conspired to prevent another such figure emerging, by weakening the office of prime minister. This was a profoundly dangerous development for Japan – the formal relegation of politics to third place at the top table, with the armed forces no longer such a distant fourth.

Tanaka's nemesis came about with surprising speed. When Takashi Tachibana, a young magazine journalist, exposed the full extent of the Tanaka machine's corruption, the *Washington Post* and other foreign newspapers took up the story. The cautious Japanese broadsheet press at last followed suit. In October 1974, faced with relentless questioning at the Foreign Correspondents' Club of Japan, Tanaka stormed out, and the following month he was forced to resign. Two years later, Tanaka was named in the Lockheed scandal then unfolding in Washington as having accepted bribes worth 500 million yen from the corporation. He was arrested and in 1983 convicted, being sentenced to four years' imprisonment. However, the appeals were expected to last for years, and he was freed on bail.

If that had been the end of the story, it would have been no more than a grisly interlude in Japanese politics. But Tanaka out of power became far more powerful than Tanaka in office. His methods, unacceptable in a prime minister, were profoundly successful in building up political support. Tanaka continued to spend to build up his faction. Members of the Diet who joined him were rewarded with office; those who opposed him were lost. Up to then the faction system had been improvised, consisting of informal alliances between a handful of leaders and their followers. Tanaka's own faction consisted of forty-four members in 1976; by 1983 it was sixty-three strong, and by 1986 it had eighty-seven members, making it easily the biggest within the ruling party.

Tanaka's revenge on his old foes was swift. In 1974 he had been succeeded by a candidate of the party elders, Takeo Miki, whose outstanding merit was his political honesty. He had a small minority faction within the LDP, and an enviable reputation in the Diet for having criticized the armed forces throughout the Pacific War. Miki attempted, quixotically, to enact sweeping internal reforms to end the faction system: he dissolved his own and the other factions were forced to follow suit, but the factions soon re-emerged under the guise of 'political study groups'. Miki then set legal limits on campaign contributions to the parties, provided for the LDP leader to be elected by grass-roots party vote and – infuriating the *keiretsu* – strengthened Japan's feeble anti-monopoly laws. Miki's reforms failed to staunch the tide of popular disillusion, and the LDP lost its overall majority in parliament. For Tanaka and the other faction leaders, this was the excuse to dump Miki, who was forced out of office.

It is true that Tanaka was too deeply embroiled in the Lockheed scandal to take power after Miki's fall: the premiership went to his long-standing rival in the party, Takeo Fukuda, an aloof bureaucrat-politician trained at the University of Tokyo Law Faculty and the Ministry of Finance. But Fukuda survived only two years, with Tanaka's faction harrying him every inch of the way. In 1978 he was replaced by an ally of Tanaka's, Masayoshi Ohira. The new prime minister campaigned for an unpopular – but necessary – sales tax to increase revenues; his party did poorly in the next election.

The following year, Miki and Fukuda had their revenge and their factions abstained on a motion of no confidence tabled by the opposition, contributing to the fall of the government and forcing a general election. Ohira died of a heart attack during the campaign, earning a sympathy vote for the LDP which now gained an overall majority. His successor was Zenko Suzuki, the opaque placeman next in line to lead the Tanaka faction. Suzuki's constant evasions, muddlings and gaffes became a major political embarrassment over the following two years, during which real power was exercised by Tanaka.

When Suzuki at last retired in 1982, it was clear that Tanaka would have to confer his seal of approval on a more articulate and independent prime minister. The 'kingmaker's' choice fell on Yasu-hiro Nakasone, who for a Japanese politician was to make a remarkable impact on the world stage. The irony is that the first Japanese international statesman since Yoshida was to be both largely the creation of Japan's indicted and corrupt political boss,

Tanaka, and the most nationalist prime minister since Kishi, and probably since the war.

No one previously would have suggested that Nakasone was not his own man. Tall, good-looking, well-dressed, not afraid to speak out in a manner that sent the mother hens of the political establishment clucking, it is not surprising that he spent his early political years as an outsider. The son of a wealthy timber merchant, he had a privileged education at the University of Tokyo's Law Faculty, from which he joined the Home Affairs Ministry, the sinister enforcer of Japan's domestic peace before the war. During the conflict he enlisted and became a lieutenant-colonel in the army.

At the age of twenty-seven, from a distance, he witnessed the mushroom cloud over Hiroshima. His wartime experience – he was the only post-war prime minister to have seen active service – was his most formative. He returned to Tokyo in August 1945. There, he later said, 'I stood vacantly amid the ruins of Tokyo, after discarding my officer's short sword and removing the epaulettes of my uniform. As I looked around me I swore to resurrect my homeland from the ashes of defeat.'

Nakasone wore a black tie in mourning for the occupation, opposed MacArthur's educational and social reforms, and in 1947 ran for parliament on an unashamedly nationalist platform, riding a white bicycle – reminiscent of the white horse of the emperor – with the Rising Sun fluttering from the handlebars. He had three pressing objectives: to expand the Self-Defence Force; to amend the 'no war' provision in the constitution; and to reactivate Japanese patriotism, particularly respect for the emperor. Nakasone set himself up, at a time when the armed forces were deeply unpopular, as the unashamed champion of their interests – a courageous thing to do.

He ploughed a lonely furrow in bitter opposition to the policies of the Yoshida government: 'I thought Yoshida's policy was based only on economism, and was making the Japanese nation lose all sense of independence and self-respect . . . I said that unless Japan defended itself, America would not come to our aid . . . I attacked Yoshida on the matters of Japanese identity and moral values, and got the message through to the public, too.' In 1951 he delivered a manifesto to MacArthur urging a rapid American withdrawal from Japan. He formed the Blue Storm School, a right-wing splinter group reminiscent of pre-war nationalist societies.

At first Nakasone was an outspoken conservative politician (a

toha) and deeply critical of the bureaucrat politicians (the *kanryoha*).
After securing control of a minor faction, however, he made his
peace with the arch-*kanryoha*, Eisaku Sato, and became transport
minister and then head of the Self-Defence Agency, advocating an
increase in Japanese military spending from less than 1 per cent of
GDP to 3 per cent, and the acquisition of tactical nuclear weapons.
In the crucial 1972 leadership election, Nakasone played politics,
the man of principle being labelled 'the weathervane' for the way he
switched sides from Takeo Fukuda to Kakuei Tanaka at the last
minute, thereby ensuring victory for the corrupt man of Japanese
politics.

Nakasone was duly rewarded with the powerful Ministry of
International Trade and Industry, where he was in the eye of the
storm in the seventies oil crisis – and proved remarkably capable.
When Tanaka fell, he was appointed to the key post of secretary-
general of the party, a stepping-stone to the very top. However, he
had given evidence to the Diet about the Lockheed scandal, although
no evidence emerged that he was implicated. In the Suzuki cabinet
he was given the job of overseeing administrative reform – a
euphemism for holding down soaring pork-barrel government
spending, which he did effectively.

When Suzuki stepped down in 1982, Tanaka with his dominant
faction – unable to take the top job himself because of his disgrace –
swung his support to his old friend and political ally Nakasone, and
crushed the candidate of his hated rival, Takeo Fukuda, in a primary
of the party's rank and file. This was originally a reformist idea of
Miki's, but instead it turned into a carnival of vote-buying on a
massive scale. Once again, as with the Suzuki cabinet, Tanaka was
the power behind the scenes: he had placed in office a man who was
undoubtedly an efficient administrator, undoubtedly cast in the
Western mould of personal leadership, but who showed disturbingly
unusual hankerings after the good old days of pre-war military
ascendency. For the first time since Tojo, the armed forces had their
man in the premiership, albeit firmly under Tanaka's thumb.

Nakasone soon made it clear that, while faithfully serving
Tanaka, he was also intending to pursue a radical cocktail of policies
on the international scene. In economic affairs, he pleased the
American administration by announcing his commitment to free
enterprise; in foreign affairs, he sought a major expansion of Japan's
profile and power abroad. His economic policy marked a sharp
departure from the bureaucracy-inspired policies of the past: having
crushed the bureaucratic faction in taking the premiership, he was

now making an outright bid for the support of Japanese big business, which had been chafing under the burden of central control and 'administrative guidance':

> I was carrying out a kind of 'improvement' of Japan's structure. For 110 years, ever since the Meiji restoration, Japan had been striving to catch up with America and Britain. In the 1970s we did catch up. Beyond that point the [state's] regulations only stand in the way of the growth of the economy. If government officials have too much power, the private sector of the economy will not grow. We had to change the system.

Tanaka, himself a successful businessman from outside the establishment, heartily approved of this. For the first time since the war, the bureaucrats had lost their leading role to the new alliance forged between business, now extremely powerful, the politicians like Tanaka, whose aims were increasingly close to business, and the militarist–nationalist tendency, personified by Nakasone. The Rubicon of Japan's march to war in the 1930s was crossed when an informal alliance was formed between the militarists and big business, crowding out the Meiji bureaucrats. Something similar was now happening, although fortunately under very different international circumstances.

The bureaucrats had no one but themselves to blame for their loss of power. Just as before the war they had sought to restrict leadership of the nation to their own elite, they were largely responsible for ensuring afterwards that democracy did not grow any strong popular roots to provide the civilian political authority with the power it needed to become dominant and independent, and to stand up to business and nationalist forces. The bureaucrats treated the political system as a necessary evil, charged with doing whatever was required to buy votes and deliver elections so that oligarchic bureaucratic rule could continue uninterrupted. When the time came, the oligarchy, represented by the haughty Fukuda, was unceremoniously bundled out of office because it lacked popular legitimacy.

Fortunately, however, events did not proceed quite as Tanaka and Nakasone had planned. Nakasone came to office in a whirlwind of activity that contrasted with the performance of most of his predecessors. He pledged grandiosely to achieve 'a final settlement of postwar politics'. He sought 'equality' in the relationship between Japan and the United States in a common struggle against Soviet communism. He set off for Washington on a first visit that established the 'Ron–Yasu' relationship. Public-relations guff of the kind natural to America's 'great communicator' seemed infectious: Nakasone remarked, 'President Reagan is the pitcher and I'm the catcher. When the pitcher gives the signs, I'll co-operate unsparingly, but if he doesn't sometimes follow the catcher's signs, the game can't be won.' (Baseball is Japan's national game as well as America's.)

In fact the relationship continued much as before – with one exception. Because the Americans felt they liked and trusted this new, decisive, plain-speaking Japanese politician, his sharp escalation of nationalist rhetoric went largely unnoticed in the West. Not in Japan and Asia, however. In his first interview with the *Washington Post*, he asserted that Japan would act as 'America's unsinkable aircraft carrier' in the Pacific; he also affirmed Japan's intention 'to keep complete control of the four straits that go through to Japanese islands, to prevent the passage of Soviet submarines' and 'to secure and maintain the ocean lines of communications'.

This, while probably a frank statement of Japan's unofficial policy, represented a major extension of its stated national goals to a huge area of the Pacific, and incensed the opposition. Nakasone was denounced as a 'dangerous militarist', and 'reactionary and militaristic'. He proclaimed defiantly: 'A nation must shed any sense of ignominy and move forward seeking glory.' His popularity plunged. After announcing his intention to secure constitutional revision of the 'no war' provision, he was forced to back down because he lacked the necessary two-thirds majority. 'I think it is right to keep the question of the country's constitution constantly under review as time goes on,' he said. 'But if you ask, is there an urgent need to amend the constitution now? – the answer is no. It would lead to a wasteful social upheaval. Still, I must say there are certain articles in the constitution which should be revised, and we should keep the matter under study.' He responded by seeking to bypass the national policymaking committee of the LDP, setting up unofficial think-tanks.

However, for this he required the support of his backer, Tanaka. In December 1983 the LDP lost their majority in the Diet. Nakasone, dangerously weakened, now depended more than ever before on Tanaka's backing for his survival as prime minister. The 'kingmaker' had, however, been weakened by the guilty verdict in the Lockheed trial, and by the efforts of one of his most trusted aides, Noboru Takeshita, to set up his own faction within a faction – a group of forty Diet members more loyal to him than to Tanaka. Nakasone tentatively tried to strike out on his own, only to be contemptuously brought to heel by Tanaka with the memorable rebuke, 'There's a fellow who thinks he's the only person fit to be prime minister. Idiot! He should stop being so impudent.' Nakasone was forced to give Tanaka's supporters a large number of posts in his next cabinet. The strong man of Japanese politics abroad was in fact only second fiddle at home.

Fate intervened, however. In 1985 the 'shadow shogun' had a stroke and, in the twilight of his power, there could be no doubt where real authority had lain in Japan for most of the previous thirteen years. The press converged on Tanaka's hospital, while hordes of photographers camped outside his residence. Politicians and businessmen rushed to pay their respects at the sick-bed. Even Tanaka's old opponent Kiichi Miyazawa, now head of Fukuda's bureaucratic faction, turned up. But Tanaka was now largely incapacitated, and his power faded fast.

It had been the longest, most corrupt and populist period of rule by one man in modern Japanese history. But in the end there was remarkably little positive to show for it except in the huge benefits that had been showered upon Tanaka's own constituency of Niigata. This snow-country province now boasted roads, two expressways, and a fine bullet-train station in the rice-fields; there he is still revered in statues and writings as a local hero.

The end of Tanaka's influence left Nakasone his own man at last, but without the powerful factional base necessary to a prime minister. He put on a virtuoso display of political activity, which after the first disastrous years aroused popular support, in an effort to walk the waters of factional intrigue. For the greatest difference between Nakasone and the pre-war right was that he had risen to power not as a force in his own right, but through playing the game in a manner none of his nationalist predecessors had succeeded in doing before. He championed the new nationalism and the commitment to free enterprise as boldly as he dared.

International events played into his hands. The West was becoming alarmed at the deployment of Soviet medium-range missiles west of the Urals, and decided to deploy in Europe its own cruise and Pershing missiles as a counter-measure. This led to growing agreement between the two to ban the missiles in the West – with the Soviets now hinting that they would redeploy the missiles in the Far East. They had crudely rattled the sabre at Nakasone, a senior Soviet official writing crassly on one occasion that Japan might be a 'likely target for a response strike. For such a densely populated country as Japan, this could be a natural disaster more serious than the one that befell it 37 years ago at Hiroshima and Nagasaki.' Nakasone, alarmed at the SS-20 threat, hastened to Western summits to insist that Japan was part of the West and must be included in any such agreement. President Reagan and Mrs Thatcher were impressed, and the Japanese were overwhelmed when they saw the prime minister standing confidently between the two leaders of the West.

In September 1983, a Korean Air Lines Boeing 747 was shot down in unclear circumstances by the Soviets. Nakasone joined the West in expressing outrage over the incident. An opinion poll showed that the overwhelming majority of Japanese were against any increase in defence spending, but Nakasone changed the government's limit on defence spending from below 1 per cent of GNP to 'about 1 per cent' – a significant shift. The defence agency wanted far better equipment: big new anti-ship and anti-aircraft missiles, and long-distance radar. Joint sea and air exercises were staged with the Americans, while anti-submarine patrols patrolled the seas. In 1986 Japan was pressed to participate in 'Star Wars' (Strategic Defense Initiative) research.

Nakasone maintained a high profile internationally, inviting Reagan to Tokyo in November, followed by Chancellor Kohl of West Germany, and the Chinese Communist leader, Hu Yaobang. All met Emperor Hirohito. In all, Nakasone's successes on the international stage were much fewer than he had hoped for. He had managed an immensely skilful public-relations exercise, and given Japanese rearmament a sharp new twist; but he had failed to override the constitutional limits to Japanese nationalism.

On the matter of reasserting Japanese nationalism at home, he proved remarkably bold. On 15 August 1985, the fortieth anniversary of the surrender, he and his entire cabinet walked in full morning dress through the Yasukuni Shrine gate, pronouncing emphatically that he was doing so in his official capacity as head of the Japanese government. The action was decisive and symbolic, reasserting as it did the government's respect for the spirits of the ancestors supposedly glorified through their deaths in war – including not just the two and a half million Japanese victims of the Pacific conflict, but the remains of the seven hanged war criminals, which had been secretly disinterred and brought to Yasukuni.

Rehabilitation for the perpetrators of the war seemed complete. They, including Tojo, had done no wrong in the eyes of the modern Japanese state. The Peking *People's Daily* roundly attacked 'militaristic-minded people in Japan's leadership'. Opposition groups charged that Nakasone's action violated the separation of state and religion as specified in the post-war Japanese constitution – for which, of course, Nakasone had only contempt. He declared without repentance, 'I firmly believe that the rainbow bridge of idealism spanning over the Pacific Ocean must not be faded with clouds and mists' (meaning that the alternative to an alliance with America was an autonomous defence capacity for Japan). 'The true defence of Japan . . . becomes possible only through the combination of liberty-loving peoples who are equal to each other . . . The matter is desired to be based on self-determination of the race.' On another occasion he said flatly, 'It is considered progressive to criticise pre-war Japan for its faults and defects, but I firmly oppose such a notion. A nation is still a nation whether it wins or loses a war.'

The prime minister also set up a commission to look at educational reform. It recommended that 'a spirit of patriotism' should be instilled in schoolchildren, and that respect for authority and for one's elders should be taught. 'Ethics education', a throwback to the old moral teaching of the 1930s, was also to be introduced. These proposals came under immediate fire from the Japan Teachers' Union, and were only partly implemented. Even more controversial were proposals for the raising of the Rising Sun flag in schools during entrance and graduation ceremonies, and the teaching of the Japanese national anthem. The Ministry of Education toughened its vetting of 'acceptable' history textbooks in schools. In 1986 the education minister, Masayuki Fujio, went so far as to justify the 1910 annexation of Korea in public. Following a storm in the Korean press, Nakasone was forced to dismiss him.

Nakasone himself did not resign, however, after making an almost equally offensive gaffe in which he asserted that the intelligence of Japanese was higher than that of Americans because 'the US has many immigrants, Puerto Ricans and blacks, who bring the average level down'. These mistakes apart, Nakasone's public-relations sense stood him in good stead: although Japan's trade surplus with America and Europe was creating dangerous tensions, he managed to foster the illusion that he was a man the West could do business with. Western leaders, fearful of stoking up protectionism within their own countries, were content to go along with this.

In the economic field, Nakasone pioneered a policy of much

closer identification with big business than with the bureaucrats. It was a controversial policy, but it had an international resonance at a time when the theory of free markets was fashionable in the West, and the Japanese establishment grudgingly agreed to go along with it. It also coincided with the views of Japanese businessmen, particularly the newer breed, who were impatient of central control and 'administrative guidance'. Nakasone launched a programme of privatization of Japan's inefficient state industries, such as the telecommunications company NTT, the Japanese National Tobacco and Salt Corporation and Japan National Railways. Nakasone dealt with the latter forcefully, firing the chairman and insisting on the loss of some 80,000 jobs – virtually unheard of in Japan.

In 1985 the Maekawa Commission concluded that Japan must henceforth fuel its growth from within, not through exports, which were so angering Japan's trading partners throughout the world. The prime minister, to his credit, went to almost comic lengths to urge Japanese to buy foreign. 'Japan is like a mah-jong player who always wins,' he argued. 'Sooner or later the other players will decide that they do not want to play with him.' He went to a department store, pursued by the full media circus, and bought an American tennis racket, an Italian tie, and a French shirt. It was all viewed by many Japanese as a public-relations exercise; while no doubt the intention was sincere, it made little difference in practice.

Nakasone came unstuck in his attempt to diminish the burden of direct taxes and introduce value added tax in an attempt to cut the chronic budget deficit. A mass of interests combined against him, and it was this, more than any other single issue, that led to his ejection from office in 1987. The first nationalist-militarist administration since the war had completed five years: Nakasone had achieved for Japan a much higher profile abroad, given the armed forces back their self-respect, and made nationalism acceptable again. Although his practical achievements were small, his symbolic ones were huge. In addition, he had set a precedent for reviving the alliance between militarism and big business that had outmanoeuvred the bureaucrats before the war.

His most positive move, necessitated by the weakness of his factional base, was to seek a measure of genuine popular support at home, playing to a more democratic gallery than prime ministers had for decades. This was to be short-lived, however: once Tanaka had gone, Nakasone had been able to act as his own man – until the factions combined to point out that he had no clothes, no real base of his own in parliament other than his own virtuoso, self-publicizing personality.

Nakasone was succeeded by Noboru Takeshita, now in unchallenged control of the huge Tanaka faction, a willy sorcerer's apprentice of the 'shadow shogun', a tiny man deeply skilled in the art of faction politics. Power was back with the money men, the professional politicians. Takeshita, like Tanaka, came from a remote province, although from a prosperous middle-class background of sake brewers. He had attended the unprestigious Wadeda University. He enjoyed much better relations with the bureaucrats than had Tanaka. Although an appallingly vague speaker, he was an excellent political fixer, and represented a return to party boss politics – this time in co-operation with the government machine. The country seemed to be set for quieter times, with the new prime minister personifying 'consensus' between the four main groups.

In September 1988, however, the Recruit affair exploded, a bigger scandal even than Lockheed. The company concerned was a publishing, telecommunications and land development conglomerate with ambitions to join the elite of the *keiretsu* (the reborn *zaibatsu*). Recruit set up a subsidiary company for flotation on the Tokyo stock exchange, distributing scores of preferential shares to influential political leaders, which soared in value as soon as the shares went public. Most of Nakasone's cabinet, as well as Takeshita himself, had benefited from Recruit transactions. As the extent of the corruption became apparent, political confidence in the prime minister plummeted to just 4 per cent, the lowest level ever recorded. In April 1989 Takeshita resigned. Nakasone was questioned in the Diet, but not indicted; he resigned from the ruling party.

As after the fall of Tanaka, the party needed a 'clean' leader. One, Masuyoshi Ito, was ruled out because he insisted on a more thorough house-cleaning than the ruling party was prepared to contemplate. Sosuke Uno, a middle-ranking member of the party, was brought in, only to fall foul of a sex scandal concerning his geisha mistress. However, he agreed to lead the party into the election for the upper house in 1989. Tainted by the scandals, he also carried the burden of pushing through Nakasone's proposal for a 3 per cent sales tax.

The Socialist opposition was for once imaginatively led by Takako Doi, an able woman leader, who made large inroads into the Liberal Democrats' traditional rural vote by proposing policies that were even more protectionist than those of the ruling party. The result was a disaster for the LDP: the Socialists won 35 per cent of the vote, compared with 28 per cent for the LDP, and forty-six seats in the upper house compared with the LDP's thirty-six. The LDP retained control of the lower house, and of the government, but seemed threatened with losing the 1990 election.

In despair, the party elders chose a comparative youngster from the Miki faction, Toshiki Kaifu, who was preferred to a former health minister as well as to Shintaro Ishihara, head of the party's nationalist wing after Nakasone. Kaifu launched a campaign against corruption within his party; even so, no one was sent to prison for the Recruit scandal (as with the Lockheed scandal). There were hand-outs by LDP bosses to the electorate on an unprecedented scale, and a scare campaign was mounted against the left; some $200 million was spent by the LDP as against $50 million by the Socialists. The ruling party won a crushing victory. Mrs Doi resigned, accused of having retained too left-wing an image for the Socialists.

Kaifu, thus equipped with a mandate, sought to introduce a major political reform by replacing multi-member constituencies, in which party factions competed for seats with bribes, with single-member ones, thus limiting the need for factions – the major source of Japan's institutional corruption. He also cut an impressive figure on the world stage as a new, honest, youthful Japanese leader. But he had no power base; he had won the election and was of no further use. In the autumn of 1991 he was unceremoniously dumped after the Socialists opposed his political reforms, amid recriminations (not altogether justified) that his government had been unable to achieve anything. A furious Kaifu insisted that he would continue the fight for reform.

The three lesser faction leaders, Hiroshi Mitsuzuka, Kiichi Miyazawa and Michio Watanabe, returned to fight for the post of prime minister: the main faction, that of Takeshita (the formerly all-powerful Tanaka faction) could not put forward its own candidate because of its connections with the Recruit scandal. It had already emerged that Takeshita himself was no more than a front for a sinister godfather figure, Shin Kanemaru. Some observers believed that Kanemaru had effectively taken control of the faction, and hence the ruling party, after the fall of Tanaka, and had effectively controlled Nakasone, Uno and Kaifu as another behind-the-scenes shogun. Takeshita, as he was shunted aside by Kanemaru, became his bitter enemy.

Kanemaru picked an old rival of the faction, Kiichi Miyazawa, as prime minister. Miyazawa, the successor of Fukuda's faction of bureaucrat-politicians, was a veteran of Japanese politics, fluent in languages and high flown in ideas. After twenty years the bureaucrats had returned to centre stage; yet they were deeply vulnerable, depending on the support of a backroom thug and manipulator. The Miyazawa administration staggered on through a year of indecisive leadership, with most predicting that it would barely survive another.

To general surprise it was the kingmaker, Kanemaru, who fell first, being forced to resign as leader of the dominant faction after admitting to taking some $3 million from a trucking firm said to be connected with organized crime. The fall of Kanemaru was followed by an unseemly three-way battle for control of the Takeshita faction between Ichiro Ozawa (the brightest of Japan's next generation of politicians and a protégé of Kanemaru's), the finance minister, Tsutomu Hata, and the former finance minister, Ryutaro Hashimoto.

Ozawa, arrogant, able and deeply unpopular, was effectively blocked, and the faction leadership went to a banal placeman, Kaizo Obuchi, a front man for Hashimoto, himself a front for the old string-puller, Takeshita. The cabinet was reshuffled to include a woman member and a thirty-nine-year-old (the average age was just sixty). Thus the prime minister was being propped up by a front man for one of the weaker LDP leaders, himself a front for Takeshita who only had any influence because the strongest man in the party, Ozawa, was being blocked by his enemies. This was like two hundred years before, when strongmen ruled at one or two removes from the shoguns, themselves supposedly subservient to the emperor. It had nothing to do with democracy. By December 1992 the government was the second most unpopular in post-war history, with a rating of just 16 per cent.

Kanemaru's downfall seemed to arouse genuine popular indignation against the institutionalized official corruption in Japan; he was even jailed for a time while police broke into his house and offices, taking away a pirate's hoard including hundreds of pounds of gold bars, and between $30 million and $60 million in cash and bonds. Later he was released on bail, and charged with tax evasion. The defeated faction of younger leaders led by the tough-minded Ozawa and former finance minister Hata sought to capitalize on popular anger by breaking away from the Takeshita faction to form their own forty-strong group. For a moment, the new shogun of Japanese politics, replacing Kanemaru, was his old rival Takeshita.

On 6 August 1993, forty-eight years to the day after Little Boy was dropped on Hiroshima, the country's thirty-eight-year-old political tradition of rule by a single party was devastated just as abruptly. It became possible to suggest that Japan was, after all, a functioning democracy. An engaging, plain-spoken critic of Japan's 'iron triangle' of rule by bureaucracy, business and politicians became prime minister, leading a small reformist party which headed a 'rainbow coalition' of opposition groups. The Liberal Democratic Party was relegated to opposition. The mighty had fallen. The will of the people had made itself felt. Or had it?

In fact, exactly the reverse had occurred of what appeared on the surface – although there is a very slim chance that events could hijack Japanese politics and result in a real deepening of democracy. The LDP lost office because its factional wars got out of hand: one of the toughest LDP bosses carried his eagerness for power to the extent of splitting the party and grafting himself onto the opposition to remain in control. The smiling young opposition prime minister, Morihiro Hosokawa, was to have his 'shogun' behind him in the person of Ichiro Ozawa, who was every bit as powerful and manipulative as Tanaka or the disgraced Kanemaru, Ozawa's own political patron.

The stage for the LDP's loss of power was set on 18 June, when the successors of Kanemaru, who had been arrested on tax evasion charges and pushed aside by Prime Minister Kiichi Miyazawa and his clique of bureaucratic politicians, defected to vote with the opposition in a no-confidence vote in the government. The rebellion was apparently headed by Tsutomu Hata, a former finance minister previously known for his incorruptibility and his colourless obeisance to his superiors (his most famous observation, in justifying a ban on beef imports, was that Japanese intestines 'were different from other people's'). In fact Hata was widely regarded as no more than the front man for Ozawa, Kanemaru's heir apparent; after his fall the latter's rival for leadership of the largest LDP faction, Noboru Takeshita, had contemptuously pushed aside both Ozawa and Hata.

The two of them had their revenge by leading some thirty-four deputies into voting with the opposition in the vote of no confidence, causing the government to be defeated by 255 votes to 220. Hata declared bluntly that 'We have to make major changes to the system to win back the trust of the people. Real political reform is our intention. I am deadly serious about it.' Ozawa, a taciturn, brooding, scowling fifty-one-year-old with a quicksilver mind is widely regarded as the most brutal of Japanese politicians, arguing through force rather than reason. Hosokawa, who left the LDP the year before and whose reformist credentials were not in doubt, commented happily that, 'It's like the Berlin Wall coming down. Politics will change because of what has happened today.'

A week later Hata and Ozawa founded the Shinsei party, with forty-four members of both houses. The defection robbed the LDP of its parliamentary majority, and also altered the factional line-up in the party: the old dominant Takeshita group, having split, was now relegated to fourth place, with Hiroshi Mitsuzuka's faction now the largest, Miyazawa's in second place, Michio Watanabe's third, and in fifth place the small reformist faction of Toshio Komoto and Toshiki Kaifu.

As Japan approached the polls on 18 July, there was a huge irony in the fact that the relatively clean administration of Kiichi Miyazawa, who had permitted the investigation that brought down 'godfather' Kanemaru was now widely regarded as representing the old, corrupt LDP, while the 'reformist' ex-party members were in fact disgruntled former members of the most corrupt LDP faction, the Tanaka– Takeshita–Kanemaru group. The election which finally drove the LDP from office in fact left the former party with virtually the same number of seats as before, 223 seats compared to 227; but with the defection of the Hata–Ozawa group, the party lacked a majority.

The real change of the election was the collapse of the Socialist party vote, down from 134 seats to 70, towards the centre factions: notably Hata's Shinseito with 55 seats, up from 36: Hosokawa's Japan New Party, which won 35 seats for the first time; another LDP breakaway, the New Harbinger Party, with 13 seats, up from 10; and the Buddhist Komeito, up from 45 to 51. The collapse of the Socialists has enormous long-term significance, because it greatly reduces the brake that the left was able to exercise upon such matters as rearmament and the government's pro-business policies: henceforth right-of-centre parties can count on almost two-thirds of the Diet necessary for constitutional revision.

Events moved swiftly after the election. For a moment, the LDP thought it could entice one of the new centre parties into a coalition. Hosokawa showed unexpected political skill as the pivot of Japan's parliamentary balance by hinting that he might indeed enter such a coalition unless the opposition picked him as its leader. Hata, his obvious rival for the job, conceded to him. The two of them set about assembling their 'rainbow coalition' based on a strictly limited political programme: they were helped in this by the collapse of the Socialist vote, which left that party uncharacteristically chastened and flexible – and in addition it scented the whiff of office for the first time in nearly four decades.

The main planks of the programme were political reform, which allowed for the end of the competitive multi-member constituency system in return for a parliament half elected by proportional representation (which the Socialists believed would benefit them) and half by a British-style first-past-the-post system. The other main plank was a promise to try and ease the grip of the bureaucracy over the Japanese economy.

The formation of the rainbow coalition made the fall of the Miyazawa government a formality. He had already been forced out as party leader on 22 July, after a bitter attack upon the party's old guard by younger LDP members, furious at their loss of office. After a ferocious internal battle, in which the old guard fielded the seventy-year-old Michio Watanabe as its Buggins'-turn candidate, the reformist former cabinet secretary, Yohei Kono, won a vote that, unusually, cut across party factions. Kono had excellent reformist credentials: he had briefly resigned as far back as 1976 in protest against the Lockheed Scandal. In fact, he was a protégé of Miyazawa, and was refreshingly anti-nationalist; his election represented a victory over the younger hard-liners grouped around Shintaro Ishihara.

Thus the LDP was now led by a squeaky-clean reformist, while the supposedly reformist opposition coalition about to take office was in fact led by a string-puller, the tough-minded Ozawa, working at not one but two removes behind the prime minister, manipulating Hata who in turn dominated Hosokawa. The latter's Fujiwara ancestors would have enjoyed the irony.

As the new government prepared to take office, the symbol of the old order, Shin Kanemaru, Japan's former political godfather and Ozawa's mentor, went on trial on charges of evading some $10m in taxes, sitting stony-faced as he was brought into the courthouse in his wheelchair under the eye of hundreds of cameras. On 6 August Hosokawa was elected prime minister, ousting the Liberal Democrats for the first time in thirty-eight years to cheers of 'banzai' from deputies. Hosokawa declared: 'I feel that an era has clearly ended and a new one begun . . . It is the beginning of a new chapter.'

The new prime minister was nothing if not engaging. Born in 1938 of an impeccably aristocratic background – his mother was a Fujiwara and his father descended from the *daimyos* of Kumamoto – he was the grandson of the then prime minister, Prince Fumimaro Konoye, and was just old enough to remember the war and the prince's suicide on the eve of his arrest as a war criminal. At the age of twenty-five he joined the staff of the Asahi Shimbun, and eight years later he became the youngest-ever LDP member of the upper house of the Diet. He led the typically dogsbody existence of a junior parliamentarian for the next twelve years, and said he was 'appalled' by a system in which members 'were mere tools of government agencies, continuing tamely to reflect the ideas of bureaucrats in party decisions'.

In 1983 his political career seemed finished when he failed to win election to the lower house, and he withdrew to Kumamoto, where his forebears had been *daimyos* for some 250 years to 1868. He was elected governor – a post with much less power than in the United States – but quickly won a reputation for energy and attracting business to the province. His background has led to his being known as 'Lord Hosokawa' in political circles.

However, the reality was of a very weak prime minister living on borrowed time. His own party was dwarfed by the Socialists and Shinsei party. At any moment, Ozawa and Hata could decide that their interests were better served by an alliance with the LDP, in which either of them might become prime minister. Hosokawa's chances of reforming the iron triangle seemed unrealizable – he was as beholden to the bureaucrats as any LDP prime minister. Faced with such a tightrope, Hosokawa clung to the modest reformist pole which the coalition agreed upon.

Hosokawa took office with a refreshing lack of formality and a 75 per cent approval rating, compared with 31 per cent for Miyazawa on taking office and 12 per cent on leaving it – a reflection of the popular Japanese yearning for change. His cabinet was heavily tilted towards Shinseito, making it not all that different in its higher echelons to an LDP government. His first public utterances suggested that he would vigorously promote political reform, and apologize for Japan's wartime acts more generously than any LPD government, but that economic policy would remain largely unchanged. Hosokawa threatened to resign if political reform was not secured.

Hosokawa declared unequivocally in August 1993, that Japan had engaged in a war of aggression, a war that was wrong. However, on economic policy he opposed any easing of the ban on rice imports and seemed reluctant to boost demand in Japan by cutting taxes. The apology immediately drew fire from the conservative newspaper, the *Sankei Shimbun*, which complained of attempts to 'convict Japan based on one-sided interpretations of history. We do not want our children to inherit fact-distorting historical views.'

Refreshingly, Hosokawa took a strongly anti-nationalist line, coming out unequivocally in favour of the Nuclear Non-Proliferation Treaty, which the Miyazawa government seemed reluctant to renew, and openly criticizing Chinese nuclear testing. On deregulation, Hosokawa announced his intention of reforming the 11,000 or so rules affecting Japanese business (and real government control is through administrative guidance, which is not even on the books), but was able to draw up a list of only 94 for repeal. In September he travelled to New York to address the UN and met President Clinton, without substantive result.

In November Hosokawa secured his first political triumph, securing passage of five political reform bills, including the new electoral system, a curb on private donations to politicians, and public funding of the parties. A number of LDP members, including former prime minister Kaifu, refused to oppose the reforms, Hosokawa had registered a success, but he still looked like a greenhorn in a roomful of gunmen, just waiting for one to decide that his time was up. The government staggered on until the following April until Hosokawa suddenly resigned following an allegation of minor financial impropriety. It seemed that the hard men behind him had grown weary of his fresh-faced approach. After an attempt by one of the LDPs dinosaurs, Michio Watajabe, to secure the job of prime minister, it passed to Tsutomu Hata, the leader of the original breakaway from the LDP, and front man for Ozawa. Few would lay bets on his chances of surviving more than a few months atop his unnatural coalition.

Japan's political revolution of last summer is a very tame affair and may result in no more than a generational change in the LDP, and its chastening. One source of major relief is that neither the LDP nor the government are in the hands of nationalist politicians; but the nationalists have not gone away. In a Diet two-thirds of whose members are conservatives, radical change can hardly be said to have arrived – much less the Berlin Wall fallen.

In a climate of economic difficulty and political upheaval, the marriage of Crown Prince Naruhito in June, 1993, provided another picturesque window on the eighth-century ceremonial at the heart of the Japanese court. On 15 April a pretty twenty-nine-year-old foreign office high flier, Masako Owada, abandoned the detail of trade negotiations with the United States to become engaged to the amiable, outdoor, outgoing heir to the chrysanthemum throne.

The daughter of the head of the Japanese foreign office, Hisashi Owada, she could only technically be described as a 'commoner', coming from one of the families at the very pinnacle of the Japanese bureaucracy. She was cosmopolitan as only a Japanese from the top drawer is permitted to be without shame, speaking Spanish, German, French and Russian and having spent time as a child in both Russia and America; like Naruhito, she was educated at Oxford.

The couple had met at a concert at the Imperial Palace, but after two years had broken off contact. Three years later they met again, and it is said that Empress Michiko personally sought to persuade her to abandon her career and marry the prince. The courtship could not have been more different from the conduct of royal affairs in Britain which, after recent troubles, the imperial household said it no longer regarded as its model. Japanese newspapers angrily denounced as disrespectful American press reports that Miss Owada had had past boyfriends; the couple, according to palace officials, met just twenty-seven times in six years, always on imperial grounds.

Miss Owada, from being a strong-willed, intelligent, humorous career woman was publicly transformed into a demure, pretty soft-spoken subordinate: at her betrothal, she appeared in a large silk kimono to perform the necessary slight bow of 15 degrees lasting precisely between three and four seconds (the bow is 30 degrees for other royals and 45 degrees for the Emperor and Empress). She was trained in preparation for the wedding in calligraphy, poetry and the imperial rice harvest ceremony. She was given the traditional imperial betrothal present of six bottles of sake, two sea bream and five bolts of silk.

On 9 June the two of them were married in the Kashikodoroko Shrine on the grounds of the Imperial Palace in Tokyo, in a secret ceremony. He was dressed in a Heian-style flaming orange kimono, she in a twelve-layer green kimono trimmed with yellow. A Rolls-Royce Corniche IV carried them through the streets of Tokyo as 170,000 people turned out for a glimpse. In the afternoon they reported the wedding to the Emperor and Empress, who by custom had not attended the ceremony itself, ritually exchanging a cup of sake, and in the evening performed another secret ceremony at the Ise Shrine at which, according to some reports, they consumed a rice cake as a prayer for an heir and, according to others, the princess stripped naked before the high priestess and her attendants who purified her with rice bran and checked her fertility. Three days of banquets followed.

The tight secrecy surrounding the royal family, which ensured such a fairytale wedding, slipped a little later in the year. Stories began to circulate that Empress Michiko, a taut, nervous person, was as at odds with the stuffy chamberlains of the royal household as she notoriously had been with the Showa empress, her mother-in-law. The fifty-nine-year-old Empress blacked out in public on 20 October, probably the result of a minor stroke or, possibly, anaemia. Curiously, a semi-open campaign denigrating her had surfaced in some Tokyo circles – a virtually unprecedented piece of lese-majesty, almost certainly emanating from within the royal household. It remained to be seen whether the new crown princess would be similarly enveloped and crushed by the overweight kimonos of royal protocol and role-playing as the Empress had been.

In a sense, Princess Asashi represented a kind of allegory for Japan as a whole. Just as in politics a comparative youngster with a cheerful smile, Morihiro Hosokawa, had broken through to the top promising reform, so it was hopeful to see a modern, intelligent career woman make it into the Imperial Palace (although matters should be seen in perspective: Miss Owada had come from Japan's foremost diplomatic family; Mr Hosokawa from two of its most ancient feudal families). For both, immediately enveloped by the Japanese system with its apparently unalterable rituals and policy priorities, the initial signs that they would make any reformist headway were not encouraging. The system seemed likely to swallow up this refreshing pair as it had countless others before them.

This whole complex web of fighting factions bears setting out because it so resembles the politics of another age – eighteenth-century England, when patronage, favours, personal loyalties and grievances shaped government policy regardless of the wishes of the people. In 1972 in Japan, nearly three decades of rule by bureaucratic politicians came to an end, and the party became the arbiter of the system. Because the party bosses were so unsatisfactory a public face for the system, it experimented with several fronts – the populist Tanaka, the nationalist Nakasone, the apparently appealing reformers Miki and Kaifu, then, strictly as a façade, the bureaucrat-politicians Fukuda and Miyazawa. But no pretence could conceal the fact that government was now from smoke-filled rooms, where power was based on favours and bribes. The political system was largely discredited, and had moved out of the hands of an elite into those of a beggars' opera, shaken at regular intervals by appalling financial scandals.

Thus the system became more undemocratic, politicians were

held in increasing contempt, the public grew more cynical and apathetic, and the real decisions came to be taken elsewhere. Both big business and the bureaucrats sought to preserve their influence through means other than participation in the political arena, a squalid spectator sport of largely ritual mud-wrestling. The extent to which democracy, always tenuous in post-war Japan, was really functioning by the last quarter of the twentieth century can be understood by a brief look at how the system actually operates.

24

THE DEMOCRACY THAT
NEVER WAS

D
EMOCRACY IS a relative term. There is no absolute democracy in the world, in the ideal sense in which every member
of society participates with full responsibility in every
decision affecting himself. Every democracy includes a considerable
measure of powers delegated to the authorities, which they claim to
exercise in the long-term interest of the people. In practice, most
democracies are societies in which popular forces, or at least the
middle classes, have wrested some genuine obligation to be consulted
by the ruling class by threatened or actual insurrection. Most are
highly imperfect systems – necessarily so, in the judgement of those
who are pessimistic about human nature, because the people governed are also imperfect and cannot be trusted entirely to govern
themselves.

The main features of any society that calls itself a modern
democracy are: that people are allowed, through the exercise of a
free and secret ballot every few years, to select the government from
an array of parties and candidates; that the press should be free, as
should the right of assembly and the right to campaign; and that the
official machinery of the state should not be employed to ensure a
government's re-election. In addition, most industrial democracies
have a strong enough parliamentary opposition to hold out the
prospect of ejecting the government from office.

Of the world's major industrial democracies since 1945, the
United States, Britain, France, (West) Germany, Canada, and Australia have all enjoyed long periods of alternating rule under two
different parties; only in Japan and Italy has one-party rule been
more or less consistent since the war until 1993. This is more
pronounced in Japan than Italy because the Liberal Democrats have

only rarely, and then with minor parties, had to resort to coalitions to preserve their power. The absence of alternation in government does not in itself, of course, mean that a system is necessarily undemocratic: voters may be so satisfied with their rulers or – as in Italy's case – so frightened of the opposition that they return the same dominant party time after time. Nor, in spite of the many defects of Japan's political system, was a victory by the opposition impossible : this happened briefly in 1947, and from time to time the government has been deprived of its majority in the upper house. With qualifications, it happened again in 1993.

All the same, there are several features of the Japanese system that lead to no other conclusion than that its democracy, while not a sham, is a very modified one indeed, a pseudo-democracy operating within an authoritarian framework. These features are, first, the enormous influence of money in Japanese politics and the favours-and-patronage system that operates largely in the government's favour; second, the limited nature of press criticism of the government; and third, the gerrymandering of constituencies, which is blatantly anti-democratic, with, in some areas, vote-rigging and the intimidation by the right of its political opponents. In addition, there is the very limited role of parliament in either enacting legislation or checking the executive, and the extent to which ministers are creatures of their civil servants rather than the reverse.

Again, it is conceivable that if none of these things existed, the LDP would still have been returned to office because of the enormous success of their economic policies. It seems more likely, however, that without these distortions the opposition would have been returned to power on two or three occasions since the war – hence the reliance placed by the ruling party on stacking the cards. For the opposition to win in Japan takes a tidal wave of support. Conversely, unless the government is wildly unpopular, the distortions ensure that it can ride out any wave of discontent.

The biggest disadvantage is money and patronage. The LDP usually spends around four times as much money at elections as all its opponents combined. This is not dissipated, American-style, on expensive television advertisements: it is paid directly to the voters in the form of bribes in a variety of guises – presents on the occasion of weddings, parties and favours. In Japan direct door-to-door canvassing is banned because it would provide the opportunity to hand over bribes to voters too easily – this has to be done in the open, and is not even technically illegal. Added to the straight-forward cash bribing of voters is the enormous quantity of money and spending that an enterprising Diet member can secure for his constituency – an advantage denied to his opponents. It is reckoned that in a non-election year a member must disburse at least $3 million in direct payments to his constituents to keep them happy – a staggering figure. In most elections, the opposition parties have simply been unable to pay to fight enough constituencies.

The system of political donations is remarkably formalized, and is far from being under the counter. Every year on New Year's Day, the top LDP politicians request donations, setting a target for businessmen; in 1985, for example, this was $10 million. The industries later apportion the amounts each is to donate. Over the next three months the director of the LDP's treasury bureau visits hundreds of large federations to collect these donations. As politicians ascend the ranks of the LDP, so the donations to their coffers grow larger. Another system is to hold 'encouragement parties' on behalf of a politician, with tickets costing anything up to a million yen (like American fund-raising parties, but on a larger scale). These donations are considered 'payments for refreshments'.

One LDP member, Tamaki Kazuo, typically netted about $2.6 million from two months of partying in 1984 to boost the $2 million plus he had received in direct donations. Another widely practised method of raising money is for businessmen to give politicians 'insider' share tips on stock about to soar in value. The banks also supply secret donations. Finally, there are individual donations handed directly to politicians in their constituencies, usually in brown paper bags.

This leads to the second abuse of Japanese politics: while members of the Diet are partially beholden to their electors – and few politicians anywhere in the world work as hard as Japanese MPs – their prime obligation must be to those who provide the funds necessary to secure their election. The party factions function to channel money from business to MPs; alternatively, MPs must raise money directly from business connections, local or otherwise. In any political system the power of the party is considerable, and business or the trade unions finance political campaigns. In Japan, LDP members are directly in the pockets of the party factions or of big business.

Such controls as do exist on campaign contributions and expenditure are easily avoided. Politicians channel individual donations of more than a million yen (the theoretical limit) to their support groups, of which there may be three or four. Kakuei Tanaka was the quintessential example of a politician using his power to lavish money on his home constituency – in addition, that is, to the direct electoral bribes. His constituency of Niigata benefited from around two and half times the average level of public investment in the rest of the country. One famous bullet train tunnel, costing a billion yen, served a hamlet of just sixty households.

The second major imperfection of Japanese democracy is the self-censorship of the press. The broadsheet press in Japan is certainly the most reserved of any major industrial democracy. It does have many admirable characteristics. It is deeply serious, clear and factually precise; it eschews trivia or frivolity. It has a huge circulation – the *Yomiuri Shimbun* prints nine million copies of its morning edition and five million of its evening edition (this paper is, in fact, slightly left of centre and critical of the LDP). Its major rival, the *Asahi Shimbun*, in particular, is Japan's solemn watchdog of any sign of incipient militarism.

Yet both newspapers, as well as the *Mainichi*, espouse no radical opposition creeds. Their views and coverage are very similar, if not identical. One British journalist seconded to a Japanese newspaper speaks with awe of the industrial attitudes to newspaper production: the newspaper had no fewer than 1300 editorial journalists, progressing up a rigid hierarchical ladder that led them from being reporters between the ages of twenty-two and thirty-five, sub-editors between thirty-five and forty-five, and editors between forty-five and fifty-one. The newspapers were obsessed with scoops, anticipating their rivals' coverage of virtually the same news by a matter of minutes; at the time of Hirohito's death, one newspaper chalked up a bill of more than $4 million for the chauffeur-driven cars necessary for the reporters camped outside the palace gates. The author and journalist Karel Van Wolferen, for one, is scathing about the practice of the *kisha* (reporter) clubs which link journalists to officials and leading politicians; there are around 400 *kisha* clubs, to which 12,000 journalists and 160 media organizations belong:

> It hardly needs to be pointed out that the *kisha* club system makes for very cosy relations between the newspapers and the people whose activities and aims they are expected to scrutinise. There is hardly any incentive for individual journalists to scrutinise anything by themselves, and no reward at all for presenting a case in a manner that contradicts the conclusions of their colleagues. But, typically, when a political or industrial scandal breaks and is

reported by all the media, Japan is treated to a verifiable avalanche of information on it, since many of the journalists were aware of the details all along.

The tabloid press is even more scurrilous and sex-orientated than its counterparts in Western countries. The press, far from being pro-government – most journalists are deeply critical of the LDP – is nevertheless fundamentally subservient, like a repressed bull terrier, gazing resentfully at its master but hostile to any outsider. It never advocates support for the opposition openly, and restrains its views to a degree that would be unthinkable even in a Western country with a proprietorial right-wing press. In many respects the press serves the function of constitutional opposition to the government – except in suggesting that there is an alternative.

A third area in which Japan is a far from complete democracy is in the gerrymandering of parliamentary constituencies. The system is unashamedly biased in favour of rural areas, where the LDP is strong: a vote in the countryside is reckoned to be worth four in an urban area. The constituencies are inherently slanted towards the ruling party, in spite of the multi-member constituency system. In the 1990 election, which was fairly typical, the LDP took 46 per cent of the vote, but 55 per cent of the seats. There is, too, some clear election rigging: multiple voting, miscounting, and intimidation are all practised and sometimes reported, but it is impossible to estimate how widespread they are. Finally, although most elections are occasions for good humour and celebration, in some areas right-wing intimidation, particularly of the press and sometimes of electoral meetings, is undertaken.

Japanese democracy is seriously flawed. It is a system with inherent and massive biases, largely through the exercise of systematic electoral bribery, much of it dispensed by the state on behalf of the ruling party. It is hard to say what would happen if there were ever any real threat to the elite's monopoly of power. The 1993 'revolution' was merely a change of elites. Would the left be permitted to take power? The ruling party is convinced that the question is entirely academic. Japan will never act in an un-Japanese way – that is, reject its masters, overturn the system. The body politic, moreover, does not control the country.

The electoral system provides the glue between politics and business. The relationship is one of mutual interdependence: business needs the politicians to secure its interests and favours; the politicians need business to get them elected. In no major industrial democracy is the relationship closer. It is certainly true to say that, while the most senior faction leaders have an influence as great as that of the business leaders, the latter, through holding the purse-strings, control the factions and the Diet members to a degree that would be unthinkable in most other democracies.

Further, in Japan there remains a concentration of business power that exists virtually nowhere else. The *zaibatsu*, reborn as the *keiretsu*, still control a fifth of all economic activity – much less than the three-quarters at the end of the war, but still a huge concentration. Beneath them, in the pyramid of economic power, are the new *keiretsu*, controlling another fifth. Two-fifths is accounted for by thousands of tiny firms, usually dependent as component or service suppliers on the big *keiretsu*, with little power of their own except occasionally at grass-roots level. The final fifth is directly in the hands of government. The senior business chiefs, who fund the factions, are in a position of enormous power. A handful of men from the hereditary *keiretsu* that have dominated Japan throughout the century, as well as a few new business leaders, are as powerful as the senior political leaders, if not more powerful. This is a profoundly disturbing and undemocratic state of affairs.

Even more so is the relationship between the bureaucracy and the government. (The third and arguably the most important link in the triangle, the relationship between bureaucracy and business, will be looked at in the next chapter.) Again, with the exception of the very senior faction leaders, the autonomous power of the bureaucracy vastly exceeds that of the politicians. The bureaucratic vice-minister is always more powerful than the minister, who is a politician. One diplomat in Tokyo told the author that on one occasion the vice-minister did not even remember the name of his minister. In any country the bureaucracy is always more powerful than junior members of parliament, although it exists nominally to serve the representatives of the people. In Japan it is more powerful than any but the most senior statesmen; decisions are increasingly taken outside the realm of politics, the product of back-door deals between the bureaucrats, business, and the interest groups.

Again, this occurs to some extent in every democratic country. In Japan it is the degree which is striking. The people's input into decision-making is virtually non-existent; the elected politicians are by far the junior of the three main decision-making groups; the ministers are subordinate to their civil servants; the prime minister is subordinate to the faction leaders, themselves easily manipulated by the bureaucracy and big business. Even such powerful faction leaders as Tanaka and Kanemaru were used by the bureaucrats as their tools in assembling an LDP consensus around administrative changes of policy.

Three large questions remain. First, does it matter that politics has remained so firmly subordinate to the other two great powers in the Japanese state, the bureaucracy and big business? After all, Japan, partly as a result of this, has been the greatest post-war economic success story in the world. Second, what is the role of the emperor, still a symbol underpinning the system, although stripped by MacArthur of his constitutional power? Third, who really runs Japan?

The answer to the first question must be that it does matter, immensely, not because democratic politics usually provides the underpinning of a modern industrial society, but because it performs an essential brake that prevents a society going off the rails – as happened in the 1930s. The dangers inherent in Japan's blithely unrepresentative system of government will be examined in the final chapter of this book. The second question will be addressed in chapter 34, which examines whether Japanese politics and society really have changed since before the war. The two chapters that follow, which detail Japan's economic miracle, will try to answer the third: who is at the controls in Japan, given that the elected politicians are not: business or the bureaucracy?

25

FLIGHT OF THE CRANE

FORTY YEARS after the Americans left Japan, the country's economy was by far the most successful the world had ever seen. Japan's manufacturing and service economy is already much bigger per capita than that of the United States. Put another way, a country with half the population of the United States provides a fifth as much per head again. The Japanese system of economic organization since 1950 should thus be regarded as the best in the world, the ideal model to follow, if possible – much more so even than America's comparatively successful free-market model, which became the standard-bearer for world economies throughout the 1970s and 1980s.

But to espouse the Japanese example is to turn most standard conservative Western economic orthodoxy on its head. As observed earlier, Japan's economy has been labelled by one outsider 'communism that works'. It is not quite that: state ownership of the means of production and rigid central planning are not features of the system. But it is an essentially government-directed economy. The government largely created Japan's economic boom through inflationary growth behind high tariff walls, state direction of domestic industry and the targeting of export markets. Even today, government still dominates industrial finance and is armed with a huge array of powers to compel companies to do what it wants.

In addition, the industrial structure of Japan mocks free-market theory: beneath the government at the pinnacle, it consists of a small group of huge cartels indulging in every major violation of the marketplace possible: price-rigging, bullying suppliers, dominating lesser subsidiary companies, trading and bartering preferentially among themselves, using their links with the banks to undercut competitors, pushing around a huge mass of tiny entrepreneurs, and heavily subsidizing a huge agricultural distribution and services sector which largely exists to disguise unemployment. This is not quite a Soviet-style 'command economy'; but it is much more like a socialist economic model than any Western one. The difference is that it works – better than any system the world has ever known.

There are two current responses to the challenge that Japan's economy presents to orthodox theory. The first is to try to insist that it is an essentially free-market system. Frankly, this is unconvincing. There was competition in Japan, certainly – often furious competition – between the giant cartels, dominating each sector of the consumer market and producing marginally different products from one another at prices kept artificially high for the consumer in order to boost profits and reinvestment. But the immense armoury of state domination has been much more in evidence, particularly during the boom years of the Japanese miracle. Only as the Japanese economy flags slightly today has the power of the state begun to ease a little. This reverses the view that state domination must equal inefficiency.

The state tells each major company what its market share should be, will initially have provided the finance for that company, and will force that company to merge with another if it deems it necessary. The fact that most of Japanese industry is in private ownership cannot alter the fact that it is the state that sets the rules and calls the shots. Japan has simply evolved a much more sophisticated form of economic planning than Soviet-style communism.

The second traditional response is to fall back on racialism and assert that the Japanese are so different from anyone else that what works for them is unique and will not work for anyone else. To say this is to contradict virtually every value America has stood for in the post-war period, in particular the view that free markets (and democratic values) are universally applicable and should be advanced around the globe. Can the Japanese really be aliens from another planet, exceptions to this rule?

The Japanese are different, more different than anyone else, in their cultural make-up. This gives them some huge advantages in slotting into the requirements of a modern industrial society – and some drawbacks as well, when it comes to creativity or flexibility. Yet that is not the same as saying that the Japanese, and only the Japanese, are capable of operating an economic system that bears little resemblance to a free-market system, or that racial superiority is responsible for their success. In fact their system, although entirely original and unique, evolved as a result of the country's extraordinary trajectory across the twentieth century, spawning many features that can be imitated – although, admittedly, societies with different historical experiences might find it difficult to do so.

How has the Japanese economic system of 'state-directed cartelism' (in contrast to Chalmers Johnson's view of it as a 'capitalist developmental state' – Japan is neither essentially capitalist, nor, today, developmental) evolved, and what does it consist of? To answer this one must look back to the maturing of Japan's economy after the surrender. A look at the history of the 'miracle' shows that it was anything but smooth. Rather, it was the product of a bitter struggle between the state and private industry, which yielded its own creative tension, and of the battle fought by state and industry against Japan's labour unions.

The economic history of the pre-war period was characterized by several distinctive periods. First, there was the introduction of a state-directed and wide-reaching modernization programme by the Meiji oligarchs. In the second stage, the state industries were sold off to private investors, largely to finance the public debt. The third saw the rise to economic domination of the monopolistic *zaibatsu*, whose concentration of wealth in a very few hands was assured when they swallowed up huge swathes of small and medium-sized industry during the Depression. The fourth stage was the attempt by the state to reverse the trend and seize control of the commanding heights of the economy for itself, ending in the agreement between the *zaibatsu* and the militarists to pursue economic-motivated agression overseas. Fifth, there was the breakdown of this agreement as Tojo's government tried, during 1943, to seize control of the economy from the *zaibatsu*, whom he blamed for failing to support Japan as completely as they should have during the war. Tojo's initiative was defeated.

The surrender, however, marked a real watershed in the continuing struggle between the bureaucrats and the *zaibatsu*. The bureaucracy survived the occupation completely unreformed. One of the members of the Blaine Hoover mission, charged with drawing up a new public service law, admitted as much:

> The proposed civil service law was submitted to the Diet in the fall of 1947. Unfortunately the nucleus of feudalistic, bureaucratic

thinking gentlemen within the core of the Japanese government was astute enough to see the dangers of any such modern public administration law to their tenure and the subsequent loss of their power. The law which was finally passed by the Diet was a thoroughly and completely emasculated instrument compared with that which had been recommended by the mission.

Moreover, the purge of bureaucrats, as we have seen, was almost totally ineffective in the long run. In fact their numbers and powers were vastly expanded during the occupation, to nearly double their pre-war strength. The position was summed up in a famous editorial of the *Uin Chua Chuo Koron* in August 1947:

> The problem of the bureaucracy under present conditions is both complex and paradoxical. On the one hand, the responsibility for the war clearly must be placed on the bureaucracy, as well as on the military and the *zaibatsu*. From the outbreak of the war through its unfolding to the end, we know that the bureaucracy's influence was great and that it was evil. Many people have already censured the bureaucrats for their responsibility and their sins. On the other hand, given that under the present circumstances of defeat it is impossible to return to a *laissez-faire* economy and that every aspect of economic life necessarily involves an expansion of planning and control, the functions and significance of the bureaucracy are expanding with each passing day. It is not possible to imagine the dissolution of the bureaucracy in the same sense as the dissolution of the military or the *zaibatsu*, since the bureaucracy as a concentration of technical expertise must grow as the administrative sector broadens and becomes more complex.

Simultaneously the *zaibatsu* went on the defensive, under criticism for their pre-war role as well as for their failure to give sufficient support to Japan's war effort. Within the bureaucracy, there had long been a sizeable body of theorists who believed in a planned economy, and they now took advantage of the weakness of the *zaibatsu* to pounce. Shunji Yoshino, a senior official at the Ministry of Agriculture and Commerce, was the patriarch of this group. As early as 1925 he attempted to regulate the small- and medium-sized sector in Japan by introducing the Exporters Association Law in order to control what was deemed to be 'wasteful' competition. Yoshino believed that:

modern industries attained their present development primarily through free competition. However, various evils [of the capitalist order] are gradually becoming apparent. Holding to absolute freedom will not rescue the industrial world from its present disturbances. Industry needs a plan of comprehensive development and a measure of control. Concerning the idea of control, there are many complex explanations of it in terms of logical principles, but all one really needs to understand it is common sense.

In 1931, partly under his influence, the Important Industries Control Law was passed. It suited both the government and the *zaibatsu*, for in effect it gave the latter the power of 'self-control' to draw up cartel agreements between enterprises, fix production and price levels, and limit new entrants to an industry; in practice, the government now had a major say in setting up such cartels. If two-thirds of the enterprises in a particular industry agreed to a cartel, the government could authorize one, forcing non-cartel members to obey the agreement. The cartel members had to submit detailed plans to the government for approval, outlining their investment and production decisions.

In spite of these sweeping government powers, the *zaibatsu* in practice continued to run their own industries, and the bureaucracy began to agitate for state control to be imposed on industry. The group of bureaucrats who favoured these measures would be the ones who remained in charge during the immediate post-war period, the formative years of Japan's 'miracle'. They conceived of themselves as Japan's 'economic general staff', a mirror image of the military general staff, committed to the total economic mobilization of Japan and to keeping the rebellious economic field commanders – the companies – in order.

In 1931 the yen's convertibility was suspended, and in 1933 the Foreign Exchange Control Law made all overseas transactions subject to the approval of the Finance Ministry. The yen was to remain unconvertible until 1964, and the government did not ease its grip on all foreign exchange transactions until the late 1960s, by which time the initial economic surge was largely over. A further portent of things to come was the Automobile Manufacturing Industry Law, passed in 1936, which required all firms in this sector to be licensed by the government, which would provide the capital for new enterprises; all taxes and import duties were waived for four years. By this means Toyota and Nissan were put on their feet, and

Ford and General Motors were driven out of business in Japan. Similar measures were enacted for other industries.

As war approached, so the central planners extended their powers. In 1937 the Munitions Industries Mobilization Law was passed to prepare for war. More important was the Emergency Funds Regulation Law, which gave the Ministry of Finance power to divert public and private capital to the war industries. Finally, the Temporary Measures Law Relating to Exports, Imports, and Other Matters gave the government power to restrict or prohibit the import or export of any commodity, as well as to control the manufacture, distribution, transfer and consumption of all raw materials – in other words, control over the whole economy if necessary. The laws formed the precedent for the legislation governing post-war planning.

In 1938 the National General Mobilization Law was passed which gave the government formal power over virtually every aspect of the economy and society through imperial decree. In 1939 the Ministry of Commerce and Industry was reorganized along new 'vertical' lines, in which bureaux were set up to shadow each industry – a major step towards the planning model of the post-war period. The following year, with the war in China faltering, the bureaucrats made their boldest move yet: the 'general plan for the establishment of the new economic structure' was promulgated, advocating the nationalization of private enterprise, the direction of industry, and limits on profits. The *zaibatsu* responded furiously, attacking it as a 'red' plan (indeed, there were supporters of Stalin, as well as Hitler, in the bureaucracy) and forcing the resignation of the minister of commerce and industry, Nobosuke Kishi.

The bureaucrats and *zaibatsu* concluded a truce and in 1941, through the Important Industries Control Ordinance, established cartels for each industry, which were to be policed by the *zaibatsu* themselves. The war period was used as an excuse by the bureaucrats for 'enterprise adjustment' – the deliberate destruction of Japan's medium-sized and small enterprises (as well as its textile industry) in favour of the giant heavy industries. Thus the precedent was established for major industries to dominate the market, subcontracting out to thousands of small dependent firms, family-run and poorly financed.

'Enterprise adjustment' was carried out forcibly, and was extremely unpopular, surplus labour being shipped off to Manchuria and China. The textile industry, for example, was all but eradicated, the number of spindles dropping from more than 12 million in 1937 to a little over 2 million in 1946, 270 textile mills being reduced to just 44. Kishi, who had returned to office as minister of munitions, was now the dominant economic bureaucrat in the government. It was his refusal to resign on Tojo's orders after the American occupation of Saipan that led to the general's downfall.

Thus the protagonists of state control in Japan were already at the helm in Japan's civil service before and throughout the war, which is scarcely surprising in a country where respect for authority and the power of the bureaucracy were so ingrained. After the surrender the bureaucrats' chief rival was weakened, and part of the civil service was willing to co-operate with SCAP to control the *zaibatsu* – up to a point.

The bosses' main defender was Shigeru Yoshida, a former Foreign Office official and therefore in traditional rivalry with the economic bureaucrats, who emerged as Japan's most prominent post-war politician and prime minister. Yoshida despised the economic planners and remarked that he was unable to distinguish an official from the Ministry of Commerce and Industry 'from an insect'.

From the first he championed the cause of the *zaibatsu*. The argument between the planners and big business (most of whose ruined factories had been temporarily 'nationalized' by the government, which assumed their obligations) might have seemed a little academic as economic crisis followed economic crisis in the immediate post-war period. The policy of the Ministry of Finance was initially to stimulate production by increasing demand. To achieve this, various payments, supposedly to compensate industry belatedly for wartime contracts, were made with paper money. This was in accordance with the 'Keynesian' view that in an economy working at very low capacity, growth was necessary to end recession – even at the cost of inflation. The orthodox American-trained economists at SCAP recoiled at this idea and insisted that company compensation settlements be terminated to reduce inflation. In June 1946 these hand-outs were ended – soon to be revived, Japanese-style, under another name.

Meanwhile, the Reconstruction Finance Bank was created in January 1947, the first of several such institutions to generate funding for industry. These policies appalled men like General Willoughby at SCAP, who sided with the conservative Bank of

Japan. Nevertheless, they worked. Japan's 'priority production system' channelled revenues into industries like coal and steel, returning them to their pre-war levels. As the immediate effect of the American-imposed decision to end subsidies to industry was a major slump in the autumn of 1946, the Americans had no alternative but to accept priority production as a means of reviving the economy. This in effect switched resources through inflation and rigged prices to the priority sectors.

By 1948 the Americans had ordered MacArthur to return Japan to self-sufficiency with a view to withdrawing American support for the economy, which on the balance of payments alone was running at around $500 million a year. The Japanese planners drew up a five-year plan for economic regeneration. However, Yoshida, with the support of the Americans, dubbed this 'socialist planning' and blocked it. Instead, Joseph Dodge, a conservative banker from Detroit, was sent to knock Japan's economy into shape. The 'Dodge Line', enacted between February and April 1949, insisted on a balanced budget and banned further spending by the Reconstruction Finance Bank in an effort to halt inflation in its tracks and make the yen convertible at the fixed exchange rate of 360 to the dollar – incredibly, a level that, absurdly undervalued to Japan's advantage, was to last for twenty-five years. Surprisingly, the austere Dodge agreed to the creation of two more state financial institutions that were to play a key role over the coming years: the Export Import Bank and the Japanese Development Bank.

In the same year, the Japanese reformed their Ministry of Commerce and Industry and their Board of Trade into a single institution, the Ministry of International Trade and Industry (MITI), which was to become the intellectual powerhouse and planning centre behind Japan's extraordinary ascent to economic superpower status. The economy was formally committed to the goal of 'trade number oneism'.

The Foreign Exchange and Fair Trade Control Law was also passed in 1949 handing over control of Japan's foreign trade to, ultimately, MITI, as well as requiring export earnings to be paid into a government account. This law was to remain in place for twenty years, the most important instrument of coercion exercised by MITI. As the economist Leon Hollerman put it in 1979, 'In liquidating the occupation by "handing back" operational control to the Japanese, SCAP naively presided not only over the transfer of its authority but also over the institutionalization of the most restrictive foreign trade and foreign exchange control system ever devised by a major free nation.' Everything was now in place for MITI to launch Japan on the greatest economic take-off in world history. These included choosing which industries to nurture, marketing their products, and limiting the number of competitors in each field. The government controlled all foreign exchange and technology, provided tax concessions and financial incentives, thus covering costs, and protected industries from foreign competitors. Chalmers Johnson concludes that 'This high-growth system was one of the most rational and productive industrial policies ever devised by any government, but its essential rationality was not perceived until after it had already started producing results unprecedented for Japan or any other industrialized economy.'

The recovery was kick-started by the Korean War, as orders for ammunition, trucks, uniforms and other products for the American effort came flooding in. The purchase of more than 7000 trucks worth $13 million got the production lines of the Japanese vehicle industry moving. The revenue from this and other orders was ploughed by MITI straight back into investment in heavy industry. By 1952–3, the Korean War was generating no less than 37 per cent of all foreign exchange. In spite of the inflow, industry was still desperately short of capital to invest in new plant to meet the American orders; to remedy this, the idea of 'positive finance' was developed by Hayato Ikeda, who as finance minister was one of the architects of the new economic order.

Ikeda established the two-tier structure of finance that underpinned the recovery. Government-guaranteed banks of last resort, like the Japan Development Bank, acted to guarantee the main clearing banks, which, enjoying this protection, provided the funds needed for the new industrial conglomerates. Naoto Ichimada, governor of the Bank of Japan and guardian of the country's financial rectitude, stood for sound-money policies, but allowed them to be bent to the extent that he permitted 'overlending' by the commercial banks to industry to be government-guaranteed. The result was a system in which the banks lent on the basis of deposits and reserves of just 2 to 3 per cent of loans – unthinkable elsewhere. Ultimately, too, the Ministry of Finance was to exert its authority over the more conservative Bank of Japan.

The overborrowing system was simple in the extreme: companies were allowed to borrow well beyond their ability to repay, sometimes beyond their actual worth; in turn the Bank of Japan permitted the banks to 'overborrow' from its funds. The interest rates charged by the Bank of Japan were very low and hence, because of industry's dependence on these funds, the government indirectly controlled industry through the banks.

The capital base of Japanese industry was transformed. In 1935 nearly 70 per cent of financing for Japanese companies came from the same source as in the West – shareholders. In 1963 the figure was 10 per cent. Bank lending in 1963 was responsible for 70 to 80 per cent of the capital of Japanese companies. There was a massive incentive for Japanese companies to go along with this (in addition to the post-war shortage of capital from other sources): income on bank loans was tax-deductible, whereas dividends on equity were paid from corporate profits after tax.

The advantage of this unique structure – apart from giving government a stranglehold on industry – was that companies which developed long-term relations with the banks were able to take decisions on grounds of long-term market growth and profitability, rather than short-term profitability in order to secure the best possible stock market prices and bonuses for their managers, as in the West. In America and Britain in particular, short-term results and high dividends determined the availability of capital and the promotion and pay of the manager. In addition, the Japanese government could control the economy as a whole through expanding or contracting the supply of bank lending, because there was so little external finance for companies (although this was to change).

The industrial structure that emerged, replacing the old *zaibatsu*, was that of 'banking *keiretsu*' – a large assembly of enterprises created around one of twelve major banks funded by the government. Some of these were merely old *zaibatsu* revived under another name, with the bank assuming many of the functions of the old holding companies – Mitsubishi and Mitsui are obvious examples. Others were 'new *zaibatsu*', similarly reconstructed. Others still were entirely new conglomerates deliberately fostered by government in key sectors. Over the course of time, new *keiretsu* like the phenomenally successful Sony were to join the elite. The club was far from being exclusive; but it remained small, and it carefully screened potential new members. Beneath the main *keiretsu* were a host of lesser *keiretsu*, jostling for entry; and then there was a huge void in the medium enterprise sector, with thousands of tiny, dependent, family-run enterprises and the agricultural economy and the distribution and underdeveloped service sectors below that.

The 'big six' banking *keiretsu* that emerged in the 1950s were

Fuji (which absorbed the old Yasuda empire as well as the smaller Asano *zaibatsu*), Sanwa, Dai Ichi, Mitsui (which re-emerged in 1955), Mitsubishi (which had been revived in 1952 after being dissolved by SCAP), and Sumitomo. Most of the new *keiretsu* also possessed their own trading companies, whose job it was to export frantically at times of contracting domestic demand. MITI worked hard to create the banking *keiretsu* system. For example, it underwrote the trading companies against bad debts abroad, and reduced their number from 2800 to just 20, each serving a *keiretsu* or small producers' cartel.

Thus had MITI more or less created the new industrial structure of Japan: a handful of dominant cartels now owed their existence to the government. This was the reverse of the position before the war, when the cartels were largely independent of the government. Moreover, the cartels were no longer controlled by family groups (although the families continued to have great influence in some), but by the banks, which in turn meant the government. Ironically, because of the immense security offered the big groups by government guarantee, they tried to compete for MITI's favours by setting up companies in all the primary areas defined by the ministry, even if this led to large-scale overproduction – a problem it had eventually to deal with.

The second great arm of state policy was the development bank. Joseph Dodge permitted the setting-up of the Export Import Bank as a worthy enterprise to push Japanese exports. In fact, this was hugely fraudulent: the main 'exports' thus financed were ships in the mid-1950s, whose construction was funded by the bank, which were then 'sold' for a day and rented to Japanese shipping companies. Between 1949 and 1953, four more major government banks were set up, the biggest of which was the Japan Development Bank with the objective of providing longer-term financing to private enterprises 'when the commercial banks were not in a position to assume the risks involved'. MITI submitted all such applications to the bank, which it effectively ran: as soon as the occupation ended, the bank was given the power to raise money directly from the market and was absolved of its loan ceilings.

The old postal savings account set up during the Meiji period as the prime and immensely successful support for small savers was turned into a 'fiscal investment and loan plan' (FILP), run by the Ministry of Finance and MITI: the first $15,000 deposited in any single post office was tax-free; as savers opened multiple accounts in different post offices, the bank had by 1980 four times the assets of the Bank of America, the world's largest commercial bank. The Japan Development Bank (JDB) was empowered to borrow from FILP and channel funds to industries approved by MITI. A loan from the JDB was taken as an imprimatur from MITI, and would serve to attract much larger funds from other sources.

Even so, the direct contribution made by the JDB was huge. In 1953, for example, the JDB directly supplied 22 per cent of all industrial capital. Government banks as a whole that year supplied 38 per cent of industrial capital. Over time these figures dwindled, to 5 per cent and 20 per cent respectively in 1961, as firms generated their own capital. Meanwhile the commercial banks, which were indirectly controlled by the government, were responsible for 49 per cent of industrial financing in 1953, and a still impressive 39 per cent in 1961. Thus in 1953, at the start of the miracle, directly or indirectly the government financed a staggering 87 per cent of internal capital, and in 1961 still as much as 59 per cent. A large proportion of this was contributed by FILP, which by 1972 accounted for some 6 per cent of Japan's total GDP.

The enormous clout of the state banks led Japanese economists to coin the term 'state monopoly capitalism' to describe the system, although 'state-directed cartelism' would be more accurate. Some critics of Japan argue that the whole structure was a profoundly risky one, owing to the over-exposure of the banks, and that it survived through sheer luck. In practice the system was safer than it looked, and highly ingenious. The banks, though over-exposed, had as their collateral the huge assets of Japanese industry; conversely, industry and the banks were guaranteed by the Japanese state. The system was self-supporting: industry, the banks and the state all propped each other up in a structure of equilibriated tension.

The model was in complete contrast to the Western one, in which the banks and conservative financial institutions hoarded money and invested it on high-return speculative stock market and property gains, while industry raised capital directly from the money markets, at arm's length from the banks. The Western banks had much less to guarantee their collateral, while they lacked adequate guarantees from the state, necessitating stronger reserve requirements. The Japanese banks had become extremely strong financially by the end of the 1970s because of the colossal wealth of the industries in which they had invested.

The 'brain' inside the 'head' that guided the Japanese economy –

MITI, working closely with the Ministry of Finance – was the Enterprises Bureau of the former. The Bureau dominated the Industrial Rationalization Council, which consisted of forty-five committees and eighty-one subcommittees covering every industry in the country. This was responsible, among other things, for introducing into Japanese industry 'quality control' and 'productivity measurement' – ideas MITI learnt in the United States, to which they were subsequently re-exported on a much wider scale. The Enterprise Bureau also set up the Foreign Capital Law, which established immensely restrictive conditions for capital imports into Japan. In 1952 another law was passed which provided government subsidies as well as tax-free status for research and development, depreciation of half the costs of installing new equipment during the first year, and large government infrastructure projects on such things as ports, roads, railways, electricity supplies, and industrial parks.

But MITI could also wield the stick as well as dangling the carrot. In 1952 it ordered ten cotton-spinning firms to reduce production by 40 per cent, apportioning quotas to each. If a firm failed to follow this 'administrative guidance' (one of the earliest uses of the term), it risked losing its allocation of raw cotton. A cartel was set up by the industry, which bowed to the inevitable. The same happened in the rubber and steel industries. Conversely, MITI, in setting up a cartel, would subsidize technologies, limit production lines, consult jointly on investment plans and get cartel members to share warehouses. At that stage, private business was happy to go along with MITI's plans: it could raise money from no other source.

The only challenger to MITI was the Fair Trade Commission, set up by MacArthur under the Unfair Competition Law. This prohibited virtually everything that was standard practice for MITI: firms were theoretically forbidden to set prices between themselves, restrict production or sales, carve up markets, or refuse to share technologies or production methods. Article Nine of the law expressly banned holding companies – but these, of course, had been disbanded; the banking *keiretsu*, however, operated under exactly the same principles. MITI nevertheless disliked both the law and the toothless Fair Trade Commission, and in 1957 began a series of attempts to do away with them. A cabinet-led committee concluded baldly that, 'the public interest is not best served by a maintenance of a free competitive order'. The following year an amending law was introduced, but was never passed because other priorities took precedence.

The new superministry of MITI had enormous powers to organize industry and direct government finance to it, and to control foreign exchange, investment, the banking *keiretsu*, and the finance cartels. All it needed now was a coherent strategy, and this was soon supplied. First, MITI decided that Japan must concentrate production in such areas as consumer and domestic appliances, rather than food and textiles; second, it was decided that the key to a massive export drive — always the foremost goal of post-war Japan — lay in creating a strong domestic market. This was the brainchild of Tanzan Ishibashi, one of Japan's most expansionist post-war finance ministers, and now minister for MITI. He argued that only by catering for Japan's large potential domestic market could economies of scale be made that would make exports attractive. MITI should work for both the domestic and overseas markets: when the balance of payments deteriorated, the emphasis would be on exports; when it improved, the emphasis would be on the domestic market.

The Ministry of International Trade and Industry did not get into its stride until the mid-1950s. By then the Korean War boom had petered out, bringing another slump in 1954 after a year in which the balance of payments deficit shot up to $260 million as ordinary Japanese, having suffered so much, suddenly indulged briefly in a consumer boom. With the economy falling into recession again, it was Hayato Ikeda who, as minister of finance, embarked upon the policies that were to lead to Japan's astonishing industrial revival. Scorning orthodox economics, he sliced 100 billion yen off income tax to stimulate domestic demand in 1956; a year later the Kishi government introduced its five-year plan projecting growth at 6.5 per cent a year (in fact the rate achieved was more than 10 per cent).

The main ingredients were an already formidable domestic market; an almost militaristic export programme combined with massive stimulation of the domestic economy; a readiness to live with budget deficits and inflation when necessary; and intensive state direction of industry, particularly by MITI. A Supreme Export Council was set up, consisting of the prime minister, the ministers from MITI, Finance, and Agriculture, the governor of the Bank of Japan, the president of the Export Import Bank, and key business leaders. It was modelled on the Supreme War Council. A new Economic Planning Agency, responsible to MITI, reported directly to the council. Another key institution was JETRO, the Japan External Trade Organization, which was nothing less than a commercial intelligence service with the object of preparing detailed information on juicy foreign markets and how to penetrate them. JETRO also had the job of marketing Japanese goods abroad. By 1975 it had twenty-four trade centres overseas, and fifty-four offices in as many countries.

Finally, MITI refined its system of incentives – as opposed to its coercive methods – in a further attempt to get industry to do what it wanted. As early as 1951, the bureaucrats had taken the decision in principle that tax breaks were more efficient than subsidies because, as one senior official coolly put it, a 'subsidy is paid in advance and does not necessarily lead to the required goal, whereas tax relief is paid after the enterprise has done what the government wants it to do'. These tax breaks were systematic, and provided a huge corporate advantage for Japanese manufacturers. Up to 50 per cent of a firm's earnings could be written off for tax purposes, a figure raised to 80 per cent by 1955. Investments in export industries could be largely written off, 'strategic' machinery was exempted from import duties, royalties paid on foreign technology could be offset against tax, and tax 'holidays' were granted of a kind that the Ministry of Finance admitted 'may not be duly justified by generally accepted accounting principles'.

Tax exemption packages were tailored for particular companies and particular goals. Sales tax was lifted for the first two years of production of Sony transistor radios, bringing the price down sharply. Taxes on television sets were raised only every two years and in stages, as mass production gradually reduced prices. So carefully planned were these campaigns that Japanese households were exhorted to – and in fact did – buy the same goods at the same time: first 'the three sacred treasures' of televisions, washing machine and fridge, then the 'three Cs' – car, cooler (fridge) and colour television. The system could be seen as a concerted conspiracy by the government to rig Japan's supposedly free market and its export drive or, more accurately, a military-style operation in which the usual rules and regulations that govern transactions were suspended in favour of emergency, *ad hoc*, priority arrangements designed to deliver victory as speedily as possible.

A typical 'incubation' of an industry would consist of the following stages: an investigation and MITI policy statement; the allocation of finance through, for example, the Japan Development Bank; the granting of licences for the import of foreign technology; the granting of land on which to build factories; the designation of the industry as 'strategic', and thus qualifying for a large cocktail of tax breaks; and finally the setting up of an 'administrative guidance cartel' to regulate the industry and exclude undesirable competition. From the beginning, these key industries were nurtured by the government, or more specifically by MITI, with the Ministry of Finance as a junior partner, in turn dragging the grumbling Bank of Japan behind it. The state did not 'own' the means of the production, because it had no need to; nevertheless, it took all the important decisions.

The goal was the creation of huge industries capable of producing goods the government had carefully prepared the public to buy, and capable of spearheading a massive export drive of (at this stage) cheap low-quality products. Japan acquired a reputation for shoddy goods, but soon introduced quality control systems which were to turn Japanese goods into some of the most reliable on the market. An artificially low exchange rate; the deliberate holding down of the standard of living in Japan through high prices, which permitted massive corporate reinvestment; a wholesale concentration on strategic industries at the expense of everything else – infrastructure, housing, social welfare, sanitation, and wages (except as judged necessary to stimulate consumer demand); the toleration of inflation and, on occasion, of government deficits; and an economy closed to outsiders: these were the key ingredients of the first stage of the Japanese economic miracle.

According to conventional economic theory, all these ingredients were bound to lead to inefficiency, failure, and corruption. Instead, the policy worked, with dramatic results. It was this stage that was to lead to charges of 'Japan, Inc.'. Indeed, it is hard to find fault with the label, which was taken up by the Japanese themselves without embarrassment. Government was the moving force behind a national mobilization to promote both domestic industry and overseas exports that was militaristic in its single-minded subordination of all other priorities.

Of course, the bureaucrats who had masterminded the assault on foreign markets were not militarists in the strict sense of the word. Few of them had served in the army, many were glad to see the back of it after 1945, and on the whole they were much more ingenious and intelligent than their often dull-witted and rapacious military predecessors. But the priority accorded the drive for growth and exports in one industry after another recalled a military operation, as did the hierarchy of the economic organizations behind the offensive: the Supreme Economic Council at the top; MITI as the main operational headquarters, with its industry-by-industry bureaucratic 'minders'; the cartels of its chosen industries as its elite divisions in the field; the mass of small enterprises (often, in the callous Japanese phrase, used as 'shock absorbers' at times of difficulty – they went to the wall, not the big boys), as the footsloggers, camp followers, and cannon fodder of the battle. The system even had its foreign intelligence service, JETRO.

The companies themselves were organized internally, after the awesome battles with the unions, in a manner that recalled the structure and disciplines of the Japanese army – although not, of course, in so spartan a manner. The export drive seemed to be a continuation of war by another name. Even the usually understated and scholarly Chalmers Johnson makes the military comparison:

> from about 1951 to 1961 the Japanese economy remained on a war footing. The goal changed from military to economic victory, but the Japanese people could not have worked harder, saved more, or innovated more ruthlessly if they had actually been engaged in a war for national survival, as in fact they were. And just as a nation mobilized for war needs a military general staff, so a nation mobilized for economic development needs an economic general staff. The men of MCI (the Ministry of Commerce and Industry), MM (the Ministry of Munitions) and MITI had been preparing to play this role since the late 1920s. During the 1950s the trumpet finally sounded.

The feudal-militarist society that had not been altered radically by defeat in 1945 or by MacArthur's occupation, and had been levelled by poverty, fell in behind the government's plans in an extraordinarily orderly manner. State control worked when it captured a mood of mass mobilization just as it had, infinitely more cruelly, in Stalin's Russia in forcing through mass and rapid industrialization in key industries. Where Stalin's enemy was the bourgeois peasant class, Japan's enemy was overseas competition. The real difficulty was to come: after the forced march necessarily reached its destination, would the exhausted footsoldiers of the economic offensive collapse under the crushing burden of the state bureaucracy? And what would happen when, as in the Pacific War, the victims overseas, having been caught unawares and forced to retreat, fought back?

26

GREATER JAPAN

T HE FIRST Japanese economic offensive really got under way
after the expansionary measures that pulled the economy out
of the 1954 slump; for the next seven years the boom went
on, unchecked. It proved to be staggeringly successful. Real GDP
increased at a rate of nearly 9 per cent in 1955, dropping off slightly
to 5.6 per cent in 1958 before soaring to 13.4 per cent and 14.4 per
cent in 1960 and 1961 respectively. Japan's unchallenged economic
advance thus lasted some twelve times longer than its Pacific War
whirlwind offensive. The reaction from abroad had begun to take
definite shape by 1959, in a call for Japan to make its currency freely
convertible, to revalue, and to open up its hermetically sealed
domestic market for export and foreign investment. It was at this
stage that the Japanese economic miracle took a crucial turn, and
the superiority of its economic planners over its military theorists
became evident. Faced by mounting international pressure, the
Japanese staged a strategic retreat.

At a crucial ministerial meeting in March 1960, two key officials,
Zen'ei Imai, chief of MITI's textiles bureau, and Taiichiro Matsuo,
were alone in arguing in favour of trade liberalization. To their
astonishment, they had the support of the one man who mattered –
the minister, Ikeda, who in turn had the ear of the prime minister,
the same Nobosuke Kishi who had done so much to create Japan's
system of state-directed cartelism. It is remarkable that a ministry
with such an intensely nationalistic culture as MITI could be steered
in this direction. To this day, MITI officials routinely use such
scathing terms as *joi* ('expulsion of the foreigners') and *iteki* ('barbarians') which go back to the shogunate itself. Japan's competitors
were referred to by the head of the trade promotion bureau as

recently as 1971 as *keto* – 'hairy Chinese'. MITI saw it as its prime duty to protect Japan's industries from 'foreign pressure'.

The dominant nationalist within MITI was Shigeru Sahashi, head of the heavy industries bureau and later MITI vice-minister (that is, the man who actually ran the ministry). He was to acquire a reputation as a very tough cookie indeed – 'the monster Sahashi', as he was dubbed by the press, 'a samurai among samurai' and 'an official who uses force' in the eyes of his colleagues. Surprising as it may seem, Japan's protected industries at the time viewed the prospect of competing with foreign industries on equal terms with something like terror, fearing 'an invasion of American capital' and the destruction of the country's carefully selected sheltered industries.

In a famous tussle with the formidable IBM, Sahashi displayed just how savagely MITI could fight its corner in keeping foreigners out of Japan. The ministry bristled with anti-barbarian devices. There was an 'informal' rule that the foreign partner could not have a controlling interest in a joint venture: they could have no more than a limited number of shares and a handful of directors in Japanese firms. MITI also had to give its express approval to each investment. IBM was a special case, however: it had organized itself into a yen-based company, and was not therefore technically a 'foreign' firm; and it had a monopoly on the patents to computer technology which Sahashi was eager to get his hands on. He declared baldly to the American giant: 'We will take every measure possible to obstruct the success of your business unless you licence IBM patents to Japanese firms and charge them no more than a 5 per cent royalty . . . We do not have an inferiority complex towards you; we only need time and money to compete effectively.' IBM backed down, accepting Sahashi's terms for doing business in Japan, submitting itself to 'administrative guidance', selling its patents and accepting competition from a carbon-copy of IBM's computer-leasing business set up by MITI itself.

The issue that broke down the door of Japan's closed economy was cotton. A major distortion had crept into the system of state control: because of the generous state incentives for producers, the main spinners were drawing upon the government-guaranteed imports of raw cotton to compete bitterly among themselves and overproduce. By May 1959, a fifth of the foreign exchange budget was going on raw cotton, while the Americans were beginning to grumble about Japan's 'dollar blouses' flooding in. Ominously, Washington called for negotiations to limit Japanese production, and introduced a 'buy American' policy for its foreign aid programme.

Ikeda and Kishi had the foresight to see three things. The first was that, without trade liberalization, Japan's growing economy could soon become inefficient and flabby: it required the challenge of international competition to permit MITI to carry out a rigorous pruning of the 'excessive competition' that had grown up, for example among the cotton spinners. Second, there was a real danger of protectionist retaliation against Japanese producers, which would have left the country no better off than before. Third, Japanese industry had nothing to fear from internationalism: it was in excellent shape to take on all comers. Only the inefficient would fail, and they were dead wood anyway. In any event, both men knew that any concerted foreign assault on Japanese markets could be blocked by subtler barriers than overtly protectionist ones.

In 1961 a trade liberalization plan was adopted just as the prime minister was hounded from office by mass demonstrations against the new Japanese–American treaty. Ikeda, architect of the miracle, took over, promising to open up four-fifths of the economy to foreign competition within three years. Pandemonium broke out in a country already in turmoil over defence issues. It was suggested that the Americans were undertaking a new 'occupation' of Japan, both militarily and economically. The far right joined the left in sharing this view. The press talked about the 'second coming of the black ships', the impending 'battle between national capital and foreign capital', and the threat of control by huge capitalist foreign powers. Sahashi, openly citing the pre-war National General Mobilization Law, called for a new 'national general mobilization'.

Paranoia had reasserted itself in a truly frightening way – hence the decision of moderate socialists to call off the protests against the Americans before the extreme right hijacked the movement and anti-American feeling became uncontrollable. To protect Japan against the expected American economic onslaught, the Asian Economic Research Institute was set up to survey overseas markets, and the Overseas Economic Co-operation Fund to administer foreign aid. In practice, both were committed to tying aid to the buying of Japanese products and engaged in export promotion; at home they were openly acknowledged as so doing. Ikeda also sought to calm domestic political opinion by going full-throttle for growth with the announcement of his 'income-doubling' plan.

Finally, MITI decided that the huge problem area of business rendered inefficient by 'excessive competition' must be tackled. The trouble was that this produced howls of anguish from the huge vested interests that had depended upon tax breaks and government allocations of raw materials over the past few years. MITI overstepped the mark, thinking itself all-powerful. Sahashi conceived the idea of 'administration by inducement', drawing up a radical plan to give special committees of government, industry and finance powers to shake up or close down whole areas of the economy so as to confront the international challenge. The law was based on what the Japanese believed to be the French concept of the *economie concertée* – co-operation between the state and big business.

However, MITI encountered truly ferocious resistance. Business, which had been put on its feet by government, now wanted to free itself from bureaucratic control. The smaller and less competitive companies feared – rightly in many cases – that they would be closed down. Like a child come of age, business tried to break away from its parents: it saw the draft law as an attempt by MITI to assert a control it should no longer be exercising. Moreover, business was now beginning to wield independent power with the politicians it bankrolled, and complained bitterly of red tape.

When, in January 1962, Eisaku Sato (later to become prime minister) resigned as minister of MITI, a political boss, Hajime Fukuda, replaced him. The real power in Japan, of course, is traditionally exercised by the bureaucratic vice-minister, and Sahashi, the overlord of MITI, had been groomed for the job. The politicians decided otherwise and Fukuda, astonishingly, passed Sahashi over – a virtually unprecedented move. MITI was stunned: the overmighty subject had been put in its place, it seemed. Sahashi's law, which had been introduced into parliament, was dropped for lack of backing from the governing party.

But MITI and the bureaucrats were not to be so easily defeated. The new vice-minister lasted just fifteen months, before Sahashi finally got the job. Simultaneously, intense pressure from GATT, the United States and the IMF forced Japan to speed up liberalization as the price of keeping its access to overseas markets. The Western chill, coupled with the problems caused by too tough a monetary policy and overproduction, caused Japan's growth to stall, taking several major companies to bankruptcy.

In this climate, Fukuda was forced to concede that Sahashi had been right all along. The special measures law would not be passed by parliament, he said, because this was unnecessary; instead, the measures would be imposed through MITI's existing reserve powers of 'administrative guidance'. Being extra-legal, administrative guidance supposedly lacked the force of law, but in practice it represented coercion. If it were refused, dire things were likely to happen to his business. A very senior overseas businessman told the author that 'we get called in from time to time and told what's what. We don't dream of straying from it.'

One contractor who ignored a directive had his water and sewage lines capped with concrete by the local city government, an action which was subsequently upheld in court. The ministry had the authority to issue directives, deliver warnings, make suggestions, and 'offer' encouragement – and foolhardy was the company that ignored them. To one outside businessman it was worse than a specific set of restrictive laws: 'it is not really a matter of Japanese competitiveness, but a marriage of impenetrable government supports and subsidies. Our people feel that whatever they do, the Japanese will just lower their prices.'

Equipped with its new powers, MITI set about economic rationalization, delayed for four years, with a vengeance. The petrochemical, synthetic textile and paper pulp industries were the first to be reorganized, their production cut back, new entrants banned, and quotas assigned to existing firms. Mergers were pushed through by the ministry. Japan's three major steel companies were railroaded into one. The Nissan and Prince automobile companies had their heads banged together.

Then MITI ran into its first recusant: Hosai Hyuga, president of Sumitomo Metals, a dependency of one of the old *zaibatsu* and now part of a major banking *keiretsu*. The issue was MITI's peremptory order that six major steel plants cut their production by 10 per cent; five agreed. Sumitomo argued that it was being unjustly penalized. At that stage the figurehead MITI minister, Takeo Miki, offered to help finance a new blast furnace for Sumitomo if the company backed down. But Miki was being too soft. Sahashi bluntly declared the following day that unless Sumitomo behaved itself, it would receive its customary coal allocation in just sufficient quantity to produce the required quota of steel. The press had a field day with Sahashi's apparent slap in the face for his nominal superior, Miki; but Sahashi won and Sumitomo backed down. Sahashi had effectively restored the powers MITI had lost when its control of foreign exchanges and trade was removed as a result of trade liberalization.

The ministry's power was resurrected, and it had shown that even Japan's giant oligarchs could still be brought to heel.

Sahashi's retirement brought MITI under renewed pressure from big business, as ever chafing at red-tape restrictions. The ministry had forced through mergers and cartel agreements in seven major industries in the mid-1960s: steel, automobiles, machine tools, computers, petrol refining, petrochemicals and synthetic textiles. While MITI was engaged in the major restructuring of Japanese industry to head off the international challenge, it also embarked on a devious programme to prevent the opening up of Japan's economy. A Capital Transfer Liberalization Counter-Measures Special Commission was empowered to draw up a mass of restrictions that would make it virtually impossible for a foreigner to enter the Japanese market.

In its decisions, the commission showed that it had a sense of humour. Full free trade was permitted in sake production and the manufacture of Japanese wooden clogs – not areas which foreigners were queuing to get into. Foreigners were allowed to buy up only 20 per cent of any one established Japanese company and were not permitted to own more than half of a joint venture. Television manufacture was 'free' to foreigners, but they were not allowed to produce integrated circuits or colour televisions, while foreign – that is imported – steel was deemed unsuitable for Japanese car-making. All foreign investment still had to be approved by MITI. In January 1967, fifty industries were opened up for foreign competition, including cornflakes, which the Japanese do not eat, and railway carriages, for which the sole customer was the Japanese government, whose policy was not to buy overseas products. All the other industries were dominated by Japanese giants. Liberalization so far was pure window-dressing.

Meanwhile, MITI's attempt to streamline the economy continued apace. In 1968, after protracted negotiations, the two biggest steelworks agreed to merge to form a huge conglomerate which would dominate the Japanese steel industry, as the Japan Steel Corporation did before the war. To MITI's astonishment, the decision provoked a genuine public furore. A prominent group of academic economists thundered that the merger was wrong, and would lead to monopoly price increases: 'What is really significant about this case is the absence of concern for the legal, economic and social implications of so large a merger, as well as the widespread belief that the acts of private enterprises are not based on their own independent decisions but on the administrative guidance of MITI.' The virtually redundant Free Trade Commission set up by Mac-Arthur at last raised its head above the parapet to insist that the new industrial giant should not force its competitors to follow its pricing purely because of its size. The commission argued that the new group should sell off its monopolistic subsidiaries: this it was forced to do by the Tokyo High Court in 1969, in an unprecedented rebuff to MITI.

Meanwhile, the ministry was now under fire for pursuing policies that had massively damaged the environment as well as the living conditions of millions of Japanese. The popular pressure for some action – by the end of the 1960s, Japan was the world's most polluted country – had been growing steadily and exploded in the attack on *kogei* (literally, 'public wound'). In 1967 the Diet had responded by passing a major anti-pollution law, which MITI had castrated by adding a clause that any measures must be 'in harmony with the healthy development of the economy'. Pressure intensified, and in 1970 the clause was repealed. MITI now boldly assumed the role of poacher turned gamekeeper, and set up its own Environmental Protection and Safety Bureau which, astonishingly, contributed to a major reduction in pollution in the course of a decade.

Another major row hit MITI shortly afterwards, this time affecting the Americans. At a summit meeting between Prime Minister Sato and President Nixon in Washington in 1969, the Americans agreed to restore Okinawa to Japan in part-exchange for a guarantee by Japan to cut its exports of synthetic textiles to America. MITI, however, had sent its own delegation to the United States which concluded that the American textile industry was thriving. The ministry prevented Sato from delivering on his promise, to the anger of the American administration.

The ministry also vigorously defended Japan against foreign investment. When the Texas Instruments Company attempted to break into the Japanese market, MITI deferred consideration of the request for two and a half years, then insisted that the American firm join a Japanese company as junior partner, and divulge its technology to local competitors; for good measure, it would have to curb production until Japanese companies were on their feet. Gulf Oil was similarly chased off – even when it sought a partnership with Idemitsu, which was told by MITI not to participate. The ministry was also determined that Ford, General Motors and Chrysler should not get a foothold in the Japanese car market, and instructed the major Japanese car manufacturers not to enter into joint ventures; meanwhile it sought to merge the companies into two giants, Nissan and Toyota.

MITI was bloodied at last by Mitsubishi, the aristocrat and also the largest of the Japanese *keiretsu*, as it had been among the old *zaibatsu*. It viewed the bureaucrats with disdain, had long had links with foreign companies, and looked upon even such eminent oligopolistic giants as Mitsui as parvenus and *arrivistes*. In May 1969, Mitsubishi announced that it had reached agreement with Chrysler to set up a new car group in which it would hold just two-thirds of the equity. Isuzu promptly did the same with General Motors; there was nothing that MITI could do without laying bare to all the world the sham of Japan's trade and investment liberalization. It seemed at last that big business was free. The MITI minister, Masayoshi Ohira, acknowledged that in place of the old 'governmental industrial guidance model', a 'private-sector industrial guidance model' had been born. Sahashi, in retirement, fumed that 'the grown son tends to forget to thank the parent for his long care'.

The fears were exaggerated. MITI still had much in reserve, even if its self-esteem had been dented. A brilliant bureaucrat, Naohiro Amaya, formulated the MITI thinking for the next step forward, arguing for a great leap from an advanced industrial society to a post-industrial one. This would require further development of the consumer goods market, as well as a mass expansion of the service sector, the large-scale introduction of robotics from manufacturing into the processing of raw materials, a cartelization process of the traditional kind of high-tech assembly industries, and a 'knowledge-intensive' drive in the media and education. In addition, MITI advocated major social spending and a large programme of industrial relocation away from the colossal Tokyo–Osaka sprawl – something MITI should have thought of before, and which was now going to be very expensive. MITI also backed Tanaka's grandiose plans for 'rebuilding the archipelago' through major investment in the regions. The ministry thus sought to regain the initiative. Big business was acting with increasing independence – although care was taken not to prod MITI into using its still formidable powers. There was public speculation as to whether its day had come.

Two things were to revive MITI from its moment of self-doubt. First, Tanaka's government permitted inflation to accelerate so as to finance his own spending ambitions; second, the oil shock of the 1970s jolted Japan out of dependence on cheap fuel. MITI was blessed at the time with one of the country's most decisive ministers, Yasuhiro Nakasone, who with a flurry of emergency powers overcame near-panic in Japan at the prospect of economic collapse. MITI swung into life, taking action against profiteers during the panic.

Meanwhile the new head of the Fair Trade Commission, Toshihide Takahashi, suddenly accused the main Japanese oil companies, which operated as a MITI-style cartel, of illegal price fixing – a remarkable charge, since that was how most of the Japanese economy was organized. In 1974 the twelve companies were brought to court. MITI hastily distanced itself from the cartel, claiming that it had been 'betrayed' by the oil companies. Even so, the principle of cartelism had been challenged for the first time. Reformers in parliament sought to promote a new anti-monopoly law, but the bill was killed by MITI and its followers in the Diet.

In response to inflation and the oil crisis, the Japanese had slammed on the economic brakes. In the first quarter of 1974, output slumped by 20 per cent from the previous quarter, while industrial production fell by 9 per cent and Japan regisered its first ever year of negative growth, at minus 0.2 per cent. Production slowed down across the nation; employees were put into part-time or 'window-watching' jobs. Bankruptcies soared to 11,000. The slump was created by Takeo Fukuda, the dry and orthodox finance minister who was Prime Minister Tanaka's arch-enemy. Thanks to his prompt action, Japan felt the effects of the oil shock before most other industrial nations, which sought to ride out the crisis and succumbed in the late 1970s. By 1975 the Japanese economy was growing again, at a modest 3.2 per cent, then by a respectable 6 per cent in 1976 and for the rest of the decade; the other industrial nations managed an annual average of barely 2 per cent over the same period.

MITI played a central role in these conditions of slowdown, creating new cartels in textiles, rubber, shipping, and petrochemicals. The Japanese adopted the same approach when the 'super-chip' – very large-scale integration (VLSI) to produce a computer with a memory of 64,000 pieces of information – loomed on the horizon. This would revolutionize the industry: costs would fall and computers' speed and memory would increase. With the news that IBM was likely to develop this chip by the end of the 1970s, the Japanese were thrown into a frenzy. MITI insisted on co-operation between the major computer firms to create a VLSI programme all of their own. MITI provided $100 million in funds, on condition that the companies act together and share their research.

To those who argue that MITI had lost its influence, this was a classic example of the ministry forcing an industry to act in concert to achieve a national goal in a manner that has hardly ever occurred elsewhere – behind closed doors and closed markets. Michiyuki Uenohara, research director of NEC, argued that, 'if the Americans were able to develop a VLSI computer, it would mean the end of the Japanese semiconductor business . . . It gave me great pleasure to see [our researchers] aiming at technological developments that would outstrip IBM.' The Americans had a shock when their pioneering firms in Silicon Valley were quickly caught up with by Japan in the production of standard items during the early 1980s. Yet the microprocessor market, which requires complex technology and sophisticated software, may be beyond Japan.

MITI also spearheaded a campaign to reduce Japan's dependence on oil from the Middle East, which was 75 per cent before the crisis. However, the ministry continued to obstruct Japan's capital liberalization: even in 1973, twenty-two industries were still wholly protected: agriculture, mining, the retail trade, and leather were four of them, the others being the new strategic industries MITI was suckling at its breast. The ministry seemed as indispensable as ever. Although not as omnipotent as in the 1950s and 1960s, by the early 1970s it had recovered from the general onslaught against it from business and public opinion. Only a real giant like Mitsubishi could take on MITI with any prospect of winning. Business in general was more inclined to argue, but ultimately had to defer.

With the post-1973 recession, MITI regained its original role in chaperoning industry. As recovery picked up steam and moved into the boom, or 'bubble economy' of the late 1980s, business also began to recover its confidence. The Japanese stock market suddenly grew into a major source of funds for industry – although never eclipsing the banks. With a mushrooming of property prices, firms found themselves awash with money and a new speculative class came into being. All of this tended to undercut the old, rigid hierarchical Japanese economic structure which had MITI at its pinnacle. Once again, it seemed that the children – and grandchildren – were ignoring the father.

The transformation of Japan's capital markets, which was based largely on the huge surplus on the balance of payments, was indeed astonishing. From 1980 onwards the Japanese banks became the world's largest foreign investors: nine of the ten largest commercial banks in the world were Japanese, as were the five top underwriters of Eurobonds, the four largest investment banks, and many of the largest insurance companies. The Japanese used the expertise of overseas investment banks like Barings and Schroders for their offshore operations, creating the illusion that they were opening up their capital markets to foreigners.

With the yen also appreciating fast, the 'bubble economy' reached a dizzying peak in the late 1980s. By 1988 the stock market had jumped to four times its level of 1983. The value of prime land in Tokyo almost doubled between 1985 and 1987; the four acres of land occupied by the Imperial Palace and its grounds were reckoned to be worth more than the state of California. In this situation, it seemed that the power of business and the markets had vastly eclipsed the regulatory power of MITI. The bureaucrats were on the run, and the political arena was now dominated by tough party bosses in the Tanaka–Takeshita–Kanemaru mould. Yet the bubble economy was to burst spectacularly, and MITI was left to mop up the mess.

27

SAMURAI, SOLDIERS, SALARYMEN

THE CHIEF ingredients of the Japanese economic miracle may be summarized under five main headings: first, the historical, social and environmental background; second, the politico-economic backdrop; third, the role of the state; fourth, the structure and culture of the Japanese company; and fifth, the Japanese system of industrial relations. Of these, by far the most important was the role of the state, but the others played major parts. The remarkable thing is how few of the ingredients in most areas can be ascribed to Japan's racial or cultural characteristics, and how many could in theory be transplanted elsewhere (although conditions abroad may make this difficult).

The social, historical and educational background is obviously the least transplantable. At least four factors are at work. The first is that the cultural conditioning in Japan makes people naturally suited to a hierarchy and seniority system; this makes an industrial structure much easier to organize than in a society which emphasizes the rights, freedoms, and talents of the individual. The head of one of the biggest overseas merchant banks in Japan told the author that the culture 'does not stimulate imagination or creativity; but it makes it much easier for those with imagination and creativity at the top to organize the tens of thousands that have none into institutions'.

Related to this is the second factor, the centuries-old emphasis on the interests of the group and of society as a whole. Workers gain their self-respect from their place of work and their colleagues: there are correspondingly fewer opponents of big corporations and big governments, fewer awkward customers at work, more of a readiness to obey orders.

Third, the education system is geared towards the assimilation and retention of vast amounts of information, as well as encouraging mathematics, and rates persistence above all virtues. From an early age, most Japanese are taught to work hard at repetitive tasks – an ideal conditioning for their future places in a modern industrial society.

Finally, for much of Japanese history, a large peasant class lived in conditions of desperate poverty and extreme subjugation, and their lives only began to improve, and then not much, in the nineteenth century. Even this century the Japanese were on the edge of starvation after the war, their cities in ruins. Although there was intense resentment against the governing class at the time, this was tempered by the belief that any attempt to overturn it was doomed, and the industrial militancy of the period soon tapered off into a readiness to work incredibly hard to rebuild Japan. Without this compulsion, and also a deep desire to build up security rather than to spend hard-earned money, the economic miracle might never have happened. All these phenomena combined to produce the kind of work ethic which was truly remarkable by Western standards.

The stories of the endurance of 'salaryman' are legion. Even today, only one Japanese worker in three enjoys a two-day weekend; civil servants are expected to work two Saturdays a month. The average number of days' holiday taken by a worker is just eight – most of them usually in mid-August, when traffic jams outside Tokyo snake out in all directions and the popular seaside resorts are as crowded as underground stations. The average Japanese works between 200 and 500 hours a year longer than his Western counterpart; it is not unusual for a Japanese worker to die from overwork (*karoshi*).

Nor are ordinary Japanese men troubled by the demands of the heart and hearth rather than the office. A government survey in 1978 reported that the most enjoyable thing in the lives of the men polled were: career, 44 per cent; children, 29 per cent; hobbies, 17 per cent; and wives just 5 per cent. For women, the mirror image applied: children were most important to 53 per cent, family in general to 13 per cent, jobs to 9 per cent, and husbands to just 3 per cent; for the overwhelming majority of Japanese still, the woman's place is in the home and the man's is in the office.

In short, the social, historical and educational backdrop predisposes Japan's workforce to be much more compliant in an industrial society dominated by large organizations than virtually anywhere else in the world. None of these factors, obviously, is readily transplantable to any other model, although aspects of the educational system could be tried elsewhere – the emphasis on mathematics and science, for example, the respect for hard work, and orientation towards skills and training.

It bears stressing too that although this compliant workforce gives Japan a huge advantage, it carries many disadvantages: lack of imagination, too rigid an application of rules and knowledge, and an inability to be flexible and innovative. Moreover, while hard work is itself an advantage, carried to excess it does not lead to better judgement or greater efficiency; studies suggest just the reverse. Any observer of a Japanese firm will see many office workers idling and just passing the time of the long working day until their section chief goes home.

One striking feature of Japanese society is that, whereas in many respects it is ordered and efficient, in others it is quite inefficient. The row that broke out over Miyazawa's claim that 'the work ethic in America' is lacking was misconceived. For various reasons, notably better management, Japanese industry may be more efficient than much of American industry. But Japanese workers are certainly not more productive, though they appear to work much harder. Japanese productivity has risen sharply, from just 17 per cent of that of an American worker in 1950 to 81 per cent in 1990; Japan has overtaken the output per worker of Germany (75 per cent), France (74 per cent), and Britain (70 per cent).

Virtually every visitor to Japan notices the slow and excessively mannered and bureaucratic approach taken by Japanese to quite simple problems. As a prominent foreign lawyer in Japan repeatedly told the author, 'The Japanese are always faffing around.' Another observer, Tom Johnson, observed that, 'When I first went to Japan, I expected everything to be extremely efficient. Like many *gaijin* (foreigners) I was surprised to find the opposite: simple things took a long time to achieve, and apparently simple decisions took ages to make.' This is because Japanese look to play by the rules, and become confused in situations outside their experience and mental conditioning.

This apparent inflexibility may be suited to modern industrial society. One top manager of a major western merchant bank in Tokyo suggests that the most important aspect of Japanese management is that 'You have discipline. The workforce is docile. It puts in the work. This is a structure in which bright people can get things done – it is not that bright people are absent.'

A recent survey in the Japan *Times* showed that 78 per cent of salarymen often felt unhappy going to work, 82 per cent said they were obsessed with work, and 67 per cent said they had insomnia because of work; 46 per cent felt there was a danger of dying from overwork.

The second prime cause of the economic miracle was Japan's battery of international advantages. The planets were favourably aligned, as it were, in the four decades of growth. Again, by their nature, this was a lucky chance, unlikely to recur elsewhere. The first of these advantages (which also applied to a lesser degree to Germany, Italy, and France, as war-ravaged nations) was that defeat and ruin were actually an advantage in 1945: they cleared away antique industries and technologies, and compelled countries to start from scratch using the latest methods. Then there was a paradox: Japan lacked raw materials of its own, so it bought from the most economical and most efficient suppliers. At that stage most commodities were cheap, so Japanese manufacturers were not compelled to buy at home for fear of offending huge domestic lobbies involved in the exploitation of such primary products.

The 1950s and 1960s was a time of unprecedentedly cheap oil – on which Japan was nine-tenths dependent for its energy needs at the time – and open Western economies. It was not until the early 1960s that Western countries, in particular the United States, which had looked upon Japan as an adolescent offspring, realized that they were being taken advantage of. The decade in which a closed Japan was allowed free penetration of Western markets proved to be invaluable in getting Japan's industries on their feet.

An advantage enjoyed by virtually no other major Western economy except Italy was that Japan had much the same government since 1948 (although Italy's ruling party, the Christian Democrats, has had to enter into many coalitions with a constellation of smaller parties in order to maintain power). The Liberal Democratic Party, while characterized by ferocious faction struggles, is a conservative pro-business party, for the most part eager to support to the hilt Japan's policies of government-backed growth. At no stage has business had to face the uncertainties of a change of government, or international speculation based on that possibility. Threats of nationalization, high taxation or workers' control have been absent for nearly half a century: the worst that happens to business is the government's occasional attempts to shake it up by threatening to withdraw subsidies. The impact of this political stability should not be underestimated: countries like Britain, France, and (West)

Germany have all feared, and undergone, wholesale changes of government. Even the United States, where both parties share much the same economic goals, has had electoral jitters.

For decade after decade, Japan has pursued growth as its main objective. Consumer spending has taken second place to productive investment; it represents only 56 per cent of GNP in Japan even today compared with 64 per cent in Europe and 68 per cent in the United States. Throughout the growth phase of Japan's economy it has been able to operate under an American defence umbrella, and it has devoted a much smaller share of its resources to defence than have most other countries with Western-style economies.

Social protection has almost always been the duty of the company, rather than of the government, which provides only a minimum welfare net of a kind that is almost shocking in a modern industrial nation, particularly one as rich as Japan. The huge governmental postal savings fund, which might have been used to provide the basis of a welfare state, goes instead to industry. For a long time, moreover, there was virtually no environmental spending in Japan; the government was unencumbered in its planning policies by environmental or consumer rights lobbies. Only in the late 1960s did the environmental lobby, in particular, begin to emerge as a force.

Japan's single-minded concentration on economic growth and exports at the expense of almost every other priority would not be possible in countries where public opinion makes itself felt more strongly, and is clearly undesirable and unattractive in its extreme version; other countries, while not enjoying Japan's growth rate, have enjoyed a much better quality of life. The lesson here may be that it is possible to concentrate resources on growth for a time, shifting the emphasis from other fields of spending, because ultimately economic stagnation will not provide the funds for other priorities.

The third major ingredient of the economic miracle, and the central one, was of course the role of the state. While stopping short of ownership of the means of production, its influence has been huge, catalytic, and oppressive: creating new industries and destroying old ones, developing industrial cults, getting up cartels and breaking them down, helping companies to organize themselves, keeping out foreign companies and targeting export markets. (In the chart, I have tried to summarize the full range of factors that so shaped Japan's post-war economy.)

Factors behind Japan's economic miracle and transferability of the model

Factor	Transferable?	Desirable?
Historical, social background		
Cultural conditioning which disposes Japanese towards accepting hierarchy	No	No
Subordination of the rights of the individual to the group or society as a whole	Partially	No
Education system geared towards both of these, as well as the rote acquisition of large amounts of information	Partially	No
Japan's history as one of a large peasant class living in poverty and subjugation, as well post-war privations	No	No
Political-economic backdrop		
Post-war ruin provided a cleared site for new technologies and reconstruction	No	No
Lack of natural resources in Japan turned to advantage: policy was to buy from cheapest suppliers, not from expensive domestic producers of raw materials	No	No
Exploitation of era of cheap oil and open Western economies	No	No
Japan has had same government since 1948, so policy backdrop is stable, predictable and pro-business. New government in 1993 shows few signs of upsetting this	Probably not	No
Government has pursued growth as its consistent, overwhelming priority. Social spending, housing, environmental spending and defence, all of which consume large resources in other countries, have been relegated to second place, giving Japan a head start. Consumption has been a distant second to production	Partially	Partially

Factor	Transferable?	Desirable?

The role of the state

Creation of MITI – small, tightly knit
directing organ for Japan's economy after
the Pacific War | Yes | Yes

Initially overt state direction of Japanese
industry through control of foreign
exchange, forcible mergers. Both Ministry of
Finance and Bank of Japan use Japan's
traditionally dependent and over-lent
commercial banking system, which is heavily
dependent on central bank, to control
industry whose primary source of capital is
from banks. Direct control through lending
from Japan Development Bank, Fiscal
Investment and Loan Plan and other bodies.
MITI control now exercised more subtly
through administrative guidance | Yes | Partially

MITI's co-ordination of Japan's export
effort remains intense. Foreign markets are
targeted, foreign aid used to promote
Japanese business. Market share is all-
important, and dumping and price-cutting
used to obtain it | Yes | Partially

Government's promotion of hierarchical
structure of Japanese business – banking
keiretsu at the top, a handful of major
newcomers beneath, and, lastly, a huge
network of smaller dependants and
suppliers, which cushion the big groups
from economic shocks and are kept firmly in
their place | No | No

Flexible, undogmatic macro-economic
policy, ready to use large budget deficits,
high taxes, and undervalued currency where
necessary to promote growth | Yes | Yes

Factor	Transferable?	Desirable?
Use of high tariffs, to protect young industries; these are only grudgingly relaxed when those companies are competitive. Internal foreign investment and competition discouraged by a variety of non-tariff methods, e.g. the distribution system	No	No

The company

Factor	Transferable?	Desirable?
Capital comes from borrowing, not equity, made possible by close ties between industry and banks. Dangerously high leverage compared with Western companies, but banks are understanding and government underwrites them	Yes	Yes
Limited shareholder power. Companies managed with sights on long-term position, not short-term profits. Accountants have little influence in companies, as do finance departments. Most investment governed by 'payback' analysis	Yes	Yes
Companies managed by self-perpetuating management elite loyal to company. Predatory takeovers almost non-existent	Yes	Partially
Growth bias, based on long-term view. Short-term profits unimportant	Yes	Yes
Ruthless competition for all-important market share, with use of loss-leading, prices set below cost initially, constant introduction of new products, use of strong capital base or ties with banks to undercut and destroy competition	Yes	Yes
Huge emphasis on company R&D	Yes	Yes
Readiness to borrow ideas from international competitors	Yes	Yes
Pioneering of just-in-time continuous processing techniques	Yes	Yes

Factor	Transferable?	Desirable?
Emphasis on reduction in factory complexity. Increasing specialization on just one or two product lines	Yes	Yes
Forward planning, e.g. massive investment in robots	Yes	Yes
Readiness to move into entirely new areas of production	Yes	Yes

Industrial relations

Factor	Transferable?	Desirable?
Lifetime employment. Confined to major companies, but probably the single most important douser of industrial unrest. Also permits introduction of new technology with little pain. Blends individual's interests with those of company	Yes	Yes
Virtual absence of serious work stoppages	No	Yes
Enterprise unions, which engage in ritual wage bargaining, based on workplace, not industry-wide, and are generally co-operative	No	Partially
Intensely hierarchical structure, but not based on class	No	No
Partial worker access to company information	Yes	Yes
Decision-making through consensus. Partly a cover for seniority system but some scope for tough and imaginative middle management	Yes	No
Buggins' turn promotion policy keeps discontent among older/ 'plateaued' staff to a minimum, although sometimes creates cautious, dead-wood management	Yes	No
Pay linked to seniority, but higher levels of salary much lower than in Western countries. Bonus system increasingly used, amounting to from a third to a half of annual salary	Yes	Yes

There can be no doubt whatever that the Japanese model has been primarily characterized by vigorous state direction and that industry, while occasionally resenting this, is still subordinate. It is a mistake to argue, as Karel van Wolferen does, that industry has now eschewed state direction or that Japan is primarily now a free-market economy. Japan's large and small industries are chiefly privately owned, but they are directed by a state economic bureaucracy within very strict limits.

There are a few who argue, and then not convincingly, that the government took little part in Japan's miracle. All agree that MITI played a crucial role in the immediate post-occupation period. However, some MITI critics like Kikkawa Motodowa believe that the role of government was auxiliary to that of big business, while others point out that trade and capital liberalization were carried out in response to foreign pressure, not government planning. The consumer, electronics and motor industries are said to owe little to government intervention. One authority (Roos and Altshuler, *The Future of The Automobile*, 1985) claims that 'the role of the Japanese government in building this manufacturing system, beyond assistance in building volume by completely protecting the domestic market from foreign products, was negligible'. This is hard to sustain on the evidence.

Can this model of regimented capitalism be transferred to other societies; and is it, in any event, desirable? The answer to both questions is, for the most part, yes. The creation of MITI was a work of genius: this small, elite, enormously powerful co-ordinating and planning agency combined all the advantages of strategic planning for Japan with a minimum of bureaucratic inefficiency and a maximum of imagination and first-class ideas.

It was right of MITI to exercise powers of direction in place of socialist forms of public ownership. In socialist countries or those with a large public sector, the pressure to keep failing industries going is immense. MITI, by contrast, has capably reorganized and managed industries in decline. Its policies of targeting strategic industries were brilliantly conceived and brilliantly executed. It was enough for Japan to concentrate single-mindedly on such industries and the creation of domestic and export markets, and it may well be right for other economies, particularly those in apparently endless stagnation or decline, to do the same.

The ministry's 'administrative guidance' provides for flexibility and is a reasonably intelligent and subtle form of making industry do its bidding. Much of this approach could be adopted elsewhere, although in Japan it borders on the extra-legal and on coercion, which is probably neither desirable nor possible in countries which have more deeply rooted legal systems. Van Wolferen alleges that MITI used sinister methods of coercion:

> A high MITI official told me that, since all companies have done something shady at one time or another, they fear exposure if they do not follow MITI's directions. The collecting of information useful in such blackmail is done at the assistant-section-chief level, and the information comes from direct investigations, competitors, clients, the police, enemies in the business community, and disgruntled employees. My informant estimates that more than half of all cases of corporate wrongdoing known to the police and MITI bureaucrats are covered up. The main leverage this gives MITI is the fear, not of legal action against the company, but of 'social punishment'. For it is considered most damaging to a firm if its name is disclosed in connection with any kind of scandal.

When such discussions hit the press, they are often for hidden political reasons. MITI's export strategy was also brilliantly executed, pioneering, and consistently one step ahead of the competition. A senior official at MITI described its role to the author recently in the following terms:

> We are not a management of companies running Japan Inc. . . . During the 1950s and 1960s, we would talk to industries, listen to what they have to say. Sometimes industries demanded crazy things or stupid things which were not rational; we might agree that a certain industry was losing money and we would discuss what we should do. We were very good at it. Some say we were very powerful, others that we were marginal, persuading industries to help themselves. The truth lies somewhere in between this spectrum.

MITI's steering role does not appear to be in doubt in this analysis.

The official went on to add that 'today we don't have legal authority; we work for the benefit of industry, giving the direction in which the Japanese economy is going. There is an exchange of information. We do not give directions or specific orders – but we sketch the big picture.' In terms of targeting export markets, he says, 'It is very rare that MITI gives specific directions because, should Japan lack competitiveness abroad, we lose GNP and jobs; we think in terms of long-term perspectives, not planning.' However, 'There is such a thing as excessive competition. The United States despise this view. But we think two industries can do harm to each other. When competitors say we must compete, and it does happen sometimes, there is a role for government to come in and say "Let's live together."' This might seem common sense; or it might seem a tacit admission of MITI's role in targeting export markets.

The view of this senior MITI official about the *keiretsu* is worth noting. Far from denying they exist, he is not even defensive about them:

> There are good and bad aspects to the *keiretsu*. If a steelmaker has good relations with a beer company, it is bad if the steelmaker's employees have to drink the beer of the beer company. They should be free to drink as they choose. But it does happen. On the other hand, if Hitachi has to raise money for a project that is difficult, and Hitachi can persuade banks because of the long-term relationship, that is a good part.

The emphasis on market share rather than short-term profitability, as well as the strategic co-ordination of industries for each potential market, is highly effective and perfectly legitimate. For countries to shout 'Unfair!' because they did not think of these methods themselves is a little absurd. Countries which lack such a strategy should try to acquire it. If free-market theorists object to this, too bad: the Japanese have found a system that demonstrably works better than the free market.

Much more controversial is MITI's shaping of Japanese industry into a hierarchial structure of cartels. While the banking *keiretsu* themselves have obvious advantages in bringing several major firms into a single conglomerate with its client bank and trading company, the disadvantages in terms of price-fixing, undermining competition, backroom deals, and generally pressuring the consumer are obvious. Nor is the system necessarily economically effective.

Rather, it seems the most convenient structure for MITI to control and dominate. It is much easier for the ministry to run the economy by giving orders to a few dominant cartels, which in turn dominate the lesser *keiretsu* and the company suppliers, than it is for MITI to regulate a more complex free-market economy. The advantage to the cartels in terms of tax breaks, their privileged access to markets, government funds, and so on is also obvious – although they sometimes chafe at this. It is far from clear that this system benefits the consumer more than a free-market one. It is in fact one of the worst features of the Japanese model, harking back to the *zaibatsu* and their crushing of medium and smaller enterprises and exploitation of the consumer, as well as blocking the emergence of a solid Japanese middle class. It is not something that should be copied.

MITI and the Ministry of Finance have proved remarkably adaptable in macro-economic policy. Specifically, while usually committed to relatively tight money and balanced budgets, they were happy whenever necessary to unleash inflation in the cause of fighting a recession (as in 1954, and again in 1963–4). Japan is not afraid to borrow. By the end of 1985 the Japanese national public debt was some 165 trillion yen, about half the country's GDP and about the same per capita as America's national debt (although most of it was held in long-term bonds rather than short-term bills). Japan has very high rates of direct taxes, which raise 74 per cent of total revenues, compared with Western countries – another slap in the face for those who equate low personal taxes with better economic performance. The government also carefully managed the currency, through refusing for as long as possible to revalue it.

In addition, MITI resorted to a classic 'interventionist' policy of protecting domestic industries wholesale while building them up, subsequently relaxing tariffs only in response to pressure, while maintaining a huge variety of non-tariff barriers. The protection of Japanese industry from overseas investment has been adhered to even more rigidly. Nothing could have flown more clearly in the face of the fashionable free-market theories of the time; nothing could have been more successful. The Japanese experience utterly repudiated the classic notion that tariff barriers make for inefficient industries – provided they have to compete abroad.

True, Japan's opening up to competition may have been helpful in bringing competitive pressures to bear when it was strong enough to absorb them, and in cleaning out dead wood. But the protectionist policy was clearly not a failure. Could other countries do the same? Perhaps – if they could get away with it in a world now alerted to such strategies – for newer industries. This would not be desirable for international competition, but international trade is a matter of stealing unexpected advantages over one's rivals.

Another imaginative but controversial MITI policy was the use of tax breaks in getting an industry on its feet. There can be no doubt that this policy was highly effective. It required immense and detailed state intervention; it broke with all the free-market proprieties, and certainly conferred an unfair trade advantage upon Japan – but while they could get away with it, who can blame them? Again, if another country can be imaginative in adopting such policies without flouting its international commitments, it should.

Tax breaks were an essential part of another MITI policy – the encouragement of personal savings. This built upon the underlying national propensity to save among people who before 1946 had enjoyed no financial security. The savings of post-war Japanese households have been running at the highest rate as a share of GDP ever reached by any market economy in peacetime. There are many incentives for the Japanese to save, including a feeble social security system, a wage system that includes large lump-sum bonus payments twice a year, and a retirement system that cuts income sharply at the age of sixty. In addition, a shortage of new housing and housing land stimulates saving to pay for it. The government-run postal savings system guarantees competitive interest rates, while until recently there has been no developed capital market or other alternatives to personal saving. The substantial exemption from income taxes for interest earned on savings accounts is another incentive. Chalmers Johnson comments wryly: 'Innate frugality may indeed play a role in this system; but the government has worked hard at engineering that frugality.'

The final key ingredient of government policy was its intelligence in showing no reticence through national pride in acquiring foreign technologies wholesale. As after the Meiji restoration, the Japanese had no inhibitions about simply going abroad, acquiring technologies or buying goods, dismantling them, and learning how to make them. Both these policies were imaginative and successful, and there is no reason why anyone else should not follow them.

The fourth major ingredient of the Japanese economic miracle is the nature of the Japanese company itself, the *kaisha*, many of which are grouped into one of the great banking *keiretsu* that are the princes, the *daimyo*, of the economy. The fifth is the Japanese system of industrial relations, which has spared Japan the enormously costly labour disputes that have affected the major Western economies – strikes, stoppages, slowdowns, excess wages. Both are interrelated, and both have worked vastly to Japan's competitive advantage.

The Japanese company is a remarkable blend of what is best and what is worst about the country. It is far too trite to write off this state of affairs as merely the re-emergence of the old feudal system in another form (authoritarian in many respects as it is) or as organized along military lines (although there are many obvious resonances of militarism). The *kaisha* is the dominant social structure in Japan, employing as it does the great majority of able-bodied men and a large minority of women. The company is the most important factor in the lives of most Japanese.

The overwhelming difference between the modern Japanese company and its Western equivalent is in its financing. In Japan, four-fifths of company financing has been provided by the banks; in spite of the growth of the capital markets over the past decade, bank lending remains paramount. The relationship between the banks and industry is completely different to that in the West, although there are traces of something similar in Germany and France. Because of the high level of lending, the banks are deeply committed to the companies they back, and will not lightly let them down; equally, they play a large role in monitoring those companies and are informed of their every significant move.

Shareholders have very little influence on how a company is run. (Managements actually pay thugs to intimidate awkward shareholders at annual general meetings.) As a consequence, Japanese companies are obsessed with long-term growth rather than short-term profit of the kind that sways the thinking of Western companies, with their eye on stock market performance and dividends. Famously, Sony's boss, Akio Morita, once remarked that 'the United States looks ten minutes ahead while Japan looks ten years ahead.'

The banks do not have such a stranglehold on the *kaisha* as might be assumed, for the assets of most of the major corporations are huge and permit them some independence. Equally, the banks are not as exposed as is commonly feared: most would have no trouble recovering their loans. Industry and the banks agree on the need for debt, high profits, high prices, reinvestment in the firm and low dividends. Interest rates are as low as possible.

Because the banks are so understanding, and Japanese companies do not need to be answerable to the stock market or to follow rigorous accounting procedures, 'finance' is not the main concern in Japan: a long-term profit-and-loss account is considered more important than a large bureaucracy seeking to control a company's current expenditure. James Abegglen and George Stalk, two of the best business authorities on Japan, explain in their book, *Kaisha*,

> Few Japanese companies employ the elaborate budgeting processes widely practiced in the West. Indeed, few Japanese companies have the massive organizational apparatus called 'Finance' which is

characteristic of Western companies. The Japanese capital budgeting analysis is often a simple estimate of the number of years
required for an investment to be paid off by profits (payback
analysis), with the cost of funds arbitrarily set at 10 per cent
annually. Japanese analysts will use discounted cash flow techniques, but are uneasy at what they see as arbitrary and hazardous
pricing and return assumptions. The simplicity of a payback
analysis allows a sustained focus on the business issues involved in
the investment and avoids the elaborate assumptions and artificial
constraints of Western analytic financial techniques.

In any event, the analysis of an investment decision in a Japanese
company is rarely done to obtain the approval of 'Finance'. The
analysis is done to help the managers responsible for the success of
the projects to make their decisions. The function of the executives
in the finance departments of most Japanese companies is to
maintain accounting standards, manage banking relations, process
capital requests, and find the necessary money. Finance does not
hold veto power over business decisions for the *kaisha*.

Abegglen argues that banking capital, rather the equity capital,
makes companies more aggressive and efficient. Stock market short-
term profitability is secondary in Japan; what matters is market share,
which leads to long-term profitability. Even Japanese shareholders
place a much higher priority on the value of the share than on
dividends, which are minimal. Abegglen and Stalk go on perceptively:

> There is a real competitive advantage in this pattern of shareholder
> relations for the successful Japanese competitor. Managements of
> the *kaisha* are freed from the tyranny of accountants, and from the
> terrible pressures throughout the US organizations for steady
> improvements in earnings per share. It is rational for US managers
> to be preoccupied with short-term earnings. Their job security
> depends on it, because the board, the top executives and the
> shareholders demand steady earnings improvements. Moreover
> their personal income and estate depend on it, because their
> principal potential asset is likely to be in the form of options and
> other plans dependent on stock price.
>
> Earnings can always be improved in the short term by sacrificing
> those expenses and investments that build long-term position. The
> Japanese manager is able to look further into the future and is freer
> to do what is necessary to ensure a successful future.

For Japanese executives, the share price is a less important objective, and for some it is not an objective at all. Companies are geared to showing results in the future rather than the present. In surveys, the Japanese have demonstrated how importantly they rate market share: in a 1982 poll, this was found to be the major Japanese corporate goal, with return on investment and new product development some way behind. In America, return on investment came first, with share prices and market share a long way behind as corporate objectives. Market share means long-term results; the Japanese are not interested in short-term results, which is largely a function of the intimate relationship between industry and the banks, and the distant one between industry and the recently booming stock market.

The advantages of this iron handclasp between industry and the banks become quite striking when one looks at companies where no such relationship exists. If a company, as in the West, is beholden to auditors and to its share price, and has a limited amount of bank borrowing at high interest rates, it is unlikely to take many risks: it is acting under tighter financial disciplines. A Japanese company barely answerable to its auditors, finance department, and shareholders, on the other hand, can be immensely bold – provided it takes the banks along with it. As the banks' own assets are tied up with those of the company, that is not too difficult; and the provision of large sums of capital means that a firm can, for example, reduce its prices well below the cost of production in order to corner a share of the market, perhaps thus incurring major debt, before raising them again – or, ideally, with rising sales leading to falling costs of production, gain victorious control of the market, and repay the banks. A Japanese businessman has merely to convince the banks of the long-term strategy, while a Westerner has to show the kind of quick profits that attract investment.

Hence long-termism versus short-termism. So why do Western companies not borrow from the banks as the Japanese do? Because Western banks are largely conservative institutions not geared to the needs of industry, not underwritten by the government, and hence charging rates of interest higher than the cost of raising money on the stock market. In addition, interest rates are a key tool of government policy in the West, often rising dizzyingly high and fluctuating, making them a more unreliable cost even than the cost of money raised on the stock market.

The next key feature of the *kaisha* is their competitiveness. The foremost goals of the *kaisha* are: first, to increase market share (rather than profitability, which is assumed to follow on in the longer term automatically); second, to invest to keep pace with the growth of the market, even if this adversely affects profits; third, to maintain low prices as a means of increasing market share – and prices can decline as costs of production decline; and, fourth, to introduce a constant stream of new products to keep the market's attention.

Competition in Japan can be absolutely cut-throat, in particular when a senior *keiretsu* is threatened with losing its dominant market position. The most celebrated case was the fight between Honda, the motorcycle giant, and Yamaha in the late 1960s. Honda had achieved its market dominance in the late 1950s through the classic Japanese strategy of borrowing massively from the banks in an effort to undercut its competitors' market share. The leader in the field at the time was Tohatsu, a conservatively managed group with twice the tax profits of Honda, and a debt-to-equity ratio about five times lower. Because of Honda's aggressive strategy, within four years Tohatsu's market share fell from 22 to 4 per cent, while Honda's soared from 20 to 44 per cent. Tohatsu was all but defeated and made huge losses. By February 1964, it had gone bankrupt.

In 1967 Honda decided to enter the automobile market at a time when the market itself was terrified of the new wave of international competition; finance, technical capability, and the best managers were put into the new venture. Yamaha, a relatively new entrant to the motorcycle field, saw its chance to stage an ambush while Honda's attention was elsewhere. Yamaha's president Koike claimed that, 'at Honda sales attention is focused on four-wheel vehicles. Most of their best people in motorcycles have been transferred. Compared to them, our speciality at Yamaha is mainly motorcycle production ... If only we had enough capacity, we could beat Honda.'

Honda's share of the market had fallen from 65 per cent in the late 1960s to just 40 per cent in 1981; Yamaha had increased its sales from 10 to 35 per cent over the same period. In new models, Yamaha had also begun to pull ahead of Honda. In 1981 Yamaha announced plans to build a factory that would allow it to double its production of motorcycles. Koike declared triumphantly, 'The difference between us and Honda is in our ability to supply. As primarily a motorcycle producer, you cannot expect us to remain in our present number two position for ever ... In one year we will be the domestic leader. And in two years, we will be number one in the world.'

The following year, Honda's president Kawashima told his shareholders without delicacy, 'Yamaha has not only stepped on the tail of a tiger, it has ground it into the earth. We will crush Yamaha!' The two methods adopted were massive price cuts of around a third on their motorcycles, and the introduction of a huge new range of models – more than eighty, while Yamaha could come up with only thirty-four – in the space of eighteen months; both companies had only produced around sixty models altogether before that. Yamaha sales collapsed by around half; the company soon had a year's stock of motorcycles unsold. It struggled furiously merely to stay afloat, not to expand as Honda had done, and its debt-to-equity ratio shot up from three to one to seven to one in 1983.

In January of that year, Koike surrendered: 'We cannot match Honda's product development and sales strength . . . I would like to end the Honda–Yamaha war . . . From now on I want to move cautiously and ensure Yamaha's relative position [as second to Honda].' He was replaced, dividends were slashed, employees were dismissed, and production plummeted from a projected four million units at the height of Yamaha's ambitions to just one and a half million. Desperately, the new Yamaha management begged for mercy as Honda ruthlessly continued its counter-attack, producing thirty-nine new models in 1983–4 compared with Yamaha's twenty-three. 'Since Yamaha is considered responsible for the present market situation, I would first like to study our position and develop a more co-operative stance towards other companies . . . Of course, there will still be competition . . . but I intend it to be based on mutual recognition of our relative positions,' said Yamaha's new president Eguchi.

The main reason for Yamaha's humiliation was that Honda had carefully waited until its rival was at its most exposed – having invested heavily in new plant that was not yet producing – before striking. Japanese companies were geared not just to producing goods but to fighting each other in almost military fashion. Yamaha had dared to challenge the natural hierarchy of the motorcycle industry, and was all but massacred. This is one of the keys to Japanese efficiency: intense competition beneath the overall constraints of government planning.

This kind of ferocity made the Japanese a quite terrifying challenge for Western companies accustomed to a much more leisurely rate of growth. For example, in the competitive frenzy between 1960 and 1980, the number of calculator companies increased from three – Sharp, Canon and Oki – to twenty-three. As the market doubled each year, companies had to double their growth just to retain their market share. Sharp managed it, but a competitor, Casio, was expanding twice as fast, and by 1973 it had replaced Sharp as market leader with 35 per cent of Japanese pocket calculators to Sharp's 17 per cent. Prices were soon falling by around a third each, which many companies could not sustain; only ten or so remain.

For a Western company growing at 20 per cent or so a year, it was a cathartic experience to compete with a rival accustomed to growing at 100 per cent a year through the most aggressive policies. With trade liberalization, Japanese companies adopted a new competitive strategy. Western companies offering new high quality products at high prices would enter the Japanese market. Japanese companies would aim for the lower end of the same market, producing lower-quality, cheaper copies for a mass market. From this bridgehead they would improve their products, challenge the Westerners at their own game, and drive them out of business.

Japan's *kaisha* also used the methods above in overseas competition: their products would be cut-price, often less than the cost of production, something Western companies – lacking their cosy relationship with the banks – could not match. In many parts of Asia, the Japanese consistently undercut Western competitors by as much as a quarter or even a third. One prime advantage that Japan had long enjoyed was lower labour costs, which were on average a quarter of the American level in the immediate post-war years; by the 1960s this advantage had disappeared. However, by that time the Japanese had started to benefit from the advantage previously enjoyed by the Americans – economies of scale. Soon, America's advantage in labour productivity had sharply diminished.

The Japanese also increasingly developed new production techniques – proving far more innovative than their rivals. One of these was 'focused production', the purpose of which was to slim down the huge variety of products on many production lines to only a handful of extremely profitable ones. In contrast to Western companies producing, for example, as many as 25,000 different types of ball-bearings for different client requirements, the Japanese would concentrate on only a handful for use by the biggest ball-bearing customers, such as car manufacturers. Through focused production, Japanese manufacturers found that they could increase productivity per worker by around three-quarters, while cutting costs by a third.

Another system which was to have striking results was the 'just-in-time', *kanban* production system, first pioneered by Toyota and adopted across the board in Japan. The essence of the system, as its name suggests, is that materials, parts and components are produced just before they are needed. Its pioneer was the legendary Taiichi Ono, head of Toyota's machine shop, who concluded that demand, not supply, should regulate production. One of Ono's workers observed that, 'If Ono found a pile of ten or a dozen doors or bumpers stacked together in one place, he would kick it with his boot as he walked past and say, "Don't make extra ones like that, just stick to making what's needed, when it's needed, okay?"'

Workers had to work much harder, and the big Japanese producers were able to force their dependent component suppliers to fit in with the system: it slashed inefficiency and inventories. Toyota's output increased tenfold, from 150,000 vehicles in 1960 to 1.5 million in 1970. Japanese car production as a whole rose from 1600 cars in 1950 to 11 million in 1980. *Kanban* was truly revolutionary because Japanese companies which adopted it could manufacture a product with only three men, when US and European competitors required four or five for the same task. Also, it relieved tension between marketing and manufacturing. In practice, the system cut the huge amount of time wasted by workers. In one department of a major manufacturer, around a quarter of workers' time was spent moving materials, and another quarter changing over from making one part to making another. Only half of their time was actually spent on the manufacturing process itself.

Another aspect of the new system was multi-machine manning: using the worker all the time on different machines, rather than leaving him on a single machine which might be idle for much of the time. This could raise worker productivity by 30 to 50 per cent, often more. Ono admitted that this caused 'problems among the workers' – probably likely to be much greater for unionized Western companies:

> Resistance from the production workers was naturally strong. Although there was no increase in the amount of work or working time, the skilled workers at the time were fellows with the strong temperament of craftsmen, and they strongly resisted change. They did not change easily from the old system of one man, one machine to the system of one man, many machines in a sequence of different processes – being required to work as a multi-skilled operator.

An immense amount of management planning must go into the just-in-time system, the kind of planning more short-sighted Western managers are often reluctant to undertake.

The fourth great characteristic of the Japanese *kaisha* is their ability to spend much more than their Western counterparts in research and development. The period of copying Western technology came to an end in the 1970s; from then on Japan pioneered technological change. For example, in 1983, expressed as a percentage of sales, Canon spent 15 per cent on research and development compared with 8 per cent for its competitor Xerox; NEC spent 13 per cent compared with 6 per cent for its competitor Texas Instruments; Hitachi spent 7.9 per cent compared with 3.4 per cent for General Electric; and so on. Only a couple of American companies like Eastman Kodak and Eli Lilley scored impressively.

Of the top twenty companies in each country, the Japanese spent more than 5 per cent of annual outgoings on research and development, compared with 3.7 per cent for the Americans. The actual annual increase in spending on research and development in Japan over the five years to 1982 was 21 per cent of industrial costs compared with 13 per cent in America. To help subsidize this, MITI and the Science and Technology Agency made funds available to assist companies in particular fields. This helped Japanese industry to gain a lead in three fields – robotics, where Japan in 1993 was ahead of all competition, new ceramic materials, where 200 *kaisha* were currently engaged in development, and biotechnology, where more than 150 companies were doing so.

The Long Term Credit Bank of Japan in 1992 summarized Japan's competitive prospects in the industries of tomorrow:

- Computers. Japan is building up strength in smaller models, but in software it will not be able to catch up with the United States for a while.
- Semiconductors. Japan's competitiveness in the field of semiconductors is expected to last. It should also be noted that Japan is highly competitive in the semiconductor manufacturing equipment industry.
- Robots. Japan is dominant in all three aspects of number of robots in operation, value of production and technological strength. [Japan had a staggering 220,000 industrial robots in operation by the end of 1989, compared with just 37,000 in the United States, its nearest competitor, 22,000 in Germany, 10,000 in Italy, 9000 in France and just 6000 in Britain.]

- Office automation. In copiers Japan has an 85 per cent share of the world market and in facsimiles its exports are growing by more than 50 per cent a year. In personal computers, office computers and word processors, Japan is still weak in software, but in hardware it is competitive . . .
- Aerospace. Developing new aircraft will be beyond Japan's power for at least another ten years. In space development Japan is said to be ten years behind the United States.
- Optoelectronics. Japan is thought to have overtaken the United States . . .
- Biotechnology. Biotechnology was developed in the United States, but Japan is catching up fast.

The list is far from exhaustive. For example, in February 1992 Japan turned down an invitation to co-operate with the European Space Agency's Hermes manned space shuttle in order to pursue its own space programme, whose centrepiece is an unmanned space shuttle named Hope to be completed by the year 2000.

The Japanese have developed a no-propeller water propulsion system which operates almost in silence if fitted with a nuclear or solar-powered engine. The Yamato One, which staged its first sea trial in June 1992, was built by Mitsubishi Heavy Industries at Kobe and has a magnetohydrodynamic propulsion system. Craft like this should be more fuel efficient than propeller-driven models and capable of much faster speeds – 100 knots or more – because they generate none of the 'cavitation' turbulence that destroys propellers at such speeds. The makers stressed that Yamato One was developed for peaceful purposes, but its military applications are obvious.

The main thrust of Japan's technological efforts for the future is in microelectronics, new materials and biotechnology. Of these, Japan is most advanced in microelectronics: in 1983 it was already Japan's biggest export. Investment in the sector was running at about $2.5 billion a year by the mid-1980s. By the end of the century, it is reckoned that some five million Japanese workers will be employed in software related jobs – around a tenth of the workforce. The electronics giants Hitachi and Matsushita seem set to be the new leaders in Japanese industry, displacing Toyota. Nikon, spotting the trend, transformed itself rapidly from being primarily a manufacturer of cameras and lenses to one supplying electronic equipment.

Two profound changes are under way in the traditional make-up of the *kaisha*. The first is the loss of market domination by the old *zaibatsu*. The Japanese insist that this took place after the war, but in practice Mitsubishi, Mitsui and Sumitomo, in particular, have remained huge and are still at the very top of the Japanese industrial hierarchy. But companies like Toyota, Honda, Hino and Suzuki in vehicles; Kubota in farm machines; Shiseido, Kao and Lion in consumer goods; Hitachi, Sharp, Sanyo, Matsushita and Sony in electronics; Fuji, Canon, Ricoh and Seiko in cameras; and Shionogi and Fujisawa in pharmaceuticals are post-war arrivals.

Another change is that even the banks that underpinned the old *kaisha* are now less powerful – and government leverage has accordingly diminished – as the success of companies has generated its own funds, and the stock exchange has found its feet. The continuing importance of bank lending should not be underestimated, particularly in permitting the *kaisha* to remain free of the tyranny of short-term profits which look good on the stock exchange. But the banks are less powerful than they used to be. In terms of control, the *kaisha* are now self-perpetuating business elites running themselves, with some interference from the banks and government, and virtually none from shareholders.

Because of the low status accorded shareholders, and thanks to Japanese laws, it is very difficult for major *kaisha* to fall into the takeover battles that are so much of the business culture elsewhere: takeovers are deeply frowned upon in Japan as somehow violating the loyalty of employees towards a firm – although this does not of course apply to compulsory MITI-engineered shake-outs of a particular sector. As in practice very few takeovers in the West have resulted in improved performance – the purpose is usually to asset-strip a firm or crush competition – the Japanese are not at a disadvantage from this.

Japan continues to lay stress on a manufacturing future, whereas the West has slowly shifted towards the service industries. Of some twenty million jobs created in America since 1980, four-fifths have been in services – retailing, catering, financial and business, transport, health and education. It is a mistake to consider that this represents a new level of economic sophistication for these economies: in fact service jobs usually pay 10 to 20 per cent less than manufacturing jobs, have low levels of productivity, offer few export opportunities – and, ultimately, are usually dependent on the health of the manufacturing sector which uses them.

Japan's success has also depended on the increasingly evident defects of Western management practices. Over the past few decades, management in the West has become increasingly self-selecting, in the absence of real shareholder control, and obsessed with creating bigger bureaucracies, empire-building and battles for turf rather than securing better results. Financial and legal backgrounds are now common for company presidents, rather than marketing and production backgrounds – at the coalface of industry, as it were. In contrast, Japanese companies routinely practise rotational training, starting their high-fliers from the bottom in order to give them the maximum experience and knowledge of the firm.

Marketing in the West tends to focus on advertising, selling, promotion and distribution. The normal way of pricing products is to produce them, and then add the necessary profit margins. The Japanese, by contrast, tend to find out what the market wants and will pay for, and then produce it, adding such customer sweeteners as higher quality, design, style, reliability, delivery and after-sales service.

Another serious adverse development for American and European management was the arrival of the corporate raider and the asset stripper, buying up undervalued companies and selling off their jewels for a profit. Many company managements focused on fighting back, rather than on improving the performance of their companies, buying off the raiders or making themselves indigestible by taking on debt to make dubious acquisitions. In 1986, for example, American companies took on $263 billion of debt, double that of the previous year, largely to foil corporate raiders: companies were consciously trying to make themselves less viable. At the same time, enormous efforts and funds were put into buying in company equity to make these companies less easy prey for takeover. In 1987, American industry spent around $80 billion to buy in equity, compared with $50 billion on new capital investments.

Virtually every one of the *kaisha*'s competitive techniques are both desirable and could be transplanted to the West, although many would take a great deal of time and effort to implement – such as a switch from dependence on equity to the banks.

This leads directly to Japan's final areas of competitive advantage: corporate culture and industrial relations. The staggering advantage conferred on Japanese industry over that of the West by the virtual absence of serious work stoppages since the mid-1960s can hardly be exaggerated. While virtually every Western economy has been plagued by stoppages, works-to-rule or absenteeism (the United States and (West) Germany less than most), Japan has been trouble-free for nearly three decades.

There are two extreme views of how Japan manages this. The Japanese version is that the country has stumbled upon a magic formula for industrial relations in which employees work happily and in harmony with their company for common goals, understand that their pay depends on company performance, are grateful to the security offered by the company and do not suffer from any form of them-and-us, manager versus worker hang-up. The other view is that Japanese companies are hierarchical, crush dissent and genuine unions, and rely on bullying and indoctrination, from company songs through to exercises and compulsory socializing.

The truth lies somewhere between the two extremes. It is true enough that unions were relentlessly crushed and Japan's powerful union federations fragmented into a mass of largely powerless 'enterprise unions', while union membership declined spectacularly. Management showed that it was quite prepared to wield the big stick. Moreover, the extraordinary success of the economic miracle in the 1960s helped to defuse discontent: with living standards rising, workers were less inclined to rebel. Yet it is also true that the Japanese system has developed a whole mass of initiatives in keeping with the country's generally paternal and communal culture that have helped to preserve industrial peace. Japanese employees are not so much terrorized and bullied (as were humble soldiers in the imperial army) as made part of a family in which they have very little say; but provided they do what they are told, they are treated relatively well.

There are at least five major elements of this 'kindly uncle' system. The first is indoctrination. The unruly university graduate is quickly taught the facts of life in what must be the most regimented corporate structure in the world. The salaryman usually joins his firm in a ceremony in which the 'company philosophy' will be enounced by a senior executive. He will soon learn the philosophy by heart. He will be dressed in a compulsory grey or blue suit, and will always be clean-shaven. He will learn to bow 15 degrees to his equals in the corridor, 30 degrees with hands held down the seams of his trousers for superiors and important visitors, and 45 degrees, with expressions of apology, when something has gone wrong. He must walk just behind superiors in the corridor, and enter the lift before a guest. He should not talk to his contemporaries in the corridor until they are all off the bottom rung. There is a right way to behave to one's superiors in cars, trains and reception rooms.

The new recruit will undergo training for the first few months. He may have to live in a company dormitory, rise before dawn, perform communal tasks, obey a curfew and go to bed by ten o'clock. He may undergo periods of mutual confession, attend endurance training in Zen temples, or train with the Self-Defence Forces. Trainees tell of being forced to go on twenty-four-hour marches with soldiers, cleaning lavatories for a day and being submerged for hours in ice-cold rivers wearing only loincloths.

The second of these elements is that Japanese companies have tried genuinely to blur the external distinctions between management and workforce: shared canteens are one example. Managers do not receive outrageously high levels of pay. A company general manager might receive $70,000 a year (to be compared with an American chief executive earning ten times that), while most Japanese workers are on the whole well-paid. Perks for the bosses are not offensively greater than for those below them. About one-third of pay is in the form of bonuses, which go to all employees, plus a stimulus for better performance. In addition it is possible for shop-floor employees to get on the board of Japanese companies – although this is not particularly common. When a company faces hard times, instead of suddenly announcing redundancies the practice is usually for executives to accept a wage cut, then encourage employees to do the same.

Another key ingredient of Japanese industrial organization is the 'quality control circle': there are about 300,000, embracing 2 million workers. It had its origins in the system used to inspect goods during the Korean War; this was later refined to 'total quality control'. Its aim broadly is to ensure that all defects are ironed out in the initial phases of production, not by inspection at the end. To this purpose, workers are encouraged to make suggestions to the management. The Japan Productivity Centre reckoned in 1987 that Japanese workers on average made 14 suggestions a year for improving work procedures, compared with 0.15 in the United States; 76 per cent of suggestions were adopted in Japan, compared with 24 per cent in America. The Japanese claim that in 1981 nearly three-quarters of all companies had at least one board member who had been a union official – although this is not so surprising in view of the tame nature of Japanese enterprise unions.

However, the unions are not entirely lacking in teeth. They stage their yearly Spring Labour Offensive, in which they co-ordinate nationally, but in practice settle at company level; the medium-sized enterprises follow the leads of the big companies and unions. Their aim, says business analyst Douglas Moore Kenrick, is 'to embarrass their managements, not to damage their companies financially'. Infrequent industrial actions consist of strikes, slow-downs, works-to-rule, sit-downs, leave-taking *en masse*, pasting posters over windows and premises and wearing arm-bands. Trade unionists sometimes enter a manager's office and shout at him, refusing to leave.

The third distinctive feature of the Japanese employment system is job security. This applies only to the one-third of the workforce employed by the major *kaisha*. The huge number of employees of the small dependent suppliers enjoy no security at all; however, unemployment is eased by state support for service industries, nominal jobs and the byzantine distribution network, which results in unemployment being no higher than 1 to 3 per cent.

The *kaisha* guarantee to an employee that he will have lifetime employment, although not necessarily in the same job or even the same industry; in return he is expected not to leave the company (although a small but growing minority do, as the size of Japan's workforce shrinks). The *kaisha* generally abide by their commitment. During the 1974 recession there were no large-scale redundancies, nor even much of a drop in wages; the companies held on to their crew and steered their craft into the wind. In 1990–94, Fujitju trimmed its workforce of 56,000 by 6000 through early retirement, lower recruitment and transferring workers to affiliates – not through dismissals. Oki Electronic Industry, NKK and Nippon Steel have done the same.

The system can provide for inefficiency – for example, Fujitsu admits that some 10 to 15 per cent of its workforce does virtually nothing – as well as lack of flexibility. However, the advantages are huge: the absence of insecurity among employees and the identification with a particular firm is probably the single biggest dampener of industrial unrest, contrasting with experience in the West where possible unemployment even among loyal workers generates greater militancy and bloodymindedness. The lifetime employment system permits the introduction of new labour-saving technology and techniques without violent controversy, because workers know they will not lose their jobs as a result. In 1992 it was reckoned that two-fifths of Japanese firms were overstaffed, keeping as many as 1.7 million 'in-house unemployed', or 'window-watchers' on their payrolls.

The fourth major feature of the Japanese employment system is a seemingly rigid commitment to seniority. Pay and promotion are closely linked to length of service. The dangers of this system of 'Buggins' turn' are readily apparent, but the Japanese operate an ingenious backroom system as well: while ageing employees are assuaged by pay and seniority, real power in fact lies with the more able executives in their own decision-making groups – even though they may lack the titles and money. These groups are often clustered around one senior figure, and are usually quite small; the mentor is usually grooming a pupil for the succession.

A fourth feature of *kaisha* culture is the enterprise union, to which all workers and many companies belong. There are no demarcation disputes, because there are no rival unions – workers can simply be transferred from one job to another. The union is permitted to negotiate vigorously with management, but rarely takes industrial action, and lacks the necessary cross-industry support to pose a threat to production.

The final feature of Japan's industrial relations system and corporate culture is its consensus style of decision-making. The central feature of this is the *ringi-seido*, a document drawn up by low-level employees and circulated gently upwards, designed to attract the support of all concerned in the decision, providing the illusion that decisions originate from below. In fact the system exists largely to obfuscate responsibility. Most important decisions are taken by key groups in a company, often at middle-management level. The bosses have the power to promote their juniors; by thus providing them with a means of consultation, they are able to voice their true opinions, which they might be reluctant to do otherwise. Senior directors are often reluctant to initiate key decisions, but their support and even tacit authorship of a decision is essential. Kenrick suggests that the system of consensus and consultation is only a token. Any decision that is reached comes only after a huge number of formal and informal meetings. Indeed, even managers hesitate to make recommendations they feel could be rejected or cause embarrassment.

> The highly stylized culture has produced a fear of originality. Unique and creative ideas are often diluted into commonplace ones in the process. Dissension is suppressed. It is better to be silent than to disagree. Silence at a conference is a minus in the West. It is golden in Japan. Consensus decisions tend towards the lowest common denominator ... Everyone is competing for his own promotion up the ladder and this does not usually come to one who antagonizes his peers or opposes his seniors.

In other words, Japan's much touted system of consensus is a rubber stamp for decisions taken by the hierarchy, as much of a sham as the ritual political circus.

These, then, are the five mainstays of the Japanese system of industrial relations. Very little is likely to be transferable to the West, where unions have much more powerful historical roots, and very little of it is desirable – except for the system of bonus payments, lifetime employment and, of course, the absence of work stoppages. This state of affairs is very largely the result of the government's relentlessness in crushing the union movement during the late 1940s and early 1950s, and of the hierarchical ordering of Japanese companies.

Analysing the overall Japanese model, Chalmers Johnson argues that it is transferable elsewhere, but that an essentially authoritarian political system is necessary – something that appeals to many Asian countries, but is hardly likely to find a following in the West. But the West will be the loser if it does not recognize the merits of the Japanese way. The Japanese miracle was born largely through the steady refinement of interventionist policies made possible by continuous one-party government and the hard work of ordinary Japanese. Many of the policy innovations have been inspired and sophisticated, and should be emulated – even if the authoritarian backdrop cannot, and should not. The fact that so little of the Japanese economic experience owes anything to free-market economics should not blind Westerners into believing that it is not highly effective.

28

THE JUGGERNAUT

T HE MIRACLE also had its downside. The dislocation of
people travelling from the countryside to find jobs after the
war was immense. To this day, Japan's provinces are underdeveloped and under-equipped, whole villages often deprived of
their male populations. (Some country areas are depleted of their
female populations, also attracted to the bright lights of the city.)
Those arriving were accommodated in flats, in the new government
buildings called *danchi*. There, in tiny, cramped living quarters, they
would congregate round the *kotatsu*, a small electric heater under a
table, keeping the heat in with blankets spread across the laps.

As everywhere else, the numbers employed on the land in Japan
have been falling, from 30 per cent of the working population in
1960 to 8 per cent in 1985, by which time only around 15 per cent
of the 4.3 million farming households relied solely on agriculture for
their income. In 1985, 68 per cent of Japanese farmers cultivated
less than 2½ acres of land, and only 2 per cent cultivated 12½ acres
or more. Agricultural production has declined as a percentage of
GDP from 13 per cent in 1960 to around 4 per cent in 1985. Over
the same period the percentage of Japan's food which is produced
for itself declined from 90 to a touch over 70. Japan still vastly
overproduces rice, which is heavily subsidized, but the overwhelming
bulk of its wheat, soya and sugar come from abroad.

Urban overcrowding, the lack of green space, the distance
travelled to work, the huge urban sprawls and the massive pollution
were among the worst in the world. By 1970, photochemical smog
was so acute that children had to stay indoors. One worker at an
industrial centre recalled that, 'The sky was very dark and often
there would be a sudden evening shower. You'd get soaked with the

little drops of black rain all over you, and the rain was full of soot. It was really dirty and would turn you all black!' In a famous case in 1960, it was found that waste from an aluminium plant owned by Chisso, which had been poured straight into Minamata Bay, had caused serious poisoning and about 350 deaths. Chemical waste at Niigata was responsible for some 70 deaths in the 1960s. By 1970, the government had to take the matter seriously, and performed a remarkable job of enforcing standards over the next decade.

There was also real, though limited, poverty in the cities, even during the latter years of the miracle: unemployment was always much higher than was officially acknowledged – figures were kept low through the sophisticated expedient of paying people low wages to do almost nothing. The Japanese put up with privations no Westerner would. Even today, many houses are not connected to main sewers and some 40 per cent of Japanese households have no flush toilets. Most electricity cables are above ground.

Yet it must be said that, given the staggering size of the population movements and economic and social dislocations, Japan has probably been the most successful society in the world to industrialize without the truly terrible conditions that usually accompany it. The miseries of the industrial revolution in Europe and Asia, much less the appalling shanty towns and slums that routinely disfigure nearly every developing country, were not to be seen in the miracle years in Japan. Pollution and poverty there was in abundance, but not malnutrition, disease, marginalization. This was a huge achievement for Japan. Japan's miracle depends, however, on its continuing to be one step ahead in the game. Many observers believe that, as Japanese society matures, there are no longer going to be the same strides forward to be made, and the country will settle into a position a long way behind the United States as an economic power. Can it possibly keep up the pace?

After all, what had been achieved by the beginning of the 1990s was staggering. To take just a few examples: at the start of the decade, Japan made about one-third of all the world's cars, steel and ships; two-thirds of all computer chips and consumer electronic products; and more than half the robots and machine tools around the world. In the 1980s the Japanese economy had continued to grow faster than any other major economy – at 4 per cent a year (although Britain briefly overtook it). Japan's trade surplus was $96 billion in 1987, a figure exceeded in 1992 when the economy was in deep 'recession' (in a slow-down, the Japanese export frantically).

Japan's target industries for the future include robotics, biotechnology, nuclear power, aerospace, computer software, high-quality synthetic fibres, high-speed maglev trains, lasers for microsurgery, organic machine memory and cars made to the specification of the buyer. Because of its huge surplus, Japan has been able to achieve an annual export total of $240 billion, a figure expected to reach $500 billion in the mid-1990s (around half the entire size of the British economy). It is estimated that by 1995 America's net debt to Japan will be some $1.3 trillion, and Japanese net investment in the United States will be $700 billion. America's share of the world trade has fallen from 36 to 23 per cent, while Japan's has risen from 6 to 16 per cent in the twenty years to 1990.

Three huge roadblocks can be spied ahead, all of which Japan has taken steps to deal with. First, van Wolferen has drawn attention to the danger that the *keiretsu* may be beyond political control, with possibly disastrous results. In practice, the restraining influence of the hierarchical Japanese state will almost certainly be able to hold the *keiretsu* in check, particularly since the collapse of the stock market deflated the ardent supporters of free-market economics in Japan. As firms turn back to the banks as their main sources of capital, the state, which controls the banks, will see its power increase.

Second, the collapse of the capital markets had dealt a mortal blow to those favouring less regulation and greater economic freedom. It often suits the Japanese state as a negotiating ploy to say that it cannot control its businesses – and this reinforces the *amour propre* of the latter. In fact, although business is on a much looser leash than, say, in the 1960s, it is doubtful that it could directly defy the government – or would wish to, if the national interest of Japan demanded, for example, that the brakes be put on the export drive.

Third, there is the problem of Japan's expensive labour force. This has been partially met by increased productivity; the main difficulties, which obsess Japanese politicians, are posed by an ageing population, with all the drains on the public purse that represents, and by the danger of retaliatory protectionism and resistance to Japanese economic penetration overseas. The answer the Japanese have come up with is the same for all three problems: the massive, deliberate, government-directed transfer of Japanese industry overseas, representing the next 'great leap forward' in the economic miracle. The aims of this are, primarily, to duck under the wire of protectionist fences, to take advantage of cheaper labour overseas, and to resolve the problem of an ageing domestic population problem through using money to make outsiders do the work for you. It is an ingenious, high-risk strategy which has worked so far, although it may not do so for ever.

The establishment of local plants overseas began in direct response to protectionism. For example, the Voluntary Restriction Agreement on Japanese car exports to the United States stimulated the setting up of major assembly plants there by Honda in 1984, Mazda in 1986, Nissan in 1987, and Mitsubishi in 1989, as well as the Toyota–General Motors joint venture. These 'voluntary' agreements limited Japan's sale of imported cars to some 2.3 million in the United States in 1987; the Japanese went for high-priced cars to circumvent this. The average price of a car in America rose by $1300 as a result.

In Europe the restrictions on car imports were much tougher. Compared with the penetration of some 23 per cent in the United States, Britain limited Japanese imports to some 10–12 per cent of the market, France to 3 per cent and Italy to just 2750 cars and 750 four-wheel-drive vehicles. In addition, the European Community resorted to more justifiable protection against dumping, imposing duties on a wide range of goods from outboard motors to ball bearings, electronic typewriters, and photocopiers.

Protectionism has been sharply on the rise. In 1975 only 8 per cent of American imports received some form of protection, but by 1984 the figure had risen to 21 per cent, and by 1986 to 25 per cent. Japan initially had very small interests overseas: only 2 per cent of its manufacturing output was produced offshore in 1983, rising to 5 per cent in 1986; then it mushroomed. The Japanese strategy was to begin by starting up wholly owned manufacturing subsidiaries using non-union labour on government-supported 'green-field' sites in economically deprived areas. Komatsu's purpose in having a $12.5 million assembly plant in Britain was clearly to avoid 26.6 per cent anti-dumping tariffs on imported excavators; Toshiba's $1.2 million video recorder plant in Britain was to dodge surcharges; and so on.

There were initially only a small number of Japanese acquisitions of overseas plant (as opposed to acquisitions of overseas real estate, which was on a much larger scale); these accelerated sharply in the late 1980s. Many of the acquisitions were in the firms supplying materials to Japanese car plants – for example, Kawasaki Steel purchased 50 per cent of California Steel, and Nippon Kokan acquired a 50 per cent stake in Wheeling Steel, Pittsburgh. The

Japanese companies have introduced radical innovation in technology in the West, which has seriously undercut local products. Among these are computer integrated manufacturing, incorporating flexible manufacturing systems; computer-aided design and computer-aided engineering; robotics; sophisticated machine tools; and sensors and telecommunications, which allow smaller batch sizes in continuous flow to be produced, without needing large inventories of components and holding huge stocks of finished product. Barrie James argues that:

> The 'new' manufacturing not only allows companies to monitor the flow of materials but also the flow of information needed to manage production from delivery of raw materials through to shipping out finished products. This helps firms to operate in smaller manufacturing plants and increasingly to customise product ranges through small production runs. At the same time they can reduce their break-even point and lower their unit costs. Labour in these highly automated systems has become a far less important component of cost. Japanese companies have been quick to spot the advantages of the 'new' manufacturing and to adopt these new techniques, which allow them to move away from countries with low labour costs to the developed consuming markets without the old penalty of incurring higher labour costs. Japanese companies have also pioneered totally new approaches to manufacturing – for example, 'mechatronics', which combines mechanics and electronics to eliminate mechanical parts by replacing them with electronic components. This has not only eased manufacturing complexity, but also provided better precision, more reliability, lower costs and led to better customer features.

In addition, backing the new overseas companies is Japan's enormous financial muscle: Sumitomo Bank, for example, is the largest banking company in the world. Japan's banks can give a major boost to Japanese companies abroad that undercuts local competition, forced to rely on more conservative methods of financing: drawing on unlimited credit, Japanese companies can produce cheaper goods in order to gain market share.

Those who criticize the Japanese presence abroad also argue that much of the manufacturing in the West is of the 'screwdriver' kind: high value-added components are made in Japan, using technologies which the Japanese refuse to share, and the bits and pieces are assembled in America and Europe using sophisticated management methods, but very simple technology, to take advantage of the relatively low cost of labour that results from the strength of the yen.

The Japanese have also been notoriously tough about driving hard bargains in the countries where they set up. By going to depressed areas, they secure no-union agreements and hire workers at below union rates (as for example Mazda in Detroit, which negotiated with the United Auto Workers' Union). Energy, raw materials, land, and labour are all more cheaply available abroad than in Japan. One Japanese company operating an assembly plant for robotics in Britain imports all its engineered spare parts, thus ensuring the least transfer of technology and the least training for the British workforce, whose jobs are limited to simple functions, in a 'colonial' style of manufacturing.

The Japanese newcomers have provided thousands of jobs, but they have also caused thousands to be lost. For example, Ford and Vauxhall announced redundancies of 2400 jobs early in 1992 because of 'significant challenges' from the Japanese. The cuts were designed to reduce Ford's workforce to 27,000 producing some 450,000 cars a year; this is to be compared with Nissan's workforce of 4500 at Sunderland, producing 270,000 cars a year, and Toyota's workforce of 3300 producing 200,000 cars. By the mid-1990s Japanese car-makers were expected to produce some 600,000 cars a year in Britain. Output per head in the British plants is roughly three-quarters that of Japanese plants. In October 1993, a report for the European Commission suggested that the European automotive components industry was only a third as productive as Japanese industry and that some 400,000 jobs should be shed as the 'absolute minimum' to make it viable in the year 2000.

In return, there can be no doubt that Japan's attitude to inward investment remains rigorously restricted. Foreign companies hold only 2 or 3 per cent of shares in Japanese companies compared with 10 per cent in America and 20 per cent in Germany, France, and Britain. The employment generated by the new plants is likely to do no more than compensate for a part of the employment lost by local manufacturers as a result of increased Japanese sales.

On a global scale it is possible for the Japanese to practise the kind of market manipulation that the *zaibatsu*, and then the *keiretsu*, have long done at home. Further, they are adept at exploiting local subsidies in depressed areas in the West: there are no guidelines in the United States or the European Community on limiting the incentives available to investors. So Japanese companies find themselves the targets of different communities outbidding each other to draw them in. For example, Britain's Department of Trade and Industry is believed to have increased its subsidy from £2 million to around £7 million in an effort to attract a new NEC plant to Telford rather than have it go to Hanover in Germany.

Such incentives are escalating. In 1982, Honda was given grants of around $16 million to build a plant in Ohio, while Toyota was given some $125 million in incentives for its car plant in Kentucky in 1985. The West has huge potential bargaining power with Japan: America and Europe together consume more than nine-tenths of its trade surplus. Western governments would be wise to insist that potential investors persuade them of the real value of their investments. This has in fact happened in much of Asia, which treats Japan warily.

The solution is for much tougher controls to be imposed on Japanese inward investment. Incentives can be linked to the level of local input and paid after a specified period to ensure that the company complies. Training grants could be made available only for programmes which create or upgrade genuine skills; the level of grants could be linked to the level accorded foreign firms in Japan. This would require massive Western co-ordination. It seems obvious that this approach is preferable to gut protectionism or exclusion, which can only create inefficiency, anger the Japanese, and reduce world trade.

It can hardly be clearer that the Japanese are determined to maintain an ever-increasing overseas investment strategy. The Economic Planning Agency stated baldly in its programme for the year 2000 that:

> In a long-term view of the future of the economy, it is inevitable that Japan will take the route from being a major trading partner to being a major power in direct investment. There are a number of forces at work, including the relatively rapid increase in international standing of Japanese companies in terms of financial, technological and management strength, and the difficulty of acceptance of trade from a single point for those major export items in which Japan has established a leading position. The increase in real incomes from Japan's relatively high rate of economic growth (a rise in wage and service prices), the possibility of a sustained increase in the yen exchange rate, and the relative increase in production costs in Japan, will be the forces making for overseas direct investment henceforth.

By 1989, Japan's direct investment abroad had grown from just $8 billion in 1975 to $154 billion, placing it third in the world foreign investment league, behind the United States with $373 billion and Britain with $192 billion. Of this, the bulk was in America and Europe. In 1990, for example, Japan invested $27 billion in North America, $14 billion in Europe, $7 billion in Asia and $4 billion in Latin America. However, the bulk of foreign manpower employed by overseas Japanese firms was in Asia – 474,000, compared with 354,000 in North America, 120,000 in Europe, and 114,000 in Latin America.

The Japanese manage their ties with Asia extremely carefully, for example reviving a once strong footwear industry there, and becoming massive importers themselves. The burgeoning economies of Asia can be divided into two groups: one is the 'four tigers' – South Korea, Taiwan, Hong Kong, and Singapore – which are buying increasingly sophisticated goods from Japan, such as integrated circuits and machine tools. They have fairly homogeneous populations which are well educated, and they use Japan's economy as a model for development. In addition they all have their populations more or less under authoritarian control. Their governments are dedicated to economic growth. All have experienced impressive annual growth rates ranging from 8 to 10 per cent between 1960 and 1990. Japan's role in each has been enormous, in terms of supplying technology and capital.

The second group consists of countries in which Japan seems also to have taken a particular interest: India, Malaysia, the Philippines and Thailand, all with large and uncontrollable birthrates, mixed and partly illiterate populations, and growing almost as fast as the 'tigers'. (Malaysia, India and Thailand grew by around 7 per cent a year between 1970 and 1983, and the Philippines by around 6 per cent.) Around a fifth of Japanese foreign investment comes to these countries; of this nearly two-thirds goes to Indonesia, with its large economic resources and population. Yet Japan has attractions even for Indonesia's traditional rival, Malaysia, whose deputy prime minister, Datoh Musa Hitam, declared in 1982:

> Presently Malaysian work ethics are somewhat without basis of direction, and if at all, are closer to those of the West. The Japanese work ethic constitutes one of the most important factors in contributing to Japan's breathtaking recovery and progress. If we can adopt or adapt those same ethics, we in Malaysia may be able to improve our performance economically as well as in other fields.

While Japan's exports to Asia have dwindled to around 20 per cent, a quarter of Japan's imports now come from the region. The whole thrust of Japan's economic policy today is towards the region where it accounts for no less than three-quarters of GDP, in spite of the success of the four tigers.

The question inevitably arises as to whether the Greater East Asia Co-Prosperity Sphere is now to be revived by peaceful means, and whether a 'yen zone' is to arise to challenge the dollar zone and the European market. The Japanese have long officially denied any such ambition, but do so no longer. Since the rise of the yen in 1985, Japan has become a major export market for the tigers: their exports to Japan increased by half in 1987 alone, particularly in such things as colour televisions, video tape-recorders and electronic calculators – the very things America finds so difficult to sell to Japan. Trade between Asian countries rose by no less than 29 per cent from 1986 to 1987. At this sort of growth rate, intra-regional trade seems set to overtake trade between East Asia and America.

What seems to be happening is that the tigers have become cheaper and more effective at producing consumer goods than Japan; and the Association of South East Asian Nations countries has in turn become cheaper than the tigers. As trade has surged, it has become normal to price it in yen, a much more stable currency than the local ones; a third of the currency reserves held by Asian central banks is believed to be in yen. The four tigers have long benefited from fixing their exchange rates against the dollar and thus depreciating as the dollar fell, yielding a competitive advantage. Japan's capital exports, as well as the creation of yen bonds in the European market, mean that, whatever the Japanese government thinks, more and more people are using the yen as their major currency. As trade with Japan begins to eclipse that with Britain and America, it makes more sense for the Asians over the long term to peg their currencies to the yen in order to maintain a stable price relationship with their main export market. So a yen zone may be slowly coming into being, even without official action.

But there are advantages for the Japanese in having one: it would increase their power over local economies and in the very long run it could reduce America's stranglehold over the Japanese. As America's largest creditor, the Japanese are paradoxically at risk: America can inflate its way out of trouble, depreciate the dollar, and thus devalue the foreign debt. If it were ever possible to lend in yen to America, this risk would be averted.

The Asian countries also have an interest in a yen zone: as the

American and European markets begin to adopt protective measures, intra-regional trade may be the only option: a yen free-trade area in Asia could vastly stimulate commerce. The chief disadvantage is that overwhelmingly the strongest partner would be Japan – on which Asian countries look with intense suspicion. When polled, more than half of Thais, 47 per cent of Filipinos, 34 per cent of Malaysians, 29 per cent of Singaporeans and 21 per cent of Indonesians feared that Japan could once again become a threatening military power in the future.

In 1992, the Japanese 'bubble' finally burst, permitting a flurry of speculation that the economy was after all a busted flush. Japan, no more than other countries, could escape economic cycles and a slowdown in growth to average world levels. The eruption was, in truth, spectacular, but whether it changed the underlying landscape, as at first appeared, remains open to doubt. By the last quarter of 1993, Japanese GDP had actually shrunk by 0.2 per cent; business bankruptcies had risen by 66 per cent from the previous year.

The causes of this were the tough monetary policies adopted by the governor of the Bank of Japan, Yasushi Mieno, in an effort to control the bubble economy of the mid-1980s. Mieno came under heavy pressure not just from the Japanese, but from abroad. Japan had been blamed for failing to help the world out of a global economic slump; but he also felt the measures were necessary to iron out the distortions in the economy. By March 1993 the Tokyo stock market had crashed to half its level two years before. Land values collapsed. Many companies suffered a severe setback in their profits – Hitachi by a third; Nissan and NEC by two-fifths; Toshiba and Mitsubishi Electric by half; and Fujitsu, Mazda, Nikkon and Daihatsu by 60 per cent; while Minobe and Japan Air Lines reported losses. Sony reported being in the red for the first time ever. Toyota plants have been working at half capacity.

The bursting of the bubble was accompanied by a series of scandals unprecedented even by Japanese standards. The biggest related to the failure of the Ministry of Finance to take action against major brokers who secretly compensated major clients for stock market losses. In fact, as part of Japan's cartel economy, the ministry had almost certainly instigated this very practice to prevent the stock market slump from pushing many companies into a full-blown recession. A related scandal was the massive frauds and losses, many of them to real-estate groups with gangster connections, funded by Japanese banks. This happened because the banks' traditional role as a supplier of funds to industry had been undermined by the latter's new flutter on the money markets: the banks have had to go out looking for customers. The most notorious example was that of Nui Onoue, a gangster's girlfriend who ran a chain of restaurants and went spectacularly bankrupt, owing a staggering $1.8 billion to her gullible bankers.

Japan's economy has become so sluggish over the past two years that some commentators consider that the miracle is over at last. It need not be – if Japan now adopts the right approach. Andrew Williams, the authoritative senior manager of Schroder Wagg's in Japan, argues that 'the main brake on Japanese recovery today is an overvalued exchange rate.' This is a consequence of the trade surplus. The knot can be untied through stimulating the domestic market, reducing the surplus, and bringing the yen down to competitive levels again. The prophets of doom are premature: a recession in Japan is a modest success story anywhere else. The Japanese economy was still growing, albeit slowly. Unemployment remained at 2 to 3 per cent, inflation at around 3 per cent, and wage increases at only 4.3 per cent. In 1992 Kenneth Courtis, the senior economist for the Deutsche Bank Group, warned that Japan is merely 'cleansing its economy and melting off the fat accumulated over the past six years of record-smashing economic expansion'.

In August 1992 the Japanese decided that deflation had gone far enough and announced a Keynesian package of rescue measures of some $85 billion in an effort to raise economic growth. With spectacular property collapses burgeoning in 1993, further expansion was necessary. The main effect of the package was to underwrite the banks, which are now in a much stronger position than they seem: although overexposed and with tiny reserves, most of their lending is still to the *kaisha*, whose underlying wealth and solvency is undoubted. The companies are now propping up the banks rather than the other way around.

Courtis points out that Japan now invests 20 per cent of its GDP in new plant and equipment; in 1991 alone it spent some $440 billion in new investment. Private sector investment in Japan totalled more than $3 trillion between 1986 and 1991, with $500 million being spent on research and development on top of that. The analysts DRI/McGraw-Hill estimate probable American growth at around 2 per cent a year for the rest of the decade, whereas Japan will be growing at between 3.2 and 3.7 per cent.

Japan's government, in its five-year plan, has specified that part of this growth must come through an improvement in the quality of life – which can only increase efficiency. The purpose is to turn Japan into a 'standard-of-living superpower'. 'Japan as a nation is wealthy, but people do not feel affected,' says a senior official. One target is to permit people to acquire housing near the big cities for around five times their annual salary rather than nine times, as at present. Sports facilities are to be improved. Spending on big construction projects is to rise from 50 to 60 per cent of the public works budget. Finally, the goal was set for Japanese to work an average 1800 working hours a year by 1993, 40 less than in 1988. It remains to be seen whether these modest social goals will be achieved.

The other side of the coin of Japan's slow-down is a concentration on exports rather than the domestic market, which in 1991 caused the trade surplus to soar to $78 billion, $118 billion in 1992, and a projected $140 billion in 1993 – $50 billion with the United States alone (largely through an increase in the surplus with Asia, rather than with America and Western Europe). There is little reason to believe that Japan is in relative decline; its growth rate seems to be slowing down only in proportion to that of the West, preserving its relative advantage. Unless, that is, unlike in the past, it has targeted the wrong industries of the future – picking the wrong winners in a costly mistake of gigantic proportions. That seems unlikely.

The only probable way to halt the juggernaut would be for the West to block Japanese exports more than it has already and fend off Japanese investment ducking in under the fence. A recent high-level academic analysis, 'Japan 2000', prepared for the CIA, provided a lurid portrait of Japan as a fully mobilized society seeking to dominate the world economically. The report suggested that Japan was essentially 'racist' and 'not democratic'. The Japanese 'mission' has been to accumulate suffcient wealth to satisfy demands at home, and:

> to create an overall economic mission that is unassailable: to be a richer Japan and to create a world in which it is possible and safe for it to continue to make money ... The Japanese economic stategy is clear: they are investing virtually all of their profits and energy to commercialize new technologies, develop new markets, improve efficiency and expand investment around the world in preparation for the next phase of economic domination.

If this seems characteristically paranoid of the CIA, there are few signs that the Japanese economy is going through more than a cyclical pause before resuming its progress. It is an astonishing achievement. And possibly a dangerous one.

PART FIVE

THE FAR SIDE
OF THE EARTH

More than seven hundred years ago, at Dan-no-ura, in the Straits of Shimonoseki, was fought the last battle of the long contest between the Heike, or Taira clan, and the Genji, or Minamoto clan. There the Heike perished utterly, with their women and children, and their infant emperor likewise – now remembered as Antoku Tenno. And that sea and shore have been haunted for seven hundred years . . . Elsewhere I told you about the strange crabs found there, called Heike crabs, which have human faces on their backs, and are said to be the spirits of Heike warriors. But there are many strange things to be seen and heard along that coast. On dark nights thousands of ghostly fires hover about the beach, or flit above the waves – pale lights which the fishermen call Oni-bi, or demon-fires; and whenever the winds are up, a sound of great shouting comes from that sea, like a clamour of battle.

From 'The Story of Mimi-Nashi-Hoichi', *Kwaidan*,
compiled by Lafcadio Hearn

29

OUTSIDERS

ANYONE OBSERVING the imperial coronation of November 1990 might have felt not just in another age, but on another planet.

Behind the society moths, the police cordons, the crowds, and the occasional terrorist bomb was a Bunraku puppet show come to life. The marionette-style figure at the centre of the enthronement tableau was dressed in a billowing rust-coloured dressing-gown, while the black forage cap on his head was surmounted by a three-foot-high plume; beside him, his tiny wife resembled a porcelain figure imprisoned in the exquisite symmetry of the five-layered kimono, heavier than her, that cascaded from her shoulders and waist.

The emperor of Japan was perched in the Takamikura, an intricately carved purple-and-lacquer stage with a canopy surmounted by a golden phoenix, representing Mount Takachiho where the Sun Goddess, Amaterasu Omikami, is said to have placed her grandson in 600 BC to initiate the dynasty that has spawned 125 emperors in unbroken succession. (Amaterasu was the goddess, in beautiful legend, who took refuge in a cave from the iniquity of her brother, the God of Storm, and was lured out by the brilliance of her own reflection in a mirror that is still a sacred artifice of the royal household.)

Ten days later, on 20 November 1990, as the celebration surrounding the imperial enthronement came to a head, the ritual known as the Daijosai, the 'Great Food Offering Ceremony', was staged. The emperor took a purifying bath, then walked along a carpet that was laid before him and rolled up behind to symbolize a passage between heaven and earth. Accompanied by two women

461

priests, he entered a bedchamber and offered the first rice of the season to the Sun Goddess; then he ate some himself, accompanied by millet and rice wine. The ceremony was secret, but according to most scholars, the emperor then lay on the bed and had mock sexual intercourse with the Sun Goddess, being reborn as a living god himself.

This man-became-god emerged in 1990 to preside over a country that was economically second only to the United States. Twice the size of Germany, it had private financial assets of $7000 billion – about fourteen times the total annual product of Great Britain – which were growing at the rate of some $800 billion a year. It owned the four biggest banks in the world, most of the skyscrapers of Los Angeles, 12 per cent of all America's loans and a quarter of California's. Its people were at the most innovative and futuristic edge of world technology, with the skills to adapt and mass-market shape-changing titanium alloys to make bra frames and water-absorptive resins to make nappies, and its industrial power's achievement in the fields of car assembly, electronic goods, photographic equipment, memory chips and robotics had turned Canon, Mitsubishi, Hitachi, Fujitsu and Toyota into household names the world over.

An ancient pagan animist ceremony causing the normally bustling streets of central Tokyo, the capital of the world's most advanced country, to be closed off by some 37,000 police was a striking but bizarre event. The temptation for most observers was to dismiss the enthronement as quaint and irrelevant: opinion polls showed that only 13 per cent of Japanese were seriously interested in their first imperial coronation in sixty-two years.

However, whatever its effect as a spectacle, the ceremony actually marked a direct reversal of the enforced renunciation of divine status undertaken by Emperor Hirohito at General Mac-Arthur's behest in 1946. While the new Emperor Akihito became constitutionally no more than a 'symbol of the state', rather than Japan's supreme governing authority, and Prime Minister Toshiki Kaifu was accorded equal status at the ceremony, the sacred Shinto rites, in the eyes of most ordinary Japanese, in whom obeisance to authority and seniority are ingrained, reasserted the throne's former supremacy. Nor was the ancient ceremony at odds with Japan's relentless obsession with progress and innovation: the views of the general public still counted for less than those of the country's perennial governing class to an extent unmatched in the major Western democracies. The consensus within that class was that the time had come to restore the institution of emperor to its former glory, if not power.

The decision could not have been taken lightly. The imperial institution enshrined, obviously, the continuity of the Japanese nation; but it also symbolized national consensus in a state in which strong leadership is virtually impossible because of the bewildering variety of powers, factions and classes. The emperor represented a Japan united only in its intense competitive defensiveness towards the outside world, and in its elaborately structured system of deference towards authority. There was no clear hierarchy between the major centres of Japanese power – the civil service, banking, industry, the politicians and the armed forces. In most constitutional monarchies, the institution was a figurehead at the apex of a structure in which the will of the people expressed through democratic elections was sovereign. In Japan, the will of the people counted for little: the formal supremacy of the emperor was necessary to reconcile the conflicting claims to sovereignty of competing interests. The danger is always that the emperor can become a pawn of one of them, as has often happened throughout Japan's history.

The reversion to tradition at the enthronement ceremony marked the growing self-confidence of newly rich Japan in its past: a self-confidence that barely recognized the transgressions that caused the Pacific War. Just weeks before the coronation, the Ministry of Education, which vets history textbooks, censored an eye-witness wartime account of how soldiers threw babies in the air and caught them on bayonets. Two years before, Prime Minister Noboru Takeshita suggested that it was not clear who was the aggressor in the Pacific War. Yasuhiro Nakasone, the country's most impressive recent leader, visited the Yasukuni Shrine in Tokyo, which glorifies the Japanese soldiers in that war. The extremist nationalism so much in evidence in the build-up to the Pacific War had not entirely disappeared either: in January 1990, the mayor of Nagasaki, Hitoshi Motoshima, was shot and injured in front of his city hall by right-wing fanatics a month after asserting that Emperor Hirohito bore some responsibility for the war.

The questions every student of the world's emerging superpower has to answer are, were the events that led to the militarist hurricane in the Far East in the middle of this century an aberration in Japan's history or a natural development? And was the Japanese system, as it regained its self-confidence, reverting to some of the old ways, or had it matured beyond them? In fact Japan has shown no sign of carrying out the necessary public self-examination, and the nature of

Emperor Akihito's enthronement suggested a disturbing regression. The three mainstays of Japan's social cohesion are a division at the top that can only be reconciled through elaborate consensus-building, the rigid hierarchy in social and working life symbolized by a divine emperor and intense nationalism and distrust of foreigners. They seemed to have survived Hiroshima and Nagasaki.

Hirohito, just after surrendering to the Allies, composed a *waka*, a short, allegorical classic verse:

> Under the heavy snow of winter,
> The pine tree bends,
> But does not break,
> Or change its colour.
> People should be like this.

It speaks for itself. Who won in the end, Little Boy or the emperor? By the time of Akihito's enthronement ceremony forty-five years later, the answer seemed much less clear than on 6 August 1945.

The Japanese are different, unique, and are so for profound historical reasons. They have gone to immense lengths to preserve their differences. And in no other country have events so conspired to preserve their uniqueness.

The Japanese are often accused of lacking creativity. Historically, this is absurd, as any glance at the fruits of the Heian period will show. Today, the most vivid and accessible expression of creativity in Japanese culture is to be found in its novels, which repay serious study. Take this extended, and extraordinary, excerpt from a short story by one of the country's most critically acclaimed best-selling novelists of the 1960s, and bear in mind that a few years after this literally stomach-churning description of a suicide pact was written, the author himself committed ritual suicide – whose agonies, as we can see, he well understood – in a similarly appalling way.

In which other country in the world could the popular, and intellectual climate be such as to permit even a framework of acceptability for such fiction, let alone such a fact? When Yukio Mishima died, the Beatles were already past their best; the student revolts of 1968 were fading memories in the West; and the age of the computer chip was about to dawn. Mishima harked back to a heroic dark age in Japan just sixty years before; the rest of the industrial world had left its medieval period at least five centuries before.

The lieutenant's eyes fixed his wife with an intense, hawk-like stare. Moving the sword around to his front, he raised himself slightly on his hips and let the upper half of his body lean over the sword point. That he was mustering his whole strength was apparent from the angry tension of the uniform at his shoulders. The lieutenant aimed to strike deep into the left of his stomach. His sharp cry pierced the silence of the room.

Despite the effort he had himself put into the blow, the lieutenant had the impression that someone else had struck the side of his stomach agonisingly with a thick rod of iron. For a second or two his head reeled and he had no idea what had happened. The five or six inches of naked point had vanished completely into his flesh, and the white bandage, gripped in his clenched fist, pressed directly against his stomach. He returned to consciousness. The blade had certainly pierced the wall of his stomach, he thought. His breathing was difficult, his chest thumped violently and in some far deep region, which he could hardly believe was a part of himself, a fearful and excruciating pain came welling up as if the ground had split open to disgorge a boiling stream of molten rock. The pain came suddenly nearer, with terrifying speed. The lieutenant bit his lower lip and stifled an instinctive moan.

Was this suppuku? – he was thinking. It was a sensation of utter chaos, as if the sky had fallen on his head and the world was reeling drunkenly. His will-power and courage, which had seemed so robust before he made the incision, had now dwindled to something like a single hairlike thread of steel, and he was assailed by the uneasy feeling that he must advance along this thread, clinging to it with desperation. His clenched fist had grown moist. Looking down, he saw that both his hand and the cloth about the blade were drenched in blood. His loincloth too was dyed a deep red. It struck him as incredible that, amidst this terrible agony, things which could be seen could still be seen, and existing things existed still . . .

Reiko did not linger. When she thought of how the pain which had previously opened such a gulf between herself and her dying husband was now to become part of her own experience, she saw before her only the joy of herself entering a realm her husband had already made his own. In her husband's agonised face there had been something inexplicable which she was seeing for the first time. Now she would solve that riddle. Reiko sensed that at last she too would be able to taste the true bitterness and sweetness of the great moral principle in which her husband believed. What had until now been tasted only faintly through her husband's example she was about to savour directly with her own tongue.

Reiko thrust the point of the blade against the base of her throat. She thrust hard. The wound was only shallow. Her head blazed, and her hands shook, uncontrollably. She gave the blade a strong pull sideways. A warm substance flooded into her mouth, and everything before her eyes reddened in a vision of spouting blood. She gathered her strength and plunged the point of the blade deep into her throat.

Yukio Mishima has of course become a loner, an embarrassment to Japan. But that was only after his suicide. While he was alive, he dominated Japan's cultural scene as its most successful author, partly because he wrote of such things as *seppuku* (as well as breaking other taboos and writing about such subjects as bereavement and homosexuality). Mishima's crime, and the reason why he was posthumously ostracized from Japanese life, was that while his fictional persona was accepted in Japan, and even internationally, his real-life act of ritual suicide was not. It shattered the carefully contrived image of post-war Japan erected by the politicians. Like General Nogi's suicide in 1912, Mishima's *seppuku* came as a rude reminder of the dark side of the Japanese character; moreover, it was performed, because of Mishima's fame, in front of the eyes of the whole world.

Admittedly, Mishima was a sado-masochistic homosexual, and a right-wing extremist to boot. But these things were known when he was alive and possessed a huge following. They do not detract from the quality of his literary achievement, which, although often unpleasant, was universal. Some was poetic, all beautifully written and most almost painfully stripping the human condition in a manner that few contemporary Western authors are able to achieve. Both in the manner of his writing and his death, Mishima drew upon the very roots of what it is to be Japanese; hence the alarm with which the establishment, always concerned when these feelings came to the surface, although not when they stayed below, viewed his death. Perhaps the key to Mishima's appeal, both in Japan and internationally, is a very simple one: although his attitudes were the most unpalatable kind of right-wing Japanese extremism, he was a romantic at odds with the bureaucratic dreariness that actually runs Japan, an individual fighting convention.

While alive he was acceptable to the Japanese political and literary establishments because of his right-wing views, obsession with emperor worship and *seppuku*. In his writing, however, he broke all the bounds of convention in form and subject matter. His prose, unlike that of so many Japanese novelists, was never stylized, elaborate or lifeless. It was beautifully sparse when required, emotionally taut yet compellingly readable and replete with brilliantly ironic plots of a kind that was peculiarly Japanese. He wrote about the subjects of his day with relentless realism – sex, violence, death, homosexuality, infertility, rootlessness, the banality of the salaryman's life – from the standpoint of a literary samurai, thus exciting approval in conservative Japanese, and none of the condemnation he would have aroused if he had been a committed left-wing writer on the same themes. In his spirit he was rooted in Japan's dark ages, but in his writing he was frontier-breaking.

The contrast between Mishima and his early admirer and patron, who must be rated Japan's best pre-war writer, is startling. While Mishima was capable of beautifully disciplined writing, much more frequently the words carried forward the story; he always appeared passionate, never contrived. Yasunari Kawabata's writing, by contrast, is as precise, taut, beautifully drawn and slow moving as a piece of Noh theatre. The masterpieces thus created are beyond dispute, in terms of description, the poetic use of words and an ironic and substantial plot. They are an exquisite tableau of place and human emotion. Yet, as with Japanese drama, there is a lifelessness, a kind of contrived and suppressed passion present that leaves an edge of coldness to stories that are in fact full of pathos and sympathy for the human predicament. Kawabata's stories are also deeply rooted in the Japanese psyche.

Three other great writers are notable for being more overtly political. Shusaku Endo's *Wonderful Fool* is an apparently light work after his two earlier masterpieces, *Silence*, about the persecution of Christians in the seventeenth century, and *Sea and Poison*, about medical experiments on American prisoners during the war. *Wonderful Fool* is a gentle, lightly written work in an almost Western hand about a wholly implausible subject: Gaston Bonaparte, a distant descendant of Napoleon, a clumsy, simple-minded oaf who arrives in Japan and befriends in turn a dog, a prostitute, a fraud, and a killer. The style of the book is extremely straightforward, thoroughly un-Japanese, and the message plainly a Christian one. Endo is Japan's foremost Catholic writer.

The book is, in essence, a picaresque voyage across modern Tokyo, a kind of Crocodile Dundee in New York transposed to a visiting Frenchman in Japan, but written by a Japanese, and thereby satirizing everyday Japanese life. Like Mishima's anger, the gentle and humorous satire is directed against the materialistic banality of Japanese life in the time of the economic miracle. Endo's target in all his works is the 'mud-swamp' of ordinary life, from the inability of ordinary Japanese to accept a Christian God to the complicity of little people, merely protecting their livelihoods, in the barbarous experiments upon the Americans.

Almost in complete contrast is Masuji Ibuse's masterpiece about Hiroshima, *Black Rain*, which recounts the aftermath of the bomb in relentless, harrowing detail as told by a number of survivors. (Ibuse draws on factual testimony.) Its most subtle characteristic is a peculiarly Japanese virtue: it shows how people survive absolute horror by carrying on regardless; routine and a certain brusqueness in the face of overwhelming tragedy are the only way of beginning to cope. The result is that Ibuse's account, which could have been merely nauseating (it often is) or sentimental (it often is), is also occasionally humorous and uplifting. Life must go on.

Ibuse, in spite of the polemical nature of his work, represents a major stylistic advance on Kawabata and Mishima. The writing is realistic, not stylized or melodramatic, virtually Western in its blend of truth and fiction, but Japanese in its observation of the minutiae of life and emotion. This Japanese approach makes a point more tellingly than more dramatic prose. Ibuse eschews the picaresque style and improbabilities of Endo to give a factual yet human-interest account of Hiroshima that rings absolutely true. If the result is less entertaining than other novelists, it is intended to be so – and is certainly no less a masterpiece.

A fifth great writer of the post-war era deserves mention: this is Kobo Abe, who wrote the intriguing *The Face of Another*. It must be said at the outset that the book is heavy going, a work about a scientist disfigured in an experiment who has an artificial face made for him. The book quickly bogs down in scientific detail, as well as in an egotistic, introverted, self-pitying monologue of the hero's plight, re-emerging as a novel with rather a good ending only in the final pages. But the book is interesting for two reasons: it is clearly a parable about Hiroshima, and it understands the Japanese obsession with face. Similarly, another of Abe's novels, *Inter Ice Age*, has a central character who, like Hirohito, is a marine biologist, and may be allegorical.

30

THE AUTHORITARIANS

FACE IS a recurring Japanese obsession. Face was all-important in the emperor's surrender broadcast and is one of the most carefully drawn of Japan's characteristics: the distinction between within and without, the latter a mere pretence to be woven around the reality inside. The demands of politeness, social etiquette and personal and social survival are such that few Japanese think ill of another if he says one thing and means quite another.

In a sense the necessity to maintain face gives some foundation for the old racialist sneer about oriental inscrutability. The Japanese go to immense lengths to conceal their true emotions from outsiders. The origins of this were almost certainly the murderously hierarchical nature of Japanese society: a man's life could be at stake if he revealed his true feelings to his social superiors. Beneath, however, most things are permissible: real emotions are even permitted to surface socially in late-night drinking binges. But at other times social decorum must be preserved.

This distinction goes to the heart of what happened – or rather did not happen – after Japan's defeat in the Pacific War, as indeed at the time of the Meiji restoration. The defeat, and even American occupation were acceptable, and ordinary Japanese showed a puzzling readiness to embrace the new American shogun as once they had their beloved emperor, because this was a matter of outside form. Within, for most Japanese, nothing had changed at all. The Meiji oligarchs embraced Western dress and technology while retaining their essential Japaneseness. In this respect the Japanese appear to be remarkably pliable and will accept outside influences while preserving an inner core of cultural attitudes and characteristics.

What is 'Japaneseness'? The question might sound racist, if

the Japanese themselves, as avidly as any of their detractors, did not insist upon it. In fact, although the Japanese have much more in common with Westerners than either they or their critics admit, it seems safe to say that they are the world's most different people.

The cause of this is partly geographical. The Japanese are outsiders, living in an archipelago on the far side of the earth to other developed nations, and on the edge of the world even for Asia – for which they were truly the land of the rising sun, being farthest East. They have always been extremely homogeneous, with only the original Ainu inhabitants, a kind of aboriginal, and the 800,000 Korean-descended community blemishing their racial purity.

In addition to the sheer cost for Westerners of getting to Japan, the Japanese yen has remained so high in recent years that it has largely deterred mass Western tourism, which was always something exotic. Most first-time visitors to Tokyo are struck by just how few foreign faces are to be seen, and how they remain an object of curiosity, just as though they have landed in some remote African country. The foreigner is *gaijin*, alien, even a barbarian to many Japanese. The civilization that was effectively cut off from the world for 300 years before 1868 has still only been marginally affected by Western attitudes, as opposed to Western technology. The Japanese still retain their own outlook on the world, their own Japaneseness within – and are intensely proud of it.

What are the principal components of Japaneseness and how have they evolved, if at all, since the Pacific War? I will attempt to sketch the unique characteristics of this very individual people, while being fully aware of the pitfalls of such generalizations. The exercise is worth doing because national traits can be identified more easily among Japanese than among most. Five stand out. Japanese society is communal, authoritarian, hierarchical, meticulously structured and amoral, defining ethics purely in terms of society's self-interest. Each of these help to define the relations between Japanese, as well as those between them and outsiders.

The communality of Japanese society arises, almost certainly, from its extreme poverty and remoteness historically. There was very little arable land to keep a large and hungry population scattered over an extensive and broadly mountainous area. The rice crop demanded an immense amount of shared labour and organization. The social bent of the Japanese largely derived from necessity. The essence of Japanese social organization is that the individual doesn't exist except as a member of society. The worst that could befall a peasant, criminal or dissident as recently as 150 years ago – in some ways worse than death – was to be made an outcast from his village.

A person's worth is measured in relation to others – to the emperor and the state, to the feudal lord (in the past), to the company today, to the family, to the clan, to colleagues in the small circles of patronage that are the nuclei of Japanese companies. Without others, a Japanese is nobody: I am, only in relation to others. The dropout, the eccentric, the man who goes his own way is traditionally an outcast, not admired for his originality or courage: even today there are relatively few individualists in Japanese society.

In van Wolferen's view, even Japan's artistic achievements are limited by the rigidities of Japanese thought:

> [There is a] notion that there is a perfect way of doing things. In learning a skill – especially in connection with Japanese music, the traditional theatre, arts, or judo, aikido, kendo and karate – the emphasis is on automatic, endless, non-reflective repetition of what the teacher does. Mastery is reached by removal of the obstacles between the self and the perfect model, embodied by the teacher.
>
> The idea that the student might have an inborn potential that is uniquely his or her own has had hardly any influence, even in the non-traditional arts. Foreign conductors and music teachers almost uniformly remark on the great technical skills of Japanese performers, together with their relative lack of capacity for personal expression.

The former American ambassador, Edwin Reischauer, provides a classical 'Japanist' apologia for Japanese methods.

> Westerners tend to look on the relative lack of intellectual creativity as a sign of inferiority, but this may be only a western cultural bias. Who is to say that truths reached by reason are superior to those attained by intuition or that disputes settled by verbal skills are preferable to a consensus reached through feeling. Hair-splitting analysis and great conceptual schemes, typical of India and the West, are not obviously better than smooth co-operation and harmony through nonverbal understanding. It is possible that a Japan standing near the forefront of knowledge in the world may come to show more intellectual creativeness than it has in the past, but on the other hand these other traits may remain more charac-

teristic of the Japanese and may continue to contribute more to their success.

'Individualism' even became a post-war term of abuse for those that followed the teachings established briefly in the schools by the Americans. Individualism was seen as the fount of selfishness and violence in Japanese society by political leaders like Yasuhiro Nakasone – ironically himself a considerable individual. In fact, in the scholar Karl Wittfoegel's seminal study, *Oriental Despotism*, the emphasis on the needs of the collective, as opposed to the individual, is to be found in most Eastern societies, including China, where irrigation, which required a rigid system of organization, is necessary to economical survival and to avoid starvation (such systems even existed in the West, in Inca Peru).

The emphasis on the collective in Japan exhibits itself in a variety of ways, which also boil down to sound common sense in a society which until recently had a very low standard of living. Japanese housing is geared to collective living, lack of privacy and impermanence. The Japanese addiction to screens, removable partitions, beds that can be stacked away against the wall and bedrooms that double as living rooms stem from the poverty of the traditional tiny Japanese wooden residence, when all those devices were very necessary. Homes are not castles: they are viewed as structures that frequently have to be rebuilt because of natural disasters, upward social mobility, or, most common, fire, which was as prevalent until early this century in Japan as in the Middle Ages in Europe.

Although the Japanese are addicted to traditional forms, they have curiously little respect for an old building as such, perhaps because of the impermanence of wooden structures. Japanese are no different from anyone else, in practice, in their enthusiasm for private property and individual ownership of, for example, the latest high-tech gadgetry. But the notion of individual ownership is comparatively recent because, until a hundred years ago, most Japanese barely possessed any goods. The Western house is described by the architect Koichi Nagashima as 'a sort of man-made cave with holes, a strongly enclosed space', and the Japanese house as 'a floating roof, a shelter from the sun unconfined by solid walls with no clear distinction between inside and outside space'.

Another unique and thoroughly practical aspect of Japanese culture is the communal bath. Members of the family first clean themselves outside the bath before sharing the water: the method is hygienic and saves on fuel: the same applies to neighbourhood baths and baths in inns. This communality applied initially to the 'extended household', which was the foundation of Japanese village life. The extended household farmed the rice crop, shared implements, and held the paddy fields collectively. This culture of social organization has transferred itself, quite deliberately, to the company or place of work, where the modern 'salaryman' has a loyalty if anything greater than that to his family, which he will see much less of.

The second great characteristic of Japanese society is its sense of deference and hierarchy, in which every member of society knows his place exactly in relation to every other. Again, this originally served a practical purpose, that of resolving differences within the extended family and within the village, at its lowest level: it was also essential in a nation with a huge warrior class with the power of life or death over others. Ruth Benedict, in her still pertinent post-war classic *The Chrysanthemum and the Sword*, summarized the astounding extent to which hierarchy extended into post-war society, with the company as the new beneficiary of the system:

Japan, for all its recent westernisation, is still an aristocratic society. Every greeting, every contact must indicate the kind and degree of social distance between men. Every time a man says to another 'Eat' or 'Sit down' he uses different words if he is addressing someone familiarly or is speaking to an inferior or to a superior. There is a different 'you' that must be used in each case and the verbs have different stems. The Japanese have, in other words, what is called a 'respect language', as many other peoples do in the Pacific, and they accompany it with proper bows and kneelings. All such behaviour is bound by meticulous rules and conventions; it is not merely necessary to know to whom one bows but it is necessary to know how much one bows. A bow that is right and proper to one host would be resented as an insult by another who stood in a slightly different relationship to the bower. And bows range all the way from kneeling with forehead lowered to the hands placed flat upon the floor, to the mere inclination of head and shoulders. One must learn, and learn early, how to suit the obeisance to each particular case.

As can be imagined, the practice of guessing another's position in the social hierarchy and performing exactly the right kind of bow

– a deeper one from a social inferior to a superior, a smaller one of acknowledgement from the latter – is fraught with social dangers. The modern Japanese obsession with business cards is primarily designed to overcome embarrassment on this score: with cards, everyone knows exactly where they stand. Both Emperor Hirohito and Britain's Queen Elizabeth II are said, charmingly, to have broken into laughter as they tried, through repeated bows, to show the right degree of courtesy to one another.

The Japanese system of deference differed significantly from that of the Chinese in that the latter belong to huge extended clans – there are only some 500 surnames among China's huge population – whereas the Japanese family is fragmented to include only immediate forebears. Until recently the Japanese had no surnames (only noblemen and samurai were allowed to possess these), and the surname still comes first as a mark of respect for the family rather than the individual member within it. Inside the broad family group, ancestor worship only goes back a couple of generations (except for the royal family and other very grand ones). In most families still the authority of the paterfamilias of the senior branch is absolute: even younger brothers of nearly the same age, or grown-up children cannot, for example, get married or decide family affairs without his approval. Women are inferior to men: wives to mothers-in-law. The system is eminently hard-headed: an outsider can be brought into the family through adoption if there is no suitable contender for the succession.

Beyond the family exists a curious structure of loyalties and allegiance to the informal groups which comprise the atoms of decision-making in the dominant feature of the Japanese business landscape, the *kaisha*, the Japanese corporation. Within each company there are a large number of intimates of anything between five and twelve people who meet constantly and are deeply loyal to each other. These small groups are often sub-sections or 'quality control circles' within a particular company, but are not necessarily so. The group usually forms part of a larger 'fraternity' which owes its loyalty to a senior member of the organization who will have picked his supporters as they joined the company: the mentor–protégé relationship is one of the central relationships in any Japanese business.

Within companies, moreover, the Japanese employee's only direct communication is with his immediate superior, rather than someone beside or above him. The informal relationship of the salaryman's work group is the only means he has of getting around this, which is why it is so important. Moreover, seniors have an obligation to consult their juniors. The extraordinary rigour of Japan's system of deference is illustrated by the fact that the Tokugawas, in their efforts to keep the feudal lords under control, regulated every aspect of daily behaviour: every head of household had to proclaim his class position and hereditary status in his doorway. The clothes he wore, the articles he bought and the house he could live in were regulated according to hierarchy. Everybody had his place.

This pyramid was not the kind of loose hierarchy that grew up in sixteenth- or seventeenth-century Europe. It much more nearly resembled that of the Dark Ages, when the king held power over a gaggle of unruly nobles, exercising immense patronage to give his favourites estates and strip his opponents of their wealth. More than traditional, the system is feudal. However, it would be a great oversimplification to leave it at that. The power play between the principal political players in Japanese society has been considered earlier: the struggle between the autocratic bureaucrats, the monopoly capitalists, the armed forces and – very much in fourth place – the representatives of the people is relatively clear.

Beneath them, Japanese society was unique in allowing, with many imperfections, a kind of meritocracy. It was possible to rise from the bottom in Japan to, if not the very top, the middling ranks of bureaucracy and industry. It is impossible for any but the very exceptional, such as Akio Morita, of Sony, or Kakuei Tanaka, to rise above that level and join the real power brokers. The existence of the meritocracy beneath the feudal pyramid structure of Japanese power makes it a more sophisticated model than the venal, incompetent control system of the old communist world. But it does not mitigate the crushing authoritarianism of the structure.

Under the surface, moreover, Japan is deeply class-ridden. The education system theoretically provides equal opportunity, but favours those with money who buy better education for their children, and bribe examiners. Children from good families already established in the Japanese elites have better prospects of going to good schools and getting into, for example, the fast stream of the Law Faculty of Tokyo University. Nearly a third of all MPs, and nearly half of those in the ruling party, are children of former MPs. The former prime minister, Kiichi Miyazawa, for example, was the son and grandson of prominent politicians, while both Japan's current strongmen, Ichiro Ozawa, and his ally, Tsutomu Hata, are the children of MPs. The former prime minister, Morihiro Hosokawa, is the grandson of a former prime minister, Fumimaro Konoye, and has a pedigree dating back to the Fujiwaras in the ninth century. Good family does not guarantee success in Japan, but it certainly helps, as the remarkable number of men from Japan's traditional clans in positions of seniority attests.

The third distinguishing feature of the Japanese system is the intense codification of the individual's role in society, in part deriving from the system of hierarchy. Various explanations have been formulated for the rigidity of such things as Japan's carefully elaborate code of obligations, punctuality and precision. The anthropologist Thomas Crump takes the view that rice-growing is its origin:

> The annual cycle of cultivation requires ever closer ... co-operation. The wet rice system requires the supply of water to be regulated for every individual *ta*, in conjunction with all the others ... Unless the level of the water is right, the rice will not grow.
>
> This poses a mathematical problem of the first order. The solution is not a rule of thumb but ritual. It is no coincidence that the great rice-growing areas of the world largely coincide with the domain of Buddhism, a religion suffused with mystic numbers and obsessed with the calendar ... The rites provide a whole series of signals, each opening the way for the next stage in the irrigation process, which involves the constant opening and closing of conduits, so that in every *suiden* the level of water is just right. With this background, it is no wonder that the Japanese set such store by virtues, such as punctuality, which are based upon accuracy.

Yet this precision is not limited to the Japanese calendar. It extends to the astonishing map of social obligations compiled by Ruth Benedict. In the system, every relationship consists of a *sendai*, senior, or *kohai*, junior. But it seems clear that the origin of this elitist system, a mixture of Japanese mysticism (Shinto), Buddhism (a more sophisticated religion), and Confucianism (an authoritarian social philosophy) lies in the absence of an overarching deity and moral system. For the rulers of Japan, this provided immense advantages: in place of a religion which might subvert the control of the state, it provides a focus for the allegiance of ordinary men and women and defines their obligations.

Naturally enough, the chief of these was blindly to serve the

477

state, through a system of inherent obligation that most Japanese have never escaped in generations. The ordinary person is still burdened by quite awesome debts throughout his life. In practice, such duties exist in any society; but such things as the tacit obligation towards a person's wife, children and parents are not codified as debts in the West; they are more a kind of duty of the heart, supplemented by morality and religion.

The Japanese have instead codified these moral obligations into a carefully constructed, almost mathematical structure. On one side of the equation are *on* passively incurred, that is the benefits that everyone has innately received from others, which must be repaid later on (there is a slight parallel with the concept of Christian original sin, with which everyone is born). These include the protection of the emperor, the care bestowed by one's parents, the care of one's lord, the *on* of one's teacher and the *on* received from those that help one during the course of one's life.

On the debit side is a person's *gimu*, the obligations he or she owes and can never repay in full, which, needless to say, is headed by *gimu* towards the emperor, the law and Japan; one's *gimu* towards one's ancestors and children; and one's *gimu* towards one's work. In addition, there are more limited obligations to repay, which can be paid off, and be mathematically calculated. These are called *giri* and include one's duty towards one's feudal lord, or boss, towards the family one marries into, towards those who have done one favours and towards one's more distant relations.

Finally there is the important concept of *giri*-to-one's-name, which is also mathematically precise: this includes the duty to clear one's name of insult or imputation of failure, even through vendetta if necessary, the duty to admit no professional failure or ignorance, and the duty to observe the strict rules of Japanese life, that is, not to live above one's station in life, to make an inappropriate display of one's emotions, to show respect for others, never to show disrespect by blowing one's nose in front of someone else, and so on.

Various points may be noticed about this system of codified social relations. First – unlike the case in China – there is no reciprocal obligation on the part of those who govern to behave properly towards the subject, or the father towards the son or daughter. In China there is an obligation of *jen*, benevolence, which rulers and parents must respect or forfeit the loyalty of subjects and children. In Japan, no matter how badly the ruler or parent behaves, the subject must show filial piety and repay the 'debt'.

One famous Japanese film is about a rich mother who steals

money collected by her schoolmaster son for charity. The son discovers the theft, but takes the blame upon himself. His wife finds out and instead takes responsibility upon herself, drowning herself. This story is considered a moral tale about the son and his wife competing to fulfil their social responsibilities. No one could hold the monstrous mother to blame. Once again, the concept is strictly authoritarian.

Second, *gimu*, the higher chain of obligation, of course applied to the emperor, to one's parents and to work. By contrast, *giri* to one's own family and friends, and even to one's boss, is in a lower category. If there is any clash, *gimu* must override *giri*, and many of the classic Kabuki tragedies are about the inevitable consequences of these clashes.

This can be quite complex. One owes *gimu* to one's parents, for example. This extends as far as the common arrangement of marriages. Most men let their parents select a bride for them, and under *giri*, the son must accept the wife chosen for him. However, it is common for a more powerful or richer family without a suitable heir to arrange for a young man to marry their daughter, adopt their name and become the heir to the family; in this case, as when a daughter marries into a family, *giri* is transferred to the parents-in-law. In the past *giri* to one's lord was more important than *gimu* to the emperor probably because one's lord was the likeliest to enforce it, but this was reversed in the Meiji era.

A third curiosity is that *giri*-to-one's-name provides the underpinning not just of Japan's peculiar code of deference, but supports such violations of the ethical codes of most other societies as the concept of vendettas and the duty to cover up and lie, if necessary, on one's own behalf (the duty to admit of no professional failure or ignorance). This is by any standards a pretty remarkable code of behaviour, and not one shared by either China or India. It enjoins Japanese to get even for every slight or slur: a man who does not do this is not fulfilling his proper obligation, has no self-respect and deserves no respect from others. In China, people who overreact to slights are deemed absurd; in Japan they must do so or forfeit self-respect. The code of conduct also enjoins absolute stoicism if necessary and acceptance of one's station is life.

The obligation not to admit a failure goes to remarkable lengths. As Ruth Benedict writes

> *Giri*-to-one's-name as a professional person is very exigent in Japan, but it need not be maintained by what an American

understands as high professional standards. The teacher says, 'I cannot in *giri*-to-my-name as a teacher admit ignorance of it,' and he means that if he does not know to what species a frog belongs, nevertheless he has to pretend he does. If he teaches English on the basis of only a few years' school instruction, nevertheless he cannot admit that anyone might be able to correct him. It is specifically to this kind of defensiveness that '*giri*-to-one's-name as teacher' refers. The businessman too, in *giri*-to-one's-name as a businessman, cannot let anyone know that his assets are seriously depleted or that the plans he has made for his organisation have failed. And the diplomat cannot in *giri* admit to the failure of his policy.

It is still deeply shameful for Japanese students to fail, which is why competition in exams is intense – and why they are so rarely held in one's progress through the education system. This extraordinary code of defending one's name and reputation also explains the extreme politeness of the Japanese. Anything less could cause offence and result, in the past at least, in a blood vendetta against the perpetrator. Japan has been defined as a 'shame culture'.

This creates an extraordinary emotional rigour and repression in most Japanese. A child is indulged when young, but by eight or nine, far from a family being a consolation for any unhappy school life, it may turn against him if he misbehaves and his teacher complains, even, in some cases, to the extent of turning him out of his house.

Etsu Inagaki described learning the Chinese classics at the age of six from a Confucian scholar:

Throughout my two-hour lesson he never moved the slightest fraction of an inch except for his hands and his lips. And I sat before him on the matting in an equally correct and unchanging position. Once I moved. It was in the midst of a lesson. For some reason I was restless and swayed my body slightly, allowing my folded knee to slip a trifle from its proper angle. The faintest shade of surprise crossed my instructor's face; then very quietly, he closed his book, saying gently but with a stern air, 'Little Miss, it is evident that your mental attitude today is not suitable for study. You should retire to your room and meditate.' My little heart was almost killed with shame. There was nothing I could do. I humbly bowed to the picture of Confucius and then to my teacher, and, backing respectfully from the room, I slowly went to my father to report as I always did, at the close of my lesson. Father was surprised, as the time was not yet up, and his unconscious remark 'How quickly you have done your work!' was like a death knell.

The memory of that moment hurts like a bruise to this very day.

She movingly chronicles her explosion of rapture when permitted the kind of freedom in planting her garden that the young generations of the West experienced when achieving sexual freedom in the 1960s. Japanese gardens are intricately laid out. Sunken rocks are carefully laid on a hidden layer of small stones, and each placed in a geometrical relationship to the stream, shrubs, trees and house. At her mission school, however, Etsu Inagaki was allowed to plant whatever she wished.

This plant-as-you-please garden gave me a wholly new feeling of personal right . . . The very fact that such happiness could exist in the human heart was a surprise to me . . . I, with no violation of tradition, no stain on the family name, no shock to parent, teacher or townspeople, no harm to anything in this world, was free to act.

She planted potatoes:

No one knows the sense of reckless freedom which this absurd act gave me . . . The spirit of freedom came knocking at my door . . . At my home there was one part of the garden that was supposed to be wild . . . But someone was always busy trimming the pines or cutting the hedge, and every morning Jiya wiped off the stepping stones, and, after sweeping beneath the pine trees, carefully scattered fresh pine needles gathered from the forest.

Ruth Benedict pointed out:

The Japanese ask a great deal of themselves. To avoid the great threats of ostracism and detraction, they must give up personal gratifications they have learned to savour. They must put these impulses under lock and key in the important affairs of life. The few who violate this pattern run the risk of losing even their respect for themselves . . .

The tensions that are thus generated are enormous, and they express themselves in a high level of aspiration which has made Japan a leader in the Orient and a great power in the world. But these tensions are a heavy strain upon the individual. Men must be watchful lest they fail, or lest anyone belittle their performances in a course of action which has cost them so much abrogation. Sometimes people explode in the most aggressive acts. They are roused to these aggressions, not when their principles or their freedom is challenged, as Americans are, but when they detect an insult or a detraction. Then their dangerous selves erupt, against the detractor if that is possible, otherwise against themselves.

Japanese repression and discipline are reinforced by the Japanese attitude to death, which is quite unique. Kishimoto Hideo, the writer, says, 'Death is not a mere end of life for the Japanese. It has been given a positive place in life. Facing death properly is one of the most important features of life. In that sense it may well be said that for the Japanese death is within life.' Ivan Morris argued that Buddhism plays its part in this concept:

> Buddhism, with its stress on non-ego and self-denial (*muga*) teaches that we can escape these sufferings inherent in the human condition only by surmounting the illusion of the self and its desires, above all the desire to survive. This reinforced the sacrificial aspects of the samurai ethos and helped the warrior accept physical hardships and eventual destruction. For many of the suicide recruits an initial period of unease was followed by a sort of Buddhist *satori* or spiritual awakening as they came to terms with their impending death.

The stoicism of the kamikaze fighters was quite other-worldly: the last kamikaze mission in the Philippines was staged using five makeshift Zero planes patched together from the remains of other damaged aircraft. Captain Nakajima, the commander, asked for volunteers:

> The words were scarcely uttered before every man had raised his arm high in the air and shouted, 'Here!' as they eagerly edged forward ... I breathed deeply and tensed my facial muscles into a scowl to keep from betraying the emotion that flowed over me.
>
> 'Since you all want to go so much, we will follow the usual procedure of selection. You are dismissed.'
>
> As I turned to enter the shelter, several of the pilots reached out to grab at my arms and sleeves, saying, 'Send me! Please send me! Send me!'

I wheeled about and shouted, 'Everyone wants to go. Don't be so selfish!'

Morris describes how harakiri came to be adopted by the Japanese:

Of all possible bad deaths none is more odious to the warrior than capture and execution by the enemy; for this means intolerable humiliation not only for himself but, far more damaging, for the reputation of his family retroactively and in generations to come. The most cataclysmic defeat will not mar the reputation of a hero or his kinsmen. Far from it: in the mystique of Japanese heroism nothing succeeds like failure . . . The soldier who allowed himself to be captured automatically lost his dignity as a warrior and could expect only the most brutal treatment: savage torture, a humiliating form of execution, mutilation of his corpse and, worst of all, the epithet *toriko* ('prisoner'). Since defeat was such a likely outcome of the warrior's way and capture such an unthinkable disgrace, it is logical that suicide should have become accepted as the honourable death for the failed hero . . .

Why did this particular form of self-immolation (*seppuku*) become established in the samurai class, not only as the standard way of avoiding disgrace and vindicating one's honour (*setsujoku*), but as an official punishment prescribed by superior authorities, the method of suicide for an attendant on the death of his lord (*junshi*), and the ultimate manner of remonstrating with an erring superior (*kanshi*)? In the first place it was chosen as an excruciatingly painful form of self-mutilation, being in fact a gratuitous infliction of torture preceding the actual death-blow, which was normally administered by a sword-wielding second known as the *kaishaku-nin*. This choice of extreme suffering was no doubt related to the strain of self-mortification in Zen (which became the samurai's religion par excellence) and also to the idea that it was incumbent on members of the elite warrior class to display their unique courage and determination by undergoing an agonising ordeal that mere commoners (or women) could not possibly endure . . .

But why disembowelment rather than some other form of self-torture? The *Hara* (abdomen), apart from being the physical centre of the body, was traditionally regarded as the locus of a man's inner being, the place where his will, spirit, generosity, indignation, courage, and other cardinal qualities were concentrated.

Stoicism, endurance, suffering; all are traits inculcated into ordinary Japanese from the beginning. Even today, the most usual form of Japanese 'spartan training' is to stand or sit in an ice-cold waterfall before dawn, or to douse oneself three times during a winter night with icy water. The object is to become so practised that one no longer feels the experience.

Executives and salesmen are often sent on courses at 'self-improvement' training schools, such as 'Hell Camp' at the foot of Mount Fuji. These bear a distinct resemblance to army training. The object, says the principal of one, is 'to break the pupil's own conception of himself'. At dawn they begin with exercises and cold showers, followed by an hour kneeling on the heels with the spine upright. Ten hours of further exercises follow, the trainees interminably screaming out slogans as loudly as they can manage. One favourite is the Ten Golden Rules of Doing Business. Long-distance runs are another feature. The 'Sales Song' composed of such lyrics as 'with the sweat of our brows, we sell products made by others from the sweat of their brows' is practised for three days at the top of the voice, to prove a trainee's 'sincerity'.

One well-known Japanese television programme celebrated the virtue of *gaman* (endurance). The young contestants travelled from country to country enduring one ordeal after another, as the writer Nick Bornoff notes in his book *Pink Samurai*:

> alternatively being starved, force-fed with unpalatable foods, confronted with wild beasts, reptiles and noxious insects and suffering a whole gamut of bizarre torments specially devised in between . . . Having imbibed a demijohn full of water, for instance, contestants were prevailed upon to refrain from urinating over 12 hours. The no-peeing ordeals climaxed in wintertime in Holland, where they sat in a tub full of ice cubes and quaffed chilled beer before standing around in sub-zero temperatures in their swimming trunks. In Thailand, they tore away the seats of their shorts as they were dragged over rough ground by elephants; they were trundled face downwards aboard a cable drum through the sands of the Nevada Desert; in Jakarta they were treated to a faceful of pepper. Contests were conducted according to a process of elimination: only those enduring one event could qualify to travel on the next.

Self-abnegation traditionally acompanies self-abasement. The British traveller U. C. L. Keeling wrote of Japan in 1880:

The Japanese are very polite . . . when speaking to anybody unless it be to the lowest classes, they deprecate themselves and extol the second person. Friends or acquaintances, meeting in the street, bow with great deference to each other, the forehead not infrequently nearly touching the knees. Those receiving their friends indoors bow and are bowed to in the following manner: the host and guest kneeling *vis-à-vis*, place their hands on the mat, and incline their heads until they rest upon them. In this position courtesies are exchanged . . . the person only rising a few inches to express thanks, good wishes or congratulations, and again resuming their humble posture.

A Japanese artist, Yoshio Markino, wrote in 1912:

I always forgive the other's anger, because it is the human nature to get into a bad temper. I generally forgive if one tells me a lie, because the human nature is very weak and very often one cannot have a steady mind to face the difficulty and tell all the truth. I also forgive if one makes a groundless rumour or gossip against me, because it is a very easy temptation when some others persuade in that way.

Even murderers I may forgive according to their condition. But about sneering, there is no excuse. Because one cannot sneer at innocent people without intentional insincerity.

Let me give you my own definition of two words. Murderer: one who assassinates some human flesh. Sneerer: one who assassinates others' soul and heart.

Soul and heart are far dearer than the flesh, therefore sneering is the worst crime.

Honour, respect and virtue are among the highest human assets in Japan. The final point about the map of obligations is that, in the absence of any religious code of conduct or morality, it remains the essential underpinning to Japanese behaviour. Thus loyalty to the emperor, the laws and Japan, as well as one's parents and one's work are the very cornerstones of Japanese morality. There is no higher authority to which a Japanese can appeal, for example, if he considers the laws unjust. The codification of behaviour is, in a sense, the natural bureaucratic response of a social system that lacks an underlying ethical base.

Many observers have ascribed this codification to the Japanese 'way of thinking' which they assert is different to that of anyone else. Few would go so far as Tadanobu Tsunoda, who argued that the left-hand side of the Japanese brain was responsive to the stimuli that triggered the right hemisphere in most other peoples; he had a huge intellectual and popular following in Japan for this thesis. But the idea that the Japanese have a unique way of thinking and moralizing is widely believed and discussed in Japan. In 1979, for example, Yoshizane Iwasa, vice-president of the Federation of Economic Organizations, expressed this eloquently:

> On the surface, we have adopted western-style clothes, food and houses and things to quite an extent, and we have become rapidly and highly westernised in many aspects. However, if you go a little deeper, the Japanese are still different. Our way of thinking, our logic, is different to those of our western counterparts. And this applies to the management of the national economy and of business enterprises where economic laws and management principles dictate one's actions.

Others have ascribed the Japanese 'way of thinking' to the enormous complexity of the language and the alphabet. Japanese, before the arrival of Chinese influence, spoke *wabun*, a non-written language. The Chinese brought writing, as well as *kanbun*, which became the language of the elite.

Only in the early twentieth century did Japan create its own written language, based on some 2000 so-called *joyo* or everyday *kanji*, adopted from the thousands of Chinese characters. Crump argues:

> The *kanji* are an example of a uniquely Japanese institution which proves the means for ranking individuals in a hierarchy in which the court – at least historically – stands at the top. There are private institutions which test their members on *kanji* proficiency, so that they can be ranked as the *dan*, or 'step' system, used in any number of competitive activities, whether they be judo, go, or ikebana flower arranging. When it comes to the court, however, there is a decisive change in content; it is not so much that the court has its own distinctive vocabulary derived from that which the court ladies used in fifteenth-century Kyoto for daily conver-

sation, but that in writing about the court, hundreds of words are used which cannot occur in any other context.

The staggering complexity of Japanese does not only accentuate the class basis of society. In order that children should learn it with any degree of fluency, systematic rote learning is essential, creating a mental straitjacket from which very few adults escape. In addition, the system of learning teaches that there is only a 'right' and a 'wrong' answer to every question. Shades of meaning, and expressions of individual opinion, are not allowed for until university level. Most Japanese are thus conditioned to an extraordinarily rigid, disciplined, memory-intensive method of categorization and analysis which in some respects is ideally suited to most of the humdrum tasks of office or factory work – but not to imaginative thinking. One Western journalist in Japan was astonished to see a small boy doing his 'art' homework: instead of doing a drawing of his own, he was meticulously copying out, four or five times, an identical drawing of a little girl.

On top of this very direct approach to language, however, lie voluminous social rules that emphasize the exact opposite – not to reveal what you think, a legacy of the times when to do so, particularly to one's superiors, could cost a Japanese his life. The writer, Masaaki Imai, confirms this:

In Japan one is not supposed to say 'no'. It is rude, impolite, uncivilised, demoralising, and hurts the feeling of the other party. Saying 'no' is a capital sin in Japan. One has to be tactful and diplomatic enough to resort to such art as euphemism and body language in order to convey his negative message. There are some sixteen ways to avoid no ... The first and perhaps most typical way of saying no is to say yes first, followed immediately by an explanation which may last half an hour and which, in effect, means no. One has to be very attentive since the tone of the response is always affirmative throughout the conversation. Don't be misled by the affirmative tone. Concentrate only on the contents and find out if you can get a firm commitment for the next step.

The second way of saying no is to be vague, ambiguous and evasive in one's reactions so that the other party becomes confused and lost to the extent that he cannot even remember what the issue was. By sending out contradictory signals, the Japanese business-man hopes that the other party will get the hint and take the initiative of calling off the talk itself. The third way is not to answer the question directly and simply leave the matter unattended. The postponement of a decision on a pending issue is tantamount to saying no, a tactic often employed by government officials. Other ways include changing the subject abruptly, criticising the other party, or suddenly assuming a highly apologetic tone.

Michihiro Matsumoto popularized the concept of *haragei*, the expression of meaning behind deliberately vague language. The fifteen basic rules of *haragei* are, he says:

1. Don't tell the truth, but don't lie.
2. Don't make friends, but maintain 'hostile friendship' (so as not to give away too much to those who may one day turn on you).
3. Don't debate.
4. Don't define yourself.
5. Don't say no.
6. Don't justify yourself.
7. Don't attract attention to yourself.
8. Don't be direct.
9. Don't ask why.
10. Don't explain why.
11. Don't be specific.
12. Don't show emotions.
13. Don't seek identity.
14. Don't be predictable.
15. Don't be independent.

He also lists the rules for saying no without saying no:

1. Avoid answering.
2. Be extremely polite.
3. Explain the situation without giving reasons.
4. Inflate the other person's ego while deflating yours.
5. Avoid the central issue.
6. Use vague language.
7. Make your argument abstract and metaphysical.
8. Pity yourself.
9. Generalise from the particular.
10. Keep the other person guessing.
11. Say 'yes, but . . .'

12. Make a scapegoat of somebody.
13. Arrange for a third party to say 'no' for you.

Kenrick asserts that non-verbal communication is important to the Japanese:

> The Japanese say, 'The eyes are more expressive than the mouth. The wise do not talk. The talkative are not wise.' They add that they do not trust words and their words are not meant to be trusted. To them sensitivity to what is in a person's mind should make speech superfluous; the use of words evidences a lack of understanding; sympathy submerges thoughtless words; verbal skill is for those at arm's length; silence is a sign of honesty and trustworthiness. To merge intimately with others, to communicate feelings that have to be understood intuitively is, they feel, more effective than verbal exchanges. The variety of these expressions indicates the strength of communal feelings and the obstacles to individualism.
>
> Followers of Zen reject dependence on words, verbal or written, for the transmission of the Buddhist enlightenment. It has been said that foreigners listen only to the words between pauses while the Japanese listen to the pauses between the words. To them silence can be pregnant. A break between words may convey a richer meaning than the words themselves. To prevent misunderstandings the single most important lesson a westerner must learn is the necessity of listening.

Sex is one major omission in Japan's moral code. For the Japanese, sex is a pleasure, enjoying the status of a human feeling, to be enjoyed provided it does not conflict with more important obligations. Faithfulness is not enjoined; men are expected to be unfaithful to their wives whom they provide with a living and rarely see. Prostitution is not frowned upon; until recently, a wife would dress up her husband for his visits to a prostitute. Such diversion is regarded as natural. Homosexuality is not frowned upon although effeminate men, as everywhere, are the targets of peer abuse among the young. Masturbation is encouraged. Drunkenness is socially accepted.

As marriages are usually arranged, safety valves are regarded as necessary. Premarital relations are not encouraged but once a man is married, he may indulge in sexual liaisons, with society's approval, although his wife may not (in practice a steadily increasing number do). Almost anything goes. One example of sexual behaviour in Nicholas Bornoff's exhaustive study of the subject, *Pink Samurai*, will suffice:

> *Nudo* theatres have many avid devotees. On Sundays, a computer engineer travels two hours on the bullet train to his favourite Tokyo strip haunt. A young representative from a chemical firm prefers rainy weekday nights: 'It's less crowded; with luck you can get up on-stage several times.' One, a rather distinguished-looking businessman who spoke perfect English, had no qualms about explaining his own particular predicament. 'I come here a lot,' he said with a sad smile. 'But just to watch. You see, I'm impotent.'
>
> . . . she tells the man to undress her, which he does rather as he might a store-window mannequin. The stage starts to revolve.
>
> Now she taps the mattress by her side, and the man obediently lies down. Mother Izumi, hardly more than 20 years old, removes her middle-aged little boy's trousers and underpants, neatly folding both and placing them to one side . . . Becoming a whore again, Izumi delves into her basket for a condom, which some strippers apply with meticulously practised oral skill. As she fusses over the motionless man with craftswomanly professionalism, she occasionally throws dispassionate glances around the rapt, silent audience . . .
>
> As her feet flail the air to the copulatory rhythm, she gradually straightens her legs and spreads her tattooed thighs to trace an arc in the air like an opening fan, a gesture quite consciously devised to satisfy enduring curiosity: this is what genitals look like when they're interconnected. Everything is explicit; nothing here is to be left to the imagination. Not a face in the audience betrays the slightest shadows of emotion.

The point about these practices is not that they occur; undoubtedly, similar experiences are repeated in many other countries. The point is that, as with Japan's abundance of pornographic and sado-masochistic comics, these goings-on are not disapproved of, except by the country's burgeoning women's movement.

The quality of Japan's 'erotic comics' quite literally beggars description. Bornoff makes a brave attempt:

In a welter of ero-manga 'erotic comics' *Erotopia, Utopia* or *Chest*, one discovers outrages suffered on the gynaecologist's couch, graphic gropings in swimming pools, gangsters poking guns up blanked-out vulvas or perhaps an old lecher raping a schoolgirl as he pushes her face into a bowl of hot noodle soup. Combinations can be highly bizarre, as a currently popular trend for combining sex and golf suggests. After peeking at lady players' crotches on the green, an elderly golfing politician lures them home to rape them. A series so popular that it has gone through over twelve book anthologies is *Rape Man*. A downtrodden Japanese Clark Kent, the protagonist, changes into a superhero whose mask and cloak costume leaves him rather uncharacteristically naked from the waist down. Trussing up female employees in dark office corridors and/or schoolgirls in toilets, Rape Man sometimes even suspends himself from high rises and swings through windows – in erectio – to perpetrate his misdeeds . . .

Repression, escapism, social backwardness, the coldly cynical permissiveness of the authorities in permitting safety valves for an intensely submissive population, all play their parts in this grisly and vastly popular outgrowth of Japanese society (although ordinary non-erotic Japanese comics and cartoons can be remarkably imaginative).

Japan is the country of the ubiquitous 'love hotel' whose rooms are rented by the hour for sex: sometimes between husband and wife because of the lack of privacy in a small home with elderly parents and children; often between client and prostitute: or between boyfriend and girlfriend. None of this is frowned upon. Some may find this refreshing, some not. But it is certainly different. Indeed, as family values break down in modern Japan and the hold of Confucianism, which has no religious force, is eroded, both men and women in Japan increasingly enjoy complete latitude sexually, limited only by what is available.

This leads directly to the issue of the 'amorality' of Japan's social order. Shinto has no conception of good and evil. It takes an optimistic view of human nature. Men are essentially good; occasionally they lapse in their social obligations and become 'rusty'. But they can be purged of this fault. Moreover, the dead automatically become *hotoke*, that is, buddhas. There is no conflict between good and evil, no heaven, purgatory or hell. Everyone becomes a god on his death, no matter what they may have done in their lifetime. This is an astonishing doctrine which holds men throughout their lives only to man-made social rules, and permits everyone to look forward to the afterlife (hence the attraction of death, historically, to many Japanese enduring a miserable earthly existence). Good and bad behaviour is judged entirely in terms of one's ability or failure to meet social obligations, which are sometimes so serious as to require suicide to maintain one's self-respect. Even cowards become *hotoke* or *kami*. Indeed, if disgraced in this world, it is often best to go on to the next.

The fourth major element of Japanese uniqueness is racialism based on moral superiority.

'The earth in the firmament appears to be perfectly round without edges or corners,' according to the Japanese philosopher Seishisai Aizawa in 1825. 'However, everything exists in its natural bodily form and our divine land is situated at the top of the earth . . . the various countries of the west correspond to the feet and legs of the body . . . As for the land amidst the seas which the western barbarians call America, it occupies the hindmost region of the earth . . . Today the alien barbarians of the west, the lowly organs . . . are dashing about across the seas, trampling other countries underfoot and daring, with their squinting eyes and limping feet, to override the noble nations.'

Racialism stems from the idea that all Japanese are descended from the gods, a chosen race related to their emperor. Minorities within Japan, such as the Korean community, are treated as stateless and have no right to a Japanese passport. Foreign residents in Japan must still be fingerprinted by law.

The Japanese practise what is little short of apartheid towards the two minorities, one racial, one social, in their midst. The social group is the two million or so *barakumin* (previously known as *Eta*, the Filth), traditionally descended from those in 'unclean' occupations like butchery and the leather trade; they live in their own villages on the fringes of Japanese society, are unable to marry outside their group and are discriminated against at every level. The racial group is around 800,000 Koreans, mostly children of those forcibly brought to Japan to work in industries during the First World War. When the American occupation withdrew in 1952, the Koreans were stripped of their Japanese nationality, which meant they were ineligible for public housing, child welfare or social security.

One spokeswoman, Yumi Lee, tells of feeling wholly Japanese until the age of sixteen when she 'first confronted the unforgettable event which occurs to Koreans in Japan: I was forced to be fingerprinted and to carry the Alien Registration Certificate at all times.' The fingerprint requirement for Japan's Koreans was lifted only in 1992. She was ineligible to play in national volleyball competitions, was prevented from becoming a PE teacher, and could not find an apartment. When Pak Ching Sok applied for a job with Hitachi in 1970, he passed the entrance exam and got in – until he was asked for his certificate of family registration. It showed he was Korean and he was rejected. He took Hitachi to court and won four years later; but few Koreans have the stomach to go down the same route. In spite of the deaths of thousands of Koreans in Hiroshima in 1945 their names were not included on the commemoratory monument. Recently they have been allowed to erect their own monument, a long way across the river, away from the Peace Park.

The Koreans are the front-line victims of Japanese racism, which is every bit as pure as the old South Africa's. The same racism insists that only Japanese-descended foreign workers can come from other lands, principally Brazil and Peru. There are around 10,000 of these, and they complain bitterly of discrimination against them by Japanese, who view them as too 'loud'. The 100,000 or so illegal immigrants doing dirty or dangerous jobs have no rights at all.

One recent example of Japanese racism affected Konishiki, the Hawaiian-born sumo wrestler known as the 'Dump Truck', who, in spite of being a second-ranking *ozeki* in the sport, could not be promoted to the top rank of *yokuzuna*. He was forced abjectly to withdraw the complaint of racism under threat of being eased out of sumo wrestling in Japan altogether.

Several *yokuzuna* had less impressive fighting records than Konishiki, but although the Hawaiian had painstakingly learnt Japanese, one senior official of the sport suggested that no foreigner could grasp its importance, which was deeply rooted in the 'Japanese people's spiritual and cultural soil'. Another official told Konishiki, 'We should never have let a *gaijin* into sumo. What would it look like if a sumo wrestler had a blond topknot?' In 1993, however, amid angry protests from some, the Hawaiian-born sumo wrestler Akebono, after defeating Japanese champion Takahanada, his twenty-third victory in ninety fights, became the first foreign *yokozuna* in sumo history.

While targeted at all other countries, Japan's sense of superiority involves constant sniping at the Americans, for example, by former prime minister Yasuhiro Nakasone and foreign minister Michio Watanabe, among others, as being less intelligent and less racially pure. Japanese girls who work for a time overseas are tainted, and have difficulty finding suitable husbands on their return.

Karel van Wolferen has labelled the modern Japanese sense of superiority and uniqueness *nihonjinron* (theorizing on the Japanese). This quite openly argues that Western values are 'dry' or 'hard', those of Japan 'wet' and 'soft'. By this is meant that Japanese are more attuned to people's needs, more community-conscious than selfish. The 'monsoon culture' in contrast to the 'desert' of Judaeo-Christianity, has produced this. The Japanese, on this thesis, are a gentle, submissive people who do not assert their rights aggressively and obey those placed over them. The obvious advantages of these theories for those that run Japan is clear.

The Japanese themselves usually emphasize how different they are racially from other people, often taking this to absurd lengths. One farmers' leader criticized imports of American beef by explaining that 'everyone knows that Japanese intestines are about one metre longer than those of foreigners'. This sort of attitude, still held by a remarkable number of Japanese, seems an extension of old-fashioned Japanese nationalism, which held that Japan is the original ancestor of all countries, the main, or 'root', country of the world. The emperor is 'the sole true son of heaven and sovereign of the world, destined to rule all within the four seas as lord and master'. (Even Hitler and Stalin had no such ambitions.)

The Japanese Foreign Ministry lays emphasis on Japan as a 'homogeneous' society, and points to the relative absence of minorities in society, as well as the image of classlessness. Some 80 per cent of Japanese define themselves as middle class; in fact, while the contrast between the middle and working classes is blurred, both sharing similar housing and income levels, there exist a small number of very well-off Japanese in relation to the general population; in addition, poverty is much greater than officially admitted. Real unemployment is almost certainly twice or three times the official figure of 2 per cent. As in the Soviet Union, unemployment is also concealed through the use of cheap labour performing non-existent jobs.

*

494

The question remains as to how much modern Japanese are still influenced by traditional ethics. The answer must be partly conjectural. Ancestor-worship is much less strong among the young. Even as modern and 'Western' an author as Shusaku Endo, a Catholic, laments the erosion of Japan's traditional values. As he told the review section of the London *Guardian* in February 1992:

> The first thing to go was the idea of the ancestor-based family system upon which the whole of society was structured. Strange though it may seem to Europeans, the social ethic in Japan weakened with the loss of the family system. Buddhism never taught us the sort of strict ethics that characterise Christianity. Rather, there existed in Japan a sort of social ethic based on the family in which ancestors were a focal point. The departure of the family system, and its reverence for ancestors, has led to the emergence of a society based on egoism.
>
> A void ensues: and people turn not to spiritual but material things in their search for the meaning of happiness. I still remember what many people in their twenties would say if you asked them what happiness meant: 'A car, a TV, a washing machine, just like the Americans.' The lives of the Americans in occupied Japan were for young Japanese a symbol of happiness beyond their reach . . .

Even the right-wing politician, Shintaro Ishihara, shows a romantic repugnance at the relentless crushing of the individual under Japan's corporate culture. He notes, with unusual thoughtfulness, that 'the poor quality of life of individual Japanese employees' is chiefly responsible for 'Japan's insatiable economic expansion'. He goes on:

> What to Westerners looks like corporate voracity actually is collective avarice to compensate for individual spiritual poverty. Workaholic behaviour is a symptom, not a cause. Enhancing the individual's life would end this sublimation, this attempt to find personal satisfaction through the corporation's success and higher profits.
>
> It should also bring a new maturity to our society. As a people, Japanese have developed a very sophisticated spiritual culture – the tea ceremony, Noh, Zen and the martial arts, to mention a few aspects. However, frustrated by the gulf between this metaphysical dimension and their mundane, uninspired daily lives, Japanese put

their energy into accomplishing corporate objectives . . . We are now at an historic turning point. We must shift from the enrichment of the corporation to the fulfillment of the individual. This will take innovative thinking about everything from politics to lifestyles.

But in spite of some aspects of Japanese society in which the controlling groups display remarkable permissiveness, the underlying ethos remains, by comparison not just with other industrialized societies but any the world over, astonishingly, outstandingly, overwhelmingly conformist and conservative. Opinion polls suggest that young Japanese are critical of the materialist ambitions of their parents; many reject the huge burdens of moral indebtedness thrust upon them by traditional culture. Japan has a thoroughgoing and engaging anti-establishment and nonconformist movement among the young, although many who reject the embrace of the system end up by espousing the equally rigid and unimaginative prescriptions of the Marxist left. Yet the ethic in most companies and in public life is much the same as it always was.

There is, of course, one key difference between the pre-war and post-war periods. There is an opposition. It existed before the war, but was ruthlessly suppressed. Today it exists in the form of a middle-class intelligentsia, plus a rather larger traditionalist socialist movement which is gradually getting its act together after decades of failure. That opposition, famously, was able to mobilize ordinary Japanese in the most serious clash of the country's post-war history, against the Kishi government's attempt to rewrite the limits on Japanese militarism. Hatred of the latter is still enough to prevent the perennial ruling class making any overt attempt to reassert Japanese nationalism.

The 1960s explosion has for thirty years prevented Japan's ruling elite from acting as it would have wanted to. But there can be no doubt that the elite, while divided between those who favour assertion and those who favour caution, with the former slowly increasing their influence, remain committed to the basic tenets of traditional Japanese control and thought: nationalism, racial superiority, authoritarianism, hierarchy, state direction, filial piety, master over servant.

Nobody who travels to Japan can conclude otherwise. The sex comics, love hotels, the proliferation of pinball and computer game parlours, the very occasional displays of eccentricity and exuberance in such areas as fashion and the arts, are but safety valves. To the first-time visitor to Tokyo the most striking feature is the armies of expressionless men and women in identical clothes – 'soldiers in suits', or, as they dubbed themselves, 'salarymen'. The ethos of hierarchy – child to father, pupil to teacher, employee to boss, manager to firm, firm to *keiretsu*, *keiretsu* to the state – is still the norm.

The real clash in Japanese politics is between the moderates and nationalists in the Liberal Democratic Party. If the hold of the traditional bosses in the party is broken, it may not be modern-minded reformists who reap the benefit, but the fearsome Japanese right, a sobering thought for those who decry the system's current inertia and corruption. There are trade unions, but they count for nothing. There is a relatively free press, but it exercises discretion in attacking the system as such or in suggesting that there is an alternative. Younger people who do not share the attitudes and prejudices of their elders are ready to criticize the system, but in practice they can only advance in life if they show the proper respect and obedience.

The system shows little sign of easing up under the pressure of modern conditions. If anything, with Japan's economic success, it is becoming more self-confident, more assertive, less ready to accommodate criticism nationally or internally. As memories of the last war fade, the younger generation increasingly in control sees less and less reason for the subtle policies of self-restraint put into practice by their elders that fuelled Japan's post-war renaissance. This significantly increases the prospects of confrontation, both at home and abroad. Japaneseness is, if anything, on the increase among those that run society, if not among ordinary people.

One observer, the journalist Bill Emmott, in his thoughtful exposition *The Sun Also Rises*, argues with passion that the Japanese are no different from anyone else, and that all the same brakes on growth – the desire of people to have higher living standards, a better quality of life, the ageing of the population – will appear and eventually reunite Japan with the slower economies. His analysis underplays the underlying authoritarianism of the system. However normal ordinary Japanese might be, the system is quite different, and much less responsive to the people, than those of the major Western democracies. Ordinary Japanese, because of their historical condition and systematic conditioning at home, school and work, are more submissive than the people of any other society in the world, let alone those in a developed society.

The remarkable difference between Japanese society and, say, a conventionally authoritarian one is that the system in Japan functions in a climate that, to most outside observers, appears free. Where ordinary people under tyrannical governments mutter imprecations as they are compelled to conform, the Japanese accept conformity without the state needing to resort to external sanction. The underlying ethos, educational system and authoritarianism in the workplace do the job of the secret police, the strike-breakers and the men with guns in other societies.

In the final chapters of this book, it is appropriate to turn back to the very foundation of that society, the institution of the emperor, the issue of Japanese war guilt, the question of how much Japanese society has changed since the war and the 'Hiroshima complex', and then draw some conclusions about the future. It will be seen that the unique status of the emperor is rising steadily; that Japanese responsibility for the Pacific War is accepted even less than before; that the system of social organization has become steadily less responsive to the Japanese people since MacArthur's departure; and that the 'Hiroshima complex' is more dominant than ever. Each of these four trends is profoundly disturbing in the country that is already the world's second economic superpower and may soon become the first, towing military and political dominance in its wake.

31

RETURN OF THE GOD-EMPEROR

THE ROLE of the emperor in the Japanese system became shrouded in mystery after he had renounced his divinity in 1946. As we have seen, this renunciation was, in fact, deeply qualified. Hirohito himself insisted upon a measure of political accountability in his late forties, selling himself to the people in a series of tours reminiscent in form, if not style, of an American presidential candidate. After MacArthur's departure, Hirohito formally reasserted the supremacy of the Japanese state and once more gently floated 'above the clouds'. As he aged, his appearance became more dignified and reserved, in keeping with his shy, repressed character. He still travelled a little, performed the traditional rice-growing ceremonies, appeared at the imperial poetry-reading, and constantly attended official functions.

Hirohito's son, Crown Prince Akihito, married Michiko, a 'commoner', that is to say, the daughter of an extremely wealthy member of Japan's business elite, as if to symbolize the new alliance between the imperial household and the business–bureaucratic class now in control of Japan, which was bourgeois by comparison with the old aristocratic elites. The marriage raised some eyebrows within the imperial household, but is not believed to have been opposed by the emperor; indeed, it was less controversial than that of Hirohito himself. But it was frequently rumoured that Empress Nagayo disapproved and made Princess Michiko's early life at court almost intolerable.

However, the tradition of the upper classes in Japan marrying beneath them in order to restore their finances is an old one; and the imperial family felt deeply exposed financially after the occupation. The impression was now assiduously given that the emperor had become a formal constitutional monarch or, even less, merely a 'symbol' of the state, as prescribed in the constitution. Nothing could have been further from the reality. In fact, Hirohito's role during the more than three and a half decades since the end of the occupation had changed significantly, but not decisively, from that exercised before the war. He no longer formally presided over the cabinet. He was no longer the object of a religious and propaganda cult. He was no longer a living god, in the perversion of the militarist-*zaibatsu* clique in the 1930s – although he remained 'divine' in many respects.

Instead, he reverted to the role performed by the Meiji emperor as the public expression of Japan's national unity, a monarch with considerable influence in matters of state, although unable to override his cabinet. This influence was exercised primarily through a series of informal contacts with the heads of Japan's power centres, the bureaucracy, the *zaibatsu* and the politicians, as well as the military, although the furore over his continued meetings with his chiefs of staff caused this connection to be stopped in the late 1940s.

He remained a high priest who still stood at the apex of Japanese Shintoism, as well as personifying Japan's superiority over other nations. He did not govern, because that was never his function. But it was far from true that the apex of Japan's authoritarianism and hierarchical social system lacked real power, either. With age, his authority over the inevitably younger politicians, bureaucrats and business chiefs grew steadily. By the time of Hirohito's death in 1989, schools, scholars and officials openly acknowledged that he possessed the same mantle of authority as the Meiji emperor.

This became apparent in a series of interviews given by senior court officials at the time of Akihito's accession and coronation. The writer and imperial authority Shichehei Yamamoto does not even mention the post-1945 constitution as in any way affecting the emperor's role: for him the formative era of the modern imperial constitution is the Meiji Restoration. The emperor had two functions under this system: to act as a Shinto priest, and to preside over the general council of state and affix his seal to imperial decisions. It is not clear whether this function does, or does not, continue to be carried out in private.

So exalted was the emperor's status in Meiji times that the Imperial House law was quite separate from the Japanese constitution, evoking the question, in Yamamoto's view,

Are the emperor and his family really Japanese? . . . This calls for a little explanation. According to Japanese law, all citizens are required to have their names and abodes officially registered with the authorities. However, the Emperor and the members of the Imperial Family lack both a family name and a family register. For that reason, when Empress Michiko married the then Crown Prince, her name was crossed off her family register.

The situation was much the same in 1615. In that era the names of all Japanese were included in census and tax registers.

All Japanese, that is, except those governed by the 'Rules for the Palace and the Court'.

Yamamoto spells out that this applies just the same for the present imperial family as for the Meiji emperor.

The implications are considerable. If the Japanese court and the Imperial House Law are detached from Japanese law altogether, indeed are laws unto themselves, the power of the emperor is in no way affected by the revision of the constitution enacted by Mac-Arthur. The monarch is not subject to the constitution. His authority does not derive from it. One might have suspected this to be the case, but here it is spelt out by a leading court authority. For Yamamoto the question of whether the emperor is a living god is a tiresome irrelevance: he is godlike in that he is superior to other people, not that he is a transcendental being capable of performing miracles. In about 1937, says Yamamoto, the idea that the emperor was a god became more widespread, but it was always false and on 1 January 1946 the emperor did not renounce his divinity because he had no need to:

The so-called 'declaration' issued on January 1, 1946, is really a misnomer. Actually, there is some mention of this matter at the end of the Emperor's speech in question, but it is devoted primarily to the argument that Japan needs to reaffirm Emperor Meiji's Five-Article Charter Oath, which was the starting point for Japan's modernisation. These so-called 'five principles' enunciated by Emperor Meiji called for public discussion on matters affecting the future of Japan and an opening up of the country to the outside world so that it could acquire valuable knowledge from everywhere. All that Emperor Showa did was to reaffirm that these five principles were the starting point from which Japan had to begin that recovery.

Then at the tail end of the message, the Emperor touched upon his relations with his subjects, saying that they should be based upon these five principles of Emperor Meiji. He added that they should not be predicated upon the false belief spread by some people during the war that he was a 'living god'. That was all he said. So this message was really only the Imperial new year's edict for 1946 and should never have been construed as a 'declaration of humanity'. Nevertheless, that is exactly how it came to be viewed, and it became famous for that reason.

There can be no doubt that Yamamoto was representing the view of the imperial household and the government on this issue. Thus another one of MacArthur's reforms was consigned to the dustbin of history.

The difference between the Japanese monarchy and the goldfish-bowl style of monarchies such as the British, where popularity is even courted and much of the mystique has been lost in an effort to establish its role in a democratic society, is all too apparent. For Yamamoto, the emperor is still 'very close' to all Japanese; his office is shrouded in secrecy; he is a priest-king; he is not bound by the constitution, MacArthur's or anybody else's; and his role and powers are broadly the same of those of the Meiji emperor at the beginning of the century.

On Akihito's accession, in a country where the written letter of the law is not very important, the authorities made a clear attempt to reassemble a legal basis for the Daijosai, the rite of offering the New Rice, which to all outward appearances clearly violates MacArthur's constitutional prohibition on the separation of church and state. The reasoning invoked by a top legal expert, Kinyo Sato, was comical in its tortuousness and complexity. Sato considered the imperial institution 'a wise and intelligent political system' in which the emperor acts as a 'kind of priest-king . . . praying for peace, safety and happiness'.

He went on to argue that, in effect, as Shinto was now defined as not being an organized religion, it was impossible to prohibit celebration of its rites on state occasions. This extraordinary argument in effect nullified the consitutional prohibition on mixing Shinto with the state, and harked back to the spurious old Meiji argument that Shinto is superior to mere religion, and hence was exempt from any restrictions on religion. Sato continued:

The Japanese way of thinking about the material world is heavily influenced by Shinto; it pervades Japanese culture. I will not deny that the Daijosai is connected to the very simple, unsophisticated reverence the Japanese people harbour for their nature and core religious feelings. But that does not have any connection to any organised religion. Article 89 deals with public expenditure for the activities of religious institutions and organisations. So it has nothing to do with the Daijosai.

By this sleight-of-hand, Shintoism escaped the ban on religion in matters of state expressly inserted by MacArthur against Shintoism, because the latter is not a religion! Even Sato was forced to admit, however, that 'some people claim that by participating in the [Daijosai] ceremony, the Emperor will acquire a divine character', although he does not accept the thesis.

Significantly, Noburo Ishihara, the then deputy chief cabinet secretary and a very senior official, offered no view as to whether, as a result of the Daijosai, the emperor acquired a divine nature: 'I am aware that there were some scholars in the pre-war period who claimed that through performance of the Daijosai the Emperor assumed a divine nature. However, the government is not in a position to make any comment as to whether the Emperor does or does not acquire such a divine nature'! He too tried to square an almost impossible circle as to whether the Daijosai represented a blending of Shinto and the state:

> in regard to the character of the Daijosai and how expenditures for it are to be handled, it is hard for anyone to deny that the ceremony appears to have the character of a religious ritual and that, moreover, it is a ritual of such a nature as to preclude the government from having any say about its contents.
> ... It is a traditional ceremony of the imperial house, which is always carried out after a new succession to the throne has happened. And since this is a traditional ceremony carried out by the imperial house, you cannot deny the fact that certain forms involved are coloured by Imperial House Shintoism. You cannot avoid having some Shinto influence on the proceedings. But precisely because of this element of Imperial House Shintoism in the conduct of the Daijosai, the question was raised as to whether it

was proper for the Daijosai to be considered an act in matters of state. And the government decided that it should not be. It will be conducted as an event of the Imperial House, in connection with the succession to the imperial throne.

This was another sleight-of-hand: the Daijosai was acceptable because it was a purely private imperial matter and nothing to do with the governance of Japan; thus church could not be impinging on state, because this was not a matter of state. Ishihara acknowledges that this view was not shared by many Japanese scholars.

In the view of the eminent historian Noboru Kajima, Hirohito derived his authority not from divinity, but out of his detachment and sense of judgement:

> the Emperor is a very learned, well-educated, intelligent person with wide knowledge and very well thought-out views. So, the opinions of the Emperor would have been very useful for rectifying the one-sided views of the military on the one hand and the civil authorities on the other.

In addition, his straightforward character, so entirely missing among his forebears, inspired respect:

> The Emperor, in the eyes of the Japanese public, is a very serious person. He will do his best whatever he undertakes. He is a very sincere person. It became clear to everyone that there is no scandal involving the Imperial Household or the Emperor. He is not interested in making money; and he doesn't go out drinking and become wild at night. He is dedicated to his duties of state, and he is a very serious student of his discipline, and maybe the only hobby that he ever allowed himself is to go and watch sumo.

Another prominent authority, Professor Mazakusu Yamazaki, saw the emperor's mystique as deriving from his position as a kind of aesthetic pinnacle (which may be close to the truth, one suspects):

> Ever since the 10th century, political rulers in this country were very obedient to a certain form of cultural authority even though unconnected with the Emperor. In other words, they knew that they could not rule this country simply by military power and economic might.

Many saints and writings attest to the fact that the Shogun's warriors as well as the aristocrats of old times were very eager to have this ability to compose poems, to play musical instruments, and to be able to appreciate paintings.

. . . In the medieval age, there are many stories that show us that the warriors had laid much emphasis on cultural matters. For instance, to be able to participate in the tea ceremony was considered to be a tremendous virtue. Sometimes, a lord or warrior traded his castle for a fine piece of tea ceremony equipment and had his life spared because he possessed such a piece. Kyoto, with its long cultural tradition, became the centre of cultural life: and anyone who wanted political power had to be a member of the 'Kyoto set'.

In other words, it was required of Japanese rulers to share aesthetic and cultural values: otherwise they were not recognised as legitimate rulers. Since the Emperor is the ultimate symbol of these cultural and aesthetic values, no ruler has ever thought of ousting the Emperor.

Astonishingly, neither authority believes that the emperor's role has really changed in hundreds of years. As far as authority is concerned, asserts Kajima, the present Emperor [Akihito] is the same case as previous emperors. 'Yamazaki asserts: As to the function of the emperor, the political meaning or the political function of the emperor as a person, I think, in substance has not changed, comparing the pre-war period with the post-war period. However, the forces that used the emperor system have changed.

I do not deny that the military used the Emperor in the pre-war period. But what was the social standing or social support of the military at the time? In any country the far right groups are supported by, one, social poverty; and, two, by the prevailing international situation of the time.'

Thus we have it: these are not eccentric voices from the far right, but mainstream spokesmen on imperial matters paraded before the foreign press. The emperor's role is no different to what it was: the emperor was used, and could be used again. MacArthur's constitution, in this key respect, may as well never have been enacted. The emperor's personal authority, while not enshrined in the constitution, remains considerable. The post-war managers of Japanese society, but not necessarily ordinary Japanese, respect him as they always did. He is enshrouded in secrecy, deference and formality to a degree unthinkable in any other of the very few major industrial democracies that retain a monarchy. In Asia, with the exception of a handful of Pacific potentates and the figurehead monarchs of Malaysia and Thailand, Japan's emperor stood alone as a remote figure of awesome respect; there are few concessions to the Western notion of popular monarchy – riding bicycles, permitting intimate television documentaries.

He is still treated with astonishing deference. Hanehisa Hoshino, one of Japan's best-known broadcasters, says ingratiatingly:

> I like the Emperor. There is nothing that I can find which is negative. There is also nothing about the Crown Prince which I don't like. I like the Crown Prince, because I think he has learned a lot from his father. And as long as the Crown Prince believes that the Imperial Family can only exist while the people of Japan welcome it, and as long as we want it to be that way, I will continued to like him.

It is hard to imagine a major television commentator in any other country saying such a thing about the monarch.

The emperor remained the prisoner of convention to a degree which even Western monarchs would recoil from. Yamazaki recounts:

> A bit before the Emperor visited the United States, I had an opportunity to give a briefing to the Emperor on the society of the United States. The meeting took place in a very simple room in the Palace. As I was sitting opposite the Emperor talking, the Emperor listened closely to what I had to say. And as he was listening to me, his knees started to open a bit. I glanced at his knees; he looked very ashamed and he looked very shy.
>
> By this I would like to say that the present Emperor has this personality which feels – that he himself felt a bit bashful or ashamed when he opened his knees in front of a university professor.

Thus Japan's official spokesmen at the time of the transition between emperors appeared both to approve the remarriage between Shintoism and state, and the notion of a 'divine' emperor. In this respect, as Japan travelled forward to the age of ultra-modern technology, it appeared to be travelling backwards from the concept of emasculated constitutional monarch to the concept of god-priest-king.

Indeed, MacArthur's attempts to separate state from church, and the emperor from religion, have been quite steadily unravelled over time. In 1953 the Ise shrine was rebuilt according to tradition and two years later the Imperial Institute for the Study of the Ise Shrine, which had been banned, was revived. In 1960 Prime Minister Ikeda said that the sacred mirror and shrine were important for the state.

A Shinto historian argued that 'the Ikeda cabinet confirmed, without any qualification, the principle of *kokutai* according to which the sacred mirror is transferred, by divine mediation, from father to son in the imperial line. The mirror is tied inseparably to the fate of the Emperor's throne. This recognition of the truth of this dogma removed all obstacles standing in the way of the further development of *kokutal'* – the essence of the nation, Japanese patriotic spirit prior to 1945, no less.

In 1966 the holiday celebrating the foundation of the imperial line by Emperor Jimmu was reinstated. In 1972 there were petitions at Ise for the reinstatement of the ceremony based round the imperial jewel and sword – the *kenjinogodoza* – arguing that 'the Emperor remains in the end a divine being and the court ceremony of the *kenjinogodoza* bears unmistakable witness to the divinity of His Majesty'. The following year the ceremony, banned by SCAP, was reinstated. The return of the Daijosai completes the process of restoring the emperor to his divinity.

For the extreme Japanese right, the 200,000-strong Uyoku, with its officially tolerated roving armoured cars and loudspeaker vans run by the All Japan Council of Patriotic Organizations (*Zen Ai Kaigi*), the restoration of the emperor to his pre-war status is the prime objective. Even as cosmopolitan a man as Shigeru Yoshida argued that 'under the new constitution the Emperor's position as that of symbol of the state and unity of the people accords with the traditional faith which has been held by the Japanese nation since the foundation of Japan. It is truly a high and lofty position. Moreoever, it is undeniable that the Emperor is ethnically the centre of national veneration.'

The level of support for the imperial system in Japan is staggering compared to that which exists for constitutional monarchies elsewhere. In January 1989 82 per cent of those polled by the Yomiuri Shimbun said the imperial system should stay as it is, 10 per cent more than three years before. Nearly 9 per cent believed it should be strengthened; only 5 per cent believed it should be abolished.

The increase in popularity of the institution may be linked to Akihito's obvious approachability. Although like his father, his hobby is a remarkably inaccessible one – he is a world authority on the taxonomic study of gobiid fishes – he also loves tennis, and is a committed naturalist. He immediately won hearts by declaring that he would be the first emperor not to bring up his children apart from their parents. As a boy he said, 'When I marry, I will live with my children, no matter what.'

Akihito met Michiko Shoda on the tennis courts. She was a 'commoner', the daugher of a leading industrialist, educated at the Sacred Heart, a Catholic girls' school. By all accounts her early married life was miserable, under fire from palace gossips for telling her children Bible stories, breast-feeding, wearing the wrong clothes and behaving in altogether too 'glamorous' a manner. She was hospitalized for four months after suffering 'great mental strain', as the palace admitted, and an abortion. Thin, shy, with a perpetually worried expression, she has captured a place in Japanese hearts.

Akihito permitted his sons, Crown Prince Naruhito and his younger brother Fumihito, to study at Oxford. By all accounts, Naruhito is an outgoing, athletic type, Fumihito more intellectual, and their younger sister, Princess Sayako, strong-willed and lively, bravely taking on minor roles as an actress. After Naruhito announced that he wished to be married by the age of thirty, there was much press speculation when this failed to happen: it was suggested that he was finding it almost impossible to secure a bride who would be prepared to put up with the agonies of life as an imperial consort.

The breakthrough came in 1992, when the twenty-nine-year-old Masako Owada agreed to marry Naruhito. She had experience as a young high-flier in the Foreign Office, and in public refused to employ the girlish falsetto which most Japanese women affect and showed no hesitation in speaking, unlike Empress Michiko. She admitted at her first public appearance, 'When I met him for the second time I enjoyed our conversation. But I knew his feelings towards me by then and, to be honest, I had mixed feelings.' Humanity seemed to have crept into the imperial institution.

Akihito's American tutor, Elizabeth Gray Vining, after describing his plight in his early teens, shaped by the privations of the occupation, concludes:

What he is not may in some ways be as important as what he is. The lack of initiative that troubled me when I first knew him, he has to a considerable degree overcome. With his great natural dignity is combined a shyness which sometimes seems like hauteur; and the ability to suffer fools gladly, which is so great an asset to any public figure, is apparently missing. The charm which is his when he makes an effort to please will bring him friends and also expose him to the resentment of those for whom it is not manifested. On the other hand, he is not facile, and he is not a fanatic, not a person of easy agreements for social purposes or of sudden enthusiasms and coolings.

He gives his faith slowly, but once he has given it he is steadfast. He is honest, with himself and with others. He has a better than average mind, clear, analytical, independent, with a turn of original thought. He has a strong sense of responsibility and a deep love of Japan and her people. He is aware of his destiny and he accepts it soberly. Cautious and deliberate, he has the true conservative's ability upon occasion to break radically with tradition. He has a sense of humour, that invaluable balance wheel and safety valve, and he has that quality without which there can be no true greatness: compassion. One of his friends wrote to me – and it is unusual for one 16-year-old to see it in another 16-year-old – 'He knows pity'.

Whatever Emperor Akihito's current virtues and status, they have nothing to do with modern monarchy as it still exists in countries like Britain, Holland and Sweden.

32

NOT SO SORRY

THE INCREASINGLY mystical and detached nature of the emperor system is not the only aspect in which Japanese society appears to be travelling backwards, permitting only acceptable social change and reverting to pre-war attitudes. Nationalism has been enjoying a steady resurgence, partly inculcated through the schools, partly through the unashamed views not only of former prime minister Nakasone but of prominent business leaders, and most strikingly, through the rewriting of history in respect of Japanese Pacific War guilt.

The process began when the democratic locally elected school boards were scrapped in 1956 in favour of centrally appointed boards. The curriculum was tightly controlled and morals teaching was reinstated in 1958 after the education minister argued that, 'It is necessary to hammer morality, national spirit and, to put it more clearly, patriotism into the heads of our younger generation.' In no other major industrial society could such remarks have been acceptable. SCAP's education plans, he went on, had been intended to weaken the Japanese race.

In 1966 the central council on education published its first 'Image of the Ideal Man' directive for local education authorities, which mapped out a blueprint of the ideal Japanese school education should produce. The 'Kimi Gayo', the discredited Japanese national anthem (described by one Japanese newspaper as 'expressing the prostration of the people before the feet of the living god, the emperor ... It was written to help ... the feudal class of Japan organize popular sentiments') was readopted as proper for schools in 1978 by the Ministry of Education; it was played at flag raising and lowering ceremonies.

Business too seemed in alliance with the conservative educational bureaucrats. Sazu Idekimitsu, the oil millionaire, would welcome each new recruit into his company by enjoining him to abandon all vestiges of 'the new-found education alien to the Japanese spirit'. In 1971 he published his bestseller *Be a True Japanese*, which stated bluntly that the educational reforms of the occupation were designed to 'pull down the dignity of the teacher', while 'the labour laws were intended to destroy mutual trust and assurance' between men and their bosses, and the constitution was drawn up to 'sever the bond of mutual trust between the Imperial family and the people'. He went on:

A Japanese has traditional Japanese blood pulsating in his veins which cannot be replaced by anything alien. It is a pure blood inherited from his ancestors, made thicker and thicker by several thousand years of peaceful co-existence. It is the blood of mutual trust which binds the people to the Imperial Family ... and therefore Japan is entirely different from nations ruled by force ... A nation based on infinite trust in the Tenno [emperor] who transcends all concepts of might and right may be said to be unparalleled in the world ... spring is coming and nothing can hold back the sprouting of young leaves.

By 1989 the orthodoxy of the increasingly influential conservative–business alliance was successfully summed up in a short bestseller *The Japan That Can Say No*, which took a sternly critical view of the tameness of post-war Japanese policy in relation to the outside world. The joint authors were Shintaro Ishihara, a prominent novelist and well-known Diet member who had inherited the mantle of nationalist leader in the LDP from Nakasone but lacked the latter's adaptability, and thus seemed unlikely ever to become prime minister; and the boss of Sony, Akio Morita, whose business abilities commanded a huge popular following, although as a self-made man he was outside the inner circle of Japan's top *keiretsu*.

The book is from the outset contemptuous of the Americans as *arriviste*, 'with their scant few centuries of history', deeply racist to boot, and in decline: 'Technology gives rise to civilization, upon which, in time, culture thrives. Nations decline when they self-indulgently let life-styles become more important than workmanship and neglect their industrial and technological base. That is the lesson of history.'

For Ishihara, the American presence in Japan is self-serving:

The numerous US bases in Japan enable Washington to project
military power from the West Coast to Capetown. They are more
important to US global strategy than to the defence of Japan . . .
Thus it is very strange indeed that our military budget includes a
multibillion dollar category to pay much of the cost of keeping US
forces here. From the standpoint of which country benefits from
the bases, Japan would be well justified in collecting user fees.

Ishihara goes on to look at Japanese–American relations in crude
terms. When an American politician suggests to him that the two
countries are married to each other, Ishihara retorts, 'Well, if we are
properly married, okay . . . a wife can talk back to her husband. But
a kept woman, afraid the man will kick her out, always has to do
what he says. Don't ever think Japan is America's mistress.'

The book is suffused with a resentment towards American
'racialism' that appears quite purblind when contrasted with Japan's
own much-vaunted notions of racial superiority. Ishihara acknowledges that 'although the Japanese were the only non-white people to
avoid western domination, it is not surprising that Europeans and
Americans look down on us too'. Western racism, he says, derives
in part from the class prejudice that characterizes their societies.

While there is some truth in his remarks about the West, the
undertone is disturbingly national socialist; it is unusual for so
committed a rightwinger to take pride in the socialism and equality
within his country, although this draws on a long-standing tradition
of the Japanese right. Nor does Japan qualify as an egalitarian
country, although it certainly has a meritocratic ethos for the bottom
four-fifths of society.

Ishihara finishes his book by cheekily offering the Americans a
118-point plan for national recovery, some of it sound good sense.
Subsequently, both Ishihara's rhetoric and prominence have sharply
increased. In July 1991 he argued in a magazine article that 'there is
nothing more pitiful than to have the capacity to assert our views as
a nation, but to be unable to do that'. Japan, he said, 'needs to have
its own global ideas and we should prepare them without consulting
the United States all the time'.

He went on to say that East Asia, two-thirds of whose output is
accounted for by Japan, is already something of a *keiretsu*, a series
of subsidiaries clustered around one big company. 'Japan', he
argued, 'is now qualified to revive its global idea, the Greater East
Asia Co-Prosperity Sphere, which had no chance before the war.'
Arrogantly, he continued that Japan had no need of military power

to enforce its will in Southeast Asia. If other Asian countries proved unco-operative, 'we can cut off the flow of technology'. This kind of rhetoric would once have brought frowns of disapproval from senior LDP bosses; but a few weeks later, former Prime Minister Noboru Takeshita appeared alongside Ishihara at a major gathering of nearly 3000 party faithful.

The third aspect in which Japanese society is drifting steadily to the right is, of course, the censoring of school textbooks and the rewriting of the history of the war. The attempt has been quite systematic, in spite of a considerable outcry from Asian countries; and there can be no doubt that it is entirely intentional. The examples are endless. *High School Japanese History*, published in 1991 as a general textbook, observes blandly of the Pacific War that, 'The war, which lasted 15 years, took about 3 million Japanese lives and severely damaged Asian nations. It ended with the defeat and collapse of the Japanese empire.' This is considered a fairly liberal text, but it fails to mention casualties on the other side, which were perhaps five times as great.

A New Comprehensive Japanese History, published in 1991, says of the Rape of Nanking, 'Towards the end of 1937, Japan occupied the [Chinese] capital, Nanking.' In a footnote, it adds: 'After the war the episode became a major issue in the Tokyo trials.' The text goes on: 'Since the Nationalist forces withdrew to Wuhan and further inland to Chonguing and continued their resistance, the Japanese government's attempts to negotiate a peace failed, and the likelihood of protracted war increased.' Thus was the war's most bestial reported massacre reduced to footnote status. In another textbook, published the same year, the Ministry of Education insisted that a passage which said 'over 70,000 people were reportedly killed by the Japanese imperial army at Nanking' be amended to a 'large number of Chinese people were killed'.

The Nanking incident remains a particularly controversial topic in Japan. Ishihara is one of a large number of Japanese who do not believe that the massacre took place on anything like the scale supposed: he suggests that the Chinese fabricated 'the concept that the Japanese slaughtered 300,000 people . . . only 200,000 people were left in the city. I don't deny that the Nanking incident occurred or that we did wrong things, but to kill 300,000 in a week is impossible.' Ishihara guesses that the true total was more like 20,000.

The left-wing historian Saburo Ienaga fought a twenty-year campaign against the constitutionality of the ministry's censorship of textbooks. Ienaga had reason to object: the meaning of whole passages of his books were completely reversed. In the first version of *The New History of Japan*, he wrote, 'The war was beautified as a "holy war", and since the Japanese army's defeats and atrocities were covered up, the people were placed in a position where, not knowing the real facts, they had no choice but to co-operate in the meaningless war.' The ministry rewrote this as, 'That the war was beautified and the atrocities occurred are, unfortunately, facts . . . Nowadays, it is accepted as common sense that the "just war" was meaningless.'

In the final version this read, 'Some atrocities took place, but they were not limited to our army. In addition an extremely complex process led to this war. To categorize it sweepingly as "meaningless" creates problems.' Ienaga was accused by the ministry of failing adequately 'to recognize the efforts of Japanese ancestors, of failing to heighten awareness of what it is to be Japanese and failing to foster affection of Japan.' The ministry also objected to the Ienaga view that the mythology surrounding the origin of Emperor Jimmu had been fabricated to justify imperial rule.

In 1984 Ienaga won a partial victory in court. But the bowdlerization went on. In 1956 a textbook denouncing the Manchurian incident, for example, ran, 'In order to find a way out of these acute domestic problems, Japan tried to monopolize Manchuria as an outlet for Japanese goods . . . The Japanese army started the war in Mukden and established Manchukuo the next year.' Eight years later the passage had been amended to, 'In 1931, due to an explosion on the railway line near Mukden, the Japanese army began fighting the Chinese army.' There was no suggestion of the undisputed historical fact that the bomb was planted by the Japanese to legitimize their immediate and massive invasion of Manchuria. The Ministry of Education has issued guidelines suggesting that, when discussing alleged Japanese atrocities, writers should use the phrases 'abnormal circumstances' or 'the full truth having not yet been determined'.

Occasionally, senior Japanese have let slip the view that the war was not wrong; the education minister in 1953, Seigo Okana, affirmed that 'I do not wish to pass judgment on the rightness or wrongness of the Greater East Asian War, but the fact that Japan took on so many opponents and fought them for four years . . . proves our superiority.' A prominent post-war critic, Jun Eto, argued that Japan's surrender had been conditional, based on the Potsdam Declaration. A historian, Takanori Irie, suggested that the constitution had been drafted by a Jew (Charles Kades), and was intended to destroy Japan as a nation. The 1930s and the 1940s are only barely touched upon in schools, and the occupation period not at all. Nakasone once argued that, 'It is considered progressive to criticize pre-war Japan for its faults and defects but I firmly oppose such a notion. A nation is still a nation whether it wins or loses a war.'

In Japanese popular culture, particularly films, Japan is always cast as the victim of the war, with Hiroshima and Nagasaki inevitably portrayed along with the Tokyo firebombs, while no mention is made of Japanese atrocities. The phenomally successful film *The Great Japanese Empire* dwells upon the horrors inflicted upon Japan: in one scene an American GI and his girlfriend play ball using the head of a Japanese soldier. The film stresses the heroism of the kamikaze pilots, the falseness of the Tokyo trials, and the brutality inflicted by the GIs after the war. Japan is defined as the victim of vastly superior forces: the American retaking of Guam, for example, is portrayed as 'one hundred cats attacking a small mouse'.

With the exception of a handful of academics, the Japanese left has continued to propagate this image and to stress the enormous suffering caused by war as such – in particular at Hiroshima and Nagasaki – as an argument against Japanese militarism. For most modern Japanese the conflict which remains such a painful memory to its survivors is a very distant one in which the issues were blurred and Japan was more sinned against than sinning. This is in striking contrast with the views advanced inside West Germany since the war.

The importance that the elites attach to the practice of rewriting history is exemplified by Japan's constant refusal to apologize for its aggressive wars in Asia, that is until the advent of a precarious opposition government in 1993. Again, this was no minor matter of historical interest to the establishment: it was part and parcel of their beliefs, and of most Japanese educated on doctored textbooks, that the country was not principally to blame for the Pacific War. Indeed, their view of Japan's swathe of destruction through China, the rape of Southeast Asia, the enslavement of Malaya, the crushing of Indonesia and the decision to attack Pearl Harbor is, why not? in view of the economic self-interest that would have been served at comparatively low cost. Japan's assertion that it feared claims for reparations if it apologized was a weak one: Japan had no intention of paying such claims, and could not be forced to do so, so an apology would have made no difference.

An apology would at a stroke have removed the prime bone of contention between Japan and its neighbours, created economic goodwill and done much to dispel lingering fears about Japan's intentions towards Asia. It would have shown Asia that Japan really had changed, that it was not afraid to accept that it did wrong in the past, and was therefore unlikely to take the same course again.

The reason why the LDP did not apologize – could not apologize – was not just out of deference to its far-right fringe: it was because it did not accept that it was in the wrong. Even Hirohito, in his first conversation with MacArthur in 1945, suggested that Japan was not to blame for starting the war. To this day, the establishment believes not that it was wrong of Japan to start the war – it had no other choice – but that it was wrong that Japan lost it. (A sizeable minority believe the army was to blame for placing Japan on the slope to war.) It is impossible to expect a country to apologize for starting a just war they feel they should have won.

Consider the way the word sorry seems to stick in the LDP's throat every time it geared itself up to utter it. The closest to an apology came in 1991 from the Japanese prime minister, Toshiki Kaifu. To the Dutch he expressed 'sincere contrition' for the 'unbelievable sufferings and sorrow inflicted on Dutch nationals in Indonesia in between 1941 and 1945 . . . The scars in their hearts do not heal easily,' he acknowledged. In Singapore he said it was necessary 'for all Japanese to be deeply conscious of what Japan did in the past and have a full and accurate grasp of history'.

Kaifu asserted to the author that these statements had settled the matter and amounted to 'a full apology'. Others do not agree, pointing to the vagueness of the language, the brevity of the sentiment, and the fact that there was no apology for the decision to go to war. Kaifu, moreoever, was one of Japan's few reformist leaders, not from the political mainstream.

Singapore's leader, Lee Kuan Yew, was to the point in response. Japan, unlike Germany, he said, had not faced up to its wartime guilt. 'There has been a catharsis in Germany. They've got rid of their sense of guilt, no longer trying to hide their past.' In Japan the issue was 'still very much a closet problem. There has been no catharsis.' Lee was downright offensive about Southeast Asia's attitude to Japan's sending peace-keeping troops to Cambodia, saying he did not accept the need for any.

The Asians, he suggested, were even unhappy about the Japanese decision to send a small group of naval vessels to the Gulf. Japanese peace-keeping was wrong, he argued, because it was 'like giving liqueur chocolates to an alcoholic. Whatever they do, they go to its limits.' He also argued that the Japanese did not 'educate its young people about the war'. If the Japanese are forced to 'take the military road, they will come out again and this time, because it is a nuclear world, it will lead to the destruction of everything'.

On the fiftieth anniversary of Pearl Harbor on 6 December 1991, an attempt by the foreign minister, Michio Watanabe, to say that 'Japan was deeply remorseful at these past acts', which sounded almost like an apology, was quickly downplayed by using the word *hansei* in the Japanese language version, which means 'deeply reflects'. Watanabe expressed 'sincere condolences' to the victims. 'Japan, for its part, should face squarely the historical fact that the Pacific War, which inflicted unbelievable suffering and sorrow on many peoples in the Asia-Pacific region, was started fifty years ago with Japan's surprise attack on Pearl Habor.'

Watanabe sounded sincere: however, parliament refused to pass an anti-war resolution prepared by the Foreign Office on the subject. 'Why must we fling mud at the history of Japan with our own hands?' asked a prominent LDP former minister. Shintaro Ishihara said, predictably, that he found it strange that Japan 'which lost the war, should apologize to the victors' . . . as though Japan had been the victim of American aggression. The chief cabinet secretary said that the government was 'in deep reflection for having caused unbelievable suffering and sorrow'. However, there were also calls by the foreign ministry's chief spokesman that America should apologize for Hiroshima and Nagasaki – which did not seem particularly appropriate on the occasion of the Pearl Harbor ceremonies.

The fiftieth anniversary of Pearl Harbor in December 1991 was marked by deep suspicion on both sides. In fact, although Japan's was a surprise attack, historians cite many occasions when, for example, the Americans staged such attacks before a formal declaration of war (among them the American strike into Mexico in 1846 before declaring war, one of five such; the French carried out 36 such attacks between 1700 and 1879, Britain 30, Austria-Hungary 12, Russia 7 and Prussia 7 according to the British historian Sir Frederick Maurice). The Pearl Harbor strategy was almost certainly based on that advocated by Britain's Hector Bywater in a book circulated in America in the 1930s when Admiral Yamamoto, the planner of Pearl Harbor, was Japanese naval attaché in Washington.

What was revealing about the anniversary was that Japan used it to issue an account that formally denied that wrongdoing was intended. A new story about Japan's famous failure to declare war was circulated. It was said that the last leaf of the fourteen-page telegram announcing hostilities was not translated until the morning of the attack because the officer in charge at the embassy was attending a farewell dinner for a departing colleague. The translation and typing was so slow that the meeting of the Japanese ambassador, Admiral Nomura, with Cordell Hull was delayed from 1.00 a.m. until 2.20, when the attack was already under way. The importance of this specious argument was that the Japanese were keen to assert that they fulfilled their legal obligation to declare war.

In a massive documentary in which ABC collaborated with NHK, the main Tokyo broadcasting station, the Japanese translation made no mention of the atrocities involved in the Rape of Nanking, although it showed the same footage as the American station. The chairman of NHK explained that between the Japanese and American teams 'there were perception gaps' about Pearl Harbor. The two sides had such differences 'that they feared they might have headed into a second Pearl Harbor'.

Japan's own television documentaries on the anniversary invariably played up 'encirclement' by the Dutch, British and American colonialists, the internment of Japanese Americans in the United States, and America's overwhelming industrial strength, and suggested that if mistakes were made, this was by the Japanese military alone. It is as though current German documentaries stressed the encirclement of Hitler by the British, French and Russians before his attack on Poland.

The emperor's formulas for 'apologizing' have been studies in opaqueness. Visiting Southeast Asia just two months before the commemoration, he expressed 'regret' about 'the unfortunate past'. On the occasion of the visit by Queen Beatrix of the Netherlands to Tokyo, he said that he was 'very sad that friendly relations should have been marred by World War II. After the war Japan resolved that it would live as a nation of peace so that it should never repeat the horrors of war.' Queen Beatrix commented acidly, 'We must not sidestep the memories of those war years.'

In October 1992 Akihito made his most sensitive trip yet, to a still-resentful China. Between 1986 and 1992, some $3.2 billion in investment has flowed from Japan, mainly into Guangdong Province and the port of Dalian. Some 200 Japanese companies are located in China. They are still forced to do deals with China's corrupt bureaucracy and are pushed into partnership with Chinese companies. The Chinese behave to them as the Japanese behave towards everyone else. The Japanese nevertheless still think the effort is worth it, although their businessmen grumble about this, as about periodic complaints that they have rekindled Chinese prostitution.

On the occasion of Akihito's visit, groups called for Japanese compensation for Chinese war victims, which the authorities untypically failed to stifle. At a banquet in Peking, Akihito spoke of the 'unfortunate period when our country brought profound suffering to the Chinese people – I deeply deplore this', according to the English language translation. According to the Chinese and Japanese versions, he expressed his 'deep sorrow', a more neutral phrase.

The emperor's visit was marred by right-wing protests in Tokyo: a smoke bomb had been thrown at the emperor beforehand by a demonstrator yelling, 'Don't go to China'. Another drove a truck laden with propane gas cylinders at the home of Prime Minister Miyazawa, while a third attempted to disembowel himself in front of the residence, all uncomfortable throwbacks to the 1930s.

A serious embarrassment occurred the same year when the prime minister, Kiichi Miyazawa, visited South Korea, just after incontrovertible evidence suggested that Japan's wartime army headquarters had officially organized the appalling brothels into which 200,000 Korean 'comfort girls' were herded, each to satisfy the lusts of ten or twelve Japanese soldiers a day; the Japanese had long denied any official involvement. Miyazawa was forced uncharacteristically to offer 'my sincerest apology' for this. In August 1992 the Japanese government formally apologized to Korea. Japan had never acknowledged its wartime medical experiments on living Chinese which, as a senior Japanese army doctor revealed in 1993, were numbered in hundreds in Shanki Province alone. Finally on 23 August Morihiro Hosokawa, atop his shaky new opposition government, expressed his government's 'profound remorse and apologized for Japanese actions', 'including aggression and colonial rule'; he referred to Japan's 'war of aggression'. Although brief, Hosokawa's statement was explicit and touched off a spate of criticism from the LDP.

Such acts of contrition are, it seems, remarkably hard to come by. No Japanese leader has made a speech like that of Germany's

President Von Weizsacker in 1985 which ranged over the whole German wartime experience and declared unambiguously: 'All of us, whether guilty or not, whether old or young, must accept the past' and 'keep alive the memories of the war'. Japan's ruling elite, by contrast, is the same as that before and during the war, with only the military demoted. The country's neo-Nazis enjoy special status, roam the streets with their vans, are in league with the police and influence government policy.

A generation has been raised without any sense of horror or atonement for the war, which caused many more deaths even than the one in Europe. Hajime Etoh, a law student, asked about the underlying causes of the war by Steven Weisman, head of the *New York Times'* Tokyo Bureau, answered, 'Basically I believe the war occurred for economic reasons. Earlier this century, Japan didn't have enough land or financial resources or colonies to compete with the United States or United Kingdom. Japan thought that war with China was the only way to survive.' His view is typical.

Carol Gluck, Professor of History at Columbia University, and one of America's top Japanese experts, asserts, 'The war appeared as a natural catastrophe which "happened" to Japan, as if without the intervention of human agency.' A British merchant banker who has lived in Japan a long time says, 'The way the Japanese see it, they were happily minding their own business when the Americans suddenly dropped two atomic bombs on them out of the blue, and they have worked to recover ever since.'

In fact, at Hiroshima's war memorial, moving and terrible as it is, there is nothing to suggest that the Japanese started the war, or even perpetrated atrocities. In 1990 the Mayor of Hiroshima apologized for Japanese aggression, referring specifically to Pearl Harbor, the first time this has ever been said on the anniversary of Hiroshima.

Relentlessly, official and popular culture drum home the message that Japan was victim, not aggressor. In *Rhapsody in August*, a hugely popular film directed by the venerable Akira Kurosawa in 1991, Richard Gere plays a Japanese American who apologizes for the dropping of the bomb on Nagasaki and for the levelling of Japan's cities; even a man like Kurosawa could not include any suggestion that the Japanese might themselves have something to apologize for.

One of Japan's most famous post-war children's stories is 'The Pitiful Elephants', the pathetic tale of how, under American saturation bombing, it was decided that the elephants at Tokyo Zoo must be put down; the elephants refuse to eat the poisoned food they are given and their hides are too tough for injections; so they are made to starve to death while the zoo keepers shake their fists at American B-20s, crying 'Stop the war! Stop the war!' The propaganda is outrageously crude, even at a Nazi or Soviet level, yet it comes from the West's 'friend', Japan.

33

RETURN OF THE MEIJI

MODERN JAPAN is an economic superpower second only to the United States, and may overtake it very early in the next century. Japan is already of enormous importance in the fields of technology, manufacture, trade, international finance, and economics. Its power extends far beyond its modest international profile and certainly exceeds that of the now defunct Soviet Union. Yet its curious political system still harks back to one imposed by feudal oligarchs in the last third of the nineteenth century. In many ways it is still deeply hierarchical, autocratic, undemocratic, indoctrinated, collective, deferential, racialist, and superiority-obsessed.

In important respects, Japan is destroying such modernization as its political institutions underwent after the last war. The emperor system is being strengthened; Japan's defeat in the Pacific War is systematically excluded from its schoolrooms; and the influential Japanese right is constantly pressing for greater national self-assertion. Patriotism, racism, and national superiority are routinely inculcated into a population which admits very little self-criticism in the media or in its rigidly hierarchical ways of business and government. All of this behaviour would give rise to serious concern in any major Western industrial country. In the context of a global giant like Japan it should be one of the most important question of the post-cold war era. Mike Mansfield, a former American ambassador in Japan, once said that the relationship between America and Japan was 'the most important in the world – bar none'. He was not exaggerating – and that was at the height of the cold war.

Whither Japan? The Dutch journalist, Karel van Wolferen, set the ball rolling in his magisterial study *The Enigma of Japanese*

Power, a ground-breaking book which argued that Japan's careering lack of direction was dangerous for the world. The most alarmist works on the subject suggest that Japan is on a course of a world economic domination and remilitarization that could provoke conflict with Asia and America. On the other side are those like Bill Emmott who argued that the Japanese are changing, their aspirations becoming more Westernized and consumer orientated, that growth is slowing down and that they will find a niche comfortably below that of America as a peaceful, democratic society.

This section attempts to set out my view of Japan's future, based on its past. I conclude that the extraordinary political system of Japan contains, as van Wolferen argues, real dangers, but that catastrophe can be averted if the inner ferment of Japanese society moves to the surface, hopefully yielding peaceful change, and if Japan's neighbours and the West adopt intelligent and sensitive policies. Japan is an immense time-bomb, but it can be defused in a manner that can benefit not just Japan, but the West as well.

The key questions to ask are, Who, if anyone, is in control of Japan? Is it likely to continue on its unstoppable growth trajectory in the long term? Are its competitors closing ranks against it? Is Japan's economic power likely to be translated into political and military superpower status? What are its military ambitions in Asia now that the Russian threat has receded? Is it moving back slowly towards nationalism and militarist attitudes? Are there safeguards in Japanese society that will prevent this? And, lastly, how should its Western partners and competitors react?

The answers start with the profoundly disturbing fact that a small, narrow-minded, nationalist, inward-looking oligarchy is in charge of the affairs of the second strongest nation on earth, and running it much more efficiently than the old elite in the Soviet Union along collectivist authoritarian lines. So who is in control? Van Wolferen argues that nobody is. He believes that while there is a group of hierachies in Japan there is no ultimate authority. 'There is no place where, as Harry Truman would have said, the buck stops. In Japan, the buck keeps circulating.' The result is that the political authorities are hard pressed to restrain Japan's economic onslaught, say that they cannot do so, and that others must take the necessary action.

Van Wolferen is very close to the truth. It is hard to doubt the thrust of his analysis when one looks at the shambles involved in securing passage of any major piece of legislation, which nearly paralyses the political system: in particular, the attempts at electoral reform, the introduction of a sales tax and the tortuous route to securing acceptance of Japan's right to send troops abroad. But it must be remembered that each of these issues were of enormous controversy inside Japan, and it may even be a sign of political health that making such decisions takes protracted debate and political arm-wrestling. In trade negotiations with the United States and Western Europe, it is rarely to Japan's benefit to reach agreement, and when this is forced upon it, the implementation is often poor precisely because it is not in the country's interests. This smacks of obstructionism, of cunning, the old negotiating ploy, 'I agree, but I have to consult my masters back home.' It is not, as van Wolferen, suggests, necessarily a sign of political paralysis. In fact, the vast majority of decisions in Japan are taken and dispatched with ruthless efficiency through the authoritarian power structure.

Nor has the system ever failed to provide a political 'boss' as supreme authority who has ultimate, if not absolute, power. The evidence suggests that now, as before the war, the main elites have much the same place in the power structure, which is pyramidical in form, with one of the elites on the top of the pyramid and the boss of that elite at the very top, beneath the mystical authority of the emperor, a ceremonial long stop whose role in society remains very much the same as before the war.

There has rarely been much doubt about which leader ran the system, as any glance at Japan's power politics shows. First there was the era of the prime ministers – Yoshida, Hatoyama, Kishi, Ikeda, Sato and, briefly, Fukuda. Then there were the bosses – Tanaka, Takeshita, Kanemaru, Ozawa – shadowy wheeler-dealers behind the throne. Each of these was clearly *primus inter pares* within the political elite, and acted as a kind of ringmaster or telephone exchange between the dominant partners in post-war Japan – the bureaucracy and big business, both themselves pyramid-ically structured.

Each elite is, in its way, more powerful than the politicians, but they need the politicians to act as a mediator between them, calming potential clashes and also providing political legitimacy. The role gives the politicians their influence. In the final analysis, too, if one had to decide which of the two great powers in the Japanese system still has slightly the upper hand, even in the heyday of business power in the 1980s, the bureaucracy has an edge. Although the power of the bureaucrats has slipped mightily since the heady immediate post-war period, the underlying influence of MITI, the Ministry of Finance and the Bank of Japan and the major development banks remains enormous.

The state still controls key sectors of the economy, and, while business believes it is in the saddle, ultimately the bureaucratic oligarchs have the last word. In fact there are rarely major clashes between the two, as in a Western system: the two operate by slight shifts in authority, usually derived from agreement at the top, about such issues as expanding Japanese exports abroad. Sometimes government attempts to tell business what to do, for example, suggesting modifying working hours and the work ethic, but with little success; and one wonders how sincere such efforts were in the first place, and whether they were intended for foreign consumption.

The problem is slightly different, then, to the one identified by van Wolferen. It is not that no one governs Japan, but that government is still, as it was in the days of the shogun, in the hands of elites barely responsible to the people or their elected representatives. As before the war, the primary blame for this attaches to the bureaucratic oligarchs, who have arrogated to themselves the power to govern, seeking to keep this as far as possible out of the hands of the elected politicians. The politicians have grabbed a fair deal of power, but, thanks to the ephemeral nature of their factionalism and the corruption of Japanese politics, are in third place, with the exception of the leaders of the most powerful factions, who fulfil an essential role in fixing compromises and determining what would be the limit of acceptability to the people (as in the past, the system goes out of its way to avoid 'peasant revolts'). Because the bureaucrats lack legitimacy, business, which actually pays for the politicians to get elected, exerts an influence matched nowhere else in the world, and now challenges the bureaucracy for power in a manner reminiscent of the militarists in the 1930s. In a showdown the bureaucrats would still probably win. But the *kaisha* exert enormous power, like the *zaibatsu* before them.

This absence of democratic accountability has huge and dangerous implications. First, the bureaucrats are in no condition to stand up against a combination of other powerful forces at the top, for example, big business and the armed forces. The bureaucrats have once again arrogantly overestimated their own strength: they and the politicians lack the popular legitimacy to withstand irresistible pressure.

Second, there is a danger that Japan is being largely driven by development economists and businessmen in a manner which takes no account of political conditions elsewhere in the world. Business-men, like soldiers, are not political sophisticates and are unlikely to appreciate that some apparently market- or business-driven actions have serious political repercussion on other people: huge trade surpluses, even if justified by Japanese competitiveness, can cause anger in the countries with corresponding deficits. The bureaucrats and politicians may appreciate this, but not usually the *kaisha*. In that respect van Wolferen may be right: it may prove extremely hard for the bureaucracy and the politicians to persuade business to soften its relentless drive for domination of foreign markets. If it is indeed true that Japanese economic expansion is unstoppable, what happens when it hits the inevitable protectionist buffers abroad?

As already explained, protectionism is not some remote danger, but a reality already. The second element of Japan's economic strategy, to get around the growing clamour for trade barriers in both America and Europe, has been the rush of Japanese internal investment to America, Asia and Europe, setting up major plants with access to their rivals' markets, thus circumventing trade barriers. Again, this has generated intense controversy: the spectre of jobs being taken from local manufacturers by Japanese low-cost 'screwdriver' assem-bly operations, putting little into the local economy, has been of major concern to many host countries.

However, that is not an insurmountable problem. There is no reason why the host countries cannot arrange packages so that Japanese companies benefit both the local economies and them-selves. It is too late to prevent the current upsurge of anti-Japanese protectionism on the import front. It is the task of Western governments to ensure that Japanese inward investment provides benefits, not disadvantages to industries in their countries. As far as Japan is concerned, the vital thing is not to react by resorting to protectionism and closing doors. Reactions of that kind in the late 1920s created the conditions for war. Once foreign markets had closed against them in the 1930s, the Japanese looked to other outlets nearer home.

Asia, then as now, was the obvious channel for Japanese expansionism when Western markets were closed. There is every sign that Asia is indeed the growing focus for Japanese investment today. A top Japanese banker told me in 1991 that:

we no longer look to the United States as our prime interlocutor. They are a long way down the road to protection. We prefer to deal with Europe, which has a closer view of the relationship between the state and the economy than the Americans have. We have more in common with Europe. But our primary emphasis must be in developing trade with our regional partners in Asia. I do not believe that there is a great deal of future in our relations with the old Soviet Union. There are certain natural resources that can be developed in Siberia. The prime emphasis must be on China, setting up simple consumer goods plants to produce for the immense domestic market there. We also must further develop our relations with Indonesia, which is very important today. We already have good economic relations with Malaysia, Thailand and Singapore. Finally, India will be a key player in the emerging Asian economy.

Thus, as in the 1930s, the combination of world slow-down and protectionism in America and Europe is causing the Japanese to look increasingly to their own backyard for the export-led growth it still seeks. Of course, this is only a trend: the huge bulk of their trade and investment remains with America and Europe. But it seems both natural and prudent for the Japanese to seek a third outlet, just as was the case in the 1930s. The difference is that this is primarily trade-led; there is no military or political component. As such, surely it is unobjectionable?

Here one must take a deep breath and look at the other main players in Asia, and hazard some guesses about the changing shape of East Asian security after the collapse of communism in the Soviet Union. Hitherto it was possible to summarize the strategic evolution of Asia in the following terms. After 1945 the region degenerated quite quickly into a communist–capitalist confrontation, with Japan as the capitalist bulwark, playing a passive military role but acting as the forward base for the Americans in the area, ranged against the Soviet Union and China after 1949, as well as communist North Korea.

By the end of the 1960s, the forward march of communism appeared still more threatening, hijacking national anti-colonialist movements in Vietnam, Laos and Cambodia, as well as lesser insurgencies in Malaysia (where they were quietly defeated), the Philippines and Indonesia; at the same time, very visible cracks were showing in the communist monolith (if indeed it had ever existed) between Russia and China. With America's defeat in Indo-China, the communist advance seemed to gather momentum. But the Nixon administration brilliantly turned the tables by exploiting the rift between Russia and China, in so doing helping to fissure communist liberation movements throughout the region. Vietnam, supported by Russia, became hostile to China and briefly went to war with it; Vietnam occupied Cambodia, crushing the pro-Chinese Khmer Rouge.

The threat of insurrection in countries like Malaysia, India, the Philippines and Thailand faded, and with the onset of a new stability, the economics of the region began to flourish. The underlying security equation had been changed. China, in quasi-alliance with America, had lent its considerable weight to stopping Soviet expansionism. In this Japan remained a useful and vital ally, along with South Korea, but was no longer quite so important.

Things stayed this way until the late 1980s, when the whole façade of Soviet might crumbled, exposing the poverty and rottenness inside. This completely shattered the security equation in Asia, although Japanese officials are characteristically reluctant to say so openly. (However, the Japanese prime minister, Kiichi Miyazawa, admitted as much in his opening speech to the Diet in 1991. He declared that 'a tremendous upheaval' was taking place in the world, 'the likes of which occur only once every several centuries'. Thus Japan's global role could 'only grow larger'.)

The long-term implications of the reduction in Soviet power are as follows. First, Japan's formidable armed forces are left all dressed up with nothing to do. The pretext for the build-up was to act as a counter to the Russians should the Americans leave the area. Now a much-reduced security force could perform the job of deterring what remains of the Soviet Union just as effectively. A senior official in the Self-Defence Forces told me in 1991 that there might be pressure for a reduction in military spending, but asserted that this was unlikely to happen, because Japanese defences had to be maintained in the face of threats from long-range Korean missiles, and so on.

In Japan there was none of the pressure and debate about the 'peace dividend' that emerged throughout the West after the implosion of the Soviet Union. It seemed that the Self-Defence forces, far from considering reducing their strength, intended to go on quietly modernizing and rearming to meet an apparently much diminished threat.

Professor Masashi Ishihara, professor of international relations at Japan's National Defence Academy, offers a soothing view:

A power vacuum would be created only if the US closes its bases in Japan and South Korea or abrogated long-standing security treaties. Japan has neither the capability nor the motivation to try to achieve a dominant position by force. For example, the 330 advanced jet fighters Japan possesses today may be impressive, but they cannot reach South East Asia unless they are refuelled while in flight. Japan has no reliable tankers. The 14 diesel electric submarines and 60 destroyers could not attack South East Asia without the protection of larger ships, which the Japanese maritime Self-Defence Force lacks. If Japan tried to invade its Asian neighbours it would turn the US into an enemy because Washington maintains security treaties with South Korea, the Philippines, Thailand and Australia. Japan could use military force abroad only at the expense of disrupting economic and political relations with the rest of Asia. So it is in Japan's national interest to maintain close and friendly economic and political ties with the region.

Second, and this provides a partial justification for Japan's position, it seems certain that over the long term there will be a reduction in the American military presence in Asia. A number of factors are at work here: why should large numbers of American troops be stationed in Japan, South Korea and the Philippines when the Soviet threat is sharply diminished? The popular pressure within America for a reduction in protection for Japan – denounced as Japan's 'free ride' on defence – points the same way.

The counter-argument is that the region is becoming more volatile with the growth of a number of prosperous economies which, under still underdeveloped political systems, may seek to translate their new status into military power. China, in particular, shows some signs of military ambitions. However, this is unlikely to cut much ice with the American taxpayer. A long-term reduction in American protection for the region seems inevitable, even if shortsighted.

A third consequence of the reduction in Russia's power is a corresponding increase in the security influence of Japan and China in particular, and to a lesser extent that of other regional powers like Vietnam and Indonesia. ASEAN (the Association of South-East Asian Nations) has also been getting its act together in a co-operative defensive posture, bolstered by Australia and New Zealand. Instead of the previous polarization between the Soviet Union and the United States, supported by Japan, with China more or less neutralized, there are likely to be three biggish, but not dominant, military powers, Japan, Russia and China, possibly in that order, and a host of smaller ones, plus a sharply reduced American presence.

In the jostling between the three, it is worth noting that China, although possessed of vast manpower, crude atomic weapons and a rapidly growing economy, remains probably the worst equipped. Russia, in spite of its problems, still retains considerable firepower and strength, as well as a major nuclear force, although these may erode over time. And Japan is not just militarily up to date and strong, but of the three has the largest economic base from which to expand its force projection both in conventional and nuclear terms.

Of the three, Japan is potentially easily the most powerful, if it wishes to be, even if China is the one flexing most military and diplomatic muscle at the moment, for example, over control of the Spratly Islands. Moreover, Japan's reasons for restraint on rearmament are fast disappearing: the Americans, far from supporting such restraint, have long been urging Japan to adopt a higher military profile. With Russia no longer a threat, Japan does not risk Soviet retaliation by rearming further.

The only remaining reason for not rearming, which admittedly is a powerful one, is that this would alarm the very neighbours it is now targeting for economic penetration. That indeed is the argument raging within Japan's ruling circles, which has yet to be settled. The argument for building up Japan's armed forces – that the region is more dangerous now that China is becoming stronger economically, while Russia may be taken over by nationalist forces in the future – is not entirely an illogical one. My own guess is that the restrainers will just win – for now. Japan will continue to build up its forces discreetly, in a manner that neither of its rivals can match economically, until it is the foremost military power in the region.

Already the quality of Japan's Self-Defence Forces far exceeds that of its rivals. Between 1966 and 1981 Japan's defence spending soared by 500 per cent; in the five years up to 1986 it increased by 40 per cent to become the third largest defence budget in the world. By the late 1980s Japan had twice as many destroyers as America in the East Asian region, and more tactical aircraft than the Americans in Japan, South Korea and the Philippines put together. The Self-Defence Forces are not actually up to their full strength, partly because of recruitment difficulties in a prosperous, full-employment society.

But the Ground Self-Defence Force, the Japanese army, consists of about 140,000 men, about the same as the British army, or a quarter of that of the American, with twelve infantry divisions and one airborne one. The navy consists of some 46,000 men, compared with its British equivalent of 70,000 and an American navy of 500,000 men. It has ten divisions of anti-submarine surface ships, four escort flotillas, six divisions of submarines, two minesweeping flotillas and sixteen squadrons of anti-submarine aircraft with about 220 combat aircraft, all of which are based on land.

The Air Self-Defence Force has around 45,000 men and about 430 combat aircraft. In equipment it is in a class of its own, with some of the most sophisticated weaponry in the world. Japan has F-15 fighters, Chinook helicopters, the Hawkeye Early Warning system and is buying six batteries of American-made Patriot missiles to deter North Korea's recently developed 600-mile Rodong-1 missiles. Japan imports more American weaponry than countries like Israel, Egypt and Saudi Arabia, but has also set up a large domestic munitions industry, mostly, though not all, under American licence. Japan's obsession with the latest equipment is set to continue. As its medium-term defence programme ending in 1990 stated: 'Efforts shall be made to improve the air defence capability of the main islands and "the capability to protect sea lines".' Japan's 1991–5 defence budget will amount to $180 billion.

In June 1992, after an agonized political debate lasting several months that threatened to explode onto the streets, an elephant finally begat a mouse: Japan's parliament agreed to set up a force of 2000 soldiers for duty overseas, for the first time since the occupation. The force was given the authority to provide logistical and medical care, aid refugees and protect hospitals and food centres and communications facilities. They will only be permitted to fire in self-defence, and will be withdrawn if a ceasefire collapses. They cannot monitor ceasefire agreements, remove land mines or disarm warring factions without express parliamentary approval.

Even so, the then opposition leader argued that the law was 'a violation of the constitution ... This is a shadow over Japan's future.' Takako Doi, his predecessor as Socialist leader, said the bill was, 'The major danger to the constitution since the war'. Writer

Ryo Otomo said, 'The West has played right into the hands of government bureaucrats who want Japan to have a glorious army again.'

The political struggle had been marked by ferocious opposition blocking tactics, including the prevention of a committee chairman taking his seat and uproar around the chamber. The preferred method was not talking but walking, making votes take as long as possible by using a slow, swaggering step to the voting box. It sometimes took fifty minutes to cross just twenty feet.

The opposition may have prevented a much more far-reaching law being enacted. Ichiro Ozawa, perhaps the most powerful figure in current Japanese politics, and probably a prime minister of the future, argued that the bill was totally inadequate. 'We cannot afford to delay on mostly necessary choices concerning our role in the world. If we are not willing to execute out responsibilities, Japan will not have respect in the international community.'

The first post-war arrival of a Japanese force abroad, in the guise of a tiny peace-keeping force in Cambodia, might have seemed risible, even effete. The 1,800 peace-keepers arrived in a tropical storm, complaining that they could not bathe: 'The water is too muddy for the pipes we brought from Japan,' said a lieutenant. His men had to wash in the river with shampoo. They had, moreover, been denied condoms after an outcry in the Japanese press about issuing them which recalled their countrymen's last military experience abroad.

If shooting broke out, the Japanese were under orders to retreat immediately to camp. In Takeo, their main headquarters near Pnom Penh, the soldiers were kept busy constructing bars, clubs, laser-disc karaoke parlours, vending machines, cinemas, libraries, installing satellite televisions, video recorders, stereo systems, air-conditioned prefabs with mosquito screens and even, possibly, massage parlours.

Following the decision to send Japanese troops into Cambodia, Japan seemed to be shedding its post-war inhibitions on defence with indecent, almost alarming speed. Shortly after passage of the bill, a senior defence forces official, Colonel Shigaki Nishimura, admitted that Japan aspired to join in a collective self-defence force for Asia. The pretext is China's military build-up: its move towards becoming an ocean-going power 'surely will persuade the Japanese people to think twice' about Japan's limited defence strategy, said the colonel.

The foreign minister, Michio Watanabe, appeared to confirm this when he asserted that Japan wanted long-range transport aircraft and ships to move equipment and men overseas. Under the 1991–6 five-year programme, Japan is to buy twenty-nine F-15 fighters, more than a hundred tanks and eight destroyers, as well as four AWAC radar aircraft. In January 1993, the prime minister, Kiichi Miyazawa, made a four-nation trip to Southwest Asia, calling for the region to 'develop a long-term vision' of regional security in view of the proposed reduction of the American presence in Asia from 135,000 troops to 110,000.

Much more ominously, the same month the LDP agreed to set up a committee to draft an amendment of the no war provision in Japan's constitution. Watanabe himself called for a constitutional revision to allow Japan to take part in collective security operations. Miyazawa himself seemed surprised by the LDP's decisions, asserting 'fifty years is a short period . . . We should not forget easily.' Hiroshi Mitsuzuka, one of the LDP's senior faction leaders, claimed that the Japanese constitution was enacted 'in a state of confusion after World War II and it was based on the orders of the commander of the occupation forces.' As Japan has been able to dispatch peace-keepers abroad even under the existing constitution, it is not clear why the constitution requires amendment, except to permit Japanese forces to operate abroad independently, or to engage in combat. In November 1993, the head of Japan's Self-Defence Forces Minister of Defence resigned after outspokenly calling for a revision of the no war clause, which aroused angry Socialist protests.

Most unsettling of all, a senior instructor in army war history, Major Syhinsaku Yanai, in an article for Japan's largest weekly magazine, *Shukan Bunshun*, argued in 1993 that the corruption of the politicians had reached such a pass that a military coup was necessary. 'It is no longer possible to correct injustice through an election in the legitimate way that is the basis of democracy,' he wrote. 'The only way left is the revolution of a *coup d'état*.' Major Yanai may have been speaking only for himself and a handful of right-wing officers, but the fact that the subject was voiced at all in a major weekly broke a taboo in post-war Japan and left a distinct chill.

It is not easy for Japan to defend its continuing military build-up at the rate of around 2 per cent a year in real terms after the collapse of its principal potential adversary, the Soviet Union. However, a pretext of sorts was recently supplied by the growing crisis over North Korea's (possible) development of nuclear weapons and a long-range missile, and China's rapid arms build-up (defence spending in China has officially soared by 50 per cent in two years). In

1993 the budget was set to increase by more than 12 per cent to around $7.5 billion; in fact most defence specialists believe the Chinese are spending at least twice that. The prospect of an arms race between Japan and China is already causing concern in East Asia, and is deeply worrying.

Yet the doubts persist. President Ramos of the Philippines has argued that Japan should improve its dialogue with Asia 'to prove that she is a friend of this part of the world'. Sending military men to Asia would arouse regional concerns in his view. Singapore's Lee Kuan Yew has argued that if America withdraws from the region, Japan would strengthen its defences, as would Korea and China. A senior member of Taiwan's ruling party, Lee Sen-Song, felt that Japan's decision to send the troops to Cambodia could upset the strategic balance in Asia. Both China and the two Koreas opposed the move. Japan's rearmament, however cautious, however justified, still arouses the most intense opposition. The only remaining restraint seems to be the MacArthur constitution, and every loophole has been opened as wide as possible.

The second overwhelming change in the East Asian equation is that the American–Japanese relationship is under severe stress, although not yet at breaking point. In January 1992, under two essentially outward-looking, thoughtful but weak leaders both being pressured by increasingly vocal domestic lobbies, the partnership hit a thirty-year nadir.

President Bush had already caused serious offence by abruptly cancelling a visit to Japan in response to domestic criticism that he was spending too much time abroad. In fact, of all overseas trips, this would have been among the most important. For the world's second economic superpower, and potentially a political and military one as well, both America and Russia have treated Japan remarkably cavalierly.

First there was the cancelled Bush trip in November 1991. Then there was the patently electioneering visit in January 1992, in which a bevy of American car-makers threw their weight about and Bush attempted to look tough on trade, gaining more cosmetic concessions and earning the epithet 'ill-mannered' from the Japanese. Russia's Boris Yeltsin followed by abruptly cancelling a trip in September the same year, because his conservative military establishment had torpedoed any concession on the Kurile Islands. In May 1993 he called off a second visit, for the same reason, only finally turning up for the G7 summit in July, and then in October, where he charmed his hosts but barely mentioned the Kuriles.

In fact, it is hard to see how a settlement could be achieved on the question. The Japanese hinted that economic aid to Russia was dependent on the issue, a stance which infuriated the Russians. The 25,000 inhabitants of the northern Kuriles, Etorofu and Kunashiri, are believed to want to stay with Russia. The islands are strategically important, commanding the approaches to the Russian port of Vladivostok, and the Japanese legal claim on the islands is shaky. Historically, the islands belong to Japan, but legally, there is little doubt that Japan renounced its claims at the 1951 peace treaty conference in San Francisco.

In 1956, when Japan resumed diplomatic relations with the Soviet Union, the southern Kuriles were returned to Japan, and the Japanese agreed to accept the weakness of its claim to the northern pair. The United States, locked into cold war confrontation with Russia, insisted that the Japanese continue to press the claim to the northern Kuriles; the deal fell through. Japan has refused to allow the issue to be referred to the International Court of Justice, for fear that its previous positions will be accepted as binding.

The irony was that Miyazawa was widely considered one of Japan's most pro-American leaders. In the immediate aftermath of his election as prime minister in October 1991, he had declared that 'the Japan–US relationship is the basic axis of Japanese diplomacy', just four months after a poll had showed that more Japanese viewed the Americans as a threat to their security than any other country: 24 per cent were concerned by the American 'threat', compared with 22 per cent by Russia, 13 per cent by North Korea, 6 per cent by South Korea and 4 per cent by China.

The storm had been brewing for some time. *Kenbei*, dislike of the United States, and *bubei*, contempt for America, have been fermenting in Japan for months. In mid-1991, the chairman of Kyocera Corporation wrote that the Japanese were growing tired of feeling that 'America doesn't like us or respect our efforts'. A prominent writer, Yoshimi Ishikawa, went so far as to suggest that 'in response to the force displayed by America [in the Gulf], there is emerging among Japanese a move from fear toward something like nascent hatred'. Kazuo Ogura, director-general of cultural affairs in Japan's Foreign Ministry, wrote that 'those on the US side are still leaning heavily on Japan, never reflecting on their own country's shortcomings. And those on the Japanese side are still bowing before the Americans' demands as if doing so was Japan's fate.' He argued that Japan and America were growing more wary of each other for three reasons: first, because of a divergence in ideals between the two; second, because as Japanese became richer they were less impressed by the affluence of the United States; and third, because the end of the cold war made the continuing massive American military presence in Japan unnecessary. Such outspokenness is extremely rare for a senior government official.

The problem of the *keiretsu* has also become a major source of friction with the United States. The Americans fail to realize how deeply ingrained they are in the Japanese economic culture. Destroy the *keiretsu* and you have to rebuild the whole economy. To the Japanese there is not the slightest reason to do this because they view the *keiretsu* as a prime component of economic success. The Americans recently pointed a finger at the Saitama Saturday Society, a *keiretsu* of sixty-six building firms which divided up bids for public works projects worth about $700 million in 1992. In Yamanashi Prefecture contracts for bridges and railway tunnels were allocated on the basis of how much companies had contributed to the campaign of the local political boss, Shin Kanemaru. Foreign companies were rigorously excluded. The American justice department warned that it might take anti-trust action against Japanese companies that prevented the Americans doing business in the country, a veiled threat aimed at Japanese companies in America.

The issue was first seriously raised by the American corporate raider, T. Boone Pickens, who bought a 26 per cent stake in Koito Manufacturing, an auto lighting manufacturer. Pickens tells a harrowing tale of how he looked for representation on the board of the company, to be turned down publicly. He then sought information about the company, and had to pursue this through the courts. At the firm's annual general meeting in 1991, the heavy brigade (in many cases this is provided by the *yakuza*) shouted down the Americans when they spoke. One of his female colleagues was met by jeers and cries of, 'What's your real job? You're a stripper, aren't you?' Pickens sold his stock the following year.

He cites the case of a Japanese businessman who set up an auto part company which became the supplier to a *keiretsu*, which was soon running his business, dictating even his profit margins. Why didn't he break away? 'No one else would buy from me. All my family wealth is in my company. It would be economic suicide.' Pickens comments: 'Cartels may be good for business, but they limit consumer choices and increase prices. Unfortunately since the competitors have to be squeezed out first, and while the squeezing is going on, prices often fall sharply, consumers are often the last to recognize what is happening. Anyone who reads the business section of a newspaper should recognize that this process is already under way in important sectors of US industry.'

The Japanese response to all this American pressure was uncharacteristically blunt. The vice-minister of finance for international affairs, Tadao Chino, said flatly that there would be no changes. Japan was 'definitely independent of the United States' and would continue its practices, including its support of Japanese financial markets and its use of foreign aid to protect its trade interests. His predecessor, Nakoto Utsumi, had bluntly suggested that Japanese companies in America would be uprooted if any sanctions were taken against Japan to open its financial markets.

Japan is intensely vulnerable on the issue of the distribution *keiretsu*. This, essentially, is a tight clinch between manufacturers, wholesalers, and retailers. As Karel van Wolferen penetratingly argues, most shops selling consumer goods are in fact comparable to the regular subcontractors of Japanese manufacturers. 'They are provided by the manufacturers with capital and, if necessary, technical know-how.' Started in the 1950s, they were deeply entrenched by the late 1980s, and, in van Wolferen's view, are 'the most effective single element for control over the Japanese market'. Price-fixing and limitations on the range of products are standard. Consumer goods produced by outsiders can only be sold through specialized outlets charging multiples of the existing market price of the product. By this means – not the extraordinary patriotism of the Japanese – foreign goods face their major hurdle in the Japanese market. Otherwise, Japan, with a high-value currency and overpriced goods, would be ripe for import penetration.

President Bush's visit, when it came at last, could not have been more disastrous. The stage had been set with a warning from the American commerce secretary, Robert Mosbacher, that stagnation in the American economy was not entirely attributable to Japan's trade policy but that 'they're exacerbating the problem' by 'not allowing US goods into Japan', a huge exaggeration, even a direct lie. 'What is lacking now in Japan is market access to US companies.'

Japan's deputy foreign minister replied that while he did not believe Japanese economic policy played any role in the American recession, Japan was trying to expand government purchases of American computers 'but there is a limit to what the Japanese government can do'. He argued that Japan bought nearly as many goods from America as from Britain, Germany, and Italy combined. While Japanese cars were voluntarily being cut back by exporters, 'American automobile companies could have modernized, expanded their factories. And somehow, that has not taken place.'

On the eve of Bush's visit, the Japanese were sarcastic to an astonishing degree. Miyazawa spoke of the need for 'compassion' for America's sick economy. 'I would like to do whatever I can to help the United States recover from its economic ills and social ills with the co-operation of the Japanese people and industry.' More patronizingly still, he remarked, 'It came as a considerable shock to the Americans that General Motors had been defeated by Japanese autos, though Japanese cars alone might not be responsible.' The Japanese Foreign Ministry put out a paper suggesting that AT&T, Sears Roebuck and General Motors were American *keiretsu*, while suggesting that the United States might benefit from the *keiretsu* system.

The visit was notable, of course, for Bush's collapse at an official dinner, which some viewed as symbolic, although almost certainly was merely a symptom of jet lag. There was also a much-publicized row between Japanese and American motor automobile manufacturers accompanying the president, notably Chrysler's Lee Iacocca. (The eleven chief executives who travelled to Japan with President Bush earned an average of $2 million in 1990. Their Japanese equivalents earned an average of $300,000 to $400,000 and paid tax of 65 per cent.) But the major achievement was a commitment by Japanese car manufacturers to buy $10 billion worth of American auto-parts, a further major step towards 'managed trade' or barter, long the enemy of the free trade principles which the United States professed. Bush was on the receiving end of further barbs from Miyazawa, who suggested that AIDS, homelessness and declining educational standards were the root causes of American trade problems.

The American president left Japan to caustic press commentary. The newspaper *Yukan Fuji* remarked, 'If American cars don't sell, maybe they should go into Tokyo Bay.' More temperately, the *Mainichi Shimbun* observed that 'the decision to buy US-made automobiles should ultimately come from the customer'. The economic journal *Nihon Keizai Shimbun* argued that 'the agreement amounted to the world's biggest and second biggest economic powers formally approving government-managed trade. This is sure to set a bad precedent.' America, it seems, was following Japan's economic example. One unpublicized agreement later emerged: just a week after the summit both the Federal Reserve and the Bank of Japan sold American dollars massively in a move to keep the dollar from rising too far and to boost American competitiveness.

The deal between America and Japan in January 1992 represented a dangerous move towards the notion of 'managed trade', that is, precise sales targets and quotas that are the antithesis of free trade. An American trade official claims that 'the fact is that in dealing with Japan targets work and nothing else does. In Washington no one really wants to admit that. But you see it in the positions we end up taking.' Shinichiro Torii, president of Suntory, the huge Japanese brewer, says, 'When you take into account employment and other sensitive issues in the United States, especially in autos and electronics, there should be moderate managed trade.' The Bush agreement on auto supplies came on top of a long-standing quota on semiconductors: that America should have 20 per cent of the Japanese market (it actually has 14 per cent).

Sir Leon Brittan, the EEC's competition commissioner, suggested that there was 'mounting evidence that the United States is drifting towards a preference for managed trade'. The America–Japan deal would 'erode' the multilateral trading system and increase trade tensions. It was wrong of America to 'demand a certain share of the Japanese market on political rather than commercial grounds. I do not believe that political ideas of this kind help to resolve the underlying trade problems or to close the gap between Japan and the United States in terms of productivity and competitiveness.' Sir Leon said he was 'disappointed and concerned . . . Already America boasts an impressive arsenal of protective trade measures.'

Worse was to follow. In February 1993, Japan's political strongman, Shin Kanemaru, issued a remarkable statement:

> Some Japanese politicians have caused misunderstanding as a result of their remarks. I told my colleagues that you have to be extremely cautious when you make remarks, you have an impact on people overseas. If we belittle the United States, there is no future for Japan . . . Japan can exist because the United States exists, but it is

not the other way around. We owe our prosperity to the United States. Many Japanese forget this fact . . . I'm concerned about this very bad state of affairs.

Kanemaru suggested that Japanese–American relations were at the edge of a cliff, about to go over. His extraordinary apology followed public repentance by the prime minister he supported, Kiichi Miyazawa, for extempore remarks suggesting that Americans may 'lack a work ethic' and that the belief in 'producing things and creating value has loosened too much in the past ten years or so' in America. 'I did not intend to criticize American workers at all,' he later amended.

There is, in fact, some controversy about Japanese labour productivity. In 1982 GDP per employee was reckoned, on a common index, at 131 in America, 111 in France, 109 in West Germany, 100 in Japan and 80 in Britain. Moreover, Japan's increase in value-added labour productivity was growing nearly two-thirds faster than America's. Japanese agriculture, by contrast, is stone age inefficient, American and British agriculture being reckoned to be four times as efficient, French agriculture two and a half times and German two times. Distribution and services in Japan also lag far behind its competitors. Where America registered 140 on a common index in 1982, France 125 and West Germany 124, Japan's score was 100 and Britain's was 78.

Kanemaru the fixer and Miyazawa the elite bureaucrat had long disliked each other; in 1991 Miyazawa had been reported as saying that he wished Kanemaru would sink in the Kamanashi River, while Kanemaru remarked that in spite of his support for the government it was sinking like a boat made of mud. However, in February 1992 the two patched up their differences in a private room at a restaurant while sitting on tatami mats, draining cups of sake, and singing folk songs. Kanemaru remarked, after being asked about the political scandals besetting Miyazawa, 'You know, politics need money. And politics is expensive. That will not change. So Japanese politicians are forced sometimes to do immoral things. That is the worst thing about Japanese politics. That is something we have to reform.'

It was no exaggeration to suggest that by February 1992, American–Japanese relations had 'declined more than at any time since the anti-American demonstrations of the 1960s', as Dick Holbrooke, former assistant secretary of state for East Asian and Pacific affairs remarked. The situation did not improve after that, and only President Bush's need for re-election, and a measure of restraint from his Democratic rivals, allowed the issue to die away, certain to return. At the time of Kanemaru's attempt to pour oil on troubled waters, a *Washington Post*–ABC News poll found that 65 per cent of Americans believed anti-Japanese attitudes were increasing, while some two-thirds were making a conscious attempt to avoid buying Japanese products. Some 60 per cent believed the Japanese were biased against Americans.

More offensive even than Miyazawa's remarks were those of the speaker of the Japanese parliament, a prominent and representative figure, who remarked that many American workers were 'lazy and illiterate and unable to produce quality goods'. He also described America as 'Japan's subcontractor'. Yoshio Sakurauchi had been addressing a domestic audience, and, after the remarks were unexpectedly picked up by American newspapers, apologized, describing the incident as 'very regretful'. But he had clearly been expressing his own true sentiments.

Shortly afterwards the Los Angeles transportation department cancelled a contract to Sumitomo for train carriages under pure political pressure. Japanese companies and Japanese Americans were increasingly subjected to vandalism and threatening telephone calls. In one isolated incident, a Japanese American businessman, Yasuo Kato, was stabbed to death near Los Angeles, possibly by an unemployed American worker who had earlier visited the victim's house complaining that he had lost his job because of the Japanese. In other incidents in the Los Angeles area, stones were thrown through the windows of a Japanese home and a petrol bomb was tossed at a Japanese couple.

The regional director of the Japanese American Citizens' League, Jimmy Tokeshi, complained of racial harassment and Japan-bashing. 'It's frightening to think what types of attitudes are out there.' The new Japanese ambassador to the United States, Takakuzu Kuriyama, was sent on a fence-mending mission. 'I don't think most people in Japan feel we are a seven-foot tall economic giant looking down on the United States. I don't think we have an image of the United States becoming a second-rate economic power.'

Bill Clinton's election was greeted with enormous interest by the Japanese public, which marvelled at so young a man acquiring the leadership of his country when in Japan senior positions are occupied by people in their sixties and seventies. The popular goodwill engendered by him, however, seemed unlikely to survive the tough attitude promptly taken by his administration towards Japan. Clinton, who has no Japanese specialists among his top-level advisers, entered office with a determination, supported by the Democrats' traditional union backers, to defend American jobs from the Japanese.

The Clinton administration took office, in particular, against the backdrop of a record Japanese trade surplus with the rest of the world of $136 billion in 1992, a third of it with the United States, which grew to $160 billion in 1993. Clinton's trade representative, Mickey Kantor, roared onto the offensive with open criticism of Japan's obstruction in the GATT talks. 'Japan continues to behave as if it had little stake in the outcome,' he declared caustically in March 1993, drawing an icy retort from the Japanese representative that the American didn't know what he was talking about.

Japan's legendary politeness seemed to be wearing very thin indeed. Privately officials in Tokyo said that if the Americans took action against the import of cars and semi-conductors, Japan would retaliate. A senior government member told journalists off the record that Japan saw America as a troubled country that had lost confidence in itself, seeking to blame others for its own defects. Indeed, Japan has now begun to resort to anti-dumping measures of its own, although these are so far confined to cheaper Chinese products. Japan's foreign minister, Michio Watanabe, was an early visitor to Bill Clinton's Washington, but the Americans actively and discourteously discouraged a visit by Prime Minister Miyazawa because of the fear that it would yield nothing but disagreement.

When it occured in April 1993, Clinton called for a 'rebalancing' of the economic relationship between the two nations. 'The cold war partnership between our two countries is outdated,' he declared. The Japanese press reacted with cold fury. 'We've entered an era of fighting with real swords,' commented the *Asahi Shimbun*.

At July's Tokyo summit for the Group of Seven leading industrialized nations, President Clinton called for a reduction in Japan's trade surplus from around 3 per cent of GDP to between 1 and 2 per cent. This was bluntly rejected by Miyazawa: 'Even if the government wants to do this or that, that cannot be translated into reality in a market economy.' A senior foreign ministry official commented: 'No one can be happy to make a loop to hang himself.' In the end, very limited agreement was reached in the kind of vague language so favoured by the Japanese because it is so hard to implement. Clinton continued to press for specific targets. The outgoing American ambassador in Tokyo, Michael Armacost, commented caustically that Japan was showing 'chutzpah' in 'touting' itself as a champion of free trade.

A formal declaration of hostilities on trade was put on hold, however, with the coming to power of the Hosokawa government. Although no real change in economic policy was expected, barring an effort to liberalize the Japanese market for rice imports, the Clinton administration seemed initially reluctant to press the fragile but popular new government too hard for fear of undermining its domestic position. A kind of calm had descended over what seemed increasingly likely to be an economic battlefield.

It is easy to be alarmist about the prospect of Japan as not just an economic, but a military superpower as well. *The Coming War with Japan* by George Friedman and Meredith Lebard, a bestseller in Tokyo, presents the doomsday scenario in the crudest possible fashion. Yet very little of the picture it paints is realistic. The differences between the current situation and the 1930s are more striking than the similarities. First, Japan's current economic success is due to business penetration in a peaceful world, not military domination, which proved so disastrously counter-productive in the past. Why throw this away in pursuit of some wild military goal? Even in the event of trade wars between Japan and America and, possibly, Europe, vast flows will continue between these three great economic groupings which would be put at risk through military rivalry.

Secondly, the trigger of the Pacific War was the choking off of supplies of raw materials, energy and materials by the Americans. This is inconceivable today: the Americans compete vigorously, but would never contemplate wholesale boycotts of an economy which is now mutually inter-dependent with theirs. In terms of energy, Japan is still heavily dependent on Middle East oil – supplying 55% of the country's energy needs.

The greatest danger to this calm arises from instability in the Middle East, and Japan has been at pains to avoid making enemies there. The reluctance of Japan to assist in the international Gulf War effort can be interpreted as an attempt to give offence to no one, until it was finally pressured into paying $13 billion by the West, which went largely unrecognized. Japan's view at the outset of the Gulf War was that any interruption in supplies would inevitably correct itself in the long term, as market pressure reasserted itself against the offending countries. Japan survived the oil shocks of the 1970s better than any other industrial power, and feels it could survive any embargo.

Meanwhile, the nuclear programme is intended to reduce Japan's dependence on foreign energy from three-quarters to less than a half within a decade. Quite simply, Japan is no longer all that vulnerable; and it is almost impossible to imagine any scenario, short of outright war, in which the West might seek to enforce an energy embargo against Japan.

Finally, although this book has shown how little Japan's political system has altered this century, one of the few important changes lies in the status of the Self-Defence Forces. Although steadily rising in influence, they still rank fourth behind the business, bureaucratic and political powers. They do not have much autonomous power to guide Japan's affairs of state. War can only be contemplated if all four powers – minus, possibly, the political – permit it. In fact, such a consensus was still needed at the start of the Pacific War, the height of Japanese militarism. The Self-Defence Forces still have to tread warily, with only 10 per cent of Japanese saying they are willing to fight for their country and a military uniform by no means generating respect or deference. Those who suggest that Japan may again go berserk in the Pacific are absurd and naive.

To argue this, however, is not to say that there is no danger of armed conflict in the Far East: rather, there is a more contemporary type of danger, of three sorts. The first stems from the political backwardness of most of the states of the region and the fact that Japan is not, as we have seen, a democratic country answerable to its people in the Western sense of the term, but one which is slowly regressing towards more oligarchic rule. The second is the interventionist role played by the Japanese state, in contrast to American-style free-market practices. The third is the immense economic power of Japan in the world that could be put to political use. These are the three prime challenges for the West and Asia over the coming decades. In order to answer the question, What could go wrong . . . we should look at each in turn.

The first potential flashpoint is likely to arise from Japan's increasing interest in Asia. By comparison with the rest of the continent, Japan is much more advanced, and much more technologically and economically strong, a relationship not unlike that between the United States and Latin America. While Asia needs Japanese investment, know-how, and consumer goods industries, there is already considerable resentment at a popular level with the high-handed attitude of Japan's businessmen in some Asian countries. It is naive not to expect anger to grow as Japan adopts an ever-higher profile. Exactly this has occurred in virtually every case of penetration by an economically dominant country faced with a weaker one, even if it benefits the latter. Again, the relationship between the United States and Latin America comes to mind: the former has always been the target of nationalist resentment because of its very presence and success.

This may or may not be a containable phenomenon. It could erupt in popular protests against Japanese business, or in Japan-bashing by populist politicians, or, more extremely, in outright attempts to control or expropriate Japanese business interests. In turn, particularly because the country does not have the normal democratic restraints, this is likely to excite a reaction from Japan, the region's strongest military power.

That is some way down the track. For the immediate future the Japanese would be deeply reluctant to respond belligerently to outbreaks of anti-Japanese sentiment in Asia. But in the long term it would be idle not to consider the possibility of Japan's racial susceptibilities being aroused by anti-Japanese sentiment in Asia. In the worst scenario, the Japanese might exercise intense pressure on governments to intervene against anti-Japanese interests, and even make military threats in the process to get them to do so. In addition, there is the more straightforward possibility of territorial arguments in Asia encroaching on Japanese interests.

What in fact are the possibilities of such a conflict of interest? On a thumbnail sketch, Korea, Japan's closest neighbour, may move towards reunification over the next decade, although the possibility of conflict exists with the nuclear crisis and the eleventh-hour assertiveness of Kim-Il-Sung. Reunification will slow down the south's extraordinary economic boom, but ultimately will result in a strengthened Korea. Of all Japanese rivals, South Korea is the one most closely emulating Japan's business methods, and is likeliest to become a major competitor in, for example, the Chinese market, as well, possibly, as the Russian market.

Korean politicians are volatile and usually authoritarian, but there is a democratic movement which may be stronger than Japan's. In view of Japan's military strength (although Korea's is not to be sneezed at) relations between the two countries are likely to be cautious in the extreme. Both traditionally dislike each other; both are proud enough to engage in nationalist exchanges if necessary. The gradual reduction in America's commitment to South Korea is likely to result in the country's adopting a more self-sufficient, nationalist foreign policy – just as Japan, for the same reason, moves in the same direction.

Japanese economic penetration of the Soviet Union is likely to be more moderate, and unlikely to arouse much resentment there. It is hard to see any regime coming to power in the Soviet Union, however nationalist (as seems likely), that is not desperate for Japanese economic support. The very Japanese reluctance to invest, contrary to the situation everywhere else, is likely to arouse Russian national ire. In practice, of course, Japan's most active territorial dispute with any country remains the one over the Kuriles.

The Russians, intent on preserving safe passage from the port of Vladivostok, seem determined not to make concessions. The opposition of the Soviet armed forces and nationalists to any flexibility on the Kuriles caused President Yeltsin of Russia to cancel his visit to Tokyo at the last moment in the autumn of 1992. It is far-fetched to see any conflict breaking out over the Kuriles, which, as one prominent Japanese told me, are 'cold and barren; it will be impossible to persuade Japanese to settle there'. Yet the islands remain a constant irritant to an increasingly nationalist and assertive Japan.

China is likely to be the major centre of Japanese economic penetration over the next two decades. The country is ready for massive investments of basic technology to manufacture consumer goods, such as very cheap cars. In turn, this could create a nationalist reaction. The Chinese political system is even more authoritarian and certainly much less predictable than Japan's, and the country is becoming more prickly. As Japanese business penetration into China grows, a potential exists for real friction, in which military force may be part of the equation. Certainly, potential sources of friction abound: China seems determined to maintain and extend its influence in a large part of Asia, including Cambodia, Thailand, Burma, Tibet and Pakistan.

Japan's adoption of a higher political profile may result in a clash with the Chinese area of influence; in particular, Japan may not consider Cambodia, Thailand and resource-rich Burma as forever within China's area of influence. Again, it bears asserting that in the post-cold war era there are two main powers in Asia, neither of which recognizes the superiority of the other (although Japan is in fact economically and militarily superior). In Indo-China Japan is flexing its muscles in a manner in a way that cannot but be irksome to China. Its investment in Vietnam, China's hated enemy in the region, is growing apace. It has dispatched troops to the UN peace-keeping force in Cambodia, which China may regard as an affront, because the main purpose of the force is to contain the Chinese-supported Khmer Rouge. There is also a long-standing territorial dispute over the Japanese-occupied Senkaku Islands as well as a quarrel over war reparations.

In Thailand, Singapore, and Malaysia, Japan has excellent business links and a financial presence. Currently, these countries are genuinely grateful for the growing prosperity brought by Japan's investment; but there is growing nationalist resentment about, for example, the despoiling of Thailand's rainforest and natural resources for the benefit of the Japanese, and their exploitation of the local sex industry. The behaviour of Japanese in Asia's brothels is becoming an increasingly live issue. Mass sex tourism organized by companies is commonplace. Manila prostitutes frankly described Japanese customers in a Japanese television documentary as 'pigs' and 'monsters'. In Japan the Association of Men Against Prostitution in South-East Asia recently put out a record whose lyrics run:

Father, when you weren't burning houses and killing people during the war, you were screwing women called 'army comfort ladies'. Brother, now you go to Asia and use your big bucks to buy lots of women. You began with what they called *kisaeng* sightseeing, just another way of saying sex-invasion. Do you understand the meaning of embarrassment and shame? Do you know who those they call the Sex Animals are? They wear ordinary civilian salaryman suits but they behave like soldiers. The time passes fast and the generations succeed one another, yet still when I walk on South-East Asian streets, as the women pass me by, they just say, 'Sex and money – that's Japan.'

Why do we so hurt Asian women's feelings? There must be something wrong with our sex life.

It is not hard to see anti-Japanese resentment erupting into genuine popular protest in the long term. Japan's relations with Malaysia and Singapore are gathering pace after a modest start, in spite of their traditional enmity towards Japan. Its presence today is still too small to stir nationalist resentment, although this could be a problem for the long term. Japan's influence is huge in Indonesia, but very largely dependent on a close relationship with the Suharto regime. This is powerful, increasingly corrupt and now undergoing the transition to the president's greedy sons; it is under threat from both Islam and the left. Its continuation can by no means be assured. If anti-Suharto forces came to the fore, Japan's close links with the current regime could lead to difficulties.

The potential for conflict and quarrelling in Asia, now that the nationalist urges of the countries in the region have been freed by the end of the cold war, is thus considerable. Few countries in the region, moreover, are constrained by the need to take electorates along with them. Japan, which might be a standard-bearer of democracy, is not. Indeed, it is in some ways the reverse. Incredibly, Japan's brand of authoritarianism with a democratic face is being looked to by some leaders as a role model in a reaction from the American example of previous decades. Moreover, there is admiration for Japan's adoption of state intervention in the economy as an economic model. Malaya's Prime Minister, Mohammed Mahathir, has said as much. The Japanese system has attractions, too, for Vietnam and Taiwan, both of which have a deep inclination towards authoritarian systems, and even possibly for Korea.

Japan's presence in Asia is everywhere apparent, with car factories and consumer goods plants proliferating on the edge of the Malaysian jungle, shopping centres and office towers in Hong Kong and Singapore, and rural enterprises in Thailand. The Proton Saga, Kuala Lumpur's ubiquitous home-produced cars, were pioneered by a team of Japanese production engineers led by Mitsubishi. In the same city, 17,000 workers turn out every morning in Japanese-style uniforms similiar to those worn at Matsushita plants in Japan and sing the company song. Mohammed Risli, a Malaysian government official, says that 'What we most want to emulate is the Japanese work ethic, the sense of loyalty to the country and the company.'

The government, like those of Singapore and South Korea, has followed the Japanese example of targeting strategic industries for growth. Says Risli, 'Japan's experience of rebuilding after the war, the way it got worker and management to co-operate and got the economy to grow in leaps and bounds, seems very Asian to me. It has much more relevance to our society than the experience of the West.' Japanese investment in Southeast Asia over the six years to 1991 was around $25 billion, roughly three times as much as American investment. Top of the league is Indonesia, with a staggering $12 billion, Malaysia with $3.5 billion, Singapore with nearly $7 billion, Thailand with $5 billion and the Philippines with $1.5 billion.

Malaysia's Mahathir has openly espoused the Japanese system, as preferable to the Western system. The model of fast economic growth accompanied by political authoritarianism and one-party rule pioneered by Japan is attractive to the tough-minded regimes of the region, who espouse it as 'Confucianism'. The Americans are shunned by these regimes for promoting such troublesome things as human rights, a free press, and independent trade unions. Singapore's prime minister, Goh Chok Tong, argues that 'the economies of the East are rising while the competitive edge of the West is on the decline'. Western scholars 'are beginning to study Confucianism as a rival ideology to western liberalism'.

Sarwono Kusamaatmadja, the Indonesian minister for administrative reform, claims that 'the West relies on management of conflict. We operate by managing consensus . . . We progress on the basis of common denominators. We always say that individual rights have a social function.' In practice, Indonesia is one of the most corrupt and authoritarian societies in the world, presided over by a military dictator and his greedy, squabbling sons. Japan is a beacon for fast-growth authoritarian regimes – as in China, Indonesia, Singapore (which nevertheless distrusts Japan's nationalist ambitions), and, to a lesser extent, Taiwan, South Korea, and Hong Kong. Only Thailand and the Philippines tilt marginally towards democracy.

The situation in Asia is hardly reassuring. China has vastly increased its military spending over the past five years. The Russians have not lowered their military presence in the area. Japan has continued gradually to increase its spending. South Korea and Taiwan have both done the same. All of these are countries which have undergone accelerated economic growth, retain fairly authoritarian systems, and are deeply suspicious of each other. Japan, with its huge economic wealth, has a host of satellite countries, but it has uneasy relations with Russia, China, and Korea, the major powers in the region and its nearest neighbours.

If Japan wishes to prosper, it must woo one of these countries, and China, since it offers excellent possibilities for economic transformation, seems likely to be the favoured one – in spite of past suspicions. Although the Americans have withdrawn from the Philippines, they still have a substantial presence in South Korea, Japan, and at sea with the Seventh Fleet. If the Americans precipitantly withdraw forces from the region, with which they do more trade than with Europe, it could plunge East Asia into instability, a regional arms race and ferocious political infighting between rich, politically immature and well-armed countries.

The Asian security map is changing faster than anyone could have foreseen. For the time being the quarrel between Japan and Russia over the Kuriles precludes any real possibility of a rapprochement between those two old enemies. Meanwhile, in 1992, South Korea and China resumed diplomatic relations after decades of enmity following the fighting between the two in the Korean War. North Korea's relations with the South have sharply deteriorated with the growing crisis over Pyongyang's apparent attempt to develop nuclear weapons. This is seen by many as the regime's last throw. South Korea, meanwhile, has also offered to develop Siberia and the Russian Far East, and even asked Moscow for fishing rights around the Kuriles. There is a real danger for Japan of the Koreans, Chinese and Russians joining forces against them; Japan has made overtures to the Chinese, and would be well advised not to make enemies of the Russians, for the sake of two barren islands settled by hostile peoples.

Increasingly, Asia seems torn between the Japanese model of nominal democracy and state direction, and the American one of democracy and free trade – to which only the Philippines and Thailand adhere with any enthusiasm. Moreover, the Japanese can argue that their system is more successful than the American one. Even authoritarian China shows some appreciation for the political stability of Japan's largely sham democracy. Francis Fukuyama's belief in the triumph of liberal democracy could not be more wrong if nothing happens within Japan to change this; a large part of Asia has chosen to rally behind the model of collectivist authoritarianism pioneered by Japan.

The third prospect of political instability lies in Japan's dominant economic power. This takes three forms: first, Japan's trade power, born of its exports, which although far from one-way, create considerable frictions; second, its industrial power, born of industries relocating abroad, which creates wealth there, but permits Japan to dominate local economies and insist that host governments meet their requirements (another major irritant); and, third, Japan's colossal financial power, exercised through its recycling of financial surpluses abroad. The Japanese have so far exercised restraint in using that muscle, although recently the central bank governor has adopted a higher profile in actively criticizing the United States for

its failure to control the budget deficit, short-termism and financial
fecklessness (all of them valid criticisms).

It is hard to put a finger on the extent of Japan's financial power,
but it is clear that the potential is huge: Japan has partially financed
the American budget deficit (and bought up a fair share of American
real estate). The flows of Japanese funding in and out of currency
and stock markets could devastate a medium-sized economy, and
even destabilize a major one, such as America's. Increasingly, if
economies behave in a way that the Japanese consider irresponsible,
they have the capacity to inflict major damage. This is real
power, which can be used in the pursuit of economic and political
ends. If a particular country is behaving in a protectionist manner
towards Japanese imports, making life difficult for their investing
companies, the threat of Japan's financial weapon is a formidable
deterrent.

One of Britain's best financial journalists, the late Jock Bruce-
Gardyne, once argued eloquently in the London *Spectator* that
Japanese financial power was largely illusory: if they ever exerted it
to destabilize the dollar, for example, the result would be a diminu-
tion in the values of their huge investments in the United States. He
was right, up to a point: the Americans could call Japan's bluff, at
considerable risk of penalty to themselves.

But the economic debate is not always run by fine bargaining. If
protectionist feeling grows too strong in the United States, a crude
attempt by the Japanese to browbeat the Americans by withdrawing
some of their funds, even though this would do some damage to
Japanese interests, cannot be ruled out. The reaction of American
voters to such pressure might be explosive, which is why the political
establishments of both countries are going to such lengths to keep
the lid on. All of this applies much more strongly to small economies.
If they don't behave themselves, they can be implicitly threatened
with financial penalties. Currency destabilization might even be in
Japan's long-term interests, for example, in delaying the achievement
of European monetary union – indeed, individual currencies can be
picked off today much more easily than a joint European currency
would.

If this sounds far-fetched, and is merely conjecture, it is worth
reflecting that virtually no decision in the world of commercial
warfare is motivated by anything other than competitive advantage,
least of all in Japan. Why not use all the weapons at your disposal?
Those who argue that Japan's economic strength does not translate
into political power are wide of the mark. If the West shrinks into

all-out protectionism, for example, the Japanese would have formidable weapons at their disposal, which in turn could provoke further reactions.

Fortunately, Japan does not have all the best cards. The country's great limitation, which is as true today as it was during the 1930s, is its isolation. It remains apart from the world to a degree unthinkable of any other major Western industrial economy. It flaunts its uniqueness, its racial superiority, over every other society on earth, and it has no true friends. It has no global ideology, like the former Soviet Union. Its Western competitors are resentful and suspicious; its Eastern neighbours are anxious to encourage Japanese money and economic aid into their economies, but are fearful of its ambitions. The more powerful Japan becomes, even overtaking the United States, the more any excessive move on its part is likely to assemble a formidable coalition against it.

If, in extreme circumstances, Japan starts killing again in Asia, China, Russia and the United States could once again form an overwhelmingly stronger alliance against it. After the experience in the Pacific War, Japan should have learnt this: only if the irrational forces in that strange society, which admittedly are much closer to the seat of power than in other industrialized societies, were to gain control would Japan be likely to repeat its miscalculation.

But the West cannot afford to make mistakes with this authoritarian, collectivist colossus. If we too can avoid the mistakes of the 1920s and 1930s, the potential for future conflict will be avoided. This requires two attitudes: first, a much firmer and tougher advocacy of the West's interests that does not lull Japanese into believing – as it half does today – that it is dealing with degenerates and fools; and, second, a much more accommodating and less knee-jerk reaction to the extraordinary contribution that this amazing civilization of the East is making to the world, and indeed to modern industrial society.

To touch on the first: Japan's economic miracle owed a great deal, as we have seen, to America's commitment to the virtues of free trade, permitting access to Western markets while Japan prevented access to its own and manipulated an undervalued exchange rate. In addition, Japan kept down its military and social spending, as well as squeezing wages. The Americans permitted this so long as Japan was not seen as a challenge. The Western response now, however, is growing protectionism; this is natural, in view of Japan's

extreme reluctance to dismantle its competitive advantages. However, the West must not go too far: raising barriers should be limited
to specific areas in which Japan itself is protectionist. Hard bargaining is right and defensible; American pandering to unions protecting
their own inefficient industries from legitimate Japanese competition
is not. The latter is not only economically wrong but will inevitably
lead to the kind of Japanese nationalist reaction that helped to
incubate the crisis of the 1930s.

Japanese industry certainly took advantage of the West's lowered
guard to construct a large number of assembly plants in the United
States and Europe that attracted the maximum in government
subsidies, that were largely 'screwdriver' operations not benefiting
the local country in terms of know-how or value added, and
undercut local producers. Again, as is beginning to happen in Britain,
the answer is not to condemn Japanese investment *per se*: this can
bring enormous benefits in teaching other countries more effective
forms of industrial organization. Instead, host countries must insist
on the kind of investment that contributes to the development of the
local economy and the host country's know-how. The Japanese will
respect countries which welcome them with hard-headed business
propositions that benefit both sides.

The second approach should seek to maximize the economic
lessons that the Japanese way of doing things has for the world. In
economics, as we have seen, there are aspects of the Japanese method
that are perfectly transferable to economies hooked on crude free-
market doctrines, and there are several ways in which the latter
would improve Japan's economic workings; dogma should be absent
on both sides. Japan's management practices, assembly-line techniques and technology can teach much to Western industry.

The West should try to assimilate the beneficial part of Japan's
experience, helping to break down the idea propagated both in Japan
and abroad that the country's economic success is due to unique
racial characteristics. It is not racialist, but a matter of cultural
development, to suggest that the Japanese may be particularly
attuned to modern industrial and technological organization in
certain ways – through their numeracy, rote literacy, their methodical and authoritarian way of ordering things, their ability to learn
vast numbers of characters, the conformity which works so well
within industrial organizations, and so on. Much of this is not
exportable, nor even desirable in other industrial societies. There are
genuine differences.

But many other aspects, such as just-in-time assembly, the

emphasis on research and development, the belief in retraining, the paternalist attitude to employees, are both exportable and desirable. In addition, there are aspects of Japan's command economy (although not every aspect) that would benefit the West. Finally, Japan needs to be allowed to fulfil its proper role as a very influential member of world organizations, such as the United Nations Security Council, the major development banks, the multilateral aid agencies, and so on. At the moment the Japanese have a good deal of power without responsibility, always a dangerous mix.

If Japan wants to remain an economic rather than a military power, so much the better. There can be nothing more dangerous and counterproductive than the current American campaign to bolster Japanese defence spending, which could seriously destabilize the Asian region. Japan is already more than equipped to take on the defensive role of America in the region. Hegemony breeds defensiveness, suspicion, resentment and regional arms races.

Japan should take its place at the top table in the world, along with the United States. To complain that Japan's political system provides too weak a leadership to perform these tasks is self-fulfilling: the Japanese political system will only change if the disadvantages of having weak prime ministers with a term of only two years become apparent internationally.

Thus on the one hand the West needs to be much sterner and clearer-minded in its approach to Japanese business: we will continue to do business with you, but only on mutually beneficial terms – then we can resist the pressure for protection. On the other hand, rather than continuing to encourage Japan to rearm, the West needs to give Japan its rightful place at the top table, so that it is not encouraged to exert its huge economic influence surreptitiously and subversively. These are the guidelines for a sensible Western approach over the next three decades.

34

THE SOFT AND THE HARD

THE OTHER great unknown is how Japanese society will develop internally over the same period. The grim conclusion is that this society is moving towards a breaking point. Its ruling class, who takes virtually all major decisions, is moving steadily to the right, while the population is beginning to acquire, in spite of their rigid regimentation, the beginnings of independent thought.

The tension beneath the surface of Japanese society suddenly and rarely exploded in October 1990 in Airin, a downtrodden area of Osaka, when some 2500 police battled with 1500 demonstrators. About 200 were injured and several buildings were burned. Airin was a typical poor quarter, where the streets stank of urine and alcohol and many inhabitants lived in $10 a night dormitories. The area is usually controlled by the *yakuza*, while police television cameras mounted on poles monitor the streets twenty-four hours a day. The riot started when police arrested an old man with a megaphone who criticized the enthronement ceremony of Emperor Akihito; a crowd attacked the police station and demanded the release of the man. The rioting lasted for three days. Can the system – today the world's most successful – survive for ever?

There is no doubt that profound change is taking place behind the rigid, unblinking exterior of Japanese society. One subtle change is that Japan has partially shed the dour salaryman image of regimented workaholics prepared to labour inhuman hours and live in tiny apartments for the sake of future benefits. Japan is a society increasingly geared towards speculation and towards the pursuit of material pleasure. Young people are changing their attitudes, seeking immediate satisfaction rather than building up their savings or status.

The population is also ageing faster than that of any other country with over-sixty-fives making up 16 per cent of the population by the year 2000, and becoming fully a quarter of the population by the year 2020. The birth rate is falling, while people are living longer.

Mariko Fujiwara, who works for the Hakahudo Institute of Life and Living in Tokyo, gives a fascinating insight into the change in attitudes of young people: their chief objectives, according to the institute's research, are stable and secure personal lives rather than the community and status; friends are particularly important to them. They are deeply opposed to the competitive ethic, 75 per cent preferring to co-operate rather than compete with other people (an image reflected in Japan's own co-operative ethic). Unlike their parents, many consider that life should be enjoyed rather than endured. Most said they had no desire to grow up.

Ms Fujiwara claims that 'there has been a dramatic increase in sexual promiscuity in the last ten years', as might be expected in a country where the only barriers to this were social, not religious and moral, and the younger generation for the first time is able to make an independent living. The old stereotyped Japanese domestic scene, with the wife having to put up with an irascible mother-in-law, is breaking down. Rather than marry, Japanese girls prefer to cohabit and sleep around, avoiding the dire traditional fate. The journalist Mitsuko Shimomura, of the *Asahi Shimbun* newspaper, also argues that Japanese lifestyles are beginning to change dramatically. She speaks scathingly of the attitude that 'diversity has to be suppressed' and of an educational system that is 'adept at inculcating technical expertise rather than in nurturing creativity' with the object of 'creating an ideal human being'.

During the upper house elections in 1992, the prime minister, Kiichi Miyazawa, for the first time, campaigned on improving the quality of life for ordinary Japanese. 'It's been said that we Japanese live in rabbit hutches and unfortunately it's true.' He pledged to bring down the cost of a home in Tokyo to five times the annual salary of worker. 'My party promises to improve the quality of life of the people.'

The elections were also unusual because of a dissident breakaway from the LDP led by Morihiro Hosokawa, from an old *daimyo* family, who campaigned for a new Japanese politics and spoke with reckless frankness. 'Everyone knows that we have a structural conspiracy in this country among politicians, bureaucrats and businessmen. Americans know it. Japanese know it.' One of his supporters, Yoshio Terasawa, a former vice-president of the World Bank's

Multilateral Investment Guarantee Agency, argued that the Japanese enjoy dismal standards of living:

> In the supermarket Tokyoites pay 235 yen for a kilogram of bananas, compared with 173 yen in Washington; 511 yen for a kilo of oranges versus 199 yen in the United States; 383 yen per 100 grams of beef compared with 130 yen there. A family dinner at an ordinary restaurant would suck several 10,000 yen bills out of papa's wallet, while an American family of four can get by for a month on $500 worth of groceries. And even if one could afford it, there is no family left in Japan any more. These days even the children don't come home until 10 p.m. – they have to attend cram schools to prepare for entrance exams. This is because only one university counts here, the University of Tokyo, known as Todai. Children begin to climb this Mount Fuji of all schools even before kindergarten, because a Todai diploma is a passport to a good lifetime career.

These are unusual sentiments to come from a former senior bureaucrat.

The miserable existence of the Japanese salaryman has often been parodied: how he rises at 5.30 a.m. every morning in the tiny accommodation reserved for a company's married couples; how he goes to the station at 6.30, catches his train to the office, joins his real 'family' there, works assiduously, has lunch in a cramped eating house, finishes work at 7.30, goes on a prolonged drinking ritual with his boss a couple of times a week, returns home at 10.00, works on Saturdays, often plays golf with the boss on Sundays, and rarely takes more than a couple of weeks' holiday a year, and then doesn't know how to spend it. In a book published in 1993, Masao Miyamoto wryly recounts the dire career consequences of taking a continuous fortnight's holiday and of seeking to get away from the office before 7 p.m.

For the vast majority of Japanese salarymen, this remains the reality and is likely to change only slowly. According to Mrs Shimomura, however, change is on the way at home. Women, who barely see their husbands, refer derisively to them as 'industrial waste'. She cites the man who returned home 'early' at ten o'clock because his boss thought he was working too hard. His wife's welcome was, 'Be quiet then.'

Some 53 per cent of women under twenty-nine are single, as are some 74 per cent of men. Women are picking their partners much more independently and getting married later, while men are more eager to do so early. In rural communities where most of the women have left, sons of farmers are reduced to seeking brides by mail-order overseas. One in eight marriages now ends in divorce, women taking the attitude that 'if they don't get on, there are many other fish in the sea'. Most women work in offices rather than paddyfields.

Mrs Shimomura is perhaps exaggerating the new status of women in Japan a little: the country is still remarkably backward in its attitudes to such things as equality in work (one employer complained in the author's hearing that he didn't like employing women because 'they cry too much – and the trouble with some young men nowadays is that they do too'), sexual harassment by *chikas*-gropers (which expatriates in Tokyo claim is prevalent in trains and on the streets), and in the home, where arranged marriages are still common and young women are still repressed by their mothers-in-law.

How far the reality of progress on women's rights in Japan differed from the hope was shown by a survey of small- and medium-sized companies in Japan in October 1991. Some 70 per cent responded that they did not understand women or the management techniques needed to work with them. A fraction fewer conceded that there were no women managers in their companies, and 52 per cent said women were to blame for their failure to achieve promotion. In another survey, 85 per cent of working women reported discrimination at work, while more than 40 per cent complained of sexual harassment. Because virtually no provision exists for childbirth, women have to leave their companies when they have children, and then return to part-time work, which amounts to hard work without the benefits. Some two-thirds of women, who make up 40 per cent of the Japanese workforce, are in such jobs. This is another reason why so many young women postpone getting married.

Bill Emmott argues in *The Sun Also Sets* that young people try to look different from one another, and even to take risks and change jobs, many opting for smaller, more creative companies in computer software, design or fashion. Even so, their noncomformity fits into curiously regular patterns.

Of course Emmott and the others are right: Japanese society is changing. But the very changes cited expose how controlled it remains. It is becoming a vigorous but conservative society, with safety valves of greater sexual gratification, love hotels, porno-sadistic comics, video games, pinball machine alleys, consumer goods and taste for fashions. At the fringes, for example, in the field of the arts and fashion and in some of the smaller enterprises, it shows signs of greater creativity. But conformity remains the order of the day for the bulk of the population, creativity being confined to such things as flashy ties in the office. Still, for the first-time visitor to Tokyo today, the most striking image must still be the sight early in the morning of the streets teeming with thousand upon thousand of identically clothed salarymen as they go to their offices. They resemble nothing so much as a huge army of soldiers in suits, to the extent that anyone, such as tourists or manual labourers, without a white shirt, tie and jacket looks completely out of place.

Japanese education is among the best in the world in terms of the high maths marks scored by schoolchildren in international league tables. However, it fails to develop the mind or logical thinking, suppresses originality and discourages pupils from asking questions. The main objective is to impart huge quantities of information. One Japanese educationalist put the purpose as 'shaping generations of disciplined workers for a techno-meritocratic system that requires highly socialised individuals capable of performing reliably in a rigorous, hierarchical and finely tuned organisational environment'.

An American who taught at college in Japan for two years, Ken Schooland, presents a grim picture in his book, *Shogun's Ghost*. He reveals that children spend two months per year more at school than their Western equivalents, that children have to study well into the night and are forbidden to go and play with their friends and that they are governed by school regulations even outside class.

The schools are obsessive about trivia. One girls' high school in Tokyo inspected its charges' underwear. Those with polka-dot or coloured panties, instead of regulation white, were made to stand in front of the class while they were denounced by the teacher for behaving like 'bar hostesses'. A girl arriving late to class was forced to sit for seven hours straight-backed.

The Japan Bar Association, in an extensive survey, found that schools were incredibly pernickety in their regulations. A middle school ordered its students 'to march to music in neat lines, eyes turned toward the teacher on a platform at the morning roll call. Standing to attention, toes should be angled at 45 to 60 degrees and fingers should be extended straight with the palms touching the body. In saluting, the upper body should be inclined forward at 30 degrees and held rigid before resuming an upright posture in a smooth manner.'

Lisa Martineau, a former *Guardian* correspondent in Tokyo, gives a vivid eyewitness account of Japanese teaching inside the classroom:

By 1 a.m. the children have been individually studying their weak subjects for four hours. Except for the sounds of pens squeaking over paper and the rustling of pages, the classrooms are still ... [the children] all have little pots of cream on their desks, which they rub on their wrists and smell. 'It is mosquito repellent', a solemn little boy tells me, 'it helps us to stay awake.' Between sniffs his eyes keep closing and his head falls back. One girl's lips are bleeding. 'I bite them to stay alert,' she says. 'The mosquito cream isn't enough.' Other children have bruises on their arms. I watch them pick up their flesh and twist it, gritting their teeth and closing their eyes until it has hurt enough to bring tears to their cheeks ...

The door creeps open and two girls sheepishly come in with their heads bowed. They are two minutes late. The teacher looks up quickly and turns on them: 'You worthless girls,' he bellows. 'How dare you come late to my lesson!' They are bent over at 45 degree angles like outstretched ironing boards. They whisper apologies. He storms across the classroom towards them: 'You have brought shame on your parents!' he screams. 'They have put their faith in you and how do you repay them? By behaving disgracefully! Come here! Kneel down!'

He points to the floor by his feet. The girls drop to their knees and collapse forward until their noses are almost touching the floor. The teacher picks up a *manga* [comic] lying on his desk. 'You are not worthy to have been born!' he howls. 'All the sacrifices your parents have made for you – and look at you – look at you!' He rolls up the *manga* in both hands, holding it like a rounders bat, and wallops the girls around their heads. They keep perfectly still. One of them digs her nails into the palm of her hands. The other children do not take their eyes from their books. The teacher throws the *manga* on his desk. 'You will stay there for the whole lesson,' he says to the girls. 'If you want to waste your parents' money, you will not waste my time.'

Beatings are common throughout the system and many parents approve. One company executive in Kanagawa says that 'when I raised my children, I asked the teachers to use corporal punishment if necessary. In training dogs and horses, they receive a treat whenever they behave and are whipped when they don't. The same stance should be taken with children. Children are animals being taught to be human . . . although brutality should be eliminated, we must trust the teachers and let our children receive the professional, loving whip of their instructors.'

Yoshio Murakami, a journalist on the *Asahi Journal*, cites many standard examples of corporal punishment: a second-year girl at high school was summoned to the headmaster's office where five teachers beat her about the head. One grabbed her by the hair and dragged her around the room; her face afterwards was puffed and swollen. Teachers express the view that, 'You have to strike while the iron is hot. Beating them can instill a strong will in them.' Just short of beating is the public scolding in front of the class. One observer described a girl offender bowing in silence before her teacher: 'The kids have to be submissive and full of remorse while being scolded, or else they risk a renewed barrage of insults. Frequently the scolding continues until they are reduced to tears and all the signs of defiance are gone. They're literally broken.'

In a survey of nearly 400 cases of corporal punishment in 1984 involving 2400 pupils, some 70 per cent of the children had received injuries and one had died when forced to practise rugby under harsh conditions as a punishment; another pupil was suspended upside down from a second-floor window of his school by a teacher. Other punishments included being made to take off their underwear in front of the teacher, being punched until medical treatment was necessary or being incarcerated in lockers. Around a quarter of those in the survey were being punished for not doing their homework properly. Bullying, *ijime*, is also rife. Some 22,000 cases are recorded a year, not all as serious as that of thirteen-year-old Yuhei Kodaida, who in January 1993 was found dead, stuffed upside down in a rolled-up mat inside a closet at school in Shinjo.

Such discipline is effective when children were young enough to be intimidated. But the sternness of the system and the absolutely unimaginative way in which subjects were taught ensured that by university level pupils were wildly unruly and unreceptive to education (as they were shortly to be absorbed into the unrelenting conformity of the salaryman's life, it is perhaps hard to blame them).

Japanese cram schools, *jukus*, have grown up in parallel to the state education system, partly to make up for its deficiencies, partly to push children as young as two and three on the first rungs of the ladder to a good job. Nearly 4.4 million children attend 50,000 to 60,000 *jukus*, representing nearly 19 per cent of elementary schoolchildren and more than half of twelve-year-olds. A child of that age will normally rise at dawn, work at school until late afternoon, then do three hours' further study in a *juku* before returning home to do two hours' homework and going to bed at midnight.

Professor Ikuo Amanon, of the sociology faculty at Tokyo University, claims that '*jukus* are harmful to Japanese education and to children. It is not healthy for kids to have so little free time. It is not healthy to become completely caught up in competition and status at such a young age.' However, many observers suggest that the atmosphere for learning with enjoyment is much better at *jukus* that in the rigidly run state schools.

In 1991 police uncovered a widespread and systematic scandal involving the hiring of bright pupils to take exams on behalf of wealthier, less talented pupils in order to obtain entrance to one of Japan's prestige schools; sums of $100,000 reportedly changed hands. In another school in Hyogo prefecture the principal and a teacher of a prestigious school were arrested for allegedly tampering with the entrance exams of fifteen pupils to make sure they would pass; the pupils were sons of old boys. The system is less meritocratic than it seems.

The pinnacle of the system is, of course, Todai, Tokyo Imperial University. In 1952, 14,836 students took the exam for the 'fast track' of the civil service and just 50 per cent of them passed. More than half were Todai graduates. Of the twenty-four who got through the exams for a place on the Ministry of Finance's fast track, twenty-two were Todai graduates. The same year the government decreed that no more than half of the fast-track graduates can come from Todai. A foreign ministry official says, 'The first thing that people want to know about you when you enter a ministry is whether you went to Todai or not. If you didn't, in a lot of ministries there are many jobs you can forget about.'

The Japanese government acknowledges criticism of the education system. It lumps this into three categories: excessive exam competition; excessive uniformity; and rigidity, as the government acknowledges:

The uniform system of force-feeding hinders the growth of powers of independent judgement and creativity and produces masses of people whose individuality is underdeveloped. This poses the danger that the nation will be unable to respond in time to important movements such as greater internationalization and greater reliance on information.

The third area of criticism is, conversely, a decline in discipline and respect in the schools:

> materialism, decreases in the educative influence of the home and community, and the wide availability of suggestive information have exerted a harmful influence on children's development. The response to this by schools and teachers has not been productive, resulting in educational disintegration characterised by bullying and the resultant aversion to going to school, school violence and juvenile delinquency.

The last two phenomena point to exactly opposite types of reform, and seriously dent Japan's reputation for having the best educational system in the world. In 1987 the Provisional Council on Education Reform, set up by the Nakasone government, recommended:

> the most important aim of education reform to come is to do away with uniformity, rigidity and closedness, all of which are deep-rooted defects of our educational system, and to establish the dignity of the individual, respect for individuality and the principles of freedom and independence, and individual responsibility. Aspects of our educational system, including curriculum content, methodology, organization and government policies, should be reviewed drastically in the light of this 'principle of putting emphasis on individuality'.

This is remarkable, coming from Japanese officialdom; it remains to be seen whether it is no more than a pious expression of concern, or will be translated into reality.

For the more anti-social kind of nonconformist, there is the Japanese justice system, which still works along modified thought-control lines. Social condemnation remains a fierce sanction against breaking the norm, let alone the law: individuals disgrace not just themselves but their families, their neighbours, their villages or towns, and their companies. A system of surveillance still discreetly exists in virtually every neighbourhood, while the night watchman is, literally, a man who keeps his eye on the doings of his neighbours for the benefit of the police.

Another enormously effective system of control, still in place, is that of the village office (in cities). The office looks after most of the usual functions of local government. More significantly, it keeps records on residence, marital status, births of children, and any encounter with the law, as well as the basic facts on each individual. All such information is entered on one's dossier, even from the most distant parts of the country, if a person has moved home. Anyone applying for a job or going before a judge has to submit a copy of his dossier; a bad entry for an individual or any member of his family is a serious matter.

The Japanese take a surprisingly lenient view of first-time infringements, in accord with the general tendency for the state to treat adults as erring children (the system has its virtues, as it prevents first-time offenders being turned into hardened criminals in jail). For the most serious offenders, however, prison is a grim deterrent indeed, as one Englishman recently jailed in Japan found out. Sigrun Falkinn, a thirty-one-year-old British teacher unjustly accused of theft and kept prisoner for fifteen months in 1991–2, provided a rare view of the inside of the Japanese prison system.

When he complained to a warder of being treated like an animal, other warders were called, and in the ensuing scuffle, Falkinn fell through a window, suffering severe cuts to his face, arms, and feet. He was then carried to 'the bunker':

> I was kicked and a wet towel was pushed into my mouth. In the bunker they stripped me naked and stamped on my arms and legs with their combat boots. One of the guards was kicking me in the ribs. They forced me into prison clothes which were several sizes too small. Only then did they drag me to the hospital to stitch me up.

He was taken first to a punishment cell and then to another: 'It had a dirty hole for a toilet. I refused to eat and drink, it was so smelly. I was taken to the hospital and assaulted by approximately six wardens.' When they attempted to push a tube up his nose, he agreed to eat and drink. After four days he was moved to the 'spy-room' which did have a proper toilet.

For the following six weeks he was watched twenty-four hours a day by a camera in the ceiling of his cell. The cell was lit night and day. Between the hours of 7 a.m. and 5 p.m. he had to sit cross-legged on the floor not touching the walls, and was permitted to rise only to go to the lavatory or to wash. He was in solitary confinement for several months and not allowed to exercise with other prisoners. Unusually in Japan, where 99 per cent of prosecutions result in conviction, Falkinn was found innocent and freed.

Due process of law is as blatantly disregarded in Japan as under any Latin American dictatorship or communist system. Most evidence consists of confessions extracted in police custody. According to Japanese lawyers, these are often forced. The Tokyo Bar Association recently claimed that twenty out of thirty prisoners forced to confess to crimes they did not commit had been tortured. All were denied food, sleep and legal access for most of their interrogation period, which included questioning sessions of more than fourteen hours a day and, for ten of them, lasted more than 100 days. Once a case goes to prosecution, the court hearing is usually a rubber stamp: out of 63,204 people being tried for the first time in 1986, only 67 were acquitted. Appeals courts only very rarely overturn convictions.

In March 1993, the death penalty was resumed after a three-year moratorium, amid Soviet-style secrecy. Three, or possibly five, convicted killers were executed in Osaka, Sendai, and maybe Fukuoka and Tokyo prisons. Relatives were not told of the executions in advance, simply informed afterwards that they should pick up the belongings of the deceased.

The Western concept of a citizen having legal rights before the state is alien to the Japanese: the law is merely a tool of the state. This was expressed by the scholar Hajime Kawakami earlier this century:

> Individuals are not believed to exist for and of themselves as autonomous entities; only the state does. In Japan, state sovereignty is heaven-granted while individual rights are bestowed by the state. The state allows limited individual rights to the extent that they further the aims of the state. Thus individual rights are always instruments of the state, not to be utilized for the aims of the individual. While in the West individual rights are thought to be granted by heaven and thus inalienable ... respect for individual rights and individual identity in the West is inconceivable for Japanese, just as Japanese respect of state sovereignty and the state is inconceivable for Westerners.

The MacArthur constitution contains explicit legal safeguards, but it is ignored. Because the legal system lacks any teeth and ordinary people do not resort to it, the constitution cannot be enforced in its provisions for the rights of the individual. Civil litigation is kept to an absolute minimum: the number of cases that go to court at all are fewer than a tenth the number in Western countries and the overwhelming majority are settled out of court, usually because the weaker party recognizes he cannot win. Judges tend to believe that anyone who pursues a case through the courts displays an inferior moral attitude. Very few cases are ever brought against the government by private individuals. The Supreme Court, which has American-style powers of judicial review, never uses them, thus placing government above the law. In business, disputes are overcome and agreements reached behind closed doors, with the law very rarely playing a part.

Another reason the law counts for so little is quite simple. The government sharply restricts the number of lawyers. All lawyers must go through the Legal Training and Research Institute. More Japanese apply for this than do Americans for law schools. But only 2 per cent – some 486 out of nearly 24,000 candidates in 1985 – succeed, although most other graduates automatically qualify in their disciplines. There is only one lawyer for more than 9000 people in Japan, compared with one for 360 people in America, and one for 900 in Britain. Simple cases take more than two years to resolve, more complicated ones up to ten years, and some up to twenty-five years.

The Japanese justify their scant regard for the law as a means of resolving matters in terms of face: in law there must be a winner and a loser, which is undesirable. The Japanese do not accept a clear division between right and wrong, good and bad, correct and incorrect. Japanese regard the law as being necessary, 'but the courts are cold and distant'. 'The law is a last resort – its significance lies in its not being invoked.' The Japan Arbitration Council has declared:

> In Japan conciliation is systematically incorporated into the judicial system ... settlement by conciliation is allowed even if such settlement deviates from what the laws stipulate ... conciliation includes compulsory features. For example, a ... party who is summoned to the conciliation proceedings is obliged to appear and if he fails to appear without any proper reason, he will be fined.

Japan's crime rate per 100,000 inhabitants is strikingly lower than in the West: murder is a quarter of the French and German levels, a sixth of the British, and an eighth of the American. Rape –

although this is said to be much under-reported in Japan – is a fifth of the French level, a sixth of the German level, a ninth of the British level and little more than a thirtieth of the American level. Robbery is a thirtieth of the German level, a fiftieth of the British level, a seventieth of the French level, and a two-hundredth of the American level. Japanese arrest rates are slightly higher than their Western counterparts in murder and rape cases, and nearly triple those in robbery cases.

The system has its methods for dealing even with organized crime through the simple expedient of permitting it to flourish under controlled conditions; tens of thousands of *yakuza*, gangsters, work for the country's thousands of mobs in such activities as protection, loan-sharking, debt collection, intimidating shareholders at annual general meetings, press ganging cheap labour and bullying small-holders into selling plots for development. The *yakuza* have their own offices, listed in the telephone directory, for these services, and until recently have been left largely untouched by the police, indeed performing services for the authorities, business and, in the latest twist of political scandal, senior LDP politicians.

Japan has more than 86,000 organized gang members, belonging to 3000 syndicates, with a turnover of more than $7 billion a year. The three biggest gangs are the Yamaguchi-gumi, the Inagawa-Kai and the Sumiyoshi-kai, each with around 10,000 members control-ling large parts of Tokyo. Under a police 'crackdown' decreed in 1992, no more than one in twenty members of mobs with a membership of 100 can have serious criminal records (the figure is 8 per cent for gangs of up to 100 members).

Recently, *yakuza* indulged excessively in the real estate specu-lation of the 'bubble economy' of the 1980s, and the police 'declared war' on them, although few believed it would be carried beyond a few skirmishes. The system thus survives by co-opting even organ-ized crime into its embrace. Again, there is nothing new about the existence of massive criminal syndicates or of corrupt police in most industrial societies, but for a system to be so amoral as openly to tolerate crime in order to control it – although not, of course, protect its victims – and even use it to protect its interests, is, again, more a feature of a severely underdeveloped society than the world's second most powerful.

The government's own polls show that ordinary Japanese are far from unmixed in their appreciation of the general direction of

Japanese society. While most Japanese replied in 1991 that their country had 'high economic power', only 13 per cent agreed entirely that 'national life is affluent'. However, 58 per cent felt that Japan was not 'a welfare society', while only 6 per cent fully agreed. Only 13 per cent entirely agreed that personal freedom and rights were guaranteed, while 52 per cent agreed to some extent, and some 28 per cent disagreed.

The Japanese remain a socially centred and nationalist people: some 41 per cent agreed that 'the people should pay more attention to state and social affairs'. More than half had a 'strong patriotic sense', and 62 per cent felt that patriotism should be further strengthened among the people, while only 19 per cent disagreed. Nearly 60 per cent felt that the popular will 'was not reflected in national policy'.

Will the gradual, but visible pressures in Japanese society ever translate into real political change? Just possibly: it is conceivable that Japanese, as they become more independent-minded, will prefer to back the genuinely reformist sectors of the ruling elite such as these headed by Hosokawa and Toshiki Kaifu, for example. Kaifu said that change must come – so as to bring Japan up to the political level of the English of 160 years ago! 'My proposal for single-member constituencies will bring Japan up to the position of the British in the 1832 Reform Act; however, it has been replaced by a less effective proposal to limit spending on political campaigns,' he added sadly.

Just conceivably, voters will really punish the LDP for its seemingly endless succession of scandals on the grandest scale, involving some of the most senior men in the party. Just conceivably the 'Rainbow Coalition' will survive or, if brought down, will be returned to form a strong non-LDP government. The government's only card has been its popularity. Hata seems less likely to retain this than Hosokawa was. Every recent Japanese scandal seemed likely to bring the system down; this time the limit may have been reached. Just conceivably.

But none of these things has happened yet. The Hosokawa government is as frail as a Japanese partition wall. Hosokawa's fall looked disturbingly like that of one of those sacrificial heroes familiar throughout Japanese history. The enormous and sophisti-cated vote- and institution-buying operation that is the LPD Demo-cratic Party still seems likely to use the power bestowed by the conformity of Japanese life to stifle political change. Meanwhile, there is a disturbing shift towards nationalist self-assertion at the top of the LDP and among Japan's elites. The drift – at a time when young Japanese are becoming individualist and hedonistic – could lead to a dramatic fissure in Japanese society one day; or the new young consumers, sated with sado-masochistic comics, computer games and designer suits, may blindly follow nationalist leaders to a more table-thumping policy.

The growth of the Japanese economy, after the shocks of the early 1990s, seems set to continue in more orderly, trimmer form. One far-sighted Japanese business chief argued with some exasperation: 'What our short-sighted companies fail to understand is that by adopting measures to improve the quality of life and to give workers more free time, they will make themselves more, not less, efficient.' The idea that a slightly more laid-back Japan would be a less efficient, more-Western style competitor seems a mistaken one.

Thus it seems best to hope that Japan can be induced towards a more co-operative political and economic relationship with the outside world through a policy of carefully inducing the country to take its fair share of the world responsibilities. If that entails accepting the reality of Japanese power, so be it; a refusal to face that reality would be infinitely more dangerous. To wait for change from within may be to wait for Godot. The position is by no means bleak, but nor is it reassuring.

The pessimistic scenario for probably the world's strongest economic superpower of the next century – and possibly the strongest political and military one as well – is not of a sudden rush to war with America, but something as follows:

Japan, with its economy of the twenty-first century and its oligarchical faction-ridden, hierarchical politics of the eighteenth century is being shut out from Western markets. Its investments abroad are becoming unpopular in the host countries. Its attempt to use its financial muscle to protect it arouse suspicion and irritation. As anti-Japanese rhetoric grows in America and Western Europe, the country increasingly turns its attention to its Asian hinterland, soon experiencing similar but sharper reactions because the countries involved are authoritarian, with a burgeoning sense of nationalism, and historically suspicious of Japan. Having built up its military strength, Japan reacts in heavy-handed fashion to civil disturbances against its interests, as well as to the territorial assertiveness of other Asian states, possibly leading to a conflict with one – China? – or more.

This heightens the tension with America and Europe, although it does not lead to conflict. Instead, a kind of 'cold war' ensues with Japan, backed by a number of Asian supporters, advocating an alternative system of authoritarian control and state direction to that of the West, possibly in competition not just with Asia but throughout the Third World. Friction ensues as countries like Korea try to maintain their independence from Japan by aligning with the West. A new arms race between the economic giants of West and East is not out of the question. Even on this pessimistic scenario, armed conflict is unlikely. It was sparked last time both by Japan's massive military advance into China – something highly unlikely now – and by the retaliatory sanctions against Japan. As long as Japan has the money, she is likely to be able to buy all the raw materials she needs.

But the world will have divided into a new political polarity between East and West, and this time one which is much more evenly matched. The prospect of such a renewed superpower competition – economic, political, military and ideological – is profoundly depressing. In the long term, Japan will probably emerge the loser because of its political isolation. That prospect, as well as perhaps imaginative policies practised by the West and the possibility of change within Japan, are the only factors that seem likely to avert a new cold war.

To return to the beginning: a country is wrenched from centuries of isolation under a military dictatorship by a far-sighted aristocratic-bureaucratic elite which then loses control of the process to a military clique once again. The elite re-emerges in control after the war, but seems to have lost the initiative to business-driven forces. The frenzied onslaught of the empty-headed suit of samurai armour in its new guise, the salaryman's suit, is rushing forward as vigorously and aimlessly as ever. In its very vigour lies the potential for economic and political confrontation; in its aimlessness the potential for failure of the kind that has dogged Japanese history.

The Japanese respect what Ivan Morris has dubbed the nobility of failure. A theme of constant fascination to them is the story of Shimabura. Some great events, not necessarily the obvious ones, act like giant signposts to their country's history. America's Civil War (rather than the American Revolution), the English Civil War (rather than the Glorious Revolution), and the French Revolution (rather than the Napoleonic period) all somehow capture the essence of a nation's past in a way that fires the popular imagination.

In Japan the crucial event was the Shimabara massacre of 1638, rather than the Meiji restoration more than two centuries later, an untypical and largely bloodless occurrence in Japanese history, even if it was the defining moment for modern Japan. Shimabara provides the key to Japan's modern history and sense of self-identity even now. The horror, ferocity, relentlessness and implacability of authority combined with the futile self-sacrifice of those involved in the rebellion illuminate deep truths about Japan.

Japan's peasants at the time lived at subsistence level; they were terrorized and bullied into working the land by their feudal lords and the huge unproductive samurai class that dominated them; yet occasionally they exploded into wild, doomed acts of rebellion against the overwhelming military might of the system. Invariably, these were viciously crushed. Such a revolt was the one at Shimabara, which looked to Christianity for its inspiration. A century earlier, Francis Xavier had arrived with his missionaries near Nagasaki, far from Edo, the centre of power in Japan. The appeal of the religion spread quickly and by the late sixteenth century the *daimyo* of the Shimabara Peninsula, Lord Arima, had himself been converted.

In 1612 the Tokugawas in Edo, increasingly alarmed by the spread of this subversive creed, launched a reign of terror against it. All foreign priests were banished or murdered, and most of the 300,000 Christians in the country were either forced to recant, or killed through hideous torture, which included being roasted alive, subjected to the water torture or the snake pit, branding, being sawn up with a bamboo saw and crucifixion. Lord Matsukura, the new ruler of the Shimabara Peninsula, was one of the most vigorous persecutors, boiling many of his victims alive in the scalding waters of the Unzen hot springs.

By 1637, Christianity was believed to have been stamped out, although in practice many continued to worship in secret. Later that year, sixteen Christians were found secretly worshipping a minor miracle and were executed. This so angered the village they came from that the people openly celebrated the feast of the Ascension. A bailiff tried to stop them and was killed. There could be no going back now. The villagers left to trek round the nearby countryside, seeking sympathizers to raise the banner of rebellion.

The nearby villages were ready to hear the message. Not only had they undergone religious persecution, they were the objects of the most fearsome economic repression as well. They had been subjected to unprecedented tax demands, such as the produce tax, the door tax, the hearth tax, the shelf tax, the candle tax and even the death tax. When peasants could not pay, the principle that they were like sesame seed was applied – 'the harder you squeeze them, the more they give'. They were tortured, often to death. A Dutch factory owner at Nagasaki gives some idea of the persecution:

> Those who could not pay the fixed taxes were dressed, by order, in a rough straw coat made of a kind of grass with long and broad leaves and called *mino* by the Japanese, such as is used by boatmen and other peasantry as a raincoat. These mantles were tied round the neck and the body, their hands being tightly bound behind their backs with ropes, after which the straw coats were set on fire. They not only received burns, but some were burnt to death; others killed themselves by bumping their bodies violently against the ground or by drowning themselves. This tragedy is called the Mino dance.

These tortures often took place after dark, so that the 'dancers' could better be seen against the night. Wives and daughters of tax defaulters were frequently stripped naked and suspended upside down, or held in icy water until they died, or, in some cases, branded with hot irons.

The combination of religious and economic oppression ensured that thousands flocked to the banner of the insurgents. Their leaders were a group of lordless samurai, *ronin*, who bizarrely chose a sixteen-year-old youth, Shiro Amakusa, as their chief. Although Shiro's mother and sisters were seized and questioned, the authorities failed to catch him. Soon the whole peninsula was in revolt, seizing ammunition stores, attacking the local feudal chiefs and winning several small skirmishes against the local militia. The armies of nearby feudal chiefs were prevented from intervening until the shogun had issued orders from distant Edo, so they merely looked on.

Lord Matsukura, then visiting Edo, was furious when he learnt of the rebellion and an elderly warrior, General Itakura, was appointed to suppress it. The two arrived with their troops in mid-January; but the rebels managed to inflict minor defeats on both their armies. However, Shiro's force failed to capture Shimabara Castle, where they had hoped to entrench themselves. He instead ordered the rebels to withdraw before the by now unified government forces to the abandoned castle of Hara. There could be no compromise because General Itakura had ravaged the nearby villages, killing the remaining inhabitants and burning alive the children he found there.

Shiro and his followers, numbering anything between 20,000 and 50,000 men, women and children, now gathered to make their last stand in Hara Castle. On 27 January 1638 they occupied the fortress. They were equipped only with scythes, sickles and spears as well as a handful of primitive guns. Huge stones were assembled for catapults. They must have known their cause was hopeless. In their 'arrow letters' to the forces camped outside they insisted that they were sacrificing themselves so that they would go to heaven; that they were dying only for their faith. Outside, some 100,000 men had been mustered by the end of February.

The besiegers resorted to a series of strategies to seize the castle. First, they tried to dig a tunnel into the castle, but, when this was discovered, the rebels filled it with smoke and faeces, which drove the attackers back. Then huge cannon balls were brought to the siege, but it seemed that no cannon big enough to fire them could be found. General Itakura, the cruel shogunal commander, then ordered an attack on the castle on 3 February, which was easily beaten back with severe losses. Another raid ten days later resulted in the loss of some 4000 men and in Itakura's own death. This was an appalling humiliation: a major defeat inflicted on an overwhelming samurai force by a rabble of farmers.

The new shogunal commander was General Mutsudaira, who proved far shrewder than his predecessor. He decided to starve the rebels out through a slow blockade, first offering them a free pardon. This was contemptuously rejected. He also conscripted a nearby Dutch ship to help him bombard the rebels, although the barrage was largely ineffective. Then he had Shiro's mother and elder sister brought. The rebel leader's little nephew was sent in with a message that all the inhabitants of the castle would be killed, while his mother and sister pleaded with Shiro to surrender. He refused.

By April, however, the rebels were very short of food and combing the beach below the castle for seaweed. The cut-open stomachs of captured rebels were found to contain only this food. On 4 April Shiro broke out of the castle with a large armed force. After inflicting severe casualties on the besiegers, he was forced back into the castle. Mutsudaira decided that the rebels were now sufficiently weak for an attack.

On 12 April samurai warriors in heavy black armour, resembling huge slow-moving armadillos, climbed the castle walls and began a frenzy of butchering and slaughter while the defenders fought back with stones and cooking pots. The rebels were burnt to death in their trenches and huts, many throwing themselves into the flames to avoid being taken alive. The remainder were then meticulously exterminated, being hunted down and decapitated. Bodies filled the rivers while heads littered the fields and ditches. More than 3500 heads were counted in Hosokawa ditch, nearly 11,000 on wooden spikes that crowded the area in front of the castle and down to the beach and more than 3000 loaded on to three ships for burial in Nagasaki. When a government retainer came across a young wounded man, he killed him and chopped off his head:

> The head ... was carefully washed and combed before being brought to the place of inspection, where it was placed among several others that had been tentatively identified as belonging to the rebel general: Amakusa Shiro's mother was now summoned and told to point out her son's head. She proudly replied that he could not possibly have been killed; he had been sent from heaven and had now either returned there, or changed form and escaped to some place like Luzon in the Philippines. Head after youthful head was presented to her, but she rejected them all until they held up the one recently taken. Then finally she broke down and said, 'Can he really have become so thin?' And she clung to the head and wept. At this point the inspectors knew, even without asking her, that they had found their quarry.
>
> Head-inspection scenes, with their mixture of horror and poignancy, were of absorbing interest for Japanese writers during the feudal period, and are included in the stories of many famous failed heroes. The present account of Amakusa Shiro adds a Christian overtone to this traditional theme by picturing the hero's mother as a Japanese mater dolorosa in a macabre version of the *pietà*.

Although around 15,000 government troops were killed, rarely in history can so hopeless and brave a rebellion have been so relentlessly stamped out. It was an awful example, a key to the crushing obeisance of ordinary Japanese, to the omnipotence of the power of the system. That, in the end, is where any struggle between Japan and the rest of the world must end, as it did in 1945: a heroic defeat against overwhelming odds. Enough surely, to give the old men who rule Japan – its big businessmen, bureaucrats and politicians – pause for thought. Or is the temptation of noble tragedy, self-immolation, still too potent a prospect?

Even if these men are still attracted by the nobility of failure, even if the middle-aged generation that is to follow them is if anything more contemptuous of the outside world, the society they control is no longer the same. Ordinary Japanese, first hypnotized by consumerism, then warmed by the stirrings of self-expression, may just be capable of insisting that Japan rejoin the mainstream of humanity. But there can be no certainty of this. And the consequences of failure would be overwhelming. At the least a new cold war between East and West, with an economic, and possibly military, power that would dwarf the Soviet Union. The remoter prospect of a hot war between Japan and one or more of her Asian neighbours, possibly drawing in the United States, does not bear thinking about. Avoiding both contingencies requires, as much as change within Japan, the most careful handling by those outside. There is no sign of this being on hand, either in Washington or Brussels.

This book has tried to show how Japan, a country with no revolution in its history, lacking a concept of individual rights, an assertive middle class, or a deeply rooted democratic tradition, has carried a feudal and militaristic outlook from the Meiji period through to the end of the twentieth century. The defeat of 1945 barely dented this, and in many respects it is being cultivated all the more vigorously today. Japan is unwilling to admit it was wrong to launch its war of aggression in Asia, and, through mass indoctrination, still considers itself above and apart from other nations.

As Japan approaches the millennium, most of the signs are ominous. The political class, always subordinate to the bureaucratic and business elites, is thoroughly discredited. Military spending, already around the highest in the world, continues to rise. Japan's economic juggernaut shows no signs of stopping, although it has momentarily overheated. In Asia, Japan may be about to enter into military competition with its more assertive, newly rich neighbours.

Most important of all, the Japanese–American relationship is breaking down, perhaps irretrievably, and trade wars between America, Europe and Japan loom on the horizon. Imagine if a Germany, unrepentant about its Nazi past, and run by the same bureaucrats that served Hitler so efficiently, were about to overtake America as the world's economic leader, and you get some dimension of the Japanese problem. If Japan resumes its economic surge, economic leadership of the globe could pass to an essentially authoritarian giant with a non-Western outlook, and a recent history of aggression and assertion that is anything but reassuring. This should surely be one of the foremost issues on the West's foreign policy agenda.

POSTSCRIPT

ABSOLUTE POWER, absolute destruction, is minimalist, like Japanese aesthetics. As modest as two tiny craft, a principal and its escort, drifting across a vast expanse of blue, the noise of their engines rising and falling in the void.

In December 1992, a small freighter, the *Akatsuki Maru*, formerly the British-built *Pacific Crane*, arrived in Japan to a noisy, organized demonstration. This little vessel was one of the most feared and shunned in history, like a ship carrying the bubonic plague from one port to another in the Middle Ages.

Its very arrival was a matter of intense relief to some, though. It had undertaken a relatively uneventful journey across 17,000 miles of ocean, usually a lonely speck in the vast sea, far from land, accompanied by just one small Japanese coastguard ship equipped with two 35 mm anti-aircraft guns, two 20 mm machine guns and two unarmed helicopters. The only incident on the voyage was when the Greenpeace yacht, *Solo*, came too close shortly after the freighter's departure from the port of Cherbourg and was rammed, without damage, by the escort, the *Shikishima*.

This apparently insignificant pair were the most carefully monitored ships in the world, being watched by American military satellites, as well as being tracked by American warships, planes and military intelligence. Their route was unknown save to those on board and a very few others. They might have gone one of four ways to Japan: around the Cape of Good Hope and up through the busy Straits of Malacca; all the way around Australia and the southern tip of New Zealand; across the Atlantic through the Panama Canal and then across the Pacific; or all the way around Cape Horn.

The ships were shunned by most of the countries with shorelines along their routes: they were barred from the Panama and Suez Canals. South Africa told the ships to stay more than 200 miles off its coast if they came that way. Chile, Malaysia and India told them to keep out of their territorial waters. In view of the danger of collision in the Straits of Malacca and the local hostility there, as well as the rough passage across Cape Horn, the likeliest routes were the long but comparatively traffic- and tempest-free loop around New Zealand or, just possibly, with American connivance, a surreptitious sneak through the Panama Canal.

Inside the *Akatsuki Maru* were large steel containers; inside them were 133 lead-lined caskets, containing altogether 1.7 tons of plutonium, the deadliest substance on earth, a speck of which can kill – enough to fuel 120 Hiroshima bombs. The plutonium was extracted from spent Japanese reactors' fuel at a plant near Cherbourg. Britain's Sellafield plant was similarly processing fuel, as part of a 30-ton consignment worth $4 billion.

The containers were designed to withstand a fire of 8000 degrees for half an hour or a ramming by a 25,000 tons craft at 15 knots. There were fears that ship fires could rage for longer and at higher temperatures, of leakage if the vessel sank in the immense depths of the ocean it was crossing, and of terrorist attack or piracy. The size of the cargo meant that there would be forty more such trips from Cherbourg and Barrow-in-Furness to bring over 100 tons of plutonium, roughly three times the amount in the entire US nuclear arsenal.

Anger focused on the danger presented by the ships. But there were even more serious questions to be asked of the country which alone has been on the receiving end of nuclear attack and has become a symbol of anti-nuclear feeling the world over. Nearly half a century after the flash-burning of Hiroshima and Nagasaki, what was the Japanese government intending to do with these relatively high amounts of the deadliest substance on earth?

The official answer was that the plutonium is solely required for Japan's nuclear energy programme, which is intended to free the country from its dependence on oil from the troubled Middle East. In addition, however, the plutonium will turn Japan into a major military nuclear power in all but name: not just any nuclear power but the world's third, after the United States and Russia. With little public debate, almost by stealth, unnoticed by outsiders, the second most powerful economy on the globe is acquiring the potential to become a nuclear military superpower; and while Japan is run by a pro-Western, more moderate regime than that of post-war Russia, it remains essentially authoritarian. That this has been barely noticed is a tribute to the skill with which the Japanese have carried it out. The country which above all others has reason to look upon the face of the atom and despair is giving itself the potential to become one of the foremost and fiercest wielders of nuclear weapons, just as other countries lay them down in the post-cold war thaw.

The ostensible purpose of the plutonium is to fuel Japan's new generation of fast-breeder nuclear reactors, which up to now have been fuelled by enriched uranium, resulting in the waste that Japan had shipped to France and Britain for processing and re-export. At the time the plutonium was bought, world uranium supplies were thought to be low. They have long since been discovered in abundance and plutonium, a far more dangerous substance, which is five times as expensive, is also plentiful as Soviet stockpiles become available for possible commercial use.

Japan has been building its own nuclear reprocessing plant, due to become operational in 1998, but is obliged to take back the plutonium it sent for reprocessing overseas. Until now, Japan only had one small reprocessing plant at Tokaimura, some 60 miles north of Tokyo, and two experimental fast-breeder reactors. The new reprocessing plant is being built at Rokkasho-Mura, on the north-eastern coast of Honshu, with the capacity to treat up to 800 tons of spent uranium a year. Planning for thirteen fast-breeder reactors is already at an advanced stage, and five more are contemplated.

Of these, eight will be along the north coast of Honshu, the main Japanese island, two on Shikoku Island across the Inland Sea, and seven along the south coast of Honshu, where the overwhelming bulk of Japan's population lives. Two more will be located on the remote northernmost tip of Honshu, and one on still remoter Hokkaido. Five of them will be within 100 miles of Hiroshima, although none will be anywhere near Nagasaki.

The proposed $6.2 billion Rokkasho-Mura plant will have more than ten times the capacity of Tokaimura. It is feared by International Atomic Energy Authority Agency inspectors, who monitor the Tokaimura plant more closely than any other in the world, that minute amounts of plutonium inside pipes or clinging to vials could amount, in the new plant, to an average wastage of 249 kg a year (at the existing plant the waste is reckoned at less than 8 kg), enough to make some thirty nuclear bombs without anyone noticing. Even a minute amount stolen in a terrorist attack or siphoned off could be used to poison a city's water supplies or to build a crude nuclear device. It is also argued that a Chernobyl-style meltdown at a plutonium-fuelled reactor could – as is not the case with the uranium-fuelled model – produce a nuclear explosion. Japan, in addition, is earthquake prone.

Nor is Japanese nuclear safety all it might be. In February 1991, an energy core cooling system was triggered at the Kansai Electric Power Company at Mihama Number Two Reactor after a steam generator pipe began vibrating out of control and eventually snapped, causing primary coolant running through it to flow into the secondary cooling system. This caused the reactor to overheat, which triggered off the emergency system. If the back-up system had failed to work, a meltdown would have occurred; on this occasion only a small amount of radioactivity was released.

In the summer of 1992 the emergency cooling system was set off at Fukushima plant, just 70 miles north of Tokyo. This time workers had mistakenly flipped a switch showing that a water pump was working when it wasn't. Fortunately, other water pumps came on automatically, continuing to cool the fuel rods, and preventing the rise in temperature that can cause a meltdown. However, many questions went unanswered: was this really all that happened, or had a more serious fault occurred? In particular, the water level should not have fallen so fast. At another plant, Takahama, no fewer than 10,000 steam generator pipes, more than half the total, were found to be cracked – which has provoked lawsuits from anxious local people.

The object of the Japanese fast-breeder programme is to increase generation of electricity from nuclear power from 26 per cent to 43 per cent and cut dependence on imports for nine-tenths of its energy. But it is clear that access to this enormous quantity of imported and domestic plutonium, which is almost certainly much more than Japan can possibly consume, will produce the raw materials for hundreds of nuclear weapons. Technologically, of course, Japan is in a position to move extremely fast towards this, in a matter of weeks rather than months. Weapons delivery systems, such as long-range missiles, would take longer to develop, but probably no more than a year.

The Japanese react with indignation at any suggestions that this is their intention. 'Such concerns are completely unfounded,' asserts Hiroyuki Kishino, head of the nuclear energy directorate at Japan's foreign ministry. Yet recently Japan criticized North Korea for its reprocessing plant, which, it said, could be used to manufacture nuclear weapons. A senior official in the Bush administration admitted in 1992 that this was:

an uncomfortable position. If it was any other country than Japan, we would look at this plutonium project and conclude a bomb was the real motive. But the fact is that it's OK for the Japanese because we trust them, and it's not OK for North Korea because we don't trust them.

A senior South Korean official states that 'obviously the Japanese have the technology to build a bomb', while Professor Andrew Mack, a nuclear proliferation expert at Australia's National University, said recently:

Japan clearly has no intention of going nuclear – it is not in their interests to do so. But at the same time it serves to demonstrate to other countries in the region that it has the capacity to if it ever needed it. Everyone – the Koreans, the Chinese, the Russians – would know that Japan would be less than a year away.

Japan is officially committed to permitting no nuclear weapons on its territory, to their non-manufacture and non-possession – the three principles spelt out by Prime Minister Eisaku Sato in 1971. The first of these was already being violated at the time, as Rear-Admiral Laroque, a retired commander of the US Seventh Fleet, made clear when he revealed in 1974 that American ships nearly always carry nuclear weapons into Japanese ports. The Japanese said that as the Americans had not officially informed them, the violations had not occurred. This drew a tart retort from former American ambassador Edwin Reischauer: 'The Japanese government had been too timid to explain the validity of the American interpretation that the ban on the "introduction" of nuclear weapons did not apply to American warships, resorting instead to evasive statements about its complete confidence that the United States would live up to its agreements.'

Former prime minister Yasuhiro Nakasone, as head of the Japanese Self-Defence Agency, advocated the building of tactical nuclear weapons, and Japanese defence theorists have always made it clear that these would not violate the spirit of Japan's constitution. The no war clause was directed against aggression: 'defensive' nuclear weapons could not be classed as such if they lacked 'aggressive' missile delivery systems. This view would presumably be extended to the concept of deterrence, under which any nuclear force is theoretically defensive, not aggressive, although it presumably would rule out a 'first strike' option. In 1993, there was strong right-wing opposition to any extension of the nuclear Non-Proliferation Treaty.

The fact remains that, without confronting the issue, Japan will have the materials and technology to assemble a significant nuclear force in under a year, and a major one in the space of two or three; moreover, its defence establishment has already considered the option, has no inhibitions about proceeding, and does not believe that this violates the constitution. Japan is to all intents and purposes a massive latent nuclear power. In the event of a crisis, several thousand fully armed nuclear warriors could spring full grown from the soil in a relatively short space of time.

The walking, peeling shades of Hiroshima have reason not to lie quietly in their mass graves. Yoshitaka Kawamoto, a survivor and the director of its peace museum, told me 1991 that he hoped others would learn the lesson of Hiroshima; his sentiment, it seems, goes unheard in his own land.

The power of the atom has come to Japan again.

SELECTED BIBLIOGRAPHY

The author and publishers would like to express their gratitude to those among the following who have kindly given their permission for the use of copyright materials. Every effort has been made to trace all copyright holders, but if any have inadvertently been overlooked, the author and publishers will be pleased to make the necessary arrangements at the first opportunity.

PRELUDE

There are a great many books about Hiroshima and Nagasaki, many of them little more than propaganda. Among the best – although almost invariably *parti pris* – are:

Akisuki, Tatsuichiro. *Nagasaki 1945*. Namara Features Tokyo. A genuinely moving eyewitness account of the aftermath of the bomb.
Alperowitz, Gar. *Atomic Diplomacy: Hiroshima and Potsdam*. Simon & Schuster, New York, 1965.
Amrine, Michael, *The Great Decision*. Putnam's, New York, 1959.
Arisue, Seizo. *Memoirs*. Fuyo Shobo, Tokyo, 1974.
Batchelder, Robert. *The Irreversible Decision*. Houghton Mifflin, Boston, 1962.
Bateson, Charles. *The War with Japan*. Ure Smith, Sydney, 1968.
Blackett, P.M.S. *Fear, War and the Bomb*. Whittlesey House, New York, 1948.
Brackman, Arnold C. *The Other Nuremberg*. William Morrow, New York 1987. A fine, passionate, pioneering and unique study of the Tokyo war crimes tribunal.

583

Butow, Robert. *Japan's Decision to Surrender*. Stanford UP, Stanford, California, 1954.

——. *Tojo and the Coming of the War*. Princeton UP, Princeton, New Jersey, 1961.

Byrnes, James F. *Speaking Frankly*. Harper, New York, 1947.

Campbell, J. W. *The Atomic Story*. Henry Holt, New York, 1947.

Churchill, Sir Winston. *The Second World War*, vol. 6. Cassell, London, 1954.

Craig, William. *The Fall of Japan*. Weidenfeld & Nicolson, London, 1968.

Feis, Herbert. *Japan Subdued*. Princeton UP, Princeton, New Jersey, 1961.

——. *The Atomic Bomb and the End of World War II*. Princeton UP, Princeton, New Jersey, 1966.

Giovannitti and Freed (eds). *The Decision to Drop the Bomb*. Coward-McCann, New York, 1965. An invaluable compendium of contemporary quotations.

Gow, Ian. *Okinawa 1945*. Grub Street, London, 1986.

Groueff, Stephane. *The Manhattan Project*. Collins, London, 1967.

Groves, Leslie R. *Now It Can Be Told*. André Deutsch, London, 1963.

Hachiya, Michihiko. *Hiroshima Diary*. Translated by W. Wells. North Carolina UP, Chapel Gill, 1955.

Hall, J. W. and Jansen, M. B. (eds). *Studies in the Institutional History of Early Southern Japan*. Princeton UP, 1968.

Hirshfeld, Burt. *A Cloud over Hiroshima*. Bailey Bros. & Swinfen, Folkestone, 1974.

Hull, Cordell. *The Memoirs of Cordell Hull*, vol. 2. Macmillan, New York, 1948.

Jungk, Robert. *Brighter than 1000 Suns*. Gollancz, London, 1958.

LeMay, Curtis E. *Mission with LeMay*. Doubleday, New York, 1965.

MacArthur, Douglas. *Reminiscences*. McGraw-Hill, New York, 1964.

Major, John. *The Oppenheimer Hearing*. Stein & Day, New York, 1971.

Miller and Spitzer. *We Dropped the A-Bomb*. Cromwell, New York, 1946.

Nagasaki, City of. *The Records of the Atomic Bombing in Nagasaki*, 1975.

Nagasaki Association. *Report from Nagasaki*. 1980.

Ooghterson, A. W. and Warren, S. *Medical Effects of the Atomic Bomb in Japan*. McGraw-Hill, New York, 1956.

Osada, Arata. *Children of Hiroshima*. Harper & Row, New York, 1980.

Osako, Ichiro. *Hiroshima 1945*. Chuko Shinsho, Tokyo, 1975.

Ota, Y. *Town of Corpses*. Kawade Shobo, Tokyo, 1955.

Takayama, Hitoshi (ed.). *Hiroshima in Memoriam and Today*. Hiroshima Peace Culture Centre, 1973.

Thomas, Gordon, and Morgan-Witts, Max. *Ruin from the Air*. Hamish Hamilton, London, 1977. Probably the most readable and comprehensive account of Hiroshima.

Togo, Shigenori. *The Cause of Japan*. Simon & Schuster, New York, 1956.

Truman, Harry S. *Year of Decisions: 1945*. Doubleday, Garden City, New York, 1955.

Trumbull, Robert. *Nine Who Survived Hiroshima and Nagasaki*. Dutton, New York, 1957.

In addition, Masuji Ibuse's *Black Rain* (Kodansha International, Tokyo, 1969), a novel based on eyewitness accounts of Hiroshima, provides the best atmospheric account of the impact of the bomb from the Japanese standpoint. It is understated, a pleasure to read, and very effective.

The description of Yoshitaka Kawamoto's experience is based on a long conversation I had with him in 1991.

PART ONE: THE MEIJI IMPERATIVE

The formative period of Japan's modern history is characterized by some superb scholarship, and very little for the general reader.

Abe, Yoshiya. *Religious Freedoms under the Meiji Constitution*. December 1969 issue of Contemporary Religions in Japan.

Akita, George. *Foundations of Constitutional Government in Modern Japan, 1868–1900*. Harvard UP, Cambridge, Mass., 1967.

Barr, Pat. *The Coming of the Barbarians*. Macmillan, London, 1967.

——. *The Deer Cry Pavilion*. Macmillan, London, 1968. Both are highly readable.

Beasley, W. G. *The Meiji Restoration*. Stanford UP, Stanford, California, 1972. A definitive and major work on the period.

Beckmann, George M. *The Modern History of Japan*. Praeger, New York, 1963.
——. *The Making of the Meiji Constitutions*. Green Press, Westport, 1957.
Borton, Hugh. *Japan's Modern Century*. Ronald Press, New York, 1955.
Boxer, C. R. *The Christian Century in Japan*. Cambridge UP, London, 1967.
Colcutt, Martin, Jansen, Marius and Kumakura Isao. *Cultural Atlas of Japan*. Phaidon, Oxford, 1988.
Conroy, Hilary. *The Japanese Seizure of Korea*, Pennsylvania UP, Philadelphia, 1960.
Crowley, James. In B. Silberman and H. O. Harootunian (eds), *Modern Japanese Leadership*. Arizona UP, Tucson, 'From Closed Door to Empire', 1966.
Gluck, Carol. *Japan's Modern Myths*. Princeton UP, Princeton, New Jersey, 1985. Probably the best academic work on the late Meiji period.
Hackett, Roger. *Yamagata Aritomo in the Rise of Modern Japan, 1838–1922*. Cambridge, Mass., 1971.
Hardacre, Helen. *Shinto and the State*. Princeton UP, Princeton, New Jersey, 1989. A pioneering work on this previously off-limits subject.
Havens, Thomas R. *Nishi Amane and Modern Thought*. Princeton UP, Princeton, New Jersey, 1970.
Hirschmeier, Johannes. *The Origins of Entrepreneurship in Meiji Japan*. Harvard UP, Cambridge, Mass., 1964.
Holtom, Daniel C. *Modern Japan and Shinto Nationalism*. Paragon, New York, 1943.
——. *The National Faith of Japan*. E. P. Dutton, New York, 1938.
Hozumi, Hobushige. *Ancestor Worship and Japanese Law*. Maruzen, Tokyo, 1912.
Ike, Nobutake. *The Beginnings of Political Democracy in Japan*. John Hopkins Press, Baltimore, 1950.
Irokawa Daikichi. *The Culture of the Meiji Period*. Translated by Marius Jansen. Princeton UP, Princeton, New Jersey, 1985.
Ito, Hirobumi. *Commentaries on the Constitution of the Empire of Japan*. Translated by Ito Miyoji. Igirisu Horitsu Gakko, Tokyo, 1889.
Jansen, Marius B. *The Meiji State, 1868–1912*. In James Crowley

(ed.), *Modern East Asia: Essays in Interpretation.* Harcourt Brace Jovanovich, New York, 1970.

Keene, Donald. *The Sino-Japanese War of 1894–5.* Kodansha, Tokyo, 1971.

——. *Japanese Culture in Landscapes and Portraits.* Kodansha, Tokyo, 1971.

Kennedy, Malcolm. *A History of Japan.* Wiedenfeld & Nicolson, London, 1963.

Kinmonth, Earl. *The Self-Made Man in Meiji Japanese Thought.* California UP, Berkeley, 1981.

Kishimoto, Hideo. *Japanese Religion in the Meiji Era.* Obunsha, Tokyo, 1956.

Lehmann, Jean-Pierre. *The Image of Japan: From Feudal Isolation to World Power, 1850–1950.* Allen & Unwin, London, 1978.

Livingston, Jon, Moore, Joe, and Oldfather, Felicia. *Imperial Japan, 1800–1945.* Random House, New York, 1973.

Lockwood, William. *The Economic Development of Japan.* Princeton UP, Princeton, New Jersey, 1954.

McLaren, Walter. *A Political History of Japan during the Meiji Period.* George Allen & Unwin, London, 1916.

Marshall, Byron K. 'Professors and Politics: The Meiji Intellectual Elite'. *Journal of Japanese Studies,* winter 1977.

Masao, Muruyama. *Thought and Behaviour in Modern Japanese Politics.* Ed. Ivan Morris. Oxford UP, London, 1963.

Mason, R. H. P. *Japan's First General Election, 1890.* Cambridge UP, Cambridge, 1969.

Mayo, Marlene. *The Emergence of Imperial Japan.* D. C. Heath, Lexington, 1970.

Minami, Ryoshin. *The Turning Point in Economic Development: Japan's Experience.* Tokyo, Kinokuniya, 1973.

Morioka, Kinomi. 'The Appearance of Ancestor Religion in Modern Japan'. *Japanese Journal of Religious Studies,* June–September 1977, Tokyo.

Morris, Ivan. *The World of the Shining Prince.* Oxford UP, London, 1964. A masterpiece of lucidity and scholarship introducing the Heian Period.

——. *The Nobility of Failure.* Oxford UP, London, 1975. A brilliant and beautifully written discourse on epic failures in Japanese history. The best episodic introduction to the history of Japan.

Murdoch and Yamagata. *A History of Japan.* Routledge & Kegan Paul, London, 1949.

Nobutake, Ike. *The Beginnings of Political Democracy in Japan.* John Hopkins Press, Baltimore, 1950.

Norbeck, Edward. *Religion and Society in Modern Japan.* Rice University, Houston, 1970.

Norman, E. H. *Japan's Emergence as a Modern State.* Institute of Pacific Relations, New York, 1940.

——. *Soldier and Peasant in Japan.* Institute of Pacific Relations, New York, 1943.

Okamoto, Shumpei. *The Japanese Oligarchy and the Russo-Japanese War.* Columbia UP, New York, 1970.

Orchard, John. *Japan's Economic Position.* McGraw-Hill, New York, 1930.

Passin, Herbert. *Society and Education in Japan.* Columbia UP, New York, 1965.

Patrick, Hugh (ed.). *Japanese Industrialization and Its Social Consequences.* California UP, Berkeley, 1976.

Pittau, Joseph. *Political Thought in Early Meiji Japan, 1868–1889.* Harvard UP, Cambridge, Mass., 1967.

Pyle, Kenneth. *The New Generation in Meiji Japan.* California UP, Berkeley, 1969.

Reischauer, Edwin. *Japan: The Story of a Nation.* Duckworth, London, 1970. One of the most readable brief accounts of Japan's early history.

——. *Japan: Government and Politics.* Nelson, New York, 1939.

Robertson Scott, J. W. *The Foundations of Japan.* Appleton, New York, 1922.

Sadler, A. L. *The Life of Shogun Tokugawa Ieyasu.* Tuttle, Tokyo, 1978.

Sansom, G. B. *Japan: A Short Cultural History.* Appleton-Century-Crofts, New York, 1943.

——. *A History of Japan.* Cresset Press, London, 1964.

Scalopino, Robert A. *Democracy and the Party Movement in Pre-War Japan.* California UP, Berkeley, 1953.

Scheiner, Irwin. *Christian Converts and Social Protest in Meiji Japan.* California UP, Berkeley, 1970.

Shigenobu, Okuma. *Fifty Years of New Japan.* Smith, Elder, London, 1909.

Shively, Donald. *The Japanization of the Middle Meiji.* Princeton UP, Princeton, New Jersey, 1971.

Smethurst, Richard J. *A Social Basis for Prewar Japanese Militarism: The Army and the Rural Community.* California UP, Berkeley, 1974.

Smith, T. C. 'The Japanese Village in the Seventeenth Century'. In John Hall and Marius Jansen, *Studies in the Institutional History of Early Modern Japan*. Princeton UP, Princeton, New Jersey, 1968.

——. *Political Change and Industrial Development in Japan*. Stanford UP, Stanford, California, 1955.

——. *Agrarian Origins of Modern Japan*. Stanford UP, Stanford, California, 1959.

Smith, Warren W. *Confucianism in Modern Japan*. Hokuseido Press, Tokyo, 1959.

Spaulding, Robert M. *Imperial Japan's Higher Civil Service Examinations*. Princeton UP, Princeton, New Jersey, 1967.

Statler, Oliver. *Japanese Inn*. Random House, New York, 1961.

Storry, Richard. *A History of Modern Japan*. Penguin, London, 1960. The best short introduction to the subject still available.

Takane, Masaaki. *The Political Elite in Japan*. California UP, Berkeley, 1981.

Tiedemann, Arthur E. *An Introduction to Japanese Civilization*. Columbia UP, New York, 1974.

Titus, David. *Palace and Politics in Prewar Japan*. Columbia UP, New York, 1974.

Tokutomi, Kenjiro. *Footprints in the Snow*. Translated by Kenneth Strong. Tuttle, Tokyo, 1971.

Totten, George O. *The Social Democratic Movement in Prewar Japan*. Yale UP, New Haven, 1966.

Wakukawa, Seiyei. *The Japanese Farm Tenancy System in Japan's Prospect*. Harvard UP, Cambridge, Mass., 1946.

Walworth, Arthur. *Black Ships off Japan*. Alfred Knopf, New York, 1941.

Waswo, Ann. *Japanese Landlords: The Decline of a Rural Elite*. California UP, Berkeley, 1977.

Yanagida, Kunio. *Japanese Manners and Customs in the Meiji Era*. Obunsha, Tokyo, 1957.

Yazaki, Takeo. *Social Change and the City in Japan*. Japan Publications, Tokyo, 1968.

PART TWO: THE DARK VALLEY

This is the most intensively chronicled period of Japan's modern history, also yielding many of the most accessible books. Even so, interpretations differ widely concerning the key events. Among the most important works are:

Agawa, Hiroyuki. *The Reluctant Admiral*. Kodansha, Tokyo, 1982.

Bamba, Nobuya. *Japanese Diplomacy in a Dilemma*. Vancouver, 1972.

Beasley, W. G. *Japanese Imperialism, 1894–1945*. Clarendon Press, Oxford, 1987. Although rather dryly written, this offers the most cogent explanation of Japanese foreign policy before the Pacific War.

Behr, Edward. *Hirohito*. Hamish Hamilton, London, 1989. A highly readable and controversial attempt to pin the primary responsibility for the Pacific War on the emperor.

Bergamini, David. *Japan's Imperial Conspiracy*. William Morrow, New York, 1971.

Bisson, T. A. 'Increase of Zaibatsu Predominance in Wartime Japan'. *Pacific Affairs*, March 1945.

——. 'The Zaibatsu's Wartime Role', *Pacific Affairs*, December 1945.

Bix, Herbert. 'Japanese Imperialism and the Manchurian Economy, 1900–1931'. *China Quarterly*, 51.

Borton, Hugh. *Japan since 1931: Its Political and Social Development*. New York, 1940.

Boyle, John. *China and Japan at War, 1937–45*. Stanford UP, Stanford; California, 1972.

Brown, Delmer. *Nationalism in Japan*. California UP, Berkeley, 1955.

Butow, Robert. *Tojo and the Coming of War*. Princeton UP, Princeton, New Jersey, 1961.

Byas, Hugh. *Government by Assassination*. Alfred Knopf, New York, 1942.

Coffey, Thomas. *Imperial Tragedy*. World Publishing Co., 1970.

Cohen, Jerome. *Japan's Economy in War and Reconstruction*. Minneapolis, 1949.

Connors, Lesley. *The Emperor's Adviser, Kinmochi Saionji*. Croom Helm, New York, 1987.

Coo, Alvin, and Conroy, Hilary. *China and Japan: A Search for Balance Since World War I*. Santa Barbara, 1978.

Cowan, C. D. (ed.). *The Economic Development of China and Japan*. London, 1964.

Craigie, Sir Robert. *Behind the Japanese Mask*. Hutchinson, London. 1945.

Crowley, James. *Japan's Quest for Autonomy*. Princeton UP, Princeton, New Jersey, 1966.

——. *Japan's Military Foreign Policies in Japan's Foreign Policy, 1868–1941*. New York, 1974.

Duus, Peter. *Party Rivalry and Political Change in Taisho Japan.* Harvard UP, Cambridge, 1968.

Feis, Herbert. *The Road to Pearl Harbor.* Princeton UP, Princeton, New Jersey, 1950.

Gayn, Mark. *Japan Diary.* William Sloan, New York, 1948.

Goodman, Grant (ed). *Imperial Japan and Asia: A Reassessment.* New York, 1967.

Grew, Joseph. *Ten Years in Japan.* Hammond, London, 1945.

Guillain, Robert. *I Saw Tokyo Burning.* John Murray, London, 1981.

Hadley, Eleanor. *Anti-trust in Japan.* Princeton UP, Princeton, New Jersey, 1970.

Halliday, Jon. *A Political History of Japanese Capitalism.* New York, 1975.

Harada, Kumao. *Prince Saionji and the Political Situation.* Iwanami Shoten, Tokyo, 1956.

Hata, Ikuhito. *The Emperor's Five Decisions.* Kodansha, Tokyo, 1984.

Havens, Thomas. *Farm and Nation in Modern Japan.* Princeton UP, Princeton, New Jersey, 1974.

Hewes, Lawrence. *Japan: Land and Men.* Iowa State College Press, 1955.

Hosoya, Chihiro. 'Japanese Documents on the Siberian Intervention, 1917–22'. *Journal of Law and Politics,* 1960.

Ikei, Asaru. 'Japan's Response to the Chinese Revolution of 1911'. *Journal of Asian Studies,* 1966.

Inoue, Kiyoshi. *The Formation of Japanese Imperialism.* Tokyo, 1972.

———. *The Emperor's Responsibilities.* Gendai Hyoronsha, Tokyo, 1975.

Iriye, Akira. *Across the Pacific: An Inner History of American–East Asian Relations.* New York, 1967.

———. *After Imperialism: The Search for a New Order in the Far East, 1921–31.* Cambridge UP, Mass., 1965.

———. *Pacific Estrangement: Japanese and American Expansion, 1897–1911.* Cambridge UP, Mass., 1972.

———. 'The Failure of Military Expansionism'. In J. W. Morley (ed.), *Dilemmas of Growth in Prewar Japan.* Princeton UP, Princeton, New Jersey, 1971.

Harries, Meirion and Susie. *Soldiers of the Sun.* Heinemann, London, 1991. This is a lucid, brilliantly researched study of the Japanese army from the Meiji period to the Pacific War that cannot be praised too highly.

Jansen, Marius B. *Japan and China: From War to Peace, 1894–1972*. Chicago, 1975.

——. *The Japanese and Sun Yat-Sen*, Cambridge UP, Mass., 1954.

——. 'Yawata, Hanyehping and the 21 Demands'. *Pacific Historical Review* 23, 1954.

Jones, F. C. *Japan's New Order in East Asia: Its Rise and Fall, 1937–45*. London, 1954.

——. *Manchuria since 1931*. London, 1949.

Kajima, Morinosuke. *The Diplomacy of Japan, 1894–1922*. Tokyo, 1980.

Kanroji, Osanaga. *The Emperor and Poems and Horses*. Shuken Asahi, Tokyo, 1967.

——. *Hirohito, an Intimate Portrait*. Gateway, Los Angeles, 1975.

Kato, Matsuo. *The Lost War*. Alfred Knopf, New York, 1946.

Kawahara, Toshiaki. *Hirohito and His Times*. Kodansha International, Tokyo, 1990. This provides a beautifully economic, if biased, insider's account of the emperor's reign, which is, on occasion, subtly critical.

Kawai, Kazuo. *Japan's American Interlude*. Chicago UP, 1960.

Kido, Koichi. *Nikkei*. Daigaku Shuppankai, Tokyo, 1966.

Kim, Eugene. *Education in Korea under Japanese Colonial Rule*. Western Michigan UP, Kalamazoo, 1973.

——. *The Japanese Colonial Administration in Korea*. Western Michigan UP, Kalamazoo, 1973.

Lockwood, William. *The Economic Development of Japan*. Princeton UP, Princeton, New Jersey, 1964.

Li, Lincoln. *The Japanese Army in North China, 1937–41*. Tokyo, 1975.

Lowe, Peter. *Great Britain and Japan 1911–15*. London, 1969.

McCormack, Gavan. *Chang Tso-Lin in North-East China, 1911–28*. Stanford UP, Stanford, California, 1977.

Maruyama, Masao. *Thought and Behaviour in Modern Japanese Politics*, Oxford UP, 1963.

Maxon, Yale. *Control of Japanese Foreign Policy*. California UP, Berkeley, 1957.

Mayo, Marlene (ed.). *The Emergence of Imperial Japan*. Lexington, 1970.

Miller, Fran O. *Minobe Tatsukichi*. California UP, Berkeley, 1965.

Montgomery, Michael. *Imperialist Japan*. Christopher Helm, London, 1988.

Morgan Young, A. *Imperial Japan*. Allen & Unwin, London, 1938.

Morley, James W. (ed.). *Deterrent Diplomacy: Japan, Germany and the USSR, 1935–40.* New York, 1976.

——. (ed.). *Japan Erupts.* New York, 1984.

——. (ed.). *Japan's Foreign Policy, 1868–1941: A Research Guide.* New York, 1974.

——. (ed.). *The China Quagmire: Japan's Expansion on the Asian Continent, 1933–41.* New York, 1983.

——. (ed.). *The Fateful Choice: Japan's Advance into South East Asia, 1939–40.* New York, 1976.

Morris, Ivan (ed.). *Japan, 1931–45: Militarism, Fascism, Japanism?* OUP, Oxford, 1964.

Mosley, Leonard. *Hirohito, Emperor of Japan.* Prentice Hall, New York, 1967. Still vigorously readable if a trifle dated.

Myers, Ramon and Peattie, Mark (eds). *The Japanese Colonial Empire, 1895–1945.* Princeton UP, Princeton, New Jersey, 1984.

Nahm, Andrew (ed.). *Korea under Japanese Colonial Rule.* Western Michigan UP, Kalamazoo, 1973.

Nakamura, Takafusa. *Economic Growth in Prewar Japan.* London, 1983.

——. *Alliance in Decline: A Study in Anglo-Japanese Relations, 1908–23.* London, 1972.

Ogata, Sadako. *Defiance in Manchuria.* California UP, Berkeley, 1964.

Oka, Yoshitake. *Konoye Fumimaro: A Political Biography.* Tokyo, 1983.

Pacific War Research Society. *Japan's Longest Day.* Kodansha International, Tokyo, 1968. A gripping thriller-like, other-worldly account of the decision to surrender, in spite of its provenance.

Packard, Jerrold M. *Sons of Heaven.* Scribners, New York, 1987.

Peattie, Mark R. *Ishiwara Kanji and Japan's Confrontation with the West.* Princeton UP, Princeton, New Jersey, 1974.

Roberts, J. G. *Three Centuries of Japanese Business.* New York, 1973.

Scalopino, Robert A. *The Japanese Communist Movement, 1920–66.* California UP, Berkeley, 1967.

Schumpeter, E. B. (ed.). *The Industrialization of Japan and Manchukuo, 1930–40.* New York, 1940.

Shillony, Ben-Ami. *Revolt in Japan.* Princeton UP, Princeton, New Jersey, 1973.

Shiroyama, Saburo. *War Criminal: The Life and Death of Koki Hirota.* Kodansha International, Tokyo, 1977.

Silberman, Bernard and Harootunian, H. O. (eds). *Japan in Crisis*. Princeton, UP, Princeton, New Jersey, 1974.

Steiner, Kurt. *Local Government in Japan*. Stanford UP, Stanford, California, 1965.

Sugiyama Memorandum. Hajime Sugiyama. Hara Shobo. Tokyo, 1967.

Swearingen Roger, and Langer, Paul. *Red Flag in Japan*. Harvard UP, Cambridge, 1952.

Takeuchi, Tatsuji. *War and Diplomacy in the Japanese Empire*. Allen & Unwin, London, 1936.

Terasaki, Gwen. *A Bridge to the Sun*. Michael Joseph, London, 1958.

Toland, John. *The Rising Sun*. Random House, New York, 1970.

Tolischus, Otto. *Tokyo Record*. Reynal & Hitchcock, New York, 1943.

Totten, George (ed.). *Democracy in Prewar Japan: Groundwork or facade?* D. C. Heath, Boston, 1967.

Tsunoda, Ryusaku. *Sources of Japanese Tradition*. New York, 1958.

Wada, Teijun. *American Foreign Policy towards Japan During the Nineteenth Century*. Tokyo, 1928.

Wilson, Dick. *When Tigers Fight*. Hutchinson, London, 1982. One of the very few studies of arguably the greatest conflict in history, the Sino-Japanese War.

Wilson, George M. *Radical Nationalist in Japan: Kita Ikki, 1883–1937*. Harvard UP, Cambridge, Mass., 1969.

Young, John W. 'The Hara Cabinet and Chang Tso-Lin, 1920–1', *Monumenta Nipponica* 27, 1972.

Yoshida, Shigeru. *Memoirs*. Houghton Mifflin, Boston, 1962.

Yuan Tsing. *The Japanese Intervention in Shantung During World War I in China and Japan*. Santa Barbara, 1978.

PART THREE: THE WHIRLWIND

The Pacific War has yielded an enormous harvest of wheat and chaff from military historians. To confine this to a few of the better ones:

Allen, Louis. *Burma, the Longest War*. J. M. Dent, London, 1984. A brilliant account.

Ba Maw. *Breakthrough in Burma*. Yale UP, New Haven, 1968.

Barbey, Daniel. *MacArthur's Amphibious Navy*. US Naval Institute, Annapolis, 1969.

Beard, Charles A. *President Roosevelt and the Coming of War*. Yale UP, New Haven, 1948.

Belote, James H. *Corregidor: The Saga of a Fortress*. Harper, New York, 1967.

Bennett, Henry Gordon. *Why Singapore Fell*. Angus & Robertson, London, 1944.

Blair, Clay. *MacArthur*. Futura, London, 1977. Highly critical but surprisingly gripping.

Brooks, Lester. *Behind Japan's Surrender*. McGraw-Hill, New York, 1968.

Burtness, Paul and Ober, Warren (eds). *The Puzzle of Pearl Harbor*. Row Peterson, Evanston, Illinois, 1962.

Busch, Noel. *The Emperor's Sword*. Funk & Wagnalls, New York, 1969.

Butow, R. C. J. *Japan's Decision to Surrender*. Oxford UP, London, 1954.

Byas, Hugh. *Government by Assassination*. Harper, New York, 1958.

Byrnes, James F. *Speaking Frankly*. Harper, New York, 1947.

Bywater, Hector. *The Great Pacific War*. Constable, London, 1925.

Chennault, Claire Lee. *Way of a Fighter*. Putnam, New York, 1949.

Clarke, Hugh and Yamashita, Takeo. *To Sydney by Stealth*. Horowitz, London, 1966.

Cohen, Jerome. *Japan's Economy in War and Reconstruction*. University of Minnesota Press, Minneapolis, 1949.

Craig, William. *The Fall of Japan*. Dial, New York, 1967.

Davis, Burke. *Get Yamamoto*. Random House, New York, 1969.

Eichelberger, Robert. *Our Jungle Road to Tokyo*. Viking, New York, 1950.

Falk, Stanley. *Bataan: The March of Death*. Norton, New York, 1962.

——. *Decision at Leyte*. Norton, New York, 1966.

Fuchida, Mitsuo, and Okumiya, Masatake. *Midway: The Battle that Doomed Japan*. US Naval Institute, Annapolis, Maryland, 1955.

Guillain, Robert. *I Saw Tokyo Burning*. Murray, London, 1981.

Havens, Thomas. *Valley of Darkness*. Norton, New York, 1978.

Halsey, William and Bryan. *Admiral Halsey's Story*. McGraw-Hill, New York, 1947.

Hattori, Takushiro. *The Complete History of the Greater East Asia War*. Hara Shobo, Tokyo, 1966.

Hersey, John. *Hiroshima*. Alfred Knopf, New York, 1946.

Higashikuni, Prince Toshihiko. *The War Diary of a Member of the Royal Family*. Nihon, Shuho Sha, 1957.

Holmes, W. J. *Undersea Victory*. Doubleday, New York, 1966.

Homma, Masaharu. *Diary*. Unpublished.

Hull, Cordell. *Memoirs*. Macmillan, New York, 1948.

Hunt, Frazier. *MacArthur and the War against Japan*. Scribner, New York, 1944.

Ike, Nobutaka. *Japan's Decision for War*. Stanford UP, Stanford, California, 1967.

Inoguchi, Rikihei, Nakajima, Tadashi, and Pineau, Roger. *The Divine Wind*. U.S. Naval Institute, Annapolis, Maryland, 1958.

Ito, Masanori and Pineau, Roger. *The End of the Imperial Japanese Navy*. Norton, New York, 1962.

Ito, Masashi. *The Emperor's Last Soldiers*. Coward-McCann, New York, 1967.

James, David. *The Rise and Fall of the Japanese Empire*. Allen & Unwin, London, 1951.

Kahn, David. *The Code-Breakers*. Macmillan, New York, 1967.

Kase, T. *Journey to the Missouri*. Yale UP, New Haven, 1950.

Kato, Masuo. *The Lost War*. Alfred Knopf, New York, 1946.

Kawai, K. *Japan's American Interlude*. University of Chicago UP.

King, Ernest, and Whitehill, Walter, *Fleet Admiral King*. Eyre & Spottiswoode, London, 1953.

Kiyosawa, Kiyoshi. *Diaries in Darkness*. Shuei Sha, Tokyo, 1966.

Kogun. *The Japanese Army in the Pacific War*. US Marine Corps Association, Quantico, Virginia.

Konoye, Fumimaro. *The Konoye Diary*. Kyodo Press, Tokyo, 1968.

——. *My Efforts towards Peace*. Nippon Dempo Tsushinsha, Tokyo, 1946.

Lamont, Lansing. *Day of Trinity*. Athenaeum, New York, 1965.

Laurence, William. *Dawn Over Zero*. Alfred Knopf, New York, 1946.

Leahy, William. *I Was There*. Whittesley, New York, 1950.

Lebra, Joyce (ed.). *Japan's Greater East Asia Co-Prosperity Sphere in World War II*. Oxford UP, London, 1975.

Lord, Walter. *Day of Infamy*. Holt, Rinehart & Winston, New York, 1957. An unsurpassedly gripping account of Pearl Harbor.

——. *Incredible Victory*. Harper, New York, 1967.

MacArthur, Douglas. *Reminiscences*. McGraw-Hill, 1964. Occasionally wordy, always fascinating, sometimes intensely moving.

Moorad, George. *Lost Peace in China*. Button, New York, 1949.

Morison, Samuel Eliot. *Coral Sea, Midway and Submarine Operations*. Little, Brown & Co., Boston, 1949.

Nakasone, Seizen. *Tragedy of Okinawa*. Kacho Shobo, Tokyo, 1951.

Neumann, William. *America Encounters Japan*. John Hopkins Press, Baltimore, 1963.

Nishino, General. *Isle of Death: Guadalcanal*. Masu Shobo, Tokyo, 1956.

Okuyama, Ryoko. *Left Alive on Saipan*. Hara Shobo, Tokyo, 1967.

Omura, Bunji. *The Last Genro*. Lippincott, Philadelphia, 1938.

Peacock, Don. *The Emperor's Guest*. Oleander, New York, 1989.

Potter, E. B., and Nimitz, Chester W. (ed.). *The Great Sea War*. Prentice-Hall, New Jersey, 1960.

Rappaport, Armin. *Henry L. Stimson and Japan, 1931–3*. Chicago UP, 1963.

Romulo, Carlos. *I Saw the Fall of the Philippines*. Doubleday, New York, 1943.

Roosevelt, Franklin D. *Papers*. Franklin D. Roosevelt Library, New York.

Saeki, S. *The Shadow of Sunrise*. Kodansha International, Tokyo.

Saito, Yoshie. *Deceived History: An Inside Account of Matsuoka and the Tripartite Pact*. Yomiuri Shimbun, Tokyo, 1955.

Shigemitsu, M. *Japan and her Destiny*. Dutton, New York, 1958.

Shillony, Ben-Ami. *Politics and Culture in Wartime Japan*. Clarendon Press, Oxford, 1981.

Shimomura, Kainan. *Notes on the Termination of the War*. Kamakuro Bunko, Tokyo, 1948.

Slim, William J. *Defeat into Victory*. McKay, New York, 1961.

Smith, S. E. *The United States Navy in World War Two*. Morrow, New York, 1966.

Spector, Ronald H. *Eagle Against the Sun*. Macmillan, London, 1980.

——. *The United States Marine Corps In World War Two*. Random House, New York, 1962.

Stewart, Adrian. *The Underrated Enemy*. William Kimber, London, 1987.

Stimson, Henry L. *The Diary of Henry L. Stimson*. Yale University Library, New Haven, 1947.

Storry, Richard. *The Double Patriots*. Houghton Mifflin, Boston, 1957.

Sugano, Shizuko. *The End at Saipan*. Suppan Kyodo Sha, Tokyo, 1959.

Sugiyama, General Hajime. *Notes*. Hara Shobo, Tokyo, 1967.

Takagi, Sokichi. *History of Naval Battles in the Pacific*. Iwanami Shoten, Tokyo, 1949.

Takahashi, Masaye. *The 2/26 Incident*. Chuo Koron Sha, Pkyo, 1965.

Taleja, Thaddeus. *Climax at Midway*. Norton, New York, 1960.

Tanemura, Sako. *Secret Diary of Imperial Headquarters*. Diamond Sha, Tokyo, 1952.

Thorne, Christopher. *Allies of a Kind*. New York, 1978.

Togo, Shigenori. *The Cause of Japan*. Simon & Schuster, New York, 1956.

Toland, John. *But Not in Shame*. Random House, New York, 1961.

——. *The Last 100 Days*. Random House, New York, 1966.

Tolischus, Otto. *Tokyo Record*. Reyna & Hitchcock, New York, 1943.

Tomioka, Sadatoshi. *The Outbreak and Termination of the War*. Mainichi Shimbun, Tokyo, 1968.

Trefousse, Hans Louis. *What Happened at Pearl Harbor?* Twayne, New York, 1958.

Tregaskis, Richard. *Guadalcanal Diary*. Random House, New York, 1943.

Truman, Harry S. *Memoirs*. Doubleday, New York, 1956.

Tsuji, Masanobu. *Guadalcanal*. Tamba-Shi, Nara, 1950.

Wainwright, Jonathan. *General Wainwright's Story*. Doubleday, New York, 1946.

Weller, George. *Singapore Is Silent*. Harcourt, New York, 1943.

Whitney, Courtney. *MacArthur, His Rendezvous with History*. Alfred Knopf, New York, 1956.

Wilcox, Robert. *The Secret War*. Morrow, New York, 1987.

Wilmott, H. P. *Empires in the Balance*. 1982.

Wohlstetter, Roberta. *Pearl Harbor: Warning and Decision*. Stanford UP, Stanford, California, 1962.

Yabe, Teiji. *Fumimaro Konoye*. Privately printed, 1951–2.

Yamamoto, Kumaichi. *Memoirs of the Greater East Asia War*. Compiled from his papers and privately printed, 1964.

PART FOUR: THE UNDEFEATED

The literature on post-war Japanese politics and economics is, with a few superb exceptions, such as Horsley and Buckley's *Nippon: New Superpower*, Chalmers Johnson's *Miti and the Japanese Miracle* and Abegglen and Stalk's *Kaisha*, either patchy or specialized or both. However, taken together, it does throw light on the enormous political tensions and vigorous economic debate underpinning Japan's miracle. Here are a few of the more illuminating works:

Abegglen, James C. 'The Economic Growth of Japan'. *Scientific American*, March 1970.

Abegglen, James and Stalk, George. *Kaisha: the Japanese Corporation*. Tuttle, Tokyo, 1985.

Abegglen, James C. *et al – U.S. Japan Economic Relations*. California UP, Berkeley, 1980.

Adams, T. F. M. and Iwao. *A Financial History of the New Japan*. Kodansha, Tokyo, 1972.

Barnet and Mueller. *Global Reach*. Simon & Schuster, New York.

Beasley, W. G. *The Modern History of Japan*. Tuttle, New York, 1990.

Bisson, T. A. *Japan's War Economy*. Institute of Pacific Relations, New York, 1945.

——. *Prospects for Democracy in Japan*. New York, 1949.

——. *Zaibatsu Dissolution in Japan*. California UP, Berkeley, 1954.

Boltho, Andrea. *Japan: An Economic Survey, 1953–73*. Oxford UP, London, 1975.

Broadbridge, Seymour. *Industrial Dualism in Japan*. Aldine, Chicago, 1966.

Bronte, Stephen. *Japanese Finance*. Euromoney Publications, London, 1982.

Buckley, Roger. *Japan Today*. Cambridge UP, Cambridge, 1990.

Burstein, Daniel. *Yen! Japan's New Financial Empire and Its Threat to America*. Simon & Schuster, New York, 1988.

Buruma, Ian. *A Japanese Mirror*. Jonathan Cape, London, 1984.

Chen, Edward. *Hyper-Growth in Asian Economies*. Macmillan, London, 1979.

Chikushi, Tetsuya. 'Young People as a New Human Race'. *Japan Quarterly*, summer 1986.

Clark, Rodney. *The Japanese Company*. Yale UP, New Haven, 1979.

Cohen, Jerome. *Japan's Economy in War and Reconstruction*. Minnesota UP, Minneapolis, 1949.

Consider Japan. The Economist, Duckworth, London, 1963.

Cortazzi, Hugh. *The Japanese Achievement*. Sidgwick & Jackson, London, 1990. A splendid book.

Craig, Albert (ed.). *Japan: A Comparative View*. Princeton UP, Princeton, New Jersey, 1979.

Crichton, Michael. *Rising Sun*. Alfred Knopf, New York, 1992.

Curtis, Gerald. *The Japanese Way of Politics*. Columbia UP, New York, 1988.

Cusumano, Michael. *The Japanese Automobile Industry*. Harvard UP, Cambridge, 1985.

Dale, Peter. *The Myth of Japanese Uniqueness*. Croom Helm, New York, 1986.

Destler, I. M. *The Textile Wrangle*. Cornell UP, Ithaca, New York, 1979.

Doi, Teruo and Shattuck, Warren (eds). *Patent and Know-How Licensing in Japan and the United States*. Washington UP, 1977.

Doi, Takeo. *The Anatomy of Dependence*. Kodansha International, Tokyo 1973.

Dore, Ronald. *British Factory, Japanese Factory*. California UP, Berkeley, 1973.

——. *Taking Japan Seriously*. Athlone Press, London, 1987.

Dunn, Frederick. *Peace-Making and the Settlement with Japan*. Princeton UP, Princeton, New Jersey, 1979.

Emmott, Bill. *The Sun Also Sets*. Simon & Schuster, London, 1989. Well-written and thought-provoking.

——. *Japan's Global Reach*. Century Business, London, 1992.

Fukutake, Tadashi. *Japanese Society Today*. Tokyo UP, 1981.

Gayn, Mark. *Japan Diary*. William Sloane Associates, New York, 1948.

Hadley, Eleanor. *Anti-Trust in Japan*. Princeton UP, Princeton, New Jersey, 1974.

Haitani, Kanji. *The Japanese Economic System*. D. C. Heath, Lexington, 1976.

Halberstam, David. *The Reckoning*. Yohan, Tokyo, 1987.

Hale, David. *Britain and Japan as the Financial Bogeymen of U.S. Politics*. Chicago, 1987.

Halloran, Richard. *Japan: Images and Realities*. Tuttle, Tokyo, 1970.

Harari, Ehud. *The Politics of Labor Legislation in Japan*. California UP, Berkeley, 1973.

Hasegawa, Nyozekan. *Japanese National Character*. Board of Tourist Industry, Tokyo, 1942.

Hata, Ikuhiko. 'Japan under the Occupation', *Japan Interpreter*, winter 1976.

Harries, Meirion and Susie. *Sheathing the Sword*. Heinemann, London. A masterly study.

Havens, Thomas. *Farm and Nation in Modern Japan.* Princeton UP, Princeton, New Jersey, 1974.

Henderson, Dan. *Foreign Enterprise in Japan.* Tuttle, Tokyo, 1975.

Hewins, Ralph. *The Japanese Miracle Men.* Secker & Warburg, London, 1967.

Hiraishi, Nagahisa. *Social Security.* Japanese Industrial Relations Series No 5.

Ho, Alfred. *Japan's Trade Liberalisation in the 1960s.* International Arts and Sciences Press, New York, 1973.

Hollerman, Leon. *Japan's Dependency on the World Economy.* Princeton UP, Princeton, New Jersey, 1967.

Horsley, William and Buckley, Roger. *Nippon: New Superpower.* BBC Books, London, 1990. A well-written and cogent narrative of Japanese politics in the post-war period that lucidly sets out the huge political clashes of the period with the seriousness they deserve. By far the best book on the subject, perhaps not taken seriously enough because of its BBC imprint.

Imai, Masaaki. *Kaizen, the Key to Japan's Competitive Success.* Random House, New York, 1986.

——. *Never Take Yes for an Answer.* Simul Press, Tokyo, 1975.

——. *Sixteen Ways to Avoid Saying No.* Nihon Keizai Shinbun, Tokyo, 1981.

Inoguchi, Takashi and Okimoto (eds). *The Political Economy of Japan.* Stanford UP, Stanford, California, 1988.

Ito, Mitsuharu. 'Munitions Unlimited: The Controlled Economy'. *Japan Interpreter,* summer 1972.

Itoh, Hiroshi. *Japanese Politics: An Inside View.* Cornell UP, Ithaca, New York, 1973.

James, Clayton. *The Years of MacArthur.* Boston, 1985.

Johnson, Chalmers. 'Japan: Who Governs?' *Journal of Japanese Studies,* autumn 1975.

——. *Japan's Public Policy Companies.* American Enterprise Institute, Washington, 1978.

——. Miti and Japanese International Economic Policy. In Robert Scalopino (ed.) *The Foreign Policy of Modern Japan.* California UP, Berkeley, 1977.

——. 'MITI and the Japanese Miracle'. Tuttle, Tokyo, 1986. A masterly analysis and narrative of Japanese economic history, with an overpoweringly persuasive thesis. Wholly authoritative and one of the few books on economics that is also a pleasure to read.

Kamata, Satoshi. *Japan in the Passing Lane.* Unwin, London, 1984.

Kaplan, Eugene. *Japan: The Government–Business Relationship*. US Department of Commerce, Washington, 1972.

Kearns, Robert. *Zaibatsu America*. Free Press, New York, 1992.

Kennan, George. *Memoirs, 1925–50*. Boston, 1967.

Kosaka, Masataka. *A History of Postwar Japan*, Kodansha, Japan, 1972.

Kubota, Akira. *Higher Civil Servants in Postwar Japan*. Princeton UP, Princeton, New Jersey, 1969.

Kuriyama, Takakazu. *New Directions for Japanese Policy in the Changing World of the 1990s*. Ministry of Foreign Affairs, Tokyo, 1990.

Kurzman, Dan. *Kishi and Japan*. Obolensky, New York, 1960.

Lebra, Takie. *Japanese Patterns of Behavior*. Hawaii UP, Honolulu, 1976.

Lee O-Young. *Small Is Better*. Kodansha, Tokyo, 1984.

Lincoln, Edward. *Japan's Industrial Policies*. Japan Economic Institute of America, Washington, 1984.

——. *Japan: Facing Economic Maturity*. Brookings, Washington, 1988.

Livingston, Jon and Oldfather, Felicia. *Postwar Japan*. Random House, New York, 1973.

Lynn, Leonard. *How Japan Innovates*. Westview Press, Colorado, 1982.

MacArthur, Douglas. *Reminiscences*. McGraw-Hill, New York, 1964.

Magaziner, Ira and Hout, Thomas. *Japanese Industrial Policy*. California University Institute of International Studies, Berkeley, 1981.

Manchester, William. *American Caesar, Douglas MacArthur, 1880–1964*. Hutchinson, London, 1978.

Maruyama, Masao. *Thought and Behaviour in Modern Japanese Politics*. Oxford UP, London, 1969.

Matsumura, Yutaka. *Japan's Economic Growth, 1945–60*. Tokyo News Service, 1961.

Moore, Charles. *The Japanese Mind*. Tuttle, Tokyo, 1973.

Munday, Max. *Japanese Manufacturing Investment in Wales*. Wales UP, Cardiff, 1990.

Nakane, Chie. *Japanese Society*. California UP, Berkeley, 1976.

Noda, Nobuo. *How Japan Absorbed American Management Methods*. Asian Productivity Organisation, Manila, 1970.

Ogawa, Terutomo. *Multinationalism, Japanese Style*. Princeton UP, Princeton, New Jersey, 1982.

Ohkawa, Kazushi and Rosovsky, Henry. *Japanese Economic Growth*. Stanford UP, Stanford, California, 1973.

Ohmae, Kenichi. *Beyond National Borders*. Kodan-sha International, Tokyo.

——. *The Borderless World*. Harper Business, New York, 1990.

——. *The Mind of the Strategist*. McGraw-Hill, New York, 1982.

Passin, Herbert (ed.). *The United States and Japan*. Columbia Books, Washington, 1975.

Patrick, Hugh, and Rosovsky, Henry (eds). *Asia's New Giant*. Brookings, Washington, 1976.

Peattie, Mark. *Ishiwara Kanji and Japan's Confrontation with the West*. Princeton UP, Princeton, New Jersey, 1975.

Pempel, T. J. (ed.). *Policymaking in Contemporary Japan*. Cornell UP, Ithaca, New York, 1977.

Prestowitz, Clyde. *Trading Places: How We Allowed Japan to Take the Lead*. Basic Books, New York, 1988.

Prindl, Andreas. *Japanese Finance*. Wiley, New York, 1981.

Roberts, John. *Mitsui*. Weatherhill, Tokyo, 1973.

Schaller, Michael. *Douglas MacArthur*. Oxford UP, London, 1989.

——. *The American Occupation of Japan*. Oxford UP, London, 1985. An enthralling analysis of the occupation, detailing the slow strangulation of MacArthur's reforms and relating this to the subsequent evolution of America's Asia policy. A fine piece of historical detective work.

Seidensticker, Edward. *Tokyo Rising*. Alfred Knopf, New York, 1990.

Shiba, Kimpei and Nozue, Kenzo. *What Makes Japan Tick?* Asahi Evening News Co., Tokyo, 1976.

Shingo, Shigeo. *Study of Toyota Production Systems*. Japan Management Association, Tokyo, 1981.

Shirai, Taishiro (ed.). *Contemporary Industrial Relations in Japan*. University of Wisconsin Press, 1983.

Steven, Rob. *Class in Contemporary Japan*. Cambridge UP, Cambridge, 1984.

Stone, P. B. *Japan Surges Ahead*. Praeger, New York, 1969.

Supreme Commander for the Allied Powers. History of the Non-military Activities of the Occupation of Japan 1945–51. National Archives, Washington, 1951.

Suzuki, Yoshio (ed). *The Japanese Financial System*. Oxford UP, London, 1988.

Takana, Kakuei. *Building a New Nation*. Simul Press, Tokyo, 1973.

Thayer, Nathaniel. *How the Conservatives Rule Japan*. Princeton UP, Princeton, New Jersey, 1969.

Thomsen, Harry, *et al. The Evolution of Japanese Direct Investment in Europe.* Harvester, Brighton, 1991.

Tonata, Seiichi (ed.). *The Modernization of Japan.* Institute of Asian Economic Affairs, Tokyo, 1966.

Trevor *et al. Manufacturers and Suppliers in Britain and Japan.* Policy Studies Institute, London, 1991.

Truman, Harry S. *Memoirs.* Doubleday, New York, 1956.

Tsurumi. *A Cultural History of Postwar Japan.* Iwanami Shoten, Tokyo, 1984.

Viner, Aron. *Inside Japan's Financial Markets.* Economist Publications, London, 1987.

Vogel, Ezra. *Japan as Number One.* Tuttle, Tokyo, 1980.

Weinstein, Martin. *Japan's Postwar Defence Policy, 1947–68.* Columbia UP, New York, 1971.

Whitney, Courtney. *MacArthur: His Rendezvous with History.* New York, 1956.

Wickens, Peter. *The Road to Nissan.* Macmillan, New York, 1987.

Wildes, Harry. *Typhoon in Tokyo: The Occupation and Its Aftermath.* Macmillan, New York, 1954.

Willoughby, Charles, and Chamberlain, John. *MacArthur, 1941–51.* New York, 1955.

Wilson, James. 'The Rise of the Bureaucratic State'. *Public Interest,* fall 1975.

Yamamura, Kozo. *Economic Policy in Postwar Japan.* California UP, Berkeley, 1967.

Yoshida, Shigeru. *The Yoshida Memoirs.* Houghton Mifflin, Cambridge, 1962.

Yoshino, M. Y. *The Japanese Marketing System.* MIT Press, Cambridge, Mass., 1971.

Zengage, Thomas and Ratcliffe, C. *The Japanese Century: Challenge and Response.* Longman, London, 1988.

PART FIVE: THE FAR SIDE OF THE EARTH

Most of the material in this section came from the author's own direct reporting and from academic papers, newspapers, magazines, etc. There are a handful of books on the subject worth reading:

Anderson, Ronald. *Education in Japan: A Century of Modern Development.* US Dept of Health Education and Welfare, Washington, 1975.

Aso, Makoto. *Education and Japan's Modernization*. Ministry of Foreign Affairs, Tokyo, 1972.

Benedict, Ruth. *The Chrysanthemum and the Sword*. Tuttle, Tokyo, 1954. This *tour de force* by an American anthropologist who never actually visited Japan, remains a classic, still shedding light on the Japanese way of thinking.

Bornoff, Nicholas. *Pink Samurai*. Grafton Books, London, 1991. An exhaustive compendium of sex practices, ancient and modern, in Japan which sheds light on one aspect of Japanese life.

Cogan, John. 'Should the U.S. Mimic Japanese Education?' *Phi Delta Kappa*, March 1984.

Horio, Teruhisa. *Educational Thought and Ideology in Modern Japan*. Tokyo UP, 1988.

Imai, Masaaki. *Sixteen Ways to Avoid Saying No*, Nihon Keizai, Shinbun, Tokyo, 1981

Ishihara, Shintaro. *The Japan That Can Say No*. Simon & Schuster, London, 1991.

Joseph, J. *The Japanese*. Viking, London, 1993. An entertaining look at Japanese uniqueness.

Kenrick, Douglas Moore. *Where Communism Works*. Tuttle, Tokyo, 1988.

Kobayashi, Kaoru. *Japan. The Most Misunderstood Country*. Japan Times, Tokyo, 1984. Perceptive and full of insights.

Martineau Lisa. *Caught in a Mirror*, Macmillan, London, 1992. Vivid and well-written.

Murakami, Yoshiol. 'Bullying in the Classroom'. *Japan Quarterly*, 32.

Nathan, John. *Mishima: A Biography*. Tuttle, Tokyo, 1974. A readable and straightforward account of Japan's most controversial post-war literary figure.

Nishimura, Hidetoshi. 'Educational Reform'. *Japan Quarterly*, 37.

Oppenheim, Philip. *New Masters*. London, 1982. Thought-provoking.

Reischaeur, Edwin. *The Japanese Today*. Tuttle, Tokyo, 1988. Highly readable.

Rohlen, Thomas. *Japan's High Schools*. California UP, Berkeley, 1983.

Schooland, Ken. *Shogun's Ghost*. Bergin & Garvey, New York, 1990.

Tasker, Peter. *Inside Japan*. Penguin, London, 1987.

Viner, P. *The Emerging Power of Japanese Money*. Dow Jones-Irwin, Illinois, 1988.

Vining, Elizabeth Gray. *Windows for the Crown Prince*. Tuttle, Tokyo, 1989.

Wolferen, Karel van. *The Enigma of Japanese Power*. Vintage Books, New York, 1989. The most powerful critique yet of modern Japan. A massive achievement. Highly controversial and sometimes a slow read, it has nevertheless opened up the debate on the nature of Japanese society.

INDEX

Abe, Genki, 275
Abe, Kobo, 468–9
Abe, Masahiro, 67
Abegglen, James, 430–31
Admiralty Islands, 259
aerospace industry, 349, 438
age-groups, 60
agriculture
  crop failure in 1932, 181
  declining production, 446
  numbers employed, 446
  providing funds for industrialization,
    124
  tax rises causing distress, 127
  post-war land reform, 313–14
  see also rice
Ainu people, 45
Airin, Japan, 555
Akahata ('Red Flag' newspaper), 331
Akao, Bin, 355
Akasaka Detached Palace, 147, 151, 166
Akatsuki Maru (freighter), 577–8
Akihito, Emperor
  approachability, 508–9
  coronation, 461–3
  Crown Prince, as, 317, 318
  marriage, 499
  resuming divine role, 499–509
  visits China, 518–19
  see also Emperor as institution;
    Emperor-worship
Akizuki, Tatsuichiro, 36–7
Alexander, General Harold (Earl
  Alexander of Tunis), 249
All Japan Council of Patriotic
  Organizations, 507
Amakusa, Shiro, 572–3

Amanon, Ikuo, 562
Amaterasu Omikami (goddess), 44–5, 166
Amaya, Naohiro, 412
Amur River, Russia, 170
Amur River Society, 300
Anami, General Korechika, xxii, 274–7,
  283–4, 289
ancestor-worship, 495
Ando, Captain Teruzo, 192, 194, 196
Anglo-Japanese Treaty (1902), 117–18,
  170
Anti-Comintern Pact, 228
Anti-Foreigner Similar Spirits Society, 300
Approved Persons Board, 301
Araki, General Sadao, xix, 173, 195,
  203–4, 234
Arima, Lord, 571
Arisue, General Seizo, 304
Armacost, Michael, 542
army
  Meiji regime: Choshu clan, influence of,
    110; Emperor, direct subjection to,
    111; First World War, loss of prestige
    following, 157; Imperial Rescript,
    110–11; *kikeitai* (shock troops), 89;
    post-samurai, 83; Russian expedition
    of 1918, 170; strength, 112, 170, 199;
    War Minister, importance of, 110–11,
    see also War Minister
  national army: class structure, 110, 202;
    establishment, 84, 89, 109; German
    model, 110, 111; indiscipline in, 220;
    organization, 110; origins, 109–10
  Hirohito's reign: coup attempt in 1936,
    192–9; Great Purpose, 193; Imperial
    Way school (Kodo-Ha), 173, 203–5;
    political power seized, 159–62;

resentment among junior officers, 202–5; training dehumanizing soldiers, 221; war with China, 209; *zaibatsu*, hatred of, 202; *zaibatsu* links, 200–201

Pacific War: civilian militia, 271; Control Group, 201–2, 205, 224, 225–6; infantry tactics, 27–8; peace terms, 275, 277–8; preparations for, 200–201; surrender insurgency, 282–6. *see also* Pacific War

peace treaty (1951): responsibility for defence, 337; self-defence allowed, 306–7

political faction, as: politicians held in contempt by, 96, 110; power of, 110, 135, 179–91

post-war: attempts to re-establish, 330; clandestine units, 304–5; collapse of Soviet Union, effect of, 528; disarmament, 301–307; general staff, nucleus retained, 304–5

post occupation rearmament, *see* rearmament

see also atrocities; militarism; Pacific War; rearmament; Sino-Japanese wars

Asahi Shimbun (newspaper), 384, 542, 556

Asaka, Prince, 223, 224, 225

Asano (*zaibatsu*), 398

Asanuma, Inejiro, 355

Association of South-East Asian Nations (ASEAN), 529–30

Asuma, Shiro, 223

atomic bombs

Hiroshima, 3–8, 14–15, 29–34, 273; casualties, 33–4; literature on, 468–9

justification for dropping, 37–9

Manhattan Project, 5, 9, 14

Nagasaki, 35–7

peace discussions following, 273–9

power structure of Japan maintained by, 39, 288–92

testing, 19–20

see also nuclear programme

atrocities

Burma railway camps, 15–17

bushido perverted, 222

China: Kaifeng, 219; Kihrien, 219; Rape of Nanking, 8–9, 210, 215, 219, 222–5, 513, 518; Wuhu, 219

complaints as to, 224–5

Control Group's involvement, 225–6

factors leading to, 219–21

history rewritten, 513–15

ordered from above, 222–5

peasants' brutal lives explaining, 220

Philippines, 22–3

press treatment of, 224

total war, 222

Unit 731, 225

Australia

ASEAN membership, 530

on ending of occupation (1951), 336

troops in Pacific War, 248, 264

vulnerability of, 252

automobile industry

Automobile Manufacturing Industry Law (1936), 392

clashes with US over *keiretsu*, 537–9

foreign inward investment, 411–12

kaisha, dominance of, 439

overseas plants, 449–55

state control of, 392–3

taxation benefits, 392–3

see also international trade

Axis Pact (1940), 229

banking system

Bank of Japan, 525

capital markets, 414–15

collateral for loans, 399

companies, banks relationship with, 430–32

financial crash and depression, 122, 176, 180–81

financing companies, *see* companies

foreign investments, 453–5

government-guaranteed banks of last resort, 396

investment criteria: long term perspectives, 426

Japan Development Bank, 398–9

keiretsu: as convenient structure, 427; replacing *zaibatsu*, 397, *see also keiretsu*

loss of power with growth of companies, 439

overlending, 396–7, 399

savings encouraged, 398–9, 417, 429

state control and support of, 448, 456

stock market crash of 1992, 455

supporting overseas companies, 450

Western system compared, 432

zaibatsus in, 126–7

Bataan, 250–52

Bates, Miner, 9, 224

bathing, 473–4

Bayonet Practice Promotion Society, 300
Beahan, Captain Kermit, 35
Beasley, W. G., 174
Beatrix, Queen of The Netherlands, 518
Befu, Harumi, 61
Behr, Edward, 224
Benedict, Ruth, 474, 477, 479–81
Beser, Lt Jacob, 6, 29
Biddle, Commodore, 65
Bikini Atoll, 343
biological warfare, 225–6
biotechnology industry, 438
Bismarck Sea, battle of, 258
Bisson, Thomas, 163–4, 271, 304, 310
Black Dragon Society, 300
'black ships', 65, 407
Blaine Hoover mission, 390
Blamey, General Sir Thomas, 256
Blue Storm Society, 348, 362
Blyth, Reginald, 317
Bock, Fred, 35
Borneo, 248
Bornoff, Nicholas, 490–91
bowing, 441, 474–5, 559
Boxer Rebellion (1900), 118
bribery, see corruption
Brittan, Sir Leon, 539
Bruce-Gardyne, Jock, 551
Buddhism, 46, 103–5
  Kiyomizu (temple at Kyoto), 51
  Sanjusangendo Hall, 51–2
Buddhist Komeito Party, 374
Buna, New Guinea, 256
burakumin (outcasts), 492
bureaucracy
  Blaine Hoover mission, 390–91
  centralized administration, 84, 96
  civil service exams, 562
  economic miracle, role in, 339, 395–404
  Emperor-worship giving legitimacy to,
    90–91
  Imperial Household Ministry, 88
  Nakasone weakens power of, 364
  obstructing post-war reforms, 326
  oligarchic elite, 97
  post-war reforms, 299
  power exceeding that of politicians, 386,
    524–5
  public office for bureaucrats, 164, 343,
    372
  pyramid of power, 84, 322
  rainbow coalition eases grip of, 375
  responsibility for war, 391
  survives occupation, 390–91

wartime decline in influence, 267–8
zaibatsu wrest power from, 169–70
Burma
  Burma road supply line, 217, 229, 231
  Chindit operations, 262
  defence of, 216, 249, 262–3
  South Burma Death Railway, 15–17
  trade with, 546
Bush, President George, 534, 537–8
bushido (warrior spirit), 134, 222
Butterworth, W. W., 328
Byrnes, James F., 24
Bywater, Hector, 517–18

Cambodia, 527, 532, 546–7
camera industry, 439
Canton, China, 213
capital markets, see banking system
capitalist classes, 63
Caroline Islands, 157
Caron, Technical Sergeant George ('Bob'),
    6, 30–31
casualties
  American: if Japan invaded, 28–9
  Japanese: atomic bombs, 33–4, 96;
    Pacific War, 27, 39, 259, 262, 263,
    270; Sino-Japanese war (1937–45),
    210, 213, 217, 228
Celebes, 248
Chang Hsueh-liang, 178, 183, 184
Chang Tso-lin, 168, 177–8
Changchun, Manchuria, 184
Changkufeng Hill, Korea, 211
Changsha, China, 216
chanoyu (tea-ceremony), 53–4
Chennault, General Claire, 216
Chiang Kai-shek
  leads Chinese nationalists, 176
  recognized as ruler of China, 178
  in Sino-Japanese war (1937–45):
    abandons Nanking to Japanese, 8,
    210; overconfidence, 208–9; poorly
    equipped, 214; refuses to negotiate,
    210–11, 213, 215; tactics, 215, 217
Chichibu, Prince, 196, 198, 212
China
  Akihito's visit, 519
  armed strength as threat, 530, 532
  Boxer Rebellion (1900), 118–19
  Britain in Hong Kong, 64
  China Affairs Board, 226
  civil war, 176
  drugs trade, 226

expansion into by Japanese, 114, 156–7, 188
Hopei-Chahar Political Council, 186–7
Japanese companies in, 519
Japanese nationalism attacked, 368
Kwantung Army, 204
military spending, 549
nuclear threat, 377
'open door' principle, 117–18, 121
Operation Ichi-go, 262
seizures in First World War, 156
trade with, 65, 170–71, 546
treaty port system, 156
Twenty-One demands, 156–7, 170
see also atrocities; Chiang Kai-shek; Manchuria; Sino-Japanese wars
Chindwin River, 262
Chino, Tadao, 537
Cho, Lt-General Isamu, 28
Chosu clan, 69, 78, 79, 87, 110, 148, 179, 202
Christianity
banned, 64, 103
Shimabara massacre (1638), 570–74
spread of, 46
unpatriotic, 108
Urakami purge, 108
post-war revival, 325
Chuan-Ying, Hsu, 8–9
Chungking, China, 213, 216
Churchill, Sir Winston
on: atomic bomb, 9–10, 20, 39; Pacific War losses, 247
relationship with Truman, 18
Citizens Council for Peace in Vietnam, 356
civil service, see bureaucracy
Clarke, Major B. L. W., 16
class structure
aristocratic clique controlling bureaucracy and army, 138
aristocrats restore Emperor's powers, 62–3
army recruitment, 110, 202
capitalist classes, 63
classlessness claimed, 494
daimyo (princes), 49, 55–6
education, 476
language and, 487
merchant classes, 56, 72–3
middle class: absence of in Meiji period, 102, 163; Hirohito's example to, 146; intelligentsia, 496; zaibatsu retard, 311
peasants, 57–62, see also peasants

pigeon-holing for life, 102
samurai, see samurai
social distinctions preserved, 474–5
status and, 73
upper class marriages, 499
Clinton, President Bill, 541–2
cold war, 326, 340, 528
colonial expansion, see foreign policy
communism
anti-American riots, 343–5
anti-communist conservatism, 335
Communist Party, 130
Japan Communist Party, 130, 331, 351
Korean war of 1950–53, see Korea
MacArthur: attacked as unAmerican, 327–9; purges communists, 330–32
nationalist, 172–3
occupation: loyalty desk, 304; paramilitary forces as protection against, 305
Patriotic Anti-Communist Drawn Sword Militia, 307
post-occupation: cold war, 326, 340, 528; fear of left, 341
security of East Asia after collapse of, 527–9
working, Japan as example of, 63
see also China; Russia; Soviet Union
companies
banks, relationship with, 430–33, 439
blackmail from MITI, 426
breaking into foreign markets, 435
budgeting systems, 430–31
capital, 430–32
competitiveness, 432–5, 437–40
consensus decision-making, 444
deregulation, 377
dominant social structure, 430
enterprise culture, 444
financing, 430–33, 439; banks as providers, 430
grouping into keiretsu, 429
hierarchical structure, 441, 475–6
individual crushed by corporate structure, 495–6
investment decisions, 431
just-in-time (kanban) production system, 435–6, 553
kaisha, power of, 525
lifetime employment, 443
long-term growth sought, 430–32
loyalty enjoined, 511
management practices, 439–40
manufacturing dominating, 439

marketing, 440
multi-machine manning, 436
overseas plants, 449–55
overstaffing, 443
profitability following market share,
432–3
regimentation, 441
research and development, 437–8, 554
retraining programmes, 554
seniority and promotion, 443–4
service industries, 439
share price unimportant, 432
shareholders' small influence, 430
social protection provided by, 420
takeover battles, rarity of, 439
tax breaks for new companies, 428
women managers, 558
see also industrial relations; salarymen
Companies Liquidation Commission, 312
computer industry
competitiveness and technological
development, 437–8
super chip (VLSI), 413–14
Confucianism, 46, 99, 103–4, 491, 549
constitution, see law and constitution
Control Group, 201–2, 205, 224, 225–6
Coral Sea, battle of, 253
Corregidor, Philippines, 251
corruption
attempts to abolish, 371–2
bribes to pass exams, 102, 562
encouragement parties, 383
favours-and-patronage system, 382–3
founding zaibatsu's wealth, 97
insider share tips, 383
institutionalized, official, 372, 568
Kanemaru, 372
Lockheed scandal, 360, 361, 363, 366,
375
purchase of votes in Diet, 97, 371
Recruit affair, 370, 371
stock exchange scandals, 455–6
Tanaka's scandals, 358–62, 366, 383–4
Yoshida's shipbuilding contracts, 353
zaibatsu's gifts to politicians, 174
court ranks, 47
Courtis, Kenneth, 456
Craigie, Sir Robert, 206
creation myths, 44–5
crime, 566–7
Crump, Thomas, 477, 486

Dai Ichi Kangyo (keiretsu), 398, 450
Daijosai (Great Food Offering Ceremony),
461, 502–4, 507

daimyo (princes)
ceremonial progresses, 49
fiefdoms, 55–6
status following Meiji restoration, 78
zaibatsu grow from wealth of, 78
Datoh Musa Hitam, 453
death
attitude to, 482–4
capital punishment, 565
see also suicide
defence, see army; rearmament
democracy
Asian countries, 549
business influence, 385–6
defined, 381
discredited political system, 379–80
gerrymandering of constituencies, 385
MacArthur's achievement, 318
military coup envisaged, 533
need for, 387
one-party rule, 381–2
people's input into decision-making
lacking, 386–7
post-war pacifist commercial democracy,
337, 340
single party rule overthrown, 372
stifled in 1920s, 171
student protest at absence of, 356
subservient press, 384–5
post-war attempts to promote, 317
deregulation of business, 377
Diet, see parliament
disarmament
armed forces disbanded, 303
atomic energy equipment seized, 303
constitution renouncing war, 301–2
difficulty of enforcing, 304
matériel destroyed, 302–3
production ceilings, 303
Self Defence Force, 303, 347
see also rearmament
Doctolero, Lucas, 22
Dodge, Joseph (and Dodge Line), 351,
395, 398
Doi, Takako, 370–71, 531
Doolittle, Lt-General J. H., 253
Doorman, Admiral Karel, 249
Draper, General William, 328–9
drugs trade
run by zaibatsu, 227
war costs financed by, 226
Dulles, John Foster, 306, 336

earthquake of 1923, 165–6
East Indies, 248
Eatherly, Captain Claude, 7
economic miracle
    bureaucracy's role, 339, *see also*
        bureaucracy
    domestic demand fostering, 401
    five-year plan, 395, 456
    foreign markets penetrated, 401–4
    government's role in: chart of factors,
        421–4; extent of, 425; state directed,
        388–94; state hand-outs, 394; state-
        motivated aggression, 390, 420. *see*
        also Ministry of International Trade
        and Industry
    growth: income doubling plan, 407;
        long-term, 430, 569; main objective,
        420; maintenance of, 447–8;
        Nakasone resists, 349; target
        industries, 448; from within, 369
    history of, 390–94
    international pressure faced, 405
    keiretsu, role of, 398
    new industries nurtured, 402–3
    pacifism and, 350
    priority production system, 395
    quality control as factor, 400, 403, 442,
        475
    reasons for: competitiveness, 432–5;
        historical, social and environmental
        background, 416–19; industrial
        relations, 440–44; international
        advantages, 419–20; nature of
        Japanese company, 429–40; state
        influence, 420–9; whether
        transplantable in West, 416, 421–4,
        425–6, 440, 445, 553. *see also*
        companies; industrial relations
    responsibility for, 339
    tax incentive system, 402
    zaibatsu's role in, 390–94
    see also economy
economy
    administration by inducement, 408
    Asian markets, 156–7, 218, 407,
        544–9, 597–8
    bubble economy of late 1980s, 415
    budget proposals, approval of, 96
    capital base of industry, 397
    concentration of power, 163
    deregulation of business, 377
    economists as decision-makers, 525–6
    'enterprise adjustment', 393–4
    excessive competition, 408

expansion by economic conquest, 171
financial crash and depression, 122, 176,
    180–81
financial power destabilizing Western
    currencies, 550–52
foreign investments, 411–12, 453–5,
    548, 553
free economy myth, 389
GDP, 349, 405, 438, 455
Greater East Asian Economic Co-
    Prosperity Sphere, 157, 218
growth: crash of 1992, 455–6
hierarchical structure: industry, 128
hierarchical structure: dependence in
    villages, 58–62
inflation causing slump (1974), 412–13
insider share tips, 383
investment in new plant, 456
macro-economic policy, 428
MITI control over, 401
Nakasone's policy, 368–9
national debt, 428
'new economic structure' (1939), 393
post-war depression, 327
pre-war, 390–94
privatization of state industries, 369
raw materials: cheap purchases, 419;
    lack of, 112–13, 156, 230; from
    Manchuria, 183, 227–8; wartime
    control, 267
recession, 138
Reconstruction Finance Bank, 394
restrictive practices and price fixing,
    400, 411, 413
scenario for future, 569–70
state directed cartelism, 389–94, 398,
    413
state monopoly capitalism, 399
steel industry, *see* steel industry
surplus labour sent abroad, 393
trade barriers: following depression, 181
trade surplus, 457
'wasteful' competition, 392
West's fears of Japan's economic
    dominance, 457, 552–4
world ranking, 462
yen's convertability, 392, 405, 454–5
Yoshihito's reign, 155
zaibatsu: government portfolios held by,
    164
see also banking system; economic
    miracle; industrialization;
    international trade; Ministry of
    International Trade and Industry

Edo, *see* Tokyo
education
  assimilation of information, 417
  bribes to pass exams, 102, 562
  bullying, 561
  censoring of textbooks, 513
  class-ridden, 476
  corporal punishment, 560–61
  cram schools, 102, 561–2
  discipline, decline in, 563
  emperor myth inculcated, 510–11
  Emperor's Rescript, 99–100, 108
  ethics, 368
  failings of, 559–63
  foreign methods studied, 76
  formality, 101
  indoctrination of nationalism, 84,
    98–101
  liberalization under MacArthur, 323
  maths, high marks in, 559
  meritocratic nature, 101
  Mori's principles, 98
  Nakasone's reforms, 368
  national teaching, 105–6
  normal schools, 98
  pigeon-holing for life, 102
  progression through system, 101–2
  reform, 563
  rewriting history books, 463, 513–15
  rote learning, 99, 487
  strict discipline, 480–81
  student protest, 356
  teaching methods, 560
  unification of system following Meiji
    restoration, 84
  universities, *see* universities
  Zengakuren (student federation), 355
Edward, Prince of Wales, 150, 162
Edwards, Professor Corwin, 311–12
Eichelberger, General Robert, 296, 305
Eisenhower, General Dwight D., 345,
    354–5
electronics industry, 439
Elliott, Private George, 245
Emmott, Bill, 497, 523, 558
Emperor as institution
  army's relationship with, 110–11
  attempts to limit absolute authority,
    187–8
  constitutional position: above law,
    500–501; on Meiji restoration, 71,
    85; powers, 43, 71, 88, 155
  emperor myth, *see* Emperor-worship

Imperial House law separate from
    constitution, 501–2
  Meiji regime: court ranks, 47; marriage
    politics, 46; weakness following First
    World War, 159
  nominal power, 85
  popular support for imperial system,
    507–8
  post-Second World War: required to
    control country, 24
  priest king, 500, 502
  sovereignty: in Emperor's person,
    159–60, 187–8; in factions close to
    throne, 85
  post-war: constitutional reform,
    315–17; renunciation of divinity, 31,
    317, 462, 499–502; reversion to Meiji
    emperor role, 500–9
  see also law and constitution
Emperor-worship
  Akihito's coronation, 461–3
  creation of emperor myth, 84
  father of the people, 88
  fuelling nationalist sentiment, 87–8
  Hirohito's coronation, 167
  inculcation of, 87–8
  legitimizing bureacracy, 90–91
  reasons for elevation in Meiji period,
    90–92
  recent myth, 92
  renunciation of divinity, 31, 317, 462,
    499–502
encouragement parties, 383
Endo, Shusaku, 467
Equipment Bureau, 200
Etoh, Hajime, 520
Eto, Jun, 514–15
exchange control
  restrictiveness of, 395–6
  yen's convertibility, 392, 405, 454–5
exports, *see* international trade

face, *see* Japaneseness
factions, *see* politics
Fair Trade Commission, 312, 413
Falkinn, Sigrun, 564–5
families
  children's upbringing, 480–90
  codified system of obligations, 479
  family group, 475
Ferebee, Major Thomas, 29
feudalism
  samurai's privileges broken, 75, 78–9,
    81

Shintoism and, 45–6
under Shogunate, 59–62
see also samurai
First World War
army's loss of prestige following, 157
munition suppliers, 155–6, 199
no active part in, 199
foreign policy
aggressiveness, 84
alliances following Sino-Japanese war
(1939–45), 117
army takes control, 179–83
colonial expansion: army expanded to
allow, 109–10; Asia, investment in,
526–7; China, see China; economic
and military debate, 170–71; First
World War, 156–7; flimsy pretexts
for, 117; Foundations of National
Policy, 207; Greater East Asian
Economic Co-Prosperity Sphere, 157,
218; Hirohito and, 169; leading to
war, 138, 162, 241–2; motives
behind, 112–13; Nakasone's Pacific
goals, 365; over-extension, 218;
popular support of, 161–2;
resentment at great powers, 173;
Russo-Japanese war adds Korea, 120;
secret societies' part in, 171–2;
Southeast Asia, 218; US response,
157, 232, 241–2; Yamagata on,
114–15
future conflict, avoidance of, 552–4
Russia, fear of, 229
trade tensions: Asia, 532, 544; Middle
East, 543–4
US relations, 343–5, 355–6, 365, 407,
494, 511–12, 534–5, 540–41
US withdrawal from Asia, dangers
arising, 549–50
foreigners in Japan
commercial rivals: excessive restrictions,
410; liberalization policy, 405, 407;
MITI's attitude to, 405–7, 410; textile
industry, 406–7
expelling, 68–9, 75
foreign inward investment: car
manufacturers, 393, 411–12; controls
on, 452; MITI defence against,
411–12; Mitsubishi/Chrysler group,
412; small share of total, 451
racialism, see racialism
under shogunate, 64
see also international trade
Formosa, 121, 259, 262, 271, 337

Forrestal, James, 305
Foundations of National Policy, 207
France
Hirohito's visit, 150–51
Indo-China occupied, 231–3, 241
shipyard management, 124
Sino-Japanese war (1894–5), reaction
to, 116
Fuchida, Commander Mitsuo, 246
Fuji (banking keiretsu), 397–8
Fujio, Masayuki, 368
Fujiwara, Mariko, 556
Fujiwara clan, 46, 206, 290, 375, 477
Fukuda, Hajime, 408–9
Fukuda, Takeo, xvi, 347–8, 361, 363,
413, 524
Fukuoka, Japan, 171–2
Fumihito, Prince, 508
Fushimi, Prince, 148
future of Japan
ultimate authority, lack of, 523
war with Asia and America, 523
Future of the Automobile, The (Roos and
Altshuler), 425

GDP, 349, 405, 438, 455, see also
economy
gaman (endurance), 484
gangsters (yakuza), 567, see also justice
system
gardens, 51–2, 481
Gascoigne, Sir Alvary, 329, 331
GATT (General Agreement on Tariffs and
Trade), 408, 542
Genyosha (Dark Ocean society), 171–2
George V, King, 150
Germany
Anti-Comintern Pact, 228
non-aggression pact with Soviet Union,
229
provides model for army, 110, 111
war guilt acknowledged, 516, 520
Gilbert Islands, 247
gimu (moral obligations), 478–9
giri-to-one's-name, 478–9
Gluck, Carol, 520
Gneist, Rudolf von, 95
gods and goddesses, 44–5, 462
Great Britain
Anglo-Japanese Treaty (1902), 117–18,
170
assistance in industrialization, 124
on ending of occupation (1951), 336
Hirohito's visit, 150

Pacific challenge lessened, 229
Pacific War: battleships sunk, 247
Second World War: Burma operations,
    216
Sino-Japanese war (1894–5), reaction
    to, 116
subsidies to Japanese firms, 452
trading under shogunate, 64, 66
Great Circuits, 85–6
Great Promulgation Campaign, 105
Great Purpose, 193
Greater East Asian Economic Co-
    Prosperity Sphere, 157, 218
Greenpeace, 577
Grew, Joseph, 224, 233, 237
Gromyko, Andrei, 337
Group of Seven (Tokyo summit 1993), 542
Groves, General Leslie, 11, 19–20
Guadalcanal, 256–7
Guam, 243, 247

Hadley, Eleanor, 310, 351
Hagerty, James, 355
Halha River, Mongolia, 212–13
Halsey, Admiral William, 262, 297
Hamaguchi, Yuko, 180
Hangkow, China, 213
Hara, Takashi, xv, xx, 152, 153, 159, 169
Hara Castle, Japan, 573
harakiri, 483–4, see also suicide
Hardacre, Helen, 106–7
Harris, Thomas Luke, 98
Harris, Townsend, 66–7
Hashimoto, Ryutaro, 372
Hata, General Hikosaburo, 271
Hata, Tsutomu, 372, 373–4, 376, 476
Hatanaka, Major Kenji, 276, 285
Hatoyama, Ichiro, xvi, 344, 353, 524
Hattori, Professor, 147
Hattori, Takushiro, 304
Hayashi, General Saburo, 204, 206
Heian period, 46–8, 52
Henderson, Harold, 317
hierarchical structure of economy, see
    economy
Higashikuni, Prince, 234, 297
Hijikato, Hisamoto, 88
Hino motor company, 439
Hiraizumi, Professor Kiyoshi, 196
Hiranuma, Baron Kiichiro, 229, 275
Hirohito, Emperor, xx–xxi
    early years: birth and as small child,
        143; education, 144–5, 147; foreign

travel, 149–51; lack of family life,
    145–6; sexual encounter, 148
character, 147–8, 153–4, 287–8
inter-war years: attempts to check
    militarists, 168, 178, 187–8, 211,
    287–8; colonial expansion, 169–71;
    coronation, 166–7; democratic
    leanings, 154; foreign relations,
    229–30; on Manchurian occupation,
    185, 187–8; marriage, 148–9, 166;
    militarists seize power under, 159–62;
    military coup attempt, 194–7;
    powerless against power groups,
    168–9; regency, 152–3; weakness in
    going along with militarists, 190
Pacific War; duties performed, 268;
    reconciled to outbreak of, 235,
    236–7; reservations as to outcome,
    269; responsibity denied, 463; self-
    respect retained, 278; spartan life,
    286; surrender broadcast, 279–82;
    surrender ordered, 25–6, 273–8
post-war years: abdication discussed,
    320–22; attacked by left wing, 318;
    household reduced, 318; MacArthur's
    fall, effect on, 334–5; popular appeal,
    319–20; renunciation of divinity, 317,
    462, 499–502; stripped of power,
    317; symbolizing national unity, 500;
    walkabouts, 319, 499; war criminal,
    as, 24, 321
scientific interests, 147, 166
Sino-Japanese war (1937–45): personal
    command of, 211–12
sporting interests, 145–6, 268
see also Emperor as institution;
    Emperor-worship
Hiroshima, Japan
    atomic bomb on, 3–8, 14–15, 29–34,
        273
    Peace Memorial Museum, 35
    war memorial, 520
    see also atomic bombs
Hirota, Koki, 205, 225
Hizen clan, 69
Holbrooke, Dick, 540
Hollerman, Leon, 395–6
Homma, Lt-General Masaharu, 250
Honda motor-cycle company, 433–4, 439
Hong Kong
    British lease, 64
    capture of, 247
    commercial ties, 453
Honjo, Shigeru, 184, 195, 196

Hopei-Chahar Political Council, 186–7
Hoshino, Hanehisa, 506
Hosokawa, Morihiro, 373, 375–7, 379,
    476–7, 519, 543, 556
housing
    cramped conditions, 446
    impermanent, 166, 473
    industrial workers, for, 128
    no respect for old buildings, 473
    reducing cost of, 556
Hsuchow, China, 211
Hull, Cordell, 233, 246, 518
Hyuga, Hosai, 409

IBM, 406, 413
Ibuse, Masuji, 468
Ichi-go, Operation, 262
Ida, Lt-Colonel Masataka, 283, 285
Idekimitsu, Sazu, 511
Iemochi (Shogun), 69
Ienaga, Saburo, 514
Ii, Naosuku, xviii, 67, 68
Ikeda, Hayato, xvi, 355, 396, 401, 405–6,
    524
Imai, Masaaki, 487–8
Imai, Zen'ei, 405
Imperial Household Ministry (Kumaisho),
    88
Imperial National Blood War Body, 300
Imperial Palace
    Kyoto, 50
    Tokyo (Edo), 71, 165–6
Imperial Way Faction, 173, 203–5
imperialism, see foreign policy, colonial
    expansion
Imphal, India, 262
imports and exports, see international
    trade
Inagaki, Etsu, 480–81
India, 262, 453, 527
Indo-China, 217, 218, 231, 232, 233, 241,
    527–8, 546
Indonesia, 547–9
industrial relations
    enterprise culture, 444
    lifetime employment, 443
    management-workforce distinctions, 442
    quality control circles, 400, 403, 442,
        475
    recruit training, 441–2
    regimented corporate structure, 441
    stoppages, absence of, 440–41
    suggestions by workers, 442
    transferability to West, 445

see also companies; trade unions
industrialization
    capital base, 397
    cities, growth of, 129
    combines established, 125, see also
        zaibatsu
    crash policy, 123
    destructive competition, 124
    financing, 124
    government nurturing, 402–3
    growth: early days, 128–9; in Meiji
        period, 138; post-occupation, see
        economic miracle
    heavy industry for munitions, 124, 200
    hierarchical structure, 128
    Industries Control Law, 201
    investment in new plant, 456
    lack of early capital, 124
    learning from abroad: samurai sent
        abroad to learn, 76
    manufacturing dominance over service
        industries, 439
    Meiji restoration, following, 75–7,
        80–81
    mergers, 124
    modern industrial society established, 84
    munitions suppliers: Korean war, 334;
        in First World War, 155–6
    over-lending, 397
    overseas plants, 449–55
    post-industrial society, 412
    post-war pacifist commercial democracy,
        337, 340
    post-war reconstruction, see post-war
        reconstruction
    privatization of state industries, 369
    productivity, 400, 540
    quality control, 400, 403, 442, 475
    raw materials, lack of, 112–13, 156,
        230
    regional investment, 411
    restrictive practices and price-fixing,
        400, 411, 413
    sales off under Transfer of Factories Act,
        1880, 125
    state intervention policy, 123–5
    suffering of workforce, 127–8
    war with China favoured, 208
    wartime controls, 266–7
    workers, treatment of, 157–9
    see also companies; trade unions;
        zaibatsu (conglomerates)
Inouye, Jinnosuke, 161, 180
Inouye, Kaoru, xviii

Institute of Life and Living, 556
International Monetary Fund, 408
international trade
  administrative guidance, 409
  Asian markets: Asian Economic
    Research Institute, 407; resentment
    against Japan, 547–8; tension over,
    544–9
  'black ships' arrive, 65, 407
  China, 546
  cut-price products, 435
  dependence on imports, 65
  East Asian business, 512–13
  export drive continuation of war, 404
  Exporters Association Law (1925), 391
  foreign investments, 411–12, 453–5,
    548, 553
  foreign inward investments, 449–55
  foreign manufacturers' difficulties,
    392–3
  foreign technologies acquired, 429
  Important Industries Control Law
    (1931), 392
  isolation abandoned, 65–6
  Japan Development Bank, role of,
    398–9
  Japan External Trade Organization,
    401–2, 404
  Japanese methods copied, 548–9
  keiretsu, role of, 398
  liberalization, 405, 407–10, 413
  Ministry of International Trade and
    Industry (MITI), 395
  Nakasone promotes growth from
    within, 369
  protectionism, 414, 428, 526, 542, 552
  under shogunate, 64–7
  Soviet Union, 546
  state directed cartels, 388–94, 398, 413
  Supreme Export Council, 401
  tariffs, 388
  trade surplus, 457
  treaty of Kanagawa (1854), 66
  'unequal treaties', 67
  United States: automobile industry,
    537–9; Clinton calls for rebalancing,
    542; Japan's sub-contractor, 541;
    managed trade with US, 537–9;
    protectionism, 542, 552–3; trade
    surplus, 542
  Western currencies destabilized, 550–52
  zaibatsu's role in, 390–94
  see also economic miracle; economy;
    foreigners in Japan; Ministry of

International Trade and Industry
  (MITI)
Irie, Takanori, 515
Ishihara, Noburo, 503
Ishihara, Professor Masashi, 529
Ishihara, Shintaro, 371, 375, 495, 511,
  517
Ishikawa, Yoshimi, 535
Ishiwara, Kanji, 183, 201
Issekikai (army secret society), 201, 224
Itagaki, General Seishiro, 183, 201,
  211–12
Itagaki, Taisuke, xix, 93
Itakura, General, 573
Ito, Hirobumi, xv, xviii, 74, 76, 88–9,
  95–6, 120
Ito, Masuyoshi, 370
Iwakura, Prince Tomomi, xv, xviii, 74, 76,
  81, 171
Iwasa, Yoshizane, 486
Iwasaki family, 97
Iwo Jima, 26, 263
Izanagi and Izanami (gods), 44

James, Barrie, 450
'Japan 2000', 457
Japan Arbitration Council, 566
Japan Development Bank, 396, 398–9
Japan External Trade Organization
  (JETRO), 401–2, 404
Japan New Party, 374
Japan Socialist Party, 130
Japaneseness
  authoritarian government, 130–31
  brain differences, 486
  codification of rules of behaviour,
    477–92
  communality of society, 471–4
  conformity accepted, 497–8
  death, attitude to, 482–4
  differences preserved, 464
  dispersal of authority, 48
  endurance and invincibility, 117, 484
  face, 274, 278, 470, 566
  geographical remoteness, 471
  individualism suppressed, 473
  intelligence comparisons, 368
  intestinal differences, 373, 494
  loyalty, 485
  persistence, 417
  politeness, 485
  racialism: based on moral superiority,
    492–97; superiority to other Asians,
    113. see also racialism

reclusiveness, 45, 62
respect for authority, 394
status-consciousness, 73
subservience and deference, 48, 58–9,
 441, 474–7, *see also* peasants; women
ukiyo (floating world), 54–5
uniqueness, Japanese claim of, 389
war culture, 54
Western values despised, 494
Java Sea, battle of, 248–9
Jellicoe, Admiral John, 199
Jeppson, Lt Morris, 5
Jimmu, Emperor, 507, 514
Jingwei, Wang, 215
Jiyuto, *see* Liberal Party
Johnson, Chalmers, 390, 404, 429, 445
Johnston, Percy, 329
Juio, Colonel Matsuicho, 257
Junshi (following the lord), 134
just-in-time (*kanban*) production system,
 435–6, 553
justice system
 civil litigation, 566
 conciliation, 566
 confessions extorted, 565
 crime rate, 566–7
 death penalty, 565
 first-time offenders, 564
 judicial review, 566
 legal training, 566
 organized crime, 567
 private rights in public law, 565–6
 social condemnation, 563

Kades, Charles, 515
Kagoshima, Japan, 82
Kaifeng, China, 219
Kaifu, Toshiki, 371, 377, 462, 516
kaisha, see companies
Kajima, Noboru, 504, 505
kamikaze attacks, 27, 83, 262, 482–3
 tradition of, 83
Kanagawa, treaty of (1854), 66
Kanemaru, Shin, xvi, xxv, 356–7, 371–3,
 375, 524, 536, 539–40
Kan'in, Prince, 212
Kanroji, Osanaga, 143–4
Kantor, Mickey, 542
Kanzo, Uhimira, 108
karoshi (dying from overwork), 419
Kase, Toshikazu, 297
Kashii, Lt-General Kohei, 196
Kataoka, Tetsuya, 346, 349–50
Katayama, Sen, 130

Kato, Takaaki, 156, 169–70
Katsura, General Taro, 119, 120, 135, 200
Kauffman, James, 327
Kawabata, Yasunari, 467
Kawahara, Toshiaki, 185, 211, 317, 321,
 334
Kawakami, Hajime, 565
Kawamoto, Yoshitaka
 as a boy at Hiroshima, 3–5, 12–13,
  20–22, 30, 31–3, 34–5
 director of Peace Memorial Museum,
  35, 582
Kawamura, Count Sumiyoshi, 143–4
Kawashima, General Yoshiyuki, 193–5
Kazuo, Tamaki, 383
Keeling, U. C. L., 485
Keiki, Shogun, 69
keiretsu (conglomerates)
 banking, 397
 beyond political control, 448
 blocking trade with US, 536–7
 cartels: convenience of, 427; dominating
  lesser *keiretsu*, 427
 contract allocations, 536
 controlling economy, 386
 distribution, 537
 US, 538
 US attitude to, 536–7
 zaibatsu reborn, 397
 see also zaibatsu
Kempeitai (riot police), 206, 309
Kennan, George, 329, 346
Kenrick, D. M., 442, 489
Kenseito Party, 169–70
Kern, Harry, 327–8
Kido, Koin, xviii, 74, 76
Kido, Marquis Koichi, xxii, 198, 230, 234,
 270, 276, 283, 285, 289
kiheitai (shock troops), 89
Kihrien, China, 219
Kijiro, Nanbu, 116
Kim-Il-Sung, 545
'Kimi Gayo' (national anthem), 510
Kimmel, Admiral Husband, 244
Kimura, Tokutaro, 307
King, Fleet Admiral J. E., 254
Kinkakuji (Temple of the Golden Pavilion),
 52–3
Kishi, Nobosuke, xv, xvi, xxiii, 267,
 344–5, 347, 353–5, 394, 405–6, 524
Kishino, Hiroyuki, 580
Kita, Ikki, 172–3
 A Plan for the Regeneration of Japan,
 196, 202

Kiyomizu (temple at Kyoto), 51
Knowland, William, 328
Kodama, General Gentaro, 121
Kodogikai (civilian military organization), 203
Koga, Major Hidemasa, 285
kohai (obligations), 477–9
Kohima, India, 262
Kojiki (book of creation), 44–5
Kokory-ukai (Black Dragon Society), 172
Kokura, Japan, 35
Komatsu company, 449
Komei, Emperor, 68, 136
Komoto, Colonel Daisaku, 178, 201
Konishiki 'Dump Truck' (Sumo wrestler), 493
Kono, Yohei, 375
Konoye, Prince Fumimaro, xxii, 173, 206–7, 209, 210, 212, 218, 225, 230, 233–6, 266, 290–91, 297, 315, 340
Korea
    absorbed into Japan, 120
    nineteenth-century conflicts, 81, 93, 110, 114, 115
    cockpit of Sino-Japanese war (1894–5), 115–16
    immigrants to Japan, racialism towards, 165, 492–3
    independence restored in peace treaty (1951), 337
    joint protectorate with Russia, 118
    Korean Air Lines Boeing 747 shot down, 367
    Pacific War; 'comfort girls', 220–21, 519
    shrines to war dead, 108
    strategic importance of, 117–18
    threatening Japan, 114
    trade tensions, 453, 545–6
    war of 1950–53: communist threat, 331; Japanese navy assists in, 307; munitions from Japan, 334; economic miracle started, 334, 396
    war with Russia over: becomes Japanese colony following, 120, 368; events of war, 118–20
Kotoku, Denjiro, 130
Kra Peninsula, 247
Krueger, General Walter, 262
kugyo (court nobles), 47
Kumamoto Soai-Sha (Mutual Love Society), 172
Kuni, Prince Kuniyoshi, 148–9, 168
Kurihara, Lt Yasuhide, 192

Kurile Islands
    partition with Russia (1854), 66
    renunciation of claims in peace treaty (1951), 337
    tension with Soviet Union over, 272, 344, 535, 546, 550
Kurisu, Hiro Omi, 347–8
Kurosawa, Akira, 520
Kusamaatmadja, Sarwono, 549
Kyoto, Japan, 7, 49–54
Kyushu, Japan, 79, 81–2

land and property ownership
    feudal system, 60–61
    land tax introduced, 124
    post-feudalism, 78
    post-war land reform, 313–14
    property collapses, 456
    saving encouraged, 429
    values in 1980s, 415
language, 486–9
    non-verbal, 489
    saying 'no,' 487–9
    written alphabet, 486–7
Laos, 527
Lattimore, Owen, 298
law and constitution
    Imperial House law separate from, 500–501
    justice system, *see* justice system
    pre-Second World War: attempts to limit absolute authority, 187–8; budget proposals, approval of, 96; centralized administration, *see* bureaucracy; council of state, 78; Emperor-worship instituted, 89–92; feudalism, 44–5; international comparisons, 91; Itagaki's proposals, 93–4; parliament established, *see* parliament; reforms of 1889, 76, 95; religious freedom, 108; sovereignty: in factions or in throne, 84–5, 187–8; suffrage, 162; weakness of, 163
    private rights, 565–6
    post-war reforms: Emperor's renunciation of divinity, 317–18; MacArthur's aims, 315–16; Matsumoto's recommendations, 315; press freedom, 323; suffrage, 317; war renounced, 301–2; Whitney's plan, 316
    see also Emperor as institution
League of Nations, 185–6, 228
Lee, Yumi, 493

Lee Kuan Yew, 516
LeMay, General Curtis, 7
Lewis, Captain Robert, 67
Leyte Gulf, battle of, 255
Liaotung Peninsula
    battle of (1904–5), 119
    ceded to Japan, 116
    leased to Japan after Russo-Japanese
        war, 119–20
    returned to China, 116
    Russia granted lease of, 117
Liberal Democratic Party
    alliance with zaibatsu, 343, 344
    constitutional amendments, 353
    factional squabbles, 339, 371–3
    gains power, 332
    kanryoha (bureaucrat politicians), 354
    leadership elections, 361
    overthrown, 373–4
    parties combine to form, 332, 344, 353
    political stability and economic miracle,
        339
    rearmament squabbles, 344–5
    reformists and traditionalists, 497
    return to old Japanese values, 347
    scandals, 568–9
    spending on elections, 382–3
    toha (career politicians), 354
Liberal Party, 94–5
literature, 464–9
living standards, see society
Lloyd George, David, 150
local government
    centralized in Department of Home
        Affairs, 96
    decentralization, 317
    village office, 564
Lockard, Private Joseph, 245
Lockheed scandal, 360, 361, 363, 365,
    375
London Disarmament Conference (1930),
    180
Lopez, Pedro, 22
Lord, Walter, 245
Lytton Commission (1933), 185

MacArthur, General Douglas, xvi,
    xxiii–xxiv
    background, 333
    defence of Philippines, 25, 250–52
    island-hopping tactics, 255, 258–9
    on: blockading Japan, 39, 260; invasion
        of Japan, 29; Pacific Command,
        254–5

presidential nomination, 330
Supreme Commander Allied Powers, see
    post-war occupation
Unit 731, and, 226
McClusky, Lt-Commander Wade, 254
McDonald, Private Joseph, 245
Maekawa Commission, 369
MAGIC code-breaker, 233, 244
Mahathir, Mohammed, 548
Mainichi Shimbun (newspaper), 384, 538
Malaya and Malaysia, 231, 247, 453, 527,
    547–8
Manchuria
    bargaining counter with Soviet Union,
        272
    Chang Tso-lin murdered, 177
    Chinese civil war threatening Japanese
        interests, 176–8
    colonial expansion in, 113, 114,
        120–21, 156–7
    developed by Nissan, 204
    Manchurian Incident (1931): events of,
        183–5; occupation following, 178,
        184–7
    Russian control, 117–20
    shrines to war dead, 108
    Society for the Ultimate Solution of the
        Manchurian Question, 300
    Soviet Union occupation (1945), 273
    see also Sino-Japanese war (1894–5)
Manhattan Project, 5, 9, 14
Manila, Philippines, 262
Mansfield, Mike, 522
Mao Tse-tung, 213, 216
Marco Polo Bridge incident, 208–9
Mariana Islands, 26, 157, 259
Maritime Safety Agency, 307
Markino, Yoshio, 485
marriage
    age of, 557–8
    arranged, 59, 558
    of Emperors, 46
    modern approach to, 556
    social obligations affecting, 479
    upper class marrying beneath them, 499
Marshall, General George, 28
Marshall Islands, 157, 258, 343
Martineau, Lisa, 560
materialism, middle class opposition to,
    496
Matsui, General Iwane, 171, 223, 224
Matsukata, Masayoshi, xix, 123–5
Matsumoto, Joji, 315–16
Matsumoto, Michihiro, 488–9

Matsuo, Colonel, 194
Matsuo, Taiichiro, 405
Matsuoka, Yosuke, 210
Maurice, Sir Frederick, 517
Mazda company, 451
Meckel, Major Jacob, 111
Meiji restoration
  aristocratic revolution, 72–3
  civil war following, 77–9, 81–2
  conservative reforms, 62
  insurrection prior to, 68–70
  modernization following, 75–7, 84
  new leaders following, 74
  reasons for, 62–3
  villages, lack of effect on, 61
  see also Mutsuhito, Emperor
merchant classes' growth of power, 56,
  72–3
Mibuchi, Shigeru, 320
Michiko, Empress, 378–9, 499, 508
Michinaga (Fujiwara), 46
micro-electronics industry, 349
Midway, battle of, 253–4, 269
Mieno, Yasushi, 455
Miki, Takeo, 361, 409
militarism
  anti-Americanism, 543
  Asian strategy, 533–4
  bushido (warrior spirit), 134, 222
  colonial expansion and, 114
  conscription following Meiji restoration,
    78–9, 81
  death in battle as honour, 108
  defence spending, 128, 531–4, 549
  disarmament, see disarmament
  emergence of military class, 97
  Foundations of National Policy, 207
  heavy industry established for ordnance,
    124
  Hirohito's attempts to check, 168, 178,
    187–8
  Kodogikai (civilian military
    organization), 203
  military coup envisaged, 533
  modern regression to, 463–4
  'nation of samurai', 78–9
  no-war provision, 517, 533
  Pacific War preparations: ascendancy in
    Pacific as aim, 207; Equipment
    Bureau, 200; 'garrison state' concept,
    200; partnership between army and
    zaibatsu, 201; Resources Bureau, 200;
    Soviet Union seen as enemy, 203
  post-war reforms: destruction of

factions, 299; education less
    militaristic, 323–4; general staff,
    nucleus retained, 304–5; rearmament,
    see rearmament; reduced status of
    military, 308
  power of militarists, 110, 120 138, 153,
    159–63
  reduction in Soviet power, following,
    528–31
  samurai resentment at Meiji restoration,
    75–9
  secret societies fostering, 171–3, 201
  seizure of power by army in 1930s,
    179–91
  Self-Defence Force, status of, 544, see
    also rearmament
  shrines to war dead, 106–8
  training and discipline taught at schools,
    98
  war culture, 54
  War Minister's role, 111–12
  zaibatsu vie with militarists, 189
  see also army; politics; 'undefeated'
    myth
Minami, General Jiro, 184, 185
mining industry, 158–9
Ministry of International Trade and
  Industry (MITI)
  administrative guidance, 409, 411,
    425–6
  blackmailing companies, 426
  control of industry, 400–401, 413–14,
    525
  establishment of, 395
  excessive competition, tackling, 408
  foreigners, view of, 405
  incentive system, 402
  long term perspectives, 426–7
  markets adjusted with balance of
    payments, 401
  pollution problem, 411
  protection of domestic industries, 414,
    428, 526, 542, 552
  regional investment, 412
  research and development assistance,
    437
  restrictive practices preserved, 400, 411,
    413
  success of, 425
  tax breaks, 428–9
  see also economic miracle, government's
    role in
Minobe, Dr Tatsukichi, 187–8
Minseito Party, 192, 351

Mishima, Yukio, xxv, 464–7
Mitsubishi group of companies
  automobile industry: foreign investment
    in Japan, 411–12
  banking interests, 397
  casualties at Nagasaki, 36
  Chrysler agreement, 412
  control, 126
  dissolution, plan for, 311–12
  faction close to government in 1930s,
    180, 351
  foundation of, 125
  keiretsu, as, 398
  power and wealth of, 126, 310, 439
  terrorist attacks, 356
Mitsui family and conglomerate
  banking interests, 397
  family council, 126
  foundation of, 125
  influence of, 56, 351, 439
  keiretsu, as, 398
  Miike coal mine, 352
  post-war plan for dissolution, 311–13
  power and wealth of, 126
  role in Meiji restoration, 69
  wealth from corruption, 97
Mitsuzuka, Hiroshi, 371
Miyazawa, Kiichi, 366, 371–2, 373, 375,
    418, 476, 519, 528, 533, 535, 538,
    540, 542, 556
Mongolia, 212–13
Moody, Sergeant Samuel, 22
Mori, Arinori, 98–100
Mori, General Takeshi, 282, 285
Morita, Akio, 430, 476, 511
Moriya, Tadashi, 221
Morris, Ivan, 46, 47–8, 80, 570
Mosbacher, Robert, 537
Motoda, Eifu, 98–9
Motodowa, Kikkawa, 425
Mukden, Manchuria
  attacked following Manchurian Incident
    (1931), 184, 514
  battle of (1905), 119
multi-machine manning, 436
Murakami, Yoshio, 561
Mutaguchi, General Renya, 262
Mutsuhito, Emperor, xvii
  achievements during reign, 137–8
  appearance, 74
  decision-making, 86
  Great Circuits, 85–6
  Imperial Rescript on education, 99–100,
    108
  Imperial Rescript to Soldiers and Sailors,
    110–11
  poems, 86
  political role, 74–5
  power regained on Meiji restoration,
    69–72
  Sino-Japanese war (1894–5), direction
    of, 86, 115
  social responsibility, 87
  visits to Shinto shrines, 104
  death and funeral, 132–4
  shrine and memorial Picture Gallery,
    136–7
Mutsukura, Lord, 572–3
Mutual Defence Association Agreement
  (1954), 307

Nagako, Empress, 148–9, 166
Nagano, Admiral Osami, 231, 232
Nagasaki, Japan, 35–7, 124, see also
  atomic bomb
Nagata, Colonel Tetsusan, xxi, 200–201,
  204–5
Nagayo, Empress, 499
Nakajima, General Kesago, 223, 224
Nakamura, Baron, 149
Nakamura, Shigeru, 197
Nakasone, Yasuhiro, xxiv–xxv
  anti-bureaucracy, 364
  background, 362–3
  economic policy, 368–9, 413
  factions bring down, 369–70
  nationalism, 364
  on: individualism, 473; nuclear
    weapons, 581
  policies, 363–4
  rearmament, 347–8
  Soviet nuclear threat, 366–7
  Tanaka's support, 363, 365–6
  US relations, 364–5
  western leaders, meeting with, 367
Nanbara, Shigeru, 320
Nanking, China, 8–9, 210, 215, 219,
  222–5, 513, 518
Narita Airport, 356
Naruhito, Crown Prince, 377–8, 508
National Police Reserve, 306–7
National Supply Agency, 307
nationalism
  communism and, 173
  Hosokawa's anti-nationalist line, 376–7
  Korean nationalists attacked, 165
  under Meiji oligarchy: Emperor-worship
    fuelling, 87–8; indoctrination in

schools, 98–101; Saigo as role model for extreme right, 83; Shintoism and, 103–4; war shrines and, 120
Nakasone's reassertion of, 362, 367–8
revolutionary ideals, 174–5
in schools, 368
supporting 'undefeated' myth, 463
terrorism of 1930s, 182–3
navy
import of raw materials, protection of, 112–13
London Disarmament Conference limits, 180
moderate wing of armed services, 112
Pacific War: anticipatory measures, 236–7; Coral Sea, battle of, 253; Java Sea, battle of, 249; kamikaze attacks, 27, 83, 262; Leyte Gulf, battle of, 255; losses, 27; Midway, battle of, 253–4, 269; post-war disarmament, 301–7, see also disarmament; US ship-building outstrips Japan's, 254
post-war rearmament, 307–8, 349, see also rearmament
Satsuma clan providing senior officers, 110
strategic and political differences with army, 121, 135
strike south policy, 230
zaibatsu, relations with, 228
see also army
Netherlands, The
Pacific War: colonies unprotected, 230, 231; East Indies occupied, 248
running arsenal at Nagasaki, 124
New Guinea, 253, 256–9
New Harbinger Party, 374
New York Times, 19
New Zealand, 336, 530
Nicholas II, Tsar, 118
Nihon Keizai Shimbun (economic journal), 538–9
Nijo Castle, Kyoto, 50–51
Nikkeiren (employers' organization), 352
Nimitz, Admiral Chester, 254, 258, 259–60, 263, 296
Nishida, Mitsugi, 203
Nishimura, Colonel Shigaki, 532
Nissan automobile company, 204, 352, 392, 409, 451
Nixon, Richard, 303, 346, 411, 528
no-propellor water propulsion system, 438
Nogi, General Maresuke, 134, 145, 146–7, 222, 466

Noh theatre, 54
Nomura, Admiral Kichisaburo, 307, 518
Nonaka, Captain Shiro, 192, 197
nuclear programme
disarmament principles, 347
military capacity, 578, 580–81
peaceful uses, 349, 543–4, 577–82
plutonium, 577–9
reprocessing plant at Rokkasho-Mura, 579
weapons: American, 343; Nuclear Non-Proliferation Treaty, 377; refusal to allow, 345, 581–2; small scale, 349; Soviet threat, 366–7
see also atomic bombs

Obuchi, Kaizo, 372
Ogura, Kazuo, 535–6
Ohira, Masayoshi, 361
oil
cartels, 413
cheap during time of expansion, 419
imports, 412
price rises causing inflation, 413
reducing dependence on Middle East, 414
Okada, Admiral Keisuke, 194
Okinawa
battle of (1945), 26–7, 39, 263
peace treaty (1951) gives control to US, 337
restored to Japan, 411
Okubo, Prince Toshimichi, xv, xviii, 81
Okuma, Shigenobu, 156
Okura family, 97
Olympic, Operation, 28
on (moral obligations), 87, 478
Ono, Taiichi, 436
Onoue, Nui, 456
Oppenheimer, J. Robert, 19, 29
optoelectronics industry, 438
Oshima, Lt-General Hiroshi, 228
Oshio, Heihachiro, 64
Otomo, Ryo, 532
overseas plants, 449–55
Owada, Masako (Crown Princess), 377–8, 508
Oyama, General Iwao, 143
Ozaki, Yukio, 135
Ozawa, Ichiro, xvi, 372, 373–6, 476, 524, 532

Pacific War
origins of: Anti-Comintern Pact, 228;

avoidable at late stage, 228; European colonies unprotected, 229; failure to foresee US reaction, 218–19; Germany, closer relations with, 228; Indo-China occupied, 232, 241; inevitability recognized, 234; raw materials, need for, 230; Southeast Asian invasion, 218, 228; Soviet Union engaged in Europe, 230; trade embargo by US, 231; war preparations in Japan, 233; *zaibatsu* and armed services allied, 227–8, 230

preparation for: austerity measures, 235–6; biological warfare, 225–6; national decision, 237; operational planning, 236; political power groupings, 207; strategy, 243; war aims, 243

Pearl Harbor: attack expected, 244; failure to declare war justified, 518; fiftieth anniversary, 517; lack of preparedness, 244–6; planning for, 237, 242; tactics used, 244–7; US ships sunk, 246

declaration of hostilities, 237

events of: air battles, 253–4, 257, 258; atrocities, *see* atrocities; Bismarck Sea, battle of, 258; casualties, *see* casualties; defence of Japan (Operation Ketsu-go), 28; early Japanese gains, 247–52; fierceness of fighting, 26–9; Guadalcanal, 256–7; hardships, 221–2; island hopping, 255; Leyte landing, 261, 270; naval battles, *see* navy; New Guinea, 256–9; Okinawa, 26–7, 39, 263; overshadowed by European war, 264; Pacific Ocean Area Command, 254; Philippine Sea, battle of, 259; Philippines, 250–52; Santa Cruz, battle of, 257; saturation bombing of Japan, 29, 217, 253, 270, 271–2, 286–7; Solomon Islands, 258; surprise attacks, 249

ending: atomic bombs, effect of, 273; civilian militia, 271; economic strangulation choice, 260–61; encirclement, 271; inevitability of defeat, 263–4; invasion of Japan, plans for, 259–60

surrender: defeat not acknowledged, 281; Hirohito's broadcast, 279–80; Hirohito's role in, 275, 277; peace talks discussed, 273–9; peace treaty (1951), 306–7, 336–8; plots and suicides following, 282–6; Potsdam Declaration, 23–4, 274–5, 301; remorse, absence of, 282; reparations, 298–9; unconditional, 24, 254, 272. *see also* post-war occupation; 'undefeated' myth

revisionist attitude to, 347

see also atomic bombs; disarmament; peace treaty; post-war occupation

pacifism

economic miracle and, 349–50

pacifist commercial democracy, 337, 340

Pak Ching Sok, 493

Palau Island, 157

Parkes, Sir Harry, 69

parliament

campaign contributions, 382–3

Diet, 317

electoral reform, 524

established under 1889 constitution, 96

gerrymandering of constituencies, 385

limited role of, 382

purchase of votes in Diet, 97

reforms: of 1889, 96; post-war, 317

suffrage, 162

tortuous course of legislation, 524

Parsons, Captain William, 5

Pauley, Edwin, 298

peace treaty (1951)

islands, 337

negotiations, 336

rearmament, 306–7, 336–7

US allies press for restrictions, 336

Pearl Harbor, *see* Pacific War

peasants

age groups, 60

brutal life explaining wartime atrocities, 220

five-man groups, 59–60

miserable life of, 57–8

oppression of, 58–62

passivity of, 61

post-war improvements, 313–14

rural unrest: brutality in putting down, 109–10; against shogunate, 62–3

saving hard-earned money, 417

superstitions of, as basis of Shintoism, 103

taxation causing distress, 127

see also villages

Peers' School, 144–5, 147

Peking, China, 208

Percival, General Arthur, 247–8, 297

Perry, Commodore Matthew C., xviii, 65
Pescadores, 337
pharmaceutical industry, 439
Philippine Sea, battle of, 259
Philippines
    atrocities, 22–3
    brothels, 547
    capture of, 247
    commercial ties, 453
    communism, 527
    defence of, 250–52
    on ending of occupation (1951), 336
    Leyte landing, 261, 270
    Luzon, 261
    Manila, 262
    Mendoro attacked, 261
    recapture, 26, 259–61
Pingxingguan, China, 214
poems, 86, 464
police
    Kempeitai, 309
    MacArthur's reforms, 309
    post-war occupation: National Police
        Reserve, 306; paramilitary forces,
        305; reforms, 299, 302
    'Thought Police', 309
politeness, 485
politics
    authoritarian power structure, 524
    Buddhist Komeito Party, 374
    bureaucrats' excessive powers, 386, see
        also bureaucracy
    corruption, see corruption
    factions, 85, 87, 173, 339, 360–61,
        369–70, 379, 463; attempts to reduce
        influence of, 371; funding of, 386;
        prime ministers' subordination to,
        386–7
    Japan New Party, 374
    Kenseito Party, 169–70
    land reform strengthens right, 313
    left wing: industrial repression leading to
        rise of, 130; socialism banned,
        130–31
    Liberal Democratic Party, see Liberal
        Democratic Party
    military dictatorship: power of senior
        military, 110, 153; during war with
        Russia, 120
    Minseito Party, 192
    money and patronage, 382–4
    nationalist communism, 172–3
    New Harbinger Party, 374
    one-party rule: bar to democracy,

381–2; business certainty, 419–20;
    overthrown, 372–3
opposition, emergence of, 496
party principles abandoned, 96–7
political power: popular consent,
    absence of, 81, see also
    totalitarianism; supreme authority
    disputed, 84–5
politicians: held in contempt, 96, 379; as
    mediators between elites, 524
post-war: American withdrawal, 354–6;
    anti-communist conservatism, 335;
    consensus government, 354; factional
    squabbles, 339, 351; pacifist
    commercial democracy, 326, 340;
    political prisoners released, 309; right-
    left confrontations, 351–7;
    subservience to US, 339–40;
    terrorism, 356
power structure: group interests, 163–5
prime ministers: chosen by factions,
    361; first commoner, 159; frequent
    changes of, 357–8; loss of influence
    of, 357–8; from rival clans, 87;
    subordination to faction leaders,
    386–7; Tojo's appointment, 234
rainbow coalition, 374–7
rearmament squabbles, 344–5
reform, economic and social changes
    bringing about, 155
right-wing extremism: appeal of, 174;
    assassinations, 153, 355; attempted
    coup of 1936, 192–9; growth of,
    171–2; post-war reforms, 300;
    samurai fanaticism, 83; secret
    societies, 171–3, 201, 300; Uyoku
    urges restoration of Emperor to pre-
    war status, 507
Seiyukai Party, 159, 192
Shinsei Party, 374
Social Democratic Party: banned in
    1900, 129–30; post-war split, 332;
    split over colonial expansion, 188
Socialist Party: 1947–8 government,
    351; 1993 collapse, 374; 1989 victory
    in Upper House, 371; factions
    combine, 344, 353
subservient press, 385
wartime, 266–72; Axis Pact, 229;
    parties dissolved, 229
zaibatsu dominance, 169, 174
see also law and constitution; Liberal
    Party
pollution, 411, 446–7

population
  ageing, 448, 556
  birth rate, 556
Port Arthur, Liaotung Peninsula, 115, 119, 145
Port Moresby, New Guinea, 253, 256
Portsmouth, England
  Hirohito's arrival, 150
  Peace Conference and Treaty (1905), 119, 129
post-war occupation
  Approved Persons Board, 301
  economic arguments, 394–5
  guilty men purged, 300–301
  MacArthur: absolute power, 298; aims, 261, 295–6; arrival, 296; democratization achievement, 318; discharged from office, 306, 334; doubts about purge, 299–300; land reform, 313–14; neutralization policy, 308; reforms ineffective, 332–3; resists rearmament, 306; trade union reform, 314; US enemies, 327–9; zaibatsu (conglomerates) attack on, 309–13, 336
  national police force, 306
  political prisoners released, 309
  rearmament, 306
  SCAP's lurch to right, 332
  US bases, 306–7, 340, 365, 511–12, 529
  war crimes tribunal, 22, 298
  ending of: MacArthur's removal, 336; right-left confrontations, 354–6
  ending of: treaty, 337–8
post-war reconstruction
  aerospace industry, 349
  anti-trust laws, 312
  arms industry, 349
  micro-electronics industry, 349
  Pauley's reforms, 298–9
  transfers to Asia, 298
  war material production allowed, 308
  see also economic miracle; Ministry of International Trade and Industry (MITI); rearmament
Potsdam Conference (1945)
  agreement on dropping atomic bomb, 10, 17–19
  Potsdam Declaration, 23–6, 274, 276, 301
poverty, 447
press
  atrocities, treatment of, 224
  identical coverage, 384–5

kisha (reporter) clubs, 384
  MacArthur's reforms, 323, 325
  self-censorship, 384
  subservience to government, 385
  tabloid, 385
prime ministers, see politics
Prince automobile company, 409
Prince of Wales HMS, 247
privatization of state industries, 369, 390
productivity, 540
prostitution
  accepted, 489
  Asian brothels, Japanese in, 547
  Association of Men Against Prostitution, 547
  Chinese, 519
  daughters sold in hard times, 181, 202–3
  Hirohito's experience, 148
  wartime brothels, 220–21
Pu-yi, Emperor of China, 185–6
public order
  civil war led by Saigo, 79, 81–3
  insurrection prior to Meiji restoration, 68–74
  Kempeitai (riot police), 206
  revolutionary violence as way to reform, 94
  rural unrest, see peasants
  samurai disenchanted under shogunate, 64
  structural conspiracy in, 556
  urban unrest against shogunate, 64
Public Peace Police Act (1900), 129
Putyatin, Admiral, 64, 65

quality control circles, 400, 403, 442, 475

Rabaul, New Guinea, 258–9
racialism
  Asians, treatment of, 16–17, 220
  burakumin (outcasts), 492
  Chinese, attitudes towards, 219–20
  descent from gods, 492
  immigrants attacked, 165
  Imperial Way Faction and, 173–4
  MITI's view of foreigners, 405
  uniqueness, Japanese claim of, 389
rainbow coalition, 374–7
Ramos, Fidel V., 534
raw materials, see economy
Reagan, President Ronald, 365, 367
rearmament
  armed forces strength, 348–9

collective self-defence force for Asia, 532
defence budget, 345, 348, 367
defence debate: in late 1970s, 347–8
defensive defence attacked, 347–8
MacArthur's neutralization policy, 308
matériel production allowed, 308
military spending, 531–4, 549
Mutual Defence Association Agreement
 (1954), 307
Nakasone and, 367
National Police Reserve, 306–7
National Supply Agency, 307
naval, 307–8
political squabbles over, 344–5
right-wing victory over, 351
Self-Defence Force: Air, 308, 531;
 creation of, 307; current security
 risks, 529–30; current strength,
 530–31; expansion of, 528; overseas
 duty in Cambodia, 531–2, 547;
 purchases of defence equipment, 533;
 standard defence force concept, 348;
 status of, 544
Reconstruction Finance Bank, 394
Recruit affair, 370
Red Swastika (Chinese Red Cross), 8–9
Reischauer, Edwin, 472
religion
 Department of Divinity, 104–6
 freedom in constitution, 108
 militarist trappings removed, 324
 state religion: established, 84, 103;
  reimposed after occupation, 502–3;
  separated by MacArthur, 323
 see also Buddhism; Christianity;
 Confucianism; Shintoism
reparations, 298–9
research and development, 437–8, 554
Resources Bureau, 200
rice
 communal cultivation, 57–8, 472, 477
 crop failure in 1932, 181
 Daijosai (New Rice rite), 461, 502–4,
  507
 imports, 376
 prices, 63, 313
 rationing, 236
 rice land payments, 47
 rice riots (1918), 159
Richards, Dr C. R. B., 15
Richardson (assassinated Englishman),
 68–9
Ridgway, General Matthew, 335
right-wing extremism, see politics

Roka, Tokutomi, 87
Rokkasho-Mura, Japan, 579
Roosevelt, President Franklin D., 18, 25,
 232, 233, 236, 237, 259–60, 264
Royall, Kenneth, 328
Russia
 expedition to Siberia, in 1918, 170, 199
 Manchuria controlled, 117–19
 Sino-Japanese war (1894–5) and
  aftermath, 116–18
 threat perceived, 114
 trading with, under shogunate, 64–7
 Trans-Siberian Railway extension, 117
 war with Japan, see Russo-Japanese war
 see also Soviet Union
Russo-Japanese war (1904–5)
 background to, 117–19
 Laiotung, battle of, 119
 Mukden, battle of, 119
 Mutsuhito's leadership, 86
 Portsmouth Peace Conference, 119
 results of, 119–20
 war with Japan, 118–20
Ryoanji garden, 51–2
Ryukyu Island group, 26, 337

Sadako, Empress, 143, 152
Sahashi, Shigeru, xxv, 406, 408, 410
Saigo, General Takamori, xv, xviii, 74, 76,
 77–83, 109
Saionji, Prince Kinmochi, xv, xx, 74, 95,
 133, 152–3, 161, 167–9, 186, 194,
 200, 205
Saipan, Mariana Islands, 26, 341
Saitama Saturday Society, 536
Saito, Admiral Makoto, 186, 192, 194
Sakhalin Island, Russia, 66, 170, 272, 337
Sakurauchi, Yoshio, 541
salarymen
 bureaucratic approach to problems, 418
 compliant workforce, 417–8
 dress, 441, 497, 559
 dying from overwork (karoshi), 417,
  419
 enjoyment of work, 417
 long hours, 417
 meritocracy, 476
 miserable existence of, 557
 negligible holidays, 417
 productivity, 418
 shedding image of, 555–6
 social distinctions, 475–6
 see also companies
samurai

culture, 53–4, 56, 59
drain on state finances, 75, 78
employment in new industries, 125
fanaticism, tradition of, 83
as *kiheitai* in army, 89
officering army, 110, 202
position in class structure, 73–4
powers of, in feudal times, 60–61
privileges broken, 75, 78–9, 81
reversion to power, 43–4, 72–3
revolt against Meiji restoration, 77–9,
    81–2
secret societies, 171–2
sent abroad to learn new methods, 75–6
Shimabara massacre, 570–74
unrest at lowered status under
    shogunate, 64, 72–3
San Francisco Peace Conference (1951),
    337, *see also* peace treaty (1951)
Sanjusangendo Hall, Kyoto, 51–2
Santa Cruz, battle of, 257
Sanwa (*keiretsu*), 398
Sato, Eisaku, xvi, xxiv, 345, 355, 357,
    363, 408, 411, 524, 581
Sato, Kinyo, 502–3
Satsuma clan, 69, 74, 77–9, 80, 87, 148
savings, 417, 429
Sayako, Princess, 508
Schooland, Ken, 559
schools, *see* education
Science and Technology Agency, 437
Scott, Robertson, 57–8
screen and panel painting, 54
Second World War
    Anti-Comintern Pact allies Japan with
        Axis powers, 228
    Axis Pact (1940), 229
    invasion of Soviet Union, 230
    preparations for, *see* militarism
    US entry, 232
    see also Pacific War
secret societies
    pre-war, 171–2, 201
    post-war: far-right, 355; reforms, 300
Seiyukai Party, 159, 192, 351
Self-Defence Force, *see* rearmament
Sen no Rikyu (tea-master), 53
sendai (obligations), 477–9
Senkaku Islands, 547
seppuku, *see* suicide
sex
    increase in promiscuity, 556
    love hotels, 491
    nudo theatres, 490

pornographic comics, 490–91
sexual harassment, 558
unfaithfulness expected, 489–90
Shanghai, China, 209, 214
Shantung Province, China, 156
Shibusawa family, 97
Shidehara, Baron Kijuro, 170, 176, 183–4,
    301–2, 317
Shigemitsu, Mamoru, 297
Shikanai, Nobutake, 352
Shimabara massacre (1638), 570–74
Shimizu, Captain Setsuro, 208
Shimomura, Mitsuko, 556–8
Shimonoseki, treaty of (1895), 116
Shinsei Party, 374
Shintoism
    above religion, 105, 502–3
    Akihito's coronation, 461–3
    arm of state, as, 105
    Daijosai, 461, 502–4, 507
    Emperor as high priest, 500
    feudalism and, 45–6
    good and evil, no concept of, 491–2
    Great Promulgation Campaign, 105
    Heian shrina at Kyoto, 52
    manifesto of 1874, 105–6
    Meiji imposition of, 103–8
    moral teaching, absence of, 220
    Naruhito's wedding, 378
    post-war reforms, 324–5
    reversion to state religion, 502–3
    shallowness of, 104–5
    shrines, 106, 378
    superstitions of peasant culture, 103
Shirasu, Jiro, 316
Shiizaki, Lt-Colonel, 285
Shoda, Michiko, *see* Michiko, Empress
shogunate
    advent of, 48
    feudalism of, 59–62
    splendour of Kyoto, 50–51
    stratification of society, 48–9
    table of shoguns, xv–xvi
    see also Tokugawa dynasty
Shoken, Empress, 136–7
Short, General Walter, 244
Showa Restoration Doctrine, 173, 203
Shrine Associations (*miyaza*), 60
shrines to war dead
    cult encourages nationalism, 120
    significance of, 106–8
silk market, 181
Singapore, 247–8, 453, 527, 547
Sino-Japanese war (1894–5)

background to, 115
Formosa ceded to Japan, 121
great powers' reaction to, 116
Mutsuhito's active support, 86
post-war Russian aggrandisement
  checked, 117–18
war won; peace lost, 115
Sino-Japanese war (1937–45)
  atrocities, 8–9, 210, 219–26, see also
    atrocities
  background to: 'ascendancy in the
    Pacific' dogma, 207; Chang Tso-lin's
    murder, 177–9; Manchurian Incident,
    183–6; Marco Polo Bridge incident,
    208–9; miscalculation by Japanese,
    208
  events of: advances in north, 214–15;
    air power, 216; Burma invaded, 216;
    Canton captured, 213; casualties, 210,
    213, 217, 228; Changsha, 216;
    Hangkow captured, 213; Hsuchow
    outflanked, 211; Japanese aggression,
    209; Operation Ichi-Go, 217;
    Pingxingguan, battle of, 214; Rape of
    Nanking, 8–9, 210, 215, 219, 222–5,
    513, 518; Russian confrontation,
    211–13; Shanghai, battle for, 209–10;
    Shanghai bombing, 214; stalemate,
    217; Tungchow rebellion, 209;
    Wuhan, 215; Xuzhou, 215
  Hirohito's involvement and
    responsibility, 211–12
  retrospect of, 217–19
  US involvement, 216
  war of punishment, 223
Slim, General William, 262
Smith, Thomas C., 61, 72
Social Democratic Party, see politics
Socialist Party, see politics
society
  ageing population, 448, 556
  communal bath, 473–4
  company: dominant social structure,
    430; providing social protection, 420
  emphasis on group and society, 416
  family group, 475
  future development of, 555
  juvenile delinquency, 563
  living standards: cramped housing, 441;
    economic growth to improve quality
    of life, 456–7; rising, 441, 447,
    556–7
  middle class intelligentsia, 496
  modern changes, 557–9

obeisance leading to totalitarianism, 84
obligations (sendai and kohai), 477–9
popular conception of, 567–8
poverty, 447
saving ethic, 417, 429
self-respect from work, 416
social condemnation of law-breakers,
  563
social relations codified, 478–9
social spending programme, 412
stratification of, in shogunate, 48–9
tensions within, 555
unemployment, 447, 456, 494
young people's attitudes, 556
post-war reforms, 326–7
see also Japaneseness
Society for the Ultimate Solution of the
  Manchurian Question, 300
Sohyo (Trade Union Council), 352
Solomon Islands, 258
South Korea, 453, see also Korea
Southeast Asia
  colonial expansion in, 218
  invasion causing Pacific war, 228, 232
  racist attitude towards, 220
  trade tensions, 532
  US demand Japanese withdrawal, 233–4
  US withdrawal, 549–50
Soviet Union
  Anti-Comintern Pact, 228
  armed strength, 530
  collapse of communism, 528
  economic aid from Japan, 535
  on ending of occupation (1951), 336–7
  German invasion, 230
  Japan seeks mediation by, 272
  non-aggression pact with Germany
    (1939), 229
  nuclear threat, 366–7
  Pacific War, intervention in, 25
  Sino-Japanese war (1937–45),
    involvement in, 211–13, 216
  submarine threat, 365
  threat, as, 188, 203, 207, 305–6
  trade with, 546
  war declared, 273
  see also communism; Russia
Spectator (London weekly), 551
Spencer, Herbert, 95
Stalk, George, 430–31
Stalin, Josef, 18, 25, 272
steel industry
  foundation of, 156
  liberalization of trade, 409

mergers, 410
overseas plants, 449
priority production system, 395
Stein, Professor Lorenz von, 95
Sterling, Admiral, 66
Stilwell, General 'Vinegar Joe', 216, 217
Stimson, Henry, 9, 11, 18, 20, 24, 26, 236
Strike, Clifford, 299
strikes, see trade unions
Sugiura, Shigetake, 147
Sugiyama, General, 208–9
suicide
    anti-surrender plotters, 284–5
    following surrender, 290–91
    harakiri, 483–4
    Junshi (following the lord), 134
    tradition of, 134, 464–7, 483–4
Sumatra, 248, 249
Sumitomo companies
    clash with MITI, 409
    dominance of, 439
    foundation of, 125
    keiretsu, as, 398
    post-war dissolution, plan for, 311
    spread of interests, 126
Sumo wrestling, 493
Supreme Commander Allied Powers, see
    post-war occupation
Supreme Export Council, 401
surnames, 475
Susanowo-no-Mikoto (god), 44–5
Suzuki, Admiral Kantaro, xxi, 25, 192,
    194, 271, 272, 274–5, 283
Suzuki, Zenko, 361
Suzuki company, 439
Sweeney, Major Chuck, 35

Tachibana, Takashi, 360
Taisho, Emperor, 133, 138, 288 see also
    Yoshihito
Taiwan, 108, 116, 453
Takahashi, Toshihide, 413
Takamatsu, Prince, 236, 290
Takeshita, Lt-Colonel Masahiko, 276,
    277, 283, 285
Takeshita, Noboru, xvi, 365, 370, 371,
    373, 524
Tanaka, General Giichi, 176, 177, 180,
    198
Tanaka, Kakuei, xvi, xxiv
    attitude to Pacific War, 347
    choosing prime ministers, 361, 524
    corruption of, 358–62, 366, 384
    exposure, 360

illness ends power, 366
inflation under, 412–13
meritocrat, 476
Nakasone supported, 364–6
Tanaka, Mitsuaki, 88–9
Tanaka, General Shizuichi, 283, 285
Tategawa, Major-General Yoshitsuga, 184
taxation
    agrarian distress caused by, 127
    cuts to increase domestic demand, 401
    efforts to reduce, 369, 376
    evasion by politicians, 373, 375
    exemptions for industry, 402
    interest on savings exempt, 429
    land tax introduced, 124
    sales tax, 370, 402, 524
    tax breaks for new companies, 428
    war profits, 312
tea-ceremony, (*chanoyu*), 53–4
Teheran Conference (1943), 258
Temple of the Golden Pavilion (Kinkakuji),
    Kyoto, 52–3
Terasawa, Yoshio, 556–7
Terauchi, Hisaichi, 205–6
Terauchi, Masatake, 159
terrorism
    left-wing extremists, 356–7
    United Red Army, 356
Teru Shigeko, Princess, 166
textile industry, 128, 393–4, 405–7, 411
Thailand, 453, 527, 546, 547
Thatcher, Margaret, 367
Tibbets, Colonel Paul W., 5–7, 13–15, 29,
    30–31
Timor, 248
Tinian Atoll, 7, 14, 35
Togo, Admiral Heihachiro, 147
Togo, Shigenori, 25
Tohatsu motor-cycle company, 433
Tojo, General Hideki, xv, xxi, 201, 224,
    231, 233, 246, 271
    downfall, 394
    military background, 234–5
    peace sought by, 273–6, 340
    prime minister, 234, 266–70
    against war with US, 242–3
    zaibatsu, failed attempt to seize control
        from, 390
Tokaido (highway), 49
Tokeshi, Jimmy, 541
Tokugawa, Keiki, xviii, 69
Tokugawa, Iesada, 67
Tokugawa, Ieyasu, xvii–xviii, 50
Tokugawa dynasty

end of, 62–4
life under, 43, 49–51, 54–6, 58–62
see also shogunate
Tokyo, Japan
earthquake of 1923, 165–6
as Edo, 49, 54–5, 570–74
Emperor moves to, 71
Imperial Palace, 71, 165, 193, 270,
286–7
saturation bombing of, 217, 253, 270,
286–7
Tokyo Imperial University, 102, 562
Toshiba company, 449
Tosu clan, 69, 78
Tottori Maru (freighter), 17
Totu, Hoshi, 97
Toyama, Mitsuru, 171–2
Toyoda, Admiral Soemu, 274
Toyota company, 352, 392, 436, 439
trade, *see* international trade
trade barriers, *see* economy
trade unions
banned in wartime, 271
early industrial militancy, 129–30
enterprise unions, 441
fragmentation of, 441
growth of militancy, 157–9
industrial action, 443
in overseas plants, 451
Public Peace Police Act, 129
Spring Labour Offensive, 442
post-war: abolition of restrictive laws,
314; MacArthur's actions against,
330, 331, 351; membership, 352;
Nissan strike, 352; public sector, 352;
right-wing victory against, 351;
strikes, 351–2
see also industrial relations
Triple Intervention, 116
Truman, Harry S.
becomes President of USA, 10–11
Churchill, relationship with, 18
decision to drop atomic bombs, 10–11,
18–20, 38, 272
MacArthur discharged, 306, 334
post-war reconstruction, 299, 328
at Potsdam, 11–12, 18–19
Tsingtau, China, 156
Tsunoda, Tadanobu, 486
Tsushima Straits, battle of (1905), 119
Tungchow, China, 209
Twenty-One demands, 156–7, 170

Uehara, General Yusaku, 135
Ugaki, General Kazushige, 170, 180,
200–201, 205–6
Uin Chua Chuo Koron (newspaper), 391
ukiyo (floating world), 54–5
Umezu, General Yoshijiro, 274, 277, 297
'undefeated' myth
apology for war, lack of, 516–21
army maintained, 304–5
atomic bombs, purifying effect of, 39,
288–92
conditional surrender only, 515
Hirohito: refusal to abdicate fosters,
321–2; surrender speech, 279–82
history rewritten, 463, 513–15
Japan as victim, 515
no wrong done, 321
popular culture, 515
revisionist attitude to Pacific War, 347
rightness of war, 514
schools' indoctrination, 510, 513
The Times on, 305
war criminals rehabilitated, 367–8
unemployment, 447, 456, 494
'unequal treaties', 67
Ungern-Sternberg, Major-General von,
199–200
Unit 731 (biological warfare development),
225–6
United Red Army, 356
United States of America
anti-American feeling in Japan, 343–6,
355–6, 407, 494, 511–12, 534–5,
540–41
anti-Japanese attitudes, 540–41
bases in Japan, 337, 340, 365, 511–12,
529
build-up to Pacific War: alarm at Japan's
colonial expansion, 157, 232; MAGIC
code-breaker, 233, 244; trade
embargo, 231; war expected, 236;
withdrawal from Southeast Asia
demanded, 233–4
'buy American' policy, 406–7
companies: corporate raiders, 440;
management practices, 439–40;
service industries, growth of, 439;
strikes, 440
fears of Japan's economic dominance,
457
future relations with Japan: war, risk of,
523
industrial strength, 264
Japanese subservience, 339–40

less reliance on, 348
Pacific War, *see* Pacific War
post-war occupation of Japan, *see* post-war occupation
racial harassment against Japanese, 541
Russian expedition in 1918, 170
Sino-Japanese war, involvement in, 216
threat perceived by Japan, 535
trade with Japan: automobile industry, 537–9; Bush's tough line; 534; compassion for sick US economy, 538; dollar exchange rate, 539; embargo, 231; Japan's dependence on, 539–40; Japan's trade surplus, 542; *keiretsu*'s defensive tactics, 536; managed trade, 539; manufacturers in Japan, 393; protectionism, 542; under shogunate, 65–7; US recession, Japan's role in, 537–8. *see also* international trade
Vietnam War, 345–6
withdrawal from Asia, 549–50
work ethic attacked, 418
universities
competition for entry, 101–2
relaxed attitude of, 102
Tokyo Imperial, 102, 562
Uno, Sosuke, 370
Urakami, Japan, 108
Ushijima, General Mitsuru, 28

Van Wolferen, Karel, 425, 426, 448, 472, 494, 522–5, 537
Versailles, Treaty of (1919), 161
Vietnam
importance to Japan, 346
investment in, 546–7
left wing demonstrations, 356, 527
War, 345–6
villages
as centre of control, 59–60, 472
depleted populations, 446
village office, 564
see also peasants
Vining, Elizabeth Gray, 152, 508–9

Wakatsuki, Reijiro, 170, 176, 184
Wake Island, 243, 247
war crimes tribunal, 22, 298
Hirohito as criminal, 24
Japanese non-acceptance of verdicts, 346
war criminals rehabilitated, 367–8
War Minister
access to Emperor, 111–12

political power, 111–12, 135, 199, 205
power struggles, 135
Yamagata's influence, 110–11
Watanabe, General Jotaro, 194
Watanabe, Michio, 371, 375, 517, 532–3, 542
Weihaiwei, Liaotung, march on, 116–17
Weisman, Steven, 520
Weizsacker, Richard von, 520
Welsch, Edward, 330
White Blood Corpuscle League, 300
Whitney, General Courtney, 296, 310
Willoughby, General Charles, 304, 306, 310, 330, 394
Wingate, General Orde, 262
Witte, Sergei, 116
women
cabinet members, 372
domestic interests, 417
faithfulness expected, 490
low status, 220
managers, 558
marriages, *see* marriage
men's unfaithfulness expected, 489–90
new status of, 558
sexual harassment, 558
subservience of, 59
suffrage, 317
in textile industry, 128
wartime rapes, 220–21
Wonderful Fool (Endo), 467–8
working hours, 417, *see also* salarymen
Wuhan, China, 215
Wuhu, China, 219

Xuzhou, China, 215

yakuza (gangsters), 567, *see also* justice system
Yalta Conference (1945), 18, 25, 272
Yamagata, Prince Aritomo, xix, xv
on colonial expansion, 113–15
formation of national army, 74, 81, 88–9, 97, 108, 109–10, 112, 199–200
Hirohito, and: marriage, 148–9; regency, 152
military dictator, 120, 152–3
socialism banned, 130–31
death, 152–3
Yamaguchi, Captain Ichitaro, 192
Yamaha motor-cycle company, 433–4
Yamamoto, Admiral Isoruku, xxii, 135, 230, 243, 253, 518

Yamamoto, Shichehei, 500–502
Yamato, Japan, 45
Yamazaki, Mazakusu, 504–5
Yanagawa, Major-General Heisuke, 223, 224
Yanai, Major Syhinsaku, 533
Yasuda group of companies
  banking interests, 126
  foundation of, 125
  Fuji absorbs, 398
  wealth and influence of, 97
  post-war dissolution, plan for, 311
Yasuda Plan, 311
Yasukuni Shrine, 106–7, 193, 347, 367
Yazaki, Takeo, 48–9
Yeltsin, Boris, 534–5
yen's convertibility, 392, 405
  yen zone, 454–5
Yokohama, Japan, 165
Yomiuri Shimbun (newspaper), 384
Yonai, Admiral Mitsumasa, xv, 274
Yoshida, Shigeru, xvi, xxiv
  American occupation, during, 306, 307, 311, 316, 332, 338, 524
  anti-unionism, 351
  army opposed, 341
  arrested by military, 341
  character, 341
  corruption ends premiership, 353
  deeply conservative, 340, 353
  Dodge Line, 351
  dominance of, 338
  economic planners despised, 394
  favouring established institutions, 342
  left wing purged, 351
  on occupation, 342
  security arrangements, 34
  United States, relations with, 339
  zaibatsu championed, 342–3, 394
Yoshihito, Emperor, xix, 136, 143, 146, 151, 155, 159, 166
Yoshino, Shinji, xxii–xxiii, 391
Yukan Fuji (newspaper), 538

zaibatsu (conglomerates)
  agreement with militarists, 163, 390
  depression affecting, 181
  Doctrine of the Showa Restoration and, 173
  economic portfolios held, 164
  establishment of, 125
  family run, 126
  founded from daimyo's wealth, 78
  gifts to politicians, 174, 359
  keiretsu as, 386
  loss of market domination by, 438–9
  narcotics trade run by, 227
  navy, relations with, 228
  Pacific War: absorbing smaller firms, 266–7; dictating politics to military, 267; influence increased, 266–7; peace terms approved, 275; resistance to, 271
  political dominance of, 126–7, 164–5, 169, 174
  post-war: attempts to break up, 310–13; Companies Liquidation Commission, 312; deconcentration, 329, 330; Fair Trade Commission, 312, 413; MacArthur and, 310–11, 336; reformers branded as communist, 327–9; reforms, 299
  power of, 164–5, 390
  reluctance to invest after Meiji restoration, 123–4
  resembling government departments, 126
  self-regulation of cartelism, 393
  swallowing small competing firms, 390
  vying with militarists, 189
  war preparations, 200–201, 227
  war with China favoured, 208
  wealth from corruption, 97
  Yoshida, alliance with, 343, 344
  see also keiretsu
Zengakuren (student federation), 355
Zenji-Roren (trade union), 352
Zhukov, Marshal Georgi, 213